The Kelly Murder Mysteries

Books 1 -3

A Penny Saved A Murder Earned

A Diller A Dollar A Really Dead Scholar

Betty Blue Lost Her Holiday Shoe

Written by S. G. Lee

First Edition 2016

SB

An imprint of *Shillelagh Books*

London, Ontario, Canada

Acknowledgments:

Sincere thanks to Jodi and Sydney, without your constant support and encouragement, this book would not be possible. You are the best friends a writer could have. I dedicate this book to my daughters, my son-in law and my husband; who have supported my writing endeavours with encouragement and love. Special thanks to my beloved mother in heaven, who taught me dreams, can come true with hard work, perseverance and patience.

Table of Contents

A Penny Saved A Murder Earned

A Penny Saved A
Murder Earned

Chapter 1 - Bloody Shoes

"A penny saved is a penny earned" ~ *Benjamin Franklin*

T he blood streaked across the floor, but he had carefully

sidestepped it. Stupid bitch! She got what she deserved. How dare she defile his Angel's property? He hadn't left a trace...had he? No, he was too clever by half.

"I didn't spot you entering. Working late? You have an early opening tomorrow." A voice he didn't recognize interrupted his thoughts.

"Wait a minute, you aren't the lady. Who are you? You shouldn't be here," the man continued clearly alarmed.

"You shouldn't be here either," the murderer insisted.

"You killed Megan. I'm telling."

"This was something you shouldn't be allowed to see."

"I'm leaving. I didn't notice anything," the man lied, witnessing the blood.

"I'm sorry pal. Wrong place, wrong time!" the killer answered.

The homeless man ran dodging racks, finally deciding to hide behind some shelving. The killer ran after him, puzzled for a moment because he could see no trace of the homeless person. The murderer then laughed, as he realized how foolish the vagrant was being, his stench gave him away. He subdued the man with a Taser gun. Waiting seconds he then pulled him from his hiding place. Taking ties from within his pocket; he fastened the man's arms and feet. Satisfied that the homeless person was now trussed up like a turkey, he smiled.

"Please! I don't want to die!" the man cried, visibly sweating and starting to shake.

The man tried to kick out his legs and arms but failed, "You've heard about fate? Well sorry but this is your fate, buddy!" the murderer explained.

"Please! Couldn't you let me go? I won't tell! I'll move to another city. Besides who would listen to a homeless man?"

"Someone would. My Angel would."

The homeless man then smiled as if to gain trust from this killer, "You won't hurt the lady who owns the store, will you?" he asked.

"I would never harm my Angel. How dare you?" the killer responded outraged.

"Sorry! I didn't mean to insult you! Please just let me go...."

"What is your name?"

"My name is Al."

The killer put his gloves back on and smoothed them and then turned his back on his victim.

"You're going to kill me now. Aren't you? Just don't harm the sweet lady who owns this store. Will it hurt?" the man asked resigned.

"I would never hurt my Angel. She is sweet isn't she? Unfortunately that makes unscrupulous people take advantage of her."

"I promise I would never take advantage of her kindness."

"I know you wouldn't and it hurts me to do this. Tell you what though, I'll make your death painless because I like you, Al," the killer offered, feeling suddenly sorry for the man. Then he checked himself.

Living on the streets was hell; maybe he was doing the guy a favour? Yes, of course he was. Taking a pill bottle out of his pocket and opening the dispenser, he placed some in a coffee cup he took from the sideboard.

Then he filled the cup with the tepid coffee from the coffee pot, stirring the pills in rapidly.

"Please couldn't you let me go? I won't tell and I'll watch over her when you're not here."

"Sorry, times up, Al. Here now, drink this coffee," the assassin commanded placing the mug at Al's lips.

Al tried not to drink and spit some of the coffee out, but the assassin plugged his nose and the cup was soon empty.

"Admit it Al, you had a crappy life. Just give in and go to the light. I hear good things wait there for people like you," the killer stated.

Al tried to fight some more, but he soon found it was losing battle. Al's breathing slowed as he slipped into a deep sleep and stopped breathing altogether. His age and living on the streets made the pills work fast.

Now what to do with the body? The killer thought. His Angel must not find this man here, bad enough he left Megan's body here for his Angel to find. This man knew his Angel; she cared, so like her to look after the homeless. The dumpster of course! The day after tomorrow was garbage day. Covered in garbage no one would find Al.

~0~

The next day

Lily

Ominous clouds replaced the morning's sunlight turning
the skies to shades of deep purple and navy blue, streaked with
gray. Lily Kelly stared at the sky for moment, and then departed
the courthouse doors in Happy Valley, Ontario, Canada, skipping
down the steps. The city looked it's age of over a hundred as the
buildings downtown looked old and decrepit. If only the town
could find some money to fix downtown Lily thought.

Then her mind turned to Amelia, her cousin and best friend.
Amelia needed Lily to support her in her grief. She had a fight with
her husband Horace again this morning about how much time he
was spending at the office. Lily was always working, and so was
Horace, so how much time was Rose their fourteen year old
daughter getting? She had won in court, but all she could think
about was her family. Everyone needed her and she felt like she
was being pulled in three different directions. Something had to
give and it looked like it was her job. She would have to cut back
on some of her work. Her family had to come first.

Lily stumbled some more over the steps only stopping from
hurrying across the courtyard to her office, when her heel broke on
her shoe. Today was supposed to be about her victory after her win
in court; but it appeared with her expensive shoe's heel breaking,
she was mistaken. They ought to get the ruts in the paving stones
fixed; that was her reflection as she cursed her bad break. What did
they say about omens? Maybe she should have taken a hint from
the heavens' darkening? She noted as her bad luck had seemed to
get worse with the arrival of some reporters.

"Ms. Kelly, give us a statement about the Rockwood case?" yelled
one reporter.

"Ms. Kelly, how does the Sulimani family feel about your victory?" yelled another.

One bold reporter stepped forward, "Crown Attorney Kelly, congratulations on your win. Was it hard to try a case which involved a council member?" asked Paul Knight from the local television station, thrusting a microphone in Lily's face.

"Anyone who commits a crime in Happy Valley will be tried by the Crown with the full force of the law, despite their office. So no, I did not find it difficult to do my job," Lily replied testily.

"Thank you, Ms. Kelly. What does the Sulimani family think about the judgement?"

"Amani Sulimani was five years old, when Zebadiah Rockwood's truck went through a red light. His truck struck the back of the Sulimani's SUV killing her. He then left the scene pursued by good Samaritans, who wished to stop Mr. Rockwood from continuing driving drunk: a pursuit caused by Mr. Rockwood's actions, which put a number of lives in danger."

"Will the family be comforted with this conviction?" queried another reporter.

"Amani Sulimani existed as their only child. Mr. Rockwood's conviction will not bring her back, but hopefully will bring some peace of mind to her family knowing he will be behind bars," Lily answered.

"Do you sense, given your own personal tragedies that you'll be able to get a sentence fitting the crime?"

"My family's history does not come into my trial cases, only the person's guilt."

"And when will sentencing take place?" asked another reporter.

"Sentencing will take place next month."

"Thank you Ms. Kelly. This is Paul Knight reporting, with an update on the Zebadiah Rockwood's drunken driving case. Zebadiah Rockwood was a long time council member here in Happy Valley. He took a leave of absence to deal with his legal issues. Mr. Rockwood was charged with impaired driving causing death, two counts of failing to remain at the scene of an accident and dangerous driving last December. When asked about the conviction today Mr. Rockwood and his lawyer issued a no comment. We will have the complete story for you at six pm. Paul Knight reporting for CHPV-TV."

Lily hated speaking on camera, even though it was part of her job as the Crown attorney, so she was glad the scrum had been completed.

She hated sounding tough and unyielding but it was all in the description of her job title. She had fought difficult challenges to get this job and she had to work hard and fight hard to keep it. After all there were aspects of her job her she loved like putting the bad people that would harm others away. The press was gone and she was now free to go to her office to file her reports and leave early. She crossed the street, entered her building and went straight up to her office.

She crossed the street, entered her building and went straight up to her office.

"Victory is mine!" Lily Kelly cried triumphantly as she walked into her office.

"So you won?" asked Colleen Finn, her administrative assistant.

"Yes, and I bested Michael Taylor. He thought he would beat me in court. He actually believed his client would win."

"Good for you, boss, I knew you would nail his lily white ass to the wall. He's such a scumbag lawyer all his clients seem to be as guilty as hell."

"Colleen! Language! But yes I did," Lily answered, showing pearly white teeth and laughing to take the sting out of the reprimand.

Colleen looked expectantly at Lily and she felt stupid did she miss something? Oh the joke! Lily hadn't laughed at Colleen's wit.

"Funny, I got it. Zebadiah Rockwood's sentencing takes place next month, but he will be held until then; no bail, no goodbyes to his favourite water hole. As the Crown, I'll recommend the longest sentence I can get. It's victories like these which make my job worthwhile. I don't know how much satisfaction this will give that little girl's family, but at least they'll know her killer remains in jail. He can't take another life again, because he will be incarcerated."

Lily went over to her desk and sat down.

"Can you imagine Michael Taylor, tried to use the defence that Rockwood was not drunk. Just tired? He claimed Rockwood drank only after the accident, while driving his company's truck; so the company couldn't possibly be responsible"

"Yes I can believe it!" Colleen agreed "I'm glad you proved he'd drank so much before getting in the truck. That proved he was legally under the influence when the accident occurred. I hope I was some help in that aspect."

"Of course were."

"Thanks, Lily."

"It's still early; only nine forty-five, and my day's clear until what, two-thirty?"

"That's correct." Colleen replied.

Colleen checked a day planner, frowning.

"Is everything okay? You seem a little down."

"Everything is fine. Amelia's grand opening starts at noon, but I promised to be there sooner if possible. If I go right now, I'll surprise her," Lily grabbed her coat to leave.

"After what happened, Amelia needs the encouragement."

"Yes, Amelia does need support. Hold all my calls Colleen. Unless it's urgent then call my cell."

"I'll do that. Tell Amelia, I hope her store has great success. What time should I say you'll be back?" Colleen responded to a departing Lily.

"Tell whoever asks that I'll be back after two p.m..."

"And if they ask where you are?" Colleen questioned.

"Tell them I'm meeting with a witness," Lily replied with a wink.

"If there's cake bring me back a piece. Please, boss?" Colleen begged.

"I ordered a cake, but it's not supposed to arrive until one thirty so we'll see. I'm leaving now. Remember only urgent calls to my cell phone." Lily cautioned, leaving through the front door.

She twisted her shimmering brown hair back up into its traditional bun. Pulling out her cell phone, she dialled Amelia's store. There was no answer.

~0~

A few minutes ago

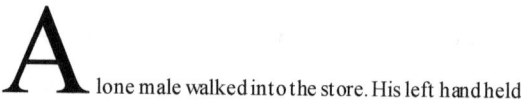

Alone male walked into the store. His left hand held a gun while his right hand steadied it. He strode in with caution. His dark brown eyes dart from corner to corner, searching for an assailant. His well over six-foot tall frame slouches. He is ruggedly handsome, with dark brown hair clipped short to his head. He is dressed in a dark blue jacket and dress pants; and a badge is clipped to his belt buckle. Finding the scene secure he putting his gun away and pulled a pair of gloves out of his suit coat pocket and a pair of booties, which he slipped on his shoes.

He checked the victim. No pulse. Advancing forward, he bent down to check the second woman; her phone still in her hand, her head bloody. He noted the second victim is still breathing, though unconscious. He looked around, as if waiting for someone. Deciding they weren't coming yet, he took out a mini recorder. He started scanning the scene and speaking aloud.

"This is Sergeant Detective Emmett Rogers. I am at the scene of a homicide, at Quirks, one forty five Maple Street. A woman lays sprawled out across the floor. The woman's arms are positioned underneath her, as if to break her fall."

"The back of her head and her long blonde hair are streaked in rusty-brown blood, as well as her clothing below the hair. Blood pools across the floor spiralling out in two long streams. Footprints are noticeable, as if someone stepped through the drying blood. The weapon appears to be a pair of scissors, found beneath the victim."

The man spoke aloud as he walked around, carefully avoiding contaminating the evidence, by stepping over a paper cup.

"A coffee cup... possibly one of those lattes is overturned. Its contents are also spilled on the floor and countertop. Coffee is spilled at the front door and possibly on the shoes. The second victim's shoes are not on the bruised victim, but on the floor. The shoes can be found near an overturned ladder, at the front door. It appears the one woman, may have been carrying a ladder and toy stock to place on the shelves, when she slipped in the blood.

The man paused to think.

"This might be a setup by the second victim to cover the actual crime. The woman, however, seemed to have the victim's blood all over her clothes and hands like she crawled through the blood. I believe there are two possible scenarios here. One the owner of the shop, one Amelia Kelly, murdered her employee and set this up to appear a perpetrator broke in and killed her accidentally hurting herself in the process. Or two... it is at it seemed and she stumbled on the crime scene."

"Is it a robbery gone wrong? It is too soon to tell. The store owner will be en-route to hospital as soon as the EMTs have arrived .Interview to follow. The time is now ten twenty a.m.," he concluded turning off his recorder. He pulled out a notebook and examined the room some more taking notes.

~0~

Now

Lily and Detective Emmett Rogers

The man's eyes turn and his vision focused completely. A woman entered the store. His eyes took in her tall and slender form and her long shimmering brown hair, pulled into a tight roll. He noted she was closely followed by the Emergency technicians and gave a sigh of relief. The woman entering the store had brilliant blue eyes. He had a feeling she often turned heads, even dressed as she was, in her business attire. But he noted something about the way she walked screamed money and upper class.

"Oh no, Amelia!" she screamed and tried to rush to Amelia, but was stopped by the man.

"This is a crime scene Ma'am. We don't want you disrupting the evidence. Let the EMTs and detectives do their job. Then you can go to ...you're er...friend?" Sergeant Detective Rogers commanded.

"Crime scene? What has happened?" Lily asked politely, wanting to be cooperative.

"Ma'am, I'll know better after I assess the scene. Until then, please remain near the front door." ordered Detective Rogers briskly.

"I promise I'll stay out of the way; but at least can I get her Adrienne Changs?"

"What or who, are Adrienne Changs?" said Detective Rogers looking totally perplexed.

"Shoes, those shoes right there!" Lily pointed to a pair of heels lying behind the yellow tape.

"You're worried about shoes? Woman! Do you have any idea of what's going on here?" Detective Rogers snapped, shaking his head.

"You sexist pig!" countered Lily under her breath.

"Men!" Losing her temper now and louder she continued "Those shoes are worth five hundred dollars! And she probably wore them for what a half an hour? And you want me to walk away and leave them to be destroyed!"

"Five hundred dollars for shoes? Is she crazy?" Detective Rogers asked dumfounded.

"No! She's not crazy. How dare you?" Lily asked suddenly outraged.

He was smug wasn't he? Handsome yes, but oh so smug, she questioned herself. That wasn't important. Amelia is injured on the floor and he questioned her? Instead of letting her go to her cousin! Why was she so worried about the shoes? They were only shoes. Amelia was injured; who cared about footwear?

"Sorry...the shoes are evidence. Name? Occupation? Address?" Detective Rogers barked, ignoring her statement.

"I want to see your identification first, and then you'll get the information," insisted Lily.

"I am Sergeant Detective Emmett Rogers," the man revealed, showing his police badge.

"Oh that's funny," Lily uttered laughing. "If you and Amelia were introduced it would be Aem and Em."

Lily followed this up by hysterically followed by crying. What was wrong with her? She never lost it like this. She always appeared a professional. She had seen crime scenes. She could handle this. Couldn't she? Amelia would be okay. Wouldn't she?!

"Get a hold of yourself Lily. You have embarrassed yourself." Lily heard a voice in her head, she recognized as her father's. Odd how her Dad's voice, came back to her now, she rarely saw him, since he lived in Prague and he only called about twice a year.

"Ma'am, what you are saying is not that funny. Are you all right? I think your friend's okay. She might have a head injury and possibly a broken leg, but she'll be okay." Sergeant Detective Rogers then turned to the Emergency technicians (EMTs) to seek confirmation demanded "Right?"

"Should be. But head injuries can be serious," the one EMT replied.

Sergeant Detective Rogers shot him a disapproving look.

"Yes, the Sergeant Detective is right. She'll be fine. She'll be taken to the hospital for treatment," the Emergency Technician agreed.

"See...what did I tell you? Now I need to see some identification and then get some answers to my questions. Name? Address? Occupation? Why are you here?" Detective Rogers barked at Lily.

"Amelia's my best friend and more. This should have been the greatest day of her life, her opening of her new store; a one of kind toy and collectibles retailer. A grand opening and now it's ruined. Who did this to her?" Lily asked, uncharacteristically wringing her hands and still trying to regain her calm, as thoughts of Amelia's demise threatened to enter her mind.

"Ma'am... she slipped in blood. She hit her head on the floor and on the ladder. No one harmed her. She did this to herself," explained Sergeant Detective Rogers.

"I realize she's clumsy, but she didn't put blood there to trip in," defended Lily angrily.

"No the blood was spilled by whoever killed the woman behind the counter."

"Someone is dead behind the counter?" Lily responded shocked and surprised.

"No comment; as I explained Ma'am this is an active crime scene. What is your name?" Detective Rogers insisted forcefully again.

"Lily Kelly-Brooksfield. My husband is Horace Brooksfield, the mayor. We live down the street on Beaconfield. Do you want the number? It's nine hundred and sixty-two." she replied condescendingly.

"If you're Mayor Brooksfield's wife... then you're the Crown Attorney." Coming to this realization, Sergeant Detective Rogers hid a sigh.

"Please update me on this active crime scene, now," commanded Lily pulling back her shoulders.

Emmett Rogers put on his professional face and smiled.

Lily just felt so angry. This cop who grinned back at her was the biggest reason. She was a married woman. She shouldn't be attracted to a cop who apparently existed to give her grief and solve a murder. She threw back her shoulders again. It was okay to look at someone attractive, she excused herself. Everyone looks, and most of the time it meant nothing. It's only if you acted on any attraction it became wrong. She would never act on the temptation. Besides he appeared to be the most annoying man she'd ever met.

"Ma'am, you know I can't fill you in on any of this case. You'll have to recuse yourself from this case, as you're familiar with the crime scene." Detective Rogers emphasized, once again interrupting Lily's thoughts.

"Why don't you just come out and say what you think. You consider me a suspect," Lily uttered.

"A lot of people are suspects in my book. I have to make a case for them committing the crime or I have to eliminate them as suspects. And don't attempt to solve this yourself; amateurs just get in the way." Detective Rogers explained, his eyes wandering.

Lily was slightly amused. Detective Rogers thought she wanted to insinuate herself into this murder investigation? She might not have before that comment, but she did now. He seemed to be focusing on Amelia or Lily as his prime suspect. Lily knew neither of them had committed this murder, so that meant she had no choice but to find out for herself who had committed this crime. She would pretend she wanted nothing to do with this situation, even as far as passing it off to her underling Barbara. After all she could always investigate behind the scenes.

Spotting the emergency technicians Detective Rogers exclaimed "Oh good, the ambulance has arrived to take the victim to the hospital. Now can we can get down to brass tacks; you can fill me in on these people and anything else you know or have held back from me."

"I want to go with her," Lily protested.

Lily pulled herself back taking several steps back putting distance between herself and this cop. It was odd, how alive she felt when she jousted with him. He was a cop investigating a murder and she was married.

"Stop this now Lily!" She told herself.

"Ma'am, I realize you want to go see your friend. Before I could release you from the scene, I need something from you. We need you to identify the other victim. Maybe you'll recognize her when I turn over the body." Detective Rogers explained, softening a little, as he slipped on another pair of gloves.

"Only if you'll stop calling me Ma'am. Call me Lily or Crown Attorney Kelly but not Ma'am. It makes me feel eighty years old."

"If it will get you to identify the victim...thank-you Crown Attorney Kelly." "Let's look, shall we?" Lily agreed.

Lily took a breath as she gathered herself to observe who lay there dead. She gasped as she stared over the counter to see the back of the woman's head. She covered her mouth in horror.

"Good grief! I never realized they appear so alike from the back," replied Lily shocked.

"Who do you think she looks like Ma'am?" demanded Detective Rogers.

"What did I say about Ma'am? Don't they give you sensitivity training at Police College? You want to know who this is? This is Megan, Megan Fowler. She's an employee of Amelia's. But she works evenings she's...is....was a college student. I can't believe this is Megan. Megan is such a sweet girl and worked part-time to be able to go to school and support her mother. Why would someone kill her? Do you think it's possible someone mistook her for Amelia?" Lily rambled, tears slipping from her eyes.

"That's a possibility, Ma'am. We will explore all aspects."

"I know the drill, Sergeant Detective Rogers." Lily gave the detective a mock salute, "Why can't you admit that they mistook Megan for Amelia?"

"We don't have any of the facts yet, Ms. Kelly," replied Detective Rogers.

"What about Amelia? Is she in any danger?" asked Lily. "If I were to speculate, I suppose that could be a possibility," Detective Rogers answered non-committally.

They both watched as the technicians gathered the evidence and blood samples and took pictures before the body was taken away.

"Will someone be assigned to guard her and keep her safe?" Lily asked getting exasperated.

"That's in motion, Crown Attorney Kelly," Detective Rogers explained, trying not to sound annoyed that she's telling him how to do his job.

Detective Rogers and Lily turned as another cop swaggered into the store. Burly and well over six feet tall, his hair was dark like Detective Rogers. Unlike Detective Rogers, this man preened like a peacock; Lily was aware of the type. Guys like him smiled with their mouths and not their eyes. They thought all women should admire them and only them. She noted his smile went as far as his lips.

"What have you got here, Emmett?"

"Nothing you need to be concerned about, Brad," Detective Rogers replied, obvious tension showing between the two.

"You should be able to get some great publicity out of this one," Brad said loudly to Detective Rogers.

Brad then strutted over to the murder scene.

"It's my case, Brad," Detective Rogers insisted.

"I'm not trying to interfere," Brad persisted walking around, "I just thought if you needed some help I would lend a hand. It doesn't look like something you could handle on your own."

"I don't need help, thanks, Brad. I don't need you messing up my crime scene." Detective Rogers declared "I've got it all under control.

"It doesn't look that way to me. I would solve this case quickly. You could use me in your corner," Brad continued.

"We don't need you. Now the Crown attorney is here, so I have it all in hand. Goodbye, Brad." Detective Rogers practically spat.

"Ah, the lovely Crown attorney Kelly is here. Can't go now," Brad exclaimed trying to sound charming but failing miserably.

"And you are?" asked Lily putting her full aristocratic chill into her voice, "I'm Brad Owens, at your service, Attorney Kelly. Sergeant Detective Brad Owens. I use to be Emmett's partner," Brad explained smiling and pointing to Detective Rogers.

Detective Rogers rolled his eyes. "Thank God you're not anymore," He stated under his breath loud enough for only he and Lily to hear.

"So what do you think, Crown Attorney? Was it a robbery gone wrong?" asked Brad.

"I'm not sure. Why do I bother to tell you this? This isn't your case," Lily commented suddenly not willing to share with Brad.

She didn't know why. Something about his smile, and the way Emmett Rogers had reacted to him made her dislike him. Brad's smile was phony, like a used car salesman. It was slick and slimy. That wasn't fair to used car sales people. Lily was sure they were more honest than this phoney, Brad Owens. Lily had come across a lot of people in her job. She certainly felt she was a good judge of character. In fact, she could spot a phoney a mile away. Detective Emmett Rogers, unlike Brad Owens, appeared like he knew his job. She'd heard of him many times, but had never run into him on the job until today. Thank goodness for the Internet on her phone. He was a dedicated cop. He had done his time and had come up through the ranks, strictly on merit. Detective Rogers didn't seem to like Brad Owens and that was reason enough for Lily not to trust him.

Emmett Rogers had an exemplary record as a police officer; she trusted his instincts and knowledge over this smarmy, Detective Brad Owens. He'd get to the bottom of this. Lily wished he would let her leave soon and check on Amelia. They had spent their teen years together and were as close as sisters. She'd always felt responsible for Amelia, being two years older. She wanted to make sure Amelia was okay.

"Okay. Well if you don't need my help, I'm leaving because I have work to do. There are other crimes to investigate." Brad answered leaving, "See you around Emmett."

"Not if I see you first," muttered Emmett under his breath.

"So am I free to go?" Lily demanded.

Emmett then offered her his pen.

"I have your address, so as long as you sign here in my notebook. "You are free to go," he said gesturing.

Lily glanced over at Detective Owens and watched him leave before reaching for the book. She then signed her signature with a flourish. Detective Rogers scanned the signature, thinking momentarily it was just as elegant as Lily. He shook his head, reminding himself to stay connected to reality.

"So I am free to go, Detective?" Lily repeated.

"I'll be checking in on your friend, of course, and I may need to follow-up with you later, but as of now, you are free to go." he smiled, already exhausted.

"I would expect nothing else from you, Detective Rogers."

As she got into her car, Lily breathed a sigh of relief she had finally been able to leave the store. She buckled up her seatbelt and put her car in gear.

Backing the car up, Lily pulled out into the street and narrowly missed getting hit by a car, she didn't view. Luckily the other driver slammed on his brakes. She noticed the male driver shouting, "Stupid woman driver" as she read his lips in her rear view mirror. He was justified in his anger. It had been her fault, but she didn't have time to dwell.

She headed down the road toward the hospital; despite her resolve her mind wandered. She thought about poor Megan's mother getting the news of her daughter's death. It would kill Lily to get news like that about her adopted daughter, Rose. What kind of monster kills a young woman? Why did, whomever it was, have to kill Megan? It wasn't a robbery, she'd read in Detective Rogers' notes, when he gave his notebook to her to sign her statement. As Lily drove, more questions flooded into her head. Was Amelia the real target? Megan certainly appeared like Amelia from the back.

Amelia didn't appear too hurt. Maybe she suffered a concussion? Concussions could be serious; she knew from her readings. The EMT hadn't said Amelia was in serious condition though. Not that the EMT could explain before Emmett Rogers got on his case. Revving the engine, she waited impatiently for the light to go green. Once Lily reached the hospital, she could reassure herself, Amelia was all right.

~0~

Chapter 2 - In Capable Hands

"Y ou're awake! I went out for coffee...I'm so glad

you're okay," Lily exclaimed, as she entered Amelia's hospital room and sat on the edge of her hospital bed.

"Who did they find, Lily? Who was killed in my store?" asked Amelia, her eyes filled with tears and horror.

"I'm so sorry Amelia, it was Megan they found dead," Lily replied with great sorrow.

"Why would anyone kill Megan? I always told her if anyone ever wanted the money in the till, give the money to them. Why would they kill her for a few measly dollars?"

"There wasn't any money missing Aem."

"No money missing? But someone killed Megan. Why did they kill her, if not for the money?"

"I'm sure they'll find out who killed her."

"I'm so scared. I crawled in blood and then realized somebody lay injured... and I couldn't save her. Now that I know it was Megan, who was dead..., this hurts even more," Amelia rambled crying.

"I'm always here for you, Amelia," Lily affirmed hugging her. "I'm sure they'll fix up your leg and send you on your way soon. As for investigating the crime...they will be caught, whoever did this."

"That will be enough, Crown Attorney Kelly. Please don't discuss this with her until I speak to the witness," Detective Rogers announced from the door breaking in on their conversation.

Detective Rogers strode in and sat down in the chair next to the bed taking out his notebook.

"Witness to what? I'm no witness! I found my dearest friend and employee dead. It doesn't make me an onlooker to the killing! I didn't see the murder or the murderer."

"Ma'am, sometimes the little things help the most. Let me introduce myself. I'm Sergeant Detective Emmett Rogers and I am in charge of this case."

"Is it true someone killed Megan, but didn't take the money in the cash register?" demanded Amelia shaken.

"The victim is one Megan Fowler. Your employee?" questioned Detective Rogers, ignoring what Amelia said.

"Yes, but I have no idea why anyone would harm her."

"We'll get back to your ideas of who would harm her later. I need details. For instance what time did you arrive?" prodded Detective Rogers.

"About nine thirty I think! I'd gotten a coffee first; one of those cappuccinos." replied Amelia.

"This would be the coffee cup we found overturned and spilled all over the floor? Good! Now can we can discount the cup as not belonging to the victim."

"No, the coffee cup was definitely mine. I think I knocked the cup off the counter, when I fell."

"Did you perceive anything different, perhaps something out of the ordinary which had been moved?"

"Well, the door slightly ajar opened easily, but I didn't notice anything out of place. I did observe the mail had not only arrived early, but was also scattered in front of the door. That was weird," answered Amelia remembering.

"The mail arriving early; that stood out as a new occurrence? This had never happened any other time?" Detective Rogers noted.

"No, it wasn't a new occurrence. Philip, who's the mailman, cares about his job. He has a set schedule and he doesn't usually get to the store until about half past ten," Amelia explained.

"We did find mail scattered all over the floor. I thought maybe you'd dropped the mail, Ms. Kelly."

"Good detective work, I did drop the mail. I picked up the mail and I tripped and let go of the letters all over again," Amelia admitted.

"I see," replied Rogers writing this all down. "Did you have any differences of opinion with anyone recently? Remember before you answer the question, if you lie to a police officer this is a criminal offense."

"How dare you?! Amelia has answered all of your questions honestly," Lily responded, outraged on Amelia's behalf.

Lily thought at this moment she had been sadly mistaken. She wasn't attracted to this Neanderthal. He had no grace or couth, he acted like a relentless robot. Lily observed the way Detective Rogers grilled Amelia and she did not like it.

"I'm trying to do my job, Ma'am. She knew the victim. She may have had words with Megan Fowler. Megan Fowler could have been a bad employee. Or Megan may have been taking money from the cash register; Amelia got angry and killed her. Then she staged the scene a little too well to cover her crime."

"You should do your job and realize Amelia was a victim here too. Whoever killed her employee managed to injure her, because she slipped in Megan's blood and hurt herself!"

Lily clenched her fists then hid them realizing she was showing him how angry he was making her. The radio on Detective Rogers' shoulder suddenly made a noise; a garbled voice, only Detective Rogers seem to understand.

"Rogers here! Yes sir, I am on my way," he replied into the radio. "I need to go. Duty calls. This conversation is not finished. I will return Ms. Kelly, Ms. Brookfield. Please, do not discuss this any further," Detective Rogers demanded, placed a card in Lily's hand and left the hospital room.

"What do you think the meaning of the call was?" Lily asked puzzled.

"Police business?" commented Amelia with a smile.

"Yes, I think so. At least the call wasn't about you."

"Why would he get a call about me? I've done nothing wrong."

"You're the prime suspect, until they clear you."

"Me? But all I did was find her," protested Amelia.

"That's right you found her!"

"He's insinuating that I am guilty? Oh no, I am a suspect. Aren't I? But what do they think I deliberately tripped? I hit my head and broke my leg, to look innocent?" Amelia realized.

"The person who finds the body is always deemed guilty first. They'll clear you," Lily replied, sounding more confident than she felt.

"They had better. Oh poor, poor Megan. Here I worry, I am considered a suspect, but she's dead," Amelia answered with remorse.

"Does she have any other family?"

"No, merely her mother."

"Oh no, her poor mother! Megan was barely twenty-one. And she's is or she was an only child."

"Doesn't matter whether you're an only child or not when a mother's grieving. As you are too aware," said Lily sadly, "Such a sweet girl. She always had a kind word for me when I called for you on the phone. I can't believe anyone would harm her, and yet someone did."

"I don't know what I would have done if you hadn't let me come live in your coach house, when Jack and Sam died. I nearly lost my mind and eating didn't even occur to me. If you hadn't brought me food and talked to me and given me a place to stay...," Amelia broke off, tears streaming from her eyes.

"You are my best friend and cousin; you would have looked after me." "You are always there for me. I'm the harbinger of death."

"Amelia, you know none of what has happened is your fault. Jack and Sam dying was an accident. Should I request an appointment for you again with Dr. Jones?"

"I'm not breaking down again. You need not worry. I'm coping, honest. If I wasn't I'd make an appointment. Thanks anyway, Lily, for caring and being my friend."

"Hey, want me to find out when they'll let you out of here?" asked Lily.

"Maybe they'll let me go home today... but I don't know how I am about to climb those stairs to my apartment in your coach house."

"You'll come and stay with us. We own an extra room on the ground floor."

"Are you sure Rose and Horace won't mind?" asked Amelia.

"Rose will love to have you in the house and Horace, well he always does what I want," replied Lily triumphantly.

"You sometimes take that man for granted."

"Never. He's always satisfied," Lily saucily responded.

"Too much information Lily! TMI!"

"The information made you smile didn't it? Now I'll go find a doctor and find out what's going on and how long you need to stay."

Lily walked into the hospital corridor, finding two interns. The first was a young woman, petite, five-feet tall, with a long white coat over green scrubs. A stethoscope hung gingerly around her neck. The second male doctor towers over her at six feet tall. He slouched to accommodate her. He too was dressed in a white coat over green scrubs. He looked nervous but tried to hide his unease.

"Hello. I'm Dr. Yvonne Stupna. I attended you, when you were first brought into the hospital. We are in charge of your case," announced the female doctor to Amelia.

"I'm Dr. Bob Stern," the male introduced himself, with confidence in his voice.

"Pleased to meet you, now can I go home?" impatiently, demanded Amelia.

"Not quite yet," replied Dr. Stupna.

"When can I go home then?"

"Let me put this in layman's terms. You've had a concussion..."

"A knock on the head." Dr. Stupna explained interrupting, resulting in earning her an annoyed look from Dr. Stern, who had tried to be subtle, but was unsuccessful in his attempt.

"A severe loss of consciousness." continued Dr. Stern interjecting, "You fractured your tibia and fibula. The tibia, a weight-bearing bone, supports the leg, so it is certainly a severe break. We put in a plate to reinforce the tibia. This is a dynamic compression plate and it will mold to the surface of your leg. This adapts to hold the tibia bone better. The plate is put in and screws lock it in place."

"You want to do surgery, on my leg?" Amelia asked sounding terrified.

"Yes, but this is simple surgery these days," Dr. Stupna reassured Amelia.

"I'm sure these doctors completed this surgery many times, to great success," Lily volunteered

"We perform many surgeries of this kind," Dr. Stern agreed smiling.

Lily just nodded her head in Amelia's direction as if to say, see.

"These are serious conditions though. We'd like to go ahead and schedule the surgery. We will see how you are healing by keep an eye on you for a couple of days. Then if we believe you're in no danger we'll send you home," Dr. Stern explained.

Dr. Stupna seemed to take issue with this and took Dr. Stern to one side. Amelia and Lily watched them whispering. Dr. Stupna seemed to be the senior doctor and she tells him "You have a terrible bedside manner. You never tell patients there is danger. Your bedside approach needs a lot of work."

Lily and Amelia look at each other; then they both suppressed a chuckle.

"We do good work you'll be fine," answered Dr. Stupna, smoothing over Dr. Stern's blunder. She patted Amelia's hand and abruptly left taking Dr. Stern.

"Doctors they are all the same," Lily claimed "They always err on the side of caution. Why don't you just rest and I'll be back to see you tomorrow."

Lily looked at her watch, well aware she had to get back to work, but hated to leave.

"I hate hospitals," complained Amelia loudly.

"I understand. I hate visiting them too. There are too many bad memories in this hospital. I'll even bring you breakfast before I head into work tomorrow. Lily promised feeling guilty.

"I appreciate how bad the food can be here,"

"Thanks, Lily, but you better check first. I may be having the surgery tomorrow." Amelia replied yawning.

Lily left the room troubled and worried. After all, shouldn't there be a police officer guarding Amelia's room? Amelia may have been the target and she was unguarded. Anyone could walk right in without being stopped. Shaking with anger, she took out the card Sergeant Detective Rogers had placed in her hand, picked up her cell phone, and called but was interrupted by Detective Rogers appearance outside the room.

"Why isn't there a guard on Amelia's door? Do you want Amelia to be killed?"

"Sorry, Ma'am, I was overruled. I was told it wasn't justified."

"Not justified? That's ridiculous." Lily claimed, "Amelia could be in grave danger."

"I agree, but with the cutbacks, they decided the cost wasn't necessary," answered Detective Rogers.

"What kinds of idiots run your department?" Lily indignantly asked.

"I'm sorry, I really did try," Detective Rogers apologetically replied.

"Well you didn't try hard enough."

"There have been a lot of cutbacks, since your husband took over as mayor. You should take up the issue with him. We've been slashed so much our budget has to be kept for policing, not guarding, I'm sorry to say," Detective Rogers replied with a sarcastic tone.

Lily thought "Stupid jerk! Now he's bringing Horace into this. How dare he? What, did he think being the mayor came easily and making cutbacks to a shrinking tax base made Horace smile? Besides Horace found extra funds for the police department. He'd told her so. Who did they think they fooled with this 'we have no money stance'? She'd tell him, he lied.

"You don't sound sorry at all. I thought you might worry about Amelia. I know I am worried about her. What if the killer comes after her, will you cite your budget cuts?" Lily pointed her finger at him, but what she really wanted to do was hit him she was so angry.

This was ridiculous she wasn't a violent person. She didn't do things like that. Why was she allowing him to make her so angry? She had to start thinking more clearly.

"Look I said I'm sorry. I am. When we can't provide what the public needs, we are just as upset as you are, or more than you are. I have no control over this. If I did she'd be guarded. I've been told there's no money for it. I explained this. I can't do anything about it. I'm truly sorry, Ms. Kelly," Detective Rogers admitted, overly apologetic.

"Thanks anyway. I know you tried," Lily acknowledged, realizing Emmett Rogers could be telling the truth, but why had Horace lied to her?

She needed to talk to Horace later about this, but meanwhile she needed to make peace with Emmett Rogers. Being adversarial wouldn't help Amelia.

"I'm going to tell Horace his budget harmed policing and how he must find funding for the police department. But I'm not promising anything; Horace is his own man. Now I'll let you get back to the case. I do, however, want a full report to my office. The information has to be sent to my colleague, the assistant crown attorney Barbara Franks. She will be handling this case, since I can't."

"I'll send you the report to you for now. You can recuse yourself if necessary."

"Thank you, Detective Rogers. I appreciate you trusting me with the report." Lily answered surprised. "I will do everything in my power to show your trust was warranted."

"Goodbye, Ms. Lily Kelly."

"Goodbye, Detective Rogers!" Lily exclaimed firmly, shutting her cell phone and went to sit on a bench to think.

She wondered if the man flirted with her. The way Detective Rogers said Lily was oddly flirtatious. He knew she remained married, to a man she loved. He stood investigating a case; did she imagine he liked her? She hoped she was. She couldn't handle a flirtatious cop.

Lily loved Horace but they had their difficulties of late. He was so distant and aloof, the demands of the job. High pressured jobs like being the mayor of Happy Valley came with a lot of responsibilities and time required, and all those money woes the city was suffering wasn't helping. If she was patient and loving it would all work out. At least she hoped it would. Horace couldn't help the time his mayoral job leached from his family. She and

Rose tried to understand but Rose suffered from Lily and Horace constantly working late hours.

Poor Rose. Lately she felt like they both neglected their daughter. Lily arranged with the office to cut back on some of the hours at work. Rose was a teen and some people thought teens could basically raise themselves. Lily knew that was ridiculous. Teens needed time and guidance. Good kids got in trouble too when they were neglected. If Lily wanted to be the mother (she promised Horace, Rose and Rose's biological mother) she would be, she must step up more and give Rose more time. Horace promised no more late nights when council wasn't meeting, but he hadn't lived up to his vow yet. When she confronted him about it last night, he promised he would fix the problem this week. She'd wait and see if he'd do it.

Should she call him and let him know about Amelia? She should call Horace, but Horace felt she spent too much time dealing with Amelia and Amelia's problems.

He'd changed so much since they got married six years ago. He used to understand and admire her devotion to her family. In fact he said her devotion to her family was one of the reasons he loved her most. Lately however he seemed so cold and distant from her; like he was mad at her. When she tried to talk to him about what bothered him he apologized and brought her roses and she would let it go. She guessed all marriages went through this. It seemed the honeymoon was over for Horace and Lily. Could there be someone else? No she wouldn't imagine things an affair on his part; he didn't have the time for someone else. He barely had time for Lily and Rose.

Marriage was work people said, so a little work was in order. They would be happy again. What they needed was a family vacation? First just a couple of days for just Lily and Horace followed by a family vacation? Why not? Summer was here and she was owed time off... but what about Amelia? Who would look after her?

Grandma Katha would! Yes, a good plan and they would all be happy again. She hoped Rose didn't find out at school what had happened, for she wouldn't get home until late. She must make up for the time she took to go to Amelia's grand opening; that didn't happen. She should talk to Horace about taking time off and tell him about what happened before he heard it from someone else.

Lily dialed Horace's cell phone. There was no answer, only his voice mail. Damn. Why didn't he answer his phone? Lily then called his private line in his mayoral office.

"Mayor Brooksfield's, private line. How may I help you?" Horace's secretary Amber Tate answered.

Something about Horace's administrative assistant rubbed Lily the wrong way, but Lily always found herself being polite. Amber constantly forgot to give Horace messages from Lily. This angered Lily. When Lily complained to Horace, he said the woman was a little ditzy and couldn't help it. Horace explained Amber needed the job, as she supported her widowed mother, so Lily tried hard to give her a little more slack. It was so hard to accept why Horace kept her as a secretary when she didn't do her job well.

"Hello, Amber. It's Lily, Horace's wife. Can I speak with Horace?"

"No, I'm sorry Ms. Brooksfield, you can't speak with him-I mean Ms. Kelly. Sorry, I forgot again what you wanted me to call you." Amber replied in her usual scatterbrained manner.

"It's just Lily, remember Amber," prompted Lily politely but hiding her frustration with Amber.

Sometimes it seemed to Lily all an act, but what would be the point of Amber faking that she wasn't intelligent?

"Oh yes, sorry, I forgot. Now, your question?" Amber absently asked.

"Is Horace there? I'd like to speak to him." Lily repeated herself, chill seeping into her voice.

"No sorry. He's gone for the day. He won't be back until later and he has tons of work to do. He told me I have to stay late and type notes from the council meeting last night," Amber whined.

Lily wanted to explain to Amber that gone for the day and coming back later weren't the same thing, but that would mean she'd be on the phone forever with Amber, so she shelved the impulse.

"I had a date too and I cancelled," Amber woefully continued complaining.

"Oh, okay, thanks for the information, Amber. Bye," Lily replied cutting off the call before she lost her temper.

What!!Did the woman think her job only took place between nine and five? Lily hadn't wanted to hear Amber's carping. The last time Amber had been bemoaning her life and job Lily was on the phone with her for a half an hour. Never again, that was one half hour; Lily would never ever get back. Lily reluctantly left the hospital.

She was still worried about Amelia. She couldn't leave her here at the hospital unprotected. What if the killer had been gunning for Amelia? But who was she to call?

Then she remembered Frank Hawk. Frank owned a security firm. Since Lily had been instrumental in putting a woman stalker who wouldn't leave him alone behind bars; they had become good friends. Frank tried everything to keep this woman from stalking him, short of taking the law in his own hands.

His stalker had been inventive and always had a reason for being nearby. Lily had been able to prove not only the stalking but Carla Carmelo's plan to kill Frank's wife Georgiana. Now his stalker Cara Carmelo served ten years for stalking and planning to commit murder. Frank was so grateful; he said if she ever needed a favour call him. This counted as a favour and Lily needed someone right away. Surely Frank would help Lily. She would happily pay a salary to whomever he sent.

"Hello, Frank? This is Lily Kelly. I have a job for your firm. Have you heard about what happened this morning? Yes... the murder at my cousin's store? Great... uh huh, that's right; I do need someone to guard her. You are a lifesaver, Frank. That would be wonderful. He'll be guarding a room at the hospital, and of course Amelia. Okay thanks, Frank, I owe you one," Lily confirmed before she hung up her phone and breathed a sigh of relief.

A half an hour later while waiting outside Amelia's room, Lily was approached by a man with shaggy red hair, tied up in a ponytail. His arms bulged with muscles and he looked like someone she would have pegged as a biker. With his tattoos and long hair, she was sure he belonged to one of the numerous biker clubs. Could this man be the murderer? Could she be judgemental and showing prejudice? No, she felt she was being fair; the man appeared scary looking like a biker.

"Hello, I'm Zachary Buchanan, the man Frank sent to guard your friend," the man explained.

Lily was astonished; she believed he was a thug. She shouldn't have judged him so harshly she thought. She stared at his muscular frame, his arms bulging from his tee-shirt. He appeared big, to the point of covering the entire door while standing in it. It was a good thing he was a bodyguard and not the murderer. This man looked and felt dangerous. Frank had come through in spades. This man would keep Amelia safe. Lily would relax and get her work finished, and she could go home to Rose. Maybe she could even have a late dinner with Rose. That would be time well spent. Family dinners had been falling by the wayside too. Rose shouldn't be so neglected, but no more of the neglect she thought. Well no more after tonight.

"I'll keep her safe. Don't you worry," Zach replied in a low gravelly voice, as if reading Lily's thoughts.

"I'll leave her to your capable hands than." Lily replied greatly relieved, with one last look at a sleeping Amelia.

~0~

Chapter 3 -
Keep the Home
Fires Burning

Lily drove home with her mind wandering; she thought about Rose. She had talked to Rose earlier to make sure she'd arrived home from school, but she still wanted to see her after such a horrific day. Lily felt guilty about not going straight home and going back to the office earlier, but Horace would be home with Rose.

The vacation she was about to surprise them with would make it up to them. When she had them both in the same room, she would present them with the vacation plans. She'd been able to rent a cottage from someone at work, who wasn't using it for the month of July. The cottage was on the beach up north, near Parry Sound, at some place called Osler's Lake. Lily had seen pictures and it sounded like an idyllic place to spend a month. They would be able to go swimming, canoeing and traipsing about enjoying nature. It would be wonderful to share family time with just the three of them. She hoped they would agree to go.

What had she been thinking? Of course they would agree to go; they would be happy to have time together. If Rose wouldn't go, they could always take Carol to keep her company. Carol was Rose's best friend and constant companion. Lily would convince Carol's parents to agree. Lily parked the car in the garage and entered the house smiling, thinking about the vacation.

Rose, her teenage daughter, fourteen years old, lounged in her pajamas in the living room. She had a bag of chips in her hand, a pop in the other hand, as she waited for her mother. Rose turned, spotted Lily, and ran to her. She pulled back as if she didn't want to appear babyish. Rose's long blonde hair streamed down her back as her brown eyes glittered with unshed tears of worry.

"So, Aunt Amelia, she's okay? Like that was scary." Rose asked flippantly, as if she didn't care, showing her true emotional state.

"She'll be fine, a little care..."

Rose interrupted raising her chin a little, "Aunt Amelia's had too much stuff happen to her. I thought she'd die when Sammy and Jack died. She didn't eat, she didn't sleep. She looked like a zombie. You're sure she's going to be okay?"

"I know you are worried, sweetie, but you must not be concerned. Aunt Amelia will be fine. She's going to be able to handle this. She's been through a lot of therapy to learn coping techniques. She will be okay. She has a bump on her head and she broke her leg, so they want to keep her for a while, but she's going to be okay," Lily replied, as much to assure her stepdaughter as she did herself.

"You're sure?" asked Rose.

Lily nodded her head and Rose continued pretending she didn't care.

"Well at least we won't have to take care of her." Rose then showed her true emotional state looking scared and confused as she continued, "Wait a minute, if someone killed Megan, what if they come after Aunt Amelia?"

"How did you know it was Megan?" asked Lily surprised.

"The news reported the victim; a college student worked at the shop. Aunt Amelia only has one college student working at her shop. It isn't the fifties where you hear everything, what two weeks later, Mom?" Rose snapped rolling her eyes, "I must have had fifty texts, from all my friends. My Spacebook and Chatter accounts overflowed; even strangers talked to me. "They all think I should be able to tell them something. I should unfriend all of them. Except now I'm popular. I think one hundred more people following me on Chatter."

"The news does get out there faster via Chatter and Spacebook. I hope you are not mad at your true friends, and you use caution talking to strangers on Chatter," warned Lily.

"Like duh! I don't talk to people I haven't met in person. Carol was the only one who didn't bug me. She came over for a while. I hope that was okay?"

"Of course I don't mind Carol came to our house. Carol is a good friend to you."

"So do you think someone was after Aunt Amelia?"

"Don't you worry; I hired someone to look after Amelia. No one will harm her," reassured Lily.

"Who did you get and from where? I hope you didn't just pick one from any place. Not all those security places are legitimate." "Who is the parent here?"

"I do grasp some things. Good grief! What am I four years old? Georgia Prentice's father hired this one firm and his place was still robbed," Rose announced as a matter of fact.

"Who is Georgia Prentice?" Lily enquired.

"She's this girl in my English class. Her dad, like has this business downtown, Prentice Pampered Pets. They sell pet foods. I'm surprised you didn't read about this. It was a big crime spree. Anyway, they hired this security firm her dad found on the internet or something and next thing you know they are robbed. They complained to the security place and they demanded money from them. Georgia's dad complained to the cops and their place went up in fire."

"Oh I remember this one Barbara Franks handled it last year. The security guard at the firm shook them down for money. We convicted him of arson and robbery, "Lily interrupted.

"So I hope you thought about who you hired," Rose announced, in all seriousness trying to sound adult.

"This firm is good; don't you worry. I hired the guard from Frank Hawk Security. They are one of the top security firms in the city, with a stellar reputation. The guard's name is Zachary Buchanan and he is muscular, so he can hold his own. He looks rough, but he's one of the good guys," Lily explained.

"Good because I think someone is out to get her. I don't understand why anyone would hurt her. Because you know, Aunt Amelia is so sweet and she wouldn't hurt a fly. Maybe she was too polite to someone?"

"She's kind and people tend to take advantage of her, but neither of us has to worry she'll be safe now. Was that your dinner? Pop and chips aren't a meal. Didn't your dad make anything or at least order some food? He knew I would be late tonight. He promised he would be here for you. He is here, isn't he?" Lily asked dreading the answer.

"No he didn't come home." answered Rose, "When I was little, before my mother went to a jail, he didn't come home early either. I'm getting used to having my evenings alone."

"Damn him!" Lily angrily replied, under her breath. Worried Rose had overheard her she continued, "I'm sorry sweetie. Your Dad has been trying hard to get home earlier and I should have come home sooner too."

"He does try, Mom. It's his stupid job," Rose defended.

"It's not a stupid job, it just demands too much of his time, and he promised to rectify the problem. It's odd though, he told me he'd be home by six, it's nearly eleven now. Where is he? If you had called me I would have been home sooner," chided Lily.

"I had some cereal. No biggie."

"It is a biggie! I'm sorry I wasn't there. You are always the first priority with me and don't let me forget. Now I'm hungry; do you want to share a pizza?" asked Lily hugging Rose.

"I could eat something." Rose admitted.

"Is pizza okay?" Lily asked picking up her cell phone "Do you want a cheese pizza?"

"Yes, cheese pizza sounds good."

As they waited for the pizza they each thought about Amelia and how much she meant to them.

"I must find someone to work at Amelia's store. Do you think any of your friends would like to work there part time?" asked Lily.

"You've got to be kidding Mom! Someone was murdered there. I don't think anyone would."

"I guess I'll head over to the employee agency. First thing tomorrow morning I'll put in an ad."

"How much would you pay per hour? I mean Carol and I could use the dough, and you would understand we were safe. Right?" asked Rose. "Carol and I found a cute bikini. The bikini fit me like it was made for me, but it costs mega bucks."

"I don't think I want you and Carol working there."

"Mom, please!"

"Well, I did think of hiring a guard for evenings to protect employees, so I guess that might work. Be sure to tell Carol the job will be alternate evenings, until nine p.m. I don't want you to get behind on your homework though, and I'll be happy to pick you up or Carol as well," replied Lily realizing she sounded overprotective.

"Gee thanks, Mom. I'll ask Carol."

Rose rushed off to call Carol, coming back a few seconds later and declared, "Carol says okay, as long as I can hang out with her sometimes as well. In fact, would you pay us to work the same shift?"

"If I did how much work would you get done? You two forget about other people, when you are together. Would you still pay attention to the customers?"

"What a stupid question. It's a job and I think if you think I'm mature enough to work there, then I'm mature enough to do the job," Rose protested.

"Sorry Rose you're right, sometimes I forget you're nearly an adult."

"Well try to remember, I'm fifteen, not five!" Rose exclaimed outraged.

"Now I must contact an employee agency in the morning. I need to find someone trustworthy to run the store until Amelia is able to come back. I still have to prepare my briefs, to prosecute the Teflon man as well. Ugh, I can't let this man get away with his crime again. I'm prepared. It will work this time, Andrew Clayton will get at the least twenty years to life," Lily explained absent-mindedly as she goes over her notes.

"Who are you after now, Mom?" Rose ventured to ask not catching the man's name. "You know I don't like to discuss my cases."

"Well excuse me for asking!" Rose muttered under her breath, and Lily ignored her as the doorbell rang.

The pizza driver arrived at the door and Lily paid him taking the pizza in. Lily glanced over at the clock noting it is now 11:30 p.m., "Dinner eaten near midnight? It was a wonder she didn't get indigestion," she thought.

Each ate their pizza, savouring each bite, both of them thinking their own thoughts, in their own little worlds. The second pizza, a pepperoni pizza was put aside and saved in the fridge for Horace.

"I have to call your dad and find out what kept him. He should have been home a long time ago," Lily repeated, becoming extremely worried.

"He probably fell asleep at his office. I told you, his job keeps him too busy," Rose complained.

"I'm sorry. I'm going to try to get him to do a little less of worrying about his job and more of spending time with us, like he promised. Would you be okay if I left you and went and check on him?"

"Mom, I'm not a little girl anymore. I'll set the alarm after you leave and then I'm going to bed. I can see Dad tomorrow. I've got choir and basketball before class tomorrow."

"Okay, sorry. Sometimes it's hard to remember you're not my little girl anymore," Lily commented.

"Try, okay? I'm growing up; I'm not a little girl anymore. You have to remember that and you don't need to keep saying it," chided Rose.

"I'm leaving the house. Lock the door and set the alarm."

"Mom!" admonished Rose, thoroughly outraged.

"Sorry."

"Okay, bye Mom," Rose replied as she watched Lily leave.

Rose went to set the alarm on the front door and the windows heading up the stairs to bed.

~0~

L ily drove quickly to city hall. She parked the car in

underground parking and took the elevator to the first floor. Lily remembered suddenly that she had forgotten to call Grandma Katha about Amelia. She would call Grandma Katha tomorrow. Grandma Katha would be a little annoyed, but she'd understand.

She rode the elevator to the first floor. She then exited and walked towards the elevator that would take her to Horace's office. In the hallway, Lily saw a security guard sitting at the front desk. He wore a blue uniform with yellow tassels on his shoulders. A badge is pinned to his chest. He was about fifty-five years old, or maybe sixty. His hair was white and his eyes blue and twinkly when he smiled and it was obvious from his wrinkles that he did it frequently.

"Hello, Mrs. Brooksfield. I believe the mayor is in his office. Working late tonight; isn't he?" commented the security guard.

"Yes, he works too many hours. Your name is Barney? Isn't it?"

"You remembered?" Barney replied surprised.

"You tell Mr. Brooksfield I said he should spend more time with his charming wife, before someone else snaps her up and takes her home."

"Okay, I will," Lily answered.

Lily laughed and waved goodbye to the guard. She got into the private elevator which went to Horace's office. As she pushed the buttons, Lily thought of how wonderful it will be to be with Horace. She blushed when she thought of what they did the last time she was in his office behind locked doors. Thank goodness for the lock on his door!

The elevator stopped and opened into the foyers leading into Horace's mayoral office. Lily turned the doorknob to Horace's office slowly opening the door. She was horrified to find a naked Horace on top of his also naked secretary Amber, directly behind his desk.

"Horace, how could you?" Lily shouted, with no corresponding answer. Lily stared at the pair confused.

Were they so into each other, they didn't realize she was there? How long had this affair been going on with Amber? Lily wondered, tearing her gaze away from their naked forms.

Puzzled she thought why didn't they bother to lock the door? Or respond, when someone talked to them?

Lily realized neither moved. Lily skirted the desk and felt Horace's wrist.

His wrist was cold and there was no pulse. She realized, with great shock, Horace was dead and so was his secretary, Amber. The whole world tilted on its axis for a moment.

She was cold to the marrow of her bones; her feet remained frozen to the floor. What sent all this into play? First Megan murdered this morning, now Horace and his secretary. Truly horrifying, this all seemed unreal. She half expected Horace to jump up and yell "I'm joking!" But as she gazed back on the scene, she saw it was all too real. Horace and his secretary had both been posed naked, as if committing the act of copulation.

Examining the bodies, clinically putting aside her horror and disbelief, Lily noted they sported identical bruises on their skulls. Looking intensely at their heads, it occurred to her this was the death-blow. This mark was in the shape of the top of the nearby lamp. She thought about it for a moment and grasped that they had been posed this way.

Horace would never cheat on me with Amber. How could I have though this for even one moment? Lily looking closer at Horace's wound there was matted blood. Did this mean a lot of time passed since they were killed?

She had seen other autopsy photos in her job; they had shown wounds such as these and they had been killed several hours prior. But how long ago were Horace and Amber killed?

She tried to put the sight out of her mind. She looked at Horace dead, but bile threatened at any moment. She swallowed, took a big breath, felt faint and yet cold at the same time. She needed to do something now. What did she need to do? Oh yes, she needed to call the police she reasoned.

Lily picked up her cell phone, gagged back the sourness coming up from her stomach and called 911.

"Nine one, one, what is the nature of your emergency?" enquired the dispatcher.

"My husband and his secretary have been murdered," Lily answered her voice shaking, and barely audible.

"Repeat yourself, Ma'am!" The police dispatcher demanded.

"I am at City Hall. I am in the Mayor's office. My husband, Mayor Horace Brooksfield has been murdered, along with his secretary, Amber Tate," Lily replied enunciating each word.

Lily felt slightly angry at this dispatcher who didn't seem to grasp the horror of this all.

"Did I hear you correctly, Ma'am? The mayor has been murdered at City Hall?" asked the police dispatcher, gasping and losing her composure for a few minutes.

"That is what I said," Lily answered angrily.

Lily then wondered what kind of police dispatcher gasped at hearing someone's been murdered. The woman sounded like she lost her calm, what did this bode for Lily? A lot of help she would be someone who didn't even understand her job.

"Are you still in the office?" The police dispatcher asked.

"Yes," Lily replied, quietly thankful the woman sounded like she had gotten back her composure.

"Is there any way the perpetrator might still be on scene?" asked the police dispatcher, as if following a script.

Lily remembered the wound and the matted hair with blood on each victim. It was so awful, but didn't mean they were probably long gone. Lily looked around scanning the room, but comprehended with heart palpitating fear that the killer could still be there. She didn't think the killer would be able to hide in this office. She could see all the spaces and no one was hiding. Lily comforted herself. She was safe. If you killed someone wouldn't you want to be gone so you weren't caught?

"I'll check to find out whether they hid in the inner room of Horace's office," Lily volunteered and regretted the impulse.

"Where is this inner room?" asked the police dispatcher.

"There is a small sort of vestibule off Horace's office so he can...er...might leave privately. It leads to his private elevator, only he has um... had a key to fit the lock," Lily explained.

Lily trembled and she felt a tear escaping her eye.

"Have you touched anything?" enquired the police dispatcher.

"I don't know. I simply don't know," Lily replied getting a little frazzled.

"Take a big breath and think. You came in the office and did what?" asked the police dispatcher.

"Ah... The door was slightly ajar. I touched the doorknob and turned it throwing the door open wider. I then walked across the floor to check on them. I touched each of their necks, checking for a pulse," Lily remembered.

"Was there a pulse? Should I be sending an ambulance?" the dispatcher demanded.

"No, there is no pulse, it's definitely too late. I can't believe any of this has happened...Why would someone do this?"

"I don't know, Ma'am. We will find the perpetrator. Do you have anything else our officers can use?"

"I don't know. I think they've been dead for a while. What should I do?" Lily demanded choking back more tears.

"What I would like you to do is to leave the office and wait directly outside if it's safe to do so. Please wait there for the investigating officer," commanded the police dispatcher, "And stay on the line."

"Okay I'll do that, but hurry, please." Lily answered, shutting her phone without thinking.

Lily shivered uncontrollably. Finishing her report to the police allowed her to think now of the finality of it all. Horace was dead. Her husband of six years was dead. It was like the icy finger of death reached out and touched her too. She felt cold, like she would never be warm again.

Lily then remembered what the police dispatcher asked of her and backed out of Horace's office trying to pull herself together. Lily did not want to disrupt any of the crime scene. She also knew she had to get away from the horrible sight of the man she loved dead. If she didn't she would never be able to answer the questions the police detective would invariably ask. Her mind began racing.

Why had Horace been posed in such a defiling way? Could this be a warning to her? Was this a way to discredit Horace and make him appear as an adulterer in his final moments? Poor Horace; he was such a wonderful man... Okay, so he wasn't perfect, but Lily loved him. How could this have happened? During the day the place was filled with security.

Lily had no idea how many security officers were assigned at night, but Barney seemed diligent. Was the only security at night Barney? Why hadn't Barney heard anything? Barney made everyone sign in at night, so how did they get in past Barney's eagle eye? Who perpetrated these crimes? First Amelia's clerk was murdered, now Horace and his secretary, Amber. This seemed personal, like someone was targeting Lily's family. Could it have been someone she prosecuted who had committed these murders?

Lily looked back through the door at Horace and Amber's bodies in totally disbelief. Horace couldn't possibly be dead. This had to be all a horrible dream. Lily pinched herself and realized with trepidation, this was no dream. Horace was dead, posed obnoxiously draped on his secretary. It was too awful to look at. If she closed her eyes this would disappear, or maybe if she shut the door? No, she would be tampering with evidence. She wouldn't do that, as much as she wanted to close the entrance.

Oh no, the press! If the press took this sight in...No, she wouldn't let whoever had done this defile his good name too, as well as taking his life.

Why wouldn't her brain work? What did she have to do? Oh yes! She had to somehow get a media blackout on this. Should she make a call to Judge Parker? No, that would have to wait until she talked to the investigating officer.

She couldn't believe the thoughts she had, she should be falling apart; her husband was dead...Murdered...with his secretary.

What was wrong with her? She needed to protect Rose. Oh no, what would she tell Rose? Rose who already lost her biological mother? How could she bear to tell Rose, her father was dead? Her mind sped from thought to thought, like a freight train going seventy-five miles an hour. She didn't want to think about what lay beyond the open door. Maybe she should call the police dispatcher back? They asked her to stay on the line and she accidentally hung up the phone. Lily heard a voice interrupting her thoughts and jumped a couple of inches.

"Ms. Kelly-Brooksfield, we meet again," Sergeant Detective Rogers announced, entering the foyer and spotting Lily in the office.

He noted she only seemed to be held up by the wall.

"Sergeant Detective Rogers. Why have Megan, Horace and Amber been murdered? Is there a serial killer on the loose?" Lily demanded.

Lily then covered her eyes trying to block out the scene in front of her.

"Hmm, you're on the sight of both my murder scenes. Do you have an alibi, Ms. Kelly-Brooksfield?" Sergeant Detective Rogers challenged from the door.

"I'm a suspect?" gasped Lily, while holding herself up against the wall. She felt nauseated, shaken and nervous. Lily breathed in a huge breath and realized how bad this all looked for her, but she knew she had not committed this crime.

"Well it looks you're husband, Mayor Brooksfield, stepped out on you. You picked up something and bashed their heads in and then admired your handy work," Sergeant Detective Rogers insisted trying to provoke her.

Lily held her hand over her mouth, as if to stall throwing up her supper.

"Don't you dare hurl on my crime scene!" Detective Rogers exclaimed, "In fact I think you should come out into the hall until the crime techs arrive."

Lily couldn't seem to take in what Detective Rogers said. None of what he articulated seemed to make sense. Shivering, Lily felt like she would throw up again. Lily then took a deep breath to keep from spewing and started to think about Horace. She wouldn't believe the husband she'd loved and had been married to for six years lay dead…brutally murdered. She couldn't get the picture out of her head, despite her closed eyes. Horace's glassy eyes wide open in object terror and the same subsequent look in Amber's eyes, were ingrained in her brain.

With Horace's hair bloodied and brain matter coming out, it seemed obvious to her, someone had bashed him hard on the head. That had to be just as clear to Detective Rogers. Yet Detective Rogers kept looking at her as if she had done this horrible deed. Why did he think she had done this?

Amber and Horace had been naked. Why? Why would someone pose them that way? When you examined them you could tell they died from head wounds, so why set them up that way? Why did they the need to stage their bodies? For my benefit, or to discredit Horace and embarrass him even in death? Lily wondered as she looked at Detective Rogers through her long hair, now hanging down in front of her eyes. And why did the annoying Detective Rogers, keep fidgeting so? Why did he hop from foot to foot? Did he think that would intimidate her, or was he nervous?

"So we get this straight, what did you do tonight after all the questioning?" Sergeant Detective Rogers demanded.

"Let see...after giving my statement to you, visiting my best friend in the hospital and arranging a guard to protect her because the police wouldn't...I went home to my daughter!" Lily replied sarcastically.

"At what time did you leave the hospital and what time did you arrive home?" Sergeant Detective Rogers asked pulling out his notebook.

"I don't know. It must have been about what ten or ten-thirty p.m.? My daughter and I ordered pizza from Pizza Pie. The pizza arrived about eleven-thirty p.m. and I left about midnight to come here. I arrived here about twelve-thirty p.m. Check with the guard Barney something. He can tell you."

"The statement from the guard, one Barney Terrell says you arrived here about twelve thirty P.M. Is that when you took the elevator up and bashed their heads in and then decided to pose them?" Sergeant Detective Rogers provoked.

"How dare you? Someone killed my best friend's employee today. Megan Fowler, a girl in the prime of her life with her future spread out in front of her, found cruelly murdered. Then I found my husband and his secretary, Amber, also brutally murdered...and you treat all of this like a huge joke?" Lily ranted angrily gulping back tears and wondering why she found it hard to breathe.

"Horace was the love of my life. I feel like I've been ripped in two. Do you want to know about Amber? Amber supported her mother. How many young people support their parent? I have known her for years. Why aren't you doing your job and finding the person who did this? Why do you stand there looking at me like I did this dreadful thing?"

"I keep looking into this, and two and two, equal the wife killed him," Detective Rogers explained. "You should have studied math a little harder. I think we are done here, Detective Rogers. I'm not speaking to you anymore without my lawyer."

Lily thought Sergeant Detective Rogers was an idiot. Why didn't he see Horace and Amber had been murdered by a person unknown? Why did he keep looking at her? Yes, the first person the police always looked at was the spouse, but it should be obvious Lily hadn't killed them. Yes, someone staged the murder scene and posed them naked but he couldn't think she had perpetrated this crime. Of course he did and he looked straight at her for this crime.

Lily suddenly realized Sergeant Detective Rogers had said something else as she reflected on all that had occurred. Now for some strange reason he started to look blurry. Lily's chest was tight, not with unshed grief, but with some sudden strain in her airways. Why can't I breathe? Lily thought with fear. She decided to tough this out, not wanting to give Detective Rogers ammunition to use falsely against her.

"Mrs. Brooksfield? Did you hear me? I asked you to come out of the office." Detective Rogers insisted looking at her strangely.

"Would you stand still? It should be obvious even to you, the great detective, that they were obviously staged… I don't feel so good," Lily muttered her hand over her mouth.

"I'm not moving." Detective Rogers insisted.

"Why are there two of you?" Lily managed to say aloud before falling unconscious to the floor.

~0~

Chapter 4 -
Media Hound

Detective Emmett Rogers looked over very surprised. Did she think faking a faint would keep him from investigating? Or did her nerves get to her? The woman seemed cool as a cucumber. If she had killed three people he would be surprised, but Emmett had been burnt before and he wasn't about to let a pretty face fool him.

Crap!

Now he had to violate protocol to check on her. He should be wearing the gear, so he didn't leave fibres. He only hoped this wouldn't screw up any evidence. He should have gotten her out of the office sooner. He checked her pulse. Yes she had a thready pulse but it was there. She didn't seem to be faking this faint. Had the stress of committing the murder got to her, or was she an innocent victim like she appeared?

"Dispatch, Sergeant Detective Rogers here. We need a bus." he said into his radio.

Emmett stared at the woman on the floor.

What the hell. Who perpetrated these murders? First this woman's cousin's employee was murdered then the mayor, Lily's husband. Were Amelia and Lily Kelly the victims, or somehow the perpetrators? Were these two women involved in these crimes? Or were they involved at all? He started to wonder why he hadn't come across Ms. Kelly. He had talked with her legal assistant, Colleen, and the assistant Crown attorney, Barbara Franks, in many cases. Now she was a piece of work. Barbara Franks. Little Miss, or should he say, 'Mrs. Butter don't melt in her mouth' Brooksfield better watch her ass. Barbara appeared to be gunning for Ms. Brooksfield's job.

This case might give Ms. Franks the opportunity for advancement. He hoped he wouldn't be responsible for that happening. He had heard good things about the job Ms. Brookfield did. She had a great reputation for working hand and glove with cops to get the perpetrator convicted.

He had been told (before being called to her friend's store) the jury had come in on the Zebadiah Rockwood case, guilty on all counts. The attorney had come through in a tough case. The slime ball, the defense attorney, Michael Taylor's reputation was for winning all his cases and people paid big bucks for him to succeed. Taylor must be spitting mad and that made Emmett Rogers smile.

This Lily Brooksfield didn't seem competent at the moment however; she had lost it this morning and now this? Of course her friend appeared seriously injured this morning...or was that now yesterday? And now her husband was dead? He should have cut her some slack, but damned if the woman didn't rub him the wrong way. She appeared incredibly beautiful, but off-limits. Not only was she married, but she stood married to the mayor. Of course she was a widow now. Emmett smiled again as he looked at Lily. What the hell was he thinking? He was on a case. She was a suspect!!!

He focused on the case again. The air appeared decidedly odd in here. The air stank like rotten eggs or something he couldn't quite peg. Maybe Lily had collapsed not from shock and his questioning, but from these fumes? Should he take the woman further out into the hall and shut the door? Why did this have to be his decision? Where in the hell were the emergency technicians?

Oh good! The EMTs had arrived, he thought as he heard the elevator ping. They would take Lily Kelly-Brooksfield to the hospital and take away this responsibility he didn't want. What could be wrong with him? He couldn't think clearly. He had to shake off the fog and start thinking with a level head. This was a big case. The mayor had been killed, and not only killed; but killed with his mistress.

What a mess; and the wife found them. Heaven knows the wife was blamed in these circumstances, so why did he have such a hard time believing Lily Brooksfield had committed the crime? Emmett watched as they took Lily Kelly-Brooksfield away. How odd, even though she still remained a suspect, he was strangely attracted to her. Something about her sassy attitude turned his insides to Jell-O. He'd had to get tougher with her, to hide the attraction he felt for her.

This wasn't right. How could he be attracted to a woman he just met, a woman who up until tonight had been married? A woman who may have killed her husband? What kind of man did that make him? Hell, if anyone knew he had this mind-set he would be a suspect. Emmett, get a hold of yourself! What could you be thinking? The woman's husband was killed violently tonight. Either the woman is a grieving widow or a ruthless killer, either way she's not for you.

Emmett looked up from his deep thoughts and saw Dr. Andrew Piper (the coroner) arrive. The tall and thin coroner had a shock of red curly hair with a streak of white right down the middle of his head. As Emmett looked closer he noticed Andrew's white hair starting to pepper throughout his hair. Why had he never detected his friend, Dr. Andrew Piper, getting older? He noted however, that Dr. Piper was jovial and smiling, even in the face of this gruesome death. Emmett wondered how his old friend could remain so cheerful.

"Say, Doc how do you stand this?" Emmett asked, "How do you stay happy faced with all these dead bodies?"

"It's either smile or cry. I give these victims their peace after such horrible acts. I help catch their killers. I must admit though seeing someone you've met is a lot harder." Doctor Andrew Piper answered, motioning to Horace Brooksfield's body.

"It never gets any easier does it?" Emmett commiserated.

"You didn't suit up, Emmett?"

"There was time to suit up and then Mrs. Brooksfield collapsed," Emmett explained.

"At least you didn't let anyone else in. We should suit up now before entering again."

Emmett quickly suited up and followed Dr. Piper.

"Say, Doc, what's that chemical odour?" Emmett asked as he entered the office again.

"Here put this mask on your face, Emmett. We need to get the bio-hazard suits in here. Come on! Hop to it! We need to get out of here. We need to leave and not come back, until we wear the proper equipment." Dr. Andrew Piper replied "Any headache, nausea, faintness, shortness of breath?"

He then handed Emmett a mask and put a piece of tape across the office door that read Bio-Hazard.

"No, just a bit of a headache, but I had one before, I even whiffed the weird smell. We've been exposed to an unknown toxin? Is the chemical the reason why Ms. Kelly-Brooksfield went to the hospital?" Emmett demanded worried.

"I think there is a toxic chemical here, Sonny. I'll know better after some laboratory tests." Dr. Piper explained "but I suspect ammonia gas, mixed with bleach. So, I would venture to guess Chlorine gas. You're lucky you appear to have no symptoms so far. In the meantime it's off to the chemical shower in the mobile unit that just arrived."

"Aw, Doc, don't tell me you're sending me to the shower. Do you know they steal your clothes and dispose of them? This is a brand new suit and those leather shoes cost me a hundred bucks," Emmett complained.

"Sorry, Emmett. We can't take chances with the toxins. I'm sure you can put a claim into the department," Dr. Piper sympathized, "If it's any consolation, I'm going to lose my clothes too."

"Have you seen the department budget? I'll be lucky to get enough money to replace my underwear. Why couldn't Brad answer this call?" Emmett complained, "This isn't my day."

"It wasn't their day either," Dr. Piper retorted, motioning towards the bodies.

"Sorry, Doc, you're right and I'm going to nail whoever did this," vowed Emmett, getting ready to leave to wait for the Hazmat truck.

Emmett and Doctor Piper went through the chemical shower and collected tee-shirts and sweatpants from a waiting colleague. Emmett left the tent to continue investigating, now dressed in a chemical suit, and ran into someone walking through the crime scene.

"Why are you here, Brad? Have you come to gloat about my loss of clothing?" Emmett asked sounding annoyed.

"I thought you might need a hand. I heard you got dosed with some strong chemicals. Those are not exactly clothes to wear in front of the media. I could handle the case for you."

"No, thanks."

"It's a real high-profile case. The mayor and his lover were murdered, and the wife finds them? It's a slam dunk case man. She killed them," Brad continued, ignoring Emmett.

"Why don't you go home, Brad, and take your media hound self with you. You barked up the wrong tree. Crown Attorney Kelly has an alibi."

"Try to do a guy a favour," Brad snarled. "Don't let a pretty face fool you, buddy boy! She knocked them off and gloated about it thinking she has you fooled."

"Get lost, Brad. I don't need your kind of favours."

"I pulled my weight as your partner," Brad complained. "I've heard what you've been saying about me. Why don't you like me? I'm a likeable person."

"I prefer being solo. You're a media hound and will always be a media hound, Brad Owens. Go take yourself away now. I didn't invite you and this is my case," Emmett announced, staking out his claim.

"As I said, try to do a guy a favour." 'Brad gripped as he left.

"Rentford, get over here," Emmett yelled over to another cop.

"What do you need, Sergeant Detective Rogers?" Constable Silas Rentford asked, all but coming to attention.

Emmett looked at his new partner with approval. He seemed to be eager; a good sign. Emmett watched Silas as he looked over the scene; Silas was quiet and methodical while he took in the entire crime scene Silas his brown hair, trimmed short to regulation style, towered over most at the scene, as his height topped out at six feet six inches. Emmett watched him and was sure this new partner would be a help to him in this case; at least he hoped so, but training new partners was never easy.

Silas had put on a protective suit and Emmett wanted to tell him the suit wouldn't be necessary. This wasn't where he needed him to investigate. Someone had to go talk to the victim's daughter, Rose Brooksfield, and inform Amber's mother, before the media got to them.

"Rentford, first I need you to start making calls and make sure I wasn't lying to Sergeant Detective Owens." Emmett commanded, "And find me a cup of coffee. This may take all night. I need you to send a cop over to inform Amber Tate's mother, one Agnes Tate, to inform her about her death. I want you to go inform the mayor's family about his demise."

"But you just told him..." Constable Rentford said hesitantly taking off the protective suit.

"I know what I told that media hound. Now find out the truth and try not to make me a liar!" Sergeant Detective Rogers barked.

"Training new partners is a pain," he muttered under his breath, but Constable Rentford heard and scurried to follow Emmett's orders.

A few minutes later he was back with a coffee he placed in Emmett's hand.

"Wow. You're good Rentford. This is exactly the way I like it, black; no sugar no cream, nothing but high octane."

"Thanks, boss. I'm off to check off the list. I'll check in later."

I can train a new partner. Emmett thought surprised. Emmett watched Rentford leave and he thought. What if this is an act Rentford seemed so subservient; maybe a little too much? He had other partners and they all ended the same way screwing up and blaming Emmett. Why couldn't they just do the job? He found himself following Rentford through the building. Emmett obtrusively watched his new partner in action as Constable Rentford passed a CSI in the hall. Silas is stopped by her as she touched his sleeve.

"Hey, Silas. Is Emmett Rogers, your new partner?" The C.S.I. technician asked, through the mask.

Emmett noted the crime scene investigator was dressed in space like gear as he hid from their view. He watched as she took head-gear off, revealing red-gold hair, pulled back in a ponytail. Her green eyes glittered with warmth and lust as she stared at Silas, her tongue sliding over her lip. Well what do we have here? Emmett wondered as he watched her. Silas has away with the ladies?

"Brandy?" Silas asked as he smiled with approval.

"Yes, it's me. So Emmett Rogers, is your new partner?"

"Yes, he is and his solve rate amazes me. Although I hear his people skills leave a bit to be desired." Silas answered "I've already seen him in action. He's quite good."

Well, what an incredible compliment. This guy might make a good partner after all. He was on the right track. Emmett thought, as he tried to mold himself into the shadows.

"Yes, well, he's gone through hell the last year. His wife, Jenna died from breast cancer. She was his college sweetheart. I feel sorry for the guy; it would be horrible to lose the love of your life." Brandy replied. "I'd make a play for him, but the guy still drowns in grief. And don't get me started on his former partner, Sergeant Detective Brad Owens. The guy is bad news. "The media is his bitch and he'll feed you to it if he thought it would get him press."

Emmett hated to be talked about in gossip. Where had this Brandy got information on him? How did she know so much about Jenna? Emmett kept to himself enough. He didn't want people to know anything about him. It was probably Brad. Why had he ever trusted his former partner? Brad was a partner but a leech who wanted all the credit for himself.

Damn, Emmett preferred to keep his information private. Last year watching Jenna die, had been the worst experience of his life, despite the impending divorce he had loved her still. Jenna had been ready to leave him, but when her lover (another cop) found out she was ill and dying, he'd dumped her.

He only hoped the gossips didn't know he had filed for divorce before that, or that she had been having an affair. He was glad Cameron Grenor had left the Happy Valley, Ontario police. Last he had heard was that Cameron had a job as a police officer, in London, Ontario. Brad would have a field day with the gossip that Cameron was Jenna's lover and he, Emmett, had been filing for divorce. Thankfully Brad hadn't known about the divorce, or that would be fodder for the grist mill too. Well good the kid liked him. He hoped he still did after his discussion with Brandy. Emmett thought.

"Brad's a bad cop?" Silas asked. "I thought he seemed okay."

"Oh, yes, Sergeant Detective Rogers pulled in all his chits to get a new partner again instead of being paired up with Brad again. You're his fifth co-worker since last year and his last for a while. His boss is fed up and declared he'll have to go solo if you don't work out as his cohort. Or maybe be assigned desk work."

"Wow, Brandy, you always know the skinny on everyone," Silas stated surprised "That doesn't sound good for me. I better get my ass in gear and get the job done. I wouldn't want to get tossed as his partner the first day."

"I guess I've heard enough." Emmett thought leaving. The kid will do his job he's even a little afraid of me and maybe that's a good thing if it gets him motivated.

~0~

Chapter 5 - Crafty Old Ladies and Mouthy Children

Silas Rentford

Silas Rentford slipped into his patrol car. He took out his

cell phone and called dispatch for information for the Kelly-Brooksfield residence. Getting the number he dialled.

"Hello?" answered a sleepy Rose, coming awake at the sound of the phone ringing.

"Is this the Kelly-Brooksfield residence?" demanded Silas.

"Yes it is," replied Rose scared, wondering who could be calling so late.

"This is Constable Silas Rentford. I would like to come by your residence in a few minutes. There has been an incident. We'd like to come over and discuss this with you," Silas explained.

"I'm fifteen years old. I don't let anyone in the house after midnight. If you'd like to discuss something talk to my mom and dad. They are at the Mayor's office downtown."

As the thought that something may have happened to her parents crossed her mind, she queried "Oh no, has something happened? Are my Mom and Dad okay? They are Lily and Horace Brooksfield."

"Is there someone with you, Ms. Brooksfield?" Silas asked.

"No but it doesn't mean you can dance around my questions. I want answers to them now," Rose insisted sounding like Lily.

"I don't want to get into this on the phone. I would like to come and speak to you," Silas maintained.

"You're not going to tell me anything except in person, are you?" Rose asserted adding, "Okay fine, go get my Great-Grandma Katha O'Malley and bring her here. She lives three doors down at nine hundred and sixty-eight. I'll talk to you and not before I see my Granny. Bye now."

Silas perceived a click, as Rose hung up the phone.

"Cheeky little brat! She didn't even give me her address. I guess I can reverse directory the address from her phone number. Poor kid! I'll have to tell her about her mom and dad and that will hurt," Silas muttered aloud, while dialling Katha O'Malley.

"Hello? Who is this? Who calls at two o'clock in the morning? This is not a civilized time to call," the old and cranky voice answered. "It's Constable Silas Rentford, ma'am. Am I speaking to Katha O'Malley?"

"What would a constable, want with me?" asked Katha half asleep. "Are you the police?"

"Yes Ma'am. I am a police officer; there's been an incident at the Mayor's office." Silas began.

"Has that ass, Horace been caught with his pants down and under a bed?" Katha barked.

"Ma'am!" Silas replied with censor.

"Ha! He has hasn't he? Poor dear Lily, she has no idea what her man is capable of. What has the heel done now? Wait a minute. Is my adopted granddaughter Rosey okay?" Katha asked.

"Ma'am, how did you obtain information on a crime that happened this evening?" Silas demanded surprised.

"Aware of what? I'm only going by your conversation young man. Lily is so in love with him, she can't see the forest for the flowers." Katha explained, "He would wink and flirt with other women.

Schmoozing he called it, but Lily didn't see the touching he did and I didn't tell her. Why didn't I tell her?"

"Explain your response to me. He assaulted women?" Silas asked excited.

"No, the ones he would touch liked it." Katha explained, "He seemed to touch ones that would smile at him afterwards. I wouldn't be at all surprised if he cheated on my Lily."

"That's impossible Ma'am. Horace Brooksfield is dead. He has been murdered."

"Someone plugged him?" Katha asked proud of herself for using what she thought was police lingo.

"No, someone hit him over the head and poisoned him," Silas replied and realized he shouldn't have said the method of death before checking out her alibi. "Aw hell!"

"Young man, you watch your language. You will not speak to me in such a manner," Katha snapped imperiously.

"Sorry Ma'am," Silas apologized, and then thought Who does she think she is? The bloody Queen?

"I'm at your front door. Could I come in please, Ma'am?" he begged.

"You wait right there, young man, while I throw on some clothes. I'm not coming to the entrance in my nightie. Keep your badge handy; I'm not opening up my door without it."

"Yes Ma'am." Silas agreed "I'll wait badge in hand."

"Well since you are so polite, I'll answer the door. This might take a moment. I have to make myself decent. It is the middle of the night after all."

Katha dressed quickly and came to the door in a lilac purple pant suit. Silas was amazed by the woman who answered the door. He had imagined a cantankerous old Biddy wizened and older than Medusa, but he found an older woman, her hair gleaming white perfectly coiffed, with brilliant sapphire blue eyes. Pearls adorned her neck. The woman could have walked out of the society pages he thought, as Katha smiled regally.

"Constable Silas Rentford I presume." She checked his identification and then waved him in the house.

"Yes, Ma'am." Silas replied. "We should go to your granddaughter's home so I don't have to explain this twice."

"Lead on my good man," Katha replied.

Katha and Silas walked two doors down to a house shrouded in darkness. Silas knocked at the door with several loud wraps. Rose peered through the peephole. Seeing her Grandma Katha she opened the door.

"Grandma Katha, I think something terrible has happened. If this is Constable Rentford, he won't tell me on the phone what it is. Is that fair, just because I'm fourteen?" Rose complained loudly.

"Rosey, he's here now to tell you."

"But he won't! He's treating me like a child," Rose claimed stamping her foot angrily.

"Rosey, my posey, what have I been trying to teach you?" Katha prodded gently.

"A lady invites guests in, sits down gracefully and gently prods for information," Rose parroted what she was told.

"Good, dear, but remember next time don't repeat the information in front of the quarry," Katha corrected.

"I'll get it right next time, Grandma Katha," Rose replied smiling.

"Hopefully there will never be a next time," Katha admonished.

"Sorry, Grandma Katha."

Silas smiled at the banter between the two. They so obviously cared about one another. He thought that must be wonderful, to have someone care for you so much.

"Ladies, if you please, can we be seated?"

"Certainly, come this way, Constable Rentford? Please," Rose asked regally, assuming lady like manners.

Silas suddenly wondered what he had gotten into with these women. The older woman, Katha O'Malley, appeared charismatic and charming, but was also crafty. She had instructed her granddaughter to pump him for information, like he would soon be the interviewee not the interviewer. He had to take charge and take back the interview. Silas waited for Rose to be seated with her grandmother and then said, "There's no easy way to say this. I'm sorry to tell you your father, Horace Brooksfield, has been murdered this evening."

He watched as the child shrank pulling her legs up to her chin visibly shrinking in age. Katha held out her arms but Rose straightened herself up and exclaimed, "No, you are mistaken. He's the Mayor. He can't be dead."

"I'm sorry Miss Brooksfield, there is no mistake. He is dead."

"And my Lily? Is she okay?" asked Katha, trying to hide a tremble in her voice.

"Is my mom, okay?" Rose also asked shaking.

"Oh, I understood she was your stepmother," Silas replied, checking his notes.

"She is my mom. She adopted me. She's okay isn't she?" asked Rose again.

"You're an idiot! This child has just lost her father and you're quibbling about whether it's her stepmother or mother?" Katha O'Malley blurted.

"Ms. Brooksfield appears to have been exposed in the office to a chemical which killed your father and his secretary, but she is under medical care at the hospital," Silas explained.

"You are a horrible man. What a way to tell a child her mother has been harmed. You, young man, should have told me immediately that Lily was harmed," Katha snapped. "Come Rose we should go to the hospital and be with your mother." she continued.

"I need to corroborate Lily Kelly Brooksfield's alibi first," Silas insisted.

"You overstep your bounds, young man. I'll have your badge." Katha asserted.

"You suspect my mom? You're crazy! She would never harm hair on my father's head!" Rose sputtered angrily "How dare you! Do you know she's the Crown Attorney?"

"I am well aware of Crown Attorney Kelly and her position, but I need to look into everyone's alibi. So where do you think Crown Attorney Kelly could be found between ten p.m. and midnight?" Silas asked Rose.

"We were together. We talked and waited for pizza, which arrived at about eleven-thirty. We ate it. What more do you need to know? I'm sure Pizza Pie would vouch for when they delivered." Rose answered.

"And before you ask me, Constable Rentford, I had a gentleman caller," 'Katha replied.

"Grandma Katha," Rose rebuked surprised.

"Who is it someone I know? I can't believe you did the nasty."

"Rose my love life is none of your business, please do not discuss this." Katha addressed Rose then turning to Silas she said, "Now look what you've done. You've made me shock my granddaughter."

"Well, don't you both be looking so surprised. I may be eighty or so but I'm not dead yet." she replied smirking "Would you like his name? It's Terrence Stewart, as in father of Chief Edward Stewart."

Silas blanched and then excused himself for a moment radioing the statements to Detective Emmett Rogers before stepping back into the room.

"I think I have enough information. I can speak to the chief's father later. Please, don't speak with him first ladies. Thank you both for your statements. I'm sorry for your loss." Silas said solemnly.

Silas worried he had been mean to a little old lady (one who had ties to the chief). His ambitions were on the line with this case he better pony up and act nicer, he couldn't afford to be in a bad light with the chief. Silas then offered, "Can I drive you to the hospital? My partner has asked me to meet him there."

"I'd appreciate the ride, young man. Thank you," Katha simpered. Rose and Katha then followed Silas to his car.

"That was incredibly masterful, Grandma Katha. Tell me how you did it later," Rose whispered.

"Quiet dear he'll hear you," Katha whispered back.

She had done it again. What have I got myself into with these two? Thought Constable Rentford, as he escorted the women to his patrol car and placed them in the back seat. These women were a lot harder to deal with then he thought they would be. The old lady appeared sharper than any young person. She seemed good at the manipulation technique perfected by the élite. He'd remain cautious with her for now. The girl was mouthy even for a teen. She obviously needed to take some more notes from Granny. He felt bad she had lost her father, especially given Ms. Kelly was her stepmother. Ms. Kelly might have committed the crime after all.

Lily Kelly was found at the scene of the crime and the wife remained the first suspect. Lily Kelly and her cousin Amelia looked good for these crimes at this time.

He would be careful with these people, however, if he wanted to remain Detective Rogers' partner; and he did want to remain his partner. Politics were always tricky.

Ms. Kelly, being the crown attorney, and now her Grandmother, being some kind of society dame, meant trouble with a capital T and then her relationship with the chief's daddy? Trouble he didn't need. Being Detective Rogers partner could be a step forward in his career and he was anxious for advancement. He wasn't getting any younger after all; he was twenty-nine years old now.

He drove them in silence to the hospital. The little girl, not like a teenager, seemed subdued now like she now realized her dad was gone. Of course she seemed worried about her stepmother; Ms.

Kelly obviously held the child's affection. Mrs. O'Malley still looked angry, like the world had better get out of her way. Silas didn't feel like stepping in her quicksand. His career had seemed stagnant, as he played the politics game, but now maybe he would see a rise in rank. Silas wasn't about to let anything get in the way of his occupation again. Advancement would soon pass him by if he didn't keep on his toes. He loved being a cop and looked forward to the day he got to be an inspector, even the youngest one ever. A guy could dream and it could happen.

"We're here, Ma'am, and Ms. Brooksfield." Silas announced, stopping the car. Silas opened the door to let them out, feeling more like a taxi driver than a police officer.

"He sounds like a chauffeur, Grandma Katha," Rose commented snidely.

"Rudeness is not appreciated, Rose Brooksfield. The policeman has been generous giving us a ride to your mother," Katha replied giving Rose a censoring look.

"Sorry, sir," Rose stated looking embarrassed.

"That's okay," Silas replied mollified.

"You are gracious with a cranky old lady, and a wounded child. Thank you for your patience, Constable Rentford. You've been more than kind," Katha said as they parted.

As they walked away, Silas felt that he had judged the old lady too harshly. After all, she had made the teen be respectful, and that had to count for something. Didn't it? While they may not have been related by blood, they did act like family. Silas respected that.

~0~

Chapter 6 - Old Bones Rattle with Tempered Steel

Katha

Katha entered through the hospital doors, going directly to the front desk to find Lily's room. Unfortunately no one was available at this time of night. Katha used the desk phone to call the emergency room enquiring where Lily had been taken.

A nurse appeared out of nowhere at the desk and said, "Please hang up the phone and leave. We are unable to confirm any information about Lily Brooksfield at this time. You can return in the morning."

"I beg your pardon?" Katha asked regally.

"I can't release any information," the nurse explained. "So you might as well come back in the morning with the rest of the press."

"I am her grandmother, not the gutter press," Katha announced leaving out the great.

"Sorry. The press called all night. Some of them are fine, but those tabloids... I guess then it would be all right to release the information, but we must be careful, like I explained. Please produce some identification. Miss.?"

"Yes, of course I do. I'm Katha O'Malley and this is my great-granddaughter, Rose Brooksfield, Lily's daughter. Rose, show them your student card," Katha commanded as she finished showing her identification.

"This would be so much easier if I owned a driver's licence. Why couldn't I be a year older?" Rose whined pulling out her wallet and showing her student card.

"Yes, your identification is sufficient. I hope you understand. The press tried to sneak their way in and we've got to be cautious. The police asked us not to release the information to anyone but family and there are privacy laws in this country which we strictly adhere to." continued the nurse, apologising some more and rambling, "I think we may have transferred her to the Medicine floor to monitor how much poison she has ingested. Let me find out all the information and get back to you."

A few seconds later after speaking to someone on the phone she said to Katha, "Yes, she's on the Medicine floor."

"Poison? She breathed in poison? I need the floor and the room number. Please?" demanded Katha sweetly, but clearly shaken by the news Lily had been poisoned.

Rose trembled, scared; as this was not the news she expected.

"The floor is the fourth floor, E-Wing; I'm not sure the room number. One moment please."

"Thank you, my dear," replied Katha as the nurse's desk phone rang. "I am so sorry. I've been called away and don't have time to look up the number," the nurse replied.

The nurse then she walked away.

"Totally unbelievable behaviour! Is this the way nurses behave now? Well how rude. Damn! Now what can we do? You didn't catch me swear, did you?" Katha cautioned.

"Hear what, Grandma Katha?" asked Rose. "I don't believe you shouldn't condemn all nurses for one nurse's actions."

"They are not helping their cause with this incident," Katha explained trying to find someone.

Katha looked around a look of dismay on her face. Rose worried Grandma Katha would have a heart attack because Grandma Katha was so upset.

"I can't believe this. Now there is no one to answer the phone. The nurses are unavailable and I don't know the room number." Katha ranted. "This hospital is badly run. Things have to change."

"Maybe we should just go to the floor and look for Mom?" asked Rose.

"Of course, I lost my facilities there for a moment. Thank you, dear. You are a smart cookie. Let's go find your mother."

Katha exited the elevator and started down the long hallway. She turned a corner with Rose in tow and then tramped loudly down the hospital corridor searching for Lily. Katha peered in rooms actively searching for Lily.

"I don't see her, Grandma Katha," Rose cried scared.

"Don't you worry will we find her. Grandma Katha will find her; never you fear," Katha replied determination showing in her face.

"Visiting hours are over until eleven a.m.," The nurse replied frostily. "You need to leave."

"Please I need to find my granddaughter," Katha stated loudly.

"Ma'am, you need to be a little quieter. Are you aware of the time? It is four a.m., the patients are asleep. Come back later in the morning," the nurse demanded.

"I am so sorry, these old bones rattle," Katha apologized, smiling a winning smile and then continued, "Please help me dear? We've news of a terrible tragedy tonight. My grandson by marriage, the Mayor Horace Brooksfield, was murdered. My granddaughter was brought here as well."

The nurse looked moved.

Katha took a huge breath and wiped away tears. "She was poisoned by the same awful person who did away with my grandson," Katha answered in hushed, anguished tones, wiping away some more tears from her eyes. "I must find her. I am so worried this poor child needs her mother after this horrendous night."

"Oh, you are the family of the mayor? It has been a dreadful day for you. Are you all right, my dear?" asked the nurse, suddenly seeming concerned with Katha's wellbeing.

"Yes, I'm sure we will be all right as soon as we know our Lily is okay," Katha continued.

The nurse at the desk looked up as they passed the desk.

"I'm sure I can help you find her. Noreen, take over here. I'm going to help this woman and her grandchild. They are the mayor's family," the nurse who had spoken to Katha said.

"I could help you find your niece. I was so sorry to get the news about the Mayor. I'm so sorry about your father," Noreen stated solicitously.

"Thank you. My father was a great man," Rose replied solemnly.

"He was indeed."

"I'm taking them to see Mrs. Brooksfield now."

"I'll hold down the ward, Linda," Noreen agreed.

"I believe the phrase is 'Hold down the fort'," Linda corrected.

"Fine, I'll hold down the fort!" Noreen agreed.

~0~

Rose

Rose wondered if she would ever able to manipulate

people to help her, the way Grandma Katha, always managed to get people to do exactly what she wanted. She wanted to be like Lily and Grandma Katha when she got older. They were smart strong women who seemed to get people to do exactly what they wanted in the nicest possibly way. They seemed to have a special power; people wanted to do things for them. Rose tried hard not to think Lily might not be okay.

Daddy was dead... Lily the only parent she had left...Deep down, she worried Lily would leave her too. Mommy (her real mother) was a drug addict and a murderess who only escaped a long prison sentence, because Lily hadn't asked for it. What kind of mother kills her drug dealing pimp in front of her daughter though? Daddy met Lily when Daddy asked for some leniency for her mother.Rose had been terrified and wanting her mother not understanding why she couldn't see her. Lily had talked gently to her and her father, explaining it all. Lily had even hastened the trial because her biological mother, asked her to do so.

Lily even made a plea deal for Rose's biological mother which meant she'd be out in twenty years. She had offered her friendship to Rose. At first Rose refused to give her any affection, feeling she betrayed her mother.

When Rose started to realize all her real mother had done she started to think how special Lily was. Lily had been there for Rose long before she had married her father. Lily had kept up with everything a mother did. Lily had taken Rose to Brownie meetings. She had been there for school functions required of a mother, even baking cupcakes for a bake sale.

Rose thought back to when Lily said she wanted to be her stepmother and how she'd begged her to stay. She also begged to be able to call Lily, Mom. Lily adopted her, so surely that meant they couldn't take her away from Lily. Provided she was okay; after all she was in the hospital. They wouldn't take her away from her family now that her father had died would they?

"Don't you worry Rosey, your mom's going to be okay," Katha reassured seeing the thoughts going on in Rose's head flash in her eyes. "She has strong genes flowing through her veins. She can survive this and she has us."

Rose peered in the hospital room. She saw her mother, lying in a bed coughing; an oxygen tube ran into her nose. Mom appeared much worse. Rose thought. Somehow in Rose's mind she thought Lily would be coming home tonight, to look after Rose, in her grief. Rose took another look at Lily.

Mom looked small and broken, unlike the strong woman who took care of her. How could Mommy look after herself let alone me? If Mom is getting better; why does she look so bad? Is Grandma Katha comforting me, and lying to me, because she thinks I'm still a child? Rose then decided Grandma Katha was reassuring her, like you would any small child. I wish I could be a kid again and not understand someone had killed her father. I'm scared, what if the same evil person comes after me as well? They hurt my mom and dad they could hurt me too! Rose looked over at her mother and thought she needed her mother more than ever now. She tried not to cry.

"I have to get home to my daughter; I can't stay here." Lily cried, struggling with the nurse who tried to keep her in bed.

"Lily, don't give the nurse trouble," Katha commanded from the doorway.

"Grandma Katha. I'm so glad you're here but it's so early. Lily then coughed and tried to catch her breath "Rose should be sleeping. Amelia's here too," Lily continued as she struggled to talk, holding out her arms to Rose. Rose threw herself gently into her mother's arms and appeared happy for a moment.

"Mommy, are you sure you're okay?" Rose cried sounding like a small child.

"What do you mean, Amelia's here?" asked Katha shocked.

"She had a little accident. I'll explain later," Lily mouthed over Rose's head, now on her shoulder.

"Rosey, my little Posey, I'll be fine. Lily then had a coughing spell. She then searched Rose's face and asked, "Sweetie, have you heard about your dad?" Rose began weeping as Lily comforted her and then cried with her.

"We'll get through this sweetie. They'll find out who hurt your daddy and he'll pay. God as my witness, he'll pay for what he's done," Lily vowed with a bitter tone in her voice.

"Now, Lily, they say 'Vengeance is mine saith the Lord.' therefore it isn't your job or this child's job to go after them. So don't you go tell her revenge is necessary. It is a policeman's job, specifically Constable Silas Rentford's job," Katha rebuked. "This child needs her mother, so don't do anything foolish."

"Don't you mean Sergeant Detective Rogers?" Lily asked, coughing again.

"No. Who is Sergeant Detective Rogers?" Katha asked.

"I suspect he's Constable Silas Rentford's boss," Rose replied knowingly, then dried her tears.

"Yes, she's correct; I believe Detective Rogers is his boss, because he is in charge of the case," Lily countered.

"Will you be okay Mom?" Rose asked.

"Of course she'll be all right. She'll get good care here and before you know she'll be home with us. We will spoil her rotten. Won't we?" Katha answered, as Lily smiled her thanks at Katha for the reassurance.

"I think you ought to go. Ms. Kelly-Brooksfield needs her rest." the nurse commanded, coming back in the room.

"But they just got here," Lily protested through another spout of coughs.

"And they can come back later today," the nurse insisted.

"We'll be going. We came to make sure you're okay. Don't you worry; I'll take good care of Rosey,"

Katha reassured Lily, and then turned to the nurse. "My granddaughter recovers?"

"You should talk to the doctor about her condition," the nurse replied evasively.

"Listen here. I want to know now how my granddaughter really is!" Katha demanded with a no refusal attitude, as she stepped into the hall.

"She'll get great care. We'll move her to a normal room tomorrow. We will keep her a couple more days; until her lungs are clearer of the chlorine gas," The nurse explained gently.

"Chlorine gas? Isn't that substance rather serious?" asked Katha.

"Chlorine gas can be very serious when inhaled. The gas dissipated and she got a reduced amount, unlike the other victims. The doctor feels she got a smaller dose then would cause serious damage."

"Oh thank God."

"I'm so glad that Mom will be okay," Rose replied and then continued, "Do you think she might be moved into the same room with her friend and cousin Amelia Kelly?

"Why are you mentioning your Aunt Amelia?" Katha demanded.

"She's here too. Aunt Amelia slipped in some blood and broke her leg. She is concussed too."

"Amelia is in this hospital? She is concussed? When did this happen?"

"Grandma Katha, it's like this..."

"What do you mean she slipped in blood and broke her leg in blood? Do you people tell me nothing?" Katha demanded rapid succession from Rose and ignoring Rose's interjection. Then taking a breath, but not calming down, Katha asked, "Whose blood did she slip in to break her leg? Is it hers? Is she okay, Rose? Why didn't Lily call me?"

"It was scary. You won't believe this, Grandma Katha, Amelia's employee Megan..." began Rose.

"Amelia's employee, Megan bled all over the floor?

"What did she do to herself?" Katha interrupted seizing on the information "I'm always telling Megan she has to be more careful when she puts stock away. Stock we can replace. Megan we cannot."

"Don't you watch the news?"

"I was busy. I didn't have time to watch the news! I meant to get to Amelia's opening too, but for some reason I thought it took place tomorrow. All these meetings of the hospital board and I don't get called about my family?"

"It's worse than that, Grandma Katha. She didn't do anything to herself. Someone murdered Megan," Rose explained.

"I don't believe I heard you correctly. Did you say someone killed Megan?"

"I didn't believe it either, but Megan was murdered."

"But why? She is...was such a sweet girl," Katha said rhetorically wiping away a tear. "I don't know why or even how, but now Daddy is dead and Amber is dead as well. I hate this! I hate the world! I want to hurt someone! Why did they hurt my dad?"

"I agree the impulse to anger is there. I shouldn't be saying these things in front of you, but you are a teenager and I think you can handle it. I'm mad and I'd like to hurt someone too, but we have to let justice take the course and trust this person will pay. I promise you, we are safe though."

"I hope they find this person soon and we are secure. It feels like they targeted our family."

"I think you are wrong. I don't think it's anything but random, but I will make sure we are protected. I still think your mother should have called me though," Katha complained annoyed.

"I think she was busy with some policeman all day...then Daddy."

""I guess Lily did have a bad day to say the least. I don't know why you didn't call me though Rose. You have a cell phone." Katha stated reproachfully.

"Sorry, Grandma Katha," Rose apologised, trying to end the conversation.

Rose wondered how Grandma Katha made her feel so guilty. Rose's father had died, poor Mommy lay hurt in hospital, yet Grandma Katha had somehow made Rose feel like it had been their entire fault for not telling Grandma Katha everything. Like they had time to share anything with her! Oh well! Grandma Katha did love Rose like she was her flesh and blood granddaughter, and she never held what Rose's biological mother had done against her. That had to count for something.

"Now you will be able to arrange for Lily and Amelia to share a room with each other. Won't you?" Katha asked sweetly of the nurse, interrupting Rose's thoughts.

"I suppose but ...," the nurse replied as if she's humoured Katha.

"Oh I didn't introduce myself, did I? I am Katha O'Malley. I'm a chair on the hospital board," Katha stated, her voice sounding cultured and demanding "And I'm related to both women. In fact, I raised them from teenagers. So I want the best for my dear girls."

"Oh, then, I'm sure we can see to them rooming together."

"Thank you, dear, where would we be without such wonderful nurses? Thank you, for taking such wonderful care of my Lily and Amelia," Katha waxed smiling. "My pleasure." replied the nurse happily.

"We will come back after some rest to see them both." Katha told Rose "Now let's go find a taxi."

Katha and Rose went down to the lobby where Katha checked for signs against cell phones. Seeing none, she whipped out her cell phone and called for a taxi. The taxi arrived a few minutes later.

Outside of Katha's, Katha and Rose peered over at Lily's home, to the sight of press trucks and reporters camped out around Lily's house. They hurriedly opened the door and crossed the threshold into Katha's home before they were spotted.

"How long do you think those press reporters will be camped on our doorstep, Grandma Katha?" Rose asked looking out at the trucks disgusted.

"They will be out there until it is old news. Your father's death is big news. They don't want to harm us they just want to do their job."

"I wish they'd do their job somewhere else. Will they find us here?" asked Rose

"Not if I can help prevent them from doing their job."

"Oh, I hate it! I hate that Daddy died and these people act like vultures at our door," Rose cried, tears streaming down her face.

"I don't like them at the door any better. Some of these press people seem considerate but I don't want to talk to them either," Katha rambled, taking Rose in her arms and pulling back her hair out of her eyes, "I'm sure this is their top story, maybe you should leave the television off for a few days."

"I don't know if I can sleep, but I'm so tired. I want to go sleep in my bed but I can't. Where can I sleep, Grandma Katha?"

"Dear, the second bedroom is all made up with clean sheets. There are fresh blankets on it as well. You can find a night gown to sleep in the top drawer of the bureau. Later, dear, I'm headed to bed too. These old bones do not like getting four hours of sleep," Katha replied yawning.

"Goodnight. Grandma Katha, I love you."

"Goodnight, dear, for what's left of it. I love you too, pumpkin," Katha replied as she too went off to bed.

Rose went up the stairs exhausted but thought I don't know if I'll ever sleep again. I wish I could go to sleep and this would all be a bad dream.

~0~

Chapter 7 - All Life's Journeys Have Secrets

"Lily? I can't believe it! You're here too? What happened to you?" asked Amelia surprised as the orderly and a nurse wheeled in Lily on a stretcher and helped her into a bed.

An oxygen tank lay beside Lily's arm on the bed.

"Yesterday was the worst day of my life," Lily exclaimed. "First I find you blooded and broken, and I find your employee murdered. I take a breather, go home and find out Horace wasn't home and hadn't given Rose dinner. Rose hadn't eaten anything but cereal all day."

"Horace didn't make it home by five p.m. like he promised?" Amelia asked, "But you said he had been so much better about not working too late."

"I know. That's why I was so surprised that he wasn't home. It was ten-thirty p.m. when I got home, and no Horace in sight," Lily said in a whisper.

"I thought he would live up to his promise. What's wrong with him? Doesn't he understand life is short?" Amelia asked.

Seeing emotions of sadness flash across Lily's face, she continued, "Something happened to you though, because you ended up here. What happened when you got home?"

"We ate pizza. It got close to midnight and he wasn't home. I told Rose I would get him. I went to Horace's office, to bring him home. I arrived at the office building and I went up in his private elevator and his office door remained closed. I turned the knob and...," Lily started crying.

"Oh no, Horace cheated on you? I'll kill the bastard," Amelia shouted.

"Someone already did kill him. Can you provide an alibi, Ms. Amelia Kelly?" demanded Sergeant Detective Rogers coming into the room.

"Gee, I don't know... my broken leg? I can't walk on it!" Amelia began sarcastically. "Wait a minute; why would I need an alibi? Oh no, Lily, is Horace dead?"

"Yes, Ms. Kelly, the mayor is dead," Sergeant Detective Rogers stated bluntly.

"You could have told her easier. She's my cousin and therefore Horace is her family," retorted Lily angrily.

"But she obviously doesn't like him. Now does she, Ms. Brooksfield? Why else would she threaten to kill him?" Sergeant Detective Rogers replied bluntly.

"You're a jerk!" yelled Lily. "Amelia thought I said Horace had cheated not that she killed him and you know it!"

"So you suspected Horace cheated on your friend Lily?" asked Sergeant Detective Rogers, zeroing in with a beady gaze.

"How dare you insinuate Amelia killed Horace!" Lily interjected shocked.

"Yes and no," Amelia answered.

"Which is it? Yes or no?" demanded Sergeant Detective Rogers.

"Yes, I suspected he cheated on Lily; but I had no proof and I wasn't about to get any proof. I didn't want to realize the truth, because then I would need to tell Lily," Amelia reluctantly admitted.

"So did she say anything about this to you?" Sergeant Detective Rogers asked Lily.

"No! Anyway, Horace wouldn't cheat on me. He loved me. I remained the wife he wanted and we were in a happy marriage. You've got to realize someone posed them like that," cried Lily protesting.

"Posed them? I don't understand. There is more than one person dead? Who is dead?" Amelia asked, trying to get more information.

"Horace and Amber are dead," Lily replied sadly.

"Horace and Amber, his secretary, are dead? Oh Lily, I'm so sorry," Amelia responded reaching for Lily's hand, then turning to Detective Rogers she asked, "Why would someone kill Horace and Amber?"

"Did you hire someone to kill them, Ms. Kelly and then pose them?" enquired Sergeant Detective Rogers.

"How could you think I had anything to do with this? Are you kidding me?" Amelia solicited shocked.

"You hide under an assumed name and I see there is an accident that occurred to someone close to you a year ago, still on the books. They never found him did they? The drunk driver who killed your husband and son were never charged."

"How dare you? The press proceeded to hound me day and night, so I took my mother's maiden name on my aunt's advice. It was my right. It is a family name after all. Do you understand what kind of pain I went through, you mean jerk?" Amelia snapped angrily and then started crying silently, hiding her face as she turned away.

"Amelia's right. You are a jerk. Do you comprehend how long it's taken her to come this far? A year ago I lost my cousin to her pain, my best friend, as well as my godson, and the best male friend I've ever known. She wanted to die too. She wouldn't drink, eat or sleep. The press camped out on her doorstep and demanded little tidbits for their daily news stories. And you throw their deaths in her face like this. That doesn't hurt her? Do have any idea what happens when you lose someone without warning? To want to die because you can't bear to feel a gut wrenching pain in the pit of your stomach any longer? Now do you?" Lily yelled at Sergeant Detective Rogers.

"I do understand that pain," Sergeant Detective Rogers answered quietly.

"You felt pain which hurts that much? I'm sorry for your loss. But nothing excuses what you've done to Amelia now. After all, you can appreciate how it is to lose someone you love, so you should be a lot nicer."

"Listen, you're the Crown attorney, so you must comprehend I need to do my job. As distasteful as the questions may be, I must eliminate or confirm suspects."

"I understand you're doing your job here so go ahead, but tread lightly," Lily cautioned. "And I remind you her lawyer is present."

"Ms. Kelly, I'm sorry if those statements hurt you. I'm also sorry I must bring up something else hurtful from your past, but I need to proceed with my investigation. Is it true when you were sixteen, your entire family was killed in a fire? No trace of anyone else found but you and your dead family at the scene? That the fire was determined to be arson and the culprit, or culprits, were never found?" Sergeant Detective Rogers continued.

"How did you know all this? How did you find out about this? It happened in a whole other city. My great-aunt adopted me and changed my name to her daughter's last name, my mother's maiden name." explained Amelia, "The publicity after the event was terrible. The pointing fingers, the pity, the ridicule, it felt like pieces of me dying. If my aunt hadn't come and rescued me and taken me into her home, I think I would have killed myself."

"No Amelia! You wouldn't have," Lily cried in a shocked voice.

"Not as long as I have you, Rose and Aunt Katha."

"Good, because we love you."

"I know, I love you all too," Amelia answered.

"Cue the hearts and flowers. While I'm enjoying this love fest; I want to get on with my questioning, Ms. Kelly. You were Amelia Cordova then weren't you?" Sergeant Detective Rogers prodded pulling out his notebook and reading.

"Yes, I was Amelia Cordova. I was sixteen years old and had a wonderful family. In one horrific night my family was wiped out, gone in an instant." Amelia stuck out her chin and steeled herself to tell the story. "My mother Aerilla was strict but always around if I needed anything. She worked part-time as a journalist for the Ravenworst Journal."

Amelia stopped to catch her breath then continued, "My mother was warm, funny and loving to all who saw her. She wrote stories in her spare time on little scraps of paper. She'd even read some of them to us from time to time. They were good and she wanted to get them published but they are all gone now. The fire took them and my families' lives. All I have left is memories and it is hard not to remember the bad ones."

Amelia hid her face under the sheet for a second, trying to regain her composure again.

"How I miss my mother. I'd give anything to see her again...the loving smile she offered us when we came home from school. She hugged me with arms that always reached me, even when they didn't physically touch me. That is what I would like to remember," Amelia sobbed, wiping away tears and continuing by telling Detective Rogers more of her family.

"My father on the other hand was a strict disciplinarian. My father, a product of his upbringing appeared cold and closed off to his emotions; though I understood he cared about me. He believed children should listen and obey their parents but he loves...loved us all," Amelia corrected, wiping away another tear.

"What did your father do for a living, Ms. Kelly?" Detective Rogers queried.

"My father, Robert worked in his own business. It was a bookstore, he inherited from his father. We all took a turn working at the bookstore during the time we weren't at school. We sold the books and cleaned the store. Daddy loved us but he expected us to pull our own weight and work hard. He always said, 'Work hard to get ahead.' He taught us a work ethic he was sure would stay with us through our lives."

"And your other family members, one Jerry Cordova and Grace Cordova? What were their personalities?" Detective Rogers asked curiously.

"My older brother Jerry was seventeen years old the summer they died. Jerry flirted and was popular with the girls. He was a bit what the kids today call a player, always with a different girl, but he was a good guy. He had a muscle car, a '67 Mustang he worked three summers to buy and fix the car. He didn't like hanging out with his younger sisters, but what seventeen-year old boy does?" Amelia voice broke here as she gulped to hold back more tears.

"Did you care about your sister, your other family members, Ms. Kelly? Or was all your love saved for your older brother?" Detective Rogers asked, provoking her.

"Are you always this cruel? Of course I cared. Grace was my baby sister. She was only fourteen years old. Of course I cared. Grace had her whole life ahead of her. She had discovered her first crush. His name was Billy I think... I remember how sweet she could be. But she also loved to torment me as little sisters do. She borrowed my best clothes without my permission."

Amelia smiled remembering, "Grace used my hairbrush, messed up my room, borrowed my make-up and she tattled to my parents about me; but I'd give anything to look at her sweet little face again and do any of those things to me."

"Isn't the truth you hated her? You said she annoyed you and told your secrets to your parents about you."

"Don't you dare twist my words! I said I'd give anything to glimpse her again and I meant every word. I loved her! I loved every member of my family! Is this all a game to you? Amelia looked at Detective Rogers beseechingly, begging him to believe her.

She couldn't understand what his problem was, why he didn't he see understand how it hurt her to talk about this.

"Oh, why don't you understand? My whole family died in a horrific fire; all of them...my older brother Jerry, my sister Grace, my mother Aerilla, and my father Robert. Everything was gone, my entire life up in flames in a matter of minutes. I awoke outside in my nightgown unconscious from smoke inhalation. I don't even know how I got outdoors. No one understood how I got out there. I wish I had protected them. I would have given my life to save them. It's like I'm still under a horrible curse and now I've let those I love most into the curse," Amelia answered, her voice filling with sorrow and horror.

She then exclaimed, "I am so sorry, Lily!"

"Weren't you suspected of committing the crime in which all your family died?"

"Not to my knowledge and certainly not by law enforcement; maybe in horrible whisper campaigns from people who love to spread unfounded gossip. Why would anyone suspect me?" Amelia asked dumfounded, "Whoever or whatever started the fire took all I loved from me."

"You were the only one alive, the only survivor. Why wouldn't they suspect you?" Emmett exclaimed.

"They didn't suspect me, because I didn't do it! You don't understand how nightmarish this was. I was a sixteen-year-old girl whose family had been ripped from her. My lungs were filled with smoke. They wheeled me down to the morgue. They made me identify the bodies. Did you read about that in your report? I stood up out of a wheelchair to stare at their bodies. People I loved. They were so burnt; I didn't recognize them at first. My mind told me I looked at cooked meat, but I soon realized with horror and dismay these were people. My family laid there, four hideous bodies, burnt beyond recognition. That was all that was left of my family. Their faces were unrecognizable. So why did they make me look at them?" Amelia asked, her face reflecting all the shock and horror of the moments so long ago.

"They wanted to see what your reaction would be; then they could decide your guilt," Emmett replied.

"Well then, they got a reaction didn't they? I collapsed and they took me to a rest home. I stayed in a rest home for six months until Great Aunt Katha came and got me."

"A rest home? Don't you mean a mental facility?" demanded Detective Rogers.

"Yes, I admit I stayed in a mental health facility. Are you happy? I suffered a nervous breakdown. Between the horrible sight of them dead and survivor's guilt, I checked out of life. I couldn't handle the stress," Amelia admitted.

"There no sin in illness, Amelia, Lily said then turning to
Lieutenant Rogers she said, "Amelia and I are cousins once
removed. Her grandmother is my great-grandmother's sister.
That's how we became great friends when Amelia came to stay
with Grandma Katha."

"All very sweet and nice, but getting back to your tragedies, how
do you explain the fact you lost all the members of your immediate
family? And you alone survived Amelia? Am I to believe that a
year ago your husband, and your young son, died and you didn't
simply because you were too sick to get into the car with them?"
Emmett demanded to know, not truly listening to Lily

"I feel I'm under a horrible curse. Do you enjoy dredging up all
this pain?" shouted Amelia.

"I'm trying to get to the bottom of this so-called curse," Emmett
replied with force. "I don't believe in curses, only evil people, and
it's my job to apprehend those people so they can't harm anyone
else."

Amelia's face was as white as a sheet, pain etched deeply into it.

"I don't want to talk about this anymore. It hurts too damn bad.
Please, Lily, make him stop talking about this," Amelia pleaded
turning to Lily.

"You don't need any more information... do you Detective
Rogers?" Lily demanded dismissively then started coughing.

"I'm done for now but...," Detective Rogers answered, as Lily
interrupted her voice a little crackling from coughing.

"I know neither of us leave town. But you, Sergeant Detective
Rogers, need to find the cretin who killed my husband Horace. I
know it wasn't Amelia or anyone close to me. You need to find
whoever did this without narrowing your field with false leads. I
want to see whomever did this pay for this crime."

"Believe me, I always get my man, or woman, as the case may be,"
Emmett retorted.

"You just keep looking, Sergeant Detective," Lily said with a
cutting glare. "My cousin and I are not your suspects."

"I'll be the judge of that, Ms. Kelly-Brooksfield!" Emmett exclaimed.

"People like you are always judge, jury and executioner," Lily sniped.

"Not in this country; there is no death penalty."

"No, you're like other cops and decide someone is guilty and build a case from supposition, even if they are innocent."

"Are you judgemental about all cops, Ms. Brooksfield, or just me?" Emmett asked surprised.

"So, you aren't going after my cousin for this crime?"

"I only go after guilty people, Ms. Brooksfield. I go where the evidence points me."

"I guess I was a little out of line, but the way you went after my cousin was cruel," admitted Lily.

"Sometimes you need to be cruel to be kind. I'd like to eliminate her from the suspect list, but I can't yet." Emmett explained, "So let me do my job."

"Fine. You do your job. Find who killed my husband," Lily repeated.

"Oh, I will, Ms. Kelly Brooksfield. You need not fear on my account." Emmett left for moment, coming back a few minutes later much to Lily's surprise. "I thought you said you hired someone to guard Ms. Kelly. Where are they?" Emmett demanded to know.

"He's out there isn't he? A big tall guy with shaggy red hair tied up in a ponytail, his arms bulging with muscles. He is kind of hard to miss as he looks like a biker," Lily stated puzzled.

"There is no one out here."

"That makes no sense. I'm paying him good money to guard Amelia." Lily said angrily, "I'm calling Frank."

"Who is Frank?" Emmett asked.

"Frank Hawk, of Frank Hawk Security, he sent over Zachary Buchanan to guard Amelia. I don't understand why Frank's man, Zachary is not in front of the door. Could he have gone for coffee?" Lily asked Detective Rogers.

Lily then dialled Frank on her phone.

"Frank, Lily here. What's up with Zachary Buchanan? He's not here. He's supposed to be guarding Lily and he's nowhere to be seen. What? I appreciate that, but if he can't do the job; frankly I don't want him back. No we'll manage without one Amelia and I seem safe now anyway. I guess that's why he left. You'll call around and find out where he's gone? Thanks Frank, but I still don't know. No, I don't want him back. I told you that. Okay, you can get back to me when you find out. Goodbye."

"So he's missing?" Emmett demanded.

"It would seem so. I guess he didn't like the job."

"Or one of you knocked him off. You seem to be good at getting rid of people," Emmett said his eyes narrowing.

"That's slander! How dare you? How did we kill him? Amelia hobbled on her crutches while I stopped every few minutes to cough, so I could breathe?" Lily replied sarcastically.

"So you hired someone."

"Did anyone ever tell you that you have a one track mind that's stuck on go?" Lily exclaimed.

"I'm doing my job."

"Fine! Go! Do what you are supposed to do. Find Zachary Buchanan. I'm sure he's wandered off from the job... and find my husband's killer," Lily demanded angrily. "While you're at it you can find the serial killer of three people!"

"Megan's boyfriend is a person of interest. We haven't been able to find him. So the two of you aren't guilty for the murder at her store, but I'm sure your friend Amelia would assist you in offing your cheating husband and his lover." Emmett taunted.

"You are on the wrong track. You know it and I know it. I loved Horace and I would have forgiven him about anything. That's what people who love each other do."

"You would have forgiven him anything, even cheating? Because if he left you he would have gotten full custody of your stepdaughter. Am I correct?" Emmett taunted some more.

"Nonsense, I don't know what I would done about his cheating, but I wouldn't harm him. We share custody of our daughter. That's right... our daughter, not step anything. I adopted her officially, right after we married. She's my child, as much as his!" Lily explained, ""Why am I continuing to talk to you? Go! Do your job."

"I'm going, but not because you tell me too. I have a great solve rate and you can bet these murders won't be any different. So if you are responsible, you better get used to those jail-bird duds," Emmett exclaimed as a parting shot and left.

"Arrogant troublemaker! You'll see we had nothing to do with this," Lily yelled after him and choked as she tried to gasp in some air, followed by coughing.

Lily then crawled back into the bed from the bedside chair. Lily had started to like him again and he thought Amelia was guilty? He believed Amelia and Lily killed all those people? Why did she remain so attracted to the man who wanted to find them behind bars? She loved Horace and he hadn't even been dead twenty-four hours and she stood attracted to someone else?

Disgraceful! She was a bad wife. Horace cheated on her, but they would have gotten past this. Wouldn't they? Lily tried everything to make this marriage work for Rose's sake. And if she didn't succeed she would have sued for custody of Rose. After all, she legally adopted her, so she had as much right to the child as Horace did. Tears slipped out of Lily's eyes. Horace died; there would be no making up for this cheating he had done. He was gone forever. Her husband was dead!

Lily sobbed quietly into the pillow lying back in the bed, finally falling into a fitful sleep. Amelia stared at her cousin. Poor Lily; she would help her deal with all of this. Even if that stupid detective thought they had done the killings. Amelia would help her, the way Lily helped Amelia when Jack and Sam were killed, but for now...sleep.

~0~

Chapter 8 - Keep to the Motto

The Killer

Why are there trucks and cars and other news vans outside of Lily Brooksfield's home? Where are Lily, Rose and my Angel? All this noise must be disturbing their rest. How dare they bother her? I had killed to protect my Angel, but I forgot how much the newsmakers were like predators. There were real journalists of course; those who acted with grace and dignity to those they interviewed. I used the predators always on the lookout for stories. I manipulated them with stories I wanted them to present, but these reporters seemed like real vultures. But maybe that was good? I certainly didn't want them to discover my part in this, but what about my beloved? The stress these vultures would cause to her made him so angry.

Huh? There's Rose, with the O'Malley woman.

Where was Lily? Was she at the morgue visiting Horace? I thought she'd be with her daughter! I had done all of this so they could be together after all. Lily personified being a good mother and deserved to keep her daughter. Horace even in death remained an unnatural father and terribly neglectful. He hardly ever spent time with his daughter. He stayed too busy with work or Amber, or both at once. He deserved his end. I did well in ending those two, now they would never harm my family again!

Why did the press continue to still linger? Did all of them want a story because of his position as mayor?

That must be it. I suppose, or was it the O'Malley woman's fault? She was in a relationship with the chief's father. What was his name...oh yes, Terrence Stewart. Surely Terrence would put an end to this fiasco and demand his son remove the trash. Should I make an anonymous call and stop all of the noise and aggravation for my Angel? No, if I did make a call I would reveal my hand. I'd stay in the shadows, continuing to watch, only taking action if it remained completely necessary. Safety first; protecting yourself, that had to be my motto. So for now I'd watch and wait. No one would harm my beloved Angel. No one!

~0~

Chapter 9 -
Slander and Lies

Katha O'Malley's house about eight hours later

G randma Katha, do you think mom's going to be okay?"

asked Rose fearfully.

"Rose, she'll be fine. And so will you. Don't you worry, my pet. You're family and we take care of family. You're a Kelly/O'Malley/Brooksfield now and don't you forget it," reassured Katha.

"Do you think Amelia's cursed and it's rubbed off on Mom?" asked Rose.

"Rose Brooksfield! Amelia, through no fault of her own, has had a lot of sorrow. It's not a curse. Don't ever let me catch you saying that again. I'm so sorry your father died, but it is not some conspiracy or a curse; someone with evil intent killed him and his secretary Amber. The police will find whoever did it," Katha claimed.

"Daddy's dead...he's never coming back," Rose exclaimed tearfully, coming to a realization that hadn't quite hit her until now.

"I'm so sorry, sweetie. I understand you're hurting. You should see a counsellor, so you can talk about what you feel," Katha insisted, concerned.

"I'm fine. I'm angry. You should be angry too! I would like to see the person who killed my Dad die, slowly and in lots of pain!"

Katha looked at Rose, gravely alarmed and frowning.

"Don't look at me like that! I'm not about to do anything stupid! I'm going to stare at some television," Rose replied stomping into the living room.

She then turned on the television to block out any follow-up conversation.

"Rose, my dear child." Katha began before a special bulletin came across the television.

"Naughty Mayor dies in sex scandal with secretary." A voiceover said.., "This reporter has learned Mayor Horace Brooksfield was found murdered in flagrante delicto with his secretary Amber Trent yesterday. Amber Trent worked for Mayor Brooksfield for the last two years. There is no comment from Crown Attorney, Lily Kelly-Brooksfield or family. Sources close to the mayor say Amber Trent had been having an affair with the mayor for the last year. The police have no comment at this time about the cause of death. Unconfirmed sources tell this reporter they died from poisoning... the same poisoning which is believed to have felled Crown Attorney Lily Kelly-Brooksfield, who is now in hospital in satisfactory condition. Mayor Horace Brooksfield leaves behind a fourteen-year-old daughter Rose and his current wife Crown attorney Lily Brooksfield. Our deepest sympathies go out to the mayor's family. On another odd note, the Crown attorney arrived at the scene of a murder at her cousins' new store Quirks yesterday."

"Store clerk Megan Fowler was found dead earlier today in an apparent robbery. Store owner Amelia Kelly was also hurt and is in the hospital. Were the two connected? Stay tuned to this station for more updates and tune in at six p.m. for News Hour for all the latest stories. Paul Knight reporting for CHPV-TV"

"In flagrante delicto? Do they think by disguising it with their fancy language, I won't know what they're talking about? Daddy did not cheat on Mom! How dare he say Daddy cheated? It's slander. We can sue him right Grandma Katha?" Rose asked.

"Right," replied Katha, not wanting to disillusion Rose and recognising she too had heard rumours of mayor's infidelity.

"Damn reporters. I can see them in front of our house," Rose said looking out the front window.

"Rose, please guard your language. I can discern these muckrakers are a pain in the neck, but we must act ladylike," Katha explained. "Besides, you have to remember there are always reputable reporters who get the story correct."

"Sorry, Grandma Katha. Oh no, I think one of them is headed to your front door."

"Dear, I think it is your friend, Carol Banks."

"Wow, I can't believe you recognized Carol before I did. Do you think she can tell I'm here?" asked Rose.

"Since she's coming up the walk. Yes, I believe your friend seemed to have figured out where you are. She's an intelligent young lady and polite," Katha declared.

"Carol is crafty; she ferrets out information. One time we tried to figure out what George Prinze hid. Carol figured it out before anyone else. He rifled through lockers, stealing the valuables and hawking them for cash. He also rifled through some teachers purses and broke into the principal's office and took some cash. Carol nailed him to the wall. He got suspended and he's in reform school now."

"What kind of school are they running? Are you sure this school is a good place for you?" asked Katha worried. "If you'd like to get out of that school I will pay for boarding school."

"I don't want to go to any boarding school; all my friends and family are here. Carol and I got rid of the riffraff, so I go to a good school now. Besides, stuff like that happens everywhere."

"Riffraff? I didn't think anyone your age recognized such an expression."

"I learned it from you," Rose replied as Katha laughed. Rose peered out the window through the curtains. "She's taking a long time to get through those reporters, Grandma Katha."

"Yes. I should shout out the door for her to run."

"Yes, go ahead, Grandma Katha," Rose agreed.

"Come on, Carol! Run!" Grandma Katha shouted.

Carol blonde-haired and blued-eyed had her long blonde hair cascading in waves down her back.. Tall and model slim and only fifteen years old she felt overwhelmed by male attention, but when standing next to Rose who could command a room, Carol felt invisible and she liked that. Rose didn't even seem to notice the admiring looks she drew, or at least she pretended not to but maybe that was better because was shy. Standing five foot eight inches Carol wore a tee-shirt with a popular television character on it. Her bottom half was covered with black boot cut jeans. On her feet are well worn black Ugg boots with three buttons on the outsides.

Carol heard Katha's call and tried to get by the reporters. She shoved through the gauntlet of reporters, jostling them with her shoulders. Carol sprinted while being bombarded with questions the whole way to Katha's house.

"Are you Rose Brooksfield?"

Carol shook her head at the reporter and continued going to the door of Katha's home. If it were anyone but Rose she would have stayed at home instead of fighting through these crowds, but Rose needed her.

"Hey kid, do you know The Brooksfield's?"

"Do you have any comment on the fact Mayor Brooksfield had an affair?"

"Do you have any more information on Lily Brooksfield's condition?"

"Do you think there is a Kelly curse and are we all at risk?"

Carol breathed a sigh of relief as Katha ushered her in the house.

"Hi Rose. I'm like so sorry to hear about your dad. I can't believe someone tried to hurt your mom too! Billy Carter said you were dead. I had to come see you and make sure they hadn't hurt you too," Carol fired rapidly at Rose. She then turned to Katha she said..."I hope you don't mind Ms. O'Malley."

"Billy Carter is stupid," Rose exclaimed.

"Yes, he is. I'm glad you're here and safe," Carol said with relief than embarrassed to be showing her feelings she added "With whom else would I watch soaps and Vampire Diaries?"

"It's more than okay, dear. I'm glad you came for Rose's sake," Katha interjected smiling. "You are a good friend to come when she needs you."

Carol blushed and replied, "She'd come to me if I needed her."

"I'm glad you're here, Carol. It has been so horrible."

"I can't imagine what you're going through with these killings. I thought it was bad when my Dad left last year, but this is so much worse."

"Thanks for reminding me," Rose replied snarling.

"Gee, I'm sorry, Rose. I don't know what to say. Please give me another chance to make it up to you. I'm stumbling here; I want to help you get through this but I don't know how," Carol said contritely. "Nobody I ever knew died except my grandmother, and she had cancer, so it was like expected.

"I'm sorry too. I don't understand why I was so angry at you. You didn't do anything. You come over here to be nice to me and I snarl at you. Sorry."

"It's okay. I'd be angry too. Someone killed your father and hurt your mom. You have a right to be angry."

The doorbell pealed loudly.

"Thanks, Carol, Grandma Katha's right; you are a good friend."

"We'll ignore them and they'll go away," Katha insisted to Rose, and Carol as the doorbell repeatedly rang.

"I want to talk to my Grandma Katha for minute...could you?" asked Rose, motioning with her eyes for Carol to go upstairs.

"I'm going up to your room now," Carol replied understanding.

"Grandma, do you think these reporters will ever go away? And why haven't they found Daddy's killer yet? It had to have been an escaped killer or something," Rose enquired angrily.

"Dear, they'll go away when the next story hits, and yes, I believe they'll find your Daddy's killer soon, but we will have to be patient awhile. They won't rest until they find him or her. Don't you worry."

"Daddy and I were so lucky when he married Mom."

"Your dad hit the jackpot when he won my Lily. Never you fear, Lily will take care of you now. She adopted you, but you are her daughter even without those papers. You are safe with your family."

The doorbell pealed again.

"Dratted people! Why won't they go find another story," Katha asked no one in particular.

"Katha it's me, Terrence. Let me in the house!" demanded the voice at the door.

"Terrence who?" asked Katha playing it dumb.

"Terrence Stewart, your beau, hopefully the love of your life," the voice answered.

"Why Terrence, come in here, quickly. Vultures are out there."

As Rose looked out, she saw several trucks, camera operators, and reporters with microphones in the distance. She tried unsuccessfully to block out the shouting.

"Ms. Brooksfield, Ms. O' Malley, any comment about the fact the mayor was found naked with his secretary?" asked one voice, as another asked, "Any leads on the killer er... killers?"

Katha ushered Terrence in and closed the door quickly. Terrence looked back at them like he escaped tigers and asked while glaring at the crowd, "Do you want me to call my son and have all of them removed?"

"Well I don't want to make difficulty for you, dear. It might be too much trouble," Katha answered demurely.

"Why my dear, it would be my great pleasure to have them removed. After all if the police chief's father hasn't the influence to get rid of those people, who does?" Terrence asked.

"Why, thank you, Terrence. A lady does appreciate such heroism," Katha said, fluttering her eyelids like Scarlet O'Hara.

Rose looked at the man in surprise. This six-foot white-haired coiffured gentleman, being manipulated into doing exactly what Grandma Katha wanted, appeared intelligent. How did Grandma Katha always manage to get what she wanted? He stood tall, about six feet, and for an older man, quite good-looking. He appeared trim, and for a senior, strong. He looked younger than Grandma Katha but Rose couldn't guess his age or Grandma's for that matter. Grandma insinuated she was eighty-five or eighty-six, but she certainly didn't appear that old. Grandma certainly understood how to pick her boyfriends. He appeared to be the police chief's father, Police Chief Edward Stewart. Rose wasn't completely surprised that he had connections. No doubt about it, Grandma Katha held a position as a mover and a shaker, and this guy was top-notch. He seemed to like Grandma Katha too. Maybe Grandma Katha would be happy again?

When she lost Grandpa Kieran she seemed so lonely. Grandma Katha lost all her spark and only recently she seemed like she had her spirit back. Did this man make her happy again? Would Mom lose all her spunk like that, now that Daddy was gone? How could Daddy be dead? Murdered! This seemed all unreal.

Rose watched as Terrence put his arm around Katha hugging her for a moment. Terrence stopped and picked up a phone and called his son. He better not hurt Grandma Katha, or she'd make him sorry.

"Yes, son, they are surrounded Katha's house. No, son, I haven't. You'll be the first to know when I'm ready to marry Katha. Sorry, so you'll remove the paparazzi? Okay. Thanks, Neddy. Goodbye, son."

"The scum should be gone within the hour. My son sent police to disperse them." Terrence told a smiling Katha, "The reporters should leave soon." "So what will your son do about the murder of my great-grandson by marriage?" Katha demanded.

"He has his best man working on the case. My son gave me the grilling of a lifetime of being your alibi, dear. He asked me if I would make you an honest woman."

"Sorry, dear! When, Police Constable Silas Rentford demanded my alibi, I had no choice, but to tell him I spent the afternoon with you. I'm embarrassed. I understood it would get back to your son, but with Lily and Amelia hurt, it went out of my head to call you," embellished Katha.

"Oh, my dear girl, I'm so sorry. How incredibly selfish of me not to think of what you had suffered. It must have been nerve wrecking and heartbreaking for you. Are you okay, dear heart? Are your chicks okay now?"

"Chicks? I think that word might be politically incorrect now."

"It's so hard to keep up with what is acceptable language. The thing is I never use the word the way they think it means."

"You'd think you would have learned in your job, Terrence."

"I'm retired from that job, which gives me a lot more leeway. Now about your girls, are they okay?"

"Lily is still in the hospital, but they say she'll get better in a few days. Amelia has a broken leg and a concussion and she is staying too."

"I'm so sorry, my dear. Neddy will get to the bottom of this don't you worry. He is the police chief after all." Terrence reassured.

"Neddy? You call a grown man Neddy? Be careful not to do call him Neddy in public, dear, it might embarrass him as chief of police." Katha cautioned, and then tempered it with praise "But I am so lucky that I can always count on you, dear."

"And this is this Rose, your great-great-granddaughter?"

"Yes, Terrence."

"It is lovely to meet you, Rose. I hope you don't mind me calling you by your first name."

"Not at all, Mr. Stewart. It's a pleasure to meet you too," Rose replied ladylike. "Well, such exquisite manners; a credit to my dear," Terrence said to Katha.

Speaking with Rose again he asked, "Would you like to call me Terrence? Mr. Stewart is quite a mouthful. And perhaps someday I'll convince your lovely grandmother to marry me and I can be your Grandpa Terrence."

"Terrence, don't put ideas in her head," Katha rebuked.

"I'll think about it," Rose replied, smiling.

"This one is a definite keeper, Grandma Katha," whispered Rose.

As she walked towards the stairs she retorted "I'm going to leave you kids alone while I watch television in the guest bedroom upstairs... with my friend. Don't do anything I wouldn't do," she said saucily, as she bounded up the stairs.

"Rose Brooksfield, you behave," replied Katha waving her finger.

"Sorry, Grandma Katha; I'll see you two later."

"I like how that child thinks," Terrence stated and kissed Katha's neck.

"Terrence, there are children in the house. Rose's friend is upstairs as well," Katha scolded.

"Sorry dear, I forgot myself in your loveliness. Are you okay Katha?" Terrence asked searching her face, "I've been worried sick. Should I stick to your side like glue?"

"I'm sure you have been; I have been too; they have to catch the evil person or persons who are behind these murders. Soon!! Drat now I better admit I'm scared and I don't scare easy. Why did people close to my girls get murdered?"

"I don't know, my darling, but I'm going to protect you and your chicks. I already asked Edward for a patrol car to swing by regularly and I'm going to hire a guard to protect your girls in the hospital," Terrence replied fiercely.

"It is sweet of you. Don't worry about the guard. Lily has already hired one. I called too. Her close friend said he already sent one. He runs some big security firm downtown."

"As long as your chicks are safe and you are safe I'm happy."

"That's why I love you. Even though you understand I can take care of myself and my love ones you step up to do so."

"Did you get any sleep last night?" Terrence asked looking worried. "You won't be any good to them if you don't rest too."

"Not a lot of sleep." Katha admitted. "Why don't you rest up against me, sweetheart, close your eyes and I'll watch over you and Rose and Carol."

"I think I might take you up on your offer," Katha replied closing her eyes and sounding extremely exhausted.

~0~

Terrence

Terrence stared at Katha's sleeping form. How did he get so lucky to meet such a dynamite lady? The woman was quicksilver when it came to pinning her. She already refused him several times but he hoped she would relent and marry him now, especially now that she saw him with her family. She worried about the age difference, but so what?

Age meant nothing. Terrence was seventy-four years old to her eighty-one. In relative terms this was not a big deal. It seemed funny how she let people think she was older and looked good for her age. Even for an eighty-one-year-old she looked far younger than she should. In truth Terrence felt she looked way younger than him. A few times people teased him saying he was a cradle robber. They were equal when you considered that according to the actuarial tables men didn't live as long as women. He would show her tender care and that despite her strength, she needed him as much as he craved her gentleness and her loving touch.

This business about the murder troubled him. Some awful person had gotten awful close to Katha and her chicks. Well they had better think again if they think they will harm anyone else his Katha loved. Katha was prideful and she worried about her reputation. Katha wouldn't let him stay. Someone had to protect them. Neddy promised him he would have a guard on the house for a few days. Surely that would give them time to find the killer.

He hoped he got to meet Amelia soon. He had met Lily a few times when she came into his court. He presided as a judge on some of her cases, but he didn't know her well. He understood how passionate Lily prosecuted the guilty, but he'd also seen her understanding for those who made a mistake. She always felt they could be rehabilitated.

He had seen a lot of those same characteristics in Katha and realized Lily absorbed them from Katha. Katha was the first woman he fell for immediately after his wife's death. It was like he had known her all his life.

He felt sure she existed as his soul mate, the woman he'd been waiting for all his life. She was the one, the original incredible, irascible Katha. The woman he always dreamed there for him. She remained a woman of immense emotions and pure pleasure to spend any time.

She was the woman he wanted to marry and be with her for the end of his days. If only he could convince her marrying him wouldn't kill him. She truly believed she held a curse on her which killed her husbands. How foolish that notion was. At first he mocked her concerns.

Katha truly believed however that her husbands, all three of them died before their time, simply because they were married to her. Even though none of what she said was true, Terrence discerned to spend even a short time as Katha's husband, a man would be extremely lucky.

All those years on the bench told him neither of Katha's girls had perpetrated these hideous crimes and there appeared something more sinister behind all this. How were the three murders connected? Terrence wasn't sure, but he knew he had to protect Katha's family. No harm would befall them while he watched over them.

Terrence heard the soft voices of Carol and Rose talking upstairs and listened in over the soft breaths of Katha sleeping. Terrence stared up to the now quiet upstairs and hoped Rose slept. This new murder sounded like someone strongly targeted Katha's family, but was it for protection or harm? He would protect his Katha at all costs. He would protect them all. Katha loved fiercely and she put everyone but herself first. This was what he loved most about her. That and her zest for life.

Katha entered a room and everyone seemed brighter, happier. She had a ready smile and a big heart. Her little courtesies, the compliments she gave out, the willing ear she lent, all of these attracted him. People would smile when they saw her coming. Total strangers would confide in her and she would listen and give advice.

Someone so giving like Katha deserved all the happiness in the world and Terrence wanted to give the world to her. He would convince Katha that she would be the wife for him and he could be the husband she deserved. Katha Stewart had a lovely ring to it after all, and it would give her his power to protect her.

~0~

Carol and Rose a short time ago

"So what happened with your dad the other day?"

asked Rose.

"I don't understand!"

"He showed up to the soccer match and you quit. Why?" Rose asked.

"Oh that," Carol said. "He didn't want to be there. So I quit, then he grew angry because I did. He said I am a disappointment. He said quitters never prosper. Blah, blah, blah."

"I'm sorry; your dad said all the wrong things. He loves you despite his attitude. At least your dad is alive and you two could mend your relationship."

"You had a better bond with your dad then I did. You had lots of years of wonderful memories."

"My dad did like to do things with me, when work didn't take him away."

"Yes, but your dad did make time for you. When did mine, except for that one time he came to my soccer game? Let's be honest, I think my dad wanted an athlete, not a daughter. Nothing I ever do or did meant anything to him. When he discovered I play soccer, he felt he could be proud of me. He would have an athlete for daughter. It's never about me."

"I think you are wrong and he loves you and doesn't understand how to show it."

"It doesn't seem like he does," Carol replied sadly.

"Adults aren't perfect. They are human and they make mistakes; besides parents always expect a lot out of you."

"Where did you get that from? Your mom? My dad wishes I would have been a boy," Carol whined.

"No, he might say it the wrong way and show you awkwardly; but he loves having a daughter," Rose reassured.

"How do you know what he thinks?" Carol sniped.

"He brags about you when you're not around. He told me you're an A-plus student and he hoped I was too."

"He did?" answered Carol surprised but happy.

"Yes, I heard him talking about you with Mrs. Pelland, the guidance teacher as well. He bragged about how smart you were."

"Here I came over to help my best friend, because she's lost her dad and she helps me. How did I get so lucky to pick you as a friend?" Carol exclaimed.

"I thought I picked you," laughed Rose.

"Remember how we met?"

"I remember those dancing toads harassed you at school. We were ten years old," Carol started.

"Yes, Priscilla, Daria, and Tina," interrupted Rose.

"They were mean," Carol admitted.

"You paid them back though. You stuck a frog, which had been preserved in formaldehyde, in Priscilla's favourite purse. What did you do to Tina and Daria?" Rose asked.

"Tina's brother put the fear in her. He liked me, so he stood up for you. He told her he would tell their mom, how she'd been bullying you. Tina's mom hated bullies and would have severely punished her."

"And Daria? Why did she stop?"

"I told her if she didn't, I would beat the snot out of her," Carol replied.

"You didn't?" Rose asked incredulously.

"I did! She backed off didn't she?"

"Thanks for sticking up for me Carol. I don't think I ever thanked you."

"Sure you did! Every time I ever needed you, you were there for me;" Carol exclaimed. "So let me help you now. Tell me about your dad."

"Someone killed him," Rose replied in a quiet voice.

"I heard that on the news," Carol insisted, "But tell me anyway."

"My dad was found dead with Amber, his secretary. Mom and Grandma Katha tried to keep it from me, that he was found naked with her. But I understood that's how they were found even before the newscast."

"It's embarrassing, but it's your father, not you," Carol insisted.

"He wasn't having an affair with ditzy Amber," Rose protested. "She couldn't even put a single sentence together. My dad likes…liked smart woman, like Lily and my mother."

"Well d'oh you'd know he didn't cheat. If someone killed him they were smart enough to pose them together," Carol agreed.

"That's what I thought, but those awful reporters made things up to report. That why you are my best friend. I knew you'd understand the truth without me even saying anything. Why can't other people realize it was staged? It's horrible that someone killed my father, but all they seem to care about is he was found naked. What about finding his killer?" Rose explained.

"Reporters are supposed to be objective. Any good reporter checks their facts."

"How do you know so much about reporters?" asked Rose.

"I want to be one someday."

"What kind? Print? Radio? Television?" Rose asked.

"I'd like to be an entertainment reporter, like the host of Entertainment Tonight," Carol explained.

"I would never do a job that you need to speak in public. I hate speaking to people and to be affected by people staring at me all the time."

"I know Rose. I think it would be a fun job for me, obviously not for you," Carol explained "It is hard work too. People don't realize how much work it is."

"I haven't a clue what job I want to do in the future," Rose explained.

"There's plenty of time. My mom says that all the time," Carol reassured "You'll figure out exactly what you want to do."

"Good imitation of your mom," Rose said giggling.

"I thought so," Carol replied looking serious. "If you need anything, I'm here."

"Thanks for realizing I can't talk about my dad yet. I'm kind of going screen saver here."

"When you want to start talking, I'll listen."

"So did you see Barry ask out Emily?" Rose asked changing the subject.

"Yes, they make a cute couple."

"Barry has liked Emily forever."

"Matchmaking again?" asked Carol smiling.

"Yes, Barry needed a little push."

"So how did you get them together?" Carol demanded.

"Barry hung out near Emily's locker again and I said to him. 'Why don't you ask her out for and cut the damn-a-rama?'" Rose admitted.

"And that worked?" Carol asked.

"Not exactly. He asked me where he should take her," Rose admitted.

"Gee, clueless much?"

"You'd think hanging around her so much he'd realize she wanted to watch she wanted to watch *Star Trek Into Darkness*. She loves *Chris Pine*," Rose replied.

"I want to see *Star Trek Into Darkness* too. So did you tell him?" Carol asked.

"I did and he said, 'But the movie is a drama and a travesty of the older version,'" Rose laughed.

"He didn't. What did you say?"

"I said it's a great movie. Check out the trailer. He liked the trailer. He said, 'I'm wrong it really takes it back to the Star Trek series, and then he decided to ask her to the movie." Rose laughed.

"I'm glad he took your advice. Like I said, they are cute together."

"They are cute," Rose agreed. "So can you stay over later tonight or do you need to bounce?"

"I can stay; my mom said I could, as long as it's okay with your Grandma Katha," Carol replied.

"It will be. Grandma Katha will say yes."

"Good. Now let's watch some *Much Music* unless you have some recorded old episodes of *All My Children*."

"You're in luck Grandma Katha has a lot of old tapes of it. I wish they hadn't cancelled *All My Children*. Hopefully they'll put it on the internet again at some point, but it's not looking good, though that could change. Grandma Katha's tapes and recordings are nice and clear," Rose said putting *All My Children'* on the television set.

Carol replied sadly, "We should watch one of the really old tapes of the show. Why isn't it on the air anymore? I miss it."

"I agree. I miss it too. Maybe we could watch some of the really older stuff later. I'm just going to close my eyes for a minute but keep talking." Rose answered.

"So I think J.r. and Annie are delecto. They look like they'll mack on each other any moment," Carol replied still watching.

Carol glanced over and realized Rose had fallen sound asleep. She covered Rose up and climbed into the other twin bed. Turning the close captioning on and muting the sound, she turned off the PVR and turned on the television setting. As she did that she saw a scroll come across the screen. Terrence also watching television silently downstairs saw the same scroll.

Fourth murder this week. Local security expert Zachary Buchanan found murdered. Story at 11p.m. with Henry Roberts. Breaking news story: Local reporter Paul Knight reported missing. If you have seen him please call your local police station with any information.

This town is damaged. Four murders in two days? Now a news reporter had gone missing? This is whack. Is this related? Poor Rose. I hope she doesn't find out her dad was such a dirty dog and cheated with Amber. I should have told her, but she was already wigged out. What kind of friend would do that? She has always been there for me. I'll be there for her. I'll beat up anyone who gets up in her grill. Carol thought, closed her eyes and went to sleep.

~0~

Chapter 10 - A
View to a Kill

Earlier that Evening

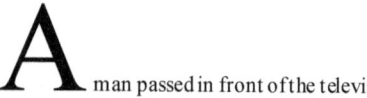 man passed in front of the television screen pacing. He

turned on a DVD recording of the news.

"This reporter has learned Mayor Horace Brooksfield was found murdered in flagrante delicto with his executive assistant, Amber Trent yesterday. Amber Trent worked for Mayor Brooksfield for the last two years. There is no comment from Crown Attorney Lily Kelly Brooksfield or family. Sources close to the mayor say Amber Trent had been having an affair with the mayor for the last year. The police have no comment at this time about the cause of death. Unconfirmed sources tell this reporter they died from poisoning... the same poisoning which is believed to have felled Crown Attorney Lily Kelly-Brooksfield, Lily Kelly who is now in a hospital in satisfactory condition. Mayor Horace Brooksfield leaves behind a fourteen-year-old daughter Rose and his current wife Crown attorney Lily Brooksfield. Our deepest sympathies go out to the mayor's family.

On another odd note, the Crown attorney arrived at the scene of a murder at her cousins' new store Quirks yesterday. Store clerk Megan Fowler was found dead earlier today in an apparent robbery. Store owner Amelia Kelly was also hurt and is in the hospital. Are the two murders connected? Stay tuned to this station for more updates and tune in at six p.m. for News Hour for all the latest stories." Henry Roberts reporting for CHPV-TV."

He screamed in anger at the television, picked up the phone and called the hospital. He wanted to discern that she remained okay.

"Please tell me about Lily Brooksfield, and Amelia Kelly. What is their condition?" he asked politely and sweetly.

He composed himself as the voice on the other end said, "I'm sorry we can't give out any information at this time."

Slamming down the phone in anger and ranting aloud, as if talking to the announcer on the television he began..., "How could she be hurt? The plan wasn't that she should be harmed. I had done it all for her. Every breath I took existed for her, my sweet Angel. Oh how I missed her. I missed looking at her lovely face. Some people can stare at a lake, watching every ripple every nuance. I look at her, and view the ripples of her emotions. Her sweetness, and kindness, the one I saw the most. How I loved her. So much so it hurt. Her happiness remained my only goal," he ranted then continued..., "You behold a great beauty. You should be bowing to her greatness."

He looked over at the man lying on the floor, duct tape over his mouth and rope over his hands and feet connecting both. He pulled the duct tape from over the man's mouth.

"Yes, she's beautiful and going to be fine," the man replied muffled licking the lips, which had held the duct tape.

"Don't get any ideas. She's mine!" the man snarled, his eyes glaring.

"Of course she's yours," mollified the man. "She must care deeply about you."

"Not yet, but she will once she knows me."

"It's like that? I loved a woman once, but she started going out with some other guy. She left me high and dry," sympathized the tied up man.

"It's not like that. I must show her I've changed and am worthy of her. I made a few mistakes in my life. Those other women enticed me to their beds. Who doesn't sow a few wild oats in their youth? I got my life back together for her. I wanted to be near her and take my rightful place at her side but others kept getting in the way. Damn them!"

"No control! Control, control! No one must comprehend this side of me. I have fought long and hard to hide in plain sight until my plan was completed and my goddess would be every day by my side," he muttered, then said louder..."You didn't hear that, did you? Let me compose myself. I'm good the interview can continue."

"Hear what?" the prisoner stated, agreeably.

"She will have my children. We will truly be happy in her home. I will allow her cousin to remain in her life if the cousin behaves. We can grow old together, just the two of us; with her family, no...our family surrounding us."

"Of course you will."

"Don't pretend to humour me. The damn doctor was wrong; I stand in control of my life. I'm in control of everything and everyone. I will have my lady by my side. My lady has shown herself to me. I will have her heart, once I revealed myself," he muttered some more.

The man began pacing back and forth, but smiled like he saw the object of his affections before him.

"She glows with a light, that beholds the goodness in everyone and oh how I need such a light. How I love her. I remembered the first day I met her. She smiled a beckoning smile at me; the smile that told me she remained mine, and mine alone. She pulled her hair back from her face with one hand and the other held lemonade for me. She cared enough to give me drink, when I was thirsty. She existed as a sight of beauty in a pale yellow sundress, with those lovely sandals on such delicate ankles. A lady of high calibre and she looked at me and smiled!"

"She sounds lovely," the captive man commented.

"She is lovely. Such beauty and warmth, my Angel has always projected. I had stared a little too long and she blushed, such an innocent. I loved the way she kept herself to herself. She captured my frozen heart on that glorious day."

"I can understand that"

"Her father, the cheap skate, paid me a mere five dollars to cut the lawn. I wanted to decline and punch him in the nose, when he refused to pay me more-than I saw her, my Angel. She came home and she brushed by me, saying sorry, swiftly entering into the house. Like a ray of sunshine, she appeared smiling moments later. A glass of lemonade clutched in her hand, offering it to me, when I stood dying of thirst."

"You mentioned the lemonade already," the man replied.

"Oh do be quiet while I give you this interview."

The hostage immediately zipped his lips with his fingers.

"Much better now where was I? Oh, how she smiled, demurely and sweetly. Her eyes cast down and she blushed. She ran back into the house putting distance between us because of her modesty. I went home and told my dying mother I met the girl of my dreams. Mother smiled. Mother glowed in happiness, as I described my Angel. She said she hoped my Angel and I would be happy together. It was meant to be. You believe me now? Even mother understood my Angel should be with me."

"Of course I believe you," the prisoner agreed. "But how did you know she was the one?"

"Terri, my former girlfriend, had also smiled, but without the blush and the honesty of my Angel's smile. Terri grinned at me, but she betrayed me instantly. She earned the punishment she received. I get turned on just thinking about it. Her body lush and willing cried out to me. How she begged for her life, pleading with me so prettily. Terri even said she had loved me. But I understood the truth, she had been with him. She offered herself to the football jock Henry. Did Henry treat her like a queen? No! He soiled her forever marking her as easy. I caught Henry bragging about it."

"Shame on Henry," the captive replied and then seeing the man's face he added, "And Terri, of course."

"Mother told me about girls like that, who put on airs of innocence but are at their hearts whores. They are liars and whores, sluts, who say whatever you want to hear. Terri had been one of these. Hadn't she offered herself again to me, to save her life? I told you I took what was offered and how she cried. She begged me to spare her."

"So you did. Right?" the hostage asked hopefully.

"No, silly! She had said we were joined as one. That I would be killing myself if I killed her. She insisted it over and over like a buzzing bee, but I understood the truth about her. She contained evil and had to die, and I cleaned myself with bleach to get her taint off myself. The blood on the power saw cleaned up nicely as well. I disposed of it and my clothes, and of course all those lovely little pieces of her body. Those delightful little pieces of flesh, I had placed so lovingly in garbage bags, for the trash she was!"

"You killed her?" the captive man exclaimed paling.

"Of course I killed her. I truly expected them to find her body but they still haven't. Foolish aren't they? You'd think they would do their job and be productive police officers. But back to my Angel, you wanted to hear all about that didn't you? Of course you do! It's your job."

"It is my job; now fill me in on your beloved Angel," encouraged the captive trying to remain useful so he wouldn't be killed.

"Now don't get ideas she's my Angel. I saw everyone mourning a whore, not knowing where she lay or how she met her fate. It was so delicious. I truly loved keeping a secret of this magnitude. I even went to the funeral and no one suspected me. Well no one except my father who hustled me off to a clinic and a doctor. My father hadn't admitted to the doctor I had killed a human being. No, Father had only said I loved to kill animals. Personally I think he was in denial but it served my purposes. He didn't stop me."

The man continued to pace wildly moving his hand while telling the story. "You know the type of father don't you? You do?" He said.

Noting the captive's nod of his head he continued, "Oh good, it shouldn't be as hard for you to understand all of this. My father abused me. His belt told me all about his displeasure. Even the doctor said that father shouldn't have struck me, or put me in the closet…that it was wrong."

"You told a doctor about your murderous tendencies and they didn't stop you?" the hostage blurted.

"Hah. good one. I do like you. The doctor wouldn't, or couldn't, understand about the murders if I told him; so I hid the real me. I learned well from the doctor how to hide in plain sight. I learned how to hide my true self, from those who would condemn it. I'd learned control, so those around me saw only the agreeable young man they wanted to view. Not even my eagle-eyed father penetrated into my core. The foolish doctor told my father I was much better with the drug and the psychotherapy I received. If people did see through the façade, I would deal with them. I've dealt with you. You understand my position right? I didn't mean to hurt my Angel. It wasn't my fault."

"You hurt your Angel? Where's your doctor now?" asked the hostage.

"Don't say that I hurt her."

"Sorry, of course you didn't hurt her," the captive agreed.

"I did kill the doctor, but only when he got to close. He wanted to lock me up in a padded cell! Me!"

"Well of course you had to. Locking you up would have been bad for you."

"You do understand. Wonderful! Now to continue with my story, my father came to me and said he knew I had killed the doctor. He didn't turn me in, but he said he could no longer pretend his son appeared normal. Normal? As if! If normal was like my mealy-mouthed father, I never want to be him."

"Who would?" agreed the captive.

"Exactly! My father told me the next day we would be going to a private clinic in Brazil, because there was no extradition there. Like I would ever be extradited; no one guessed my crimes but my hawk-eyed father. Mother had been right when she said all his cheating with his secretary made him stupid. How dare he cheat on the lovely lady, my mother? He never guessed what I planned for him. Too bad he died so quickly, clutching his heart. I felt bad for a few minutes. I even sought help after the incident. I listened for hours on end to a simple-minded shrink who blamed all my woes on my father. Why didn't he understand I loved my Angel? She makes me whole, instead of the shattered pieces he made me without her."

The man then clutched his hands to his heart and seemed to be carried away with his thoughts. His captive grew alarmed he had to keep him talking. He smiled at the man hoping to connect with him.

"Where was I? You are listening, aren't you, Paul? I love your newscasts by the way, even when they anger me by mentioning my Angel. Of course those same stories brought my Angel back to me, so I forgive you. I understand you have to do what you are told. It's your bosses I blame. But enough about you, back to my reasons for all I'm doing."

"Thank you... I think you were speaking of about your shrink and your father...," Paul commented, but was interrupted.

"I think you need the tape back on your mouth. You're ruining the interview," he exclaimed, placing duct tape over Paul's mouth again.

"You understand why I had to do this. Don't you? Why all this was necessary? Why I had to bring you here? After all you get a great story out of it. Enough, enough about your story though, and of course dwelling on my conquests, my triumphs, I need to focus on the work at hand and getting my beloved to love me. I think she will finally perceive me as the man she wants as her partner. Don't you, Paul? My psychiatrist was wrong. He said my Angel was an unattainable woman. Silly man! What did he know? But I believed in my Angel; all she needed was to meet me again. Then she would smile her smile and love me. I will be the man she will call her hero, her knight in shining armour."

"No, I'm getting ahead of myself. Quit making me rush, rush and ruin my plans. I need to stick to my plan, slowly advance and win my fair maid. This interview is over, Paul. I have a lot of work to do. A man like you should understand."

Paul couldn't conceal the angry look which came over his face. Paul knew what this meant if he didn't get the interview, he would be killed.

"Don't you dare make angry faces at me! I'm doing my job, you just do yours!" Paul tried to signal that he would do his job by bobbing his head but the man ignored him and he was forced to watch as the man called the hospital yet again.

His Angel lay injured in a hospital room. At least she had her cousin for company. She was safe. Take a deep breath, the man thought and he began to pace and rant out loud again.

"Those damn girls. Those whores! They tainted both sweet cousins. It is why they were in the hospital; I shouldn't blame myself. Should I, Paul?"

Paul nodded.

"I tried to save the innocents from the taint. Hadn't I slain to get rid of the taint?"

Paul nodded again and hoped to once again convince him the interview was necessary.

"Okay Paul, you want an interview on why I killed?"

Paul nodded frantically.

"Certainly I'd be happy to give you an award-winning interview. I am so careful after all this. These stupid cops will never discover me. What? Well certainly I killed. I didn't leave any evidence of myself there. I snuck up when her back was turned to me. Megan! What a slut. I had viewed how she let her boyfriend in after closing hours. How they had soiled the countertop at Quirks. How dare they? She had to die. She fought back too easy and I had to kill her brutally... all that blood."

"It was her fault my Angel slipped. The boyfriend will die too. His turn will come. Slowly and more painfully, it won't be as easy as her death. I saw him take from the till while the slut cleaned up herself at the store. First, though, I plan to let him suffer, mourning the whore. I'll bide my time and kill him too. Or I'll let the cops think he committed the murders. Oh the irony that would be. You agree, Paul?"

Paul tied with rope, sat somewhat slumped in a chair, directly in front of the killer. Duct tape now covered his mouth again, but he nodded.

"Of course you do! I'm brilliant. He will pay... oh yes... he will pay for his treachery. The whore Amber, who screwed Lily's husband in his office? She deserved what she got. What, you think she was just his secretary, Paul? Oh no, she was his paid whore! I watched as she strutted and tempted Horace; but he was married to sweet Lily. So why did he cheat? Some men don't understand how fortunate they are."

Paul shook his head trying to get free of the duct tape.

"Don't shake your head at me! What? You want to understand why I wasn't identified? No one saw me arrive through the basement. The guard during the day is an idiot. I snuck up the back stairs and spotted them. Those two rutting like farm animals. I waited patiently, until they stopped falling all over each other; snuck up and first hit him on the head, then her. She shook then. Oh I truly scared her! I loved that part! It was so delicious! She ran but I caught her and hit her on the head. I posed them so everyone would recognize their crime. I was simply brilliant."

Paul moved his head; he was finding it hard to hold it in this position listening to this man drone on, but the killer moved his head back and forth as if Paul was agreeing.

"Why thank you, Paul. Yes, I have to admit it was brilliant. So you wanted to see how I created the gas?"

Paul bobbed his head in agreement, anything to keep this man talking.

"Chlorine gas is such an easy fix for me to make. After all, I excelled at Chemistry in high school. So, I remembered the quantities. Like I said, I my memory is excellent. They used this substance in the First World War. Our poor troops were harmed irreparably. Some of them out right killed with various gases they used. But why am I telling you this? You are a journalist and well-educated; you'd comprehend all of this information.

"Now where was I? Oh yes...in fact, if truth were to be told, I have a photographic memory. Like my Angel, these were truly a match. It was so much fun to mix and watch the chemicals take root. I cleaned up at the scenes, leaving no trace of me. I'm good at cleansing. I still can't quite believe the Ravenworst police haven't clued in about the chlorine gas."

Paul struggled to get some more to get free at this point, but the killer took it as if he'd asked him a question.

"What? You want to know why they didn't clue in Paul? The investigators in Ravenworst were underfunded and too proud to ask for outside help. Lucky for me! It does seem the Happy Valley Police investigators are more thorough. They identified the gas. Damn that Coroner Andrew Piper. He is too smart for his own good. As for the investigating officer, Emmett Rogers, scrutinized too close at my Angel. As long as he doesn't threaten her, I will allow him to pretend to investigate. The widow Lily likes him despite her protests. But believe me, Paul, I will fix him, or any police officer who threatens what is mine. I noticed the way he looks at Lily Kelly, when no one is looking. Don't you think it would be kind of funny if he became a relative and never discerned any of my crimes, Paul? Oh how glorious that would be, flaunting my crimes in front of a police officer. Now wouldn't it, Paul?"

Paul tried to nod but his head wouldn't bob anymore.

"You understand how it is, being in front of the cameras all the time. Emmett Rogers is an upstanding man, fit for a family member. So I think he would be acceptable for her. Don't you?"

Paul managed to nodded again, trying to make himself agreeable once more to the killer.

"Well, of course I was worried about my dear, sweet Angel and her cousin, though it hadn't occurred to me though that Amelia would slip and Lily would be gassed. I blamed those whores just thinking about it again. Yes the whores are to blame; at least now their taint is stopped. They can't harm my Angel. I'll continue to watch over my sweet Angel keeping her safe. Those damn paparazzi stalk my Angel's house. Can't you do anything about the paparazzi, Paul? I appreciate you hate their ilk too. They give reporters a bad name. If they don't leave her alone, they will suffer the consequences. And you know what that means, don't you Paul? And if the cop dares to threaten my Angel, I'll stop him. One day soon my Angel will appreciate me and she will comprehend all I had done for her."

"Quite the story," Paul retorted as the killer took the tape off his mouth again and offered him a lukewarm coffee.

Paul readily drank, his throat parched from the exposure to the tape.

"Do you want me to feature you on the news? We should get this all on camera for a special series. It will be on tomorrow."

The killer didn't respond and Paul grew frightened.

"You will you let me go now?" asked Paul.

"No, we may need to have another interview. Aw, I can't lie to such a trusting face. The truth, though, is now you know about me... I can't let you go," the killer answered putting the tape back on Paul's mouth, "It's too bad you won't be available for the story at six p.m. Isn't it, Paul? It's too sad; you are so much of a snoop, you caught onto me. You'll have to explain how you did later, when I return. In the meantime, those pills I slipped in your drink should be taking hold soon. Nighty, night, Paulie. Oh, and sorry about the tight space. You can't be found. Don't think about making any noise. I've soundproofed my apartment, including this closet."

The killer upended Paul like he weighed next to nothing and placed him into the hall closet.

"Please..." Paul begged groggily through the new duct tape, begging for his life.

"Sorry, Paul, I'm going to the hospital. Nothing and no one will get in my way. I must grasp for myself, my Angel is okay. I can't have done the unthinkable and seriously hurt my Angel. I would never harm her, ever. I blame those evil people who made me kill them. Why did they get between us?"

He shut and locked the door to his apartment after changing into the police uniform. That uniform would make them tell her how she was. He got into his car, driving straight to the hospital. When he arrived at the hospital, he became angry to find a man standing guard outside her hospital room door. Who is he? Why did he keep me from my Angel? How dare he come between us? He thought.

He went to the cafeteria and purchased two coffees. Taking two stir sticks, he placed sugar and his. He reached into his pocket for the pill bottle he no longer used. With no one watching, he put pills into the other coffee and waited as they melted into the cup. It was ready. He went up in the elevator to the floor he seen the man on. Making small talk, he began..."I'm Detective Barnes sent to protect Ms. Kelly and you are?" he lied.

"Zachary Buchanan, I work for Frank Hawk Security Services. I was told there were cutbacks and you weren't able to guard the lady." protested the man.

"We'll get this killer, you need not worry. But it certainly is a relief to find Ms. Kelly is protected. The station sent me to check on Ms. Kelly."

"But that isn't what you said a minute ago." Zachary Buchanan protested.

"A slip of the tongue, forgive me I've had a long shift today. Now you were hired by whom?"

"Lily Brooksfield hired me. I know what that's like to work along shift, I was supposed to get some relief an hour ago so I could get lunch."

"Oh, where are my manners? I have two coffees, here have one." the killer offered.

"Thank you. That hits the spot."

"Listen, see that cop down the hall?"

"Yes," Zachary answered.

"Excuse me for a minute while I'll speak to him and get him to take over while you go to lunch."

"That would be great."

The killer went down the hall and appeared to speak to the cop then returned, "We can go now. Come on I'll treat you to lunch."

"Wow, they pay you that much?"

"No, but I won fifty bucks in the office bet, so I can treat you."

"Well thanks; I'll take you up on that." Zachary gulped down his coffee in the elevator and the killer pretended to get a call, which he had to answer in his car.

"Say, can you go to my patrol car for a minute, I have to check in before lunch.

"I could just meet you in the cafeteria."

"I might be called away and then I couldn't tell you. Come on it will only take a few minutes," begged the killer.

"Okay, sure." Zachary agreed.

How easy it was to trick someone using a police uniform. It just initiated such trust. At least someone had the use of those pills, he thought laughing to himself...two some ones. He chuckled. How he hated that they clouded his mind. He led the man to his car.

"Wait a minute I feel dizzy. What did you do to me?" Zachary asked already swaying on his feet.

The gun was stuck in the man's side with no resistance, the drugs already cloudy the man's mind. He made the man get in the trunk and slammed it shut. At first he heard banging then silence as the man succumbed to the drugs effect. He was mad at Lily before, but he understood now. She took steps to protect his Amelia. How could he fault her for helping his Amelia?

The killer drove, thinking about the man in his trunk. Obviously Lily had hired him sight unseen, a repulsive brute which could harm my Angel. If he hadn't shown me his security badge, I would have thought him the dregs of society or one of those gang members.

My Angel shouldn't be tainted with such burgeoning evil. I must get rid of him before he blemishes her, or makes a move on my poor Angel. In her grieving state she's fair game for predators like him. Don't worry my darling; he shan't get near you again.

He reached his underground parking spot and opened the trunk. Damn the man wasn't moving yet another body to get rid of. He drank down the coffee in one gulp and reached for the protective suit in his back seat putting it on.

Oops, I must have put too many pills in to the cup.

Who understood that many pills would kill? That damn doctor! He had been trying to kill me? Well, I'd fixed him first. I'd have to remember that for future reference those little pills did so much. But it meant the body must be dumped sooner.

Where could I put him? Think. Somewhere he wouldn't be found too soon? The Beyer building downtown? Undergoing renovations to be sold... it would be perfect! I will find some place to hide him somewhere in the building. The car rocked and he worried about the body in his trunk.

Watch the road and follow the laws. I must not give the cops a reason to stop me. Good, I'm here at the rear entrance of the Beyer Building and no cop in sight. I must not leave evidence of myself on him. After planting him there I must strip him bare than redress him.

Damn! There is someone there. That asshole real estate agent, Herbert Weatherthorpe prowled around the building. Guess it's a dumpster for old Zachary Buchanan. There's one nearby. I'll strip him, then redress him with the clothes I brought and toss him in the bin. I hope this would be a lesson to those who would try to take advantage of my Angel's good nature.

Her cousin obviously shared some of her good nature or she wouldn't have hired this man sight unseen. If she caught sight of the man she wouldn't have hired him. Lily had been there when he couldn't be for his Angel and he wouldn't forget the cousin. She deserved his familial devotion. He would grow to care for her. She was like a beloved sister-in-law. After all, she would soon be family. There, no one saw this remote location of the dumpster and pick up is tomorrow. Zachary would soon be lost at the dump, like Terri.

I'll throw away the plastic liner and vacuum the trunk when I get home. No fibres could be found from Zachary Buchanan. We are safe, my Angel, safe. He tidied himself, took off his protective suit, and then placed the suit in the back seat. He had to clean the police uniform at the cleaners. He then got back in his car and peeled away quickly from the curb.

Chapter 11 - Family Ties

“T he ad should read...**SALES ASSOCIATE**

WANTED MUST BE PREPARED TO WORK EVENINGS AND WEEKENDS. RE-ENUMERATION ACCORDING TO EXPERIENCE...and the phone number I gave you,” Lily repeated still with oxygen in her nose.

“Lily shouldn’t you be resting? Who did you call?” asked Katha, coming in their hospital room.

“I was calling to place an ad, so we could reopen Amelia’s store again.” Lily explained, “I thought Rose and Carol could work at the store, but I’m not prepared for the girls to work there anymore. Not after the guard disappeared which I had hired to look after Amelia. I called the office to take over my cases for a while; a month or two until they figure out who killed them.”

Katha noticed Lily was careful not to mention her husband was one of the victims and Katha worried about Lily. Katha recalled how Lily avoided grief, by keeping busy and fretted this time she would not be able to do avoid the inevitable.

“Lily, I already hired someone. I interviewed earlier today for the position. There were several excellent candidates, but the best one was a lovely college girl Susan Terrell. She’s the daughter of Barney, the security guard at City Hall. She is a black belt and experienced in sales. She worked all through high school at George’s Toys.”

“Didn’t they go under?”

"Yes, unfortunately the toy shop was taken over by a big conglomerate and they closed it when George died, a few weeks ago. So she needs a job. I offered her the job and she happily accepted. Today the cleaning crew came in to fix the place, so the store can open tomorrow. I think the store should be strictly a nine to five operation for a while, until Amelia can be more hands on at the store."

"You hired someone to work at my store, Aunt Katha?" Amelia asked with a touch of anger and surprise, "And now you're setting the hours in my store?"

"I hope I didn't over step my bounds," Aunt Katha countered innocently.

"No of course, you didn't overstep," Amelia claimed swallowing her anger.

"Thanks Lily, thank-you, Aunt Katha. What would I do without you?" she said sarcastically under her breath, but Katha heard her anyway.

Amelia then hugged Katha despite her misgivings.

"You'll never find out, because family is always here for you honey," Katha replied taking it for a compliment, then turning to Lily she said. "Do you want to talk about Horace?"

"I don't want to talk about this!"

"Lily, you like to avoid things you don't want to face," Aunt Katha began.

"I'm grieving, that's how I'm doing. I'm madder than hell, that's how I am," Lily cried.

"You won't do anything stupid will you?"

"I never do anything stupid. I'm the poster child for good behaviour," Lily replied.

"No, you do go off the rails from time to time. You bumble into places no one should go. Like last year with that horrible man who threatened you, and years ago with that other man." Katha commented, "They could have killed you."

"Ian Turner was a maniac. I think he would have killed you. Thank god he's in jail. Horace was terrified for you. Oh I'm sorry, Lily, I shouldn't have brought up Horace," Amelia apologized.

"No, it's good for me to catch his name. I can't believe he's gone. Horace was so wonderful. He was a good father and a good man. I'll be damned if I let his murder, take all those memories away from him and his family," Lily cried, wiping tears away from her eyes.

"Let the police handle this." Katha begged, "They will work hard to solve this crime. They'll find out who did this and they'll pay."

"She's dating the police chief's father," Amelia announced conspiratorially to Lily.

"And you didn't tell me? When did this start?" asked Lily looking surprised.

"Oh about two months ago I think. I came over early one morning and he was still in her house," Amelia replied smirking.

"I'm still in the room girls. Do you mind not talking about my love life? It's unseemly," Katha retorted annoyed, "And we've been dating for a year."

"Is he handsome? I've never met him, only his son Edward," Lily asked of Amelia, ignoring her grandmother.

"He is extremely handsome. He's kind of Sean Connery meets Edmund Gwynn," Amelia commented, "He wears top of the line, fitted suits too."

"He is a hottie, isn't he?" Katha agreed. "And he's got charm to spare."

"Well he better understand what he has in you," Lily commented.

"He does," Katha admitted.

"Ladies, good afternoon," Sergeant Detective Rogers exclaimed, stepping in the hospital room. "Better now ladies?"

"Hello, dear. You solved the crime all ready?" Katha asked innocently.

"We are still actively looking at the crime scene, Ma'am," Detective Rogers admitted, then turning to Lily he demanded, "I'd like to talk to you alone, .Ms. Kelly-Brooksfield."

"'I don't think so. Lily, don't speak to him without us, or at least another lawyer," Katha claimed angrily.

"Don't say a word to him, Lily. He wants the crime to be committed by one of us, so he can close the book on this case!" Amelia agreed.

"I am a lawyer, remember?" Lily answered.

"Listen to me, Ms. Kelly. You're still a valid suspect in my book."

"You will not bully my cousin! Is that clear, Sergeant Detective Rogers!" Lily demanded, "My husband has been murdered and we had nothing to do with either murder!"

"Then you won't mind answering a few questions will you?" Sergeant Detective Rogers commented.

"Fine, I'm innocent, so go ahead," Lily said.

"I believe your first husband died in a car accident? Sorry, correction, I understand the investigating officer believed it to be a drunken driving accident?"

"Dredging up what you think are skeletons will not solve my husband's murder! My first husband died crossing a street. The police thought someone leaving the bars had too much to drink and had killed William. One day we will find the drunk driver and he'll pay. William Wentworth was a great man, a great Crown attorney. I became a Crown attorney based on my own merit, after his death," Lily cried. "My life is an open book. I have no skeletons."

"It would seem to me you're a black widow and so is your cousin. Wasn't there gossip that he had been cheating on you?"

"Do you believe everything you overhear? That must be a real drawback in your job," Lily snapped sarcastically.

"So was he?" Sergeant Detective Rogers demanded.

"No, he wasn't. I'll never believe he cheated on me," Lily shouted.

"I found documented proof he was having an affair with one Cecile Grimes," Emmett confirmed.

"I don't believe any vicious gossip. She's a lawyer in my office. He spoke maybe two words to her."

"The affair has been documented, I'm sorry to tell you. It's too bad you're a head in the sands kind of girl. We've confirmed Horace had a long-term affair with Amber by the way. Two husbands, two cheats, two dead men! Suspicious wouldn't you say?" Sergeant Detective Rogers needled.

"I think you've said enough young man. I'll be talking to your superior about this!" Katha spit angrily.

"You go ahead, Ma'am, but I need to solve a murder. I am looking at every angle to solve the case," Sergeant Detective Rogers explained.

"Well since you've now discovered I had nothing to do with the crime, you can now move on and figure out who killed my husband," Lily demanded.

"Goodbye, Sergeant Detective Rogers," Lily dismissed him.

"Goodbye, for now, Ms. Kelly-Brooksfield," Sergeant Detective Rogers retorted, than added as a last parting shot, "We'll be in touch."

"That man is rude. I don't like him!" Katha bristled, "How dare he talk to you like you were a suspect?"

"He's doing his job. You do understand that, don't you, Grandma Katha?" defended Lily.

"I may perceive he has a job to do, but I don't need to like the way he does his job," Katha grumbled, "I have half a mind to complain to his superiors."

"Don't worry, Aunt Katha, it will all blow over once he realizes he's got the wrong person."

"If you say so, my darling Amelia, but if you change your mind let me know. I'm heading out my dears. Get some rest."

"We will. Goodbye, Grandma Katha," Lily replied.

"Goodbye, Aunt Katha," Amelia added. "I got strange vibes from Detective Rogers; despite his bringing up all that garbage, the man likes you," commented Amelia smiling knowingly after Katha had left.

"Oh be quiet!" replied Lily only half kidding.

"Well he is kind of cute; don't you think?" asked Amelia.

"He is positively handsome in a rugged sort of way." Lily replied, then thinking of Horace, she continued, "He's also looking into two murders and seems to think we had something to do with the crime. Besides, I'm not looking at any man. I lost the love of my life to murder."

"Sorry, Lily, losing Horace must hurt like hell. The only thing which got me through, when my husband and child died was you, so lean on me, cousin, I'm here, bum leg and all."

"Thanks, Amelia. Do you think Horace cheated on me?" asked Lily.

"I'm sorry Lily; I didn't know how to tell you," Amelia explained.

"Did you see something which made you think he had an affair?"

"I saw him kissing Amber at a local restaurant. I followed them when they left right to a motel," Amelia admitted. "I had planned on coming over to tell you today."

"I can't believe this. I thought he loved me. Why did you do this Horace? Why?" Lily asked.

"If it helps in his twisted way, Horace loved you Lily. You were the woman he held on a pedestal. He loved you."

"Yes, he loved me enough to sleep with Amber," Lily said bitterly, "Was she prettier than me? Is that the reason why?"

"No and I take what I said back; Horace was a fool. You did everything for Horace and he didn't appreciate any of it," Amelia exclaimed fiercely.

"Thanks, Amelia. What would I do without you?"

"You'll never need to find out how to live without me."

"I seem to have heard that," replied Lily smiling.

"We're family and we support one another through thick and thin right?" Amelia answered. "Right! We keep having these weird tragedies though. Could Sergeant Detective Rogers be on to something?" asked Lily.

"People die. We can't read things into this. It's not mysterious. We are not cursed. At least that's what Dr. Jones has been telling me."

"But most people don't have two dead husbands at the age of thirty. Do you think William was murdered like Sergeant Detective Rogers suggested?" Lily asked.

"No, some idiot with too much to drink killed him. It was unintentional, unfortunate, and tragic, but not a deliberate murder."

"I understand he has to investigate, but I wish he'd quit bringing up the past and all it entailed. I hope he doesn't mention Rose's mother in front of her," Lily commented.

"She still doesn't know does she?"

"No, she has no idea her mother is in a mental facility for the criminally insane," Lily replied.

"Do they treat her well?" Amelia asked.

"Yes, I check up on them all the time. She's treated with gentle care. She's been there six years now. The doctors have great hopes she can be cured. But I've seen no sign of her recovery."

"What exactly is wrong with her?"

"She doesn't recall her crime. It's a self-defence mechanism. She thinks she works at the hospital and Rose is a doll she carries around with her," Lily explained.

"Oh how awful, to live with the knowledge you killed someone; even to defend yourself and your daughter."

"I tried my earnest to get her off, but my supervisor overruled me. I had gotten her a twenty-year sentence when she became catatonic. She was languished in a jail cell, neither eating nor sleeping. She didn't respond to anyone. I finally got them to move her to the centre with the judge's permission."

"If Rose knew she would be grateful that you'd looked after her mother so well. So what happened since then?"

"Cordelia started responding to voices but she didn't recall me or her crime. Horace took her a doll of Rose's to remind her and snap her out of her fugue, but she declared Rose was a doll. Horace didn't want Rose to have any knowledge of her mother's condition. He made me swear only to tell her about her mother, if necessary. Horace didn't even want his mother or anyone else to know she wasn't in jail but in a forensic psychiatric facility."

"That's like a jail thought too. Right?"

"She has access to her shrinks; but yes she's kept securely so she can't harm anyone."

"Why are you worried about that? Do you think she'd harm Rose?"

"Horace thought there might be more to the story. Something may have happened to Rose, but we could never get the story out of her. Rose doesn't remember that night," Lily admitted.

"But what did you tell Rose?"

"Rose thinks she's in jail and she isn't allowed to visit. I hate lying to her, but as I said Horace insisted she should never comprehend what her mother did."

"Isn't it better Rose doesn't know? She's already had a difficult life and now losing her father..,." Amelia asked.

"Yes, that what I thought too." Lily replied, "But I still feel guilty."

"Don't beat yourself up about protecting Rose. You are the best parent you can be."

"Thanks, I love my little girl, okay not so little girl, so much. I hope I can be the best parent for her now she doesn't have her dad," Lily replied sounding worried.

"You will be Lily. You mother everyone, even me. Rose is the luckiest kid alive. She has you!" Amelia reassured.

"I love you Aem."

"Enough with the mush. I'm tired; I'm going to take a nap now. You should get some rest too."

"Goodnight, Amelia." Lily replied closing her eyes.

Then sneaking a glance under her lids, Lily smiled. She noticed Katha watched and listened from the doorway. Amelia closed her eyes and she thought, how she'd like to go back to that time when they were the teenage girls Katha raised. Those rebellious young teens Katha took in had bonded like sisters, through the tragedies that touched their lives. The bond was still tight and would remain so. They would all get through this. They were Kelly's and family was there for each other.

~0~

Chapter 12 - Ghosts of the Past

T he next day Lily awaited the doctor. She had to get

permission from her physician to leave the hospital. She had a lot to do. Horace needed to be honoured befitting his status as mayor, but she wished she could have a funeral for family only. Well why not? Rose had been through enough, so she wanted a simple funeral. Others who wanted to give their respect would come to the wake and do so. She would make a quick appearance at the wake and leave. There. Plans made, unless that stupid cop Emmett Rogers decided to arrest either her or Amelia. He wouldn't, would he? No, he had no grounds.

A model thin woman polished looking, with honey blonde hair in a twist at the back of her head entered the room. She wore a dress which would be worn to high society tea. She was followed by an older woman about sixty-five years old, with short dyed black hair. She too, was dressed in a high society tea dress.

"I found you! You rotten bitch! You thought you could hide and play the poor grieving widow. But I know what you did it and you'll pay."

"What?" Amelia answered.

"I warned him my poor Horace. I knew you'd be the death of him. How could you?" demanded the first woman bitterly.

"Why haven't you got on handcuffs? You did this, Lily Kelly. I warned my son about you. I told him you were trash! After all, you are related to Katha O'Malley, and Lord knows she's a piece of work!" the older woman yelled, "Katha O'Malley goes after anyone in pants. I understand she's after Terrence Stewart now. God save the man!"

Lily sitting in a chair beside her hospital bed, looked up in surprise.

"Who are these people Lily?" Amelia asked.

Lily smiled a bitter smile and narrowed her eyes. and then smirked, "You've met my mother-in-law Cheryl, Amelia, and this woman is Horace's first wife Renée,"

Amelia caught on quickly and asked acting puzzled, "But I thought his former wife rotted in jail for life?"

"Oh Amelia, I do love you. No, you're thinking of his second wife, Cordelia." Lily replied laughing, "Cordelia is Rose's mother."

"You killed him, you evil bitch. Don't think you can get away with this act pretending you were poisoned!" Cheryl commented viciously. "I warned Horace he shouldn't marry you. I told him you were a black widow."

Cheryl then paced near the hospital room door.

"Oh gee, where have I heard those lies before? Have you talked to Sergeant Detective Rogers recently?" Lily asked sarcastically.

"We weren't about to let you get away with killing dear Horace. He chose to take sustenance elsewhere because he wasn't satisfied with you. You evil bitch! That didn't mean you had the right to kill him," Renée sneered.

"I talked to a pleasant young cop. I told him what kind of woman you are," Cheryl expounded. "He won't let you get away with this."

"You two are so repetitive it's boring. As to this cop what did you say? Did you tell this cop that your son didn't talk to you anymore? Did you tell him you assaulted your son? You have a file? Did you tell him you aren't allowed to associate with your granddaughter, because you obtained a record? That you are forbidden to associate with children less than sixteen years of age, because of a conviction for child abuse? Isn't that right, Cheryl? You have a child abuse record dating back to when Horace was young?" continued Lily twisting the screws.

"Simply a misunderstanding!" Cheryl complained.

"I don't call a child of three, getting a broken arm from his mother a misunderstanding!" Lily replied angrily.

"Horace lied. I never touched him! That wicked nursery school I sent him to made Horace tell such wicked lies." Cheryl whined.

"Right and your husband didn't divorce you and sue for custody to get away from you and protect Horace," Lily said bitterly.

"If anyone has motive here, it's you two. I should enlighten the police officers about you two. Right, Renée? Funny how you were charged with stalking! Didn't your dad get your record expunged?"

Renée's face grew purple and looked extremely angry. She stalked to Lily, raising her hand as if to hit her.

"I wouldn't do that, Ms. Harrow," demanded Detective Rogers coming upon the scene. He pulled back Renée's hand as she was about to hit Lily.

"I wasn't doing anything!" Renée protested.

"Would you like to lay charges against this woman, Mrs. Brooksfield?" asked Sergeant Detective Rogers.

"No, I think I'm okay for now. But I'd like them to leave," Lily replied forcefully.

"Not before I speak with them. Ms. Harrow, Ms. Waverly if you please, I'd like to speak to you both in the hall?" demanded Detective Rogers.

"I guess we can discuss this in the hall. I can give you an earful about this evil siren," Renée replied to Detective Rogers, then turning to Lily she shouted, "But this isn't over bitch. We know you killed Horace. You wait, you've got a whole lot of hurt coming your way."

"I said enough, Ms. Harrow. You can go out into the hall instantly or I can file a harassment charge against you, and perhaps throw in a stalking charge," Detective Rogers commented.

"Renée we must not sink to her level," scolded Cheryl.

"Thank you, Mother," Renée answered sweetly.

"But I'm worried about him, Detective Rogers. He's taking her part. What about justice for our Horace?" Renée continued motioning at Detective Rogers like he was a chair.

"Got another man twisted in your web, do you, Lily?" Cheryl cried viciously, "Is he the reason you killed my boy? He waited in the wings? What do they see in you?"

"Enough! You two leave this instant. I'll be back shortly, Mrs. Brooksfield," Detective Rogers exclaimed.

"Wow! He does like you. I told you so. Did you see how he defended you with those witches?" Amelia commented, "His kind of chiselled good looks make you warm all over."

"Amelia, quit trying to set me up with him! I just lost my husband. Or did you forget I'm in mourning?" Lily protested, "I loved Horace."

"Horace wasn't good enough for you. I'm sorry to say. You deserved a hell of a lot better than a man who cheated, using you for a place to eat and sleep and a mother for his child," Amelia retorted angrily.

"Amelia, please, I'm begging you, I just lost my husband."

"Sorry, Lily, I understand how awful it is to lose someone you love. I want someone I consider closer than a sister to be happy." Amelia commented, "I wish you would get over the hurt faster."

"I love you too, Aem," Lily responded.

"You're closer than a sister to me too, but I loved Horace and I need time to grieve."

"I want to know what they are saying," Amelia insisted.

"Okay, then will both listen," Lily replied.

Amelia then used her crutches and went with Lily to hear the interrogation from the doorway.

"So, Ms. Harrow, where were you between hours of eight p.m. and twelve a.m. on June fourteenth?" asked Detective Rogers.

"We're suspects? Try looking beyond your hormones. That bitch killed my Horace, just when he decided to come back to me," Renée screamed loud enough for Lily to overhear.

"It would have been so wonderful when Horace married you again. I'm sure you would have talked Horace into talking to me again," Cheryl said regretfully.

"Ms. Harrow, is this all your imagination? Or did Mr. Brooksfield say he would leave his wife to return to you? And remember this is an official police statement, which means if you give me false testimony, you can be charged! Are we clear?" Sergeant Detective Rogers demanded.

"Well, he hadn't come right out and said he was coming back to me, but I read between the lines he would have come to me. I know he loved me. Even my brother said so," Renée claimed.

"And who is your brother?" asked Detective Rogers curiously.

"Sergeant Detective Brad Owens. We had different fathers so he's sort of my half-brother," Cheryl explained "I'm sure you've seen him, he's a cop too."

"Renée," cautioned Cheryl but didn't elaborate.

"Well isn't that interesting," Sergeant Detective Rogers said slowly drawing it out, empathizing it didn't matter to him. "Now your alibis, ladies?"

"Well I chaired an event. The People Against Drunk Driving charity ball. I lost a child to a drunk driver! My sweet, Cheryl-Lynn Rose. I went out of my mind when she died. I admit I was a little too forceful with Horace but I regretted it," Cheryl admitted "I attended from six p.m. until after two a.m. I'm sure many people saw me as I spoke as the main speaker at the podium. Roberta Anderson, Barry Pike, and John Nevelson. Oh, and Gregory Hanks will vouch for me. I'm sure you're familiar with Greg; he is the CEO of Hanks those grocery stores across the country?"

"And you. Ms. Harrow?"

"Well I watched television, by myself. That's an alibi. It was *The Bachelor* on *TiVo*. I had to catch up on a few episodes," Renée expounded.

"Sorry, but unless someone can substantiate your alibi, it won't convince me. Now will it?"

"But I watched television. Can't you just check my *TiVo* and tell?" Renée stammered.

"No, Ms. Harrow. You could have left it playing while you went out and murdered Horace and Amber," Detective Rogers declared.

"Why aren't you observing Lily Kelly? She had more of a motive. He cheated on her. Glare at her! The woman is a black widow! Her first husband died mysteriously. Look at her, not me!" whined Renée stamping her foot.

"We are looking at everyone at this point, Ms. Harrow, but you just moved up on my suspect list," Detective Rogers declared.

"Me? I moved up on your suspect list? I didn't kill him. I loved Horace. I hate you! I'm going to tell my brother about you and then you'll be sorry," Renée whined, stamping her foot like a child.

"Don't leave town Ms. Harrow. Now I expect you both at the police station, you and Ms. Waverly, at one p.m. to sign your official statements."

"I'm not coming. I refuse. You can't make me. You just want to grill me," Renée complained. "I could arrest you now."

"No, please," Renée begged.

"If you're not there at one p.m., I'm issuing a warrant for your arrest," Detective Rogers declared.

"You will be so sorry! I'm going to get my brother to get you fired. He's popular and he'll make you pay," Renée threatened.

"He's already tried and failed big time, but please, be my guest, go whine to your brother," Detective Rogers replied breezily.

"Come on, dear, drop this tact. You'll just rile up the officer. Once he understands what she's like, he'll go after Lily; you wait and watch. He can't be blind to her evil, even Horace wasn't. was about to drop her like a bad shoe," Cheryl insisted pulling Renée's arm and leaving.

~0~

The next day

Emmett

E mmett stared after the departing women. How did a

caring person like Lily Kelly-Brooksfield get mixed up with two witches like those two? Horace must have been a piece of work. Being involved with that woman Renée, and being brought up by Cheryl Waverly, probably made him the person he became. He learned some bad things about Horace Brooksfield in his investigation. The man collected women like they were disposable; nevertheless he obtained a loyal wife like Lily Brooksfield? He must have entertained some decency and yet someone murdered him.

Those women were piranhas. The way they were involved with Horace Brooksfield, made them definite suspects in his mind. He'd check out the mother's alibi, but Renée's alibi couldn't be verified. It didn't make her necessarily guilty, but she did have a strong motive. She was the jilted ex-wife, after all. What a story! Horace planned on getting back together with Renée? Given a choice, what man would pick that shrew Renée? But the victim Horace sounded like an idiot. He had been having an affair with Amber, when the woman was by all accounts mindless. The story that Renée told bore checking. Brad was not a good source. The man remained treacherous; it didn't matter if he was a cop.

He'd lie to back up his sister. He wanted to believe her cousin, Amelia, hadn't done this; but the first rule of being a cop in homicide, suspect the spouse. He needed to make a quick trip to visit Dr. Piper. He would get the autopsy reports and then he would check out Ms. Waverly's arrest warrant and her alibi. He had begun to experience something for Lily Kelly Brooksfield a little too much. He must get back his objectivity. What if she and her cousin were serial killers in those sweet packages?

~0~

Chapter 13 - Home Sweet Home

Amelia slipped her crutch up higher, trying to balance on her crutches, as she entered the foyer of Lily's home.

"So great to be home, I won't even complain it's your house," Amelia commented, stepping into the living room and settling into the dark blue sofa, propping up her leg.

"My casa is your casa. Besides how will you get up those stairs anyway?" Lily asked. "The guest room is down the hall there."

"Thanks again."

"Consider this your home."

"Have you talked to the funeral home yet?" Amelia asked.

"Yes, I arranged a simple private service Friday morning at ten a.m. I can't bear to have all those people there," Lily answered. "I can understand you wanting a quiet funeral," Amelia replied.

"A good thing I've already changed the arrangements for the funeral," Katha commented coming in the room.

"You did what?" Lily screeched. "You didn't! Did you Grandma Katha?"

"I had to, dear. If you have the small simple service you want, everyone will think you're guilty and you'll lose your job," Katha explained.

"She's right Mom. Some of my acquaintances called the two of you, the Cousin Killers. I say acquaintances, because I no longer consider them friends. Some would call them frenemies, but they are just a bunch of haters," Rose commented.

"I'm sorry honey. None of this is fair. You lose your father and they now blame your adoptive mother for killing him. For the record, I didn't kill him. I loved your father."

"I know you didn't kill him Mom," Rose replied sounding annoyed. "Why do you think I was so mad at my so-called friends? Carol has stood by me though. She's shown she's my true friend. She came over to Grandma Katha's last night and spent the night."

"Carol is a true friend," Lily agreed.

"It's going to be a little rocky for a while, but we will get through this. At least school is out for the year. I'm glad school started in August last year. We should go away, somewhere fun. But where?" asked Lily

Mom!!!" Rose protested. "We can't leave! Are you cray, cray?"

"Cray, cray? Does that mean crazy?" Lily asked, amused by the slang.

"Lily, think of how guilty you'll appear." Katha complained, "Partying, vacationing while your husband is dead."

"Grandma Katha, I would never...," Lily protested, hurt by the accusation.

"That's what people will say and think Mom. People like to gossip," Rose agreed.

"Do you think we are not aware you would never do that Lily? People judge others; it's not fair, and not right; but you're in the public eye as Crown attorney. They will be scrutinizing your every move," Katha explained.

"I guess you're right, but I don't have to like it."

"I love you all and I will do all in my power to protect you from the paparazzi and keep all three of my girls safe. We are strong and we are Kelly's, descendants of Boudicca and her name means..?" Katha demanded.

"The word means Victorious," all three women answered in unison.

"That's right. We shall triumph. We shall overcome adversity and no man shall ever dominate a Kelly woman!" Katha announced

"Amen to that!" all three women replied.

"The funeral is Friday at ten a.m. just like you wanted. Now, though, there will be some dignitaries and some other prominent people."

"Thank-you then," Lily commented meekly.

"Now that's settled, my story is on and you know I love my soaps, I missed it yesterday. *General Hospital* is okay too but it isn't All My Children. *Young and Restless* is fine, too; but *All My Children* was my soap," Katha complained. "So wonderful, seeing some of the actors from my favorite soap on *The Young and Restless*, and sometimes *General Hospital* though. I'm so glad they are still working."

Rose meanwhile was surfing her computer and watching the television at the same time.

"Oh no! Grandma Katha, Mom, and Aunt Amelia; the news on Chatter is mindboggling. You'll never guess the terrible thing that has happened," Rose interrupted.

"Are you sure you're reading a reputable source?" Katha asked, "I'm forever reading some celebrity died when they didn't because of some hoaxer."

"No this is being widely reported by news organizations, I'm afraid," Rose commented.

"What has happened now?" asked Lily like she doesn't really want to know.

"They found a body in the dumpster near Aunt Amelia's store this morning. The body has been there since the first murder. They only found it because they came to pick up the garbage today and one of the garbage men noted blood under the dumpster," Rose stated shocked.

Lily gasped and held her hand to her mouth. Amelia also, gasped.

"My store? They found a body at my store, again?" Amelia exclaimed, shocked.

"You read that on-line? I try to only read the only headlines on Chatter; all the rest of the stuff is too depressing. In my day you'd read that kind of bad news the next morning in the paper. Now when your mom was young, you'd see a special bulletin on the television. Another body found? What in the world is going on in this town? I'm going to get Terrence to get his son working on this a little harder," Katha rambled, "So we are all safe."

"Why didn't anyone call me? It's still my job! Does Barbara think I'm unaware that she tried to make people think I'm the guilty party? I know Barbara is after my job. She's not fooling me," Lily angrily shouted, then coughed.

Katha glared at Rose for telling Lily and Amelia bad news.

"Don't you dare get yourself all worked up and tied up in knots Lily. She won't succeed. You have something she doesn't, common sense, decency and morals," Katha stated consoling Lily.

"Grandma Katha's right; besides she's weird," Rose exclaimed.

"Rose, we don't call people weird," Lily admonished.

"Even when they are?" Rose exclaimed.

"Hush Rose, don't upset your mother. Our world has been turned upside down. I can't believe there has been another murder in this city!" Katha continued.

"Why would someone kill and put them in the dumpster near my store?" Amelia asked.

"It is so bizarre," Lily commented.

"It's the curse; it has to be the curse," Amelia announced.

"Amelia, what did Dr. Jones say about curses? There are no such things. Isn't that what you told me?" reminded Lily.

"But if that is true, why do I feel like I am under one?"

"Sweetie, there is no such things as curses. Life gives us challenges. Sometimes too hard to bear and get through; but we soldier on and live our lives. Now put all this curse talk aside," Katha explained.

"Yes, Aunt Katha," Amelia meekly answered.

The doorbell pealed loudly. Rose looked out the peephole in the door to see Sergeant Detective Rogers on the doorstep.

"Mom, Sergeant Detective Rogers is here and he doesn't look happy," Rose said in a sing-song voice.

"Hello Ms. Brooksfield, is your mother, and Ms. Amelia Kelly, here?" Sergeant Detective Rogers asked stepping into the house, as soon as Rose opened the door.

"Mom, Aunt Amelia, he wants to talk to you," Rose yelled. Lily walked over and Amelia hobbled over on her crutches.

"We just heard the awful news," Amelia commented. "So the murderer killed twice?"

"Yes, the murderer did. I'm sorry Ms. Amelia Kelly but you are under arrest. You have the right to remain silent, anything you say can be held against you in a court of law. You have the right to consult with an attorney, and to have that same attorney present during questioning. If you are unable to afford an attorney one will be provided for you," Sergeant Detective Rogers announced clipping a handcuff through her crutch and onto her one wrist.

"What? You're arresting me? Lily he's arresting me. Help me!" Amelia screamed, horrified and turning to Lily.

"Don't say a word. I'll take your case until we can get you another lawyer. Now, Sergeant Detective Rogers, who is Amelia supposed to have killed?" Lily demanded.

"The charge is murder in the first degree of Megan Fowler and Albert Young," Sergeant Detective Rogers answered.

"Quit kidding! It is not funny! I didn't kill Megan and I don't know any Albert Young," Amelia protested.

"Quiet Amelia! Don't volunteer anything." Lily cautioned, "As your lawyer, I'm telling you don't say a word."

"But I don't know any Albert Young!" Amelia protested again.

"Ms. Kelly, you're going to lie now?" Sergeant Detective Rogers commented with disgust.

"Albert was his name?" Amelia questioned. As a thought crossed her face she continued, "Oh no, not Al! It's Al? Al's dead?"

"Ms. Kelly that's an award-winning performance, but we have you dead to rights," Detective Rogers replied clapping.

"Sergeant Detective Rogers, I advise you to keep your opinions to yourself. My client is innocent!" Lily demanded and turning to Amelia she cautioned, "Are you okay honey? You can tell me later who this Al is. But don't say another word in front of this police officer, do you understand?"

"Did anyone tell you Al was homeless?" Amelia angrily asked. "I helped him. I offered him a job but he wouldn't take it. He said he would watch over my store. He was so sweet; he just needed a little help. I used to give him money for breakfast every morning. How can Al be dead? Who could do such a thing?"

"Homeless? The guy was homeless and no one thought to tell me any of the information?" Sergeant Detective Rogers commented sounding shocked.

"It looks like your department isn't being entirely helpful. Listen to me please. Look at my cousin. Amelia is innocent. She would never hurt anyone. She doesn't even have a record," Lily protested "She likes to help people though and she helped Al. Just because she is a good person, it doesn't mean she's a murderess."

"Counsellor, you are aware people can surprise us; but I'm inclined to believe you, something about this doesn't add up to guilty. She doesn't have a clear motive. I thought when I came in here that Ms. Kelly was guilty but...," Detective Rogers began.

"You say they think my client is guilty? Tell me what you evidence you think makes her a suspect as a favour. Please?" Lily begged.

"I shouldn't be telling you this, but I think from my own instincts and her reaction she's being set up for the crime."

"So tell me."

"She was aware of both victims, but that shouldn't get a person convicted. The reason the assistant crown attorney made me make an arrest..." Detective Rogers began before he was interrupted again.

"The assistant crown attorney? My employee who works for me? Barbara Franks?" Lily interrupted, "I was appointed by the attorney general, not her."

"I am well aware of the way you were appointed, but Ms. Franks insisted to my boss that I had to arrest Ms. Kelly. I had no choice," Detective Rogers explained.

"On what basis did she want you to make an arrest? Was it because my husband was the deceased?" Lily asked continuing, "Or because Amelia happened to be near the murder scene and she had seen them both?"

"Amelia's hair was on the Mr. Young's body," Detective Rogers replied. "I'm sure the hair got there as transfer, but Ms. Franks insisted it is crucial evidence, and proof of Ms. Kelly's guilt."

"Well of course my hair was on him. I hugged him yesterday. He was such a sweet man. He always looked out for me." Amelia explained, "I can't believe he's gone."

"All of this is circumstantial evidence. Don't worry Amelia. I'll get you out on bail by this afternoon." Lily replied, "And you, Detective Rogers, you know this is a bad collar; so why are you listening to Barbara Franks?"

"Ms. Kelly-Brooksfield, she might be safer in jail. I think someone has set her up and possibly you for murder. I think you're both in danger until we catch this killer," Detective Rogers commented sounding worried.

"Why do you say we are in danger?" asked Lily.

"It just feels too personal, these killings. Call it a hunch, but I feel like someone is watching my every move and yours too. This killer is smart and seems to be one step ahead of us."

"You think someone watched your every move? Don't you think you're being a little paranoid?" Lily asked.

"No, I don't. It's only paranoia if you're wrong and I'm not wrong. Someone is pulling the strings, but whoever it is I will find them. Now I'm sorry Ms. Kelly, but we need to go. I must take her in; it's my orders."

"And you always follow orders," Lily replied grimly.

Emmett looked at her apologetically and said, "You can follow my car if you want Ms. Kelly, or meet me at the main police station." he explained. "That's where I'll be taking her for the booking."

"Grandma Katha, will you watch Rose? I'll be back soon."

"Mom, do remember I'm not two years old, but bring back Aunt Amelia," Rose commented.

"Of course, go!" Katha answered.

"Adults, you're such a pain sometimes! I'm fifteen," Rose stated to Lily's departing back.

Detective Rogers, Amelia and Lily left through the front door. Emmett placed Amelia into the back of his patrol car and drove away as Lily followed.

"Grandma Katha, will Aunt Amelia really be okay?' asked Rose after they leave.

"Of course she will child. Your mama is a bulldog as a lawyer. She'll get Amelia, home by dinnertime," Katha reassured Rose.

"I'm kind of worried about something Detective Rogers said though. He said he thought someone set up Aunt Amelia "

"Nonsense! Why would anyone set up Amelia? They've made a mistake and they'll rectify it. Amelia will be home tonight. You just wait and see."

"He also said the person pulled the strings behind the scenes and was one step ahead of him. Are you sure we are not in danger?" asked Rose looking around as if to see the person.

"Not to worry dear, whoever it is doesn't know who he or she's dealt with; we are the Kelly's and we triumph over adversity and evil."

"Thanks, Grandma Katha. That does make me feel better."

~0~

Chapter 14 - Your Place or Mine

Violet and Brandy

Violet a tall thin woman resembling Olive Oyl with glasses, sat at the front desk of the Happy Valley police station. She perused the police roster on her computer, only looking up as Constable Brandy Calders came through the metal detector at the front door.

"Where's Rentford today?" Brandy Calders asked before she had even reached the desk.

"Rentford? Who is that?" Constable Violet Garden enquired.

"Silas Rentford, the cute new cop, who works with Sergeant Detective Rogers," Brandy Calders answered stopping at the desk.

"Oh, that man. He's not new. He's been around for years. I just didn't recognize his name when you said it. He called in sick. Must be a bug going round. Sergeant Detective Brad Owens called in sick too," Constable Violet Gardens commented.

"Oh? Do you know if he has a girlfriend?"

"You like him too? What does Brad Owens hold out the *'I'm available'* sign?" Violet probed.

"Not Sergeant Detective Brad Owens! I'm speaking about Constable Silas Rentford. He's cute and his eyes are like a puppy dog, all soft and sweet," Brandy replied dreamily.

"Silas Rentford? You like Silas? But he's so shy."

Violet looked at Brandy, a pale red-head, slightly overweight, dressed in a police officer's dress uniform. If only she wear some make-up and lose some weight.

"He's not gay is he? My Gaydar did go off like it usually does." Brandy asked.

"No, I don't think so. I've seen him ogle Tricia, when he didn't realize anyone looked."

"Tricia, who's she?" Brandy probed, nervously shifting from foot to foot.

"Constable Tricia Peters. She has all her uniforms form fitted so her assets are observed," Violet replied cattily. "Let us not forget Kendall, the iron lady, I won't get into her."

"Kendall sure has been promoted a lot. Has Silas Rentford been here long?"

"He's been here for a few years. I think he came here, what about six years ago?" Violet replied. "Or was it five years?"

"He has been here that long? I didn't realize."

"He is kind of cute, I guess if you like that type," Violet admitted, "So you like Brad?"

"Yes," Brandy responded.

"But I thought you dated someone else," Violet commented.

Violet then looked around as if she was being watched, as if she was afraid she'd be seen slacking off.

"I was, but it didn't work out because he wasn't exactly faithful. You had better be careful; Brad changes partners all the time. He might not be any better with you."

"I think people misjudge him. He's sweet and just a little insecure," Violet exclaimed. "But any woman getting in between us, had better watch out; I'm a little possessive."

"Do you think he'd like some chicken soup if he's sick?"

"Brad or Silas, or both?"

"Both," Brandy answered.

"I think they would. Do you think we could get a discount at the soup place around the corner, the Soup Queen? I'd like to take some soup to Brad after my shift ends," Violet requested.

"When is your shift finished?" Brandy asked.

"I'm off in a half an hour, but if it's busy at the desk I'll need to stay longer to work.

"Well if you give me Silas' address, I'll go get us both some chicken soup for our guys and when you get off you can give it to him. I'm sure he'll love you for it," Brandy offered smiling widely.

"I'm not supposed to give out any personal information, but I guess I'll make an exception. Seeing as you're not after my guy. Thanks. This might be my chance to win him. We girls have to stick together against women like Tricia and Kendall."

"Thanks, I know this will help," Brandy answered, pulling out her notebook and a pen to write.

"Just go get the soup, here's the address for Silas,"

Violet wrote out the address and gave Brandy the piece of paper.

"Good, I'll be back shortly with the soup. Bye now! See you soon."

Brandy excitedly looked forward to bringing Silas his soup and making him feel better. Granny Calders always said the way to a man's heart was through his stomach. Now if you provide a man with medicine and chicken soup when he's sick, he would love you forever. Brandy would be that woman if it killed her. She would get chicken noodle. It was the best soup for cold and flu. Should she pick up some medicines too? No, she didn't want to look too obvious. Soup would be enough. When he was well again, she would make him her raved about famous turkey lasagna. Everyone loved her lasagna. Silas would too. She had him in the palm of her hands; he would be hers soon. She wished Violet as much luck with her delivery.

~0~

The Killer

In the shadows in his apartment a man listened to a radio, "*And in local news, Reporter Paul Knight, remains missing. Anyone who has information is asked to call your local police station. In other news Amelia Kelly, owner of Quirks and cousin of Crown Attorney Lily Kelly, was taken in to custody today as a person of interest in the murder of Megan Fowler and Albert Young. Megan Fowler and Albert Young were found murdered near Quirks two days ago. Crown Attorney Kelly's husband, the Honourable Mayor Horace Brooksfield, was found murdered in his office two days ago. Police Chief Edward Stewart has told this reporter an arrest is imminent.*"

What!?What!? Were these police officers fools?

His Angel, and her cousin, were the victims. Yes he killed, killed to protect his incredibly lovely Angel's innocence. These people were vermin and vermin you killed. They blamed his beloved Angel and her cousin? If they looked at them they would know they were angels sent from above for him. It had to be all the fault of the assistant Crown attorney's fault. She wasn't like his Angel's cousin. A pit-bull when it came to her job.

Barbara Franks, even her name, ugly, not at all lyrical like his angel, or her cousin. Barbara coveted Lily's job. Don't think he didn't understand her motives, but she wasn't going to get the job.

He suspected she wasn't strictly on the up and up, but she hid it well. Barbara, extremely sneaky, managed to elude him, an unheard of occurrence in his world.

No one eluded him, until now. She appeared up to something again. When he found out what he would use it to his advantage. Barbara better watch her step. She annoyed him, her constant barrage of Lily, one more step out of line and it was curtains for her. Curtains...

Ha, Ha, Ha! He'd use the curtains to strangle her in her office... er Lily's office. Wouldn't it be funny, even ironic? She was totally out of line; that bitch Barbara Franks. Her britches were too big, his daddy always said.

He awarded Lily a job, to benefit his beloved Angel and her beloved cousin. He rid the world of a crooked Crown attorney, who cheated on Lily. Lily still did not understand the lengths trash like Barbara could do, but he did. He protected her from that knowledge too, but maybe he hadn't done her a favour by protecting her from William Wentworth's cheating ways. Lily had found another man just like him in Horace. It had been simple matter to tamper the car of the stranger and make it appear a drunken driving accident. Lily trusted just like her cousin. In some ways she exuded the same innocence, so he protected her. Her bad choices should not harm his beloved Angel.

He had arranged a simple accident, and poof Wentworth appeared a traffic statistic. A reason pointed out not to drink and drive. The bottle of scotch he offered the driver convinced all, the driver drank and drove and ran over Wentworth. Okay, so he put the bottle of scotch within the man's reach. The drunk driver had chosen to drink it after all. He didn't feel any remorse. Why should he? The driver deserved to die anyway. He'd seen him two days before driving drunk.

The driver sat before the wheel, striking an old lady crossing the street. The man left her to die, broken and battered in the street.

The man had explained to the killer, he needed to drink, but he promised he wouldn't again. He would go to rehabilitation. And the killer let him go; thinking he would give the man a second chance, but the man threw it all away. So the man sobered up for two days. So what!

The man fell off the wagon again. The man would have killed someone else, once more! He patted himself on the back. After all, hadn't he just saved a lot of pedestrians and other drivers from Wentworth and this drunk driver? A vermin like William Wentworth, out of Lily's life, and the drunk driver killed himself. All painstakingly tidy, he was good at his craft.

Wow! It was surprising that it had been seven years ago. Seven years ago, Lily, the brave little widow. She lobbied for the Crown attorney. A word here, a word there, and he got a lot of people to rally for her. Her success hadn't been totally on her own merit. She remained, however, the perfect woman for the job. Despite worrying someday she might be obligated to arrest him, he respected her. She stood tough on criminals, something he admired. He wasn't a criminal, just a person who acted as a judge and punished the wicked. He did something valuable for society. After all, society needed judges to keep order when the courts failed. If it wasn't for his feelings he had for his Angel, she might hold his heart. She needed as much looking after as his Angel did. She was a great mother to Rose.

Rose existed as a testimony to her. A modest girl, not flashy, and given to flirting with the opposite sex. Lovely girl Rose! Kind and sweet, everything a girl should be. Lily? She trusted too easily. She got mixed up alongside Horace Brooksfield, right after that disaster William Wentworth he excised. It must be the kid which made her fall in love with such a cretin. She was a natural mother who needed a child. Neither of those two worms gave her a child of her own.

Lily treated the child as if she was her own. He hadn't been able to stand for such a sweet trusting woman, as Lily lived, to be cheated on repeatedly, while she mothered that lovely little girl. More women should mother as she did. Simply put...Horace had to die.

Look how Lily looked after his Angel. Oh sure, Rose's real mother Cordelia was no prize, but then she obsessed over drugs. Cordelia did the right thing and protected Rose from danger. He respected that about her. Lily took the child after the incident, right after the poor deluded woman Cordelia lost her mind. Lily made sure the child felt safe and loved. He felt sorry for Cordelia. She lost her child. He understood sometimes people needed a break from reality after a great loss. He needed one when Sam died.

No, concentrate; don't go to the bad place. It wasn't your fault. The fault lay at Amelia's husband. Jack's door; he shouldn't have taken Sam in the car. He started humming. It calmed him. He didn't want to think about Sam anymore because it hurt too much. He needed to think of something else. The time came to put his plan into action. The boyfriend would be blamed.

Albert the homeless man had gotten in the way. Albert would have told Amelia. One plus one equals two; simple arithmetic. Albert had seen the murder, and Albert died painlessly. He was homeless after all and he probably wouldn't have survived long anyway. He was guiltless in Albert's murder too. That made him feel much better.

Planning was always crucial. The culprit was all picked out for the other murder of Horace Brooksfield, ready to be framed. He'd kill two birds with one stone, as well as get rid of that insipid ex-wife of Horace's, Renée. Or should he go with the mother-in-law; after all, both of them dared to threaten Lily? How dare Renée threaten his real family? After all when he married his beloved Angel, his darling Amelia, we would all be family.

Amelia needed family, with all her losses to be made whole again. He would be her rock. She would be his family, the one he'd always needed, and he would be hers. He'd planted Renée's hair at the scene. He wondered whether they'd tested the hair yet and if it would be traced back to Renée. The trashy, vulgar woman thwarted him at every turn. He thought about killing her, but this was so much more delicious. She would go to prison for the murders, and the inmates might even take the job of killing her for him. If not, then she would suffer. Truly suffer, like she made Lily, his Angel's cousin suffer, through her vulgar accusations and her constant attentions to a married man (Lily's husband).

If Andrew Piper stood truly as good as he claimed, he'd find the hair. Renée, such a bitch, with a wicked tongue; Daddy would have called it forked. She lied as easy as she breathed.

They had better free his Angel soon. If they didn't fix that rapidly, Assistant Crown Attorney Barbara Franks would see some roses too and a tombstone together with her name on it.

How he hated that horrid woman Barbara! He'd like to rip her head off like you would a Barbie doll. Wouldn't it be a lovely sight for Andrew Piper, or a sight for the lovely Brandy Calders? He put Rogers off his trail, but he should be polite and ask his help. Yes, the plan would work.

The doorbell rang. Who could be at his door? They found him out and knew his crimes? No he remained far too clever for that.

Dimwitted Barbara Franks and the idiot Emmett Rogers thought they were so smart. Luckily Paul had been disposed of in a place that wouldn't be traced back to him for the murder. No trace of him left here. How dare he deny him exclusive control of the interview, after everything he contributed to his career?

He should have supported the woman reporter. She did her job better. What was her name, Holly Hollis? She was just so forward and in your face, qualities he disliked in a woman. Holly Hollis wasn't a female he trusted, but then he should never have trusted Paul Knight.

Oh well, live and learn. Sadly, he hated to take care of Paul. He had drugged him and then disposed of his body.

He would just be another celebrity who died tragically by his own hand. Paul's body had no restrain marks, the special cream he'd put on first before the ropes, erased all traces of the restraints. Chemistry never failed him. Only the track marks from the drugs remained. Paul's stint in rehab a couple of years ago might convince them. Stupid ass!

Why did Paul make him take this step? They could have had a long profitable relationship. If only Paul hadn't wanted an exposé on all his crimes. His Angel must never find out all he had done until she married to him. Why couldn't Paul have understood? He paced a little; checking once again; to make sure the place remained clean of any traces of Paul Knight.

Damn! The doorbell rang again, and he didn't answer it. No, don't get angry. He mustn't show any anger to whomever appeared at the door. He'd better answer the door quick, though, and find out who was there. He wouldn't want to be too obvious. He hurried to throw on a robe over his boxers. He answered and found a woman holding soup.

"I brought you chicken soup." she cried, "I hope it makes you feel better." "I'm sure it will but I wouldn't want you to get sick."

"I'm hearty. I hardly ever get sick. Let me come in and help you."

"Thanks, but I'd never forgive myself if you did." he said gently, "Besides I'm sleepy. It's the cold medication."

"Yes, right, see you tomorrow." He said quickly, closing the door and thinking 'In your dreams honey.'

Soup! Yum! He loved chicken noodle; too bad the woman longed for him. She stood a sad, pathetic, sort of thing. He couldn't be mean to her. She wasn't one of those women to betray him. No, rather like his deceased mother, she was sweet, down trodden and perhaps a little forward but not too forward. Kind of like a puppy dog you wouldn't kick when it was down and injured. He had standards after all, rules to follow. One of his rules was to treat women who are chaste and innocent correctly. If he wasn't so sure his Angel remained the one, this woman might have been a good substitute. But that would never be... He would never betray his Angel.

~0~

Chapter 15 - The S.O.L.F.B.O. Club

"Amelia Kelly is out on bail. Wow that was an incredibly quick release from jail yesterday. Must be nice to have connections," Violet exclaimed straightening the front desk of the Happy Valley Police station.

"The Crown attorney was her lawyer though," replied Police Constable Fourth Class Jenni Hayes, getting ready to leave.

"Nepotism!! Told you so! So did any more evidence come in on the case?" questioned Violet.

"No, the hair is hers, Amelia Kelly; but it could have been transference exactly as she said. She met him every day and hugged him, which might have ensured hair transmission. It's not like homeless people change their clothes frequently."

"If Amelia Kelly didn't kill Albert Young, Megan Fowler, Amber Tate and Horace Brooksfield, who did?" queried Violet.

"Damned, if I know!"

"Anything I should be on top of today?" Violet asked.

"No, the duty roster is done," Jenni replied yawning. "I'm so tired, I think I'll walk home, but I'm going to shower first. I don't think I'm awake enough to drive."

"Good thing you live close to the station. Why do you drive here anyway?"

"Sometimes I like to go to the place around the corner for breakfast. It's too far by foot."

"I wonder how Brad is today. Have you heard from him?"

"Brad Owens? The hottie? Brad, the guy who all the recruits, straight and even those who weren't drooled over him? What's his name...Brad Owens?" Jenni joked.

"Right, make fun of me. I took Brad some soup last night. Poor thing; so sick, all he wanted to do was sleep. He was in his bathrobe when he took the soup and then just said goodnight."

"It worked. He's on the duty roster and he hasn't called in sick."

"Well good," Violet countered, not sounding so sure.

"Here he is now." Jenni commented, "Good day, Violet, and if you get a date later, don't do anything I wouldn't do!"

"Jenni quiet! He'll hear you," Violet admonished.

"No he won't. He only has eyes for you."

"Hello Violet. You look lovely today. Did you get a new hairstyle?" Brad flirted.

"Why yes, it is," Violet replied her eyes shining and happy.

Brad responded playfully. "I feel so much better, where did you find such ambrosia?"

"You're welcome. I made it by my own two hands," Violet lied blushing.

"Later Vi," Brad replied smiling and going went into the locker room.

"Wow, he called me a pet name," Violet said to herself aloud.

"Are you okay? You are speaking, but you make no sense, Violet!" Brandy queried, coming into the locker room.

"I'm fine. Brad called me a pet name."

"I'm impressed, what did he call you?" Brandy solicited.

"He called me Vi."

"Oh how sweet. So did you get Silas to notice you last night?" Violet queried.

"No! He liked the soup but he took it and sent me away in his bathrobe no less," Brandy replied. "But I hope to meet him today. Even get him to like me as Brad did you."

"He'll remember the soup you brought. He is on today's roster."

"Oh good! They'll remember we brought them soup and then we'll be their girlfriends," Brandy claimed.

"Granny always said the way to a man's heart is through his stomach."

"I certainly hope Granny's right," Violet remarked.

"I think he liked it, and he's better today, but let's not get ahead of ourselves."

"Ladies, if someone does appreciate you for yourselves they aren't worth it. I don't know what you want with them," Jenni commented coming out from the shower area.

"I thought you'd gone home," Violet admonished.

"Besides didn't you also take soup to a certain male someone yesterday?"

"I took a sick friend soup, which just happened to be male. He's much too old for me. There's nothing romantic about that. Barney Terrell used to be a cop and he was sick. I'd do it for any fellow officer. I'll go home in a moment. My shower's broke and the landlord hasn't fixed it yet. I need to be awake enough to walk home anyway." Jenni answered, "You two need to value yourselves more. Let the guys run after you. Bye now."

"Good grief! She insists we are running after guys, but she's not?" Brandy whispered.

"Just ignore her. That's why she doesn't have a guy... she lies," Violet answered cattily.

Jenni gave Violet a dirty look as she left the locker room, and as a parting shot she said, "Try to lead a horse to water..."

"Why did she call us horses?" questioned Violet, "Is she insulting our appearances?"

"No, she's not insulting our looks. It's an old saying;" Brandy explained. "She may be right about letting them chase us."

"Oh no, he spotted me alright. He called me a pet name. He remembered the soup; it won't be long before he starts thinking of me in a different light," Violet replied with a dreamy appearance on her face.

"Well I hope Silas thinks of me too."

"Silas will think of you. When we land those two you and I can double date."

"I'm sure it will be fun," Brandy replied.

"We will go to the movies and dancing. You will be the maid of honour at my wedding," Violet waxed dreamily.

"And you can do the same for me."

Brandy then began twirling around like she was dancing with a partner.

"Someone will see you!" hissed Violet.

"Sorry, guess I was carried away," Brandy commented. "I'm just so excited."

"It's a great plan," Violet agreed. "But I think you'll need to lose a little weight to fit into your wedding dress or my maid of honour dress. I don't think they sell size sixteens, and the way you're putting on weight that's all you're going to fit in."

"Forget about being my maid of honour. You're fired!" Brandy retorted angrily.

"Like Silas would ever marry you anyway. Brad, on the other hand, would love to marry me."

"Dream on Violet. He thought to be kind. More than likely he threw the soup away in the garbage."

"You take that back bitch!" Violet shouted.

"No, I won't! He's stringing you along; he doesn't give a damn. I have seen him with many women within the last year."

"He didn't recognize me until now," Violet claimed.

"You need to go on a diet for your own good and none of the purging I observed you doing earlier."

"I don't purge. Something I ate disagreed with me," Brandy explained. "Besides Silas likes me the way I am."

"Yes Silas does. Sorry if I was harsh. People commented on my being too skinny and I hated it."

"You were too skinny last year, so I said so I said that you didn't look so hot and you appeared sick," Brandy commented.

"I appreciated your concern. That's why we are friends. You were the only one who was honest. Everyone else just said you are too skinny. Or wow, you lost weight, which I took to me you look great. Anorexia deceives you," Violet admitted.

"I'm glad I helped you."

"You should recognize just because your guy, Harold dumped you as his mistress, doesn't mean you need to let your body go to seed," Violet continued.

"I've never been anyone's mistress. Why would you say I was someone's mistress? I'm insulted!" Brandy cried angrily. "And I'm not fat."

"You can hide it from some people but not from me honey...oh no you're not fat you're pregnant! How far along are you?"

"This time you are wrong. I'm not pregnant. Do you honestly think that? I know I put on a few pounds but…"

Violet looked Brandy up and down as Brandy straightened her dress short the short gaping at the bust line. She noted Brandy left her top button undone on her dress pants and then threw a jacket obviously too small, over the shirt to try to conceal all.

"Sorry, but you know I can help you get a bigger uniform without anyone knowing."

"The uniform fits fine. I must go get ready for roll call. Sorry about earlier, are we still friends?" Brandy asked mollifying Violet.

"Yes, sure we are friends. If you need help let me know. Silas is one of the good guys; he'll still like you even if you are pregnant."

"I am not pregnant!" denied Brandy.

"Sorry. I sometimes let my mouth get away from me but I mean well."

"Okay, I'll forgive you too. Don't spread around the rumour I'm pregnant though. I must go before the big boss gets mad," Brandy explained.

"Yes, you better. Chief Stewart gets angry when you're late for roll call. Besides I need to go too. My phone will be ringing off the wall," Violet explained, "Everybody wants to know when we will catch the mayor's killer. What about the other two women? Why aren't their killings important to the people? The same person likely killed them."

"You think the killings are connected?" probed Brandy. "From the paperwork I saw the homeless man Mr. Young. Amber what's her name, the mayor's hottie, and the store clerk they were all murdered by the same person."

"Wow, that's weird. Honestly, a serial killer? What a difficult case. I hope my Silas solves the crime. I'm reporting for duty before I'm late. Later," Brandy replied, checking her watch and opening the door to leave.

"Silas won't solve the case, and don't count on that nitwit Rogers. My Brad will run rings around both of them and solve it first. You'll find out and apologise," Violet yelled after Brandy.

Detective Sergeant Emmett Rogers walked in to the police station in time to overhear this but preferred to ignore it. "Hello Violet how's things?"

"Fine," Violet informed him. "Did you hear they found the news anchor Paul Knight dead?"

"Paul Knight? Was he murdered? Who got the case?"

"No, can you believe it? He hid; that he was a closet junkie. He more than likely offed himself, but Brad Owen nailed the case, so he'll find out the truth."

"Hmm," Emmett replied trying hard not to comment and say what he really thought of Brad.

"Oh, I forgot Alan Barnes tried to find you earlier," Violet remembered.

"Alan was looking for me?" queried Emmett

"I don't know. You should be careful talking to him. He deserved to be demoted last month. He didn't show up to the job and blamed his partner Brad Owens," Violet cautioned. "What a nerve he has. He is a backstabber, so watch your back Emmett."

"Violet, you should be a better judge of character." Emmett explained, "Brad isn't who you think he is."

"Brad is a great guy," Violet protested.

"Sorry, I haven't seen the great guy. The guy is a hotdog and he always wants the press to write him up, just so he can advance his career," Emmett said angrily.

"And if anyone gets in his way say goodbye to your job."

"You aren't being fair Emmett. I'm surprised at you. I thought he offered to help you with the murder of the mayor."

"He wanted to help himself right into the press. The mayor's murder is a high-profiled case, but the joke is on him. Chief Stewart handled the press aspects anyway," Emmett said angrily.

"You can't know him all that well. He loves helping."

"He was my partner. I recognize him better than you do Violet. Be careful that you don't cut off more than you can chew," Emmett cautioned.

"I think you've read him wrong, but I am aware this comes from a mistaken place, so I'll let it go," Violet retorted, but still gave him an angry glare.

"I tried Violet. You need to learn to think for yourself."

"Hey buddy, I've been searching all over for you," Alan Barnes cried, walking in to the station.

"So I hear," Emmett answered. "How can I help you?"

"Can we discuss this where we can't be overheard?" Alan whispered.

Alan motioned first to show Emmett; Violet listened in and then gestured to the men's locker room.

"Sure," Emmett replied.

They both walked into the men's locker room and sat on the bench.

"My career is in the toilet and I hoped you would give me some tips on how to fix it," Alan explained.

"How did you get demoted? Did this have something to do with that asshole, Brad Owens?"

"It's a long complicated story but I'll shorten the tale. I'm too damn trusting and I shouldn't always trust and cover for my partner."

"So what did 'Mr. Hotdog' do this time?"

"He kept disappearing and I'd cover for him. One day I went to look for him, but Brad overheard that Chief Stewart was at the crime scene so he hurried to the call. He got there before me. He told Chief Stewart that I was late because he searched for me. Brad went on to say he'd been covering for me. The lying bastard! He convinced him easily. Chief Stewart bought his act. The Chief thought Brad had an exemplary record. He said I should be grateful he covered for me. What did he discern of me? Only what Brad told him. Brad even backed up this position by writing vague reports, like he had been covering for me. Of course the Chief believed him."

"Wow, that's rough. If I didn't distinguish all the bad points about the guy, I'd be tempted to believe him too."

"How can I rectify the chief's opinion of me?" Alan questioned. "I don't want to be a patrol officer forever."

"Keep your nose to the grindstone. Accept all calls and all requests. Sooner or later Chief Stewart will comprehend your worth in the department," Emmett counselled.

"I hope so."

"Later, Alan."

"Have a good day Emmett, and call me please if anything breaks on the case. I recognize I'm hot dogging, but I need the collar," Alan pleaded.

"Don't worry, I'll call you. The guys in the club, meaning us, need to stick together," Emmett replied cryptically getting up to go.

"You mean the blue-collar?" asked Alan.

"Yes the blue-collar too but I'm taking about the S.O.L.F.B.O. club."

"I still don't get understand," Alan stated puzzled.

"I'm talking about the Shit out of luck from Brad Owens club," Emmett explained, laughing as Alan joined in.

After they left Silas Rentford stepped out of the shadows and went to his locker to get his report book. Silas glared at their retreating backs. He then left to get on with his day. Brad Owens too has also been hiding in the corner and he laughed. They talked about him.

"Too funny," he spoke aloud, "You'll be a patrolman forever Alan; you might as well accept your future. And latching your star to an idiot like Emmett Rogers will get you nowhere. Why do you think I'm not his partner anymore? I'm going places neither of you will ever be able to achieve. So play your games, but I'll still be chief one day. You'll grasp how you should have revered me. Did you tell him about your disappearances Alan? I don't think so. Let Rogers realize what a backstabbing little know-it- all you are. Then he'll appreciate what a worm you are." Brad laughed when he realized he was talking to himself. He then left to get in his squad car.

~0~

Chapter 16 -
The Kelly Curse

Lily paced back and forth in her room trying on one

garment after another, as she prepared for Horace's funeral anything to postpone the moments ahead.

"Lily, you saved my life," Amelia pronounced while she put on a black dress that Lily handed her.

"I still need to get the charges thrown out of court," Lily declared, finally settling on a black suit.

"Mom, Aunt Amelia's right. You rock," Rose articulated as she entered the room without knocking.

"Glad you think your mother did well, but we must do more to do to get Amelia free," Lily answered.

Lily then checked her notes on her dresser. Exiting the bedroom they went into the living room; Rose following behind them. Amelia sat down on the sofa, slipping her foot into one shoe and then trying to manoeuver into the other one.

"Do these look all right?" Amelia asked. "I can't wear heels with my broken leg, but these slip-on shoes are easier to walk in and get on."

"They look fine Amelia," Lily answered.

"I've been thinking about my dad recently, Lily. Do you remember much about him?" Amelia enquired changing the subject.

"I remember him being strict and having a bit of a temper," Lily cautiously replied. "But I also remember he loved you so much."

"The one thing I remember about my dad is that he had this money clip. He played with the money clip all the time. He'd rub his fingers along the gold inscription of the R. Do you remember?"

"I do remember. Uncle Robert used to strip dollar bills out of the clip and hand them to us for the ice cream man."

"Did you realize my Grandfather Cordova made the piece for him? I think it was the last gift he ever gave him. I still remember the stones, all our birthstones. Mine, Grace's and Jerry's birthstones were all on it. Dad treasured that money clip."

"I loved when my dad and Grandma Katha let me stay for the summer to spend time with your family. Your mother, Aunt Aerilla, used to make us picnics," Lily recalled.

"And Grace always imitated us." Amelia revealed sadly, "I still miss them."

"I know. I miss them too," Lily replied softly.

"Your dad, Uncle Peter, is still at the embassy in Prague?" asked Amelia changing the subject.

"He focused heavily on his career. His job was all he had after Mom disappeared."

"He had you too. I know you don't like to talk about this, but do they have an idea what happened to Aunt Heather?"

"I went to school. We lived in Prague and I attended an English language school. Dad's job played big bucks for me to be there. Mom dropped me off at school," Lily replied.

Lily paced a little and she sniffed back tears threatening to surface.

"You were how old? Nine or ten?" prodded Amelia.

"I'd really like to know what happened. No one ever told me and you don't talk about it."

"I was nine. Excited about a part I had in a play. I had the part of Wendy in Peter Pan. Thrilled to play, but I never got to portray the part." Lily's voice broke, but she continued, "Mom drove me to school and dropped me off after kissing me goodbye. I observed her drive away her little Volvo. My dad came by at noon. He took me out of the classroom, and at first gently asked me when I'd last seen my mother. I told him I had seen her in the morning before school. He told me not to worry; she must be shopping and hadn't gotten in touch. We got in the car and we went to our house. Time went by quickly that day and my father paced back and forth, waiting on a phone call that never came. They discovered her bloody vehicle the next day. The police came and I caught the whole story, despite their hushed tones. My mother wasn't in the car but her purse remained and there was a lot of blood. Her blood was throughout the car. There were bullet holes in the driver's side door panels. They had no idea whether she was alive or dead, but they insisted there was so much blood she couldn't be alive.

Amelia gasped.

"You can't imagine how scared I was, Amelia. We were all devastated. No one told me anything. My mother was missing, feasibly dead, and my dad didn't say anything to me, not even an encouraging word."

"Not one word?" Amelia commented. "Uncle Peter must have been out of his mind with fear."

"My dad appeared shell-shocked. I swear he kept expecting Mom to come back through the door. Sleep appeared to be the last thing on his mind. He made me food, but I don't remember eating much. The first week went fast. I was sure she would come through the door. Grandma Katha finally came to us. Dad had broken down and called her explaining about my mother being missing. Grandma Katha comforted me. She made me eat even small amounts of food and put me to bed at night."

"Where was your dad?" Amelia asked.

"Dad spent more and more time at work. The police came to the house, his office, and took him in for questioning. They seemed so focused on my father. They kept him for hours, questioning and re-questioning, but Grandma Katha hired a terrific lawyer and he came home, set free."

"Why did they suspect your dad?"

"They always suspect the spouse first. It's the first rule of police work. Anyway, they seemed to stop focusing on my dad once he proved he had an alibi. Dad became lost in meetings amongst fifty people the morning Mom disappeared. They understood he couldn't have done killed her, at least not by himself."

"Well of course not. I knew part of the account, but not the entire story. Uncle Peter wouldn't have harmed Aunt Heather! Stupid cops, always judging others!" Amelia exclaimed.

"You know that and I know that, but they didn't seem to believe him innocent. One cop insinuated he had hired someone to murder her, but the lawyer made short work of him. Grandma Katha consoled me, talked to me, stayed by me in Prague about six months. My mother never reappeared. My dad became more and more immersed in his work. I saw little of him, but lots of Grandma Katha. Grandma Katha thought my dad should pull himself together and take care of me. Dad stated he didn't understand how to look after me. Grandma Katha talked to my Dad. Ill-equipped to keep me he gave me to Grandma Katha who took me to Happy Valley. You know I only saw him about once a year. Grandma Katha has truly been like a mother to me since all of this happened."

"Me too! What would we do without her?" asked Amelia.

"I remember when she brought you home, and even though I lived in Ravenworst and you lived here, we've acted like sisters ever since, in every way. Indeed, what would we do without Grandma Katha?"

"I don't ever want to find out how being without Aunt Katha would feel," replied Amelia.

"Mom, is our family cursed?" asked Rose.

"No, we've had a lot of tragic things happen, but it doesn't mean we are cursed. Bad things happen to good people once in a while. We are strong Kelly women," Lily reassured. "What doesn't break us makes us strong."

"But I was not born a Kelly," Rose protested.

"You are my daughter! I have the adoption papers to prove you are a Kelly! You couldn't be more family, even if I gave birth to you," Lily admitted.

Katha and Amelia then left the room a moment to give Lily and Rose some time to talk.

"So you don't regret you adopted me? I mean you had Dad before and he's gone," Rose whimpered before breaking into tears.

"Never ever doubt that I love you. You are my daughter in my heart and mind. Adopting you and making you officially my daughter was the best thing that ever happened to me," Lily fiercely replied.

"I love you, Mom. I'm sorry you lost your first mom too."

"Thanks honey. We miss them they are still in our hearts and it is okay,"

"So you don't mind that I think of her as my mom sometimes?" Rose timidly asked.

"Of course not I'd be disappointed if you didn't."

"I do love you, Mom," Rose articulated again. "I love you too, pumpkin."

"Mom, I want to go to the mall today and meet my friend Carol after the services and the Wake for Daddy. Daddy wouldn't mind that would he? I need to get away and go out with my friend Carol," Rose enquired.

"Rose, if that will make you feel better then I think you should go be with Carol. Your dad would tell you the same thing," Lily replied, dabbing her eyes and pretending she had something in them instead of tears.

"He was always a great dad. He always went to my plays and my games. I miss him too, Mom," Rose answered, trying hard not to cry.

Rose adjusted her pantyhose and her dress and then put on high-heeled shoes.

"Is this outfit okay? Would Daddy like this dress?" Rose asked while smoothing her skirt.

"Yes, the outfit is perfect. I can tell you do but we're going to take one day at a time starting with this ordeal today. We're about to put on our manners and mourn your father."

Katha entered the room and surveyed their outfits without saying a word. Katha then smiled and Lily was relieved that she found them acceptable.

"Will there be a lot of people there?" asked Rose.

"There will be. Your father was well-loved."

"He could be a little gruff at times but a decent person. Other people ought to have seen that in him. Do you think they'll talk about the way he was found?" asked Rose.

"Crass people will talk about him, dear. The thing to do is hold your head up high and pretend you didn't hear them because what they need to say doesn't matter," Katha advised.

"Aunt Katha is right! Ignore any ignoramuses," Amelia counselled.

"See, we all agree," Lily replied smiling.

"I love you all! I'm so glad I made you my family." Rose declared looking around at the three strong women in her family, "With Daddy gone you are all I've got."

"You always have me. We love you too!" Lily reassured.

"Make that three," added Amelia.

"No, four," replied Katha interjected, "One for all and all four one!"

"That's from The Three Musketeers Grandma Katha," protested Rose.

"My dear haven't you seen the movie with Chris O'Donnell. There are four of them!" Katha explained winking. "Chris O'Donnell is still hot. Have you seen NCIS: Los Angeles?"

"Grandma Katha," admonished Rose.

"Well, I may be older, but I'm not dead yet." Katha laughed and then continued, "Okay then, one for all, and all for one. Ladies, time to put on your best manners. We will do Horace proud."

Katha then put on her coat as she steered the women out to the waiting limousine to travel to the funeral parlour.

~0~

Chapter 17 -
Goodbye Is Not a
Word I Want To
Say

Arriving, the women faced a huge room filled with

people. Lily felt surprised, since the funeral would not take place for another half hour. The big, accommodating, funeral home held all the dignitaries who arrived for Horace's funeral. The men wore black suits with sombre ties, the women black or navy blue dress. Lily found this all so surreal. How could she be at a funeral for Horace? It seemed not long ago she attended a funeral for her first husband, William Wentworth. How could she have lost yet another husband, in such a short time? And Horace had been found in such a way?

Horace had an affair with his secretary? Amber seemed like a lovely woman...ditzy, but polite. But does a courteous woman sleep with your husband? Lily hadn't wanted to believe it, but Emmett Rogers confirmed through his investigation Amber had been having an affair with Horace. Why Horace? Why did you do this? Why wasn't I enough? Who killed you? No one, not even someone who cheated on me like you did, deserved to die.

Unbelievable, how had women in her family lost all their husbands in such a short time. Was there a curse at work here, or something more sinister? Odd how both her husbands were dead! Two mysterious deaths, one deemed a traffic accident, the other murder. Would they ever find out who killed Horace and Amber? How did these murders relate to Megan's killing and the homeless man Mr. Young? All these questions raced through Lily's mind. She looked around noticing a lot of people here, to say their final goodbyes to Horace. There must have been two or three hundred people there. A lot of them were politicians wanting publicity, understanding the press would be here, always ready for the photo opportunity, a sound bite to get them elected or re-elected.

Lily noticed the awful Harold Crimshaw. *How dare he? Horace hated him.*

He said the only reason he ran for mayor, was to keep an opportunistic bastard out of the City coffers. Horace also said if Harold Crimshaw ever got to be mayor, there would be a lawsuit from every female employee in the mayor's office vicinity. She thought Horace had been exaggerating, but the man did seem a little smarmy. She only hoped the people there, would give her a few minutes alone at Horace's grave to say goodbye.

Both she and Rose needed privacy to say goodbye. She wanted a private graveside ceremony, not a photo opportunity, to observe the grieving widow and her daughter splashed on television and the front page of the paper.

Lily sat down with Rose and Katha and Amelia followed. She found her mind wandering to wonderful times with Horace. She remembered times when she and Horace went on holidays at the beach with Rose. He encompassed all the qualities of a good father, but had he been a good husband?

So many times she complained to him that he needed to spend more time with her and Rose. She remembered all their holidays as wonderful, but had she idolized them? She recalled the first Christmas they spent together when Horace, not realizing Rose was too old to believe anymore, dressed up as Santa. Rose guessed at once her dad was in the costume. Rose went along with the disguise, realizing how much it meant to him. Rose was such a thoughtful child, even at nine years old. It was a good memory and the memory she wanted to keep of Horace in her head. Not the image of the way she found him. Lily realized with a start the service had been concluded. It was time to say goodbye.

She wasn't ready. Would she ever be ready? Oh how weary, she felt, like she was cold and would never be warm again. She shivered pulling her coat she hadn't taken off, closer to herself. Did Rose appear cold too? Lily thought, as she glanced at Rose and leaned in hug her.

"Thank goodness the service is completed," Lily said aloud.

"Excuse me, dear, but you need to go up and announce the wake afterwards," Katha whispered, prodding Lily.

"I'm so tired Grandma Katha. Do I have to go to the wake?" Lily whispered back.

"I know, sweetie. The worst part is near over and you can soon go home, take a hot bath and rest," Katha promised.

"I don't ever think I'll sleep again," Lily whispered.

"It will get better Lily. Do you want to go visit my Doctor? He can help. I can call him for you," Amelia whispered.

"No, but thanks, I appreciate the thought Amelia."

Lily sauntered to the podium and spoke to the room, "Everyone please feel free to join us for a celebration of Horace's life, at the Pope Hotel, in the Rose Room. Light foods and refreshments will be provided. We will be holding a private graveside service for Horace, for family only. Thank you all for coming; this concludes the service for today."

People slowly wandered out making their goodbyes. The four Kelly women also left, and headed for the graveside ceremony.

At the cemetery, after getting out of the limousine, Lily looked around at Horace's grave site. This was a lovely spot to be buried in, even if the cemetery at the edge of town marked the official end of Happy Valley. Lily wiped away a tear as she felt guilty for even thinking of this. Horace need to be buried, whether she liked the thought, or not and this spot had been carefully picked. Lily glanced around and saw a lovely full-grown maple tree nearby, with a bird's nest. She noted it also held a bird feeder. The other graves close were well-tended and flowers were on them. The graves adjacent to those that crept up a tall hill were well tended as well. Lily wandered how they mow the grass, so evenly when it went up such a huge hill. Those graves were cheaper but not ideal. They hadn't sold the ones higher. The fact that some of the graves would be situated beside the fence next to the Canadian Shield rock face high above the hill made them undesirable. The igneous (pink and some say red in colour) Canadian Shield face rock flowing from the great lakes to western Canada resulted from volcanic ash which had covered the area eons ago. The Canadian Shield rock face left a gap in the cliff face above, where a chasm would make anyone climbing there, fall about one hundred feet to a valley below.

The fence preventing that from happening was often broken and defaced by the town's teenagers, making the place dangerous. Horace had campaigned to have them build a better fence and hired guards after one of the teens fell and needed to be rescued. The teen was lucky; he survived the fall and spent two weeks in the hospital.

The minister began to say a few words over Horace. Lily felt cold and out-of-place. It was like she wasn't at this tomb. She understood unfortunately this remained the truth not an illusion; she stood beside Horace's final burial-place. A tear slipped from her eye and she wiped it away before anyone could notice. The coffin hung on winches about six feet above the ground. Lily watched them get ready to lower the coffin.

"May we take a couple of minutes before you lower it?" Lily inquired.

The one man looked reluctant and frowned. Lily looked at the other man expectantly, hoping he'd change the other one's mind.

"We can give the lady ten minutes, Bob. The body is the mayor. How much time do you think the lady has had without prying eyes to grieve?" declared the other man, "Besides, it only takes one of us to lower it."

"Fine. I will come back in ten minutes, Mrs. Brooksfield. We are so sorry for your loss," Bob replied.

"Yes, Bob can do this on his own," the other man replied.

Then the two men walked away towards the chapel on the grounds.

"Mom, someone is watching us," Rose fearfully retorted.

"It's probably one of those muckraking reporters from the tabloids. We'll say goodbye quickly and leave. Then they won't have a story," Lily explained annoyed.

Ten minutes passed quickly and Bob returned. As they watch the coffin being lowered into the grave a shot was heard. All the women duck for cover. Bob, who had been lowering the coffin by machine, jumped out of the cab of the backhoe and ran for cover as well.

"Keep down all of you," Lily commanded taking charge and dialling her cell phone.

"Nine-one-one. What is the nature of your emergency?" requested the voice.

"I need the police. Now!"

"Police operator, what is the nature of your emergency?" solicited the police dispatcher.

"Shots fired at Westside Cemetery, the south side of the cemetery. We're under fire here, please hurry," Lily screamed into her phone as a bullet whizzed by her.

The bullets rang out fast and furious. Lily found herself pushing Rose into the open grave under the still hanging coffin. She took one arm of Katha and one arm of Amelia and pulled them both into the burial plot, dropping her cell phone, and hanging up the phone by accident. Just as she did so a bullet pinged overhead. It had hit the metal wench holding the coffin. The coffin was now hanging precariously over their heads in a downward angle.

"Mom, someone shot at us again! We're all going to die."

"It will be okay honey. The police will come and stop whoever this is. And we will be protected here under your dad's coffin," Lily reassured her daughter, while still searching for the cell phone she dropped.

More bullets rang out over their heads. They heard poof sounds; as the bullets hit the dirt and some of them narrowly missing the coffin above them.

"Yes right, keep telling yourself we'll be fine. Bullets are coming our way, there isn't a cop for miles, and only Daddy and his coffin is all that protect us. Oh no, they'll put holes in Daddy's coffin. Daddeeee," Rose complained hysterically. "And his coffin is falling down on our heads."

"Your dad is protected us even in death, Rose. The coffin won't fall. Now pull yourself together. You can't fall apart now. We will beat this gunman," Lily answered.

"Rose is correct, we're all going to be killed, Lily," Amelia cried.

"Oh, for Pete's sake pull yourself together, Amelia. Set a better example," Lily sniped.

"You're squishing my foot," Katha complained to Amelia.

"My leg, oh my leg. The crutch stuck into the dirt and I'm falling over in soil," complained Amelia.

"Good grief, someone's shooting at us, we could all be killed and you two complain about being cramped?" Rose shouted annoyed, "Get a grip people! We could be killed here."

"Well if she'd get off my foot with that crutch...," Katha replied annoyed.

They heard sounds of running across the graveyard and then more shots ringing out. Lily picked up the phone and went to dial the police again and realized they were still connected.

"Hello Ma'am, are you still on the line?" enquired the police dispatcher.

"Quiet. I can't hear the police operator," Lily cautioned.

"Can you spot the shooter Ma'am? Is it just one shooter?" probed the police dispatcher.

"No, I can't glimpse the shooter. We're trying not to get hit by the bullets," Lily explained exasperated.

"No need to take that tone, Ma'am; you demanded my assistance. Please stay on the line. Police are on the way," the police dispatcher cautioned.

Lily tried to quiet her family, "Quiet all of you. Would you all quit squabbling! I must hear this woman. I told you all that."

"You've taken cover? Where can the policemen find you when they arrive?" demanded the police dispatcher.

"Believe it or not, we've jumped into my husband's grave to get away from the shooter. His coffin dangles above our heads and it could fall with the right shot." Lily explained, "Please hurry! My daughter is here, too, as well as my cousin, and my great-grandmother. And my cousin has a broken leg from last week."

"They're on the way, Ma'am. Do you hear the sirens?"

"I hear them mom," Rose claimed.

"Yes, I do now. Thank you so much." Lily answered.

"As long as it not an ambulance!" Katha announced.

"Why would it be an ambulance? None of us are hit!" Amelia stated.

"Please give me your name for the officers," demanded the dispatcher.

"I didn't give you my name? Oh, I am sorry, this is Mrs. Horace Brooksfield," Lily replied proudly. "And what is your name, so I can thank you later."

"No, thank you is necessary Ma'am, but my name is Violet Garden. I believe we spoke the other day," answered the dispatcher.

"Thank you, anyway, Violet. We appreciate all of your help."

"Mom, they take forever and you thank her? What if the shooter comes here and shoots down at us. We are sitting like ducks waiting to be plucked," Rose complained.

"More flies with sugar Rose," Amelia muttered under her breath.

"We're being shot at here, not throwing a tea party," Rose exclaimed.

"My hip, oh dear it's stuck again. I don't know how I'll ever get out of here. I don't think they made artificial hips for crawling into graves," Katha complained, trying to distract Rose.

"Are you okay, Grandma Katha? I've never known you to complain. I guess it would be okay if Daddy protected us up in heaven like Mom said," Rose said pointing to her father's coffin.

"Daddy won't let anything happen to us."

"That's right sweetheart," Lily agreed approvingly.

They listened intently but heard no more shots filling the air with sound and fury.

"Do you think it's over, mom?" Rose asked.

"Mrs. Horace Brooksfield?" a voice asked, hovering above the grave.

"Yes?" Lily said cautiously, hiding her daughter beneath her just in case.

"Police, Ma'am."

"Can you pass down your badge?"

"Lily, just let the man help us out of here. I'm getting filthy," demanded Katha. "I don't know how we can go to the wake like this."

"I agree with Mom. Don't listen to the two whiners. Mom, please, just take a look at his badge before we trust him," Rose insisted.

"I did, Rose. His identification is legitimate."

The policeman reached down and helped them up out of the small space pulling Lily up first, followed by Amelia and Rose and Katha.

"Why Brad Owens, is that you?" questioned Amelia surprised as the police officer pulled her out gently.

"Amelia Cordova! As I live and breathe. It's wonderful to see you again," Brad Owens said sounding pleased.

"You know Sergeant Detective Owens?" asked Lily shocked that Amelia had smiled at him.

"Brad used to come by my house when I was a teenager before the...before the accident," Amelia stuttered.

"So you were aware of my cousin as a teen?" Lily enquired.

"Did I? We were all in love with Amelia. She was the prettiest girl in Ravenworst. She was the one who got away." Brad answered, with deep feeling in his voice turning to Amelia he said,

"So this is where you got to, I was so sad to hear about your parents and your siblings."

"Thanks. I moved in with my Great Aunt Katha when they died," Amelia explained, trying to change the subject.

"I've been here about six years," Brad commented.

"Six years? How odd, I've never even run into you."

"A police officer has a busy job. We don't have a lot of time for anything else. It is a bigger city now," Brad explained. "It's wonderful to see you," Amelia said sweetly. "I'm so glad you answered our call. We're safe now aren't we?"

"I sent another cop to check the perimeter, but we should probably take cover until he comes back." Silas Rentford appeared suddenly looking haggard and with his gun still drawn.

"For Pete's sake, put your gun away. You could harm the ladies. Did you find the shooter, Rentford?"

"Yes and I called it in, she's dead."

"What? How can the shooter be dead? You say it's a she? Did you return fire?" enquired Brad puzzled and angry.

"No sir, I did not," Silas denied. "But she's dead all the same."

"People don't up and shoot themselves. It has to be another shooter, or she shot herself," Brad insisted.

"Why, what is this old home week?" Amelia said suddenly, looking up after hearing Silas' voice.

"Silas Rentford, is that you?"

"Amelia Cordova?" Silas asked looking surprised, "Wow, it's so incredibly wonderful to meet you again."

"It's lovely to see you too, Silas," Amelia replied blushing. "Did you know someone shot at us from the graveyard?"

"I was sent to find the active shooter here in the cemetery. Are you okay? You don't have any wounds do you?" probed Silas worried, looking like he wanted to personally check her over for bullet holes.

"No, I'm fine, and is everyone else here," Amelia answered.

"Gosh, it's great to spot you, Amelia. When you disappeared after the fire we were heartbroken at school," Silas continued, grinning wildly at Amelia.

Lily looked at both men. They seemed enthralled with Amelia; no one else existed for them.

"Silas talk with the lady on your own time!" Brad then mouthed 'Sorry' to Amelia and then ordered, "Back to your report Rentford. Did you examine the body?"

"Yes sir, she's dead. Woman about sixty, sixty-five years old, dyed short black hair, society matron? Wallet in her purse says she's one Cheryl Waverly."

"No, it can't be Cheryl. You have to be mistaken. She's my mother-in-law. She wouldn't shoot at me. Not while her granddaughter was nearby," Lily protested shaking her head, "Even she would shoot at family."

"Oh no, you are wrong. It couldn't be Grandma. She wouldn't shoot me or anybody," Rose cried, also shaking her head.

"No, I'm not sorry, Ms. Brooksfield. She looks like her driver licence picture. No room for doubt about the shooter, it was the deceased woman, Cheryl Waverley," Silas replied unequivocally.

"Excuse us ladies we'll be right back we need to check the perimeter again," Sergeant Detective Owens said frowning at Silas.

Silas and Brad then left.

"Good Lord. What kind of people do I come from that my grandmother shot at me?" demanded Rose disgusted.

"Watch your language, missy. We do not take the name of the Lord in vain," Katha retorted.

"She was my grandmother and she shot at us. I have a right to be angry," said Rose dejected and hurt, "She could have killed us."

"Obviously, the loss of her daughter obviously broke her mind and Horace's death (before she could make up with him) put her completely over the edge," Lily agreed. "If she had been truly thinking I know she would never put you at risk. The woman adored you."

"Is it true she broke his arm when he was little?" Rose probed, "Do you think she killed Daddy?"

"I know she didn't kill him. She loved him, no matter what. Yes, it's true she broke his arm. She became unhinged slightly when she lost her daughter, but losing your father must have made her even more unbalanced.

"I hate her! How could she do this? And at Daddy's grave! It's like slapping Daddy. I don't want to be a Brooksfield."

"You are upset dear, but you must not talk that way. As for the people you come from, you are of my blood now, so you come from good Irish stock," Katha expounded.

"That's right, Rose. You are a Kelly woman remember?" Amelia agreed.

"I remember."

"Come on Rose; we have to go."

"Great, now I've got dirt in my hair. Must we still go to the Wake? I've already said goodbye to Daddy," questioned Rose, changing the subject.

"Yes, but only for a short time. We need to leave now," Lily explained.

"I need a drink," Katha announced. "Preferably a gin fizz, or a fuzzy navel."

"Me too!" Amelia agreed.

"Me three," Lily exclaimed.

"I need one too," Rose announced.

"I hope you're talking about pop, because you're getting a drink over your mother's and my dead body. Oops, poor choice of words, but you get the drift right, Rose?" Katha exclaimed.

"I do, Grandma. Pop sounds good. I feel like I must have a ton of dirt in my mouth. Ooh, decaying body dirt. Yuck!" Rose fretted wiping her tongue.

Amelia hid a laugh. Suddenly Sergeant Detective Owens appeared again at Amelia's elbow. Silas looked chastised Lily noted as if Brad had yelled at him.

"Can I escort you ladies to the wake?" asked Sergeant Detective Owens sounding boyish and nervous.

"I'm finished all my paperwork and I'm off duty. Can I escort you Amelia?" requested Silas, also smiling "And we could catch up on old times with you?"

Brad frowned again at Silas.

"While you gentlemen made kind offers, it wouldn't be seemly for you to escort me to a wake," Amelia answered prettily, side stepping both offers. Amelia turned to each of them and smiled a sweet endearing smile, "But please, feel free to come to the wake."

"We'd be happy to. Wouldn't we, Brad, I mean Sergeant Detective Owens," Silas chimed.

"Correct. At least let us see you safely to your limousine?" agreed Brad, "You are lucky the chauffeur guy didn't panic and take off when he overheard the shots. He called us too. He is still parked over near the front gates of the cemetery."

"Seeing us safely to the car would be wonderful. Thank you gentlemen," Lily agreed, but neither seemed to register that Lily was even there, until Amelia nodded her head.

The chauffeur then drove away with the ladies inside only after a lecture from Brad and Silas about keeping the ladies safe.

"Home please," Lily requested from the driver.

"We don't have time to go home," Katha stated annoyed.

"Well I'm so glad you're done with your cops," Lily said cattily to Amelia.

"I can't believe they were more interested in you, Aunt Amelia, than the fact that Grandma tried to kill us. Did they really say Grandma was dead, Mom?"

"I'm sorry, sweetie," Lily replied sadly.

"This is ridiculous. I can't believe any of this happened. If Grandma tried to kill us, then who killed Grandma?" asked Rose.

"I don't know. The whole business appears strange and the body count keeps rising," Katha exclaimed.

"There's a lot of stuff going on in Happy Valley I don't understand. I understand the news anchor Paul Knight killed himself. I for one do not believe it. I met him once; he seemed like a focused man and not the type to kill himself."

"Paul Knight the television anchor?" Rose queried, "Who cares about him? Grandma tried to kill us. Why?"

"I don't know why. She must have a screw loose. I met Paul Knight a couple of times. He seemed like a nice young man. I can't believe they are reporting his death on Chatter," Katha explained holding up her I-phone.

"When did you get an I-phone? Mom won't buy me one of them. She claims I'd always be on the phone. And you own a Chatter account?" asked Rose surprised.

"Doesn't everyone have a Chatter account? I'll get an I-phone for your belated birthday present and the data plan as well. Then you can use Chatter a lot more," Grandma Katha offered whispering.

"I already have a Chatter account, but I'd love an I-phone," Rose exclaimed.

"Don't encourage her, Grandma Katha. She's not getting an I-phone, as much as she wants one. She'd never get her homework done, always surfing on the thing," Lily admonished.

"Yes, I will. Please, Mom?"

Katha gave Lily a look that conveyed to Lily that this could make Rose feel better.

"Well if Grandma Katha chooses to give you one for a belated birthday present and you don't abuse it, I guess I won't stop her."

"Thank you, Lily. Now I hope it won't upset you but, we just do not have time to stop at home. We are late as it is. We'll need to stop at the washroom and tidy up before we go. I own a lint brush."

Katha held up the lint brush from her purse and began brushing off soil from her dress. She then passed it to Amelia.

"A lint brush? You're going to clean yourself up and go to the wake? My husband's been murdered. We've been shot at by his mother, but we're still going to hold up appearances and go to his wake?"

"Mom is correct. Let's just go home."

"Lily and Rose, this has been hard on all of us, but we can't let the murderer win. If we don't go to Horace's wake then we haven't truly said goodbye. I know it didn't really make me start to feel better until I realized how many people loved your great grandfather."

"Fine, then! Can I borrow the lint brush after you, Amelia?" requested Lily.

"So we're going?" Rose asked her mother.

"Yes," Lily answered.

"We can all use the lint brush," Katha replied generously. "I think some soap and water is also in order for our faces. You have a dirt mark, all down your neck Rose."

"Why didn't you say something sooner? What if someone saw me like this?" Rose replied sarcastically.

She then scrubbed at the dirt despite what she said.

"Quit rubbing it in, Rose. It makes it worse." Katha claimed.

"Who cares? I'm sick of this all. My dad is dead. My grandmother is dead. I just want the world to go away." Rose answered.

"It will get better," Katha stated.

"How can it ever? My mom is in jail...my family is gone."

"No, it is not. You have your mother, Lily me and your Aunt Amelia and we are your family Rose and we love you."

"I love you too, Grandma Katha. I'm sorry I'm such a pain," Rose replied wiping tears away.

"You're never a pain. To me, your aunt, and your mother, you are our pride and joy. Now, dry your eyes. I have some wipes in my purse, I'm sure they will do as well, to wipe the dirt off."

"Always prepared aren't you, Aunt Katha?" Amelia stated.

"I certainly am," Katha replied and then turning to Rose she asked, "Are you okay now?"

"No, but I want to forget about all of this and just remember Daddy for a while."

"You do that Rosey," Amelia, Lily and Katha all said.

"Please, stop near here," Rose instructed the driver, "It's City Hall. It has a washroom, a huge one, where we can clean off the dirt...Oh no, we can't. Daddy was killed upstairs,"

Rose remembered and bit her lip so she didn't cry. But it didn't work as tears escaped from her eyes and she rushed to wipe them before anyone noticed.

"Your father would understand and want us to get cleaned up to represent him best."

"Okay, I do look bad. Daddy would hate my dress appearing dirty," Rose said dabbing her eyes.

"We'll make it through this," Lily insisted taking Rose's hand.

"Driver, stop here, for a few minutes," Katha advised.

The driver parked the limousine in front of City Hall. After the ladies excited the vehicle, they entered the City Hall foyer where Barney Terrell greeted them.

"What happened to you all?" Barney asked and then observed, "You are all covered in dirt. It's obvious something happened, but I thought you'd all be at the wake by now."

"We had a little incident at the gravesite. Someone shot at us," Lily replied not admitting it was Cheryl, her ex-mother-in law.

"Someone shot at you? Good lord, are you all okay? Should I call the police?"

"Not necessary. The police have been informed, and other than a lot of dirt, we are fine."

"Mrs. B., sorry that happened to you, especially after Mr. Brooksfield's death. I wanted to go to the funeral but I don't get off for a few more minutes. I did plan on paying my respects at the wake. Horace Brooksfield was a fine man and deserves my respect," Barney explained.

"Thank you, Barney. Horace was fond of you. He spoke highly of you."

"Thank you Mr. Terrell, Daddy spoke well of you. He said you were the best at your job here," Rose responded, changing the subject.

"I believe Mayor Brooksfield was a lucky man. He has a lovely wife and daughter. He spoke lovingly of you, Miss Rose. He said you played basketball like a pro and had a real talent for mimicry and acting."

"We need to get cleaned up before we go to the wake, Barney, but since you're off in a few minutes would you do us the honour of accompanying us to the wake?" Katha invited impulsively.

"I would be truly honoured, Ma'am," Barney replied smiling.

"Please excuse us now while we clean up the dust," Lily said.

"Sure. I'm sorry that I kept you, Ma'am."

Barney watched their departing backs, his gaze never leaving them until they went into the washroom. This made Rose feel slightly uncomfortable, but since she didn't want to upset her mother she said nothing.

"You were awfully good to him, Grandma Katha," Rose said.

"Well he seemed like a pleasant man, and your father liked him, although he didn't like Amber..."

"How do you know that?" Lily asked.

"I came to visit Horace to arrange a surprise birthday party for Lily last year and I saw him glance at Amber with such malice when she flirted with him," Katha admitted.

"Are you sure you didn't imagine it?"

"No, she brushed him and he pushed her away and then he yelled at her to quit flirting with every guy who had legs," Katha admitted.

"We should tell Detective Rogers," Lily insisted.

"Fine, I'll do that after the wake." Katha exclaimed continuing to brush her hair and replace her make-up, "There, all fixed. We all look decent now. Let's go, girls."~0~

Chapter 18 - The Awakening

Arriving at the Pope hotel they entered into the Rose

ballroom for the wake. Barney helped Amelia in, earning a dirty stare from both Silas and Brad.

"Hello, Lily. I'm so dreadfully sorry about Horace. He was a lovely man," Colleen Finn lied.

"I know you didn't like him much, Colleen, although you never hesitated to put him through to me on the phone at work," Lily replied.

"I'm still sorry he's gone, Lily. I recognize how much you and Rose truly loved him," Colleen answered.

"I appreciate you coming, Colleen. How is the office?"

"I'd rather not get into it; you have enough to worry about today," Colleen commented.

"Is Barbara that bad?"

"She is different than you are to work for in the office. But you quit worrying about the office. I'll manage until you come back," Colleen explained.

"I appreciate you holding down the fort until I return." Colleen scanned the room and seeing a crowd gathering waiting to speak to Lily she said, "I better let you go; it appears like there's a line of people who want to speak to you."

"Thank you again, Colleen, I'll see you later," Lily answered.

"If you need anything you tell me, Lily," Colleen insisted touching Lily's arm, and then walked away.

"My dear Mrs. Brooksfield, I am so sorry to hear about your loss and troubles," Gregory Hanks said as he came up to Lily and took her hand. Gregory Hanks was a tall gentleman, whose blue eyes sparkled with life.

"Have you met Mr. Hanks, Rose?" Lily asked politely.

"Yes, of course, Mom. You own Hank's, a huge grocery conglomerate across North America, don't you Mr. Hanks?"

"Yes, little ma'am, I do," Gregory Hanks admitted.

A man came up and whispered in Mr. Hanks' ear and Lily discerned the man objected to Mr. Hank's speaking to her. He must be his campaign manager. Lily had been told he ran for parliament. Why had he even allowed him to come here? Was it because Horace had been the mayor? Lily wondered.

"Should you be seen speaking to me?" Lily asked, "I understood you thought of running for office. A member of Parliament wasn't it?"

"Wow, you certainly have great sources, my dear. My mind isn't made up yet. I've known you since you were a child, at one time I had hoped to be your great-grandfather. Of course, I can be seen with you. I would never turn my back on you, parliamentary seat or not," Gregory Hanks expounded.

"Thank you, Mr. Hanks."

"My dear, call me Greg," Greg Hanks replied congenially.

"Thank you again, Greg."

"Your grandmother appears so sparkling and extremely lovely. Like a fine wine. Does the woman never age?" Greg stated with a leer in his voice.

Lily was always amazed at how easily Grandma Katha seemed to collect eligible, interesting admirers. She only hoped she'd be able to do the same in her old age.

"No I don't think Grandma Katha does age. It's part of her charm."

"It certainly is. I've missed the dear lady." Greg announced, "Damn Kieran for swooping in and grabbing the prize. A blast from the past and then he pounced regaining her heart."

"Speaking of the love of my Grandma Katha's life; if you recognize what is good for you, you'll guard your tongue around her when you speak of my great-grandfather Kieran."

"Who's hanging around her now?" asked Greg, sounding peevish and jealous.

"His name is Terrence Stewart. He's the police chief's Dad," Lily explained.

"Oh..." Greg replied sounding dejected.

"I'm sure she'd love to hear from you," Lily responded devilishly.

"I think I'll go speak to her." Greg announced, "My nephew took over the business, so I'm going to have a lot of time on my hands."

Katha spotted Greg, smiled, and waved.

"Look, she's smiling. Go talk to her."

Greg sauntered over to Katha as Terrence frowned. Lily watched from across the room, trying not to laugh. She scrutinized around for Rose, only to find her standing behind her.

"Mom, where is Aunt Amelia?" asked Rose. "I don't see where she went."

"I can't tell," Lily answered and looking around she added, "Oh there she is."

Lily pointed. Rose then walked over towards her Aunt Amelia. As Lily gazed around, she was happily surprised at how many people came to honour Horace. So many people kept coming up to her and telling her how sorry they felt that Horace was gone. No one mentioned the way he was found, although Lily had caught some quiet whispers stop when she circulated the room.

A few people had offered to start a scholarship in Horace's name for law students, a wonderful idea and something she had planned on doing for Horace's memory. Rose would be happy to have her father honoured this way. Rose wandered back to Lily's side interrupting her thoughts.

"Mom, Aunt Amelia is embarrassing us. You'd think this was a party not my dad's wake. Look at her; the men kowtowing to her every wish or command."

"Why, whatever do you mean?" asked Lily.

"Look over there, Mom, near the window. Those two police officers grovel all over her every word, and observe how they keep chasing the other men away. There's something odd about them."

"I'm sure you are mistaken. Why would they grovel? They hardly know your Aunt Amelia."

"Watch them. The guy in the blue suit came over to speak to her. He speaks to Aunt Amelia and bam he's turfed," Rose stated watching intently.

"Sweetie, Amelia said she met them when she was a teenager. Aunt Amelia lost her family to a fire; this has brought back some lovely memories for her, instead of the horror of their deaths," Lily explained, not believing this but trying to appease Rose.

"But, Mom, I don't think she has a clue those men like her."

"Rose, you're quite right, she doesn't have a clue, but it is harmless enough. I do however appreciate you watching after your Aunt Amelia. We both understand she is a special person."

"Mom, I love Aunt Amelia. I'm not judging her when I say this, but she's awful naïve for her age."

"Aunt Amelia is inexperienced. Despite all she's gone through, she trusts like a child, "Lily agreed.

"I understand, mom. She doesn't see what is right in front of her." Rose explained, sounding worried, "And sometimes people take advantage of such trust."

"We can all be blind to other's motives. I hope Amelia never loses her zest. Sweet people like Amelia lose their innocence becoming bitter, confused and lost," Lily reassured. "But I promise I'll keep an eye on that pair. Thank you for letting me understand."

"So you'll keep an eye on her too?"

"Yes, I promise I will, sweetie," Lily agreed.

"Will you be okay?" Rose asked searching Lily's face.

"We both will, sweetie, but I want this wake finished," Lily admitted.

"Can I go, Mom?" Rose asked. "I need to get out of here."

"Going to the mall with Carol?"

"Yes, she's over there," Rose pointed to Carol, who was flirting with a waiter who couldn't have been more than eighteen years old.

"Okay, take your cell phone and make sure you are home by four p.m. Promise me, no flirting with older boys. They can't be trusted."

"Good grief, Mom. Can you be any more embarrassing? A. If I was to flirt with older boys I don't think it would be your business, and B, I'm not the type to flirt with older boys at the mall. Don't you understand your own daughter?"

"Sorry, what could I be thinking?" Lily replied sarcastically.

"Mom!"

"Fine. Do you need any money? Of course you need money. Here, is a hundred dollars. Spend the money and find something lovely to wear, but nothing too short or too trashy. Got it?" Lily ordered knowing that she gave Rose too much money.

"Thanks, Mom. You're the best," Rose replied, changing her tune and hugging her mother.

"Like, I'm so sorry, Mrs. Brooksfield, you know about your husband. And I don't believe what the press said," Carol proclaimed as she stood in front of Lily.

"Hush, Carol," Rose exclaimed, poking Carol in the ribs.

"What? What did I say?" Carol asked dejected.

"Ah, thank you, Carol," Lily said a little flustered.

"Don't you worry! Rose and I will go hang out at the mall and do some window shopping. Retail therapy is good for the soul," Carol explained.

"It is, isn't it Carol? Have fun at the mall you two," Lily laughed.

Carol had been hanging around so much for years. She was like part of the family, so it wasn't a stretch to say she'd changed a little. Lily thought. Carol appeared more outgoing now she had turned fifteen, more so than Rose. But wasn't that a good thing? Rose needed to come out of her shell and not worry so much about what people thought all the time. Carol would distract Rose although she should worry about Carol.

Carol seemed a little more boy crazy than Rose. She hoped Rose would stay as sensible as she was now and not follow Carol's lead. This was difficult for them both to bear and Rose had already been through so much in her short life. It was good Carol and Rose would go to the mall. A little retail therapy would distract Rose, for a few hours. Lily looked forward to a little shut-eye while Rose was gone, if she ever got away from this wake and never-ending crowds.

"Lily, check out Amelia. Those policemen are a little too forward with her," Katha interrupted Lily's thoughts.

"You want me to check on her too? It is harmless enough, Grandma Katha. She's just chatting with some old friends."

"She might think of them as old friends, but those boys have designs on her and I don't trust them," Grandma Katha replied perceptively.

"Fine, I'll check on her then," Lily answered, appeasing her Grandma Katha.

Lily went over to Amelia and listened to part of the snippets of the conversation, going on with the two policemen. Barney Terrell stood nearby, fingering a money clip in his pocket and listening to the conversation.

"Do you remember when your dad hired me to cut the lawn?" Brad said touching Amelia's hand and fingering a money clip in his pocket as well.

"You cut the lawn too?" Silas blurted frowning. He too fidgets, fingering a money clip in his pocket.

"You both did," Amelia admitted.

"I used to slip out and bring you lemonade. Daddy used to get mad. He said it was wasted on the help. I'm sorry he was mean to you."

"He was a tartar wasn't he?" claimed Brad.

"He was abusive; I saw him hit you," Silas insisted.

"I did too," admitted Brad.

"My father had the right to discipline me." Amelia defended, "He didn't like it when I talked to boys."

"Do you remember when you slipped out to the dance?" asked Silas

"Do you mean the one where I danced with both you and Brad? It was such a magical night, until I got home. I went to sneak in the window and my dad caught me. He was so mad. I barely sat down for a week. He wouldn't let me out of the house for a week either except to go to school," Amelia remembered. "I thought he would kill me. He was so mad."

"I wanted to take you to the Prom, but you disappeared," Brad explained.

"I did too!" Silas piped in like he didn't want to be forgotten.

"I was ill after the fire. It was a terrible time. You understand I don't want to talk about it," Amelia explained quietly, not elaborating.

"So gentleman, how do you know my cousin?" Lily interjected, changing the subject.

"Yes," both answered in response to Amelia, not hearing Lily.

Both men continued to stare at Amelia. Lily noted that Barney Terrell stepped a little closer, trying not to appear like he was listening as well. All these men seemed too interested in Amelia. Amelia suddenly seemed to be a man magnet. Amelia had been sending out vibes she wasn't interested, since Jack and Sam died. Now it was like some kind of light switch had been turned on and it was on high neon.

"Thank you for allowing me to honour your husband, Ms. Brooksfield. Like I said Mr. Brooksfield was a fine man that will be greatly missed. I need to take my leave now. I wasn't feeling to well the day before yesterday and I'd like to go home and rest,"

Barney exclaimed taking Amelia's hand, earning a frown from
Brad and Silas.

"Goodbye, Barney, and thank you for coming," Lily commented.

"Barney, did I meet you before today?" asked Amelia.

"Yes, I used to live in Ravenworst and we may have run into each
other a time or two then as I use to come to your dad's store; but
my daughter Susan also works for you now." Barney answered.

"Oh, so that's it. Susan is wonderful, a simply fantastic help to me
at the store. But you look too young to be her dad."

"She was my wife's daughter. My wife was considerably older
than me. Before she died, I adopted Susan," Barney explained.

"Oh, how sweet," Amelia stated earning Barney another frown as
he sent a triumphant grin their way.

"Well, it was lovely to be with you again, Ms. Kelly. Goodbye, for
now," Barney replied.

Barney kissed Amelia's hand and left. Lily was disturbed that was
kind of weird. Why were all these men fawning over Amelia? And
why did they all come from Ravenworst?

"Awfully presumptuous of him," Brad complained, watching
Barney's departing back like a hawk.

"Yes, I don't like him either. Are you okay, Amelia?" asked Silas
solicitously. "I don't understand what you are asking, but I'm
fine."

"So gentleman, how do you know my cousin?" Lily asked again,
this time a little more forcefully.

"I met her a long time ago. She lived in Ravenworst. Silas and I grew up in Ravenworst," Brad answered, as Silas jabbed him with his elbow.

"It's been a long time. We did some catching up of old times and memories," Silas answered, smiling at Amelia.

"It must be enjoyable to meet with an old friend," Lily replied gauging them.

"Yes, it's always wonderful to be with an old high school classmate," Silas answered, taking control of the conversation.

"We are sorry about your husband, ma'am," Brad stated solemnly.

"Please call me Lily," Lily said speaking to both Silas and Brad.

"Thanks, Lily," Brad and Silas stated at the same time.

"I'm so sorry you were harassed at the station," Brad exclaimed.

"And I for one don't believe you're guilty of anything, other than being at the wrong place at the wrong time," Silas cried, as Brad glared at him.

"I tried to get on the case, but Rogers has it in for me. I know you are innocent Amelia. I was so angry, when I heard he had arrested you," Brad announced smiling and offering his hand, earning him another elbow from Silas.

"Can I get you something to eat?" asked Silas of Amelia.

"No please, let me."

"No thank you, Brad, Silas. I don't feel well," Amelia stated appearing wan and limped on her crutch. She then asked, "Can we leave soon, Lily?"

"Oh, I'm sorry, Amelia." Brad sympathized, "We are awful of us not to realize how tired you would be standing on your bad leg."

"Let me say goodbye to Grandma Katha," Lily said solicitously, walking away for a moment.

"I will drive you home," Brad offered as Silas glared.

"Thank you both. Lily and I would love a ride home, but first we need to go make sure Aunt Katha doesn't need a ride."

"Okay, then," Brad replied smiling. "Let me do the chauffeuring."

"Thank you, Brad. I'd be happy to take you up on your offer," Amelia answered.

Lily approached Aunt Katha, who held court with her current beau Terrence Stewart; beside him his son, the chief of police, Edward Stewart, and Greg Franks held a deep conversation.

"Grandma Katha, we're going to head out now," Lily announced.

"Oh well, I guess I should be leaving now. Excuse me, gentlemen," Katha retorted.

"Please, couldn't you stay a little longer?" asked Greg, "This is truly a wonderful conversation."

"You just remember she's my woman now Greg!" Terrence said glaring.

"I don't see a ring so she's fair game," Felix challenged.

"Gentlemen, I'm right here. As to staying I don't know. Terrence and I had some plans too," Katha answered.

Terrence grinned, because Katha made it clear she was with him.

"Well played, Terrence, well played," Greg exclaimed.

"I believe you and I need to talk about this kind of behaviour, Terrence Stewart," Katha admonished.

"Sorry, dear. You are correct; I'm acting like a cave man. Forgive me?"

"Since you ask so nicely, I will."

"Grandma Katha, please talk with your friends and have fun. I'm going home for a nap. I'll see you later, Grandma Katha," Lily said ready to walk away.

"All right, you can come to supper. Terrence and I will bring something to eat at six p.m. So don't you dare cook."

"Thanks. I don't think I have the energy or inclination to cook, so your offer will be wonderful."

Lily then walked across the room taking care to walk beside Amelia in case she needed help with her crutches. Lily and Amelia climbed into the car with Brad to drive home. Silas and Brad, Lily noted, continued to chatter all the way home to Amelia, like two old friends, but Lily noted each one persistently vied for Amelia's affections.

Arriving at the front of Lily's door, Amelia got out of the car first. Amelia scrambled for her crutches. Brad assisted her placing them carefully under her arms. Lily climbed out feeling totally ignored by all of them.

"Please come in Lily's house for coffee," Amelia invited Brad and Silas with a smile.

Entering the house ahead of the party, Lily noticed disarray. She could not believe it, but it was obvious someone had been in the house. She was terrified. Someone had broken into the house. Everywhere she stared things were moved, and thrown around the room. The sofa cushions were shredded and their contents spread across the carpet. The lamp had been thrown on the floor; its cord appeared frayed and broken. The kitchen was not much better she noticed as the fridge door was open and food had been flung all over the countertops and floor. Why? Why would someone do this? Lily thought with great dismay.

"And they say you can never find a cop when you need one," Amelia commented looking at the mess.

"We'll be happy to call this in Amelia," Brad reassured.

"Thank you so much, Brad. We would certainly feel so much safer," Amelia said.

"Who could have done this?" asked Lily, still in shock.

"Sorry, Ms. Brooksfield, I mean Lily. People read about these things in the notices and break in when people aren't home. We should have thought of this and posted a guard. I am so sorry the police department failed you," Silas apologized.

"I can't believe this. First the cemetery where people shoot at us and then this? Are we safe here?" Amelia asked, sounding scared.

"Don't you worry, Amelia. We will keep you safe won't we, Silas," Brad reassured.

Brad then put an arm around Amelia, which earned him a frown from both Lily and Silas.

"Thank you. I feel so much better now. Don't you, Lily?"

"Yes, I guess. Thank you, gentlemen. Now could you call this in while I check to see what appears to be missing?" asked Lily, wanting them to be gone and for this to have never to have happened.

A few minutes later a team of police officers arrived to check for fingerprints, but Lily began to think it was odd she couldn't find anything missing. Why had someone broken in if they didn't want anything here? Had someone slipped out the back door when they arrived? As the policemen scurried around, Lily realized how tired she is. She wished the policemen would all leave, so she could sleep. All the sleepless nights she'd been having had caught up with her. She wanted to have a short nap before Rose came home. They take forever to make a simple report, she thought. Amelia had already gone to her room. Amelia got to sleep. Lily wished she was.

"Are you finished yet?"

"We have completed our investigation, Ms. Brooksfield. You seem tired. I'm sorry we kept you," Brad stated solicitously.

"Good. I'm glad to hear that. It's been a trying day with little sleep."

"We will check back later, but for now we leave," Silas announced.

"Thank you, and good afternoon," Lily replied; shutting her front door and breathing sigh of relief to have them go.

~0~

Chapter 19 - Stirring the Pot

Flashback to the morning before the funeral

Cheryl Waverly and the Killer

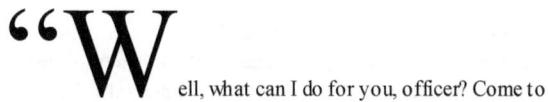

ell, what can I do for you, officer? Come to grill me some more? Why you police officers need to ask and re-ask all your questions, I don't know! Well don't stand looking like a hound dog, come in the house," Cheryl Waverly retorted, opening her door to a police officer in uniform.

"Thank you," the policeman answered. The police officer unconsciously fingered a money clip engraved with the initials R.C. in his pocket.

"Would you like coffee? Here," she said, shoving a cup at him without waiting for an answer "Cream or sugar?"

"Nothing thanks, I like my coffee black," the policeman responded. "I prefer it cold, but this will be fine."

"Well, I don't hold with those newfangled drinks. I think cold coffee is so disgusting. Now what do you want from me?"

The police officer didn't answer quickly enough for the impatient Cheryl so she snapped at him, "Spit the information out! What do you want? I'm a busy woman. I've got a club meeting to go to and tomorrow I have my son's funeral. Lily Kelly or not, I'm attending the service. He was my boy and that bitch killed him. You know she did, so why haven't you arrested her?"

"Lily Kelly will not be charged with killing your son," The officer began before being interrupted.

"And why not? She's as guilty as sin. The black widow killed my boy. She did! Even if she has political connections, does that mean she should get away with murder?"

"I agree her family always uses clout to get out of crimes. They are criminals, those Kelly's; I have no doubt. Are you aware years ago Katha O'Malley ran over a little girl while drunk and she got away with the crime?

"What do you mean? When did this happen? Why wasn't she charged?"

"In the summer of nineteen hundred and sixty eight, a child played out the front of her home. A car came out of nowhere, mounted the curb and struck the little girl. The mother had stepped in for a second to get her child a drink. The mother came out and found the car gone, her little girl lying broken, dead in the grass," The police officer explained, deliberately creating a picture of the day to invoke anger.

"No! The bitch and her evil spawn killed both my children? How did you become acquainted with this knowledge? Where's your proof?" Cheryl demanded suspiciously.

"Your daughter was Cheryl-Lynn Rose Brooksfield?" asked the officer consulting his notes.

"Yes, my baby was only three years old when she was murdered. She was Horace's twin," Cheryl explained dabbing her eyes "It was July the eighth, 1968. They told me she was killed by a drunk driver. My Cheryl-Lynn Rose lived as an angel, such a sweet good-natured child. She obeyed without question. I thought she would be out of harm's way, but she wasn't. She stepped on the road. She was so good. Not like her brother, Horace. I loved Horace, but he loved being a naughty boy. Horace had such bad taste in women, although he did give my granddaughter his sister's middle name."

"Hmm, the date of Katha O'Malley's drunken driving cover-up is the eighth of July nineteen hundred and sixty eight," the police officer lied, pretending to consult records; Katha O'Malley went to a party. She was seen inebriated, stumbling around and entered a car taking the wheel; not more than a block away after the accident. Her car appeared on the stolen vehicle list the next day."

"You believed Katha O'Malley killed my baby Cheryl-Lynn Rose? Lily killed my other baby, Horace, and neither paid! There can be no justice when they get away with killing my babies," Cheryl begged crying loud sobs, "Why does an evil family like the Kelly's get to exist? Why? Someone should stop them."

"There is no accountability if someone isn't charged, Ma'am. A person who abused their power to get away with killing a child is beyond comprehension," the police officer waxed. "If I had a child that was killed by a drunken driver, I think I would want revenge. I'm not advocating taking justice in your own hands though; that would be just as wrong."

"You're a good boy. Your mother must be proud," Cheryl replied, wiping her tears away.

"I hope so, ma'am, but my parents died a long time ago. I grew up in foster homes, and a good family took me into their hearts and adopted me," the police officer confided, fake tears falling from his eyes.

"Oh you poor dear boy! Horrible places those foster homes, and cesspools for the worst dregs of life. Were you aware Horace was removed from my home and taken until his daddy was found? Why they thought I broke his arm, I'll never know!" Cheryl raved.

You did break Horace's arm, you monster. You go through life harming others and think no blame should come your way. You did not get your daughter a drink, but got yourself a snout full of booze. Cheryl-Lynn died because you are a neglectful, unnatural mother. Why shouldn't there be payback? Payback is a bitch, and you'll get yours. You dare to insinuate I'm not good enough for your company, simply because through no fault of my own, I was in a foster home. Of course I'm lying, but you don't know that you arrogant, rich, bitch!

*How dare you go through life judging others? 'Judge not lest you
be judge' is what the good book you carry around says. Well,
you've met your judge, jury and executioner, and she's starring at
you in the mirror. Be careful, son, you're in the home stretch now;
don't show your thoughts on your face and tip your hand. He
thought.*

Cheryl looked at the police officer as if he wasn't listening to her
but continued anyway, "Did you ever hear the like of it? They
pointed the finger at me! Would you believe it? They accused
me...of harming my child. I would never harm a hair on his head
even though he was a worthless wastrel."

"Why anyone could see you would never harm a child. But I
thought Horace had a job as the mayor? A job so prestigious
doesn't make him a wastrel!"

"Quite true, I certainly would never harm a child. As for him being
the mayor...well I had to use all my connections to get him such a
prominent position. A good mother does what she can for her
child."

*Liar! Even though your son was a cheat as a husband, he earned
his position as mayor.*

"Well you'd never be aware of your upbringing; obviously
someone did something right by you. You certainly act like you
have breeding. Such a kind man, you should meet my ex-daughter-
in-law Renée. She's a delightful woman," Cheryl ranted on
oblivious.

Anger flashed briefly across the police officer's face but then he
smiled sweetly, "Why thank you, ma'am. It wasn't my fault or my
parents' fault; a drunk driver killed them."

"Oh, you poor, dear boy. Did they find the evil person who killed
them?" Cheryl asked, offering him a fresh-baked chocolate chip
cookie.

"Yes I found her, but the crime was swept under the rug. Katha O'Malley drove drunk and she killed them too," He answered nibbling the cookie edges.

"You are telling me that Katha O'Malley, or her family member, has killed three people and no charges have ever been laid? Katha O'Malley's family continued on living their lives, like nothing ever happened being happy and earning lots of money? Katha O'Malley and her family have much to answer for their crimes," Cheryl demanded angrily.

"Katha O'Malley and Lily Kelly might have much to answer for, but their family is blameless in the crimes. If only I had the guts, I'd make the two of them pay. I would..." Cheryl finished.

"Someday...,"The police officer said sadly shaking his head.

"Someone should make them suffer. They are totally evil. Katha's spoken to me many times over the years, no hint of the evil she has created. She saw me grieving and said nothing," Cheryl snarled under her breath.

The police officer heard this and hid a smile.

Cheryl pounded the table in anger, and then composed herself dismissing him, retorting loudly, "Are we done here? I'm sorry, but I must not be late for my committee meeting."

"Yes, sorry, Ma'am. I needed to confirm your alibi."

"If you did your job, you'd know I signed a form yesterday to confirm my alibi. Nail Katha O'Malley, she most likely helped kill my boy too," Cheryl said firmly, walking the police officer to the door.

"Thank you, Ma'am. I can't tell you how much I'd like to make them pay. If there is any way I'll try, but she has political clout...Well I've made it my life's mission, but she still gets away with her crimes," The police officer replied, in a last parting shot, leaving the house.

He got into the car and smiled. His plan appeared to be working. The silly woman had fallen for the scheme, hook, line and sinker. She believed Katha had harmed her child, not only that but both of the Kelly's had killed her children.

It was simple physics you stir the pot and the pan boiled. Cheryl Waverly appeared sensible, even normal, but she was an evil, vindictive bitch. She thought she loved her children, so to sooth her moral compass she must seek revenge. She thought it okay to harm her own child, like his father had done to him.

He remembered how his father had locked him in closets and beat him black and blue. He had told him to keep all the abuse a secret, or he'd find himself back in the closet or in one of those foster homes again. The dark still held great fear for him. He still slept with the light on because of the monsters in the dark. His doctor had tried to tell him nothing would harm him if he turned out the light, but the doctor had never seen the demons which came in the night.

The doctor hadn't had the devil wage war against him, in the guise of his father. Call him names he'd like to block out and burn his ears with them. He didn't feel the soft whispery breath of the demon's drink, as he lashed out, and smacked you against the wall of the closet. He hadn't caught the sound of the door's lock click, and understood the door wouldn't open for hours. No parent should harm their child.

Even if Cheryl hadn't been such a threat to Amelia's beloved cousin, he would have had to stop her. She would have harmed others; this behaviour was her way. He felt justified in his actions. Much like an avenging angel he righted wrongs and protected his Angel. If Cheryl Waverly took the bait and came after Katha, she had signed her own death warrant. It would then be a necessity to kill her. He wouldn't let her harm one hair on any of his Angel's family. Cheryl Waverly was an insipid woman who believed the world revolved around her. Well, she would soon found out it did not!

He would be merciful, however. One quick shot to the head provided she didn't try too hard to kill Katha. She had better not move one strand on that shock white head of hair. Any endangerment of his sweet Angel, in any way, or her family, all bets were off and she would suffer a fate worse than death. She'd die sooner and less humanely. They would soon be his and no one harmed his chosen clan.

Never ever again would he sit back and let the demon win. People would not push his family around anymore. He would keep following his plans. Soon, his sweet Angel would be all his.

~0~

The afternoon before the funeral

He stood outside the house listening to the bug, he had planted. She had swallowed the bait and ran with it. He listened as Cheryl picked up the phone.

"Bob, do you still own a twenty-two rifle? Why? Oh I thought I'd go away for a few days after the funeral and go on a hunting trip in Saskatchewan. Piffle, no I don't possess a licence but you'll loan the gun to me, won't you? You won't? Please, Bob, can't you expedite a permit for me? You will give the rifle to me? Fantastic! I knew I might count on you. Thanks, Bob, I'll owe you. Goodbye, dear."

The bullets she obtained would all be blanks, but she would never find out that the gun wouldn't harm anyone...at least until the last-minute. He would never take the chance she could harm his beloved Angel, or her family. He'd watch her and when she shot at Katha, like he understood she would, her life would be extinguished. He would claim he shot her in the line of duty. Threatening his Angel and her cousin was not to be accepted. He read the transcript. She had gone too far. The woman was dangerous. He stopped the other woman Renée. The police would soon find Renée's hair in the samples taken at the murder scene; but this woman would not, could not be tolerated any longer.

No doubt of the signs; she would snap and harm his Angel. The seeds planted, she would come after Katha. Killing Cheryl would be no great loss.

The woman annoyed everyone and was an evil child abuser. She abused her own son. She was not fit to be near his Angel or Rose. So she would not live another day. He listened into the chatter at his cousin Lily's house, well... not his cousin yet, but soon. The bugs he planted worked perfectly; even if they were the bugs the department classified, as out of date. The bugs would never be missed and the wiretaps still worked like a charm. He enjoyed spending time amongst his family, even if he only heard their voices.

He would get someone to break in while everyone attended the funeral and remove them. No he decided he should do it himself! There'd be enough time before he went to the Wake. He'd be on duty and slip away. They must not be found in the house. As much as he wanted to leave the wiretaps, if he didn't find all the bugs, all would be lost. He might get someone to remove the bugs, but then someone would enter the home and he couldn't allow them to soil his Angel's domicile.

The only solution was for him to do the job himself. He would see the way his family lived and touch their things.....touch Amelia's, his Angel's things.

~0~

One half hour before the funeral

"Good, the family is gone. Time to put the plan in place," he muttered to himself as he entered Lily's house.

He searched eagerly for the wiretaps he had planted. He took the bugs out of the phone, but the lamp would not be found. He searched frantically for it. Where was it? He could not remember where he had placed some of the other bugs. Could he find them all?

Where did he leave them? What if the wiretaps were found? He searched frantically while his fingers lovingly touching the money clip in his pocket. Calmness filled his body as he fingered his trophy. His Angel was nearby, he felt her, as long as he had her father's money clip. He thought the token wasn't needed anymore, and yet knowing her birthstone was on it, filled him with such happiness.

All he could think about when he touched it was her beauty... her eternal goodness filled him with such joy and euphoria. Peace! He felt an utter calmness come over him. He then touched a scarf belonging to his Angel. He pulled the stole to his nose smelling the garment. A sweet floral scent filled his nostrils. The scarf smelled of her. How glorious! It was like being next to her in a meadow of flowers.

His other hand stayed on the money clip, as if transferring her being into the clip. He closed his eyes and remembered dancing with his Angel; only in his dreams, but soon this would be reality, in his visions, his beloved wife and she adored him, a dream come true. All he needed to do was follow his plans. He must protect his Angel at all costs. She would be his family. Her cousin and her daughter would welcome him into their family; especially after they knew the lengths he went to protected them all. However, if her cousin found those bugs, she would misinterpret what he meant to do for her, his Angel. She would seek to turn his Angel against him.

Where were those damn wiretaps? He manipulated the money clip, not finding the smooth gold comforting. The bugs traced to him, so it was imperative that he find them all. He continued frantically searching for the bugs. Finally he found a bug in a lamp. Had he found them all?

Of course he did!

Breathing a sigh of relief, he slipped his hand out of his pocket and got ready to leave before the family came home. What the man did not realize was that when he pulled his hand out of his pocket the money clip fell out and then he inadvertently kicked it under the sofa. He completed his sweep for his bugs, tossed the rooms in anger, and then headed to the funeral and his Angel.

~0~

Chapter 20 - Caught In the Wake

Rose and Carol

As Rose and Carol ate at a table in the food court, Rose decided to bring up something that was bothering her.

"Did you get creeped out at the funeral, too?" Rose asked. "Those two cops threw themselves at my Aunt Amelia like they were her last meal."

"I saw them. Yuck! I like Bobby Bradford, but you can bet when I'm as old as your aunt, I won't remember him. Or if I do I won't be hanging all over him," Carol replied.

"It's gross when old people drape all over each other. Your Grandma Katha had men fawning over her too."

"I saw Gregory Hanks of the Hanks grocery stores; he was all over Grandma Katha."

"Your Grandma Katha sure has some choice guys for older men though," Carol answered.

"She does. Aunt Amelia on the other hand ought to be careful. I think those two cops were creepers," Rose responded.

"But they're cops, so that makes them okay," Carol protested.

"Just because they have a badge, that doesn't make them perfect.
I'm getting bad vibes from one or both of them. Remember when I
got bad vibes about the new kid Kyle, and it turned out he was an
arsonist?" Rose asked.

"Like intuition?"

"Yes, like intuition. I keep getting a creepy feeling something is
wrong with them. I want to check out more about those two cops.
It's strange they ended up in the same town as Aunt Amelia, when
she used to live thousands of miles away," Rose explained. "You
should leave it alone. "No harm and no foul, as the saying goes."

"I would if it weren't for those bad vibes from those two," Rose
continued. "Besides don't you find it odd they end up in the same
place as my aunt?"

"So they moved here. Just because they lived in the same town as
your Aunt Amelia, that doesn't make them guilty of anything."

"I should tell you about my aunt. Can you keep a secret?"
demanded Rose.

"Sure, I'll even pinkie swear," Carol promised and then upon
Rose's hesitation to speak, Carol pressed, "Spill it already, would
you?"

"Well, okay, but it is a bit of a long story. My aunt grew up in a
town about one hundred kilometres from here, a place called
Ravenworst. She had an ideal life, two parents and siblings; her
younger sister Grace and an older brother Jerry."

"She has siblings? I was never told she had siblings. Where do
they live?" Carol then looked at Rose hurt and angry.

"Don't look at me that way. I'll explain."

"Then do so, Rose."

"Anyway at sixteen, or seventeen years old, Aunt Amelia had
taken a babysitting job. She was supposed to babysit overnight. All
went well until she became sick. She threw up and stuff. She came
home after calling the parents of the kid and went to bed shivering
and sick. She fell into a deep sleep, after taking cold and flu

medicines of some sort." "Something weird happened; when she woke up she was outside in her nightgown."

"Whoa! What happened? Did she like, sleepwalk?" Carol asked, popping a French fry in her mouth.

"No, she wasn't sleepwalking. Let me finish the story please. Aunt Amelia found herself choking. She felt the grass underneath her. She opened her eyes disoriented and looked around and saw her home burning and huge flames shooting from the roof. The house was ablaze and burned quickly to the ground. She tried to crawl back to the house, but she had inhaled smoke and her lungs felt like they were burnt. Aunt Amelia collapsed and when she woke up again she was in the hospital. She was told her whole family had perished in the fire. Her father Robert, her younger brother Jerry, her sister Grace, and her mother Aerilla could not be found. The puzzling thing for her was she wasn't aware of how any of it had happened."

"How was that even possible? Shouldn't she have felt someone carry her outside, or did she go on her own?" Carol demanded, enthralled by the tale as she ate.

"She still doesn't remember. Anyway, someone had called an ambulance for her. The police interrogated her since she was the only survivor. They even made her look at the remains."

"Well how cold. It's not like she could identify them, might she?"

"No," Rose stated. "And to this day no one knows who it was that called the ambulance either."

"What a bizarre story!" Carol said while finishing her taco meal. She then reached for her share of the fries.

"Where do you put all that food? If I eat tacos I gain weight," Rose stated.

"I think you worry too much about calories. You're way too skinny."

"No, I'm not." Rose rolled her eyes at this comment.

Carol then retorted "So tell me more of the story. There is more isn't there?"

"Poor Aunt Amelia lived through all of the tragedy. Last year she lost her husband and her son to a drunk driver. And now her employee Megan and a homeless man were murdered. My dad and his secretary are also murdered. What does all this have in common?" asked Rose mysteriously.

"Amelia Kelly?"

"Right again. People get stalked. Anyone who they feel tarnishes their obsession is just in their way," Rose said knowledgeably. "I think someone fixated on Aunt Amelia and will keep killing until she's with them."

"Rose, how do you come up with this stuff? Don't you think that's an exaggeration? I mean, just because she has a few bad things happen to her," Carol insisted, "And would you eat some fries? I can't eat them all myself."

"I'm not hungry, but I'll take a couple of fries."

Rose picked two of the smallest fries on the plate and tossed them in her mouth. She then raised her brow and said while chewing, "There, are you happy now?"

"No. I'm worried you make up stuff to distract yourself from your dad dying."

"I'm not making up any of this story. I've snuck into my Mom's office and read some case files over the years. These things happen. Crazy people get fixated. I think that's the word and they think the person loves them. You know how those Hollywood stars get stalkers? Well, I think Aunt Amelia has one. I know she does," Rose explained with confidence.

"Didn't your mom get mad when you snooped in her office?" asked Carol.

"No, silly! She thinks it is all password protected. Too bad she uses such an easy password," Rose boasted.

"You better hope your mom doesn't catch you. If my mom caught me snooping on her computer, I'd be dead meat," Carol exclaimed "My dad uses complicated passwords you would need to hire a cryptographer to figure out."

"What or who is a cryptographer?" Rose asked.

"So you don't know everything. A cryptographer deciphers (figures out) his password. During the Second World War, they used them to keep secrets from the enemy with passwords," Carol explained.

"How did you find out the information and I didn't?"

"As I said, you don't know everything, Rose! Just because you do well at school, you think you know all. My great-grandfather told me all about cryptographers. He said he dated one, but she wouldn't talk about her work, so he married her."

"He sounds interesting."

"He is," Carol answered proudly. "And so was my great-grandmother, but she died."

"I am sorry, but she must have been mega-old."

"She died when I was little, so I don't think she was that old though she was older than him. And my great-grandfather is only seventy-four," Carol commented. "He married some other woman. I didn't like her, but they are divorced now. Thank goodness."

"Oh, well, I got into my Mom's files and there are lots of crazy stalkers out there."

"If your mom catches you using her password you'll be in so much trouble, I'll never see you again."

"I'm careful. Mom hasn't a clue I read her files."

"If your aunt has a stalker, how will you realize who he is?"

"I think the stalker is one of those cops. They are here from Ravenworst. They creep all over here and they seem predatory."

"Predatory? They didn't seem that way to me," Carol said faking, as if she actually understood the word.

"Hmm, you don't even understand the word. They want Aunt Amelia completely to themselves. You only exist in their eyes if you are in their view of her... that is predatory," Rose insisted.

"They did drape themselves all over your aunt, but they are cops. Cops aren't criminals; you are imagining things," Carol protested.

"I'd like to believe that, I really would. But I've seen in my mom's cases, people whom you would never suspect of being criminals. The worst of the worst ones are those who hide in plain sight," Rose explained.

"You mean like the janitor at our school last year, busted for being a pervert?" asked Carol.

"Yes, exactly like him. So I figure I need to access information about these cops. We need to find out where they were born, who their families are; or whether they've ever committed a crime, even if it's been sealed."

"Sealed?"

"Yes, when you are under age, sometimes you can get your record hidden, so no one can find out," Rose explained reaching over and ate another fry. "We must find these things out to keep my family safe. If what I suspect is true that one of those cops is a serial killer."

"I don't want to be involved in this."

"Well d'oh, who else can help me, Carol?"

"I don't want to get in trouble. We shouldn't be involved," Carol protested. "You won't get in trouble."

"Fine, but I think you should check out the security guard who found your dad. I saw him watching Amelia too. He's a creeper too."

"Okay, I'll put Barney Terrell on the list."

"How will you find out the information?" Carol asked.

"I'm going to sneak into Mom's office downtown and you're going to help me so I am not caught."

'I am not sure that's a good idea. I don't think I want to go to your mom's office. You should tell your mom what you think," Carol advised. "Besides, I'm supposed to be home soon. I'm going to get in trouble."

"Come on, Carol, don't be such a chicken. Please, you can be a heroine!"

"Would you please just tell your mom, Rose?" Carol pleaded.

"My mom would not believe vague suspicions, especially about a police officer," Rose explained. "If I can get the information we need, she will believe me. Grandma Katha dates the police chief's father."

"She is? Really?"

"Grandma Katha can do something, or at least look into his background more. Please Carol, help me. I'm begging you."

"Wow, your grandmother dates the police chief's father? I've met him; he's an interesting guy but I'm still not doing this," Carol laughed, like she understood something Rose didn't.

Rose looked hard and long at Carol with a beseeching stare.

"Fine, I'll help, but we better not get caught. It won't look good on my college transcript," Carol reluctantly agreed.

"We won't get caught. We will be careful," Rose promised. "Okay, let's hurry. I have to be home at four p.m."

"Fine, it shouldn't take long. Besides, you owe me. Remember when I snuck out to your locker, and got your homework. I have gotten a detention." Rose replied, piling on the guilt, "We aren't supposed to go to the lockers during class, but I did for you."

"I said I do it, now quit making me feel guilty. Let's go already." Rose and Carol waited patiently for the bus and got on.

~0~

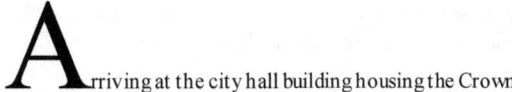rriving at the city hall building housing the Crown

Attorney's Office, Rose and Carol entered the building. The guard passed by into the other part of the building and they snuck down the hallway. They quickly hid behind a pillar at the sound of the guard coming back.

"We're going to be caught," Carol whispered.

"Quiet or we will be caught." The guard passed by again.

Rose breathed a sigh of relief and uttered, "My mom's office is down there, around the corner. We will make it."

"We almost bit it there," Carol complained. "But we didn't get caught. We are safe as long as you watch while I go in my mom's office," Rose claimed.

Rose crept to the office door. Finding it locked Rose frowned and jiggled the door.

"Don't shake the door. It's locked and the guard will know we are here. Do you have a bobby pin? I think I can pick the lock," Carol explained.

"You can pick a lock?" asked Rose.

"Sure, my dad taught me how to pick a lock."

Rose pulled a bobby pin put of her long hair and handed it over to Carol. Within five minutes of Carol attempting to pick at the lock with the bobby pin, the lock made a clicking noise. Carol turned the knob of the door, ushering them in the dark room.

"See, I told you I could do it," Carol boasted as she turned on a lamp.

"You keep watch while I check out the files and once the computer is on, we turn off the lamp."

Carol kept watch for the guard as Rose peered at the computer screen. Rose keyed in her mother's password and began searching through files. Soon she realized it might take a while.

"Sorry, I realize I'm taking time, but I'm scanning through a lot of files," Rose explained.

"Hurry! I think I heard the guard again. I don't want to be caught." Rose finally managed to access the file on the fire in Ravenworst.

"Here it is. I found the file," Rose cried loudly.

"Hush! Do you want him to hear us?" Carol stressed.

"Hurray up and find the information."

Rose scanned quickly through it realizing nothing jumped out at her. She ran another program to access police sealed juvenile records, on both policemen and Barney Terrell. Carol glanced in.

"I'm still looking. Keep watch," Rose demanded seeing Carol out of the corner of her eye.

Looking intently at the screen, Rose unrelentingly searched for the information. She gasped as she found something. Continuing to read she printed off a copy of the record.

"I found the information. Come on Carol, we have to get the evidence to my Grandma Katha," Rose insisted, as she dialled her cell phone "Drat! No answer. I'm going to try again."

"Tell me," Carol demanded. "I put my neck on the line. Share with me."

"There's nothing bad on Barney Terrell, but you won't believe what I found on that police officer! It's like this..." Rose lifted a finger while she dialled her Grandma Katha's phone number again. She then spoke into the phone and left a message, "Grandma Katha, I'm coming over there. I must talk to you! Don't open the door to anyone, except Terrence or his son."

"You should call your mom and your aunt," Carol demanded "The man could be a serial killer, and he's a cop. He's dangerous."

"No. I'm going to Grandma Katha's. I can find the spare key, let myself in and wait for her. Thanks, Carol. You should go home. I promise I'll tell you before anything happens."

"I don't think it's a good idea to leave you to tell your Grandma Katha alone. What if she doesn't believe you? I should go with you," Carol insisted.

"You will get in trouble if you are not home in time, I'll be fine."

"I can't ditch you. My dad will have to wait," Carol asserted.

"It's perfectly safe. All I have to do is to get to Grandma Katha's and she'll get her boyfriend's son to send out the other police officer to nail him," Rose contended. "Now go. You know how your dad gets when you keep him waiting."

"Okay, fine! But call me in a half an hour okay? I have to know you are safe."

"Don't worry, I'll call you. Hurry, so you are not in trouble."

Rose left to catch her bus, leaving Carol to go home on her own. Carol knew she had to be home on time. Her mom insisted she be early the nights her Dad, Gerald picked her up to go to his house. Carol began to worry though. Should Rose be going to her Grandma Katha's by herself? Rose should have shared more information with me. If anything happens to Rose, what am I supposed to say? It's short trip to Rose's grandmother's house, so she'll be okay. Wouldn't she? Carol then felt that she was just being a worry wart. He mother always accused her of being one.

"Rose will be just fine," Carol thought out loud. Yet the idea to go find Rose still lingered, even as Carol boarded the bus to go home.

Carol rode the bus, all the while feeling that Rose could be in danger. What kind of a best friend remained more concerned with herself getting in trouble than protecting her friend? Carol was a terrible friend. She checked her watch and decided she should call her friend and thought, Rose should be there by now. Rose's phone rang four times and then went to voicemail. Carol then decided that she could not allow Rose to remain in danger while she rode the bus home.

Carol got off at the next stop. She was determined to find Rose. She would go to her best friend's house and then Rose's grandmother's house. If Rose was in trouble she would save her. If she wasn't in trouble, then why didn't Rose answer her cell phone? Carol contemplated; I'm going to back up Rose's story to Uncle Edward and help apprehend this awful person. Carol had never told Rose that the police chief was her great-uncle. Maybe it was too late to tell Rose, but Carol felt that her Uncle Edward would listen to her. As Carol walked down the street she heard the wail of a car horn. She turned around and noticed her mother's car pull over to the side of the road next to her.

"Carol I've been looking for you. You were to meet your father over twenty minutes ago. Now get in this car now," demanded Carol's mother, Francine. "Are you aware of the grief I would get if you weren't there on time? Your father will lecture me. Ever since he's been dating Alana, he's been impossible."

"But, Mom..."

"Get in this car now! Don't argue with me! If you get in this vehicle now, we might be in time for your father."

"Mom, please," Carol begged.

"Did you hear anything I said? He blames me when you're late and keeps threatening to take custody of you. He could go to court. See how much attention you get from him. Your father has the attention span of a gnat," Francine complained.

"Fine, I'm coming," Carol retorted angrily under her breath and then stated, "It's on your head if anything happens to Rose."

"What did you say?" Francine asked, her eyes narrowing like she thought Carol had something bad about her.

"Nothing," answered Carol.

Carol prayed nothing would happen to Rose. She would go along with her mom, but as soon as her dad's back was turned, she would leave to look for Rose. Nothing and no one would stop her from saving Rose.

~0~

Chapter 21 -
"Mom It's me,
Rose"

Lily rose slowly from her bed. She had been so tired earlier, she had lain down and fell straight asleep, but somehow she still felt exhausted. Getting Silas and Brad to leave hadn't been easy. The two policemen jumped into action, after finding Lily's home tossed. Lily thought about how odd it was. There appeared to be something suspicious about the break in at the house, though nothing seemed to be missing. All of this was strange and the two police officers acted odd. It was strange how the two policemen continued to fawn over Amelia and never once spoke directly to Lily about the break in at her house. They kept reassuring Amelia, like Amelia's house had been broken into instead of Lily's.

Amelia's coach house hadn't even been entered. All of this seemed surreal, like Lily didn't exist as the homeowner or even in their minds, in any form at all. The two of them didn't seem to want to leave Amelia's side either, but Amelia inviting them to dinner this evening seemed to work. Amelia also said she felt tired and suddenly they had been all solicitous, saying them later. Weird and yes a little creepy, how much they fawned over someone they hadn't seen in years.

The pair of them needed looking at closely. She hated being suspicious of people but so much had happened lately. Those two cops set off warning bells inside of her. Amelia didn't need to be afraid on top of everything else. Did Amelia have a stalker, or two? Wait a minute...would a stalker explain everything that had happened?

These men had recognized Amelia, from a town one thousand miles away. How unusual that they should appear in the same town as Amelia... hmm at the same time things had happened to her and her family? Lily felt like she might be onto something here. Amelia came to Happy Valley as a teenager. She changed her last name, so people would not connect her with her family tragedy. She now shared the same name as Grandma Katha. So what were the odds they'd show up in the same place and find her? One of them stalked her? Had she missed something here? The tragedy! Of course someone killed them. Those men knew Amelia's family. They said they'd cut her lawn for Uncle Robert with disgust in their voices. Had Uncle Robert done something to start all of this? Might it have been some little thing Uncle Robert did, or didn't do? A normal every day thing people did, which triggered something only a psychotic person would take offence to and react?

Aunt Katha said the police had always questioned how Amelia had gotten outside in her nightgown. What if her stalker saved her?

Amelia had been safe at the Freidman's babysitting; he wouldn't comprehend she had come home. So he might have set the fire thinking she was safe. If the killer did, which one of these now police officers had done the crime or crimes?

A year ago Amelia lost her husband and child. A stalker killed them and made the crime look like a drunk driver? That was certainly a bit of a stretch to think the crime happened in that manner. Although, trying to connect all of the murders were as well. Even a crazy serial stalker wouldn't kill a child. Would he?

And what motive did the stalker have for killing Megan? And the homeless man, Mr. Young? And if she followed the reasoning a stalker had killed them, might she take the deduction one step further and suggest the stalker killed Horace and his secretary?

What could connect complete strangers, who were now gone...murdered? Amelia...Amelia appeared to be the connection. No wonder the acting Crown Attorney had gone after her. If Lily had been thinking clearly, instead of focusing on her grief, and protecting Amelia she would have seen the associations. Barbara didn't understand Amelia the way Lily did.

She hadn't seen the connections Lily now looked at in retrospect. She needed to get to her office tomorrow and research those two. Until she could do the research, she would pretend she didn't suspect them and keep smiling in their presence. Don't alert them or make them suspicious in any way, which might be dangerous to them all. Hmm, what was the saying? Oh yes. "Keep your friends close, and your enemies closer." The Sun-Tzu Chinese general and military strategist from four hundred B.C. sure had that right, she thought looking up in her favourite quotes book.

She wondered what time the clock said. The sun appeared down in the sky a lot lower than four p.m. It couldn't be so late, could it? She glanced over and noticed the power had gone off at some point as the numbers flashed on her alarm clock. How odd. She pulled out her cell phone. Remembering she had turned off her phone earlier for the wake, she turned it back on glancing at the time. Good grief! Six o'clock. They'd all be here for dinner soon. Good thing Grandma Katha always brought enough food to feed an army.

"Rose?" Lily called aloud, looking around for her.

Where could that girl be? She should have been home two hours ago. Lily fiddled with her cell phone and realized she missed a message.

"Mom, it's me, Rose. I shouldn't have, and you can get mad at me later for my actions, but I accessed some records at your office. We're all in danger. Those two cops Constable Rentford, and Sergeant Detective Owens, I thought both of them were trouble. But only one of them is a serial killer, who stalks Amelia. I'm on my way to tell Grandma Katha. She can do something, her or her new boyfriend's son, the chief of police. By the way the man I suspect is...the phone message broke off here."

Lily tried urgently to call her daughter back, but only got the call answer feature on Rose's cell phone. She repeatedly called getting the answer machine. She stared at her phone in disbelief. She had missed an important message from Rose. Rose didn't go after them herself did she? No, Rose said she went to Grandma Katha's, but that was hours ago. So why hadn't she called since the first initial call? As the dawning realization Rose might have gone after them herself, Lily became frantic with worry. Katha entered the house, her hands filled with food from a takeout Chinese food place.

Grandma Katha was here. Rose would follow Grandma Katha, Lily thought breathing a sigh of relief. The minutes ticked by and still no Rose. Lily's heart turned over, but she dared ask, "Isn't Rose with you?"

"Why would Rose be with me?" enquired Katha.

"She said she was headed to your house in a message I received about two p.m.," Lily answered.

"I wasn't home all afternoon. I got in some afternoon delight at Terrence's place," Katha replied winking and setting down the food on the kitchen counter.

When Katha realized Lily appeared serious she asked, "You haven't seen Rose at all?"

"No and I'm worried."

"This is not like her. She usually comes home promptly. And why did she tell you she came to my house?"

"I promise I'll explain later Grandma Katha. Right now please call those two cops, Constable Rentford and Sergeant Detective Owens."

"Reporting Rose missing?" asked Katha.

"No, I won't explain anything to those two men. Please just tell them Amelia has a headache and get rid of them. Just get them not to come to my house," Lily begged urgently.

"I don't understand what's going on with you. Why don't you trust them? Is Amelia okay?"

"Amelia's fine. I promise I will explain fully later. Right now I'm going to your house and see if my daughter is there," Lily said, hoping her maternal instinct which told her Rose was in danger, was wrong.

"Okay, honey, I'll do as you ask," Katha promised.

Lily left immediately, going out the front door, hoping to find Rose next door. Lily hurried to Katha's house and let herself in the domicile. Everything looked normal. All looked untouched. Nothing looked disturbed, oddly though the phone was on the hook. But where was Rose? Why had her message stopped? Had Rose's cell phone simply died? Was Rose in the spare room? Lily ran down the hallway and opened the closed-door to the bedroom of the spare room. She found a perfectly made bed. The spread, a beautifully crochet blue and white blanket, lay thrown pristinely across the bed. The pillows were fluffed and the sheets light blue in colour, crisp clean, and nothing appeared disturbed.

No one had been here since this morning. No one slept in the bed. So where was Rose? Panic seized Lily as she thought of what may well have happened to Rose. Was it one of those policemen, a serial killer? Rose was in grave danger; though her mind refused to go there.

She needed to do something, but what? How could she keep her daughter safe if someone took her? Grandma Katha...she needed Grandma Katha. Rose's voice was all she could think about hearing. Lily dialled Katha.

"She's not here!" Lily screamed in horrified tones, "I can't find her."

"I'll be there in less than ten minutes. You can explain to me why you sound so frightened, and what happened." Lily paced the floor waiting for Grandma Katha to arrive.

It seemed like an hour before Katha arrived, however Katha arrived in less than five minutes and immediately hugged Lily.

"Amelia will keep the food hot. Now tell me what happened?" Katha demanded.

"My phone was turned off, but Rose called me. I fell asleep when she needed me. I'm a terrible mother." Lily cried. "Grandma Katha, what will I do if anything happens to my baby?"

"Lily, the first thing you will do is pull yourself together and make some sense. What did Rose say to you? And I want it word for word!" Katha demanded.

"Rose phoned me and because my phone was off the cell phone went to voice mail. I got a voice mail from her." Lily explained and played the message as Katha listened.

"Mom, it's me Rose. I shouldn't have, and you can get mad at me later for my actions, but I accessed some records at your office. We're all in danger. Those two cops Constable Rentford and Sergeant Detective Owens, both of them are trouble. One of them is a serial killer who is stalks Amelia. I'm on my way to tell Grandma Katha she can do something, her or her new boyfriend's son the chief of police. By the way the man I suspect is..."

"Oh my God! She didn't! She broke into your computer? The child is in danger. You think she didn't get here?" Katha asked shocked. "She seemed to think she discerned who the killer was. Was it one of those two policemen? Policemen have guns... Oh no, my great granddaughter is with a serial killer."

Katha took a huge breath and closed her eyes. Opening her eyes she said, "Sorry, I lost my calm for a moment, Lily. We will get her back safely. It has to be something simple, like she went somewhere else, because I wasn't home."

"Perhaps she left a message on your phone? May I?" Lily asked, reaching for the home phone.

"I'm sure that's true. She's at Carol's house," Katha repeated, breathing sigh of relief.

"There are no new messages, no saved messages," a computerized phone message said.

"But that's impossible! I left a memo to myself. A reminder about picking up the food in case I forgot. There were saved messages. I saved one from the funeral director about the costs, a few messages from friends and condolence messages from the hearts of our friends. Someone has been here and erased my messages. But why would they do that?" Katha asked puzzled.

"Oh no! You don't think Rose..."

"Left a message on my machine?" Katha completed Lily's thought.

"Yes, and whoever has erased the message has Rose?" Lily finished, her voice breaking up in fear.

"Why would someone who's stalking Amelia take Rose? I'm sure she's fine. She forgotten to tell us she went to Carol's," lied Katha unconvincingly.

"Didn't you hear the message? She suspects both police officers, but she understood one of them was the serial killer. Do you think she was talked about Megan Fowler; Mr. Young's and even Horace and his executive assistant, Amber, as his victims?"

"Rose says in her message a police officer is a serial killer. How can a serial killer be a police officer? Serial killers don't start as adults, do they?" Katha asked.

"No, the studies I've read said they start in childhood."

"And those two said they had known Amelia since she was a teenager."

"You mean she thinks one of them killed Uncle Robert, Aunt Aerilla, Jerry and Grace?" Lily demanded, getting more horrified by the minute, "And this person might have my little girl? Oh no, my baby. What can we do?"

"First of all we remain calm and don't jump to conclusions, Lily. Like I said, perhaps she's at Carol's house."

"Yes, right! She must be at Carol's house. Someone broke in to your place and erased your messages and they didn't take my daughter," Lily replied sarcastically.

"Sarcasm is unnecessary and beneath you, Lily. We will find her."

"She may already be...," Lily's voice broke off and she started crying.

"We'll find her. Terrence will help us. He's a retired judge. And as you well recognize he's the police chief's father," Katha insisted positively. "He has to be careful. If one of them took my daughter, and a police officer understands we are on to him, the man might do something drastic before we can find Rose."

"I know that, and somehow we must protect Amelia without letting him know. Because if Amelia even suspects one of them it will show all over her face," Katha cautioned. "Now I'll call Terrence. He should be to your house anyway."

"Call Terrence. I'm going to use your computer and access my files. If I can find what Rose found, maybe I can pinpoint which one is the killer," said Lily excitedly.

"Okay, Lily. Please, go ahead, dear." Katha agreed, "We will get Rose home safe; believe me, Lily."

"I know we will," Lily agreed, clicking with her mouse as she started to search files on the computer.

"Terrence, dear, can you come to my house before we go to Lily's? I need to talk to you privately and urgently," Katha requested on the phone. "Oh thank you, my dear. See you soon."

"He's coming, Lily. He'll be here soon and our little girl will be safe," Katha reassured Lily.

"From your lips to God's ears," Lily replied.

~0~

Chapter 22 -
Keep Your
Enemies Closer

Rose and the Killer

At the killer's home, Rose was bound and gagged. Her
feet were fastened tightly to the chair with yellow household rope.
Her arms and hands were also bound with the same type of cords.
She had a white tee-shirt gagging her mouth. Rose began rocking
back and forth attempting to knock over the chair to no avail. Her
eyes searched for him, as the door to the bedroom opened.

"You are a clever girl aren't you?" He retorted chuckling, "You
tried to get free? You are so like her, my Angel. Odd, considering
you don't share the same blood. I'm not going to harm you. I
promise you. Don't struggle now. I'll remove the gag and you
won't scream. Nod yes or no." the man demanded.

Rose ignored him struggling to get free but her head moved
slightly.

"I'll take that answer as a yes. Sorry, but I'm not going to untie
your feet and hands yet. This should make you more comfortable."

"So where did you take me? Will you kill me?" probed Rose
bravely.

"Kill you? Why would I kill you? You are family," declared the man astonished.

"Oh, okay then. Good," replied Rose, trying not to appear puzzled.

"Oh you don't understand? I thought you would. It's okay though, I'll explain. It's quite simple."

"Explain what? You executed my great-uncle and his family? They were kinfolk."

"No, no they were not. They didn't act like family. They only pretended to share the same blood. They didn't protect Amelia, not like your mother and you do," The kidnapper explained.

"Family doesn't harm you."

"Why did Aunt Amelia need protection? What happened to her that was so bad?" solicited Rose, trying to get him to talk and see her as a real person.

"She was a little older than you, and her father would beat her...every day. I noticed the bruises. I know teachers did too." The man exclaimed, "No one helped her, my poor Angel. They turned their eyes away and did nothing to aid her."

"Her father hurt her? What a rotten creep! What kind of man was Uncle Robert, that he would beat his own child?"

"Yes, you understand?" he asked with a smile and cocked his head "Somehow I knew that you would."

"No one should harm a child, let alone their own child. Poor Aunt Amelia, what a horrible thing to be raised by a parent who would stoop to harm their own child."

"You are like my Angel. I thought so. She defended her dad. She would tell people she bumped into doors. But it was her father. Do you want to understand about her brother Jerry? Why he had to be killed?" His voice drifted, as if weighing whether or not he should tell her.

"What did Jerry do?" Rose inquired, trying to get him to talk.

"I love that you call him Jerry for he doesn't deserve the title of honorary uncle like my Amelia being your aunt. That scum defiled women!" The man said with anger, "He had sex with my girlfriend, after Henry did. He slept with many innocent women at school."

"I'm sorry, that must have hurt. What a dreadful man Jerry was. You must have really loved your girlfriend. How could she have done that to you?"

"I did love her, until I saw her for the woman she was. Amelia showed me that she alone was the real thing, an angel and vision of kindness and sweetness, untainted by evil surrounding us."

"Aunt Amelia is special. So you protected Aunt Amelia? How did you defend her?"

"I watched over her. I saw what they did to her. I told Jerry to leave her alone. I told him he was not to raise his hand to her again. He looked at me with scorn as if I was beneath his notice."

"What a jerk," Rose commented.

"Yes, he was a jerk and I lost my temper and struck him. I was skinny and had no muscles then and Jerry snorted with laughter as I didn't hurt him at all. Jerry pummelled me, knocking out my front tooth. He told the principal I started it all. They believed him, not hearing me at all."

"How awful."

"The fight resulted in a punishment...mine! I got two weeks suspension and a beating from my father. I spent three days in a closet."

"Closet? You were trapped in a closet? Who put you there? Was it your father?" Rose asked

"I don't want to talk about the closet. The only thing that matters is that when I got out, I vowed revenge. I planned on telling his father what Jerry had done .I went over while Amelia wasn't home."

"What did Uncle Robert say?" Rose asked, trying to get the rope off her wrists without him noticing.

"Don't call that cretin uncle!"

"Sorry," Rose apologised.

"You'll understand why when I finish this story. Robert Cordova laughed at me and applauded his son. He congratulated him for knocking me down. He called me an interfering wimp! He thought I was lying that Jerry had been sniffing around your sister. He threatened that Jerry would knock my block off in the next five seconds if I didn't get out while I could."

"Did Jerry attack you?"

"Jerry raised his fist again and knocked me off my feet breaking my nose. Do you notice the scars?"

"Is that why your nose is a little crooked?"

"Yes it is," he admitted. "I grew even angrier, when it took my nose so long to heal."

"Is that when you decide to kill them?"

"Of course it was. Her family didn't cherish and protect her, my poor Amelia, my beloved Angel was in torment and I could save her. Amelia at her babysitting job, I made my plans to pay them back for their treachery. I started a fire and to get rid of her family. I dispatched Grace first, smothering her, as she lay sleeping in her bed."

"Why did you kill Grace?"

"I eradicated Grace because I had seen her evilness. She'd kick Amelia, hit and lash out at her. She deliberately told lies about Amelia to incite her father Robert to hit Amelia. That wasn't what a sister did."

"No, she didn't act like a sister, but Aunt Amelia must have loved her."

"Amelia was better off without her. I saved her," he protested, angrily.

"Of course you did. I'm sorry." Rose replied, worried she'd angered him, "Please, tell me more."

"No, I need to think."

The man then paced the floor, stroking his fingers through his hair.

Rose was sure that the man was now convinced she didn't believe him, which meant any bond she had made with him would be severed. She couldn't allow him to think she didn't believe him her life depended on this.

"Please I'd like to hear more. I think I'm beginning to understand" Rose insisted.

"Okay, but don't interrupt me again." the killer said tightening the bonds on her feet.

Then he sat down in a chair near her and began his story again. "I crept up the stairs to Jerry's room. I hit him over the head with a lamp as he slept and smothered him in his bed. Maybe I should have harmed him more, but I didn't have the heart."

"Of course you didn't you are a good person," Rose said mollifying him.

Rose was rewarded with a smile from her kidnapper.

"I went to her parents' room. I gagged Aerilla and tied her to the bed he slept on, the demon who called himself Amelia's father. Aerilla begged me with her eyes to spare her. I ignored her. I clobbered that devil, Robert over the head. When he awoke, I had tied him to the bed hand and foot. He begged me to let him go kill Aerilla and the rest of his family and let him go."

"No, a father wouldn't!" Rose exclaimed, then seeing the sad shaking of the killer's head she replied shocked, "He did? How truly evil!"

"The arrogance, the selfishness Robert displayed made me realize he had to go. I asked him if he wanted me to kill Amelia. He said go ahead, like to him she was a worthless daughter, no better than a piece of trash. I told him she was worth hundreds of him. I hit him on the head again for the pain it caused him."

"And then what happened," Rose probed softly.

"I don't want to talk about this anymore. I only want to talk of my Angel. All of this reminds me of how she disappeared after the fire."

"Please, tell me what happened?" begged Rose.

"Talking is good for the soul," he quipped.

"So true... please continue."

"You are a good listener. As much as it hurts, I'll continue. The pain was my punishment for starting a fire that might have killed my Angel. Luckily I got her out in time, and then I hid after calling for an ambulance. They had to take her to the hospital and I couldn't find her. When she reappeared six years ago, it appeared a sign from God that my Angel needed me. I watched from afar and she looked happy. Truly happy! How could I interfere with true happiness? If she had remained that way I wouldn't have. If he had been good to her I would have left them alone. I would have."

Rose tried not to reveal the revulsion she was feeling, but her up-curled lip gave her thoughts away.

"Don't look at me that way."

"I know you would have let her have her happiness. You love Amelia," Rose agreed trying to appease him.

"Please tell me more."

"Okay, that husband of hers, Jack, the lucky man who held her heart, cheated on her. He told her he went to work and he ducked into a motel with his mistress, a married woman. I wanted to kill the evil woman who dallied with him through carbon monoxide poisoning. She had hurt my Angel, even if Amelia remained unaware. The woman lied to her husband so I should have slayed her, but I recognized her all too well, so she lives still."

"Uncle Jack? You murdered him too? But you didn't kill the woman because you recognized her?" Rose inquired, trying to keep him talking to make sure he identified with her as a person.

"I admit it. I felt angry with him. He had a treasure beyond measure, and yet he had cheated on an Angel. Why would anyone hurt her like that?"

"I don't know why anyone would hurt Amelia. Uncle Jack cheated on Aunt Amelia? I don't believe it," Rose retorted shocked.

"I saw them together so make no mistake he cheated on Amelia. Jack had been blessed with a child with her; the child should have been ours...and he did that? Amelia's beloved son Sam was his to cherish and love. Sam was such a cherub. How could he? Sam should have been mine and Amelia's."

"But he wasn't."

"I thought Sam had stayed with her when I tampered with the car and I drove my car right into Jack's. The child went with Jack in the car, to my ever-loving shame and revulsion. Jack deserved to die. Amelia's son Sam did not. I took his life. I am a horrible person for murdering a child."

"You killed Sammy. Little Sammy?" Rose cried covering her mouth in horror.

"I blame Jack! He made me do it... If Jack hadn't cheated and made me punish him..."the killer sobbed, "I cried so much and my Angel, Amelia was devastated to lose her son. I became overcome with shock and pain to find out what I had done. I had to rest in the hospital after the accident."

"You stayed in the hospital? You sought help from a shrink?" Rose inquired surprised and feeling sick, but wanting to keep him talking to her, so he would see her as an extension of Aunt Amelia.

"I wanted to die when I discovered how I harmed my Angel. But the drugs and the doctor convinced me it was all an accident. I hadn't made her sick with the flu after all. The flu had made her unable to look after Sam, not me. Jack had taken the boy. He hadn't properly strapped him in his car seat, so he murdered him, not me," The man rationalized.

"You told the doctor what you did and he let you go?" demanded Rose, now wondering what doctor in his or her right mind would let this nut job go.

"No, it is my secret, and you'll keep my secret won't you?"

"Of course I will, you didn't mean to harm Sammy," Rose lied.

"I didn't tell the doctor. He wouldn't understand. I only said I felt unhappy. I said I had hurt the one I loved, and I wanted to die," he explained.

"Aunt Amelia wanted to die. She didn't sleep and she didn't eat. Do you understand how you harmed her?" Rose exclaimed angrily, "I thought she would die and that would have been your fault."

"I understand she hurt from the loss, but she found Doctor Jones. Now I can forgive you and thank you for talking to me in such a stern way because of Doctor Jones. Doctor Jones is a genius. I love everything about my Angel. We even shared the same shrink," he boasted.

"How sweet!" Rose replied sarcastically, without thinking.

"I love how you stood up to me for Amelia," he replied thinking what Rose had said supported his position. "Family is so important. You'll be my family too and you'll love and support me."

"Why did you kill my father?" inquired Rose in a small voice. "I didn't want to at first. I wasn't going to harm him, for your sake, but he wanted to leave your mother Lily, for a slut. Yes, the one I executed him with Amber. Silly, stupid Amber."

"Amber wouldn't do that and neither would my father," Rose protested.

Rose realized with surprise she had the ropes off her one hand. She ducked her face down to hide her triumphant smile.

"Oh dear, I shouldn't have said such a word in your presence, little Angel. I'm sorry for sullying your ears Rose. Forgive me, little Angel," he said thinking she hid her face because she believed him. "Now back to my story about Amber. She had convinced him to leave your mother Lily. Your mother is a divine woman. She's a woman of exceptional strength and character. She is more a mother than the woman who bore you, and yet he took up with that slut Amber. He was an evil bastard not fit to be your father," he said manically.

Rose couldn't help the tears that ran down her face. Rose feared that she would never get away from this madman and that she too would die.

"Please don't cry, Rose. I'm sorry I made you sad. I never wanted to that."

"I'm sorry but this is just all so sad," Rose responded trying to stop crying.

"Please, you don't know everything!" He protested as Rose couldn't stop two more tears from falling, "He had decided to take you from Lily and that would take you away from Amelia. You are more Lily's child than his."

Rose shook her head.

"No, he really was going to take you, Rose, and divorce Lily. Allowing him to go ahead with his plan, he would take your home away and you. So I'm sorry, but he had to die," he explained and smiled warmly at her.

Rose found it very creepy; it appeared he thought he would now be a father figure to her.

"But Daddy loved Lily," Rose protested, before she stopped herself.

"No, he didn't. He loved himself. I told you why aren't you listening? Pay attention to me!" he yelled. "Horace planned to leave Lily and remove you just to hurt her because if he cared about you he would have made more time for you. Amelia loves you, and Lily does too. If he took you, he would be hurting her."

The man paced back and forth swinging his fists into the air which scared Rose.

"And Amelia's store clerk, and the homeless man...why did you kill them?" questioned Rose trying to hide her fear and revulsion, worried he would become more agitated.

"She dared to defile Amelia's store. Al said he would tell everyone I killed Megan. Now was that fair? He had to go. You know he did. I killed him humanely. He was collateral damage," The man screamed. "It wasn't my fault. It wasn't!"

He then stomped his foot like a child.

"It's okay; of course you had to kill them. They tried to harm those you loved," lied Rose, trying to get on his good side and calm him.

"Do you mean what you just said? You don't think it's my fault?" the man replied excited.

"Of course I don't. We must protect Aunt Amelia," Rose reassured, as the man smiled at her.

"We can be family. But forgive me if I must keep you here for a while tied up to the chair. I trust you, I do, but we must convince your mother you are safe. Once Lily is convinced she likes me, Amelia will love me, too. I am convinced she will. And we will be family. You will be my honoured niece. You can be the flower girl at our wedding," the man replied beaming.

"Aunt Amelia will be upset, because they can't find me!" protested Rose.

"We must make her believe you visit a friend or something won't we? Now you will write out a letter for her, exactly as I tell you to write it. We wouldn't want Amelia to worry, now would we?" the man commanded expecting an of course we wouldn't.

Rose nodded her head in agreement.

"Here you go," he said handing her a pen and paper, "And tell your mother to tell Amelia not to worry on this one."

He then untied Rose's hands, but not her feet.

"I can't write two letters. My mom would be suspicious if I sent two letters," Rose complained setting down the pen.

"Fine then, write one, but remember no funny stuff. I will be reading it," he cautioned.

He smoothed out the paper and placed the pen in Rose's hand.

"Don't worry; I want you to be my uncle," Rose lied again.

"Good, now write," he demanded.

~0~

Chapter 23 - The
Best Laid Plans

L ily and Katha heard the front door open of Katha's house

and close and at first they hoped that Rose was somehow safe and coming in the door but they knew that was impossible. They had to search her whereabouts.

"Oh, hi, Lily, I just came from your house. No one answered," Terrence stated entering the kitchen.

"Sorry dear, I should have told you the plans changed," Katha apologised.

"Quite alright, my dear. By the way, I found this letter addressed to you on your stoop, Lily," Terrence said, noting Lily's tears he turned to Katha and probed, "Katha, my dear, what is the matter?"

"You found a letter? May I see the letter, Terrence?" Lily demanded, holding out her hand and all but snatching the letter from his hand.

"Sure here you go. Now as the kids say, spill it. What has happened?"

"The letter is from Rose. Why didn't she text me? She wouldn't send a letter. This makes no sense," Lily cried.

"She's okay. The person who broke in here...didn't take her?" probed Katha, ignoring Terrence's question.

"Someone broke in your house?"

"Yes, but the matter is handled," Lily claimed.

Terrence bent over and began to look under furniture and under the lamp shades.

"What is wrong with you Terrence?" asked Katha.

"Nothing! I'm sitting down and resting. But maybe I'll walk around and get the kink out of my leg," he said with a finger to his lips.

Terrence continued complaining about his leg as he walked. Using nonverbal clues, Terrence showed Katha and Lily a listening device he had spotted under a table. He continued to search for more and found one in the phone. He also found one in the kitchen cabinet and one even in the bedroom lamp which the killer had somehow missed. He put all of them in a glass jar he filled with cotton balls.

"Read the letter quickly and then we will spin it differently to whomever listens," Terrence requested whispering.

"What if he already knows we think he took her? Lily and I talked about Rose," Katha answered worried.

"We'll convince him, but first, as I said, I must read the letter," Terrence reassured.

Lily read the letter aloud, "Mom, I sent you a letter to tell you and Amelia that I am at my friend, *Daisy Adair's*. You remember her. Don't you, Mom? Please reassure Aunt Amelia, all is well. Oh and *Daisy's* friend *George* says ' Hi.' I'll be home tomorrow."

"Daisy Adair? Wasn't that a character in the show *Dead Like Me?*" Katha queried. "It's one of Rose's favourite shows. I bought the DVDs for her for Christmas. *George* is the main character."

"Yes, Daisy Adair is a character from *Dead Like Me* which means she is sent me a message that she is with one of these men. I think I know which one, but proving it will be difficult. We set a trap. But what can we use to trap him?" enquired Lily.

"Did you lose your money clip, honey?" Katha questioned Terrence as he spotted and picked up a money clip off the floor.

"It's not mine," insisted Terrence.

"Oh my, you found Uncle Robert's money clip. How could it be here?" Lily asked puzzled.

"You don't think the person who took Rose killed Robert and the others do you?" asked Katha.

"Nonsense! How do you know it's your Uncle Robert's?" commented Terrence.

"All my cousins' birth stones are on it. Grandpa O'Malley fashioned the money clip especially for him. Remember, Grandma Katha? I recall Uncle Robert taking it out to buy us ice cream (a rare occurrence) from the ice cream truck the week before he was murdered," Lily explained.

"The money clip has stones on it," Katha agreed.

"Are you saying the man who murdered your uncle, aunt and cousins kidnapped Rose?" Terrence queried.

"What can we do?" demanded Katha. "We need to save Rose."

"Follow my lead. We will catch him in the act. As soon as he claims the money clip, we can name him as the murderer," exclaimed Lily.

"We will find our Rose." Terrence took the listening device out and all of them gathered around it.

Lily read aloud the letter again from Rose.

"Well isn't that lovely, Rose is visiting her friend *Daisy*. It is lovely she can have fun with friends. She went through such trauma today. She deserves some fun."

"It was bad enough we buried her dad today, but her own grandmother shoots at her at the cemetery," Katha exclaimed. "It's good that she can spend time with her friend *Daisy* and forget all of this," Lily continued.

"Yes, it's pleasant for kids her age to have friends," Katha improvised.

"I found this money clip outside in the street. I wonder to whom this money clip belongs," Terrence said offhand with a wink.

"We should place an ad in the paper," said Katha continuing to improvise.

"The law states you must call the police and report found money, especially if it's more than twenty dollars," replied Lily.

"We need to go now?" asked Katha.

"No, it can wait until later tonight."

"I guess I could take the clip to the police in the morning. For now let's go to my house and eat dinner. The two fine policemen will be coming for dinner. We could give the clip to them," Katha retorted.

"Sounds good to me." Lily answered.

"I did try to cancel because Amelia seemed tired, but I wasn't able to get in touch with them, so the two men should be arriving soon," announced Katha.

Katha mouthed to Lily, Sorry I didn't cancel.

"Okay, let's go back for Chinese food. Amelia's at my house," Lily declared, sounding a little wooden.

"Yes, let's go. I'm hungry," Katha replied.

Katha, Lily and Terrence left through the front door of Katha's home.

"Do you think who ever planted those bugs listened to us?" queried Katha, while walking over to Lily's house.

"No doubt about it. I'm sure they eavesdropped," Terrence said.

"I want Rose back," Lily cried.

"We will get her back. He has made a mistake dropping the money clip and we will find out where he has Rose," Terrence reassured.

"Excuse me while I bring Edward up to date on this," Terrence explained, as he entered the kitchen of Lily's home.

Amelia, oblivious to the conversation in the kitchen or their suspicions, answered the doorbell the trio failed to hear. Emmett Rogers was ushered into the house. Amelia then went back to her room.

"Hello, Ms. Kelly, Ms. Mallory, Mr. Stewart," called out Sergeant Detective Emmett Rogers, as he walked into the kitchen and they all seemed to jump a foot.

"Why are you here?" asked Lily puzzled. "We didn't call you."

"Rose called me. She said she had something to tell me and she invited me to dinner," Sergeant Detective Emmett Rogers replied smiling.

"You can't be here, you'll spoil it all young man," Katha retorted.

"I think he can be a big help, dear," Terrence exclaimed as he turned to Emmett.

"So you see, Emmett, we believe this money clip belonged to the dead man," Terrence tried to explain.

"It's simple; I believe it is a clue." "But we're not sure which of them has my great-granddaughter," Katha interrupted.

"You alleged one of two policemen committed a horrific crime. A money clip is all you require to find him guilty? Lots of money clips are similar," Emmett protested. "I think you need more evidence if you want to find Rose."

"This money clip is special, Detective Rogers," protested Lily, showing him it wrapped in a Kleenex as to not pick up fingerprints, "You see, this clip was specially made for my Uncle Robert by a jeweller, my Grandfather O'Malley. Grandfather O'Malley made this money clip and a jewel encrusted tie clip to complete the set. The tie clip also has a ruby, an emerald, and peridot for my Uncle Robert's children's birthstones. Amelia has the clip in her jewellery box. I've seen it," Lily replied, continuing to show him the clip.

"You said you believe the clip is the same one...the money clip that belonged to your Uncle Robert? You're speaking of Robert Cordova, who was murdered in a fire in Ravenworst?" Emmett demanded.

"Yes, and one of those policemen dropped this when they grabbed Rose. You have to do something to save her," Lily commanded.

"I'll help find Rose and if it is one of those two we'll find her. Now I know I've seen a tie clip like that and recently. But where, and whom?" Emmett probed thinking hard.

"You have? You've seen the clip then, young man? Where did you see and who had it?" inquired Katha.

"Grandma Katha, please be quiet. Let the man think," Lily snapped exasperated. "I don't want to believe a cop could do all this, but cops are people too. People are flawed, so cops can be too. I do recall seeing a money clip recently. It had been held in either Owens' or Rentford's hands. They rubbed the clip, like the clip held a magic Genie or something. That is why I remember the incident. I saw the clip in one of their hands, but I'll be darned if I can remember which." Emmett retorted.

"We'll figure out which one it is. We have a plan," Lily explained.

"Plans are good and if I think your plan is a solid one, we will go ahead," Emmett replied.

"I'm glad we have your approval but son, your boss, Chief Edward Stewart has already approved my plan. Your agreement is just a formality," Terrence announced, grinning to take out the sting.

"Fine! Then we'll go ahead. But call me Emmett, please, all of you, since I'm working with you."

"Please, Emmett, just get my daughter home safe." begged Lily, not even realizing she called him Emmett.

"One more thing you need to know, Amelia doesn't know anything about our suspicions. Don't let on to either of them before the trap is sprung."

"It is about time you called me Emmett, Lily. It sounds nice from your lips." Emmett replied smiling then turning to Terence he agreed though he sounded annoyed, "Don't worry, since you got my boss to okay this action and this is highly unorthodox, I will follow the plan to the letter."

Emmett quietly found a place to hide in the house, cautiously avoiding any recording devices.

~0~

Chapter 24 - A Penny Saved A Murder Earned

half an hour later Emmett waited in place for the

culprit to come, so the trap would be sprung. Lily jumped up to answer a knock at the door.

"Where is Amelia?" Brad Owens asked, as he was ushered into the house.

"I'm sure she feels better after her rest," Lily answered.

"I'm so glad Amelia is rested," Brad replied.

"Me too!" replied Silas who had arrived as well.

"But where is she?" Brad demanded like he'd said nothing.

"She'll be down in a couple of minutes. Please, come in and take a seat. Can I get you a drink? Tea coffee, beer?" Lily offered.

"Beer, please and thank you," They both answered.

"We're off duty now."

Katha limped into the room and took a seat in the living room in a swivel chair.

"Oh how lovely to visit with you both again," Katha exclaimed.

"I don't understand why you'd say it's lovely to visit with us again. You saw us a few hours ago at the wake," admonished Brad

"Oh so I did. Forgive my forgetfulness in my old age," Katha explained preparing to spring the trap.

"It's okay old...er...people forget," Brad replied "Excuse me a moment, I need to use the facilities," Silas commented, but Terrence didn't catch the words.

"Talking about people forgetting, you'll never believe what I found out in the street," began Terrence.

"So what did you find?" asked Brad.

"I found a money clip, and look...someone's money." Terrence said pausing for effect and trying to appear normal, "I know what you're thinking. Don't you worry; I'm turning it into the police station. I'll go down to the station after dinner and give it to them."

"You don't need to take it to the station," explained Brad. "It's mine, I must have dropped it at some point."

Brad took off his coat, revealing a tie clip, a ruby, an emerald and peridot stone, glinting in the light.

"Brad?" asked Amelia, as she entered from the garage.

"I thought Lily said you were upstairs?" Brad commented puzzled.

"Why, Brad, where did you get that tie clip? It's just like the one Grandpa O'Malley made Daddy to match his money clip," Amelia's face contorted by confusion.

Brad looked horrified and in the next instance grabbed Katha. Pulling a gun out of his holster and held the gun to her throat.

"Brad! What are you doing?" Amelia cried out, oblivious and confused, "Why are you holding a gun on Aunt Katha? You'll hurt her!"

"I don't want to hurt her. I understand Katha's been good to you, and like a mother. But I need you to listen to me Amelia."

"Don't listen to him, Amelia!" Katha screamed, "He's not who you think he is! He's a serial killer!"

"Shut up you crazy old bat! What I did, I did to save Amelia," Brad shouted.

"I don't understand. Why are holding a gun?" inquired Amelia, still appearing perplexed.

"Oh, my darling, my Angel, of course you don't understand, but you will," Brad promised. "Do you remember the summer I cut the lawn?"

"I do, but what does that summer so long ago have to do with you holding a gun on my aunt? Why are you arresting her? She didn't kill my family!" Amelia cried, still sounding puzzled and sitting down on the sofa.

Terrence whispered to Lily, "Is she really that stupid?"

"Quiet! She knows what she's doing," Lily whispered back.

Brad focused so hard on Amelia and her reaction that he didn't hear Lily or Terrence.

"No, of course I'm not. Katha hasn't done anything wrong. I know how loving she can be to you. She tried to look after you years ago. She even went to the police about what your father had done to you. She told them he beat you! She even sought out a lawyer and tried to get custody. Unfortunately no one would listen, as the cops were friends of your father. You need not worry though; I've dealt with those police officers."

"My father lived as a good man and father, so he disciplined me. I wouldn't listen to him. I was a know-it-all teen," Amelia exclaimed defending her father.

"When he called you a slut, because you spoke to Silas and me, then he thrashed you! Did that show fatherly love? He left bruises on your beautiful skin! Was that discipline?" questioned Brad angrily.

"He was my father." Amelia exclaimed, "He had the right."

"He was a terribly abusive man and father. Your mother didn't stick up for you. Instead she avoided it all, by falling into the bottle," Brad complained.

"I loved my parents."

"I understand you felt affection for them, but it was so hard to see them harm you day after day. I couldn't bear to see them hurt you anymore," Brad begged Amelia by his eyes to accept and praise him.

"You killed my family? You murdered my mother, my father, my sister and my brother?" Amelia demanded, tears pooling in her eyes.

"I didn't know had come home! I had made sure you went to your babysitting job, but I didn't see you come to the house. I would never have hurt a hair on your head," Brad apologised.

"You killed my family? Why?" demanded Amelia.

"They harmed you! Your father beat you, while your mother drank. Your brother brought his slutty women home, and your sister hit you, belittling you, calling you ugly. This was not a family for an Angel. This family came from hell. You deserved better, my Angel, my pet. I couldn't allow this anymore, and when your father came out to me and said…"Your money for cutting the lawn, five dollars, in pennies. I grew angry because he owed me for the summer. He owed me ten weeks, at five dollars a week and yet he had offered me a total of five dollars for an entire summer's work. He even laughed at me as he stated 'A penny saved is a penny earned. Save your pennies and you'll have more money!"

"Daddy gave you five dollars for the whole summer?" Amelia asked astonished.

"Yes, in pennies. Do you believe it? He gave me five dollars' worth of pennies. He threw the money at my feet... like I was an animal. He laughed at me again. He told me to stay away from you. He'd seen the looks I'd given you all summer. He saw how I felt. But he said you weren't for the likes of me. He had sicced Jerry on me. Jerry beat me up as he, your father, held me down on the ground. Jerry broke my nose, the bastard . . . oh, forgive me, my Angel! I should not use such foul language in front of you." Brad began to pace... "I waited for you...When they were all in their beds, I started my plan. I snuck in and tied them to their beds. I won't sully your ears with your sister's and your brother's killings, except to say, I remained merciful."

Amelia gasped but Brad didn't hear her and continued explaining what he had done.

"I tied your parents to their beds too, but mercy was not on my mind. Not with those excuses for parents. They begged for their lives, not yours, or your siblings, theirs! She offered up herself in exchange for her life, not his. I mentioned your sister and your brother were easy prey. She didn't seem to care. She told me they didn't matter. I grew so angry, I dispatched her first.

"You killed my mother?"

" I told you I had to dispense with her. I talked to your father for some time before I took his life. After all I had to give him a chance to tell his side. I won't tell you what he said about you. That would be too cruel. I did however tell your father my new saying, before he died."

"You had a new saying?" enquired Amelia, trying to humour him and keep him talking.

"I did indeed. Your father inspired my new saying, '*A Penny Saved A Murder Earned*'. I told him my new saying as he slithered and writhed beneath the pillow I held over his face. He stopped fidgeting and I left the room."

"You smothered my father?"

"Of course I did. I smothered them both."

"You smothered them both?" Amelia cried.

"But they really deserved it!! You know they did. They were so evil. I then set up the chlorine in the house. The chlorine caught on fire much too soon though. It burnt much too bright. I ended up burning the house down to the ground," Brad waxed bragging. "The flame was so beautiful; I watched as the colours of the fire rose so high in the sky. I seemed to touch it."

Brad seemed to go into a trance talking about the fire.

"How did the fire occur then?" demanded Lily, but he ignored her and she motioned to Amelia to ask him.

"How did the fire happen then? Did you find me and save me from the fire? Is that how I got outside the house?" inquired Amelia.

"Yes, but the fire didn't happen until after I took you out of the house. I couldn't believe it. You'd come home when I had killed them. You slept in your bed and you were unconscious. That was my entirely my fault," Brad responding to Amelia's voice.

"Tell me, Brad, why did the fire start?" Amelia prodded. enunciating each word.

"I set the fire to cover my crime, but you were safe. You didn't burn. I'm so sorry about your accident. Chlorine got into your lungs. That too was entirely my fault."

"So I got on the lawn, because you carried me?" Amelia softly requested.

"Yes, my Angel. I became scared because you vanished. They took you away from me. My punishment for my miscalculation was the absence of your beautiful smile. Lost, so totally lost, as if I was put in the closet again, by the devil himself, I tried to be good, like you'd want me to be. I did try hard, Amelia, my beloved Angel," Brad said mournfully.

"You tried to be good for me?" replied Amelia, still in shock how Brad had fooled her and murdered her family, but somehow she wanted this monster to explain it all.

"I joined the police. I went to the police academy in Ravenworst after I got out of the hospital. For once father had pride for me. I had joined the side of the good." Brad explained, "My father claimed you were my curse. But I was so miserable without you. Working for the Ravenworst Police force and not being near you, my beloved, sweet, Angel, seemed the curse."

"You worked for the police force there too?"

"Yes I did. Like a sign right out of blue you appeared in front of me. I had found you without even trying. The story appeared on the news all about Lily, and you emerged there, Amelia, comforting her. My dear Angel, my dear Amelia, helping her cousin. You needed me so I came to Happy Valley."

"You saw me and found me from a television story?" Amelia asked shocked.

"Of course I did. A single glimpse of your cousin on the news, and I found you. Some guy kidnapped Lily; poor Lily, working as a lowly employee in the Crown attorney's office. In the background of Paul Knight's story, you cried hugging Lily. I wanted to take you in my arms but you were here and I resided there. I thought and I applied to the Happy Valley Police Department."

"They were anxious to get someone like me. They needed skilled police officers. I moved up quickly through the ranks. The department was damn glad to get someone of my calibre here. I could be happy; I could watch over my Angel again."

"Six years ago? You've been a cop six years?" demanded Amelia, connecting the dots in horror.

"Maybe a little less time, than six years; but enough about me you were residing with your husband Jack. You didn't even take his name, but you had the boy Sammy. So if you loved him, why didn't you?" Brad said accusingly.

"I loved him, but I didn't want to change my name again," Amelia claimed softly.

Brad eased up a little with the gun, but still held the gun to Katha's side, as he paced across the room.

"But he didn't love you, the bastard. If he had I'd let you go...even if it hurt, just to make you happy," Brad coldly exclaimed. "But I watched him. He cheated with another woman in a motel."

"How dare you! You're lying! He would never cheat on me. He loved me," Amelia protested.

"You and Lily both know her. The woman he cheated with was Renée Harrow," Brad said smiling.

"You believe he slept with Renée?" Amelia protested. "I don't believe he would cheat with her. Why do you continue to lie to me?"

"Believe me, he slept with her. Renée sleeps beside anything on two legs. She even tried to proposition me when I threatened to arrest her for the murder of Horace Brooksfield."

"I thought she was related to you!" Amelia exclaimed flabbergasted.

"She's not related to me. Can you believe she told some people I was her brother? And she tried to kiss me, on the lips. Disgusting!"

"But she said she was your sister," Amelia protested. "The woman claimed kinship by being my half-sister, but the truth is she was married to my half-brother, Titus. Titus died and any relationship with her died too."

"Did you kill your brother Titus too?" Amelia demanded.

"No, I didn't kill Titus. He disappointed Dad in the end. He died in a bank robbery. It seemed my pretty boy, do no wrong brother, financed his lifestyle robbing banks," Brad laughed.

"Did you kill Jack and Sammy?"

"I didn't mean to kill your boy. Please believe me, Amelia; I would never harm your son. I almost killed myself when Sam was killed. I didn't know he was in the car," Brad confessed with horror on his face begging her to believe him.

"You killed my baby? You monster! I hate you. Did you hear me you creep? I hate you!" Amelia screamed hitting his chest.

Brad sought to cover his head and Katha saw her move. Katha managed to break free and kicked his feet from under him kicking the gun away as well. Terrence and Lily then managed to tie him up quickly with Terrence's belt.

"I did all of this for you, my Angel, my Amelia, don't hate me. Please don't hate me," Brad pleaded. "I loved our little boy Sammy."

"Ours? He wasn't yours. Don't you dare say his name, you cretin."

"I'm sorry. Please, Amelia, my Angel, forgive me. I tried to kill myself after your boy died. Fate intervened and my cousin saved me. He told me if someone loved you, then they could forgive you and Dr. Jones told me the same thing. It was like I was reborn. Of course my cousin didn't know it was you though," Brad explained, "You do forgive me, don't you my love?"

"Of course she does, Brad. Don't you, Amelia? Since we are all family now you'll want to tell us where you took Rose," Lily replied, appeasing Brad and patting Amelia's hand.

"He took Rose? He has Rose?" Amelia demanded.

Lily nodded.

"I forgive you Brad. You love me, correct? So you wouldn't want me to be unhappy. Now would you?" Amelia winningly asked.

"I do love you, my Angel. You are my reason for living," Brad replied smiling happily, bathing in his Angel's light of goodness.

"You'll bring Rose to me, won't you?" Amelia ordered, "She's like my daughter."

"I know she's like a daughter to you and I'll bring her to you I promise. I didn't hurt her. She likes me. She wants me to be her uncle soon."

"You were at it again," Silas exclaimed angrily, interrupting the conversation as he came in with his gun drawn.

"Hello, cousin. Not to worry; everything is all right now. You see, you were right. Amelia loves me, so she'll forgive me," Brad replied.

"She didn't say she loved you. You fool!" protested Silas waving his gun.

Lily, Amelia, Katha and Terence looked on in surprise.

"Well don't look so shocked. Sit all of you," Silas demanded.

"I'm already sitting young man," Terrence complained. "And so is Lily."

"Then you two sit, Katha and Amelia," Silas commanded, "And you two remain seated."

"You are his cousin?" probed Lily and Katha shocked.

They had seen no resemblance to Brad and they now worried about the gun Silas still had drawn.

"I guess I can answer some of your questions. Yes, Brad is my cousin. Did he tell you he is adopted? My uncle dallied with another woman and the result was Brad. My uncle adopted him with my aunt. My aunt never had a clue that he was her husband's spawn, but enough family history. It's too bad we've come in on a murder-suicide. It's too hard as a police officer to come upon these scenes," Silas smirked, than sadly shook his head.

"What does he mean he came in on a murder-suicide?" asked Amelia.

"What, you think you can get away with murdering us all, and making one of us the killer? Who do you plan to make the murderer?" demanded Lily, trying to stall so Emmett could come out into the room.

"Looking for that nitwit police officer, Rogers? You're going to be waiting a long time," explained Silas laughing. "Let's put it this way. I didn't use the facilities. I checked on my earlier handy work. Emmett Rogers is still out cold, and will be another of your victims, Crown attorney Kelly. It's a terrible shame, how you hid your homicidal tendencies all this time and then snapped."

"No one will believe this. Why did you do this anyway? I thought you were one of the good guys?" protested Lily.

"I am one of the good guys. I was entrusted by my Uncle Kelvin to look after my cousin and I do my job. He needs looking after and he's family."

"If you looked after your cousin, how did he murder so many people?" Lily inquired with sarcasm, "You say you were entrusted to look after Brad by your uncle? What happened to him? Did Brad murder him too?"

"Don't be ridiculous, Brad wouldn't kill his father," Silas argued, as he looked over at Brad for confirmation.

Seeing Brad's head go down in shame, he continued, "Oh my God, she's right! You did kill Uncle Kelvin."

Silas looked thunderstruck and extremely angry. That worried Lily.

"What the hell is wrong with you?" Silas questioned, "Does family mean nothing to you? After everything we've done to protect you? Is all of this about your obsession with my girl? You understood how I felt about Amelia. How could you?"

"She is mine. I told you she's my Angel!" ranted Brad.

"Your Angel? The one you always rave about? Amelia's that Angel? When did you decide she was your Angel? Was it the summer Amelia and I met? Did you decide then and there you needed to have what I wanted?" Silas angrily exclaimed.

Pausing trying to get his anger under control but not succeeding Silas continued, "Of course it was you. You always wanted what I wanted. You took my best toys when we were small and claimed they were yours. I let you keep them. Anything you wanted was yours for the asking. I loved you like a brother. I felt sorry you were stuck with your father and Titus, the wonder boy. Now I must clean up your messes again. Why, Brad why? Why do you push me this way and test my loyalty? It isn't necessary, you are my family. I'll pick you. Always! Now because of your foolishness Amelia's going to die, and not just Amelia, but all of them. Does cleaning up after you never end? Now I must kill a teenage girl to protect you. I assume she's back at your apartment?"

Brad nodded strangely submissive. Silas then untied Brad and held the gun on Lily, Katha and Terrence.

"It's time for me to finish this. I'm sorry, Amelia, I did love you. I'll make your death as painless as possible."

"No! No she won't die! If Amelia dies, I die!" exclaimed Brad. Brad had only registered the words that Amelia would die. Brad then grabbed Silas' gun as it went off with a huge bang.

~0~

Chapter 25 -
Slipping the
Bonds

*A short time ago at Brad's house, one
street over from Lily's*

Rose and Carol

Rose slipped the bounds off her feet and wrists. She

rubbed her wrists, as she felt the rope burns. She unfurled herself slowly, and walked to the door, seeking a way out of the house. She hesitated at the door for a moment looking both ways for any sign of Sergeant Detective Owens. Startled when she heard a noise in the other bedroom in the home, Rose cautiously peered into the room. She wondered... What if Brad hid in the shadows? She looked blinked and realized; yes, she saw Carol tied up on a chair.

"Carol, how did you get here?" Rose asked, and then realized Carol had a gag across her mouth.

Rose sneaked over, removed the gag, and began to untie her friend

"Rose, are you okay? The cop grabbed me after I came to make sure you were okay," Carol explained, "I'm supposed to be at my dad's house, but I left right after I got there. I told my dad I was sick. No one will look for me or you for that matter. You didn't tell anyone you went to your Grandma Katha's did you? We must get out of here before he comes back."

"Brad grabbed me too, right in Grandma Katha's house. Can you berate me later, so we leave before he does come back?" Rose replied annoyed.

Carol began sobbing and between sobs she asked "Are you sure you're okay?"

"Yes, silly, we're both okay."

"Well he sure moves fast. He had me all tied up and knocked out in about five seconds. We need to get out of here. He'll come back," Carol repeated worried.

"You wouldn't believe the story he told me. The guy is wacko. He is so obsessed with my aunt, I think he's killing people he believes will taint her." explained Rose, "Besides, I must go tell my mom, aunt and great-grandma before he does something else."

"Tell me about it!" demanded Carol.

"There's no time. Come on, now."

Rose peered into the hallway to see if Brad concealed himself in the passageway.

"Is the coast clear?" asked Carol.

"I think he's gone, but we better keep our eyes open," Rose replied, looking both ways again.

"Let's run over to your house now."

"Oh no, I'm not making a mistake again. I'm calling Mr. Stewart, Terrence's son, the police chief. I'm telling him everything," Rose announced.

"Well do it fast, while you walk outside to your place," Carol demanded.

Rose scanned the room and found her cell phone on the table. She grabbed it and pulled Carol with her out the front door of Brad's apartment to find they were only three houses away from Rose's house. She phoned the number she had seen Terrence dial only a few days ago.

"Hello, Mr. Stewart, Rose Brooksfield here. Uh huh... sorry, Chief Stewart...Oh, good! Then this should be easier, "Rose exclaimed. "I need some help. You won't believe what happened to Carol and me. We were kidnapped! What do you mean you knew I was missed?"

Carol urgently pulled at Rose's arm, but Rose continued to listen to what Chief Stewart said on the phone and didn't acknowledge her.

"Rose, listen to me. I remember the car parked in your driveway. The car is Sergeant Detective Owens' blue Honda accord. He drove the car in the parking lot at the Pope Hotel. My dad has an Accord too, so I can distinguish what kind of car it is," Carol urgently insisted, as they continued walking to Lily's house.

"What? What did you just say, Carol?" Rose asked, as part of what Carol said registered.

"I said the car belongs to Sergeant Detective Owens. The blue Honda parked in your mom's driveway is his. Which means Brad probably has taken everyone in your house prisoner," Carol exclaimed worried.

"You're sure? Of course you are," Rose exclaimed then she said into her cell phone before hanging up. I know who the serial killer is, and he is at my house...No! I'm not waiting...Sure, you can send your force to wrap this up, but by then I will have stopped him. I'm not letting him kill anyone else in my family."

"You shouldn't speak to the police chief that way, when you want his help."

"What was I supposed to do? A bad cop is here, in my house. There is no time to waste; he could be killing everyone in my family," Rose cried, sounding terrified but determined.

Rose lifted the garage door halfway, being careful not to make any noise and then quickly ducked under.

"Why are we in the garage?" asked Carol whispering following her in.

"My dad has a gun safe hidden in here. He showed me one time. There's a gun and bullets in here."

"Are you crazy? You can't use a gun! Wait for the cops."

"I can't wait. I'm not going to let Brad kill my mom too. I already lost a mom to prison because she was a drug addict and now a dad to this freak show. He's not killing my mom, Lily as well."

"You don't even know how to use a gun. You could be killed. Please, Rose, wait."

"I know how to use a gun. My dad believed in equality and he thought I should be able to shoot a gun. I'm going to stop him."

Removing the gun from the safe, Rose loaded it with bullets. Rose looked down the barrel as she pointed it in Carol's direction.

"Hey, watch where you point that thing," Carol exclaimed. "For the record I'm still against this, but I'm coming."

Rose and Carol crept in through the back door. Rose motioned for Carol to be quiet and cautiously follow her. As Rose and Carol neared the living room, they stopped and listen to the conversation.

"Looking for that nitwit police officer Rogers? You're going to be waiting a long time." explained Silas laughing, "Let's put it this way. I didn't use the facilities. I checked on my earlier handy work. Emmett Rogers is still out cold, and will be another of your victims, Crown Attorney Kelly. It's a terrible shame how you hid your homicidal tendencies all this time and then snapped."

"I'm not going in there. Someone has to stay outside and get help if needed. That's where I'm headed now," Carol insisted, whispering.

"Fine, then go to outside near the garage and keep watch," Rose whispered back. "I can handle Brad Owens. Direct Chief Stewart to me when he arrives.

"I don't want to leave you alone," Carol protested.

"Come out with me and wait. Please Rose it is too dangerous. Wait for Chief Stewart!" "I'll be fine. I have the gun and someone has to stop him."

"Fine, but I don't like you doing this alone, so be careful," Carol advised, leaving extremely quietly.

Rose glanced around and found Emmett Rogers. His head was blooded and he was out cold. She slapped his face, managing to rouse him as he blinked his eyes.

"What happened?" he whispered to Rose while he rubbed his head.

"Silas hit you over the head is my guess. They are both in on it. Silas Rentford is Brad Owens' cousin, and he has been covering up for him all along while he committed crime after crime," deduced Rose.

"How do you know this?"

"It's a guess... maybe more like a hunch. But I'm sure I'm right. He'll make a move. We need to stop him now," exclaimed Rose, waving her gun.

"Where did you get the gun? You shouldn't brandish a gun you're only fifteen. Give it to me," demanded Emmett.

"I'll be able to make a perfect shot. My dad believed women should be able to protect themselves, so he used to take me to the pistol range. You don't need to worry," replied Rose whispering.

"I can't even see straight. I'm seeing double, but I can't let a child take a suspect into custody. Give me the gun."

"I'm not a child and I'm not giving you a choice.

"You said it yourself, Detective Rogers, you can't even see straight. And if you think for a moment I'm going to let those psychos harm my family anymore, you can think again. Besides, as Grandma Katha says, I'm a Kelly, and Kelly women are brave," Rose whispered, and then they both remained quiet for a moment to overhear and see the rest of the conversation.

"If you looked after your cousin, how did he murder so many people?" sarcastically inquired Lily. "You say you were entrusted to look after Brad by your Uncle? What happened to him? Did Brad murder him too?"

"Don't be ridiculous! Brad wouldn't kill his father," Silas argued, as he looked over at Brad for confirmation.

Seeing Brad's head go down in shame, he continued, "Oh my God, she's right! You did kill Uncle Kelvin. What the hell is wrong with you?" Silas questioned, "Does family mean nothing to you? After everything we've done to protect you? Is all of this about your obsession with my girl? You understood how I felt about Amelia. How could you?"

"She is mine. I told you she's my Angel," ranted Brad

"Your Angel? The one you always rant about? Amelia's that Angel? When did you decide she was your Angel? Was it the summer Amelia and I met? Did you decide then and there you needed to have what I wanted?" Silas angrily exclaimed.

Pausing trying to get his anger under control but not succeeding Silas continued, "Of course it was you. You always wanted what I wanted. You took my best toys when we were small and claimed they were yours. I let you keep them. Anything you wanted was yours, for the asking. I felt sorry you were stuck with your father and Titus, the wonder boy. Now I must clean up your messes again. Why, Brad, why? Why do you push me this way and test my loyalty? It isn't necessary, you are my family. I'll pick you. Always! Now because of your foolishness Amelia's going to die, and not just Amelia, but all of them. Does cleaning up after you never end? Now I must kill a teenage girl to protect you. I assume she's back at your apartment?"

Rose saw Brad nodded strangely submissive. She then saw Silas untie Brad and hold the gun on Lily Katha and Terrence.

"It's time for me to finish this. I'm sorry, Amelia, I did love you. I'll make your death as painless as possible."

Brad registered the words that Amelia would die. He then grabbed Silas' gun as it went off with a huge bang.

Rose heard Brad yell, "No! No, she won't die! I won't let you kill her!"

Rose took a firing stance and the gun went off just as Silas' gun also fired. Rose looked on in horror, hoping against hope, that her bullet wasn't the one which seemed to hit Silas' chest. Silas lay profusely bleeding, his heart pumping the blood out of his body. His body shuttered a death rattle and he ceased breathing.

Brad cradled his cousin in his arm crying, "Wake up, Silas! Quit fooling around. You can't leave me. You are my only family. You look after me. Who will keep after me and make me good? Don't die, Silas! Please, don't leave me. Don't you die on me! Please Silas don't die! Don't go! You always looked after me, even when we were kids, and father would lock me in the closet you'd get me out of the dark. I should have picked you. You should come first, but we can change all of that if you give me a chance. Please, don't leave me in the dark, Silas," begged Brad.

Brad continued anguish in every tone as he begged, pleaded, and cajoled Silas to no avail. He began rocking Silas's body in his arms back and forth, a pitiful figure sitting on the floor, his chest covered in blood from Silas' wound. His arms clenched in an unbreakable hold around Silas' body, as he pulled him to his chest.

"Give it up, Owens. He's dead," Emmett yelled.

An eerie howl emitted from Silas' lips, as he realized what Emmett said was true. Silas was unmoving and therefore dead. Brad looked stunned and unseeing, as Emmett then said in a moderated tone grabbing Brad's hands behind his body he recited, "You have the right to remain silent and refuse to answer questions. Do you understand?"

Brad said nothing; he just continued staring at Silas' body.

"Anything you do say may be used against you in a court of law. Do you understand?"

Brad continued to stare at Silas.

"You have the right to consult an attorney before speaking to the police, and to have an attorney present during questioning now, or in the future. Do you understand?"

Brad continued staring at the body of his now dead cousin not responding, beyond perceiving sound. He moaned a low pitiful moan from time to time but no reply is heard from Brad.

"If you cannot afford an attorney, one will be appointed for you before any questioning if you wish. Do you understand?" Emmett continued, "If you decide to answer questions now without an attorney present, you will still have the right to stop answering at any time, until you talk to an attorney. Do you understand? Knowing and understanding your rights as I have explained them to you, will you answer my questions without an attorney present?"

"Mr. Owen appears out of it. I don't think he understands anything you said," Rose explained. "Did I kill the other one?"

"No, Rose, the bullet came from a trajectory which could only have come from Brad's gun. Glance at the wall there and you'll find your bullet."

"How could I have missed?" demanded Rose pretending that shooting off a gun was not a big deal, "Not that I wanted to be the one to kill anyone, but I thought I was a better shot."

Rose's speech was interrupted by Lily who ran at Rose with her arms wide open and hugged her.

"Rose, oh Rose," Lily cried with joy at seeing her daughter in one piece safe and home.

"I'm okay, Mom."

"I was terrified, baby. I'm so glad you are okay," Lily exclaimed wiping back tears and then running her hands down Rose's arms to convince herself Rose was real.

"Rose, oh my, I was so worried when Lily told me he had you," Amelia expressed hugging her niece.

"Baby girl, we're all glad you're okay," Katha exclaimed.

"Did he hurt you?" Lily asked checking Rose's face.

"No, Carol and I now own a few rope burns, but we will be fine."

"Rope burns? Let me see." Lily demanded, "Oh, my poor baby. You must have been terrified.

"I was fine. I told you I was fine," Rose claimed, "Besides; I was the one who tried to save you."

"So you did," Lily acknowledged.

Katha exclaimed, "You came through, like all Kelly women do in a pinch, because we are all or one…"

"And one for all!" Katha, Amelia, Lily and Rose responded at the same time, hugging one another.

"Can an old man get in on this family hug, Katha?" begged Terrence.

"I guess we could include you a little, Terrence. Sorry you felt left out of the loop," Lily apologized.

"Yes, sorry, dear," Katha apologized hugging Terrence "But you'll have to get used to it when we Kelly women are together we are one."

"I wouldn't have it any other way," Terrence responded hugging Katha back.

~0~

Chapter 26 - Life Goes On

Emmett tried to march a despondent Brad Owens to a

waiting police car. Brad inconsolable screamed and cried, fighting to stay with the body. Emmett with great difficulty got him in the back of the waiting car.

"Patrolman Barnes, Sergeant Detective Owens has confessed to the murders. He has been read his rights but he has not responded. He is to be taken to hospital for a mental evaluation. He will be treated with the utmost respect. This case won't be thrown out because of any police wrong doing. Is that clear?" demanded Emmett from Alan.

"Yes, sir. Good work, sir. The Police chief has told me to relay this message, sir. I'm repeating the edict word for word, so do not blame the messenger."

"Get to the hospital for a scan and medical attention now. You are to go with Patrolman Appleton now. Is that clear?" reiterated Patrolman Barnes. "Then I expect a full report on why a fifteen-year-old girl, fired a gun to protect an officer."

"Totally clear. Please tell the chief I'm on my way," Emmett acknowledged realizing he had no choice but to obey.

"You're in a bit of hot water, Emmett. Can I do anything?" Alan inquired.

"No, but thanks. Point me in Patrolman Appleton's direction," Emmett answered.

"Tell the chief and Patrolman Appleton I'm driving him instead," Lily exclaimed after overhearing this.

"What about your daughter? Doesn't she need you?" probed Emmett worried about Rose.

"Quit making excuses and get going, Sergeant Detective Rogers. I'm fine with Grandma Katha, Amelia, and of course Mr. Stewart," Rose demanded crossing her arms, appearing remarkably like her mother's stance.

"Kid, you can call me Emmett and so can your mother. I think you have earned the right. Are you okay, Quick Draw McGraw?" asked Emmett, "Maybe you should be checked out too."

"Who's Quick Draw McGraw? Oh wait a minute, that is from an old cartoon. Mom quotes him too; I prefer Annie Oakley. I'm fine, Emmett but thanks."

"Are you sure, pumpkin? I had planned on making a run to the hospital with both of you," Lily commented.

"Mom, I'm fine besides I'll stay with Grandma Katha. She needs me."

"Are you sure?" Lily asked.

"I'll be fine, Mom."

"Okay, we're leaving now. I'll be back soon," Lily said feeling reluctant to leave her daughter. "I love you, Rose." "Would you just go make sure the hero is okay?" Rose exclaimed. "Bye, my little heroine," Lily said to Rose.

Lily mouthed to Katha 'Keep her safe'.

"Rose, I was so scared, but I stayed in the garage. Is the drama all over now? Are we safe?" Carol enquired, coming out of the garage as Emmett left with Lily.

"Oh, I am sorry, Carol. I forgot you were there."

"You forgot I was there? Thanks a lot. I could have died for all you cared."

"Sorry, Carol. It's all over. Emmett arrested Detective Brad Owens. Don't go in the house though. Detective Silas Rentford is dead," Rose explained.

"You shot him?" Carol queried shocked, her hand to her mouth.

"No, I tried, but I missed. I was so scared I didn't shoot straight. I thought Silas would kill them all and it would have been my fault, since I missed."

Rose started crying.

"Rose, my baby doll, you did save us. You distracted Silas," Katha cried overhearing.

"I did?" asked Rose sounding surprised.

"Yes, you did," Katha answered.

"You are a hero, Rose, or is it heroine? I can never remember," Carol responded trying to cheer up her crying friend.

"The word is heroine, Carol." Katha informed and then announced, "And you are right, Rose is a heroine."

"What can I tell my parents?" Carol asked, "They will be so mad at me,"

"Tell them the truth Carol. When they hear you were kidnapped, they'll forget most of the rest," advised Katha.

"You still didn't explain how you wound up Brad's prisoner."

"That's your fault, Rose," Carol claimed.

"My fault? How is it my fault?" Rose demanded. "I was worried about you and came to make sure you were safe. He grabbed me outside of your house because you didn't call the police," Carol explained.

"I guess then it was a little my fault. You can blame me when you tell your parents if you want, but what really happened to you?"

"Considering it was entirely your fault, I think I will," Carol insisted. "Anyway, I got off the bus to come back here; when you didn't answer he grabbed me. Was that because he had you trussed in the chair?"

"Yes, I think he had me by then. I wasn't in Grandma's house more than five minutes and he had me tousled up like a turkey," Rose replied. "And then what happened? How did you get back here?"

"I got off the bus like I said and my mom was there, she made me go home and go to my dad's."

Carol then related to Rose and Katha, what happened when Carol got to her dad's.

"Daddy said that he had to go out and I whined that I had just gotten there, but Daddy did his spiel like he always does:.. And you'll be here when I get back. The office needs me. I've got more security contracts; I have people depending on me. I have to go to work .he complained. So I told him... Okay goodbye. I don't matter. You don't want to spend time with me. So Daddy, offered to bring me a present. Like presents were all I wanted? Why doesn't he understand I want to see him more often?" Carol bemoaned.

"Parents don't always understand that work takes time away from loved ones. They think there will always be time for family. I'm sure Gerald loves you, Carol," Katha answered.

"He did promise to take me to opening day at the fair, this weekend. I hope his work doesn't get in the way ,again!" Carol answered, "After he promised me to take me he said he loved me and he would come back for me in a few hours. Do you think he'll be so mad he won't take me to the fair?"

"I'm sure he'll be so happy you are safe and he'll let all the anger go," Katha reassured.

"What Grandma Katha means is she will make sure he does," Rose said conspiratorially as Katha smiled.

"So what happened next, Carol?"

"So after my dad left I called a taxi. I took the cab to your grandma's house. Brad said you were hurt and needed me. I was such a fool to believe him. I tried to get away but he clocked me. When I woke up I was tied to a chair."

"Carol, I think we need to get you checked out at the hospital, if you were unconscious." Katha insisted, "I'll tell your parents to meet us there."

"I don't want to go to the hospital," Carol complained, "I don't need to go there. My head hurts a little, but I'll be fine."

"Head injuries can be more serious than people know. I think it's a good idea. Besides think of the case it will make with your mom and dad. They'll see you were kidnapped and hurt, making them reconsider becoming angry. They'll forgive you leaving without telling them."

"Fine, but I'm doing this under protest."

Katha drove them to the hospital and they found themselves there within twenty minutes. They were met by Gerald and Charlene Banks, two worried parents who stood together arm-and-arm.

"Weird they haven't got along not since the divorce, Rose."

"They were worried about you. I called them before we got in the car. Your parents love you," Katha added.

"Mom, Dad I'm so sorry, but I had to try and save Rose. That man could have killed her."

"No, we are sorry baby. If we hadn't been fighting and worried about our own concerns, you could have told us what worried you," Francine replied, poking Gerald.

"Your mother is right. Honey, are you okay? Katha said you were kidnapped and hit on the head,"

Gerald probed searching her eyes.

"Gerald, she should go in and get checked into the hospital. We're keeping her from being checked out."

"Sorry, of course you are right, Francine."

"Come on, sweetie. Let us go get you checked out by a doctor."

"Thank you, Katha. I don't know how I will ever thank you for saving my daughter," Gerald replied, shaking Katha's hand.

"The person you have to thank is my great-granddaughter. She untied herself, got free, and untied Carol, then she saved her entire family from that crazy police officer," Katha answered.

"See, what did I tell you, Gerald? Rose is a perfect friend for Carol. She's sweet she's kind and she saved our daughter."

"She wouldn't have gotten into any of this fix if it wasn't for Rose and her family."

"Gerald, Rose saved her. Take that back. Now!"

"Francine is right; you are a wonderful friend to our Carol Thank you, Rose," Gerald answered then turning to Francine he said, "Happy now, Francine?"

"I promise we'll talk some more later," Francine said to Katha.

"See you later, Rose," Carol declared, smiling as Rose gave her the thumbs up sign.

~0~

Chapter 27 -
Epilogue-Should
I or Shouldn't I?

Three months later

"Rose, the brief commitment trial is completed. Brad Owens will be locked away for the near future. He will be taken to Pinecrest and get a suite in the forensic unit. I don't think they'll be along drawn out trial."

"Good, but what is Pinecrest?" Rose asked.

"It's a hospital for the criminal insane, here in Ontario. I do think, however, that his mind is broken. Losing his cousin Silas was the last draw for him."

"He's a serial killer. I have no pity for him. Do you want me to be sorry for him Mom? Why? He killed Dad," Rose asked shocked.

"Actually, I do feel sorry for him. What came out in his commitment trial was horrific. The terrible things that happened to him as a child and young adult broke his spirit."

"None of that excuses his behaviour. Lots of people have troubled childhoods, and they don't go crazy and kill people," complained Rose.

"I don't condone his actions, Rose, but I can still have empathy for him. Compassion is always possible."

"You are a better person than I. I don't want to ever think or hear about him ever again."

"School starts the weekend after next, which means we have two glorious weeks to have some fun, "Lily began before being interrupted.

"Can we go somewhere now, Mom? It's been so hard staying here. People still give me odd looks and frown. When they see me, they start talking in quiet whispers," Rose complained.

"The whole thing has been hard. This has been horrific, on all of us," Lily commented, looking at a vacation brochure.

"I wish Emmett would come around again. I liked him."

"You call him Emmett now, instead of Detective Rogers?" Lily asked hiding a smile.

"Yes, you heard him he told me to call him Emmett. He came around so many times to see you after the shooting. Did you say or do something? Emmett isn't coming around anymore."

"Well. yes, I did, he appeared interested in me but I'm mourning your dad," Lily admitted.

Rose stared at her mom, noticing, for the first time how sad she looked. Rose felt guilty for not realizing her mother had been suffering too. She decided her mom's pain needed to be acknowledged too.

"Mom, I've been selfish thinking about all my own pain. I know how much you loved Daddy. We both miss him so. But if there's ever a time when someone wants to like date you... you should go for it."

"I think it's too soon, but thank you, baby doll. Did anyone tell you, you are one of the most considerate, sweet daughters around?" replied Lily hugging Rose.

"Don't call me baby doll in front of other people, you make me sound five years old. Besides some people think it is a sexist comment. Please don't tell anyone I said you could date again either; it would ruin my reputation," Rose replied with a wink.

"Would you like to spend two weeks in a beautiful beach cottage with your Aunt Amelia, Katha, Terrence and say, your friend Carol and I?" questioned Lily with a smile.

"Really, Mom? Two weeks at the beach? And Carol, can come?" Rose requested excitedly.

"If her parents say she can go. Carol has been an incredible friend to you."

"No kidding, she is the best friend ever. She told off Billy Robertson and Nathan Patel," Rose admitted "She has one mean tongue. Her backhand is solid too."

"Why did you mention Carol's backhand? She didn't hit them?"

Rose nodded.

"What did Billy and Nathan do? Why did she get so mad?"

"Billy joked and said all the women in my family were black widows; even if we didn't kill we got others to kill for us. I hate him. I wanted to punch him too," Rose admitted.

"Rose, you know violence is never the answer." Lily was appalled at Billy's behaviour but worried about Rose's reaction to this kind of bullying.

"I do understand that, Mother. No hitting, no matter what, unless your person is threatened and you can't find another way," Rose parroted.

"Well, yes."

"Well, don't get mad at Carol and not let her come with us, but she threw her drink at Nathan."

"Why did she do that?" solicited Lily. "Nathan tried to cop a feel of my breast, but before I could do anything, Carol had thrown her drink at him and implied he committed a criminal offense. She requested whether she should be calling Sergeant Detective Rogers. Nathan got scared," Rose laughed.

"Nathan should have known to commit a sexual assault on someone is a criminal offense. How dare he touch you like that?" Lily replied with a furrowed brow I'll pick up the phone and..."

"Mom, it's handled. Besides, Billy appeared angry too. Billy made him apologized to me. Then he gave Nathan a black eye."

"I hope you're not glorifying a black eye. I mean, I know I'm angry, but to hit someone..."

"Violence is never the solution," repeated Rose sounding less than enthused.

"Thank you for telling me this, Rose. I appreciate your confidence, but I think you should lay charges. He could do this to someone else."

"No worries, it's all good now Mom. But if it will make you happy, I could tell Emmett and see what he thinks," Rose answered, "Can I go call Carol now and invite her?"

"Sure, go ahead and call Carol. We leave the day after tomorrow," Lily yelled after her. "Make sure you tell Carol's mom and dad we will be home after Labour Day."

"I'll do that, Mom."

The doorbell rang and Rose ran quickly past Lily, pushing her out of the way to answer it. She found Carol on the doorstep, followed by Sergeant Detective Rogers.

"Come in, Sergeant Detective Rogers." Rose invited politely, spoiling it by yelling, "Mom, your cop is here!"

"Rose Brooksfield!" Lily exclaimed waving her finger at Rose.

Rose brought Carol into the living room and they began to talk in excited whispers giggling.

"Rose?" Lily called. "Yes, Mother?"

"Grandma Katha brought over some homemade molasses cookies at noon. They're in the cookie jar. Help yourself to two cookies, but leave room for dinner. Please ask Carol if she'd like to stay for dinner too, if it's okay with her folks."

"'Kay, we're going to my room."

"Brad Owens will remain under criminal psychiatric care for the rest of his life. The sentence to keep him there came down today," Emmett stated without preamble, as he stepped into the room.

"One of my colleagues called me and told me," Lily confessed.

"One less worry for you now; it's all over. He can't harm your family anymore."

"How's the head doing? I haven't seen you since you came by those few times, after the ordeal," Lily exclaimed with reproach.

"It's much better, thanks. I'm sorry I didn't call. I wanted to give you space," Emmett answered, hanging his head in regret.

"Why? Because you kissed me in the hospital waiting room?"

"Let see... your husband had just died, a serial killer, a killer – who happened to be a cop – had taken you and other family members' hostage and I kiss you? I felt like a heel for forcing my attentions on you," Emmett replied sheepishly. "And you didn't seem all that welcoming when I came to visit afterwards."

"You didn't force anything on me. I liked it," admitted Lily as Emmett smiled.

"Good," Emmett replied looking around for anyone. He then requested, "Is Amelia here?"

"You too?" asked Lily sounding disappointed at the thought of Emmett being attracted to Amelia.

"I don't think you understand!" Emmett insisted.

Lily stared at him and frowned. "You don't, do you? You like Amelia. Why did you kiss me? Go! Get the lady you want. Amelia is at her store."

"I wanted to make sure no one was around to interrupt us, when I do this," exclaimed Emmett passionately kissing her full on the lips.

Lily swooned for a moment, melting into the kiss. Drowning in the moment, she couldn't sense where she stood. It felt like she stood on thin air, or on a cloud. She deepened the kiss and so did Emmett. The whole world disappeared. She felt like tearing off her clothes then and there, but reality set in and she felt guilty. This was not right! She remembered Rose upstairs and her dead husband, Horace. She pulled out of the kiss. Her lips were swollen and she felt the need to kiss him again, but Lily was terrified. It was too soon wasn't it!? Her body was now at war with her mind. What am I thinking? My husband has been dead for only three months. I have Rose to think of, to put first. I can do this... No! I shouldn't do this! Should I? No, I shouldn't. It's just not right.

"It's too soon, isn't it?" probed Emmett, sensing the change in Lily's mood.

"Yes," Lily babbled breathlessly. "Er... uh no, it isn't. Hell, I don't know. This is all too soon. I can't believe I'm even considering having a relationship with you."

"I'll take this one day at a time. We can find out all about each other. Please? I'm attracted to you, Lily. Give me a chance? Give us a chance," Emmett pleaded boldly.

"This came totally out of nowhere. I'm a widow, I'm supposed to be thinking only of my dead husband, grieving for him, not thinking about another man." Lily complained, exasperated with herself, "I loved Horace."

"But you are attracted to me, despite yourself aren't you?" Emmett persisted taking her hand.

"Yes I am. I like you, too and yes, I'm attracted to you. If we start down this road dating, we will have to take it slow and keep it quiet for a while. I won't have any more gossip hurt my daughter, or the rest of the family," Lily answered, pulling her hand away from Emmett's, "I can't believe I'm even considering this. My husband died only three months ago."

"I wouldn't hurt them or you for the world," Emmett explained. "I respect you and them too much."

"I'm going away for two weeks for a family vacation. Rose needs this vacation and so do I. We can't begin any relationship until after our vacation."

"I think I can wait until you get back," Emmett answered hugging her again.

Emmett soundly kissed her again. Lily felt like she was flying, soaring high in the sky. Her limbs turned to Jell-O and she felt like she never had before in her lifetime. Neither Horace, nor William, had ever made her experience the world this way. What did that mean? She felt more alive in this kiss; it caressed every neuron ping in her body. She was truly lost in this moment, as the whole world faded away.

"You owe me five bucks. I told you Sergeant Detective Rogers appeared interested in my mother," Rose bragged smugly.

"You implied he was interested in your mother. You didn't tell me your mom might be interested in him," Carol complained, staring at Lily and Emmett kissing,. "Wow! Talk about a sizzling kiss. Someday I want someone to kiss me like that," Carol concluded. "It reminded me of the way Damon kissed Elena, on the Vampire Diaries."

"Well, even if she is interested in Emmett, she still loves my dad. She just needs someone to be her partner and hold her hand," Rose replied offended.

"He wants to do more than kiss," Carol answered.

"Yuck, Carol! Please don't talk about my mother that way," Rose admonished. "And she's still in love with my dad."

"Sorry. I do think he is attracted to her though."

"I had a dream about my dad."

"That's a good thing?" examined Carol worried.

"Yes, I think he wanted to tell me something important."

"What did father want to tell you?" Carol asked.

"My dad seemed so alive in the dream. He smiled the special smile he had only for me, which said he loved me. He motioned for me to come closer to him. I went. You don't know how incredibly wonderful it felt to see him again. I've missed him so much. He told me..."I'm dead, Rosey." I nodded and he continued. "You know this is a dream. I don't have a lot of time to talk to you. I love you sweetie, you and your mother Lily. I want you to listen to me. I was a heel. Your mother Lily, I betrayed her horribly. She was so good to both of us and I made your mother suffer. She needs to be happy."

"I don't want your mom to be lonely ever again. Let her find what she needs…who she needs. Rose. Give her a chance to be happy when it comes."

Carol cocked her head and then shook it as if she couldn't believe what she was hearing then seem to accept it as she said "Wow! Amaze balls. I mean, he talked to you from the grave."

"He also said he sent someone for her. Do you think he meant Sergeant Detective Rogers? I think he is someone who might make her happy. Someday! He told me I should call him Emmett. Emmett will be good to her. He'll treat my mom well and make her happy… at least I hope so. But he's not my dad!"

"I liked your dad, Rose, but he wasn't kind to your mom, maybe Emmett will make her happier.

"You know, Carol, although, Mom can take care of herself, I guess it would be great if someone else that could do that for her once in a while."

"It would be wonderful for your mother," Carol exclaimed. "You are generous to your mom's needs. Most kids would have hated their mom thinking about dating so soon."

"Yuck! That sounds icky!"

"That isn't what I meant to say!" Carol complained.

"Like I said, Dad wants her to be happy, so why shouldn't I? She took me on, and became my mother when she didn't have to make me her daughter. I suppose it's the least I can do," Rose continued, like she struggled with the idea, but wanted to do the right thing.

"So did you dream anything else?"

"Yes. My dad told me that he loved me again, and called me Rosebud. It was his favourite name for me. He said have a good life, be happy, and suddenly he was gone."

"Your dad is correct. My mom would be lost without my dad to do things for her. Even though they're divorced, he still comes over to fix things," replied Carol, clearly misunderstanding the comment.

"That's not quite what I meant, but I guess it's good too," Rose replied. "Let's go and leave them. This is kind of gross and liable to scare my psyche if we talk about it anymore."

Rose and Carol scampered up the stairs laughing and went to Rose's room.

"I'm excited about going to the beach with you and my family. Isn't it cool Mom requested that you come with us?" Rose exclaimed.

"I wonder how many guys will be at the beach? I'm taking my tiny red bikini," Carol commented."

"You hope the guy that was at the beach last time we went looks at you again," replied Rose giggling.

"Like you didn't like the way Giorgio looked at you?" laughed Carol.

"Did you see that loser Derek stare at us? I overheard him say to his friends we were hot."

"Yah, like we'd ever look at that guy." Carol laughed again.

"Do you remember Rebecca's slip?"

"Slip? The girl grabbed for her bikini bottoms. I felt sorry for her, but tie it in a knot, or knots," Carol answered cattily. "Remember the fireworks for Canada Day?"

"Yes, and I remember the moves Kyle tried to put on you." Carol started laughing, like she couldn't stop.

"Yes, it was funny. The way he laid afterwards in the sand. You really pushed him," Rose replied also giggling.

Downstairs Lily and Emmett heard the laughter.

"It's wonderful to hear Rose laughing again."

"She's been through a lot. Have fun at the beach. Remember though, I'll be waiting when you get back, I'll be waiting," Emmett promised. "Goodbye for now."

"Stay for dinner. I'll order Chinese, but this time, we'll skip the serial killer," invited Lily laughing.

"I'd be happy too."

THE END OR IS IT?

Look for Emmett and Lily further adventures and the rest of the Clan Kelly's fun in Book 2 of the Kelly Murder Mysteries - A Diller a Dollar a Real Dead Scholar, on the next page.

~0~

A Diller A Dollar
A Really Dead
Scholar

Book 2 of the Kelly Murder Mysteries

A novel

Written by S. G. Lee

Copyright 2016 © Sheilagh G. Lee

First Edition 2016

Published at CreateSpace

Copyright © 2016 by Sheilagh G. Lee

ISBN (13): 978-1-987977-06-6 (paperback)

ISBN-10: 1987977068

ISBN 978-0-9936531-4-8 (e-book)

A Diller A Dollar A Really Dead Scholar

Chapter 1 - Real Life Is Worse than a Movie

'A diller, a dollar, a ten o 'clock scholar; what makes you come so soon? You used to come at ten o 'clock, but now you come at noon!'~Nursery Rhyme, Author Unknown

Rose

Rose arrived early for choir with Carol, by her side. She wasn't aware of what she would have done without her constant side kick, and best friend Carol in the last few weeks. Carol had amazingly defended her making her proud to be her friend. However, the calendar said the second week of school and the whispers still continued. Gossip was continually passed around about the murders but especially at school.

Rose was tired of all of the innuendoes and speculation, she thought. Her father had died, no not simply died; he had been murdered by a serial killer. This should have garnered some sympathy, for both the circumstances of her father's death, and the manner, but all she caught was jokes about the position he had been found. Rose guessed finding him naked with his secretary; who he'd been having an affair with led to the gossip, but she was so tired of all of it. If that wasn't bad enough though, everyone had to find out this serial killer had killed many people. He had killed Rose's Great Uncle Jerry, Aunt Aerilla, and her cousins Robert and Grace before Aunt Amelia came to Happy Valley. Last year he had murdered Aunt Amelia's husband Jack and killed her little boy Sam.

Continuing on his killing spree, he had killed Aunt Amelia's employee Megan and the homeless guy Mr. Young. All of this simply because he was obsessed, horribly obsessed with Aunt Amelia, all of so senseless and stupid. She grew tired of talking about the incident. Who did she kid? She couldn't even talk about her father's death to the shrink, her mother made her visit. People came up to her at school and wanted gruesome details. Or they wanted to know more about the capture of the serial killer. Grandma Katha called him the cop in wolf's clothing, and some other names Rose didn't care to repeat.

She wanted to scream. Tom Rose hated and loved Happy Valley, Ontario, both at the same time. It was after all the place she was born, but the buildings were old here and the town was dying as prosperity had flown along, with a number of businesses that employed people. Would there even be a job for Rose when she wanted one? With the loss of jobs, people's attitudes had changed or maybe they'd just revealed themselves to be small minded and frankly she was tired of it. As soon as she could she was going away to university and then she'd live in another city when she graduated, visiting Lily, Grandma Katha and Amelia regularly.

Rose just wanted to be Rose Brooksfield again...not Rose Brooksfield whose father had been murdered. Wasn't it bad enough that her mother Lily Brooksfield, or Lily Kelly as she had always called herself, Mom now dated the cop, who had investigated her Dad's murder.

What did it mean about Mom's true feelings for her Dad, Horace, that she had moved on so quickly? Rose had encouraged Mom, but she had been rash. Mom should be thinking of her Dad not this Emmett Rogers all the time.

Now all Rose ever heard from Mom was Emmett this and Emmett that. What about Dad had she forgotten him? And if she had forgotten him...what did that mean for Rose? After all she was Lily's adopted daughter not her flesh and blood. If Mom got married to Emmett, would there be room for Rose? What would happen if Mom decided to have children with Emmett? Rose bit her lip she had to stop thinking this way as Grandma Katha declared this borrowed trouble, but still Rose worried.

Rose looked over at Carol as she flicked her long blonde hair out of her eyes. Rose thought that Carol dying her hair blonder had made Carol's eyes look bluer and her fair skin even more ivory looking. Carol seemed to be getting a lot more looks from guys too. What was up with that? Maybe Rose should cut her long hair? She didn't want to look exactly like her best friend from the back. Maybe she should make her hair reddish brown like her mom, Lily's. Then they'd be more alike, with hair and eyes matching in colour.

Rose suddenly looked up from her thoughts as she noticed the light bulb appeared out in the hallway near the gym. How odd she thought she wished the janitor would change the bulb quickly. It was creepy here at six a.m., even with Carol at her side. As they reached the choir room, Rose was relieved to find the light on in the room. But where was Mr. Scholar the choir teacher?

"I don't understand why Mr. Scholar called a six-thirty a.m. practice and can't be here when we get to the room," complained Carol loudly. When Rose didn't answer right away she whined. "Aren't you talking to me yet?"

"I had to catch my breath, besides my leg hurts and I have a cramp in my leg. All the fast cycling on my bike pulled a muscle or something in my leg, and now my stomach hurts."

"Why don't you walk around the room and get rid of your cramp? I'm going to sit here and snooze. Wake me up when someone comes. I don't want anyone to catch me sleeping," Carol replied.

Rose walked around the room. The cramp in her leg, didn't seem to ease and neither did her stomach cramp. Rose's shoe slipped and she surprised herself, stepping into something sticky in a dark corner of the room. Great, now something was on my brand new shoes. Icky she thought. She glanced down, that looked like blood. It couldn't be? Could it? Did someone get a nose bleed, perhaps Mr. Scholar?

She peered behind the desk looking for the source of the blood and saw to her great shock Mr. Scholar lay dead. A knife protruded in the place where his heart should have been. Rose stared for a moment, not believing what her eyes saw. How could Mr. Scholar be lying dead, his chest bared open and nothing inside of him.

It seemed so unreal, like one of those movies she watched at Anna's. If her mother had known she viewed a chop movie, Rose would be in so much trouble. As it is she'd observed the movie with her hands over her eyes but this.... This was real....Mr. Scholar had obviously been murdered brutally murdered and his organs were gone. Was it his heart? Because Rose was sure that's where the teacher had declared it was in biology. Oh my God, what if the killer was still nearby? Rose scanned the room with her eyes seeking out all the spaces in the room where someone may hide. How could Carol be sitting dozing in a chair? Carol slept waiting for the choir teacher, while he lay dead near her.

"Rose what's wrong with you? Why did you gasp?" asked Carol, waking up and noticing Rose stillness and alarm at the same time.

"Carol he's dead," Rose indicated.

"I appreciate your dad is dead and we are all sad, but why bring that up now Rose?" Carol retorted exasperated.

"Mr. Scholar is here."

"I don't see him."

"That's because he's behind the desk. He's dead," Rose replied in a whisper.

"What did he have a heart attack or something? He's awful young for that, but I understand lots of people have sudden heart attacks," rambled Carol.

"Carol can you be quiet?"

"Well good grief, blame me like that it's not my fault the guy decided to have a heart attack!"

"He didn't have a heart attack, someone has killed him and I think they took his heart."

"Don't joke around Rose. It isn't funny."

"I'm not joking."

"Oh my God and we're still in this room alone. The killer could come back and get us, if he isn't in here all ready. I want my mother!" wailed Carol texting on her cell phone and getting no answer.

"We have to get out of here. People should be in the Gym, this time of morning they practice for basketball," Rose replied thinking on her feet. "I want my mom, too."

"Call her. Call your mother. Ask her what to do! She's always got an answer," demanded Carol.

"Let's lock the door first and put a chair in front of it. No one is in here now, but they might have a key for all we know."

"I did that already. I'm calling my Mom," stated Rose dialling.

"Mommy...,"cried Rose, as Lily answered.

"What is wrong Rose? What has happened?" demanded Lily.

"Mommy," Rose began incoherently through sobs.

"Take a deep breath now. Speak slowly and clearly. Tell your mother what is wrong," demanded Lily.

"Mr. Scholar the choir teacher is dead," Rose told her through the sobs.

"What? Did he have a heart attack? Are you okay? Of course, you're not okay. Do you want me to come to the school, baby? I can be there in ten minutes." Lily exclaimed quickly.

"Mommy he's bee....nnn he's bee....nnn mur...dered. Someone took his heart I think," Rose hiccupped.

"What? Who is with you? Are you safe?" demanded Lily.

"No one's here. It's just me and Carol. We are so scared, mom. I want you here."

"It will be okay baby, tell me everything, but first is the room safe you're in? Is it locked, and blocked?"

"Yes, we locked the door and blocked the door as well for now, but I don't want to stay here Mommy. It's icky and the killer might come back."

"What did she say? What did she say we should do?" demanded Carol.

"Quiet. I want to understand what my Mom said," implored Rose to Carol, and then speaking to Lily she replied.

"Sorry, go ahead mom."

"So tell me what happened," Lily demanded.

"I had a cramp in my leg, because I rode my bike to school fast. We raced then I won. I didn't see Mr. Scholar at first. I walked over near his desk and slipped in something sticky. Mommy, his blood is all over my new shoes. It's all over my shoes!" Rose answered in horror.

"Then what did you see?" prompted Lily trying to calm her daughter.

"I saw him. His chest is wide open and it is empty. There's nothing there, but tons of blood around and in him. I think his heart is gone. A knife is stuck in his chest," Rose sputtered a torrent of words, tumbling out of her.

"Okay, here is what I need you both to do to do. First, did Carol get near the body, or step in the blood?" demanded Lily.

"No. Lucky girl, Carol's shoes are fine. Mine are a total loss."

"Okay, did you track much blood, across the floor?" inquired Lily "And does the door own a lock that you can turn?"

"Blood?" Rose asked shock setting it as she stared at her shoes.

"Focus, Rose. I know it's difficult but you need to focus."

"Okay. Yes, we blocked the door I did track blood across the floor, since I had my shoes on, and yes the lock turns and then you can shut it behind you."

"Okay then carefully. Now take off your shoes and leave them on the floor. Be careful to walk only where blood isn't in your sock feet," Lily advised. "Walking to the door, I want you unblock the entrance, and then run don't walk, where people congregate. Also remain on the phone until you observe lots of people. Then take Carol's phone, while you still talking to me and call the police."

"I will Mom. We will run to the gym. They practice basketball there, early in the mornings."

Rose and Carol then flew down the hall and burst into the gym.

"Ladies, we are practice basketball here, would you like a detention?" shouted the coach.

"There's been a murder and we want to be with people," Carol shouted back belligerently.

"Carol Banks, if you made up something...," threatened the coach as he then saw Rose who spoke into Carols' cell phone.

"911. How can I direct your call?" asked the Operator 'Fire? Ambulance? Police?"

"Police, please?" Rose demanded, as she felt an eerie calm come over herself and heard herself give the details from far away.

"There's been a murder at Happy Valley High school. It's the choir teacher Mr. Scholar. He's be murdered in the choir room with a knife. Oh no, I sound like a clue game and it's not funny. It's horrible! He's dead," Rose stated horrified, a chill coming over her. She suddenly felt light-headed, and with blurry vision, quickly fell to the gym floor.

~0~

Chapter 2- But I'm the Crown Attorney

Lily arrived to the school. Her pale white complexion,

notable even more pasty showed fear in her every movement, as she ran up the steps and straight into a policeman guarding the front door.

"What do you mean I can't go in the school?" demanded Lily.

"It's a crime scene, Madame, so unless you're on staff here we have advised all parents to go and wait for their children at Pierre Elliot Trudeau Public School," the policeman stated. He was tall over six feet, muscular, and very broad across.

"Do you know who I am?" asked Lily imperiously.

"No, Madame, now as I said you needed to wait at Trudeau...," began the policeman before being interrupted by another plain clothes police officer.

"Let her through Alan. That's the Crown attorney, Lily Kelly," Sergeant Detective Daniel Brown explained. Daniel Brown was like Alan very tall, but closer to six feet five. They must do weight training in their off time Lily thought, noting he too had large muscles and chest. He had the look of a descendant of Scotland and Lily could imagine him in a kilt the way he moved. She then wondered how she had thought of anything else, but getting to Rose in those few minutes.

"I'm terribly sorry, Madame Crown attorney!" stated patrolman Alan Barnes.

"That's okay, simply let me in there, now!" Lily pleaded, and then she added, "Please."

"We've called an ambulance," Alan explained.

"I thought the victim was dead? Shouldn't we merely have had a coroner's van?" Lily asked puzzled.

"Lily, I'm sorry but it's for your daughter, Rose," 'Dan replied.

"What do you mean it's for Rose? What happened? Did someone hurt her? Tell me she's going to be okay!" demanded Lily panicking.

"She collapsed. She was unconscious, but she's awake now. I'm sure she'll be okay once they take her to hospital," Dan replied in soothing tones.

"What? Take me to her now!" Lily commanded.

"She's in the gym. I'll take you there."

Lily ran down the hall as fast as she could towards Rose. Entering the gym her eyes searched spotting her daughter lying on the floor, she sprinted towards her.

"Baby, it's okay, mommy's here," Lily comforted."

"Not a baby.... It hurts... Oh God, it hurts. Make it stop mom, please! Make it stop," winced Rose, barely opening her eyes and sweating profusely.

"Where does hurt Rose?" asked Lily.

"Left side! Oh, please make it stop hurting. Why does it hurt?" demanded Rose as Lily feels her side asking where it pains. Lily presses down on her left side Rose says it hurts on the right. When she presses down on the right side lifting up her hand it doesn't hurt but when Lily took her left hand off Rose screamed in pain.

"I think you might have had an appendicitis attack Rose," Lily replied in full mother mode.

"You think I have appendicitis? Doesn't that mean an operation? I don't want an operation," stated Rose complaining loudly. "Forget I said that if it means cutting out the pain tell them to do it! It hurts bad mom.'"

Rose then threw up all over her mother's shoes.

"I guess we both need new shoes," Lily said as she cleaned her shoe off, with tissues offered by Dan.

"The ambulance is here sir," Patrolman Alan Barnes advised.

"I need a statement from Rose about the killing apparently the other child with her, one Carol Banks, only saw the shoes. She didn't see the body of the victim," Dan stated.

"Dan my child is ill. I understand, you need a statement but I wish it could wait," Lily said forcefully.

"I'll make it fast, Lily. I know she's in pain."

"Then do so, she needs to go to hospital. Now!" Lily replied exasperated through clenched teeth.

"Are able to you give me a statement Ms. Brooksfield?" asked Dan as the paramedics tend to her and radio in that they also suspect appendicitis.

"I'm in so much pain I feel like I'm dying and you want to know what happened? Okay, fine, in a nutshell, I came to school on bike....went to choir room. I got a cramp in leg, a stitch in my side walked around the room to get out."

Before this point Rose's voice appeared calm but now it shook with terror, "I felt like I stepped in something looked down ....and oh my god it was blood. I followed the path with my eyes and saw first his feet and then his body. I couldn't do anything someone had murdered him. They took his heart out. It was a terrible sight like someone had hallowed out his chest. A knife stuck out of him. I think I'm going to be sick again."

"Take your time and try to pretend it's a horror movie and you want to tell your friends," Dan coaxed.

"I don't want to remember. It was so awful. I don't even watch scary movies because they are so gross and scare me to death," Rose commented grimacing again as a wave of pain washed over her.

"One quick question before the paramedics take you to the hospital did you or Carol hear anything as you came in the school or in the choir room. Anything different, or out of the ordinary?" asked Dan.

"The light was out in the hallway and it was darker than usually, but that was because it was early?"

"The hall appeared eerily quiet, when we came in, and then I heard rustling like someone was there in the hallway. I saw a blur of someone, but I have no idea what or even who that was," Carol interrupted.

"Thanks Ms. Brooksfield, Ms. Banks. I hope you feel better soon Rose," Dan exclaimed as the paramedics took Rose to the hospital.

"I have to go Carol. Will you be okay?" Lily asked.

"She'll be fine Ms. Brooksfield we will make sure she gets home safely," Dan Brown interjected.

"Good, it's that okay with you, Carol?"

"Yes, as long as I'm not alone," Carol replied. "I've never been so scared in all my life. My mom didn't answer my text, I'm glad you answered the phone. Mrs. Brooksfield," then turning to Rose she asked, "Are you sure you'll be okay Rose?"

"She'll get good care. I'll call you later Carol," Lily promised.

Lily drove to the hospital following the ambulance. When she arrived to her surprise she found her Grandma Katha already there.

"Hello, Lily, my dear. Some hospital board worker came upstairs to my office and one of the staff members, said Rose had been brought in," Katha explained. "What happened?"

"Grandma Katha, I'm so glad you're here." Lily cried with relief.

"Where else would I be when my granddaughters need me?" Katha stated, "It will be okay honey. Now tell me what happened."

"I hope so Grandma Katha. It's been all so awful Grandma Katha. Rose found her teacher brutally murdered and then she collapsed. And I couldn't get to her," Lily replied, as her great grandmother took Lily in her arms hugging her like she was a child again.

"This isn't fair. That child scarcely lost her daddy a few months ago, and now this. Lord almighty! But they have her in examining her. I'm sure they'll find out what's wrong with our girl. It probably is her appendix." Katha stated reassuringly, "Our Rose is a strong girl. No little useless organ can beat her."

"Mrs. Brooksfield?" enquired a doctor.

The doctor is a man of about six feet tall about twenty nine years old with a thick accent from India. Lily wondered why she noted this, as only his skill as a surgeon was important and you couldn't tell that by looking at someone.

"Yes I'm Mrs. Brooksfield," Lily replied Lily followed the doctor into Rose's hospital room.

Katha followed too. Rose appeared to be sleeping fitfully in the bed.

"Ms. Brooksfield? I'm Doctor Patel. I'm an intern looking after your daughter. I believe your daughter has a ruptured appendix. We'd like to do surgery immediately," Doctor Patel explained. "Then we will have to transfer her to the medicine floor.

"But shouldn't you do some tests to confirm it?" Lily stated shocked that she was right "And why would she go to an adult medical floor?"

"The children's surgical wing undergoes some changes and is not available, so we transfer children fourteen and up to adult wings this week. There are some caveats of course that they be placed in single rooms, or with other children. Now we did some preliminary tests and they give us a good idea that Rose may have a ruptured appendix," expounded Doctor Patel.

"Ruptured? Did you say ruptured?" Katha demanded registering what the doctor said.

"Yes."

"But isn't that serious?" asked Lily.

"Yes, that's why we need to get in there and remove the appendix and flush the area before more bacteria gets into the bloodstream,

"Doctor Patel agreed "Surgery is needed. We need to perform a full exploration and lavage of the area and to remove the offending appendix.""

"Oh okay," Lily said, not sure why she replied so calmly when she shook inside.

Lily put her hand to her mouth and took a deep breath before asking "Will you do the actual surgery?"

"No, I will assist Doctor Thomas who will perform the actual surgery. Don't worry! The man has performed literally hundreds of these surgeries," Doctor Patel reassured as he produced the surgery papers for Lily to sign.

"Will Doctor Thomas perform the surgery soon?" inquired Lily.

"He should be here soon. Doctor Thomas was called in a short time ago." answered Doctor Patel.

Lily saw another man dressed in green scrubs about forty five years old with short cropped, clipped, curly brown hair entering into the room. Tall, handsome and very self-assured with a dazzling smile that lit up his olive coloured skin, he breezed by Doctor Patel and grabbed the clipboard from Rose's bed.

"Doctor Thomas, I send this patient to O.R. one for you,'" Doctor Patel stated.

"Thank-you, Patel. I'll take over now," Doctor Thomas replied briskly.

Doctor Thomas looked at the paperwork then asked "Do I have all the paperwork?"

"Yes, Doctor Thomas," Doctor Patel responded.

" Would you care to assist me?" asked Doctor Thomas surprising Doctor Patel with a smile.

"Yes, thank-you sir, for this opportunity," Doctor Patel replied happily with an answering smile.

"Don't let it go to your head we operate as a teaching hospital."

"But I thought you said ...,"Lily interrupted, but neither doctor appeared to hear her.

"Are you the mother?" demanded Doctor Thomas looking at Lily, finally.

"Yes," admitted Lily.

"Did Doctor Patel explain to you it wouldn't be possible to do keyhole surgery, given the severity of the appendicitis?"

"No, he didn't. What is keyhole surgery?" requested Lily "In keyhole surgery the appendix is removed through a small tube, leaving a tiny scar. That is not possible in this case. We will make an incision length wise and go in and fix the problem," explained Doctor Thomas.

"You've done lots of these surgeries?" queried Lily.

"I've done many, many surgeries a lot of them more complicated than this." Doctor Thomas bragged, "You'll be able to see her soon and follow her progress to the recovery room on our board in the waiting room through these doors. Her number is patient 443."

Doctor Thomas then pointed to the waiting room nearby. Lily thanked the doctor and then watched as the orderlies wheeled Rose down the hall and into through the operating room doors. Lily paced back, and forth, awaiting the conclusion of the operation. She wished she could go in with her, but that was not possible. Katha joined her a few seconds later offering cup of coffee, she gotten from the Tim Horton's in the lobby. Lily began to pace.

~0~

Two hours later Lily asked, "What is taking them so long? Shouldn't they be done? I don't see her listed in the recovery room just in the operating rooms."

"They must take their time. We want our Rose healthy again," Katha reassured.

"I think it's too long something is wrong," Lily insisted.

"Now dear don't borrow trouble. Like I said they are thorough," Katha replied.

Pacing again Lily couldn't believe it took another hour for Doctor Thomas, to come out of the operating room entrance doors. It was kind of him to come straight to them even before she saw Rose's number come up on the board as moved to recovery.

Then Lily saw that Doctor Thomas' scrubs seemed to be covered in Rose's blood. Lily noted his face did not look like the surgery went well. She steeled herself for what he would tell her.

"It was a difficult surgery. Rose's appendix had erupted causing peritonitis," Doctor Thomas began, "We cleaned out as much of the infection we could, but the wound must be left open for a few days so we can excess it all."

"Peritonitis, that doesn't sound good. That's bad isn't it?" Katha interrupted, "Wait a minute, leaving the wound open, isn't that dangerous?"

"No, it is often the course of action in this type of infection. It is mild peritonitis which can be handled. If we had waited a few hours longer, I don't think Rose would be here. She will continue on a strong course of antibiotics overnight and fluids intravenously. I won't kid you, peritonitis can be a serious infection; but we fight the infection with all we've got." Doctor Thomas explained, "Then we will close it up in a few days."

"My daughter might die?" Lily demanded to know, feeling faint.

Katha put her arm around her to hold her up.

"There's no doubt it is serious, but we believe we were able to get a lot of the infection out. Now we will fight it in the blood stream and wait it out," Doctor Thomas continued.

"So how long will that take hours? Days?" Lily asked.

"As I said we wait it out flushing the infection with antibiotics and fluids," Doctor Thomas continued to explain, "She will be taken to four West."

"But why will she be on an adult floor? She's a child," Katha protested.

"Because of renovations to the children's wing we will transfer Rose to an adult surgery floor, but rest assured she will not be sharing a room with an adult," Doctor Thomas explained.

"Thank-you, Doctor Thomas," Katha replied as Lily took all this in.

Doctor Thomas then left. Lily assumed he was on his way back to the O.R. rooms or some other patient; frankly her mind was only on Rose.

"You should go home Grandma Katha. I'm staying overnight," Lily insisted.

"Of course you are. And I should stay right here too," Grandma Katha stated.

"Please, Grandma Katha, you need to go home and get some rest. One of us should. I'll go up to Rose's room and wait for them to bring her there from recovery."

"This is my granddaughter. I love her too Lily," Katha said quietly.

"I know you do and I love you too. But you need some rest. I'm going to need you tomorrow, and so will Rose. So please Grandma Katha, go home now and come back in the morning. I promise we'll call, if we need you," Lily exclaimed.

"Fine you win, but I'll be back by six a.m."

After Katha left Lily followed the orderlies as they transferred Rose to her bed on Four West. After the nurses settled Rose and left Rose asked, "Mom it's all over?"

"Yes, honey. You simply have to mend now."

"Don't go," Rose begged.

"I'm not going. I'll be here when you wake."

Lily sat beside her daughter's bedside, watching her sleep, worried Lily couldn't believe this had happened to Rose. Suffering from appendicitis? The poor child should have fun and time with friends, not seeing dead bodies, and dealing with ill health and serial killers.

What a terrible thing for Rose to see. Her teacher's heart had been cut out. Why had someone killed her choir teacher, anyway and so brutally? It wasn't Lily's worry right now, only Rose getting better mattered right now. Barbara could hold down the fort for a few days at the Crown Attorney's office. Barbara was the assistant Crown attorney after all.

Rose slept peacefully; Lily could close her eyes for a moment. After all Lily would awake at any sound from Rose.

~0~

Chapter 3 - Whose Boyfriend is Vincent?

E arly the next morning, after falling asleep in the chair next

to her daughter and awakening, Lily stood up and stretched. She glanced over at her daughter Rose, noting that she wasn't as pale and her skin tone pinked up. Surely this was a good sign? She reached over and gently touched Rose's forehead. It felt cool. Thank-you, God, Rose was now on the mend.

Lily stomach rumbled. She hadn't eaten since lunch yesterday. Lily thought about how nice it would be to have coffee and some breakfast. She then heard some noises in the hall.

One nurse wheeled a cart, the other walked along side. They stopped at the nurses' station outside Rose's hospital room. Lily listened as she heard the two nurses talking.

"Can you believe it? Doctor Thomas was on call yesterday but it was certainly hard to reach him," the one nurse began.

"I know, I thought the chief would have a fit," said the other.

"What was his excuse?" asked the other.

"He said his phone was dead and that he also had a flat tire and had to have his tire replaced at the garage," the other nurse replied.

Well, wasn't this interesting where could Doctor Thomas have been? Lily wondered. Lily then peered out hoping not to be seen to get a look at the nurses.

"He better watch himself brilliant surgeon or not the chief hates it if you're not available when you're on call," the other one commented. "You know his wife is an unholy terror. This is the right expression, correct?"

Lily peered out some more to see the one nurse counting pills into little cups as the other watched.

They seemed animated in their conversation as it continued, "With that expression you're dead on. He is an excellent surgeon, but I understand his personal life is going to the dogs. That wife of his is a biotch. She's always calling here demanding to either know where he is or when he'll be home," Mary expounded. "She actually asked me if I was had an affair with him. Is she jealous much?"

"You shouldn't speak of him that way he is a brilliant surgeon. He is still on top of his work," defended the other nurse. "He saved the Georgas boy. That child would have died without the bowel surgery he performed. He did a good job on that Brooksfield girl as well, Mary. He saved her life too."

"Poor, kid! She's been through a lot," Mary commented.

"Her dad died and that horrible way he was posed with his mistress. Do you know she confronted a serial killer?"

"I don't understand what you speak of. What is this about serial killers? Did you fall asleep Mary and dream about some movie? Not to worry, all is well. Our patient, the child seemed better when we checked on her an hour ago," the other nurse exclaimed.

"Dayita, don't you know who she is?" asked Mary sounding surprised.

"Is she someone famous?" Dayita asked.

"Infamous, is more like it. Rose's father was the Mayor. He was murdered about two months ago, him and his secretary. A serial killer stalked her Aunt. He killed a number of people. That little girl tried to stop him herself when he took her aunt, mother, and grandmother. He even injured a policeman. Course he was one too," explained Mary.

"One what?"

"A cop, silly! The serial killer was a cop."

Day it a stopped putting pills into the cups.

"I heard nothing of this. Happy Valley is a small, sleepy town.
That is why my parents allow me to live here. It cannot be that a
policeman was a killer."

"Not only a killer, but a serial killer. I can't believe you didn't hear
about this."

"When did this happen?"

"In the early part of June, I think."

"I was in India with my parents in May and June. They tried to
marry me off to Vanajit Rapal."

"They tried to force you to marry?"

"I barely got away from my obligation. Only my mother kept my
father from forcing this upon me, and only because I agreed that I
would marry a man of my choosing (of my native soil and religion)
within a year."

"Good lord, how archaic. You have a choice. Don't let them force
you into anything."

"You don't understand. It is my duty. I cannot let my family down
by marry outside my religion. A lot of people misunderstand my
religion."

"You have a duty to yourself to marry someone you care about."

"I would not speak of this with you. We need to marry someone
who is of Muslim faith, no one else. The punishments for marry
outside the faith are harsh for those in my family."

"Why would you subject yourself to such abuse? Leave and marry
who you will."

"It is my religion and I obey. You grew up in a culture that allows
that kind of freedom. I did not. I must not shame my family," the
woman tried to explain.

"But I thought you came from Pakistan? A lot of people I know
who are Muslim still marry whom they wish. My family came
from Lebanon originally and we honour the past. I think you
should think long and hard about this before you ruin your life. As

to my family, I'm mixed with so many different cultures and backgrounds you shouldn't judge that I have any culture."

"You are white and a westerner, are you not? And of the British Isles background from the colour of your skin. You wouldn't understand my culture. We are respectful of our religion and our elders."

"My family comes from all parts of the world. We also have indigenous people in our background, but most of all I am Canadian. So, I do understand that you are being exploited."

"You understand nothing. Maybe you should visit the mosque and study the ancient text of my religion, before you come to these sweeping conclusions. My religion is my life, just as Catholicism is yours. It will be difficult to remain friends with you if you persist in enforcing your values on me," Dayita said softly.

"Please Dayita, I meant no offense. I'll drop this conversation for now."

"Then you'll now explain about the child and this serial killer remark?"

"The child was abducted by a serial killer got free and came after the kidnapper/serial killer saving her family."

"How could a child stop him?" asked Dayita horrified.

"The child was ready to shoot if necessary. Luckily she didn't have to," Mary continued.

Lily thought about interrupting their gossip but something inside her made her want to listen to more.

"That's amazing, not what you'd expect from a teenager. It sounds like she's genuinely brave. Everything should be fine for her now. She's on the mend from her appendicitis. She can still be a child, despite all her recent tragedies," Dayita stated.

"You'd think so would you? My brother Paul is a cop and he says that the girl found her choir teacher brutally murdered at her school yesterday. She then collapsed with appendicitis symptoms," Mary cried.

"What a horrible thing to happen. That poor child," Dayita exclaimed. "Let's be particularly nice to her, so she feels safe. Now I need to get this pills sorted, they have to be given out soon."

"Did you hear who the teacher was that was murdered though?"

"And do we know him?"

"It was someone we both know well! It was Vincent Scholar," Mary replied sadly.

"No, it can't be Vincent? Your boyfriend, not that Vincent?" Dayita exclaimed, a strange strangled sound in her voice.

"Yes, it was Vincent," Mary stated quietly.

"Are you okay? Why didn't you tell me sooner? You've been working all night and you didn't say a word. Why do you still work?" Dayita asked.

"It turns out he wasn't my Vincent. We broke up a week ago, when I found him with another woman," Mary replied, sadly. Mary then began crying softly.

"He was with another woman? The man was a pig dog!" Dayita then looked at Mary's face and backtracked, "But you still cared about him. I'm so sorry Mary."

"I'm sorry too. More than I can say. I gave him back his ring too. I wish I'd kept it now. It would be nice to have something to remember him by."

"You wish you had it to remember him? Why? If he betrayed you?" asked Dayita.

"Because I love him still; frankly I blame that woman for taking him away. I wouldn't put it past that simpering biotch to have killed him. He wanted to come back to me, I know he did. She had the nerve to tell me he lied about working at the University of Vienna. He taught music at the University of Vienna. She's the liar," Mary explained.

"If you sincerely think that she is evil, you should tell the police. Especially if you know who she is," Dayita stated her eyes narrowing.

"That biotch is the police. She works as a 911 operator," Mary spat out angrily.

"Please Mary, your language. You do not want to sink to her level. She's a cop? That is a exceedingly good reason to tell them that she's a suspect," Dayita insisted. "She shouldn't be able to use her position to get away with murder."

"Her name is Violet Garden and she looks like Olive Oyl."

"Who is Olive Oyl?" Dayita asked.

"A stick figured cartoon character with glasses. Violet will turn it around on me. I don't have an alibi for most of the day, probably not for when the murder took place either. I live alone who can alibi me? I got ready for work and came here but who would believe that?" Mary explained, and then continued, "Then there is that other woman who works at the police station she claims she's pregnant with Vincent's babies. Her brother is a cop too! And you know how cops stick together."

"I'm so sorry, Mary. I know how much you cared about him."

"Women were always making play for him too. Silly twits! You always been a good friend you never did that," Mary rambled on.

"Why would I do that? He was your boyfriend," Dayita asks surprised. "I still think you should call them about that woman 911 operator, Violet and that other woman, even if they know other cops they should pay."

"Yes, she does. I'll call them anonymously. She deserves a little payback anyway," Mary replied. "That man stealing biotch!"

"I wish you, not to use such language. It is crude and taints the ears. I am sorry to tell you this, since he has died, but I saw Vincent with Doctor Paula Yates the day before he was murdered. She kissed him."

"Doctor Yates? But isn't she married?"

"I heard she sued for divorce, Dayita answered, "Her husband is not a nice man and extremely jealous."

"So he killed my Vincent?"

"It is possible. Doctor Yate's husband shook her arm, the last time I saw her with him. He pinched her nose and bruised her neck. I should have said something. She had a black eye as well and insisted that she had walked into a door. But I believe he harmed her. Yet he dated other women telling them he would get divorced."

"We should tell the police about him?" Mary asked.

"I have no wish to speak to the police. If you wish to do so go ahead. I will say no more of this. We must start handing out the medicines now," Dayita answered.

"I know we don't want to get behind. We'd get in so much trouble. I'll start on that end of the hall, you take the other end okay?"

Mary began pushing the cart down the hallway and Lily moved away from the door. Lily peered down the hall again wondering when Grandma Katha would get here to relieve her.

Coffee called to her. Good grief, she thought it was closer to eleven am, but it was only seven am. She couldn't believe the conversation she overheard. What were the chances, that two nurses looking after Rose would know Alexander Vincent Scholar? She had to get in touch with Dan Brown, since he investigated and inform him of what she heard.

What could she be thinking? She wasn't on the job right now except as Mom. Rose needed her as Mom, not the Crown attorney at work. She'd slip away for few minutes when Katha came and make a quick call. Thank-you God for Grandma Katha, or she would have gone out of her mind yesterday. Rose looked so much better now. Looking back over at Rose she knew she couldn't love her daughter more if she had given birth herself. Lily closed her eyes for a moment.

When Lily opened her eyes again time had passed looking at her watch she couldn't believe it said nine a.m.

Lily got up to stretch and glanced again down the hall. There she saw a tall man striding towards her. His hair was brown and clipped in military cut close to his head. The man stood about six feet tall, and seemed to have his arms full of goodies. His right hand held a teddy bear holding a Kevlar balloon. The balloon's greeting was 'Get Well Soon' and a small bear was attached to it with ribbon. In his left hand he clutched flowers and two small boxes about the size of chocolates and another flat package.

"Emmett is that you?" Lily asked.

"Hello, Lily. Long-time no see," Emmett exclaimed.

"It looks like your hands are full," Lily replied smiling.

Emmett blushed and said, "I thought Rose would appreciate some presents."

"That was so thoughtful of you Emmett. I should have called you yesterday. How did you find out that we were here?" Lily inquired apologetic.

"One of my buddies at work, let me know," Emmett answered pointedly. "Are you okay?"

"I'm honestly glad that you're here."

Lily then hugged him carefully, but awkwardly as not to crush what he carried.

"Emmett it isn't even visiting hours yet."

"But you're glad to see me?"

"Yes,"

"Rose is better?" Emmett asked.

"She seems much better, but I'll know better once the doctor sees her." Lily replied.

"She's one tough little girl," Emmett stated "She may not be of your blood, but she's picked up her mother's grit."

"Thank-you, Emmett. I'm sorry I have to cancel our date tonight. I should have called you sooner," apologised Lily.

"Can I have a rain check?" asked Emmett.

"Of course you can. I looked forward to our date though," Lily confessed.

"I was too," Emmett admitted.

"Emmett, I mean Mr. Rogers you came to visit me?" Rose inquired from the bed now awake.

"Yes, of course I did. And as I told you before, it is okay to call me Emmett."

"Did you bring me presents?" Rose asked, awakening on cue and greedily spotting his full hands.

"Yes." Emmett replied laughing. "Here you go Rose. Flowers, a balloon, and a beanie bear. By the way, he says 'Get well' too. Oh and this and this," Emmett exclaimed handing her two wrapped packages. This one is for your mother."

"Wow! Thanks Emmett," Rose said dutifully, and began opening the first package. "Chocolates? Thank-you, Emmett, I'll eat these when I feel better and the doctor allows me to eat."

"Oh, sorry Rose, I should have thought about that. Do you want me to put it in the drawer for now?"

"Sure, thank-you."

Rose began opening the other package to reveal Emma by Jane Austen.

"Thank goodness this isn't a Twilight book. Everyone loves that dippy book but me. I can't keep a straight face when they talk about shiny vampires and baseball playing vampires and the movies. Don't get me started," Rose stated, scrolling her eyes. "Do you know everyone at school has read that book, but not plays by Shakespeare, or books by Jane Austen?"

"Should I have bought that book instead?"

"Oh, no, I already own that one. I'm looking forward to reading this book."

"I knew you'd appreciate good literature," Emmett stated.

Lily arched an eyebrow.

"Okay, so my sister, Suzy helped me pick out the book," Emmett admitted.

"Thanks again Emmett, this was all so nice of you." Lily stated, "Here, take a seat."

"I'm sorry, but can you wait in the hall? The doctor would like to examine his patient," Dayita explained coming into the room.

"Yes, of course we can do that," stated Emmett and Lily getting up to leave.

"'You can stay if you want Mom,'" Dayita commented.

"I'll wait in the hall until you're done," replied Emmett and then stepped into the hall.

~0~

Emmett

Waiting up against the wall outside the door, Emmett answered his ringing phone, "This is Detective Emmett Rogers. Yes sir, no sir. Yes, sir, I will be happy to come in and make a statement this afternoon at one p.m. Yes sir."

Emmett began to worry. His boss wanted him down at the police station right away. It was obvious they wanted to question him. He needed a lawyer. He didn't murder Alexander Scholar, but he had to admit he wanted to. The bastard had played games with women, master manipulator that he was he juggled too many women all at once.

Damn it! They should be looking at those women's husband's boyfriends and family not him!

He grew angry with himself for losing his temper and actually thinking about setting the man straight the morning of the murder. Suzy's pain had been all he thought of. His baby sister Suzy was his responsibility for so long. He raised her since she was sixteen. He'd only been twenty four, when their parents had been killed in a motor vehicle accident.

Twenty-four years old, he been so young, Emmett thought looking back.

Freshly home from his tour in Afghanistan and suffering from post-traumatic stress disorder, he had been thrown into a family drama. His sister Paula had followed in her older sister Dianna's footsteps and gotten pregnant a sin in her father's eyes worthy of expulsion from the family home. His wife grieving for the loss of their child and had found herself barren, if that wasn't enough for Emmett had been no match for parents who had been bent on suicide before succumbing to a cancer demise.

Emmett knew he hadn't been ready to lose both parents in one fell swoop. And his sister Paula hadn't been any help. Let's be honest though Dad had kicked her out when he learned of her impending motherhood. Emmett had done all he could to get her to live with him but Paula had married the joke who had gotten her pregnant and it hadn't gotten better since then. Her husband was a career soldier and when he was home Emmett felt he brought the job home with him. He argued incessantly with Paula and made her miserable, but Paula wouldn't hear a word against him. Speaking out against Jason had caused a rift. Paula barely spoke to him something that hurt Emmett deeply. Emmett kept reaching out trying to repair the rift but so far with no success. She didn't even speak that much to Suzy.

Poor Suzy she lost her parents eight years ago and her sisters and was stuck with him. He stepped up pulled himself together, taking care of his mental health and become the cop he was today simply because Suzy needed him to look after her. His post-traumatic stress disorder was under control. He hadn't had any episodes in years. He breathed in and out. Saying his mantra to himself, everything will be okay.

Suzy wanting to be a cop like him was a compliment. Could he help it that he had been glad so far she hadn't been able to pass the weight requirements of the test? Unfortunately a few months ago, she began weight training, so she could pass the test the second time and she passed.

Emmett was so incredibly angry when he thought about Alexander Scholar. Suzy, young and vulnerable and only twenty-three years old had been taken advantage of by that bastard Alexander Scholar. He had dated her wooed her, strung her along like the other women in his life. Poor Suzy thought she was the only one. When she questioned his commitment Alexander Scholar gave her a ring and said they were engaged. The ring, like his promises were glass. Suzy had come crying to Emmett after she had taken the ring to a jeweller to get cleaned. She thought that Alex had gotten scammed.

Emmett investigated and found out the man had a whole string of women, whom he juggled and had given glass engagement rings. Emmett had never been so angry. He had cooled off then gone to talk to Suzy. She needed him so he could choke down the anger and forget about Alexander Scholar. Emmett advised Suzy to forget him and move on. However a week before the murder, Suzy had told him tearfully, that she was pregnant with Alex's baby. Emmett had totally lost it then. His baby sister, the little girl he had raised since nine had been cruelly betrayed.

She needed someone to be there for her and the baby and Alex Scholar could never be that man. He had comforted her told her that all would be all right. Emmett promised he would help her raise her child, if she wanted to keep the baby. She had begged him to promise that he would not tear Alexander limb from limb. He had promised that he wouldn't, Suzy's feelings came first. He had however been bound and determined to tell Alexander that he had to stay away from Suzy for good.

He wanted Alexander to give up all rights to Suzy's child in writing. He kept putting it off though because he wanted to keep his vow. Emmett had gotten angrier and angrier as the time passed He almost let it go, but then he went with Suzy to her doctor's appointment the day before the murder. Seeing Suzy like that scared and alone made him so angry.

He stewed about all night and then (even though he knew it was a mistake to go into the school) he went to meet Alexander. Arriving Emmett thought better of his actions. He hadn't wanted to make anything worse. So he'd sat in his car until he calmed down, deciding to handle the matter with a lawyer, rather than waste words on Scholar.

When he told them his alibi, they would look closely at him for this crime. The fact that he was at the murder scene probably about the right time would get him thrown in jail, for a crime he didn't commit. He needed a lawyer fast, but where could he get one? The only lawyer he knew was Lily and she was the Crown attorney. She couldn't take his case in fact she might be the one to send him to jail.

His thoughts were interrupted by Katha. Katha took one look at Emmett and asked, "Are you okay, Emmett?"

"Do you know any lawyers Katha, besides Lily?" Emmett answered looking worried.

"Do you need a lawyer Emmett?' asked Katha surprised.

"Yes," 'Emmett confessed.

"You're in luck give me a dollar."

"Here you go!" Emmett said handing her a looney (a Canadian dollar coin).

"Let's take a walk," Katha replied, putting the coin in her pocket.

When they reached an alcove where no one sat, Katha took Emmett in and requested, "Sit."

"What did you want the dollar for coffee? I've got some more change if you need it," offered Emmett.

"No, silly! I'm a practicing lawyer. I don't take too many cases anymore, but consider me your lawyer. Now tell me all about why you think you need one," replied Katha.

"It's like this...,"Emmett began and told her all about Suzy his sister, her troubles and how and why he doesn't have an alibi.

"Everything will be fine. Don't worry Sonny. I'll represent you. When we go downtown to police headquarters only answer questions they ask when I nod my head. They'll try to trick you but if you follow my lead I'll get you out of this," Katha stated.

"Thanks Katha," Emmett replied relieved. "It is at one p.m."

"One it is then, I'll be there. If you need me before that here's my card," Katha advised, advised, "Now let's head back."

Emmett and Katha arrived back in time for the nurse Dayita to come out to look for them.

"You can come back in now," Dayita stated interrupting.

Emmett breathed a sigh of visible relief, as he and Katha entered Rose's room.

"Mom, you and Emmett should get breakfast in the cafeteria. Then come back and see me," Rose commanded

"Yes, your majesty," Lily replied laughing and taking the arm Emmett offered.

"See you later Annie Oakley," Emmett stated.

"In a while crocodile," Rose countered.

"You're a good teen," Katha told Rose. "You're sure you don't mind Emmett dating your mom?"

"I don't know, on one hand I resent her moving on so quickly. My dad hasn't been gone that long, but I know I can't stop her moving on and it's only a date after all, not marriage. I messed up their date tonight. So it's the least I can do. Besides mom needs to eat and she can't in front of me."

"So how are you, truthfully?" Katha asked.

"I have some pain killers. I'm bored though; does my being a good teen rate a television?" Rose pleaded.

"Yes, I think that could be arranged," Katha replied hiding a smile.

"Thanks, Grandma Katha, you're the best. I hate missing Vampire Diaries," Rose explained. "So how is your boyfriend Terrence?"

"I don't want to talk about this."

"Did you split up? I'm sorry Grandma Katha. I thought he was the one for you. Grandpa O'Malley always said you should love again."

"He did?" Katha asked shocked.

"When he was dying, he told me to encourage you to love again. He said he'd wait for you in heaven, but you needed to be loved until then. He's the reason I thought I should butt out of my mom's love life."

"Aw, that man. No one will ever live up to him; as for Terrence and I, we haven't split up. I have some thinking to do," Katha answered.

Katha got up and stretched her legs and took out a brown paper bag from her briefcase.

"I got you some magazines. Here they are. There is Entertainment Weekly, People, and some teen magazines. See, this one has One Direction and that Harry Styles all the girls are raving about. He's extremely popular, I'm given to understand."

"Thank-you Grandma Katha, but One Direction is for much younger kids and Harry Styles is not my type. They've also broke up," Rose stated politely. "But it was nice of you. Thanks again."

"That's funny, Carol likes Harry Styles," Katha replied.

"She was in love with him," giggled Rose. "Ouch, that hurts. Don't make me laugh again Grandma Katha."

"Is that the real reason why you don't like Harry Styles?" Katha inquired.

"No, Rose has moved on to Drake. He's Canadian and has loads more talent. He's a quadruple threat."

"Quadruple?"

"Yes, he has dancing, acting, singing and comedic abilities. Did you see him on Saturday Night Live?"

"No, I don't believe I did."

"Oh, sorry, not your show."

"I've seen SNL but not that one," protested Katha, "So you like this Drake, too? Should I buy you his album on CD?"

"No, Grandma Katha, if your best friend likes some guy you don't like him too, but I do like his music and if you like to buy me an I-Tunes card I could put it on my I-Phone...," Rose commented rolling her eyes.

"I can buy this card at the drugstore, right?"

"Yes, and just about any other store. Can you bring my cord for my I-phone too. It's almost dead and I want to text Carol," Rose answered rolling her eyes.

"I'll get you a card and bring the cord for your phone then. Between you and me, who is that you like?" enquired Katha.

"I like Brad Pitt."

"Isn't he a bit old for you?" Katha asked worried.

"Ooh, yuck. I don't like him like that. He has a girlfriend who might as well as be his wife. You know, Angelina Jolie. They're going to get married anytime now and they have what, six kids?" Rose answered rolling her eyes again, like Katha has lost her mind.

"Oh, sorry, I got that wrong dear." Katha stated mollifying Rose, "I liked Cary Grant when I was young myself."

"But he was so old...and he's dead. Oh sorry Grandma Katha, of course he's wasn't that old," Rose retorted backtracking.

"He was older, but he's matinee good looks and his smile made me melt," Grandma Katha admitted.

"Yes, sorry. I kind of like that guy that plays Damon on Vampire Diaries, too," Rose said changing the subject.

"Yes, he's an extremely handsome young man," Katha agreed.

Rose looked through the magazines but fell quickly asleep, the magazine with Harry Styles still in her hands.

Katha tenderly took it out of her hands and tucked the covers gently around Rose. Katha glanced at the magazines while waiting for Lily to come back. Lily arrived in the room, after a mere half an hour and Rose hearing her step awakened as Katha left.

"I beg your pardon? You want me to meet whom at the police station?" asked Lily into her cell phone a conversation that seems to have been going on awhile, "Fine, but I'm not happy about this there are other people that work in my office. My daughter is ill, and I'm needed here. Why can't Barbara Franks meet with this person? Okay, okay, as I said I'll be there. But this bloody well better be important."

Lily turned to Rose and said, "Rose, I have to go to work for awhile, but I'll be back in a couple of hours. I have to meet Sergeant Detective Daniel Brown about some work."

"Go Mom, I'll be fine. Aunt Amelia gets back today doesn't she from her buyer trip?" Rose asked.

"Yes, and she said she'll drop by."

"Knowing Aunt Amelia she'll bring me a present," Rose replied with glee.

"Rose Brooksfield is that all you care about, presents?" asked Lily admonishing her.

"No, but they are nice," commented Rose. "And it makes the pain easier."

"Pain? You're in pain? We can call the nurse and get her to give you something." Lily exclaimed worried.

"Mom, I could push this button for the morphine, but I don't want to get addicted so I haven't been pushing it," Rose admitted.

"Push it when you need pain relief. You won't get addicted and you won't keep it that long. Now get some rest honey. I'll be back in a couple of hours."

"Okay, but if I get addicted..."Rose stated hesitantly.

"Use it, see you later pumpkin," Lily stated leaving then to the nurse, "I'll be back in a couple of hours take good care of my little girl. I convinced her to use the pump but you might want to check on that."

"Don't worry. She's a joy to look after we will take good care of her," the day nurse answered.

Lily then departed and smiled as she passed a parcel laden Amelia, who didn't seem to notice Lily. Lily didn't say a word but hurried out of the hospital and to her appointment with Dan Brown

.~0~

Amelia and Rose

"Is there a Rose Brooksfield here?" asked Amelia, as she

stood in front of the nurses' station

"Yes, her room is right here, but it's restricted to relatives," Dayita insisted.

"I'm her Aunt Amelia."

"Then go ahead, but please don't stay too long she needs her rest," Dayita cautioned and then watched as Amelia entered and Rose acknowledged her.

"Hello sunshine. What this about a dead body and you winding up here to get your appendix out?" Amelia scolded.

"Aunt Amelia you're back," Rose replied.

"I got the first flight back when Aunt Katha phoned. You look pretty pink. That's a good sign," Amelia commented coming in and looking at Rose.

"Did you get all of your buying done?" Rose enquired.

"I did. I ordered some especially, unique items for the store. I also brought you a few presents," Amelia stated.

"What did you bring me?" Rose asked greedily.

"Here," stated Amelia handing her a package.

"Oh, Aunt Amelia, this is perfect. I hate this scratchy ugly hospital gown they made me wear," Rose replied taking a soft peachy coloured nightgown out of the box Amelia handed her.

"There is this too," Amelia replied handing her another package.

"An E-reader? You got me a Kindle?" Rose asked excitedly.

"It's loaded with books too, that I bought from Amazon. I bought you two paranormal novels, Love's Labours Won and A Tiger's Heart Wrapped in a Player's Hide by S. G. Lee. There's also a romance novel that I bought also for mine Jodi Langston's Always. It's a romance though, I shouldn't have bought it for you," Amelia stated.

"Oh, don't be an old fuddy-duddy, Aunt Amelia. I've read lots of adult romance novels. I am fifteen you know not twelve," Rose complained.

"It's an adult story, but I guess it will be okay for you. It's a wonderful love story. There are other books lots of mysteries, and a couple more romances. It should keep you busy," Amelia stated.

"Thanks, Aunt Amelia, it will give me something to do. I'm so bored. Grandma Katha's getting the television set up so I can watch Vampire Diaries tonight. Want to come back and watch?" Rose begged.

"I'm going to go get something to eat at the cafeteria and I'll make sure that television has been set up. I'll come back tonight after I check in at my shop. In the meantime, while I'm gone you get some sleep, okay?" Amelia stated.

"You promise to come back?" Rose asked.

"I promise now rest up. So we can see what Elena, Stefan and Damon, is up to now," Amelia replied smiling. "Goodnight sweetie, see you soon."

"I'm only closing my eyes for a minute," Rose protested, and then spoiled it all by falling into a deep sleep.

Amelia then tiptoed quietly out.

~0~

Chapter 4 – Life Is Full of Surprises

Lily arrived at the police station and ran up the stairs and into the old brick building. The police station seemed to be falling apart with its peeling paint and crumbling brick walls. Horace should have gotten the council to approve the building of a new station. Everyone thought the new mayor would do that, but somehow Lily doubted they would. The room she was instructed to meet Daniel Brown in was down the hall. She noted the old fashion institutional lighting that made the hallways darker than they should be. The whole building seemed to need an overhaul. Lily tramped down to the interview, her heels clicking on the granite floor loud and angrily. Daniel Brown appeared outside the room and ushered her in.

"So, what was so urgent that I had to leave my daughter's sick bed?" demanded Lily.

"I have a suspect and we wish to question him. I thought you might like to watch through the glass," Sergeant Detective Daniel Brown responded.

"Who is this suspect? And what kind of hard evidence do we have so I can prosecute?" Lily asked.

"This guy was outside of the school in his car before the murder. His sister was impregnated by this guy and he wanted revenge," Dan explained, "He has motive, means, and opportunity."

"It may seem like a good motive, but I've been hearing about lots of other people with motive. This seems a little too soon in the investigation to find a suspect. Why should I even be here? You can send all this to my office."

"This is intel from a solid investigation and believe me you want to be here. Don't let the fact that he's a cop trouble you. We both know good cops, that can be turned, or hide a bad side," Dan stated.

"This is a cop? Again? You better be damn sure of your work. The last cop we had to arrest was a PR disaster for your department, and a danger to my family!" stated Lily. "What kind of police station do you run in this city?"

"Why don't you ask your Grandmother's sugar daddy? His son is the police chief," Dan angrily replied.

"How dare you? You've overstepped your bounds. Don't ever bring my family or my Grandma Katha into this. Even if she's dating someone, it's truthfully, none of yours, or even my business. It has nothing to do with this crime," Lily retorted.

"Gee! Ask a question and get it shoved down your throat. Sorry, I asked."

"Is something bothering you, Dan?"

"Nothing I want to talk about. It won't interfere with my job."

"See that it doesn't. Can we get to the question at hand, another murderous cop?" asked Lily.

"We haven't arrested the cop yet, so we haven't been able to nail him yet. That's why he is here for questioning," Dan stated annoyed.

"Like I said let's get on with it then. I'll watch through the glass."

"Okay, interview room one," Dan stated leading the way to the room and then entering by himself.

Lily peered through the one way glass and gasped. What the devil? Why was Emmett here? Dan investigated Emmett? Why didn't Emmett say anything to her? This had to be all one big mistake. That stupid cop Daniel Brown hadn't done his due diligence and was about to a career mistake. Emmett was not guilty. Lily peered through the glass again.

"Wait a minute, Grandma Katha was in there? She acted as Emmett's lawyer? Lily thought as she listened in and heard through the speaker...", "This is a formal statement. You have the right to remain silent and refuse to answer questions. Do you understand?"

"Yes," Emmett replied.

"Anything you do say may be used against you in a court of law. Do you understand?"

"Do we have to do this Dan?" Emmett continued.

"We'll do this by the book, Rogers. Now, you have the right to consult an attorney before speaking to the police and to have an attorney present during questioning now, or in the future. Do you understand?"

"Fine, let's get his over with," Emmett answered.

"If you decide to answer questions now, without an attorney present you will still have the right to stop answering at any time until you talk to an attorney. Do you understand?"

"Yes, I read these rights to perps every day and my attorney is right here! Meet Katha O'Malley, Dan."

"Do you have the right to practice in this state Ms. O'Malley?" Dan asked looking shocked at Katha's age.

"I hope you don't allude to ageism, Sergeant Detective Daniel Brown! I could sue you for that. For your information, I have a law degree, and am up to date with the law society."

Lily laughed when she heard that; trust Grandma Katha to put Dan in his place.

"Oh, okay then, shall we begin? Your name is Emmett Rogers?

"Yes, you know it is," answered Emmett with a nod from Katha.

"So, Emmett, where could you be found on the morning of September ninth, at six a.m.?" Detective Daniel Brown demanded.

Emmett glanced at Katha again and she nodded. Emmett then answered, "I was parked outside of the High School."

"What high school would that be?" asked Dan.

"I was at Happy Valley High School, in downtown Happy Valley. Satisfied?" Emmett replied.

"And so we are absolutely clear, this would be at what time?" Dan enquired.

"Six a.m.," Emmett mumbled.

"Excuse me, can you repeat that again for the record."

"Six a.m. Okay?"

"And you know the exact time because..?"

"I looked at my watch and the clock in my car," Emmett replied.

"And what were you doing outside a high school at that time of the morning. Have you got a thing for the kiddies?" Dan provoked.

"How dare you? That is so sick!" Emmett yelled, jumping up from his seat.

Katha motioned for him to sit down and explain. Emmett felt foolish that he fallen for one of the tricks in an interviewer's book. Emmett took a huge breath to calm himself sat down and answered, "Sorry, for losing my temper, but your accusation was vile. I wanted to speak with Alex Scholar, so I went to the school."

"And did you and then plunge a knife into his chest and scoop out his heart?"

"No, I never got out of my car."

"And do you have any witnesses to that fact Lieutenant Rogers?" Dan demanded.

"Actually I do, a teacher at the school Teresa Brown saw me sitting in my car. Teresa came over and talked to me for about twenty minutes and then I left," Emmett explained. "She also kissed me."

"Teresa Brown? My sister, who teaches at the school? That Teresa Brown?"

"Yep."

"You're lying!" Dan shouted.

"Five foot six, brown hair, blue eyes, kind of curvy? Pretty and kisses like a dream? Yes, I would say that's your sister, Teresa Brown." Emmett provoked.

"Don't talk about my sister that way."

"I respect Teresa. A bit troubled, but she's a sweetheart," Emmett countered.

"You stay away from her Emmett Rogers. She's barely out of a relationship. She doesn't need to get mixed up with the likes of you," Dan said his teeth gritting and his hands clenched.

"I know she did, and funny thing that relationship was with Alexander Scholar. Small world isn't it? You've been hiding a valuable lead. It seems you might have a motive too!"

Katha whispered in Emmett's ear.

"My attorney and I will be leaving now," Emmett stated, getting up from his chair.

"I say when the interview is over," Dan shouted angrily.

"I'm his attorney and I say charge my client or we leave," Katha demanded.

"Interview ended. Time eleven sixteen a.m." Daniel Brown looked angry and waved at them as if to say leave.

"Hmm, I thought so. Come Emmett, we are out of here," Katha cried, triumphantly.

In the hallway Emmett turned to Katha to thank her, and saw Lily. Lily stood straight and tall her long blonde hair in that twist. He longed to pull out and run the strands of hair through his fingers while making love to her. The physical aspects however, had not progressed that far in their relationship. So far it had been two steps forward and two steps back. He hoped she hadn't seen the interview, before he could explain to her or she'd never speak to him again. He smiled at her but she hadn't noticed him yet.

"Lily, why are you here?" Emmett asked.

"My job, Emmett, I am the Crown attorney," Lily answered, angrily.

Emmett flinched, he knew Lily was angry, if only he could get her to hear him out then she'd understand.

"I thought someone else would be handling this case."

"You did, did you? I would love to have stayed with Rose, but I had to come down here and find out you were the suspect. Why didn't you tell me any of this Emmett?"

"I didn't have the chance."

"You didn't have the chance? Nonsense! You could have told me. Instead you kissed another woman."

Katha attempted to get between them to stop them from arguing without success.

"You couldn't have given me a heads up that Dan wanted to question me?" asked Emmett sounding hurt, "I thought we were friends."

"I am the Crown attorney, if I'm doing my job then no one, comes before it. Not even so-called friends," Lily exclaimed.

"Somehow, I thought things were different between us. I thought we were more than friends."

Emmett then walked away, appearing angry.

"Emmett, be fair," pleaded Katha chasing after him, "You knew her job was important to her."

"You want to be fair? She blindsided me," Emmett shouted, looking discreetly, to see if Lily listened.

Lily watched them walk away and grew angrier. Good grief, she had to do her job. She had no idea that Emmett was a suspect.

What did he want from her? Did he want her to ruin her career for him? Had she been that mistaken about him?

And Grandma Katha must have known but all of this, and yet she had said nothing. She knew she was being unfair there were other people who were viable suspects but they should have told her Emmett was a suspect. Emmett kissed Teresa Brown, he claimed her as his alibi. Lily thought they were exclusive...that Emmett had started to care about her, but he kissed Teresa Brown who used to bully Lily at school. He had even had Grandma Katha keep secrets from Lily.

To hell with them both!

She'd think about this all later, but for now she was headed back to Rose.

~0~

Chapter 5 –
Strange
Bedfellows

Emmett and Katha

Emmett frowned as he walked down the hallway with

Katha.

"You were awful to Lily, Emmett. I thought you cared about her? Was I wrong about you?" asked Katha.

"I'm protecting her. I'll explain it to her later," Emmett answered.

"I think you should explain it to me right now!" Katha demanded angrily.

"She's the Crown attorney and the sole breadwinner, now that Horace is gone. She can't appear to be favouring me in any way, or they will take her off the job again. And heaven knows she can't afford to have that happen again. She barely back to work," Emmett explained. "She can't afford to be seen as compromised, especially by me."

"I don't know Emmett I think you should have let Lily in on this one. She's not going to take this well. I wouldn't be surprised if she's mad at the both of us."

"I'll make it up to her. What would you suggest Flowers? Candy? Jewellery?"

"Oh Emmett, you have a lot of discovering to do," Katha stated hiding a laugh.

"She doesn't like candy or flowers or jewellery?" Emmett asked puzzled.

"Lily will want a lot more than pretty gestures," Katha admonished. "You've hurt her. She also has trust issues due to those two husbands of hers, and you may have made that worse."

"I'm in trouble, aren't I?"

"Oh boy, are you ever," answered Katha, "How would you like a distraction?"

"Shouldn't I go after her now?"

"No, it looks like she's leaving without either of us."

Emmett watched Lily turn around and stalked by him. She then went out the front door of the police station without saying a word.

"No! Lily runs hot, when she's angry. She needs time to cool off,' Katha stated. "Let's get a coffee. There's a coffee shop around the corner."

Emmett and Katha walked over to the shop and then entered.

"So, do you want double cream, double sugar in your coffee? Or nothing in your coffee, like mine?" Emmett asked ordering two coffees.

"Double, double, please," Katha answered, finding and sitting down at a table.

Emmett picked up the coffees from the counter and took them to the table. Sitting down Emmett asked, "You look distracted. Did I create a huge rift between you and Lily?"

"No, we'll kiss and make-up. I'm about to announce something this afternoon to the press and I could use a cute guy by my side. What do you say?" enquired Katha pretending to flirt.

"Me? Why me? What happened to Terence Stewart the police chief's father?" asked Emmett looking uncomfortable.

"We had a little tiff. Can you believe he thought we should get married? I just wanted to live in sin."

Emmett spit out a mouth of coffee, laughing and then added, "He obviously cares about you."

"And I care about him but marriage? I've been married three times, before. I'm not sure I'm ready to give up my independence again."

"You've been married three times? I thought you were only married to Mr. O'Malley."

"Kieran O' Malley was my third husband, and the love of my life. We met when we were in public school. We were much too young to declare our love, but we spent all our time together. Of course then he went off to war and I never heard from him again until fifteen years ago," Katha coyly replied.

"That would be the Second World War?" Emmett interrupted.

"Of course, you silly boy. How old do you think I am? Don't answer that, if you value your life. He joined up when he was fourteen. He lied and said he was eighteen years old. I thought he died in the war, that's what I was told by his mother. Of course by the time the family found out he had been a prisoner of war, I had left London, England, with my first husband, Edward Kerr and gave birth to my daughter, Florence. I didn't see him for many years later. I attended a fundraiser for the hospital."

"My escort Gregory Hanks cancelled because he was ill. I sat down there and then he walked in the room, He looked like he did, when we first met. I swear time stood still as he walked across the room like in some kind of dream come true. My heart almost beat out of my chest when he walked up to me. I thought I had imagined him but there he was. He opened his mouth and said, "Katha Kelly, where have you been most of my life?"

"That sounds like a real line!"

"It worked with me. I kept that part of my heart sectioned only for him, and it opened up like a flower bursting forth for him, from that moment on."

"Did he treat you like the jewel you are?"

"Of course, he did. He was a charmer that man. We spent every day together after that chance meeting. In fact we were married three weeks later."

"Wow! That was fast."

"Not especially, we'd lost all that time together and we relished in every moment we had. He gave me flowers every day. We were married and I never tired of him telling me, that he loved me."

"He sounds like a great guy," Emmett commented.

"Kieran was incredibly sweet and fun. He had a sense of humour that wouldn't quit. He never failed to make me laugh. He would cook for me and bring me breakfast in bed. "Every day was so comfortable, so enjoyable. We enjoyed each other's company, so much. I foolishly thought we would die together in extreme old age." Katha continued, her voice going quieter here and sad, "One morning (three years ago) I awoke turned to him and found him dead beside me. The silent killer snatched him from me. My heart shattered and pieces if it still haven't recovered. I don't know if I could survive Terrence passed away, if I married him."

"Katha, he could die anyway. Wouldn't you like some time with him as his wife?" enquired Emmett, "Wouldn't you like some time carved out for the two of you?"

"Yes, but marriage... it's a huge step. I don't know if I want to take the plunge again. Kieran was a gem, but Edward and Charles were difficult men to live with. Terrence is a lot like Kieran too, but he is also set in his ways. He's been married twice before and neither of those marriages worked out. That's not a lot in his favour.

"Did Edward and Charles die?" questioned Emmett.

"Yes, but if they hadn't I would have divorced them. They were dreadful men and even worse husbands. Too bad I didn't see that, before I married them."

"You didn't do something to them?" Emmett kidded.

"No, they both died from natural causes," Katha giggled.

"Then how can you hold two marriages against Terrence. Could the fault have lain with those two men and not Terrence?"

"I know your right Emmett... that I'm looking for an excuse. Terrence can cook like a dream. He loves cooking and I hate it except for baking. He's charming and sweet and opens doors for me, even when I don't need it."

"Aren't those the qualities women look for in a man?"

"I guess. His stubborn nature may outweigh everything else. That's what I've got to consider," Katha answered, sipping some coffee.

"Being stubborn can be considered a good quality," Emmett stated "Besides he's not the only one who is stubborn."

"In whose world would that be, that stubbornness is a good quality?" Katha quipped.

"He must have some exceedingly, good qualities," Emmett stressed.

"Like I told you Emmett, he cooks. He is sweet; he likes to surprise me. He is a good man. He's loyal and loving," Katha replied.

"And do you love him?"

"Yes, I believe I do," Katha replied surprising herself.

"Then marry him," Emmett replied matter of fact.

"So says the man who's never taken the plunge, but I'll think on it."

"While you're thinking about it, think about this I have been married. My wife died."

Katha reached out towards Emmett and patted his hands in sympathy, and then said, "I'm sorry Emmett."

"You move forward but you never forget. You carve a piece out for them, to remember them and then you can find new love, at least that's what I'm told. I'm trying to balance that and move on with Lily."

"Don't hurt Lily. Thanks for the advice, Emmett. I will think on Terrence's proposal and weigh all you've told me before making a decision. In the meantime, I've something to ask you."

"Shoot."

"Should a policeman being saying that?" laughed Katha, "Seriously though I've decided to run for mayor. Could you be at my side in an hour, while I announce that I'm running for mayor?"

"You're running for mayor?" Emmett asked shocked.

"Someone's got to be the mayor and replace dear, dead Horace. Why shouldn't it be me?"

"Sounds good to me. You'll have my vote," Emmett answered.

"Good, I've got a lot of work ahead of me, especially if I win. I want to shake this town up and fix what needs to be fixed. Do you know I heard a real estate developer might be manipulating the city government? I think Horace must have been asleep at the switch," Katha stated.

"If Horace colluded with him, you have no proof. You ought to watch your speech Katha someone could hear you. So what's this developer's name?" Emmett asked, whispering.

"Okay, it's hearsay, until I have written statements, but I heard about Horace helping him. His name is H. Weatherthorpe. I don't know what the H stands for, but if he did manipulated the system to make money, when I get done with him as Mayor, his name will be mud.

"You really don't like this man."

"Something about this man creeps me out and I don't know why. But I hate his politics even more," Katha whispered back, so no one in the coffee shop would overhear.

"Do you think the city is that bad?"

"It's not that bad, but I aim to change that. And make the city better. Now let's go," Katha replied determined.

"I hope I have bitten off more than I can chew," Emmett muttered, following behind Katha.

~0~

Chapter 6 - Homework, Really?

Carol arrived to Rose's hospital room, walked in and slammed down her school bag.

"Way to get out of school. Principal Thomas has been such pain. She made it so no one can leave the classrooms during class. You have to get a hall slip to go to the washroom." Carol began the minute she came in, "And every two minutes people ask me did Rose and you find the body? Did the murderer hit Rose? Is she dead? What about me don't they care about me?"

"And hello to you too. Do you feel better? Did it hurt to have your appendix removed?" Rose asked, sarcastically.

"I'm getting to that. You're so ungrateful. I came on my lunch hour purely to see you even after you didn't answer any of my texts."

"Thank you for that, but my phone is dead," Rose responded.

"Do you mind if I eat in front of you?" Carol enquired, not waiting for a reply and eating her sandwich in front of Rose.

"I can't eat yet you know," Rose protested.

"Oh sorry, I hope you can eat soon. Did it hurt much? Can I see your scar?" Carol demanded.

"No, it doesn't hurt much now. And I'll be able to eat soon. I guess you can see my scar," Rose answered, "Draw the curtain and I'll show you."

Carol drew the curtain and then seeing the open wound she commented, "It's not so bad. You can still wear a bikini when it's healed it won't show much."

"You're sure?"

"Yes, I am sure it will heal nicely. It will be a thin white scar once they sew it back together. Besides you know the guys like you. Billy Robertson was especially worried about you. He cornered me to ask how you were. I think he might send you flowers. He wanted to know what room you were in. If Bobby Bradford asked after me like that I'd be thrilled."

"Billy asked about me?" asked Rose, surprised and pleased.

"Yes, he texted me. That stupid Nathan Patel and his friend Jack Heinz came over and spoke to me," Carol exclaimed.

"Yuck, I hate Nathan Patel and his friend Jack is worse than he is. I heard Jack slipped some girl roofies," Rose stated.

"Who told you that?"

"Kristy she said that her friend couldn't prove it but Jack did it."

"I'm staying away from that guy," Carol declared.

"Yes, me too."

"Ms. Brown gave us a ton of homework. I brought yours."

"Gee, thanks! You get sick have an operation and you still have to do homework?" Rose complained.

"Yes, it doesn't seem fair. Neither does the rest of your homework I brought. Here it is! Sorry to have to give the work to you, but I promised I would."

"You brought French homework, and math? Teachers annoy me. I hate homework," Rose replied angrily.

"We study integers and some other math stuff. It's all there," Carol stated.

"It's not fair. I'm not doing my homework, until I feel a bit better," Rose stated.

"I wouldn't either. I've got to get back to school or I'll get a detention again."

"Detention again?"

"I was late this morning, sue me. See you later."

"Goodbye, Carol," Rose cried after her.

Rose started the homework and finished it quickly finding herself and wondering what to do with herself. She pulled the television over hoping it now worked. Turning it on to see Grandma Katha in a flash alert the announcer said…, "Local resident Katha O'Malley chairwoman of our local hospital, lawyer for the underdog has a big announcement that could affect you. Tune into Channel seven for more details at noon."

"Mom, I'm glad you're back you won't believe what I saw on the television," Rose cried as Lily came into her hospital room.

"A new music video?" asked Lily.

Rose shook her head.

"What was it? A blurb on the music channel; something new from Lady Gaga or Beyoncé?" Lily continued.

"No, Mom, but at least it's nice to know you have been listening to me." Rose replied, "Grandma Katha and Emmett were in one of those flash alerts thingies about an upcoming story."

"Why would they be on the news? Oh no, Emmett complained about his questioning down at the station?" Lily complained, "What the hell is wrong with that man?"

"Emmett was questioned Mom? Why? Was it Mr. Scholar's murder? Is he a suspect?" fired Rose rapidly "He'd never harm anyone.

"Well…,"Lily broke off.

"Mom, don't tell me that is why you left? You went to go grill Emmett. I thought you cared about him. How could you do this to Emmett? How could you do this to me after everything I've done to try and accept you moving forward?" Rose cried, angrily, "I'm sure Daddy would have liked him, too. I like Emmett and if you screwed up this relationship..."

"Me, do this to Emmett? What about him?" Lily replied, not believing that Rose took Emmett's side.

"Mom, I know that this is your job but shouldn't you recuse yourself when someone you care about is involved?" asked Rose.

"I didn't know you even knew the word recuse and Rose quit blaming me, I didn't know. I got to the station and there he talked about being outside when Mr. Scholar was murdered." Lily stated exasperated.

"So he was there he didn't kill him. There's more to the story though isn't there? Spill the full story, Mom," Rose demanded.

"He said he sat in his car outside the school. He had a motive, because he was angry and he wanted to harm Mr. Scholar because he'd hurt his sister," Lily hesitated to tell her deciding whether not to tell Rose more.

"Oh no, she's pregnant isn't she?" Rose demanded.

"Emmett's sister is pregnant with Mr. Scholar's child," Lily admitted.

"What? No way! Poor woman, you should have seen Mr. Scholar with his several girlfriends. They were always coming to the classroom the last two weeks." Rose acknowledged, "I thought they must not have a lot of esteem."

"Your right they probably were lacking esteem but what kind of school do you go to; that a teacher can parade his paramours past his students?" asked Lily disgusted.

"What does paramour mean?" Rose puzzled.

"It means his girlfriends," explained Lily.

"Mom, people date all the time, big friggin deal!"

"You know how I feel about foul language."

"Sorry, mom, but it's not a swear word. i use it in my texts all the time."

"It is in my book and don't use it in front of me again."

"So, I can use it anywhere else?" Rose asked cheekily.

"No, you can't. Now tell me who you saw at the school with Mr. Scholar over the last few weeks."

"I saw the history teacher Ms. Brown, the Spanish teacher Ms. Vasquez, the principal Mrs. Thomas, and the head librarian Mrs. Abrams all kissing him in the last week," Rose stated.

"Well that man never heard the phrase that you should soil your own nest," Lily replied without thinking.

"Oh like Terrence says, 'Don't shit where you eat! ', " Rose answered knowingly.

"Rose your language is atrocious and getting out of hand," Lily admonished, "I'm going to talk with Terrence. That's an inappropriate way of talking in front of you."

"Terrence is a nice man and I'm almost an adult why can't I talk anyway I want to?"

"You are not an adult and I hope that when you are an adult you will choose your words carefully."

"I'm sorry Mom, but please don't say anything. Please don't embarrass me, besides Grandma Katha likes him you don't want to wreck that," Rose begged.

"I won't, but you better not repeat his inappropriate comments again," Lily scolded.

"Mom, you should hear the way they talk at school and the texts I get. That's nothing."

"Well I would rather you didn't talk like any of them and maybe I should be checking these texts."

"Fine, invade my privacy, but I don't think you're being fair. I don't swear like the rest of the kids and if all I've heard was true Mr. Scholar was awful," Rose complained.

"Mr. Scholar did not treat those women well but...," Lily replied changing the subject.

"It's true Mr. Scholar doesn't sound like a nice man," Rose agreed.

"Even people who aren't nice, don't deserve to die," Lily stated.

"I never said...oh just you never mind! What Emmett's alibi was that he sat in the car?" Rose inquired.

"He kissed Theresa Brown in his car," Lily admitted angrily.

"Ms. Brown, the history teacher?" asked Rose astonished, "Yuck! No wonder you're mad."

"Apparently she's also Dan Brown's sister," Lily explained.

"Dan Brown the investigating officer?" Rose asked.

"Yes," Lily replied.

"Now I get it. Emmett didn't tell you about being there and kissing another woman. Maybe you should have staked your claim."

"Staked my claim? That's ridiculous and old fashion and I am not jealous. I barely know the man and I still mourn your Dad," Lily answered."

Rose exclaimed, "You do like him, or you wouldn't be jealous."

"I am not jealous. I barely know the man and I still mourn your Dad," Lily answered.

"Me thinks the lady does protest too much." Rose cried laughing, "Besides Daddy would approve."

"Do you quote Shakespeare at me now?" asked Lily.

"You have to admit it fits, Mom."

"I'm glad you read great literature," Lily stated.

"Oh no, you don't Mom. You can't change the subject. You like him don't you?" Rose insisted, "That's okay as long as you still love dad. You do love Dad still, don't you?"

"I still love your dad and I like Emmett, but I'm mad at him. I didn't think he would kiss another woman when he's dating me," Lily complained.

"He seems like a good guy I don't think he'd do that. Mom, did he knew you were dating? You've been playing the guy kind of hot and cold. Besides she kissed him."

"I can't believe I'm discussing this with my teenage daughter. But I have to admit you give good advice," Lily said smiling.

"Of course I do. I've had a good teacher who gives me good advice all the time," Rose stated.

"Well thank-you Rose," Lily proudly replied.

"Mom, I'd like to give you the credit, but a lot of his advice comes from Grandma Katha." Rose reluctantly explained, "For someone so old, she's pretty smart."

"Your Great Grandma Katha always gives me good advice but for your own sake don't call her old," Lily admitted.

"She's pretty kewl," Rose responded.

"Kewl? What the heck does that mean is that the same as cool?" Lily asked

"Gee mom, you have to learn some new slang," Rose replied "That one has been around for so long that I'm a little embarrassed to use it even for you."

"Sorry, I'll remember my place," Lily replied sarcastically.

Rose then turned to the television and gasped.

"Mom, Grandma Katha and Emmett are on the television now. Turn it up," demanded Rose.

Lily leaned in and turned up the volume.

"We are here with Katha O'Malley a prominent attorney, activist, chartable contributor, and Hospital board member and here in town and Sergeant Detective Emmett Rogers of the Happy Valley police force. Katha O'Malley has called us here for a reason.

What would that reason be Ms. O'Malley?" asked the reporter on the television.

"This town was rocked with tragedy two months ago as you all well know. My grandson by marriage was brutal murdered by a cold blood serial killer who stalked my family. Incredibly because of my great-granddaughter, Rose and the bravery of this man here beside me that killer was apprehended. The reason I am here today is to give back to this city," Katha answered.

"I have participated in many charities and have served faithfully on the school board and on the hospital board for many years now. I want to put that all too good use to help this city and run this city as the Mayor. I know that I can see this city balance their books and make this city one of the nicest places to leave once again," Katha avowed.

"Thank-you, Ms. O'Malley. So there you have it, another candidate for Mayor on your November ballot. Stay tuned to this station for your evening news and updates in the investigation of the murder of Alexander Scholar at Happy Valley High two days ago."

"Wow, mom, Grandma Katha wants to be the Mayor. It's about to get interesting in Happy Valley," Rose commented.

"It does seem that she wants to be the Mayor. They would be lucky to get her. She would be exceedingly good for this city," Lily exclaimed.

"She could shake up council. That's for sure," Rose answered.

"But I hope she understands the mayor can't get everything done without council agreements. I wonder why she didn't tell us a head of time that she ran for mayor?" Lily cried a little hurt.

"I think she may have broken up with Terrence. She'll deny it Mom, but she was a little down in the dumps," Rose explained.

"Terrence seems like a nice man I'm sure whatever the problem is she'll sort it out," Lily soothed.

"I hope you are right mom. I'm going to sleep now I'm tired." Rose cried suddenly, "Wake me up when Aunt Amelia gets here. I hope Grandma Katha remembers my cord my I-phone is dead and then I want to watch Vampire Diaries."

"Sweet dreams, baby doll," Lily said, "I'll sit here and watch you sleep."

Lily watched a now sleeping Rose and breathed a sigh of relief. She had been so worried, but now Rose was on the mend, she would be going home soon. Emmett kissing that woman was unbelievable, but that was the point. Emmett was a good man he would never cheat on her she had to learn to trust that. William and Horace had strayed so obviously that had left her with trust issues.

She wasn't going to ruin this blossoming relationship with those old insecurities. She knew she had to make this relationship work and teach Rose that not all relationships were doomed to fail. After all we mimic what we see from our parents and Rose had seen plenty of incidents that no child should ever see with her birth mother, Lily had to do better. Without Horace Rose's father Lily was all she had. Well I guess that's not true. Katha and Amelia are also there for Rose but they didn't have that much a better track record then Lily did at love.

Now Grandma Katha wavered from staying with Terrence; like loving him like it was a bad thing. She had such a love with Grandpa Kieran. Lily had thought Grandma Katha gave up after he died but she pulled herself together and went on helping Amelia cope when she lost her family.

Were the Kelly's doomed to love and lose? No, Lily was determined that would never happen again, at least for her but it seemed that she couldn't get past that kiss. Kissing someone meant you cheated, no matter what anyone else said. He had to prove to her it meant nothing then they could go on and work out a relationship. Emmett shouldn't have kissed Teresa, but did he, or was it that entire woman's fault? Needy grasping woman tend to go after nice men.

~0~

Chapter 7 - Actions Speak Louder than Words

One Week Later

Rose lay on the sofa at her home. Cranky and out of sorts, Rose kicked the blanket off and sighed. Lily then absentmindedly reached over and put the blanket back on Rose.

"I'm fine and the blanket made me hot. Mom, you have to quit fussing over me." Rose complained, "I'm glad they stitched me shut again. Where's my I-phone plugged in I'm missing all the text messages."

"I'm not fussing. Okay, I guess I am. Sorry, Rose. I'm so glad to have you home. Here's your phone."

"Me too! Hospitals are a real pain."

"Yes, literally.'" laughed Lily, as Rose joined in.

"Don't, oh that hurts," Rose cried, holding her side, but still smiling through the grimacing. Rose then began scrolling on the I-phone for messages.

"Is this a party, or can anyone join in?" Emmett asked.

In Emmett's arms were roses, candy and a book.

"Emmett? Hello. Did Aunt Amelia let you in?" asked Rose putting down her phone, "Darn those are for mom aren't they?"

"They are for your mom, and yes, Amelia let me in," Emmett answered Rose, while turning to Lily he asked, "Can I have a couple of minutes of your time?"

"I suppose I could give you a few minutes, excuse us for a second Rose," Lily replied.

"Don't take his head off mom. Listen to his explanation. He's called several times in the last week, Grandma Katha said," Rose whispered.

"I wasn't home," protested Lily.

"You are now. Talk to him, mom, please? I feel sorry for the guy."

Lily stepped into the next room and shut the door. Rose slowly got up from the sofa, and walked over to the door. Rose pressed her ear against the door and heard..., "Here, this for you Lily."

"Candy and flowers? What do you think I am a heroine in a book that needs to be wooed?" Lily asked sarcastically.

"It's my way of saying, I'm sorry."

"You didn't tell me you were being brought in for a murder inquiry," Lily exclaimed, sounding hurt and annoyed.

"I know and as I said I'm sorry Lily. I should have told you, but I thought if I did it might put you in a bad position. You're the Crown attorney and the man you're dating is a suspect? I know we agreed to keep our relationship quiet for a few months to protect your reputation and here I was blowing it wide open," Emmett explained.

"It worked out well for you," Lily countered.

"How can you say that? You are mad enough at me to spit nails, so how did I benefit?" Emmett asked.

"I don't know it must have been nice to have Theresa Brown fawn all over you and kiss you," Lily stated.

"Oh, so that's what you're mad about. You're jealous," Emmett stated knowingly.

"What is this high school? Where you put your lips, is no never mind to me."

"For your information she kissed me and I told her I was involved," Emmett replied hurt and annoyed.

"Sure, then that makes it all better," Lily answered sarcastically.

Lily breathed in and then smiled and turned to the box of chocolates opening them, "What kind of chocolates are these?"

"Creams. A little birdie told me you like cream filled chocolates," Emmett answered, not sure why Lily had changed her tune.

"Thank-you for the flowers and chocolate," Lily said, for the record I like chocolate with nuts too. Goodbye now."

"Goodbye? Do you forgive me?" Emmett asked, realizing that Lily was still angry.

"Forgive you for what?" Lily asked sounding surprised.

Emmett wondered if he ever understand women. Was she mad or not? He decided she wasn't, the chocolates had worked.

Rose smiled behind the door and went back to lie on the sofa before Lily opened the door and caught her. Lily swept through the door and Emmett closely followed behind her crying, "Oh, okay, so you're not mad. That's good."

"Boy do you have a lot to learn," Rose stated under her breath, but Emmett heard and looked surprised.

"Are there any leads on the killer?" Emmett asked thinking that was safer topic.

"Even though you have an alibi, I can't discuss this with you," Lily exclaimed.

"Is it true that Dan Brown has been taken off the case?" Emmett persisted.

"That wasn't done by me. Chief Stewart took him off the case and replaced him with Sergeant Detective Kendall Evans," Lily protested.

"I don't think I've met him has he been on the force long?" Emmett asked.

"Kendall is a woman and she transferred here from another city," Lily replied. "I think she recently made Sergeant."

"Is she good?" asked Emmett.

"I haven't actually met her, but she seems to be. She's weeding through the information," Lily answered. "I've talked to her on the phone, but as I said I can't share any of the information with you."

"But I'm not even a suspect anymore," complained Emmett.

"Okay, I guess I could share a little with you, but you didn't hear it from me. Understand? Alexander "Vincent" Scholar was a busy man with the ladies. He seems to have women coming out of the woodwork. Some of them know him as Vincent, others as Alex, or Alexander, some as Zander. As Grandma Katha would say he was a heel. He seems to have been involved with a number of women at the school and the hospital and numerous other places in town. How he juggled them all, I don't know!"

"So any leads? Do you have anyone without any alibi?"

"Plenty! None of them seem to have an alibi. Most of these women live alone."

"Surely motive will filter them out," Emmett commented.

"They all have motive, that's the problem. The man was contemptible. He asked a lot of them to marry him. He gave out numerous glass engagement rings. We found a whole drawer full of rings at his apartment," Lily explained.

"That explains the ring he gave my sister," Emmett answered. "It was definitely glass. At least that's what the jeweller said where Suzy took the ring to be examined."

"How is your sister?" asked Lily.

"She's getting bigger every day."

"I hope you don't tell her that."

"No. of course I didn't. I want to keep my body all in one piece. The doctor said she's expecting twins. She's on complete bed rest, until the babies are born."

"I understand she was in the hospital the day of the murder." Lily said sympathetically.

"They thought she would lose the baby, er... babies. They found out then she's having more than one that day."

"But she's feeling okay?"

"She's doing much better. I hired someone to look after her though, when I'm not at home."

"You're a good brother."

"Our parents were killed when she was sixteen and I've looked after her and my other sister ever since then, I'm not about to stop now. Uncle Emmett will always help her with the babies," Emmett insisted.

"How far along in her pregnancy is she?" asked Lily.

"Almost six months. I don't know how she hid it so long carrying twins. I guess it's because she so tiny to begin with. She looks like she has this big beach ball out in front."

"So have you, or one of her friends planned the baby shower?"

"I have to throw a baby shower?" asked Emmett looking panicked.

"You have a month or two to wait, but with twins they could come sooner," Lily answered. "Of course you could wait until they were born."

"They can come sooner?" Emmett blanched.

"Sometimes they are born earlier. Would you like some help Emmett? Rose, Amelia, Katha, and I are experts at parties, and I'm sure we could prepare a lovely baby shower. You could wheel Suzy in and we could shower her with gifts for the babies."

"I'll help this should be fun," commented Rose.

Emmett looked away from Lily to Rose, suddenly realizing Rose was in the room.

"You know about Suzy?"

"Mom told me, but I didn't tell anyone," Rose replied defensively.

"You'd do that for Suzy? Throw her a party so she'd feel good about the babies? But you don't even know her," Emmett exclaimed.

"No, we don't know her, but we would love to get to know her. She's you sister, so she's got to be pretty special," Lily answered. "But this doesn't mean I'm not still mad at you."

"Of course, you are not over your mad." Emmett replied, slightly confused, "Thanks Lily and Rose, for the offer of the baby shower. Suzy would appreciate that and so will I."

"What are friends for? So what do you have there Emmett?" Lily asked motioning to the book.

"A present for Rose. I should go give it to her?"

"I thought you said you didn't have anything for her?" Lily stated looking surprised.

"I wanted to talk to you first, and then surprise Rose."

"Rose would love a present. That's a thoughtful idea, go ahead and give it to her," Lily commented hiding a smile as he handed it to Rose.

"Here, Rose."

"Thanks Emmett, I haven't read this one. The title of the book is Jane and the Unpleasantness at Scargrove Manor? Is this about Jane Austen?" asked Rose.

"My sister Suzy highly recommended it. She says it's written in the Austen style," Emmett replied.

"I can hardly wait to read this," Rose answered excited, then continued, "You'll never believe what I heard on the television."

"I don't know how you heard anything on television when it's clear you were listening in on us," Lily answered.

Rose blushed.

"What did you hear now?" asked Lily and Emmett together.

"There's some big meeting at the high school, apparently parents freaked out saying their kids aren't safe. They even had the nerve to bring up Daddy's murder."

"How dare they use Horace," cried Lily angrily.

"I'm sorry they did that Rose and Lily," Emmett sympathized.

Emmett and Lily's text message sounded on their cell phones rang simultaneously.

"It looks like we're being paged to the meeting. I don't want to leave you alone Rose," Lily stated checking her phone.

"I'll be fine I'll keep my phone handy and Carol can come over and stay with me."

"Please, phone Carol now, and see if she can come over," Lily demanded.

"I'm calling her," Rose replied annoyed.

"Make sure she can stay for awhile," Lily insisted.

"Carol, it's Rose. Can you come over for a couple of hours? You can? Wonderful, yah, my mom has to go out to a meeting. I know moms can be a pain. Your mom will drive you? Sure, I'll tell her. Tell your mom I said thanks, and so does my mom. Bye. See you soon," Rose commented concluding her conversation.

"Carol will come over? Will you be okay for few minutes, until she gets here? I have to go now," Lily stated looking worried.

"I'll be fine now. You can go."

"See you later," Emmett and Lily stated at the same as they left out the front door.

"In awhile crocodiles."

Rose breathed a sigh of relief at her freedom. Carol arrived a few minutes later, letting herself in the house, with the key under the mat. Carol plopped herself down on the sofa beside Rose, jarring her a little bit, and making Rose wince.

"Sorry, I didn't mean to hurt you. Did you get your homework done? I can take it in for you tomorrow," Carol offered.

"I got it all done. I still think it's unfair."

"Don't kid, a kidder, Rose Brooksfield! I'm your best friend. We've been friends for a long time. I know you. You love homework. And you love getting A's best of all," Carol exclaimed

"I do not. I like to do my best work and they reward me with A's."

"They reward you with A's because you like to study and write long essays."

"I guess, but if you'd apply yourself a little more you could get them too," Rose argued.

"I work hard. I don't see why I should spend all my time doing work for school."

"Gee, you're saying I'm a nerd?" Rose demanded.

"Ah, no. Let's change the subject I don't want to fight with you," Carol says "So do you have Vampire Diaries, or did you already watch?"

"I have the show and no, I haven't watched it yet. I fell asleep," Rose complained.

"So how are your mom and her new boyfriend, Emmett?" Carol asked, as Rose cues up Vampire Diaries on TIVO.

"Mom isn't dating him. Mom sensed my reluctance and that's why she pushed him away," Rose lied.

"I don't understand it. Your mother seemed to like him," Carol complained.

"They are supposed to be adults, but they fight about the stupidest things and I messed up their date with my appendicitis." Rose replied sadly.

"Yes my parents were like that before their divorce. So fix it."

"How can I do that?"

"You've watched All My Children or General Hospital for how long?" asked Carol, "Do you remember when Zach kidnapped

Kendall on the yacht, and they had a fabulous time? And look how Pete convinced Cecilia to go to New York with him in the reboot."

"Look how Pete and Cecilia turned out and the show isn't on anymore. What does this have to do with my Mom and Emmett? We don't have a yacht and I can't fly them to New York."

"Gee, and people say you have a romantic nature. Why didn't you think of this Rose? You don't need a yacht. You need to plan a date and have those two go on it. Send an email from your Mom to Emmett, telling him to meet her here at a certain time. Make sure he's all dressed up and when he gets here. Get your Mom to get dressed up and go to the restaurant you pick. Then make sure you reserve dinner there," Carol replied. "Now can we watch Vampire Dairies?"

"I think that might work but Mom won't go out and leave me alone. Do you know how hard it was to get her to go for work tonight?" Rose complained.

"So get your Grandma Katha to help. She can pay for the restaurant ahead of time too," Carol explained.

"Sounds like you thought of everything. I think Grandma Katha will go along with this. She likes Emmett too."

"Being an All My Children fan comes in handy, even if the show is in limbo," Carol stated grabbing some chips and throwing them in her mouth.

"Hey, give me some chips, before they are all gone. Let's fast forward and get to the good parts."

"Is this a private party, or can anyone else join in?" asked Amelia coming in.

"Come on in and watch Vampire Diaries," Rose replied.

"Oh, good, fill me in on what I missed," Amelia asked setting herself down in a nearby chair.

"Emmett made my Mom mad and they aren't speaking."

"Actually, I wanted to know about the show, but Lily is mad at Emmett? Why?" Amelia demanded surprised.

"Our teacher kissed him," Carol offered.

"And did he kiss her back?" demanded Amelia, looking angry, "I'll fix his wagon."

"I don't think he kissed her back, but Mom is annoyed."

"Oh...Lily did have two husbands that cheated. She'll take her time before she commits."

Rose looked angrily at Amelia.

"Sorry Rose, no offence to your father but he did stray and that hurt your mom," Amelia stated.

"He loved Mom. I know he did."

"He did love her, but he hurt her too. Lily doesn't trust as easily anymore."

"I can understand that, but Carol and I have a plan to fix it all," Rose stated.

"I'm not sure that you should interfere."

"Do you want Mom happy or not?"

"I want Lily happy."

"Me too, so even if I don't like her moving on so quickly I'm going to grin and bear it. Mom deserves to be happy."

Rose and Carol then lay out their plan and Amelia nodded and agreed to help and get Grandma Katha on board as well.

~0~

Chapter 8 – Whose Bed has Mr. Scholar's Boots Been Under?

L ily crept into the back of the Happy Valley High School

auditorium at first checking out the gathering crowd. Her boss had been manipulated by the acting Mayor Harold Crimshaw and had deemed it necessary not only for her to be here for this town meeting but to actively participate. Lily thought that Mayor Crimshaw insisting that she give a speech, totally unnecessary. Lily however had no choice she knew that until the election of a new mayor, Mayor Crimshaw had the power to fire her.

He manipulated everyone through some antiquated law still on the books. So she would provide a speech if that would keep him happy. Lily liked her job and wasn't in the market for a new one or for scanning the partnerships to become a lawyer at a firm.

Frankly she hoped someone beat the man in the election and Grandma Katha would be a good choice even though it would be odd working for her.

"Hello, Lily," Emmett exclaimed, suddenly appearing behind her.

"You scared me you shouldn't creep up on a person like that." Lily answered, "Were you sent here too?"

"How did you guess? I'm to meet my new partner until this case is solved Sergeant Detective Kendall Evans. I don't suppose you could point her out to me could you?" asked Emmett.

"Sorry, Emmett, I've only talked to her on the phone. Remember I told you that. She's been good about keeping me in the loop though via the phone." Lily admitted, 'Besides I'm preparing for the speech I have to make."

"Joy. You too, have to make a speech? Well I guess I'll have to hope she knows what I look like."

"Good luck, Emmett. See you at the podium," Lily replied to his departing back

Lily listened intently as she heard groups of people simultaneously start talking about Alexander Scholar.

"He dated my sister you know. She is such a stupid bitch. He snowed her good. She actually thought he would marry her. Did she ever look in the mirror?" asked one person.

"While I heard he had affairs with a bunch of the teachers here at this school," the other person continued.

"Tell me more," said the other voice.

"None of them knew he had it on with the others, because he told them they had to keep it on the down low or he'd get fired or they'd get fired. No teacher interactions in their contracts so he used that," replied the other.

"Those poor children what kind of a man uses all those school rooms that way?"

"May I have your names please and identification," demanded Lily, pulling out her Crown Attorney identification.

"Well, I never. We were having a private conversation here you have no business listening in," the one woman complained.

"Didn't anyone ever teach you it is bad manners to eavesdrop?" the other woman asked outraged.

"She's a lawyer. She doesn't have any power over me."

"There are no private conversations when someone has been murdered. Now let me see some identification now!" Lily forcefully demanded once more.

"Sally Potter, see," replied the first speaker showing identification from her wallet.

"Renata Parsons." the other replied showing her driver's licence "But you are not a police officer. I don't have to cooperate."

"Ms. Parsons, would you prefer we took this to a police officer and have a formal interview with one of them at the police station," Lily stated angrily.

"That won't be necessary will it Renata?" Sally urged.

"Thank-you Ms. Potter. Now you Ms. Potter you were saying your sister was involved with Mr. Scholar what is her name?" demanded Lily

"Now there's no call for getting my sister involved in this. She may be foolish, but she's my sister," Sally complained loudly.

"I'm sure you wouldn't want us to find out later that would look bad for your sister if you can give us her name we can eliminate her from our inquires."

"Well I guess her name is Margaret Hearst. She's a math teacher at the school. She lives at 300 Hunt Drive," Sally admitted, "She's sweet but that's what makes her such a target for unscrupulous people like Alexander Scholar."

"Thank-you Ms. Potter. Now you, Ms. Parsons, where did you hear that he had these affairs with several teachers? Do you have names?" Lily demanded writing furiously in a small notebook.

"I heard about it in the supermarket I picked up some brisket for dinner, and then I couldn't find the cabbage. This woman stood next to it crying," Renata answered.

"A woman cried next to the cabbage?" Lily inquired puzzled.

"Yes. So I say to her. What's the matter? And she says I've been had literally and figuratively. Well I didn't understand that so I said so and she says that she's an English teacher at the school and that her boyfriend is a cad. He's been sleeping with numerous other women. I said I was sorry that she'd been treated that way and she said you and me both. She said he slept with many women at her school and probably had tricked them the same way. She said she'd been tricked with promises of marriage a glass ring and protection. The only thing she got out of it was secrecy for their relationship, so she wouldn't get fired," Renata explained.

"Did you get a name?" asked Lily.

"No, it was one of those chance encounters; where you comfort someone because they need it. You know?" enquired Renata.

"Could you describe this woman?" Lily asked.

"Let me see.... five foot three inches tall give or take an inch. She had blonde curly hair short to her ears and blue eyes. She wore a blue dress, too," Renata answered.

"Thank-you both, you've been helpful to the investigation. I hope you appreciate that we need you to keep this quiet, so as not to alert anyone of the seriousness of this information," Lily cautioned.

"I was that helpful?" asked Renata puffing up like a peacock.

"The information collected will be analyzed and hopefully point us to the killer," Lily stated.

"Wow, we may have helped find a killer," Renata exclaimed turning to her friend.

"It sure looks like it," Sally answered. She then turned to Lily and said, "Nice meeting you, Ms. Crown attorney Wentworth."

"I don't think that the name she goes by that was her other husband's name. I think her name is Crown attorney Kelly, right Ms. Kelly?" Renata asked.

"That's correct, Ms. Parsons. Thank-you both for your time I must get up to the podium and officer may be in touch with you later to take your statement again and or follow up on the information," Lily stated as turned to leave.

"Nice lady. I'd vote for her again. She sure does her job," Renata stated.

"You don't vote for Crown attorney in this country. They are appointed. Don't you pay attention what and who you vote for?" asked Sally annoyed.

"I pay attention some of the time I voted for William, Horace, or was it Harold, for Mayor?" Renata complained.

"Good grief, William Wentworth was her first murdered husband; Horace was that woman's second murdered husband. Harold Crimshaw acts as the mayor, now," Sally explained rolling her eyes, "Kind of hard on her husbands isn't she?"

"Hush, she'll hear you," Sally cautioned.

"If I could I'd vote for her. She's doing a great job," Renata stated.

"Me too, even if she is pushy woman have to be pushy in that sort of job." Sally whispered.

Lily heard every word and smiled at least they thought she was doing her job she only hoped her employers thought she did a good job. Lily reached the door to the back of the auditorium opening it to hear..., "And so I want to assure you as acting Mayor that our city is perfectly safe. Our police work diligently to find the culprit who killed Alexander Scholar. The police believe this may have been a domestic dispute," Acting Mayor Harold Crimshaw stated.

"What the hell?" Emmett whispered to Lily, "We never said any of that, to my knowledge."

"He's pontificating trying to win the election," Lily explained angrily, then taking a breath to calm herself she continued, "But we can use this to our advantage."

"Sorry, I'm late did I miss anything? I'm Sergeant Detective Kendall Evans," A tall statuesque Nordic looking blonde asked holding out her hand to Lily.

"Hello," Emmett all but gushed straightening up and holding out his hand, "I'm Sergeant Detective Emmett Rogers."

"You're my new partner. It is so nice to meet you. And you are Lily Kelly, the Crown attorney," Kendall exclaimed with a smile, still looking at Emmett.

Lily is taken back by this as the smile seems more for Emmett then her.

"It's nice to meet you," Lily exclaimed, then went onto explain what Kendall had missed in the speech from the mayor, "His worship the Acting Mayor tells us not to worry our pretty little heads that it was a domestic dispute gone wrong and the killer will be found shortly."

"What an idiot!" Kendall cried loudly then covered her mouth, lest someone have heard her.

"We can concur, but we can use this to our advantage," Emmett said like it was his idea with a frown from Lily, "Sorry Crown attorney Kelly, it was your idea, you can explain it."

"It could be a domestic dispute a crime of passion; it has all the signs of a planned killing. They brought the weapon and cut out the heart. That hasn't been revealed has it?" Lily asked.

"Of course not, that would be poor policing we haven't revealed anyone all the details of the killing. You and your daughter only know because you were one of the first people on scene," Kendall explained.

"Then I think we can use that to our advantage," Lily explained.

"I'm sure we can right Emmett?" asked Kendall, starring at Emmett like he looked like ice cream.

"Yes... er Kendall," Emmett gulped. Emmett then turned to Lily and said, "You're up Lily, time to make your speech."

Lily sauntered up to the head of the podium and took hold of the microphone still watching Kendall and Emmett. The two of them had their heads close together. They had better fill me in later. She thought I don't like the way she looked at him like his chocolate she has to have. Putting away her thoughts she calmed herself as the mayor introduced her.

"Ladies and gentleman I assure you, as the acting Mayor did that the police are on top of this crime. I assure you we're treating this crime with the utmost care and attention. Here is our crown attorney Lily Kelly to brief you on more. Lily?" Harold Crimshaw introduced.

"We work diligently to find and apprehend the person responsible for this hideous crime," Lily fiercely claimed, "I want to warn you, whoever you are, we will find you and you will pay for this crime."

"That is absolutely correct, thank-you Ms. Kelly. In fact two detectives are now on this case. If you would give a warm welcome to Sergeant Detective Emmett Rogers, and Sergeant Detective Kendall Evans brilliant detectives who have been assigned to this case," Harold Crimshaw said with flourish. Emmett and Kendall Evans nodded to the audience.

Principal Jane Carol Thomas, a five ten inch tall woman with short curly brown hair stood up and said, "Thank-you Mayor Crimshaw, Crown Attorney Kelly, Sergeant Detective Emmett Rogers and Sergeant Detective Kendall Evans for your hard work. I'm sure the parents now all feel much better about their children's safety in our school. Lieutenant Evans you wanted to say a few words, so without further ado I give you, Lieutenant Evans."

Principal Thomas then sat down. Lily noted she appeared a little over weight in a black pantsuit that clung too tightly to her abundant curves. Lily wondered if she acted catty, simply because she felt jealous of Kendall's looks and now looked at all women standing near him suspiciously. What was wrong with her that she acted this way? She wouldn't act this way she wouldn't. Lily had to concentrate on this case and put aside her foolish emotions. Lily then realized she had not been listening to Kendall's speech and started to listen to the rest.

"You will not succeed in getting away with murder. I and my colleague will find you. This I promise," Kendall stated looking fierce and then sat down.

The principal then stood up again and concluded the night with her last speech of the night, "This school is safe. We will be keeping a police presence here and everyone will be searched as they were tonight when you entered this auditorium. To those of you who say this violates your civil rights; please note that under city bylaws the police have the right to do this to keep your children and yourselves safe. Goodnight and to reiterate Our Crown Attorney, and the investigating officers, we will find you. Goodnight ladies and gentlemen, this concludes this evening's meeting,"

Mayor Crimshaw then turned to Lily and said, "Well I think that went well."

"Yes, sir. I have to leave now. I have an early morning start to get on the information coming in about this crime, plus I have to prepare my briefs for the Georgic case tomorrow. I want to win," Lily explained wanting to leave and get back to Rose.

"All is ready for that case you will convict that mobster?" asked Acting Mayor Crimshaw.

"Yes sir, it's practically a slam dunk," Lily reassured him.

Mayor Crimshaw then left.

"Bet your glad that idiot is gone," Emmett exclaimed.

"I hope Katha wins against him," Lily answered, "Because I don't want to work for him to long."

"Me too! I think she'd make a great Mayor. She's got guts and grit."

"That she does in spades," Lily agreed.

"So did you bring your car?" Emmett asked stepping closer to Lily.

"Amelia dropped me off. Her car is the shop and I didn't want to leave them without a car," Lily explained, "She went home to be with Carol and Rose."

"Can I give you a ride?" Emmett asked.

"I like that," Lily replied smiling.

"Oh there you are Emmett. I thought we could go out for coffee and discuss the case," Kendall flirted with Emmett.

"I already promised Ms. Kelly a ride home. I'm off the clock we can meet in the morning," Emmett answered.

"Oh, I guess I was mistaken I thought you'd like to get up to speed on the case," Kendall needled.

"I'm up to speed Kendall. I've already accessed the entire case. I guess they didn't tell you I'm the senior officer on this case. You're here to help me!" Emmett laid it out for her.

Lily hid a small smile at the rebuked but watched as this sunk in and Kendall got a distinct pout on her face that marred her looks, which Kendall then took pains to hide.

"So can we meet in the morning then to discuss the case?" Kendall asked.

"Goodnight, Kendall. See you tomorrow morning six a.m. sharp at the station," Emmett stated forcefully.

As Emmett left with Lily, Lily could have sworn she heard Kendall groan which made Lily smile. She couldn't help it. Emmett had chosen Lily, not Miss Beauty Queen, Kendall Evans.

~0~

Chapter 9 –
Dating is fun!
Really!!

Rose lay on the sofa looking towards the front door

jumping at every sound.

"Expecting someone?" asked Lily, "Is it Carol? Is she on her way over?"

Rose chose not to answer.

"Rose, I'm speaking to you. When you don't answer that's considered rude," admonished Lily.

As the doorbell rang, Rose tried to get up, but leapt up too quickly and gasped in pain.

"I'll answer it. You stay put. Carol can wait," Lily insisted

Opening the door, Lily is surprised to find Emmett dressed in a dark blue tailored suit, a red tie and shiny black patent leather shoes.

"Emmett did we have an appointment? Why are you here? I wasn't expecting you, was I?" Lily stated.

"I don't understand you emailed me and told me to be here," Emmett stated.

"No I didn't. Rose Brooksfield what have you done?" demanded Lily.

Emmett stared hard at Rose then a smile came over his face. Rose smiled back a huge conspiratorial smile.

"Rose, I'm speaking to you. What have you done?" repeated Lily.

"You two are pigheaded and you still haven't gone on your date so I arranged a date," Rose admitted.

"Come on Lily. It does seem sweet gesture on Rose's part," Emmett replied.

"But it does mean she got in my private email. Haven't you learned your lesson? No more of that Rose Brooksfield," Lily admonished "My computer is not yours to use. Haven't you learned from what happened before? Do I have to change all my passwords, again?"

"Sorry, Mom. Now go up and get ready Mom. Put on your prettiest dress," Rose encouraged.

"I can't leave you all alone. You are recovering from major surgery," Lily complained.

"Good grief, I'm getting better besides Grandma Katha will be here in ten minutes. So no more excuses Mom. Go get ready to go. So you can look your best." Rose commanded, "Dating is fun. Really!"

"You've got this all planned out don't you?"

Rose nodded.

Lily saw how determined Rose looked and she cried, "Oh all right. I'll go get ready."

Lily ran upstairs quickly. Emmett smiled to himself, as he noted that Lily seemed actually happy to go out with him. Even if the date wasn't her doing, there was hope yet.

"So, I have you to thank for my date with your Mom tonight, Rose?" Emmett enquired.

"Well...," Rose replied a little sheepishly.

"Great work, kid. Now where do we go on this date?" Emmett asked, "Or should I make reservations now?"

"I thought that restaurant Trivotti's on Hunt Drive. It's got great reviews. I made you and Mom a reservation," Rose explained.

"That's a little pricey on a police salary. But I'll swing it," Emmett answered.

"That's the other thing. It's a present from Amelia, Grandma Katha, and I," Rose explained. "Oh, and I don't want to forget Carol. She gave me the idea."

"I don't know if I should accept such an extravagant gift. It was nice of you, but I can't believe you talked to Carol about me and your Mom," Emmett perturbed and slightly embarrassed.

"You have to accept it's a gift. We talked about you a little, but nothing bad, only that me getting sick ruined your date."

"Rose, you could never ruin anything for your Mom and I. We would have eventually made up our date."

"Now you don't have to. You two can go out now."

"I guess if you put it that way how can I refuse, besides your Mom owes me a date," Emmett answered.

"Good because as I said everything is arranged your reservation is at seven o'clock."

"Oh good, Grandma Katha here and it sounds like Mom is almost ready." Rose stated, "There she is now."

Emmett turned and saw Lily come down the stairs. He thought her a vision of true loveliness, in her dress of brilliant blue. The dress made her blue eyes shine like diamonds. Her hair usually in a twist was out. It was long and hung to her waist in curly red gold corkscrew curls. Emmett had to admit he loved curly hair on a woman and something about Lily's hair made him want to run his hands through it and kiss her senseless.

Emmett check himself there was a child here, an impressionable teenage girl, who counted on him to treat her mother like a queen. Their first time together would be spectacular, but running his hands through Lily's hair and over her body would have to wait. Lily was like a spooked horse and needed tender handling. No matter what his desires he would rush her, not if he had any hope of keeping her love.

"Do you like my dress Emmett?"

"It's lovely, you're lovely Lily."

"Why thank-you, kind sir."

"Shall we go?"

"Let's," Lily replied putting on her fall coat.

Lily noted the falling leaves and the changing colours of the trees and said to Emmett.

"Aren't the trees lovely? I think fall is my favourite time of year, all those pretty red and orange leaves create a beautiful picture."

"It's my favourite time of year too."

"Something else we have in common."

"That's true."

"So where do we go?" asked Lily.

"We'll go to Trivotti's on Hunt Drive. It's supposed to be a four star restaurant, or is it five star? Either way, it's supposed to have great food. I hope you like Italian food."

"I love Italian food. How did you know?"

"I have to be honest I didn't. Apparently Rose thought of everything and made the reservation. In fact she insisted that your Grandma Katha, Amelia, and herself, pick up the tab."

"Wow, that's my girl," Lily commented. "She such a thoughtful girl, sometimes I worry she acts too old for her age and she was never a child."

"She seems like a well-adjusted teen. You've done a great job with her Lily."

"Thanks Emmett, it's nice to hear that," Lily replied.

"She's been through so much in her life."

"And yet she's a sweet understanding girl," Emmett finished.

"Like I said thanks Emmett you're good for me."

"I hope so. I like to be good for you," Emmett answered playfully.

"Oh, oh, oh..." Lily blushed.

"Here we are my lady."

Emmett then pulled up to the curb, parked the car and went around to the passenger door to open the door for Lily. As they went into Trivotti's, Lily noticed the beautiful tables with lace table cloths. She saw flowers at every table and a roving violinist. "It's almost like a parody of the perfect restaurant, but somehow it works," Emmett commented.

"I'd have to agree. It is a lovely restaurant. So what is your favourite colour?" Lily asked.

"Blue is my favourite colour, especially when I see you in that dress."

"My favourite color is blue as well. So do you have any siblings besides Suzy?"

"I have one other sister, I had another, but she's gone. I don't like to talk about the circumstances," Emmett stated.

"I'm sorry Emmett. I don't have any siblings, but it must be difficult to lose one. Amelia is like a sister to me," Lily answered.

"So you were married before Horace?" asked Emmett.

"You know this. My husband was William Wentworth he was the Crown attorney. I met him while working with him and we married."

"I'm surprised you don't have any kids besides Rose," Emmett commented.

"I wanted them my husbands didn't," Lily explained.

"I'd like some kids someday."

"I might too, with the right father. I still have time," Lily replied warming up and then blushed.

Their conversation was interrupted as a beautiful woman in a tight red dress, with long blonde hair and blue eyes, stopped by their table.

"Emmett is this, your sister?" the woman asked, then turning to Lily she explained, "Emmett and I work together and we dated about three months ago, or was it four? I've been assignment since then."

"Cara, what do you want?" asked Emmett, sounding shocked.

"Let me see. I'm having dinner with my sister Mandy and I noticed you here."

"When did you get back from your assignment with the R.C.M.P.?" Emmett inquired.

"This morning and boy did I miss you," Cara replied planting a passionate kiss on Emmett's lips.

"Cara you are mistaken...,"Emmett began, "We broke up a long..."

"Don't let me stop you. We're only on a date." Lily interrupted.

"A date? You moved on all ready?"

"I...,"Emmett protested, "We hardly even know each other."

"Emmett didn't you break up with this woman?" Lily asked disgusted.

"Tell her Cara. Tell her how I said goodbye, when you went out of town," Emmett begged.

"Silly me, I didn't know that we were done. I thought you understood that I'd be back and we see each other then," Cara said a tear in her eye.

"Emmett I'm leaving," Lily stated angrily.

"Please don't Lily. Cara exaggerates. We had one date and I told her we didn't click. I hate to be mean to people, so I said goodbye to her when she left," Emmett protested, "She means nothing to me."

'I'm sorry I thought...,"Cara answered, "Sorry for interrupting, please enjoy your date."

Then Cara walked away.

"Do you have any more of those that will come out of the woodwork?" Lily demanded.

"I don't think so, but I'm not a monk."

"I guess I believe you then. I'm not a monk either, after all I've been married twice. Okay, then, I guess we can continue or meal and our date," Lily agreed.

"I'm going to have lasagne what will you have Lily?"

"I love lasagne too. I think I'll have that too," Lily answered.

"Since I'm driving, I'm not drinking. I only want milk, but you go ahead order whatever drink you want," Emmett explained.

"Thank you, I think I'll have some milk too. I've kind of got in the habit of drinking it with meals, so Rose will drink milk too."

"I understand they have fabulous desserts here," Emmett answered looking at the dessert menu.

"Mmm, Tiramisu. I'd like to have that for dessert if I have room."

"Order it anyway. If you don't have room you can take it home and eat it later. In fact why don't we take home an extra piece for Katha and Rose."

"That's great idea Emmett. I'll do that."

Lily thought about how sweet Emmett was to think of Katha and Rose. She is a little troubled by this former girlfriend Cara. No matter what Emmett might think this woman doesn't seem done with him. Emmett did say he was done with her though, so she couldn't hold this against him. He was a handsome, intelligent, sensitive man, a real catch, as Katha used to say when she was a teen. She would take this slow and see where it led, because she had more than her own heart to think of, she also had Rose's to think of. Rose and her needs had to come first.

"Did you enjoy your meal?" asked Emmett.

"I did thanks. I think I will have to take that dessert home after all."

A short time later Emmett drove Lily home.

"It's being a wonderful evening despite my old girlfriend, I hope. Sorry I can't resist," Emmett stated.

Emmett then bent down, taking Lily in his arms and kissing her passionately on the lips. Lily lost in the kiss, felt warm all the way down to her toes. Rose looked out the window moving back the curtain to see Emmett and Lily them kissing. She smiled and then thinking of her dad and frowned.

"Rose quit looking out the window."

"I'm not, I promise, Grandma Katha."

"Don't spy on your mother and Emmett," stated Katha.

Katha then glanced out the window herself.

"Perfect, she looks happy now let's get away from this window before she catches us. Turn on the television quick," Katha commanded.

Rose ran to the television and turned it on.

"What should I put on?"

"Put on the television whatever you'd normally watch."

Lily entered the house with Emmett in tow and Rose snickered that they hadn't noticed Rose at the window.

"Did you have a nice time?" Katha asked.

"I did and here's some dessert for all us I didn't eat any."

"Cool. It's tiramisu, Grandma Katha," Rose cried looking at the contents and getting a plate.

"You two, had a good date?"

"Yes."

"Good, then I'm off to my house. Bye, Rose, Katha and Lily."

"Aren't you going to eat dessert before you go?" Lily shouted after him at the front door.

"No, eat it and think of me," Emmett exclaimed getting into his car and then pulling away from the curb.

Lily then went back into the kitchen.

"I think you should keep the dessert you could use a few more calories. You've lost a few calories since Horace passed," Katha stated.

"Only a few that I could stand to lose," Lily commented.

"No, Grandma Katha's right. You need to gain some weight. Mom eat the dessert," Rose commanded her mouth full of tiramisu.

"Yes, mom," Lily stated, laughing and picking up the fork Rose offered her.

They all ate the tiramisu savouring each bite.

~0~

Chapter 10- Things you'd like to forget

Two days later

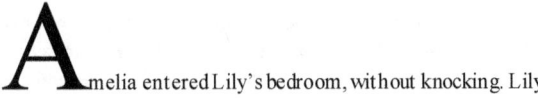

melia entered Lily's bedroom, without knocking. Lily

getting ready for work gave her a dirty look. Then looked at her expectantly knowing Amelia had something on her mind.

"Lily, I have to talk to you."

"I don't have a lot of time, since I need to get to the office, but you know I'm always here for you Aem. Spill! Quickly!"

"I...," Amelia then lowered her head to her chest.

"You can tell me anything Amelia. Now start talking."

Amelia bit her lip and then admitted, "I wanted to tell you before you heard this from someone else. I dated Alexander Scholar months ago, but he always called himself Vincent when he was with me,"

"Then you didn't know he was the murder victim?"

"Not at first..."

"Okay. Now he called himself Vincent, not Alex, or Alexander?" Lily prodded.

"He did, but I found out he saw other women, so many other women. So I dumped him."

"But you didn't know he went by other names?"

"No, not until recently when I heard some people calling him something else."

"They called him other names?"

"He seemed to use many different names with these women. Some called him Vinnie; others called him Alex, Alexi, and Zander. You get the picture," Amelia explained, "I'm so embarrassed and I should have told you sooner."

"It's not your fault Amelia. He was a real huckster. But how did you know about the other women?"

"Vincent and I met at the coffee shop and he wanted to stop at his house and get something before we went on a date. He excused himself to use the facilities and while I waited, I heard several messages on his phone," Amelia explained.

"And how did you happen to do that?" Lily asked trying not to laugh.

"Okay, I admit it. He'd been at the gym when I ran into him at the coffee shop. He said to wait in his living room, while he would have a shower. He took so long, I started listening to his messages mainly because I was bored," Amelia answered sheepishly.

"And can you remember any of the names of these women that left messages?"

"I don't know it was six months ago. I have an exceptional good memory but..."

"What did you eat for breakfast that morning?"

"Cornflakes," Amelia responded.

"See, you do remember. Now try to recall what the first message said."

"Okay. The first message was from... a Mary... she said something about working at the hospital. I recall she called him Vincent. She said something about working as a surgery nurse. She said she had to help out with some late night surgery and would see him about ten p.m. Then a woman named Paula called. I think she may have been a doctor at the hospital. She said something about working late covering the emergency room diagnosing patients..." Amelia paused here to recall, looking into space then she continued, "The next message the woman said her name was Karen...no Carol. She talked about working late at school. So I thought she appeared to be a teacher at first, but she said something about working late. That she had to supervise teachers and do some paperwork. Carol mentioned she wasn't free this evening because her husband would be home around nine. Her husband must be a doctor because she said he worked at the hospital, performing surgery. She went on to say she would leave work early to meet him at the Dixie Motel, room three-forty-five."

"How do you remember all this Amelia? You always seem to remember so easily," Lily asked amazed at what Amelia has remembered from six months ago.

"I don't like to talk about this, but when I was young, I was told I had eidetic memory. Except for the night of the fire, it has never has seen me wrong. If I think about something it's like I was back there. I recall images, sounds, or objects, like I was still there." Amelia explained, "Apparently the events of the night the fire started, made my memory fail." Amelia then started pacing.

"I'm so sorry you had to go through that Amelia, but it is better you don't remember parts of that night. I thought that having an eidetic memory must be nice to have but I'm not sure now," Lily replied.

"There are things you'd like to forget and you can't," Amelia answered sadly.

"I'm sorry Amelia. How thoughtless of me, of course there are plenty of things we'd all like to forget," Lily apologised reaching out to Amelia with her arms.

Amelia didn't move into the hug but smiled at Lily and then continued, "I don't share this, because when I was little people found out at school and they either wanted me to do all of their work, or they thought I was a freak."

"I'm sorry you were treated that way Amelia," Lily stated angrily.

"It's the past. Even with my memory you should try to forget the past, forgive, and move on. At least that's what Doctor Jones says," Amelia stated.

"Has Doctor Jones been helpful?" asked Lily, worried that Amelia saw her psychiatrist so regularly again.

"Don't worry Lily. I needed some help dealing with what happened two months ago. I mean he killed because he was in love with me. He ruined both your life and mine, and all because of me," Amelia stated crying.

"Amelia you know it wasn't your fault any of it. You did not encourage him. He decided he loved you. He was mentally ill!"

"Then you aren't mad at me?" asked Amelia.

"Is that why I haven't seen much of you since then? Amelia, you are a silly goose. We are closer than sisters. I love you. I do not blame you for any of this. We both lost ones we loved to that animal. He's locked up for good, so let's not waste our breath talking about him and giving him any more power over us. So we put that behind us, live our lives and don't let him take anything else away from us okay?" Lily stated passionately.

Amelia wiped away her tears.

"You're the best you know that Lily. I love you too."

"I kind of think you're the best too. We are Kelly's after all. Like Grandma Katha says, Kelly women are brave, strong, invincible, and together they love deeply, defeat all evil and persevere."

"Brad Owens won't get out of Pinecrest anytime soon though. Will he?"

"No, not if I can help it he'll live out his life there, or some other psychiatric hospital." Lily exclaimed, "I've tried to forgive him but I can't. I never want to see or hear about him again but that's impossible. So I'm going to fight to keep him there."

"Some other hospital? They're closing Pinecrest? I heard some rumours."

"It may be closing but they'll find room for Brad Owens somewhere else. I'm also campaigning for a bill they have in the commons to prevent him from ever getting free."

"You mean Bill C-54 which would designate him in high risk category? I heard about that and told my member of parliament, I supported that too," Amelia asked.

"When I'm done that's what I hope for; but you know the bill didn't get past the senate. I guess I do hope it gets revived. I don't ever want to see him free again; but the Canadian Psychiatric Association objected to the bill. They told the committee that most people with mental illness do not commit crimes and that one in five Canadians are affected by mental illness, so they too need protection. Maybe they do, I'm somewhat torn."

"What about those that do? We need protection I don't want him out and what if Rose's birth mother, Cordelia gets out?"

"I don't like to see people get extra freedom either, but people with mental illness have to be treated."

"But not at our expense," Amelia protested.

"We will be safe from Brad and Cordelia. They are not getting's out any time soon. Even if she did I have full custody of Rose. She can't get custody of her."

"But she could harm her."

"She won't. She loves Rose. Now we need to get back to Alexander Scholar's messages. I need some insight into his private life."

"Okay, I've remembered a few more of the calls anyway. The next person to leave a message was a Suzy, I think...she called him Vinnie and said she had to work at the police station late. She sounded young though, like twenty, or twenty-one years old. At least her voice sounded that young. She said she was pregnant and that the baby was his. And why didn't he call her?"

"That would be Emmett's sister. She's pregnant with Vincent Scholar's babies."

"Babies, plural?"

"Yep. We need to organize a baby shower for her in a couple of months."

"His poor sister. That man was a cretin. Is that why they questioned Emmett at first?"

"Yes."

"I've got plenty of ideas for a baby shower we'll give her a great one."

"Good, but getting back to Vincent Scholar's messages any else you can remember?"

"I heard someone named Maggie, call him Zander. Maggie said she was free and could he meet her for dinner at eight, at Chez Mark's. That's about all I heard on his answering machine. I got mad and left, not even saying a word to him. He called me later, but I told him to go call one of his harem," Amelia remembered.

"Wow, he wasn't nice Amelia. I hate to ask this but you were out of town the morning of the killing weren't you?" asked Lily.

"What day was that?"

"Monday, September ninth," Lily answered.

"Was that two weeks ago, the Monday, after Labour Day?" asked Amelia.

"It was," stated Lily.

"No problem, you can mark me off your list. I was in Chicago at a toy convention."

"I thought that was in February."

"The main conference was in February, but a bunch of us got together and out together a conference in Chicago. You can confirm that I stayed at the Hyatt Regency Chicago," Amelia answered, "Oh, and I took Georgette Davidson with me, so she was with me the whole day."

"Sorry, I had to ask Aem. I have to eliminate people and be impartial."

"No worries, it's your job. I have another problem though, that I wanted to talk to you about."

"Tell me, Amelia."

"There's this man...I'm genuinely attracted to him. He's especially sweet and charming and..."

"So, what is the problem? You deserve to be happy. Date him," encouraged Lily.

"He's going through a divorce," Amelia stated.

"A divorce? He's married? You should wait until that's final."

"But Doctor Henry Thomas is so nice."

Lily looked at Amelia shocked. Amelia dated Rose's surgeon as well?

"He is. You should get to know him you'd genuinely like him," Amelia protested, misinterpreting Lily's surprise.

"Doctor Thomas, the doctor who did Rose's surgery. That is the Doctor Thomas, you dated?" Lily asked incredulously.

"I said so. I dated that other doctor too. But he was mean and dictatorial. He tried to tell me who I could speak to. He grew jealous of a male waiter."

"What other doctor?"

"Raj Patel he's a doctor, but he's not on the level, my Henry Thomas is."

"You dated both of them in this small span of time?"

"You make me seem like a serial dater."

Lily didn't know what to make of this. Amelia was not only dating, but dating three men so quickly? Wait a minute did Amelia say Patel was bossy? "Doctor Patel seemed dictatorial and possessive to you?" Lily asked.

"He wanted me to dress a certain way, act a certain way, as well. He made hints that I should convert to his religion. I've known lots of other people who practice the same religion and they weren't so extreme about their being of the Muslin faith. They were kind and considerate of others faiths and they didn't try to convert me. Amir Sarraf was sweet, gentle and considerate unlike Doctor Patel. If I had been ready to date when I met him, he would have been a great choice. Doctor Patel however, made me feel indecent and not worthy of him, like I had to change to be his date."

"Well, isn't that interesting. It sounds like he's abusive."

"I don't know about that, but I dumped him. So it doesn't matter."

"It does matter. The guy treated you badly. It raises red flags that the man insists a woman behave a certain way."

"I'm glad you care, but it's water under the bridge. Now, I think Henry's cute, don't you?"

"He's married. You need to think about this more," Lily stated forcefully.

"I wanted to have fun again and have someone pay attention to me. Why won't you support me?" Amelia pleaded.

"Don't we both. But we should take it slow. Given what we've been through."

"Pot, call the kettle black much? A little birdie told me that you were dating again," Amelia commented.

"How did you know? Emmett and I went on a date last night."

"So how was the date?"

"Wonderful at first, but then his last girlfriend showed up."

"No, she didn't!" Amelia cried.

"She did. This woman he works with Cara, something came over to our table. She claimed she thought I was his sister Suzy...," Lily related.

"She knew you were on a date and tried to wreck it," Amelia stated."

"Do you think so?"

"And you think I'm naive?" Amelia asked.

Lily rolled her eyes.

"Don't roll your eyes. I know you do. Believe me Lily; you are naive about women like that."

"I am? I guess I am. She did stare at me for a reaction."

"And did you give her one? Did she get satisfaction?"

"No, I dismissed her and she sat down with her sister again," Lily explained.

"Good for you Lily. Way to put her in her place. So, did you have fun?"

"I did, but I feel guilty, like I cheated on Horace," Lily admitted.

"Nonsense, Horace would want you to be happy," Amelia stated, "And he would like the fact that Emmett is so good to Rose."

"He is good to Rose. We got dessert for her and Katha last night. It was his idea," Lily replied.

"He is sweet then."

Lily worried about Amelia's heart getting hurt, but she knew that the worst thing she could do was to let Amelia know how she truly felt about her date. Amelia opening her heart was a big step, but did it have to be a married man, who still wasn't divorced? Lily had to be supportive not judgemental.

"So you try to move on too... with Doctor Thomas?"

"I am. I know he's married for now but as I said he's getting divorced," Amelia stated, again seeking Lily's approval.

"If he can make you happy then go ahead," Lily answered, "But go slow and don't get hurt okay."

"Thanks Lil, I knew I could count on you."

"I have to leave soon but know that I always support you."

"As I do you Lily," Amelia answered back.

"Come into the kitchen. Rose is taking so long we have time for a coffee."

Lily then walked with Amelia to the kitchen made a coffee which she placed in front of Amelia and then sat waiting for Rose. A half an hour went by and still no Rose. Lily glanced at the clock if Rose didn't hurry they'd be late. Lily had taken the morning off to take her to her follow-up appointment with the doctor, the least Rose could do was be on time.

"Rose hurry up, we'll be late. Your appointment is at nine -thirty a.m.," Lily yelled up the stairs.

"I'm coming," Rose yelled down then complained, "Mothers, they always rush you."

"Rose, you have five seconds to get down here."

"Gee whiz, I said I'd be down. Take a chill pill."

Seconds later Rose appeared.

"Look I'm here now let's go," retorted Rose.

"Bye Amelia. See you later," Lily retorted.

"Bye Lil. I'll finish my coffee then I have to head to work too but I'll lock the front door, Amelia answered.

"Bye, Aunt Amelia," Rose stated.

"Bye sweetie, see you later," Amelia replied.

Rose then put on her coat and darted out the front door. Amelia smiled at the two of them. Sometimes she wished she had a daughter like Rose. Who knew if her relationship progressed with Henry, they could have a daughter, and a son...someday. She'd have a family of her own and she'd be whole again.

~0~

Chapter 11 – Alexander's Conquests

Lily and Rose arrived at the hospital and headed to the clinic floor. As they exited the elevator, they overheard a conversation taking place, behind an open door.

"Why didn't you tell me Dayita? Why, do you tell me lies?"

"I didn't lie."

"Yes, you did, but not telling me he was dead!" whispered the angry voice, which Lily recognized as Doctor Patel.

"Raj, it is none of your concern. We are divorced, no one will connect me with Alexander Scholar," the other voice replied.

The voice sounded familiar to Lily, but she couldn't place it.

"I didn't even know that was his name. I thought his name was Vincent," Doctor Patel admitted, "Now I have had to clean up your messes. It's bad enough you married him."

"I thought I loved him."

"But you will marry with in our faith next time and our parents will never know of this man and his many names."

"The man was a cheat. Imagine my surprise when Mary started dating him after our divorce. I didn't want to tell her I was married to him."

"If you married a man in our religion and he strayed it would be your fault. A woman must cater to her man to keep him. But you speak of Mary Brown? Isn't her brother a cop?" asked Doctor Patel.

Hmm... Mary Brown was Dan's sister too? Daniel Brown's sisters were both involved with Alexander Scholar. Did Theresa Brown talk to Emmett and distract him with a kiss to protect herself, or her sister? Who was this mysterious ex–wife the man was speaking to? Wait a minute the man called her Dayita. Wasn't the name of the nurse, looking after Rose, Dayita? Her voice sounded the same, Lily thought.

Lily continued to listen.

"Do you think I should go to the police and reveal that I was his ex-wife?" Dayita asked.

"The police would have to promise not to let the press find this out. If our parents found out that you had been married not once, but twice, and to a man who is not of our faith. No, I do not think they, the police, would keep this to themselves. The press would find out and the family would shun us. You cannot tell anyone."

"I divorced him, did I not?" Dayita admitted, "It is if it never happened."

"That's what you think, but if Father finds out...,"Raj countered.

"You won't tell him will you?" pleaded Dayita, "Father must not find out."

"No, I won't tell him. I like my head. He entrusted your welfare to my care. I have failed and you fall prey to this awful man. Father would be angry. He might even cut off the payments for my studies. I must finish them, and become the great doctor I am meant to be. I will make Father proud."

"But you're an intern, a great doctor now, surely you don't need Father?" Dayita asked surprised.

"Are you under the impression I receive money for this? I must pay my student loans," Raj explained. "But one day I will pay my own way when I become a surgeon instead of an intern."

"So you won't tell Father?" Dayita begged.

"I have said I would not. It benefits neither of us for him to find out of your indiscretion," Raj admitted. "Now you too, must promise to say nothing to the police."

"I do not think this is a good idea, but I will keep silent," Dayita stated. "For myself, as well as you."

"Me? This has nothing to do with me," protested Raj.

"You know I found him with her, don't you?" asked Dayita, changing the subject slightly.

"Who did you find Vincent with?" asked Raj.

"A slut!"

The sound of a slap was heard and Lily wondered whether she should intervene. She peeked in and saw Dayita holding her face.

"Dayita you were not raised with such language you will not speak this way," Raj admonished, "Who did you find him with?"

"Carol, the biotch." Dayita replied.

"Dayita Patel, you will not speak thus. It lowers you. She may be unclean, but you will not use such language. What would Father say?" Raj replied angrily, his hand raised again.

Lily wanted to intervene but she wanted to hear what they were saying more so as long as Doctor Raj Patel didn't strike out again, she wouldn't burst in.

"You are a good brother Raj. I bid you forgive me. I know you are correct, that I dishonour my family by lowering myself with such bad language. I do think however that one of his women could have killed him. Alexander searched constantly for his next conquest. Conquest...that is the right word, no?" Dayita admitted sadly.

"You should come forward, before they find out and think you had something to do with his death," Raj reconsidered.

"Me, kill the man? I have ceased to care since I divorced him," Dayita stated. "What about you? Did you do something Raj? You were late to work that morning your shift began at six o'clock and you didn't get here until six fifteen a.m. and you are never late."

"You dare to question me?" declared Raj, "Whoever has killed this camel dung has done the world a favour."

"Then you did kill him?"

"We will not discuss this. The subject is closed."

Raj then walked away. Rose motioned to Lily to quit listening and hurry up or they will be late.

"For Pete's sake Mom I'm going to be late for first my appointment and then my afternoon class," whispered Rose urgently.

"Rose, I need to question the two of them with Emmett. We have to get this appointment over with and then you'll have to go back to school with your Aunt Amelia," Lily replied her mind feverishly thinking ahead.

"Right, dump the sick kid. She's not important," Rose replied, peevishly.

"You are important Rose, but I have to find a killer. You know how important that is, before he, or she, kills again."

"Yah, I know your work is important but shouldn't I come first?"

"You always come first, but would it be okay, if Amelia got you after the appointment is over?" Lily begged.

"Fine! Let's get this over with. I have a Spanish test his afternoon and I want an A plus," Rose answered.

Lily called Emmett and alerted him to the two new suspects so they wouldn't get away. Rose's appointment soon got over. Doctor Thomas' other intern, Doctor Rosenberg, told them Rose healed nicely. Lily was grateful to hear that Rose's scar would be almost invisible. Rose loved her bikinis. Amelia arrived to take Rose back to work and Lily headed to her office, sure that Emmett would handle the Patel's and their interviews. ~-0~

That afternoon

Lily sat at her desk and looked over the lists of suspects; frankly she couldn't make heads, or tails, of the number of people suspected in this case. Everyone wanted Alexander Scholar dead, and no one seemed to have an alibi. If there had been more than the precision cut in the chest she could almost believe this was a case like an Agatha Christie novel. The coroner however believed that the cuts were made by only one or possibly two people, not a great number. Why had this person, or persons, taken his heart and where was that heart. Was it a souvenir? Were they dealing with the first kill of a serial? Lily hoped not. One serial killer in the form of a Brad Owens was enough.

Why would anyone take a heart out of someone's body? Jealousy? Dr. Patel had shown that side to Amelia. He was mad about Alexander's Scholar's treatment of his sister, or worried that his father would find out about his sister's brief marriage? Lily could believe the way this case consumed her life, and time. She was a single parent now she had to find more time for Rose. That little worm acting mayor Crimshaw had made her office life unbearable. He called at least at least three times a day for an update and if that wasn't bad enough now he taken to phoning at night interrupting family time with Rose.

Lily missed Horace. She still loved him, despite the fact that he had so cruelly betrayed her. What was wrong with her? She should hate him, but all she felt was sad about the time that she had lost with Horace. Emmett was ready to be her boyfriend, and all she could think about was Horace and the past. She was conflicted. Emmett seemed nice, great boyfriend material in some ways but he was so attractive he seemed to draw women to him like a flame.

Could Lily really trust him to remain true to her? Lily had been twenty-four years old, when she had met Horace. Young, and determined to move her way up in the Crown attorney's office, Lily had worked twelve hours most days, and had no time for anything except her work. Then she had met Horace, his ex-wife Cordelia, and their daughter Rose. Cordelia had fallen into something that had made her a total mess. She became a drug addict, a prostitute, and at the time of meeting Lily, a murderer.

Horace had been trying to save his ex-wife but had gotten nowhere. Everyone he'd talked to wanted Cordelia to face life imprisonment. Lily had looked over the case, when it had landed in her lap. She felt sorry for the family and for Cordelia. What everyone else who had looked at the case hadn't seen was the reason for the murder. Cordelia had gotten her life together left the life of a prostitute and married Horace. She's given birth to Rose and lived the life of a businessman's wife. Cordelia stayed home as a mom for Rose, but then Cordelia started drinking and became an alcoholic.

Horace had divorced and got full custody of Rose. Cordelia started going to alcoholic anonymous and begged to be allowed to see

Rose again. Horace had relented, because Rose begged for her mother. Horace began to share Rose with Cordelia. She'd spend three days with Cordelia then four days with Horace. The arrangement seemed to be working and then Cordelia's former pimp found her.

The man began drugging her, getting Cordelia addicted. Cordelia continued to drop Rose with Horace, and appeared normal, but she turned tricks and exposed Rose to unsavoury characters. Cordelia finally broke when the pimp tried to force himself on her. Cordelia didn't seem to understand what had happened, but Lily's boss wanted the longest sentence possible. Lily had put her career on the line, making a deal with the lawyer which Horace had hired to save Cordelia. Cordelia's final sentence had been fifteen years, but she hadn't served it in prison. The past seven years Cordelia had been in Pinecrest, a mental facility for the criminally insane; the same place where Brad Owens was now housed.

Cordelia's mind was broken by the drugs and the crime she committed. At her sentencing Cordelia collapsed completely, recognizing no one. They had taken her to Pinecrest for evaluation and decided Cordelia needed to reside there. Shortly after the sentencing on the advice of her doctors, Horace brought her a doll. Cordelia called it Rose. The doctor's seem to think that was a good sign, but Cordelia now lived in the world where no one existed but her doll. Horace didn't have the heart to tell Rose that her mother languished in a mental hospital and would never recognize her again. He allowed Rose to believe her mother was in prison instead and would someday get out. He told her because of her age and the crime that she wasn't allowed to visit. Lily worried that someday Rose would find out the truth. But Horace had been correct to protect Rose with mistruths after all Rose had gone through.

Horace had asked her out Lily had refused. Horace had been persistent and even using his daughter Rose to woo Lily.

Rose had captured Lily's heart with pictures and gestures, and her need for a mother. The two of them, Horace and Rose had needed Lily and she found herself in need of them. So they had quietly married and she became a mother to Rose, and a wife to Horace.

How she missed Horace, his counsel, his loving touch. Despite the fact he had strayed, she knew in her heart he had loved her. He had kept secrets, big secrets and she hated that. She hated secrets yet she had been left with the secret that she now had to keep from

Rose; the secret that Cordelia was not in jail. Rose had no idea. She thought her mother refused to see her in jail. Horace was afraid that it would hurt Rose irreversibly if she found out that her mother didn't even recognize her. Lily wasn't sure what to do, but she was sure that whatever she decided would hurt Rose. So she had picked the lesser evil to lie by omission. Hopefully if Rose ever found out she would forgive Lily.

"Earth to Lily."

Lily looked up to find Emmett standing in front of her office door.

"Emmett? Why are you here? Did we have an appointment? Or did Rose set me up again," Lily asked.

"No, but I thought I could convince you to come have a late lunch with me."

"What no Kendall?"

"She's off running down some leads," Emmett answered. "Of course, they'll probably be like the other leads, more of the same, no alibis, and lots of suspects. Besides I'd rather eat lunch with you."

"I've plenty of work to do here besides Scholar's murder. I hope what I overheard helped," Lily stated.

"I don't know how we will ever sift through all of them and figure out who did the actual killing." Emmett admitted.

"Kendall tells me the coroner believes that this killing may have been done by two people, not one. Of course that is just a theory," Lily explained.

"At least he has a theory. I haven't one at all," Emmett replied, discouraged. "There are so many people that we have interviewed who hated Alexander Scholar, but they all have alibis."

"You don't have the acting Mayor calling you all times of the day, and night to get updates."

"No, I've got the chief of police telling me I have to wrap this up soon. Dan Brown has been taken off the case. And all of that this looks bad for the police department because of the Owens' case." Emmett replied, wearily then realizing that bringing up Brad

Owens might hurt Lily he added, "I'm sorry Lily, I shouldn't have mentioned him."

"Don't worry about that Emmett. He's safely behind bars at Pinecrest. Right now, put this behind us and focus on finding this killer, or killers. It doesn't help that the victim was despicable. Does it?"

"No, it doesn't. But no one has the right to take someone's life," Emmett stated, vehemently.

"You are absolutely correct Emmett. They don't. Did Kendall tell you about what I overheard Doctor Patel and his sister say?"

"Yes, I was a little disappointed you didn't call me."

"I did call you. Kendall answered."

"Oh, sorry. This does look like a viable lead will do some back checking and then bring them in for questioning."

"We'll get this person. They can't escape us for much longer," Lily answered.

"At least the meeting last night may have brought us in some new leads. Violet Garden has been fielding calls, and has great tips from the public, all morning and we'll check out every lead. I don't want to rush in and arrest the Patel's without enough proof or rush to judgement that they are guilty. Everyone looks guilty in this case."

"That will help us."

"I certainly hope so. Now about lunch..."

Lily looks at the time on her computer.

"Good grief it is two thirty p.m... It's way past lunch."

"But you haven't had lunch yet. Have you?"

"No, but Rose gets out at three p.m. and I promised to pick her up. In fact I should be leaving now. I want to spend a couple of hours with her and get back here to finish the work on the Collins prosecution."

"Why don't we go to the school pick up Rose and have a meal with her," Emmett replied. "Then if you have to go back to work we can call Amelia, or Katha, to keep her company. I know since she's been ill you haven't felt like leaving her alone."

"That's great idea. Let's go we can make there before three p.m. and get her. You don't mind sharing time with Rose?"

"Of course not, she's your daughter. Do we have time for a quick kiss?" Emmett asked, playfully seizing Lily and kissing her.

"Emmett someone could see us. This is my office, a workplace," protested Lily.

"Let them. I want everyone to know how I feel about you," Emmett replied.

"Well I don't!"

Emmett looked at Lily like he was hurt.

"Don't look at me that way Emmett Rogers. It's only been a few months since Horace died. We shouldn't do this not here. I have to be careful to keep an image of being a professional in my workplace," Lily explained.

"All right we will do it your way and take it slow," Emmett agreed, "So let's go get Rose and eat a late lunch."

"It sounds exceedingly good to me. Let's go then."

~0~

Chapter 12 – Connections

Lily and Emmett arrived at the high school, awaiting the final bell. Lily watched as Rose came out the front door and Lily waved to her from the car. Rose, however didn't see them, and continued walking. A young girl her hair dyed black with blond roots showing practically flew out the front door of the school. Her green eyes were fringed with black and her lips were adorned with black as well. She was clad all in black from head to toe down to the vintage Doc Martins she wore on her feet. The young woman was taller than Rose and solidly built. She looked like she worked out Lily noted. The young teen jumped on Rose's back, knocking Rose to the ground and began to pummel her with both fists. Her repeated blows hit their intended target, as Rose retreated into a ball to avoid the blows.

Lily and Emmett opened the car doors and jumped out of the car in a flash. Emmett sought to reach the young woman before she was able to strike again.

"Police freeze," Emmett shouted as the girl, but she still continued to hit Rose.

Emmett reached out to grab the girl's arm but she swung again at Rose.

"I said, police, freeze. I suggest you quit hitting Rose and stand up young lady," Emmett repeated.

"I wasn't doin' nothing, pig," The young girl commented, straightening up.

She then hit out at Emmett and tried to run. Emmett caught up to her, placed handcuffs on her putting her hands behind her back and then brought her back to Lily and Rose.

"I saw what you were doing. I know what you did to Rose. What do you have to say for yourself?" Emmett asked her.

"Biotch deserved what she got."

Turning to Rose Emmett asked, "Are you okay Rose?"

'I'm okay," Rose responded, glumly.

"You have the right to remain silent. You may refuse to answer questions. Do you understand? Anything you do say may be used against you in a court of law. You have the right to consult an attorney before speaking to the police and to have an attorney present during questioning now or in the future. If you cannot afford an attorney, one will be appointed for you before any questioning if you wish. Do you understand?" Emmett continued.

"Yah."

"If you decide to answer questions now without an attorney present you will still have the right to stop answering at any time until you talk to an attorney. Knowing and understanding your rights as I have explained them to you, will you answer my questions without an attorney present? You have the right to have your parent present during questioning. Do you understand these rights as I have read to you?"

"Yes I understand; but why am I being arrested? I told you, that bitch deserved a comedown and more. Her nose is always up in the air like she's the freakin' Queen. Who does she think she is anyway?" the girl answered, and then turning to Rose she spat, "I'll get even with you, for this. Cassandra told me what you did. You just wait and see."

"I don't even know a Cassandra," Rose commented perplexed.

"F you don't know Cassandra knows you. She saw how you clung to my boyfriend."

"You're out of your mind."

"Don't talk to her Rose." then turning to the young woman Emmett demanded, "Now you what is your name, young lady?"

"I don't have to tell you my name. I know my rights," the girl stated defiantly.

"I'm sure you know you do. As a police officer, I demand you identify yourself," Emmett explained.

"Fine then, I'm Daria Brown. My Dad is Daniel Brown. You will be so sorry now that you messed with me. He will whoop you're ass." Daria boasted, then she glared at Rose, and said, "You whinny little piece of trash. You can't even fight your own battles; you have to get mommy and mommy's boyfriend to handle your problems. You better watch your back Rose, because I'll be out before five and mommy can't protect you forever."

"Are you always so violent and mouthy?" asked Emmett.

Daria struggled to get free of Emmett.

"Do you want me to add resisting arrest to the charges? You've already assaulted a police officer."

"F-Off pig, I did not assault you. You hurt me and twisted my arm that charge won't hold up in court. I could lay charges of police brutality against you."

"Calm down, Miss Brown," Emmett insisted.

Emmett then used his cell phone to call for a patrol car.

"I'm not violent. Don't you firm up your fictional case by lying."

"You are using foul language. That is considered violent behaviour."

"Swearing is not a crime, nor does it make you violent. Rose's mom murdered someone. Why aren't you arresting her? Or are you so in love with the skank you can't see that?" asked Daria.

"Let us see Rose walked minding her own business and you came up behind her, knocked her over, and then started using her for a punching bag. Have I left anything out?" Emmett asked sardonically.

"She did what?" asked Carol exiting the school and hearing the conversation.

"She looked at my boyfriend. I told the biotch not to look at him." Daria defended herself.

"I wasn't looking at him. The guy is ugulee," Rose replied "Your so-called boyfriend annoys me. He pesters me and keeps trying to get me to go out with him. He's gross. As if..."

"Shut-up you lying biotch. I knew you were after him. I should have fixed your face a long time ago."

"You just try Daria. I'll make you pay," Carol shouted.

Rose rolled her eyes.

"Rose and Carol, go stand over there and let me handle this," Emmett insisted.

"Yah, you go over there you little chicken, Rose and hide behind your beard, Carol," Daria insisted.

"Shut-up Daria," Carol shouted.

"Do you know how ignorant you are?" asked Rose.

"Just because you got a cop doing your Mom, doesn't mean that these charges will stick," Daria shouted.

"Don't you dare talk about my Mom that way!" Rose shouted back.

"F-off. I'll talk about her anyway I please. It's a free country," Daria retorted, "Really mouthy when you have mommy's sugar daddy defending you. Aren't you?

"It won't matter what you say, you'll go to jail anyway." Rose insisted, "You assaulted me and I have witnesses."

"Dream on, Rachet. You are such a child who can't even swear in front of mommy."

"What are you merked? Is that why you attacked me?" Rose asked

"Oh, the baby knows some slang. My mains will get you biotch."

"Do you honestly threaten me with your stupid attempt at sounding tough? You sound ridiculous," Rose countered.

"I suggest you quit talking to Rose, before you get yourself in more trouble," Lily insisted.

Lily then took Rose's arm to pull her away, but Rose broke free and Carol went after her pulling her back.

"My Grandpa won't let me do time, either! I've got major connections," taunted Daria.

"Really? Who is your grandfather?" demanded Rose.

"Acting mayor, Harold Crimshaw. So watch and learn, Sasquatch, " Daria taunted, "You should shave above your lip, your mustache is getting big."

Rose rolled her eyes at this. Emmett and Lily heard about Daria's connections with trepidation, wondering and worrying how Crimshaw would react at Daria's arrest.

"Be quiet both of you please. And no more slurs, Daria. You'll dig a bigger hole for yourself," Emmett exclaimed, and then commanded, "Rose, go and stand by Carol. Please!"

"Fine! I know when I'm not needed," Rose cried dramatically, "Gee, you'd think she was the one that had been hurt."

Rose then ran over to Carol. Lily noticed she had an animated conversation with Carol. Then Carol glared at Daria and hugged Rose. Daria just crossed her arms and glared some more.

"Lily, go get the cop inside the door to come out. I need him to take some witness statements. The more witnesses, the less chance Daria can wiggle out from the charges that she assaulted Rose."

"Okay."

"It won't work you know. It doesn't matter who you get because I've got power with my dad and grandfather. You should stop babying Rose. She's so backward for her age that she has to run to mommy all the time," Daria continued to taunt.

Daria then laughed even as the patrol car arrived to take her to the station.

"Patrolman Barnes, it's nice to see you again. Please take good care of this young lady; it seems she's the Mayor's granddaughter and apparently Daniel Brown's daughter as well. The charges are as follows...assault, and resisting arrest. I'll be down in a couple of hours to begin the questioning. Make sure the parent, or a child advocate, is available by then," Emmett explained turning Daria over to him.

"I'll be happy to Emmett. Has she had her rights read to her?" Alan asked.

"I did."

"Okay, see you later, Emmett."

"This isn't fair!! Rose had it coming. She was after my boyfriend and she probably killed Mr. Scholar. Everyone knows she is a death groupie. Her whole family is a bunch of black widow spiders." shouted Daria loudly as she was put in the car, "My mom said her whole family is toxic."

"That girl is a real bully," Lily commented.

"Sometimes bullies are people who have incidents in their lives they can't control. Others just enjoy being bullies," Emmett answered.

"Which do you think she is?" asked Lily.

"I'm not sure, yet!" Emmett stated shaking his head.

"What a piece of work, that girl is."

"She's an example of a lot of kids we see now. Spoiled and feeling entitled to do anything to get what they want. Frankly, I think if the kids had a parent who would spend some time with them, they'd be better off."

"Oh dear, I hope I'm spending enough time with Rose," Lily cried looking over at Rose talking to Carol.

"You spend enough time with her. You take time with Rose talking with, and to her. It makes all the world of difference to her behaviour and attitude," Emmett replied "In the meantime we need to get Rose to a doctor and have her checked out for injuries." "She won't be happy about that. She's fed up with doctor visits as it is. But I agree, she's going."

"We'll bribe her with a dinner of her choice with Carol included. That is if Carol's parents agree. They'll even let Carol come with us, while Rose gets checked out at the hospital. That is if you step away from work that long."

"There's no question of that. Rose comes first. I'll work into the night if I have to from home. But I'm so angry at that girl Daria. She hurt Rose. I'll either have to recuse myself and get someone else on the case to prosecute." Lily stated.

"We have to do that in our jobs, it's never easy."

"Did anyone tell you you're a nice man?"

"I appreciate the vote of confidence. Now let's go corral Rose and Carol and get her looked over."

~0~

Chapter 13 – Compassion

Rose waited to see the doctor at the emergency room when

Daniel Brown suddenly burst into the cubicle. He looked hesitant then he spoke looking contrite, "Can I speak to you and your daughter? I mean, before the examination makes you mad?"

"That's up to my daughter." stated Lily angrily.

"I'll listen to him Mom, if only in the interest of fairness," Rose admitted, "But I won't like it."

"Thank you Rose, for hearing me out. I don't condone my daughter, Daria's, actions. What she did was despicable. However, they happened because of mitigating circumstances. This morning, Daria overheard a conversation that the treatment hadn't worked for her mother's cancer. Her mother hasn't long. I should have gone after her. Instead I comforted my wife and thought we could talk after school. Unfortunately Daria acted out all day and then she attacked you. It is so hard for her right now. Frankly I haven't been there for her. I've been either with my wife, or at work. Daria needed someone to talk to, listen to, and be comforted by. I'm so sorry for the fact that she attacked you Rose. That wasn't right. But I'm begging you all for some compassion for Daria and me."

Lily looked at Rose and saw Rose's injuries. She wanted to make Daria pay for hurting her daughter, but Dan's speech had made her feel bad for Daria. The poor girl acted out of fear of losing her mother. That was hard for anyone to take. Let alone a vulnerable fifteen-year old. No, Rose had been hurt. She could have been seriously injured. No sympathy for that little witch. Lily glanced over at Rose to see how Rose felt; after all no matter what Rose was the only one whose feelings mattered. Rose put her chin up and got a determined look in her eyes.

"Mom, I hate that she hurt me. I'm not that hurt though, it's a few bruises."

"Daria seemed angry. I don't like that," Lily insisted.

"Me either, but I guess I can understand Daria being angry. If I wasn't seeing Doctor Jones after Daddy died, I would have acted out. I felt like hitting objects and people, but Doctor Jones helped me. We should help Daria. She deserves to be with her mom at the end and not in jail. Or at least her mom deserves to have her there," Rose stated with great maturity and compassion making Lily proud.

"Do you truly feel this way Rose? Or do you feel pressured by Detective Brown?" asked Emmett.

"I do feel this way, Emmett. To think about losing a mother... it hurts. My mom going to prison and then refusing to see me, hurt. It was like she died. It hurt so badly. Yet, I know she's alive and even though I have Lily as my mother, I miss her. Daria doesn't even have that. Losing my Dad still hurts dreadfully. I can't imagine seeing my mother ill and dying and not being able to do anything, but watch," Rose answered.

"Rose, you are an extraordinarily compassionate person. I'll take it from here though. You stay here and get checked out. You had surgery a short time ago. I want to make sure that you haven't injured anything," Lily replied as the nurse came into the room calling Rose's name.

"I'm going in by myself. Don't finalize anything without me. Don't worry, I'll tell you what the doctor says. Besides Carol will be with me," Rose demanded.

"But..."

"Mom, I'm not a child."

"I promise I'll look after her, Mrs. Kelly-Brooksfield," Carol reassured.

"Okay, go you two, but I want an update."

Lily watched as Rose and Carol left with the nurse following her.

"She's a pistol that one," Emmett commented.

"She is," Lily admitted, "and Carol's a good friend."

Dan shifted his feet back and forth and Lily remembered he was still there.

"What?" Lily asked.

"Will you help my daughter?" begged Dan.

"Sorry of course you needed an answer. I think we can work something out, provided of course that Rose has no lasting injuries and Rose agrees," Lily answered, "I am the Crown attorney after all."

"Thank you, Lily," Dan stated. "And please, thank Rose for being so compassionate."

"What kind of punishment do you feel is necessary, Lily?" asked Emmett.

"I think Daria should see a psychiatrist. Talk over her feelings. She'll have to have a restraining order too. She would have to stay five hundred feet from Rose, at all times, unless Rose decides that that is unnecessary and tells me. She must also complete anger management classes and two hundred hours of community service, within two years. If she does this I think this could end all this. She will not have a record and will not go to jail."

"Wow, you think fast on your feet," Emmett commented.

"Daria can do all that," Dan agreed, "I'll make sure she complies with all of this."

"Daria is the one that has to agree. She has to agree and sign that she will abide by these terms," Lily explained.

"I know she will." Dan said, "She doesn't want to go to go to jail, despite her tough talk. You don't know how much this will mean to my family."

"I think we do," Emmett and Lily both say.

"I'll go ahead and call the station, so you can get Daria released into your custody tonight, Dan," Emmett stated then turning to Lily he asked, If that's okay, Lily?"

"That will be acceptable, provided tomorrow Daria comes with you present, Dan and signs the agreement with her lawyer. You also have to sign Dan since she's underage," Lily explained.

"Thank-you, so much, Lily and Emmett. You genuinely don't know, what a compassionate thing you and your daughter has done for our family, and Daria. Please, thank Rose again, for me too. She's a true testimony to your great parenting Lily," Dan replied leaving.

Emmett excused himself and went to use a phone to get Daria released. Doctor Patel came in the room and spoke to Lily, followed by Rose and Carol. Rose sat down beside Lily. Carol on the other side.

"Mrs. Brooksfield, Rose seems fine. Her stitches and the area of her incision have healed nicely. However, Rose says that someone pushed her down. She has sustained a black eye and some small bruises on her back from that assault. Nothing of any consequence though," Doctor Patel stated, thoughtfully.

"That is true. She was pushed down then pummelled. She's okay then?"

"As I said she is good. She has a few bruises, but they will heal."

"Oh, I'm so relieved thank-you, Doctor Patel," Lily answered.

Doctor Patel then left. Lily proceeded to fill Rose in on the deal she's put together for Daria. Rose stood up and paced back and forth appearing troubled. Lily wanted to hug her, but felt that Rose would object at that moment so she resisted the urge. Rose suddenly stopped and turned to Lily.

"So she can't bother me? She has to stay five hundred feet from me?" demanded Rose.

"That's correct Rose. Under the agreement if she violates that she goes to jail. She can't threaten you in any form." Lily explained, "Thank-you for showing compassion Rose, after all her mother lies dying."

"Poor Daria! Don't tell her I said that though she'd hold that against me. It doesn't excuse what she did but I can understand her being so angry. But I'm also mad that she hit me. I feel sorry for her, but she can't hit people. I didn't hit people when Daddy died. Even though I felt like I wanted to punch someone. Maybe she doesn't have any friends with her attitude."

"You agree to the terms though, Rose?" asked Lily "Because if you don't we can change them, slightly."

"It seems like you thought of everything. I agree to it all as long as she stays away from me. I don't have to see her to sign anything, do I?"

"No sweetie, you don't. Emmett went to call the station. She will be released tonight into her father's custody. Then tomorrow she'll come to my office and sign the plea agreement," Lily reassured, her daughter.

"Good! Simply because I don't want her to go to jail, doesn't mean I want to see her again."

"I understand that Rose. That's why I'm putting the restraining order in place. I don't want her anywhere near you."

"I just want to put my two cents in and let you know that I think you're being very generous to Daria. You could have made her go to jail. That's why I like you so much Rose you're a great person. I'm glad you're my friend," Carol commented.

"Thanks Carol. You're a good friend," Rose answered, then turning to her mom she said, "I love you, mom."

"I love you too," Lily answered.

"Now that we're done being sappy shall we go home?" Carol asked.

"Hey, are my favourite ladies ready for an early dinner?" asked Emmett coming back into the room.

"Dinner? We're going to dinner with you?" squealed Rose excited, "Where?"

"Anywhere the lady wants to go," Emmett answered, smiling.

Lily whispered to Rose, "Remember the man makes a police salary."

"Is Bobby's Pizza too expensive a place to eat?" asked Rose.

"Not at all Rose," Emmett answered, smiling, "And Carol can come too if her parents approve."

"Gee, thank you Mr. Rogers," Carol exclaimed.

"Thanks Emmett. You are the best," Rose stated.

Rose and Carol walked a short distance away to the outdoors and Carol dialled her parents. Emmett and Lily heard whispering and giggling and then Rose returned to stand beside them.

"Is it okay if she meets us there? Her parents said it was okay but she has to go home first," Rose asked.

"Sure that's fine," Emmett answered, as Rose told Carol.

Carol then left.

"Thanks, Emmett. I love their Venetian pizza."

"I don't think I've ever tried that."

"It's good you should try it, Emmett," Rose insisted.

"I will."

Lily smiled at the camaraderie between the two as they got into the car to go to the pizza restaurant. Lily began to think about Emmett. He was a good man one of a kind in this day in age. She imagined what it would be like if they were together. Emmett would make an incredible father for Rose. Emmett might be a good man, but Lily had such bad luck with husbands, not only were they murdered, but they both cheated on her. Not an especially good track record. Could she trust her instincts when it came to Emmett? And Emmett had a job that could certainly cause her to be a widow once again. Cops got murdered every day.

Would it be wise to investing him in her heart? Emmett was a sweetheart though. He not only supported her, but he was good to Rose, at every opportunity. Surely three times the charm? She remained angry at Horace she couldn't deny that. He had lied to her. He had been having an affair with Amber of all people, his ditzy secretary Amber...Amber who could barely type. That should have put up red flags for Lily; instead Lily had trusted them both. Fool that she was! Lily had been friendly with Amber and thought she respected her, but Amber obviously hadn't. It had come out at Brad Owen's murder trial sentencing, that that they had a long term affair accumulating over years.

Had Horace used Lily, only to be a mother for Rose? It wasn't purely to have a mother for Rose, so he didn't have to bother with Rose, was it? No, he loved her. Didn't he? She loved Rose. She felt Rose was a part of her. She was a great mother to Rose, and yet had Brad Owens been correct. Horace had planned on divorcing her and taking Rose. He'd filed the papers the day he was murdered. She was Rose's mother since the day Cordelia had been committed. How could he have done that to her, or Rose?

"How could you Horace? How could you hurt your child?" Lily thought, as she stared at Rose as they got out of the car and entered the restaurant. She should stop thinking in permanency? She should stand on her own two feet and not rely on a man. The need to have someone always by her side had gotten Lily into to trouble. She'd take this relationship slow.

~0~

At the Crown Attorney's office the next day Lily finalized

the details of the deal for Daria. Lily noted aloud and for the record that Daria and her father Dan and her lawyer had arrived right on time.

"Do you understand the details of this deal Ms. Brown?" Lily asked in her professional mode.

Daria looked at her lawyer and nodded.

"For the record, Ms. Brown, we will document your responses to this plea deal," Lily commented indicating the recording device.

"I object!" Daria's lawyer interrupted, forcefully.

"The recording will be destroyed, if and when the sentence is fully completed," Lily explained.

"That's acceptable then," the lawyer agreed.

"Now Daria, do you understand these terms? You must attend anger management classes. The number of classes to be determined by your psychiatrist, in conjunction with this office." Lily stated, then turning to Daria's lawyer, George Perrod she asked, "Has a psychiatrist been chosen?"

"Crown Attorney Kelly, a Doctor Robert Hayward will see her," stated Mr. Perrod.

"Number two, you will have at least three appointments a week, with your psychiatrist; until he determines you need less. Number three, you will stay at least five hundred feet from Rose Brooksfield at all times. If you have a gym class with her, you will stand on the opposite side of the gym if possible. You will not partner with her for any gym exercise. If asked to do so you must take the teacher aside and explain the restraining order, or be in violation. Number four, you will complete five hundred hours of community service. Is this acceptable?" demanded Lily.

"Aw, do I have to? Five hundred hours of community service?" whined Daria, "That's way too much. Big deal, so Rose got a few licks."

Lily frowned and cleared her throat. Daniel looked at Lily worried as if she'd change her mind, then turned to his daughter and asked exasperated, "Daria Jane Brown, show some contriteness. Would you rather go to jail?"

"No Daddy, but five hundred hours of community service? That's so much time to give away." Daria whined, "Why do I have to do five hundred hours?"

"Because you committed a crime," Dan said under his breath.

"It's not fair," complained Daria as her lawyer also tried to shush her and whispered in her ear.

"I'm sorry, I'm like, totally behaving badly," Daria exclaimed.

"Apology accepted Daria. Shall we continue with the plea deal?"

"Yes, please," Daria answered.

"Can she pick where she performs the community service?" asked Daniel Brown, ignoring Daria's outburst.

"I guess if we approve the choice," Lily responded, bending a little.

Daria then whispered in her Dad's ear.

"Daria wants to know if she can volunteer in the hospital as a candy striper?" asked Daniel.

"That would be acceptable," Lily agreed.

Daria signed the papers with her lawyer then she whispered this time in her lawyer's ear.

"You have something you'd like to say Ms. Brown?" Lily asked, wondering what Daria whispered.

"Ms. Brown has told me she has some evidence she like to tell you about an open case," George replied, "My client is not sure if this is important to your case, or even that you needed to know. But she wishes to tell you; provided of course it will not impact her sentencing. You of course can pass this along to the investigating officer."

"Please go ahead, Ms. Brown. As long as it doesn't involve a crime committed by your client, I will hear her out."

"First of all I want to apologise sincerely for my behaviour yesterday, and to hope that you will convey my apology to Rose, since I'm forbidden from doing so. This was like totally out of character for me, and I'm truly sorry for any harm that I did to Rose," Daria took a huge breath here, after saying what seemed like a well-rehearsed speech.

"Thank-you Daria. Now you had something to tell me about an open police case?"

"On the morning of September ninth, when Mr. Scholar was killed, I was there."

"What time did you arrive at the school?" Lily prodded.

"I got there about five forty five a.m. I couldn't sleep so I went in early. I wanted to join choir. I love choir. I hoped to be lead soprano this year...Oh no, if they start up choir again and Rose is in it, can I go?" Daria demanded.

"Daria, as long as you don't stand directly beside Rose and don't speak to and or taunt her, I'll allow it," Lily answered.

"Okay, thank again. I got there at five forty five a.m. I couldn't sleep so I went early. It was exceedingly odd. The hallway was creepy and so dark. I hurried along; when I heard raised voices yelling. I was kind of scared, but then I thought, I heard two people arguing. It was nothing to do with me. I wanted to get into the classroom as quickly as I could, but then I realized the voices were in the choir classroom. I didn't want to hear it so I walked away from the choir door and went down to the vending machine around the corner. I was thirsty, I wanted a drink," Daria explained.

"Then what happened? What else did you see, or hear, Daria?" coached Lily

"The corridor was dark, but the voices were raised so loud. But I couldn't understand what they said, or whether it was man, or a woman yelling. I thought I heard swearing, and a voice saying, "I hate you". I also thought I heard the door slam, but then I heard raised voices again but I didn't hear what they were saying," Daria replied sounding confused.

"Did you see anyone?" asked Lily.

"I saw someone come out of the choir room, but only from the back. They were dressed all in black. They even had a black wool cap on their head," Daria explained.

"Could you tell if it was a man or a woman? Or their hair color?"

"I'm not sure. I couldn't tell though what their sex was. They were tall, five-feet-ten inches, or more. I saw some hair coming out of the cap but I couldn't tell whether it was long or short. It was brown and curly I think. A light brown, coloured hair, it wasn't dyed," Daria answered. "Oh, and they had bloody tennis shoes on. I noticed that because they were white with red splotches on them. Of course it wasn't until later I thought that might be blood but only after I heard about Mr. Scholar's murder. The person that came out of the room had big feet. However "I know some women have size ten shoes, so I'm still not sure whether it was a man or woman."

"Are you sure they didn't move in a way that would indicate they were man or a woman?" demanded Lily getting up from her seat and pacing a little.

"Gee haven't you been listening at all, stupid? I couldn't tell at all who, or what they were," Daria stated.

Lily stood in front of her office window turning around she stared straight into Daria's eyes.

"Can you think of any other details Daria?"

"Gee, I told you. Then with a look from her father and her lawyer Daria replied, "No, I didn't. It was terribly dark, and so early."

"Why weren't you in the choir room when Rose came to school?" demanded Lily sitting down at her desk, "Since you said the voices left?"

"I felt sick from the drink I got and I went home." recalled Daria then she added, "I didn't realize I had gotten Orange Crush from the vending machine. I pressed Doctor Pepper."

"Orange Crush makes her sick," volunteered Dan, "She's intolerant to it."

"Did you see anyone else outside of the school when you went home?" asked Lily.

"Do I have to tell her everything Daddy?" Daria demanded.

"Tell Lily everything so you don't get in anymore trouble."

"Fine, then let me see. I saw my Aunt Teresa kissing some guy in his car. I almost went over, but I didn't want to embarrass her. I saw her kiss that guy Emmett Rogers, the one that arrested me. That was weird, two days before I'd seen her with Mr. Scholar."

"You saw Teresa Brown with Mr. Scholar?" demanded Lily.

"Yah, but my aunt didn't have anything to do with this murder. You can't blame her just simply because she was there. I told you the truth she kissed your boyfriend. She couldn't have been with Mr. Scholar," Daria defended, "I saw Ms. Vasquez, the Spanish teacher sitting in her car crying. She listened to some weird music from the sixties I think."

"What song did you hear and did you see anyone else?" Lily asked.

"The song kept singing, 'Why does the sun go on shining,' or something stupid like that. Then there was Ms. Abrams the librarian in her car she listened to her car radio, because I heard Queen's music, 'Bohemian Rhapsody', coming from her car. She also read a book."

"Okay so let me get this straight. You saw Teresa Brown your aunt, and Mrs. Vasquez the Spanish teacher, and then Ms. Abrams, the librarian. You didn't see anyone else?"

"You want to know everyone I saw?"

"Yes, Daria, everyone."

"Okay, I saw Ms. Hearst, the math teacher, after that the librarian, Ms. Abrams, she looked at some papers... I think. I saw some man I've never seen before in a suit and tie. I also saw some kids outside Bobby Forest, Jerry Gilliam, Sherry Tyrell, and Gina Lloyd. The four of them were talking like crazy. They seemed to be waiting for something too. Maybe they were joining choir too? Oh, and mommy, because she dropped me off. I went over to her car and told her I wasn't feeling well and she drove me home," Daria recalled. "Mommy didn't feel well either. That's why she was still there."

"Thank-you Daria. That's everything you remember?" asked Lily, "And you are sure you didn't know this man?"

Daria shook her head.

"For my records what did he look like?"

"That's all I remember. The man in the suit looked East Indian or something, no turban though. He had dark hair and black beady eyes. It was probably him. He looked sketchy," Daria stated, hesitating for a second almost like she hid something else.

"Thank you, Daria. If you're sure you can't tell me anymore. I think were done here and thank you for the information. If we have any follow-up questions we will get in touch with you."

"Thank-you, Mrs. Brooksfield. I'm going to live up to my agreement, as Daddy says. Cause I don't want to go to jail and I am truly sorry," Daria commented.

Lily waited for them to go out the door then called Emmett.

"Emmett, I got some information this morning for your investigation. Could you swing by my office and I'll give you the information I collected?" Lily asked, leaving a voice mail for Emmett.

Where could he be? Was he out with his new partner Kendall who obviously had the hots for him? She sincerely disliked that woman. Kendall Evans was such a predator. Like a lioness ready to track her prey, and it was obvious who her prey was. Emmett seemed unaware that she made the moves on him. How long could a viral man resist such a nubile young woman? Kendall worked with him and was a beautiful intelligent and a fellow cop. How could Lily hope to compete with that? Ick she was being ridiculous and untrusting. What in the hell was wrong with her? She had to stop this!!

Lily knew she let her insecurities get to her. Emmett seemed amused rather than flattered by Kendall's obvious interest. She had to put that out of her head. And she would. She couldn't let this relationship die, simply because she was jealous. She was jealous? Good grief she was!! What happened to taking it slow?

She didn't care about Emmett, did she? He had wormed his way into her heart, in such a short time. With his lopsided grin and his big doe eyed smiles he'd made her care. She had wanted to take it slow since it was so soon after Horace had died, but he snuck into her heart. She would make this relationship work. She had to, she couldn't bear any more heartache.

~0~

Chapter 14 –
Speechless

Rose lay on her bed talking to Carol. Carol stood by the

bedroom window looking out.

"So I told Bilal, that he was nice, but I wasn't interested," Carol stated.

"You didn't! What did he say?" asked Rose, "And turn around, so I can see your face when you tell me."

Carol turned her face around and Rose saw she was blushing.

"He asked me if it was because he was of Muslim faith, that I wouldn't date him."

"No, he didn't!" Rose commented, shocked and then asked, "And then what did you say?"

"I wasn't ready to date anyone, but that he was nice," Carol explained.

"Is that true?" asked Rose.

"No, but it's better than him believing it was because of his faith. You know that wasn't the reason. He accepted that only because he knows I'm Catholic. The fact is he doesn't interest me and not because of his religious beliefs. I don't care about that; unless he were say a Satanist," Carol explained.

"I know what you mean. Yuri asked me out."

"No, you're kidding? Ooh yuck!"

"I know he's tall, gangly and he never bathes and slaps on too much cologne. It's so gross," Rose exclaimed.

"So what did you say to him?" asked Carol.

"I was nice at first, but then he wouldn't take no for an answer, so I was mean."

"What did you do?" Carol asked.

"I told him I wouldn't date him if he was the last guy on Earth, and then I swore at him," Rose exclaimed.

"You swore? Miss I'm so shocked if anyone says a bad word?"

"I said the F-word," Rose admitted then blushed.

Carol's phone then rang interrupting them.

"I can't talk now. I'll call you back," Carol exclaimed, cryptically into the phone.

"Who is that on the phone?" asked Rose, as Carol held up one finger to say in a minute.

"No, I can't, I'm with Rose. Don't go there, I'm warning you."

"Who is it?" demanded Rose.

Rose genuinely wanted to know who Carol talked to.

"Uh huh. What? No! You're kidding right? The shoes were where? You saw the shoes where, Daria? Okay so you saw them at the hospital when you did your community service? No, you should tell someone else," Carol continued.

"What you're talking to that biotch Daria? You know what she did to me! Hang up," demanded Rose angrily.

"I've got to go. You be careful the shoes belong to someone and they are liable to come back and get them," Carol replied, "Oh, so they were in the shoes? Did you see who? Okay, fine I'll talk to you later, but be careful. Bye."

Carol then hung up her cell phone as Rose glared at her.

"I don't know why you wouldn't let me hear what she said. Gee whiz, Rose," Carol stated annoyed.

Rose clasped and unclasped her fists then breathed in and out, counting slowly to twenty. But it did no good she was still furious with Carol.

"How could you Carol? You are supposed to be my best friend? You know what that girl did to me!"

"You let her off the charges. You got that plea agreement for her. How was I supposed to know you were still mad?" protested Carol.

"Gee, I'm kind to her because her mother is dying and you hold that against me? That stupid evil biotch sneaks up behind me, knocks me down and sucker-punches me and then accuses me of ogling, her ugly, no good boyfriend. Why wouldn't I be mad?" asked Rose sarcastically.

"But Rose, what she had to say was important. She saw the killer at the hospital while she did her community service. She bent down to pick up something she dropped, and she saw the shoes of the killer again," Carol explained, "They were right there in front of her."

"When did the Drama Queen see them the first time? She's probably lying. She likes all the attention. She loved being the aggressor against me. She loves the reputation she got from beating me up. Do you know after I was nice enough to get her a plea bargain, so she didn't have to go to jail, she spread lies around school that I had to get my mommy to fight my battle? I hate her! I hope she comes within five hundred feet of me, I'll send her ass where it belongs, to jail!" Rose stated angrily.

"I don't like this side of you Rose. You sound like your dad," Carol commented.

"How dare you? I hope I do sound like him because my Dad was a wonderful man," Rose declared.

"Rose, I don't want to fight with you. Your dad wasn't perfect and you've been my best friend for years. Are you jealous of her? Because you don't need to be!"

"Jealous are you freakin' kidding me? I'm not jealous! She's a mean spirited evil biotch and she's out to get me and my so-called best friend takes her side. Don't you dare bring my dad into this!!"

"No one is perfect. Your dad could be cruel too, like when he fired that janitor, just because he moved some papers on his desk."

"He gave him the job back the next day," Rose protested, defending her father.

"That's not the point and you know it. You aren't thinking about this. You are reacting like your Dad always did."

"I hate you Carol Banks. I think you should go home now and don't come back. I don't know if I want to talk to you ever again," Rose declared angrily, stamping her foot. "You are so unbelievable. You go around insulting my father and cavorting with my enemy..."

"Big words ...pulling out the big guns now? Guess what, Rose Brooksfield? I don't have to take your crap. I'm leaving. Don't call me again, unless it's to apologise."

Carol then slammed the bedroom door and then the front door as she left. Rose ran downstairs after her to fight some more, but by then Carol was gone.

"Why did Carol slam our front door Rose? Did you two have a fight?" Lily asked.

"Don't mention Carol to me. She's dead to me," Rose declared dramatically.

"You might feel better if you talked about it."

"She talked to Daria on her cell phone," Rose explained.

"And?" asked Lily.

"That's not enough? Daria has been spreading rumours of me all over school and then my best friend takes a call from her? Like it's nothing to cavort with the enemy," whined Rose.

"Do you want me to put a stop to her rumour mongering?" asked Lily angry, at the thought of Daria doing this, after the sweetheart deal Daria had gotten.

"Do you want the school to all believe it is true and that I'm a bigger dweeb then they think I am now?" asked Rose, "That my mommy does have to fight all my battles?"

"What do you want me to do?" asked Lily.

"I don't know. Just don't embarrass me, anymore," Rose claimed frustrated.

Lily wondered what it would be like to live with a normal teen it seemed she was about to find out.

"Did Carol go home? Should you go after her and apologise?" asked Lily without expecting an answer.

"I don't know home? I'm not chasing after her. She can come back and apologise to me," Changing the subject Rose asked, "Carol said that Daria she saw the murderer. You didn't tell me that."

"It was only from the back, besides you know I like to keep my cases private." Lily replied, and then she thought about it and asked, "Why and when did this come up in conversation I told Daria not to talk about this."

Rose looked uncomfortable and then decided to tell Lily, "Daria told Carol that she saw the shoes of the murderer. I should have told you that right away, but I thought she lied for attention. You know what? She probably still is lying!"

"Did she say where she saw them again?" asked Lily.

"She's working at the hospital as part of her community service. I only heard Carol's side, but it sounds like she saw the person's shoes, not the rest of them," Rose explained.

"I'm going to have to have to speak to Daria about this."

"Sure, go talk to the drama Queen. You're wasting your time. She's probably making all of this up for the attention." Rose sniped.

"This conduct makes me speechless. Rose, you don't sound like yourself. You should go up to your room and think about this behaviour. Then when you're done thinking, go over and apologise to your best friend," Lily demanded.

"Right take her side. Everyone is against me."

Rose then went up to her room and slammed her door.

"Now who's the Drama Queen?" exclaimed Lily out loud, and then called Katha on her cell phone.

"Grandma Katha, could you come over here? I need someone to watch Rose for awhile. I have to warn you though she's out of sorts." Lily then explained Rose's behaviour expecting sympathy.

"The start of the teen years can be difficult, so she's overdo," Grandma Katha stated knowingly, "I wondered when that perfect daughter of yours, would feel comfortable enough to act out."

"So you expected this? Why didn't you warn me?" asked Lily surprised.

"They all do this Lily. You did it. Amelia did it, and now Rose does it. It's a part of growing up. At least she isn't sneaking out to concerts."

"You knew Amelia and I did that when we stayed with you?" asked Lily shocked.

"If you had looked back two rows, you would have seen your Grandma Katha watching over you," Katha admitted.

"I love you Grandma Katha. Thank you, you are always there for us."

"Where else would I be?" Katha asked, "I'll be there in a flash, then you can go get your business done. Don't worry about that daughter of yours either, Grandma Katha's Johnny Cake will get her in a sweeter mood."

"Will you save me a piece and some of your homemade strawberry jam?"

"Of course I will. Are you off to your office?"

"Thank you for taking care of Rose for me," Lily responded.

"It's a joy. Never forget that our children are joys," Grandma Katha said. Lily heard it both in her phone and at her elbow.

"Thank you for coming so quick. So is their Grandmother Katha." Lily replied.

Lily then left through the front door. Rose waited then stamped into the kitchen.

"Good, she's gone," Rose griped.

"I don't think you appreciate your mother and all she's done for you," Katha exclaimed.

"I do too. She took Carol's part."

"Did she? Or did you want her to agree with you, so wouldn't feel bad about how you treated Carol," asked Katha calmly.

"I didn't treat Carol badly. She treated me badly. She talked to the enemy."

"Do you control Carol? Do you own her?" Katha asked.

"I didn't say I owned her." Rose complained, "But she talked to Daria."

"But she's not allowed to be friends with anyone but you, or people you approve of. Is that okay? Would she do that to you? Would it be okay if she said you couldn't talk to Billy Robertson?" Katha asked.

"How did you know...?" Rose replied, then backtracking she continued, "I guess I did treat Carol badly."

"And?"

"I was so mad. I was wrong, I guess. How is it that you always make me see things like this? And mom doesn't."

"You're a teenager; you're adversarial to your mother. I'm a disinterested party. So, how will you make this right?"

"I'll apologise to Mom later. I'll think on how to make it up to Carol," Rose replied, reluctantly.

"The Johnny cake will be ready in about ten minutes."

"Thank-you, Grandma Katha, you're the best. The cake will help me think how to make it up to Carol," Rose exclaimed, happily, "Especially if I can have some of your homemade strawberry jam with it."

Katha smiled, a knowing smile, Rose would make everything right again after this talk. Her girls would be okay. Amelia on the mend from her heartbreak, Lily realizing her interest in Emmett Rogers, it would work out. Emmett was a fine man. He reminded her of Kieran O'Malley, her beloved husband who had died. He was a man to be proud of. Lily could find her happiness with Emmett and then Katha could spend her time finding someone special for Amelia.

They'd never know that she worked on this for them...her three girls, all lights of her life would be happy.

~0~

Chapter 15-
What's One
More?

C arol arrived at Happy Valley hospital and met with a

shaken Daria.

"So what was the big hurry? Why did I have to hightail it all the way over here Daria?" Carol demanded.

"I told you. The day Mr. Scholar was murdered I saw the murderer's shoes; today I saw those same shoes. I'm scared," Daria admitted.

"You should have gone to the cops. I hope you're happy, because you called me I may have lost my best friend." Carol replied.

"That's no great loss. She's an uptight low-life," Daria snarled.

"I think I'm leaving like now. Pick up a phone and call the cops."

"Defend the biotch and desert me, why don't you?" Daria whined.

"You have no right to insult Rose. She's never done anything to you and then spread vicious lies about her, punch and hit her? Who do you think you are Daria Brown? Rose could have said put you in jail and they would have in a heartbeat. Do you know that?" Carol cried angrily defending Rose.

Daria looked alarmed and then resigned she decided to apologise.

"I'm sorry Carol. I know she's your friend though I can't for the life of me understand why. Rose gets up in my grill. I'm so angry and Rose is always there in my face." Daria confessed, "I hate her I'm so special outlook and the way she looks at me and yet she's so nice to people. It kinda makes me angrier. You know? Her father was murdered, doesn't she care? "

"Daria, you have no idea how hard that was on Rose. She was close to her Dad. She misses him terribly. I don't know how many times I've comforted her when she's cried. Simply because she doesn't wear her heart on her sleeve, doesn't mean she doesn't care," Carol answered.

"That's a weird expression 'heart on her sleeve'. I think you've been hanging out with those Kelly's too much!"

"I heard that expression from Rose's Grandma Katha." Carol explained, "That woman is kind and she cares about people."

"She's awful old," Daria commented.

"Grandma Katha isn't old, not in the real sense. She knows lots of stuff and she listens to me."

"You call her Grandma Katha. She's not your Grandma Katha. I'm your family not them!" Daria complained.

"Sometimes I wish they were. They are exceptionally loving people, and sometimes all our family cares about is themselves and their own stuff. Besides didn't I come when you called?" Carol retorted.

"I guess so, sorry." Daria replied, reluctantly, "But I'm family, she's not. I don't know why Rose Brooksfield is your friend. She's so stupid and mean."

"That's the point. She's my friend! My best friend! Get to the point, why did you call me? Now where did you see these shoes?" Carol demanded.

"The shoes were walking by. I dropped a book from the volunteer cart and there they were walking by. However by the time it registered the shoes were gone, along with the person wearing them," Daria answered.

"So you didn't really see who it was?"

"Hey, Daria!" a voice said interrupting.

A skinny young man, about seventeen years old and over seventeen years old, put his arm around Daria. He had a scruffy goatee and mustache, and greasy black shoulder length hair worn down around his face. His clothes were all black and he wore a leather jacket and eighties styled combat boots.

"Paul, I told you not to come here when I'm working. I have to finish my volunteer work satisfactory. Your interruptions could make a black mark against me. Do you want to visit me in jail?" Daria complained.

"Sorry, Daria, I forgot. I wanted to see you, babe. Do you want me to fix that little bitch, Rose Brooksfield's ass? I can make matters difficult for her," Paul stated.

"Paul! Don't go there. You'll get me in more trouble."

"I said I was sorry. I need to protect my girl. You know how I miss you. This job sucks and it's Rose Brooksfield's fault," Paul replied, touching her arm and hugging her possessively.

"Paul any retaliation against Rose is out," Daria cautioned.

"What does retaliation mean?"

"It means you do nothing to her. You don't even speak to her. Get it?" Daria demanded.

"I don't like it when you talk to me like I'm dumb," Paul complained and twisted Daria's arm behind her back leaving marks.

"Who are you and why do you think you can hurt Daria?" Carol asked.

"This is my boyfriend, Paul Decker... Paul my cousin Carol," Daria introduced.

"You can do better Daria." Carol commented.

"Your cousin is kind of cute, but she has a nasty tongue. Some guy should straighten her out. If she got some she wouldn't be so jealous."

"Daria he's a winner." Carol retorted sarcastically.

Daria looked back in disgust at Carol.

"Thanks coz," Paul replied misunderstanding.

"I am not your coz, or anything related to you," Carol stated.

"She is quite feisty maybe we should consider a threesome Daria,"
Paul commented.

"You'd better be kidding Paul," Daria answered, as Carol rolled
her eyes and bit her tongue.

"Try to make someone feel they are wanted and important,"
muttered Paul.

"You're gross. Can you go away? We are discussing something
important here, the killer's shoes," Carol retorted.

"Are you still going on about shoes? Daria nobody cares about a
pair of stupid shoes," Paul complained.

"Dense much?" Carol cried rolling her eyes

"I told you I saw the killer that morning." Daria explained, "At
least his shoes."

"So big deal, you saw some shoes. I didn't tell you this because I
didn't want to freak you out, but I saw someone before that come
out of the choir room," bragged Paul.

"Did you recognize who it was?" asked Carol excited.

"I wasn't talking to you Carol. I'm speaking to someone who
appreciates me; but I'll answer your question anyway, I recognised
both of the men and women that came out of the room." Paul
boasted.

"You should tell the police," Carol demanded, "That is if you
know who was in the room, before Rose and I got there, Paul. Tell
me what you saw."

"I did see someone. Daria and I were macking in the hall. She's so
sweet and I was getting into the kiss, you know?" Paul began.

"Not that part Paul. Good grief, do you think I want to hear that
about my cousin and you?" Carol asked, disgusted.

"I heard raised voices, with loud yelling and crying. I thought about going in, but I thought I'm not getting in to that shit... er sorry crap. I get enough of that yelling at home. And believe me you do not want to get in the middle of a couple who is laying down," Paul continued.

"They were laying down? Yuck. Gross," Carol misunderstood.

"No, not laying down, laying down. You are so naive and you insinuate I'm stupid? You know like fist to cuff?" Paul explained, but broke out laughing at Carol.

"So explain some more then," Carol insisted.

"So first, Mrs. Thomas came out of the room. You know the principal?" Paul says and then continued, "But then we went to the vending machine and Doctor Thomas her husband came out. I knew it was him, because I met him once. Then some few minutes later Doctor Patel went in and out."

"How did you know it was Doctor Patel?" Carol demanded shocked.

"I knew it was him, because my Mom works with his sister and so does Daria's aunt. I saw him there a couple of times, with his name tag on his chest. Then while I was thinking about taking Daria into an empty room and....well you know. Ms. Vasquez went in and out followed by that new librarian, Mrs. what's her name?" Paul answered.

"Do you mean Mrs. Abrams? She is filling in as a librarian. She's a teacher. She doesn't have a degree in library sciences. Did you have to tell my cousin what we were going to do?" Daria stated outraged.

"I should be bragging baby, since we did it right after that in the Math room," Paul says "And you were hot for me, babe. Don't deny it. Want to go into that closet for moment or two and have me refresh your memory?"

"Paul must you? That was between us. I thought you cared about me! She'll think I'm a slut," Daria then wiped tears out of her eyes then threatened Carol, "You had better not spread this all over school."

"As if I would tell anyone what you did!" Carol shrieked, "You should be embarrassed though. You did it in the school and with that Neanderthal? Haven't you any self-respect?"

Paul glared at Carol.

"Don't glare at me Paul. You're a user and I better not see any more marks on Daria, or I'll make you sorry you were born."

"Don't you threaten me, Carol Banks," Paul shouted waving his fist at Carol.

"Look I'll put this simple Paul," Carol cried putting Paul in a headlock in seconds, "Lay off harming my cousin, or I will hurt you."

"Okay, okay. I love her. I wouldn't harm Daria," Paul stated, "Let me go before someone sees this."

"Please, Carol, don't hurt him."

"Fine I won't hurt him I'll let him go." Carol replied letting Paul go.

Paul straightened himself up and looked awed at Carol.

"She's tough," he claimed.

"She's black-belt," lied Daria.

Carol hid a laugh and then thinking some more she said, "I'm sorry about Aunt Denise, but value yourself more, Daria. You can do better than this slime ball..."

"Don't you call me slime ball Carol," Paul stated angrily.

"Don't you, even, unless you want to be put in a chokehold again," Carol replied, putting her hand up as Paul starts getting closer to her again.

Paul backed off and then put his arm possessively around Daria who cuddled closer.

"Please don't tell anyone especially my mom," begged Daria.

"I want tell Aunt Denise, but the police have to know who Paul saw," Carol stated seriously.

"They don't even know he was there I never mentioned him. So they don't need to know at all," Daria argued, "You know my Dad was there at the Crown attorney's office, when I did my plea bargain. I told them I was there that morning, but I wasn't about to let him know what we were doing. He'd freak out to know we were kissing. If he heard what we were doing...he'd kill Paul."

"Are you ashamed of me, baby?" Paul asked misunderstanding again.

"I'm not ashamed of anything. It's no one's business, but ours. And don't call me baby, you know I don't like it," Daria cried, angrily rolling her eyes.

"I thought you loved that movie Dirty Dancing. That's what Patrick Swayze calls her. He even sings Baby, oh baby you're the one," Paul charmed.

"I hope you used protection. One of him is enough in the world," Carol commented.

"Oh shut-up, Carol," Daria replied, smiling at Paul thrilled about the Patrick Swayze remark.

Carol rolled her eyes.

"You'd better tell them the truth, both of you, before they think you killed Mr. Scholar together," Carol insisted as her cell phone rang.

"Hello," Carol cried angrily into it, "Oh, it's you. What do you want? Okay, I guess I could come to dinner. Yes, but ...okay then got to go."

"Paul, you and Daria should go talk to Ms. Kelly at her office. She needs to know what Paul saw. If the murderer finds out what you saw he could come after Paul and then you. So tell the police!" Carol stated turning back to Daria, "Since you're safe with Paul. I'm gone. I've got somewhere to be. See you later."

In the shadows the killer overheard and wondered what to do. The killer picked up their cell phone and made a call. "Darling, you know I love you more than life itself, but we have a problem. The brats heard and saw everything. I know you're scared. Me, too! I promised I'd protect you and I will. I know I know, but as I said there were witnesses. Don't worry, I will handle this. Oh, okay. Goodbye, dear," the voice cried, hanging up the phone.

Alexander Scholar was a worm, a cretin of the highest order. If they hadn't killed him someone else would have but it was unfortunate that it had been them. The bases had all been covered up to now, this was simply a wrinkle. It could all be fixed, no need to panic and worry about exposure. However now there was a witness. No strike that...witnesses, Paul and Daria. They had been using the school as a bedroom.

What was wrong with children these days? The killer thought. They had changed since the killer was young. Now they were mouthy and would never shut-up. They talked back to adults like it was their right. They treated everyone badly and their school was a bedroom? An anonymous phone call would have to be made to warn them off and if these two didn't listen well then they brought it all on themselves. They'd have to have an unfortunate accident. These two had to be prevented from talking, from speaking with the police, or Ms. Kelly at all costs but what about the other one? She might have to be dealt with too. If they wouldn't be warned off then something had to be done. What was one more, or two, or even three, more after all?

~0~

Chapter 16 - Love and Marriage

Lily paced back and forth, her ear to her cell phone. She

repeatedly called Amelia and got no answer. Where was Amelia? Katha had declared a family meeting and she couldn't find her.

"Hello, Amelia? Where are you? I know you're not at Quirks, your store. Anyway, this is the fifth message I've left you. Grandma Katha, (your Aunt), has called family meeting. She claims she's got an important announcement to make. Call me back when you get this message. I'm starting to worry," Lily stated, leaving a message yet again on Amelia's cell phone.

Lily wondered if Amelia was with Doctor Thomas. How she wished Amelia hadn't gotten involved with a married man. Dating him before the ink had dried on his divorce, didn't seem right. Even if the man was serious about Amelia, he was still attached. He should back off until the divorce was final. This was the first man Amelia, had been serious about, since her husband and child had died. And he was married.

Married men often lied telling their patsies that they were going to leave their wives. Lily didn't trust him. Why couldn't he wait to date Amelia, if he told the truth? Lily saw nothing but disaster ahead.

"Mom can Carol come to dinner?" Rose asked.

"This is a family dinner. Carol is not family, even if she spends more time with us, then with own her family," Lily responded.

"Please Mom? Carol is truly angry with me. I have to make it up to her and I already invited her to dinner," pleaded Rose.

"Why do you ask me, if you already told her she could come? You shouldn't have told her to come to our house before asking me; but since you did, I won't take your invitation back," Lily retorted.

"Thank-you Mom. You're the best mom in the world."

Rose then ran up to her bedroom. At least this makes me better in Rose's eyes, Lily thought.

Lily pulled the hamburger out of the fridge. She started dicing the mushrooms, and onions. She put the lasagne noodles in the boiling water, with a little oil so they don't stick. She wiped tears from her eyes, as the onion smell wafted up. Why couldn't they make a tearless onion? She thought as she wiped her eyes and then re-washed her hands.

She cooked the hamburger, throwing in the diced onions and mushrooms. Then slowly layering mozzarella cheese, she cut thinly; she began to make the layers of lasagne. She then placed the finished product in the oven to cook, at three hundred and fifty degrees, for the forty five minutes, it needed to cook. Lily cleaned her kitchen counter, when she heard the doorbell ring. As she went to answer it, Rose came running by, answering the door before Lily.

"Oh, hello, it's you Emmett. I thought you were Carol. But it's good to see you. Can you stay for supper? We're having lasagne Mom made," Rose cried, talking a mile a minute.

"I'm looking for Carol Banks. Have you seen her today?" asked Emmett.

"She was here about noon but we had a fight, and she left. I think she went to talk to Daria Brown," Rose snarled.

"Rose, I'm sorry but this isn't a social visit. Carol has gone missing her parents expected her hours ago. They've tried her cell phone repeatedly, but got no answer. We've issued an Amber alert," Emmett replied sounding professional.

"Carol can't be missing. We have to make up. Besides don't you have to wait twenty four hours, or something before you can look for people officially? So she can't be missing. Can she?" Rose rationalized.

"I'm surprised that Carol never told you. Her great-uncle is the police chief," Emmett answered.

"What? But wouldn't that make Terrence, her great-grandfather?" asked Rose.

"It does."

"She didn't tell me! Why? Didn't she trust me? I'm so mad at her. I'm going to shake her when I see her. How dare she keep something so epic from me?"

"Rose, put those feelings aside for now. I need to know have you any idea where Carol could be?"

"How do I know where that stupid Carol could be? She's mad at me, so she's ignoring her texts, thinking it's me. And most of our argument was entirely her fault. Although she said she'd come here for dinner, when I finally got her to answer her home phone."

"She answered her home phone? Today?" Emmett asked.

"Yes, but she's not answering anymore. She's not answering my texts either. She's late, so she's getting even by not coming. She must have changed her mind," Rose explained.

"What time did you talk to her?" Emmett demanded.

"I don't know, four p.m.?" Rose stated, "Do you want to check my cell phone? The call should be there and then the repeated texts."

"She'll probably show up here any moment, but apparently her mother is worried and called her uncle who sent me," Emmett reassured.

"The police chief's worried? That can't be good," Rose commented.

"She's missing. If you can help me with my enquiries in any way...."

"Here you go here's my cell phone. Take it and find her. No matter how mad I am that she didn't tell me about her family, I wouldn't want anything to happen to her. She's my best friend."

Rose then handed her cell phone to Emmett.

"You phoned Carol at three p.m. not four and talked to her for about a minute," Emmett explained. "That means she has been unaccounted for approximately, four and a half hours."

Rose bit her lip and took a deep breath. She then seemed to grow calm.

"She probably went out to buy something. Carol loves to shop." reasoned Rose trying to convince herself, "She will be here soon. See, there's the doorbell. That's probably her. She's fashionably late."

Rose went to answer the door and admitted Katha and Terrence. Rose looked behind them, disappointed that Carol didn't follow them.

"Is she here? Is Carol here?" Terrence demanded, his eyes searching the room with hope.

"No. I'm so sorry, Terrence. Carol hasn't come here yet," Lily replied, becoming alarmed herself.

"She'll show up Terrence. She's has to," Katha reassured, "After all she's my great-granddaughter too now and I want to shower her with the same gifts and love other family members get."

Lily turned to Katha a look of astonishment and hurt on her face.

"You and Terrence got married? When did this happen?" Lily asked.

"You got married Grandma Katha? Why didn't you invite us?" Rose cried, also looking upset and hurt.

"Oh, I guess I let the cat out of the bag. Didn't I, Terrence? It was kind of last minute. We went to city hall yesterday and we were married after Terrence caught me at a weak moment. Terrence convinced me that we were meant to be and we thought...why not marry now?" Katha explained.

"Can I help it if I make you weak at the knees and you melt at my every suggestion?" Terrence quipped back.

Katha patted his arm.

"Oh, you! You better watch yourself old man, with that kind of talk. I am woman, hear me roar," Katha answered, annoyed.

"Sorry, dear, you know I like my jokes. I wanted everyone to know what a fortunate man I am, to have the most beautiful, intelligent, modern woman in the world. I am truly a lucky man to have this worldly woman, love me and marry me," Terrence waxed.

Terrence then threw his arm around Katha.

"You better believe that old man, because you're stuck with me now," Katha quipped, smiling and flirting.

"Stuck like glue and don't you forget it my dear," Terrence exclaimed as he smiled back.

Rose and Lily looked on. Seeing the love in both faces, they knew this would work out despite their disappointment at not being at the wedding.

"I'm disappointed that you didn't invite Carol, Mom and I, but I'm glad you got married now, Carol and are not friends, but family. I love it! Carol would love this," Rose cried.

"I don't understand why she's not here," Katha commented.

"But where can Carol be? She should have been here by now," Rose worried "And I guess I was mean to her. What if something happened to her? She's my best friend."

"I'm sure she knows you didn't mean it Rose," Lily reassured.

Terrence looked alarmed and shifted his feet before settling in a kitchen chair, looking dismayed.

"My great-granddaughter is usually on time. If she said she'd be somewhere she's usually early. Where can she be?" Terrence demanded.

"We'll find her," Lily comforted.

Terrence turned to Katha and said, "Katha, this puts a lid on our celebrating. We can have a big celebration later. But right now I have to stay by the phone to learn about my great-granddaughter...I mean our great-granddaughter."

"As if I could celebrate when my beloved great-granddaughter is missing," Katha stated miffed.

"I'm sorry sweetheart. It's coming out all wrong. I'm just so worried."

"I know dear, it's terrible, but we will find her. Emmett won't rest until we find her. Why don't we eat the lasagne Lily made and keep up our strength until we hear something," Katha comforted.

"You smelled my lasagne?"

"Of course I did Lily, dear. Didn't I teach you how to cook it that way?"

"I'm already losing my Denise. Where could Carol be?" Terrence muttered.

"The police will find her dear."

"You believe they'll find her? Do you know a number of women went missing here and in the surrounding area in the early eighties and nineties?" Terrence exclaimed.

Emmett went noticeably pale. Lily put her hand out and rubbed Emmett's arm in a comforting manner. He must have known someone who went missing Katha thought. Katha vowed to find out who Emmett had lost in that time period.

"Hush, darling man. That predator is probably long gone. Don't scare the children and don't borrow trouble. You watch, Carol will come through that door any minute now."

"I hope, and pray, she does."

"We'll find her Terrence. Emmett, you'll find her won't you?" begged Katha.

"I'll do my darndest. I may have to leave soon to check out the hospital and find out who was the last person to see Carol. If you hear from Carol in the meantime, please call me," Emmett insisted

Emmett's radio went off and he left the room coming back a few minutes later.

"I've had a call I have to go, now," Emmett said after taking a call on his radio.

"Carol?" Katha asked.

"No, it's not about Carol. I'll promise I'll talk to you all later and we will find them. Save me some lasagna, please, Lily."

"I'll do that. Let us know if you hear anything about Carol."

"I will. Bye all," Emmett exclaimed leaving through the front door of Lilly's house.

"What can we do, mom?" asked Rose.

"We'll eat and then make some calls and wait here. Emmett will call here with news, so we will wait here," Lily answered.

Lily worried that they wouldn't find Carol in time. She had many cases over the years where people had gone missing but not all of them had good outcomes. Rose couldn't suffer another loss. God wouldn't do that to them would he?

~0~

Chapter 17- Scream if you want to

In The Killer's basement, a windowless, soundproof room,

Carol scared and trembling is tied to a chair. A person walks in front of her telling her, "Go ahead and scream if you want to. No one will hear you," the killer exclaimed, "I built this room with my own two hands. I'm a craftsman in all things. Handymen, have nothing on me."

"What will you do to me?" Carol asked.

"I'm not about to kill a kid, especially a good kid like you. Can't say I didn't think about it, but I'm not that kind of person. I guess I'll have to put my plan into place. When we leave the country, I'll tell them where you are and you can go free," the Killer stated.

"Please, I won't say anything. Please, just let me go home, now!" Carol begged.

The killer narrowed their eyes and stared hard at Carol. Then suddenly flashed a smile that scared Carol. If Carol had met them before she would have taken as innocent and sweet, but she knew better now this person was dangerous.

"Sorry dear. I'm not going to jail," the Killer admitted, "I wouldn't last two minutes there."

"I wasn't going to call the police when you took me," Carol explained.

The killers rolled their eyes and then turned their back to Carol, for a moment composing themselves. Carol grew afraid.

"Child, I know you were calling them. I saw you dial the first two numbers," the first Killer claimed in a chilling voice.

"I called a friend," Carol lied.

"You were calling a friend at 911? I don't think so. But don't you worry. You'll be quite comfortable here. I'm not heartless. See, I have a sense of humour. Now I've hooked up the cable so you have television. What would you like to watch? Here's the remote but I wouldn't watch any news programs if I were you. They are all depressing."

"Gee, thanks," Carol replied, sarcastically, but the killer smiled broadly, taking it as a compliment.

"I'll bring you some dinner in a little while," the Killer stated, "Don't take my kindness as an invitation to try any funny stuff. This lock is full proof. You can't leave, until I want you to!"

The first Killer then swept up the stairs and Carol heard the lock being turned. Carol reasoned that making yourself human to a kidnapper would keep you safe. She would make him like her so he would see her as a person, then he couldn't kill her. Surely Grandpa Terrence would get Great-Uncle Edward, to send out his cops to find her and when they did, this person would pay big time. This killer wouldn't harm her. That was a good plan. It worked for Rose, when Brad had taken her. She would be safe and free soon. Wouldn't she? Carol was scared, but she sucked back the tears that threatened. She had to keep herself alert and ready to escape if she got the chance.

Why did she fight with Rose? This was all that stupid Daria's fault. Oh no, Daria. Was Daria in danger too? Rose said Daria was trouble...Rose was correct, but Daria was her cousin. She had to go to her, when she needed help. She should have told Rose they were cousins, and then she would have understood why she had to talk to her. Why Carol couldn't ignore Daria's plea for help. Would Carol ever be able to tell Rose her side of the story?

Carol grew afraid that she would die, no matter what that person said. As long as she knew what and who the killer was, then the killer would have no choice but to silence her. Was it terrible that she wished her best friend Rose was here to save her? But Rose wasn't here and that was good, especially if Carol didn't get out of here. At least Rose would live out her life. No! She couldn't keep these morbid thoughts. She would get out of here! She would formulate a plan to get out of here. She was strong and she would survive. She was after all a Stewart. She could pick the lock. She was good at that.

~0~

The next day

Rose bound down the stairs looking tired and wan, Lily sitting at the kitchen table didn't look much better.

"Where can she be? She still doesn't answer her phone. Amelia and Carol are both missing. Where could they be?" asked Rose talking a mile a minute, "Did you know Daria, was actually related to Carol?

"Slow down Rose, we'll find her and no, I didn't know Carol was related to Daria," Lily answered.

"Carol was anxious to discover some information for you, mom. She also wanted to help Daria. I shouldn't have yelled at her over Daria. Who cares about Daria? Wait a minute; did the police talk to Daria?"

Rose jumped as the doorbell rang.

"That's them," Rose exclaimed, "Oh it's you."

Emmett was at the door and looked tired.

"Hello, Emmett," Lily commented, "Come in to the kitchen and I'll get you a coffee."

"Did you talk to Daria? Did she tell you when she last saw Carol? Or what she did to her," Rose demanded, before Emmett had even entered the kitchen and took his coat off.

"Rose, let the man sit down and have a coffee first."

"Sorry, I'm just so worried," Rose explained.

Lily put a coffee in front of a grateful Emmett who took a swig, swallowed and then explained, "Daria and a young man were found unconscious late last night. They are suspected overdoses and were rushed to the hospital. Do you know anything about Daria and her boyfriend? We haven't been able to identify him yet. He had no identification on him and no parents have reported him missing. Do you know anything about the drug scene at your school? Could Carol be into drugs?"

"What? Carol would never take drugs. And Daria has a boyfriend? I never saw her at school with a boyfriend, or drugs, and she didn't hang out with the people who raved," Rose stated.

"She had a boyfriend and his name is Paul Decker," Emmett answered.

"Paul Decker? He's a douchebag I think he's eighteen. He trolls for younger girls. Daria is stupid to fall for him. She's annoying, but she would never use drugs. Will she be okay?" Rose demanded.

"They don't know at this point. They are both in critical condition."

Rose motioned for Lily to pour her a cup of coffee too and Lily taking pity on her complied. Rose took a huge swallow of coffee and sighed.

"I can't believe this. I'm actually worried about Daria," Rose exclaimed, "What's wrong with me?"

"You have a good heart." Lily commented.

"No word about Amelia?" Emmett asked.

"No, there isn't any word Emmett, and it isn't like her. I don't care about the stupid rule that you have to wait forty eight hours. It didn't matter when you started looking for Carol. My cousin went missing and I want her and Carol both found," Lily griped.

"I'm going upstairs and making some calls to some kids at school someone has to have seen Carol and Aunt Amelia, too."

Rose then ran upstairs.

Lily knew the odds of either of them being okay, were slipping away with every minute that passed. Where could they be? Had they found something out and the killer had taken them? Were they together? Were they safe? Where were they?

"Are you okay Lily?" Emmett enquired.

"What a ridiculous question, Emmett. Carol has been over her so much, she feels like my second daughter, and Amelia is my best friend, as well as my cousin. So how do you think I am?" Lily asked sarcastically.

"I'm sorry Lily. I'm worried too. We will find them. I need to get back out there to find them."

"Have you had anything to eat since yesterday?" Lily asked.

"No, but I have to keep searching."

"What does Kendall do?" enquired Lily.

"She's interviewing some of our suspects for the murder and eliminating some of them." Emmett replied.

"You can't search on an empty stomach. Your brain won't function well that way. We haven't had breakfast I'll make some." Lily invited then added, "We need some food too. I'll call Rose back down when the food is ready."

They heard the front door open and slam shut, then Katha walked into the kitchen laden with baskets, containers and bags.

"Hello, I brought muffins, pancakes and waffles," Katha stated, "It's still warm. Dig in."

"I smell food," Rose cried running downstairs.

"Thank-you, Grandma Katha. You think of everything," Lily exclaimed.

"When I'm worried I cook. Why where is our Amelia? I thought she'd be here too. Is she out looking for Carol?" Katha asked, her eyes searching the room for Amelia.

"She's missing Grandma Katha. She didn't come home yesterday," Lily blurted.

"Amelia's missing too? What? You should have called me! Why didn't you call me? Where have you looked for her?" Katha demanded, panicking.

"Everywhere. We've looked everywhere for both of them," Rose cried sounding defeated. "I haven't slept a wink. They have to be okay. I couldn't live with myself if something happened to Carol, after I was so mean to her. And now Aunt Amelia appears to be missing. Do you think the same thing happened to both of them?"

"I hope nothing bad happened to either of them," Katha cried wearily sinking into a kitchen chair.

"What if I never get the chance to say I'm sorry?" Rose whined.

Rose then started to cry. Lily put an arm around Rose and Rose dried her eyes.

"Oh for Pete's sake, pull yourself together Rose and think who could have taken our girls. We need to be strong and fearless. That's what got us through the Second World War. Who do they both know?"

"You will get the chance to tell her, honey. I asked Doctor Thomas, but he hasn't seen Amelia either," Lily answered.

"Why did you ask Doctor Thomas?" asked Rose and Katha at the same time.

"Amelia's been dating him," Lily admitted.

"But he's married to my principal," Rose protested.

"She's dating a married man? That's not like the girl I raised but it's a lead," Katha cried upset.

"How?" Lily asked.

"A married man has much to cover, maybe he took Amelia."

"We'll look into it," Lily answered, but didn't mean it. She thought Grandma Katha was being ridiculous. Emmett looked embarrassed, but leaned over to listen more intently like he needed to hear all this.

"She said he'll get a divorce," Lily continued, trying to mollify Grandma Katha.

"Divorced men can be nothing but trouble," Katha commented, "Maybe Amelia is with another friend."

"I thought I knew all her friends and I've called them."

"You should have called me, but we will find them, Lily. Amelia is a Kelly and Carol is an honorary Kelly, because she has such grit. They are both intelligent. If God forbid they have been taken. I have no doubt they will hold on until we find them. Besides we have Emmett looking for them and Emmett is a bulldog. He'll find them."

"Thank-you Katha I am trying," Emmett commented.

"Oh, sorry, Emmett I didn't notice you there," Katha admitted.

"Just fueling up before I go back up again."

"Then please eat some of this food," Katha invited.

Katha then started dishing out the food into plates and serving them to Rose, Lily and Emmett.

"Where's Terrence?" asked Lily.

"Terrence is with his children. They are all out looking for Carol."

"Carol's parents must be freaking out," Rose bellowed.

"Gerald Banks loves that girl, but the man is neglectful. He is lives in the moment. That's why he left Carol's mother for that young woman," Katha commented.

"Grandma Katha you shouldn't talk that way," Rose cried through waffles.

"This will bring them together," Lily exclaimed.

"They're back together, at least they are dating. that's what Carol told me," Rose admitted, but neither, Katha or Lily heard her.

"Would you have taken Horace back after he cheated on you with Amber?" asked Katha.

"I loved Horace. I think I would have forgiven him, but I'll never have the chance to know," Lily stated.

"Emmett will find the girls and everyone will be fine. You'll see," Katha continued.

Rose stood up and thought about leaving the house and going to look for Carol herself, but she didn't have the gun she'd used to shoot at Brad Owens, the police still had it. Somehow, she thought if someone had taken Carol, then she'd need a weapon. But where could she find one. If not a gun then what weapon could be used? A bat? A hockey stick? Should she attempt to find them? Of course she should! Carol did the same for her when she went missing. Rose wouldn't let Carol down she'd find her and save her.

~0~

Chapter 18 -
While You Were
Sleeping

Carol awoke and looking over surprised to see Amelia

lying beside her in the basement of the killer's. Carol shook Amelia trying to awaken her.

"Amelia? Amelia? Wake-up! You have to wake-up now!" Carol cried shaking Amelia.

"What? I'm up. I'm up," Amelia answered, then looking around she demanded, "Where am I? Why are we here Carol?"

"She brought you in. He dumped me here yesterday," Carol answered.

"Who dumped us here?" asked Amelia.

"You'll see. Here comes one of them," Carol cried, cryptically. "Probably with a drugged breakfast. He tricked me last night by drugged me with the soup he gave me."

"We need to get out of here," Amelia exclaimed.

"We will we have to wait until they leave, then we can figure out how to get out of here," Carol explained. "I've got a few ideas."

"Why did you bring her here?" asked the voice, that Carol and Amelia could hear through the vent.

"For the same reason you brought the other one. We have to protect ourselves," the other voice cried.

Carol hadn't seen his face, but she knew her kidnapper was a man.

"What can we do?" asked the first voice.

"I thought about killing her and the other one, but I can't kill a child," exclaimed the voice of the person, who took Carol.

"I have no such compunction," the first voice said chillingly.

"Our safety and freedom comes first. I know that! I have a plan which doesn't involve another murder or murders." the voice of the kidnapper that took Carol said, and then continued, "You should have read the local paper online. I did."

"Why?" asks the other voice.

"It seems we've bungled again, my dearest. Those two people that we kidnapped two days ago are related to the police chief." the voice that took Carol replied then continued, "This is serious business. We appear to be in grave danger of being caught and going to jail."

"No. That can't be! How is that possible? It's all Vincent's fault. That worm should have died a thousand horrible deaths. What he did to me..."

"Don't think of it. Don't think of that evil cretin. I'm glad that I cut out his heart after he made advances to you."

"And you gave the heart to me. I have the heart in the glass heart-shaped box you gave me."

"As a reminder of who actually holds your heart and has your best interests at heart as well."

"Dear, you always look out for me and help me."

"That is why I took the child. But if she is the grand-niece of the Chief of police, that complicates events. And now the other one, Amelia, her Great-Aunt is married to the police chief's father."

"Families are so incredibly complicated."

"Definitely complications we don't need but you're missing the point. They will be searching that much harder for the pair of them. We must advance our plan and move to somewhere with no extradition."

"I don't want to move. I'm happy here now."

"Are you my dear? Will you be happy to go to jail, and then spend the rest of your life on death row, waiting for your execution?"

"There's no death row in Canada."

"Okay then, you'll die in a police shootout, or linger in a jail cell, the rest of your life just staring at prison walls."

"Must you be so sarcastic?"

"If we stay here we will die or go to jail!" the man insisted.

"I don't want to die or go to jail."

"And you won't, and neither will I. We will make plans to go to Argentina. They have no extradition. But in the mean time we will act normally, feed the prisoners and get ready for our new life. Now since we have two prisoners, how will we open the door without them rushing us and escaping?"

"I purchased this earlier. If those two try to escape again, this will stop them."

Carol and Amelia heard crackling sounds like electricity.

"That's why you're my partner, dear. You do help fill the gaps."

"This stun gun should do the trick. That stupid, Amelia, hurt me yesterday. She pushed me over and that child ran by," the other voice complained loudly.

"And they've learned their lesson. I'm sure they must be hungry by now."

"My idea to not feed them and then drug their drinks worked beautifully."

"They will be weaker now and easier to manage," the voice responded.

"I'll give them easier to manage," Amelia muttered, angrily.

Amelia then flexed her fists as if to hit them.

"Go along with them, please Amelia. They have a stun gun now, and I'm hungry. Besides I have another plan to get us out of here."

"They'll drug the food again, we can't eat it. What's your plan, pass out after eating?"

"My father is an electrician and I've gone around with him and watched him fix objects since I was little. I think I can open that door, when they are not here. We have to wait them out."

"You sure you won't electrocute yourself?" asked Amelia, worried.

"I'm sure. It will work you'll see and we will be free," Carol says confidently.

"So, cooperate until then?"

"Yes."

"Okay, but I don't want to," Amelia cried.

"As long as you follow my lead will get out of here. Understand?"

"I said I'd do it."

"Smile, now then, they're coming," cried Carol.

~0~

Chapter 19 - Rudeness Is in the Eye of the Beholder

At her office, Lily shifted papers on her desk. She wanted

to take the day off, but they were cases she needed to prepare, plus she had promised Rose she take her to her office for take your daughter to work day. She had Rose copied some papers, anything to keep Rose's mind busy. Lily's attention focused on the phone, hoping it would ring with word of Amelia and Carol. She was sure that's where Rose's thoughts were too. Her intercom rang and she answered.

"Lily, Detective Kendall Evans, and Detective Emmett Rogers are here. Shall I send them in?" Colleen declared.

"Go ahead, Colleen. Send them in," Lily responded.

Kendall waltzed in her head held high in a military stance. Emmett followed.

"Sorry, Lily, there's no sign of them," Emmett announced.

"There's no sign of them? You're absolutely sure, Emmett? Of course you're sure. I just want them back." exclaimed Lily.

"We all do Lily," Emmett answered.

"It has to be one of the suspects for the murder. Amelia and Carol must have found something out, but who could it be?" Lily asked.

"The suspects are endless, and if only Daria would have talked. I think she must have known something she didn't share," Kendall announced.

"You're instincts are good Kendall. I'm starting to wonder if someone gave Daria and her boyfriend, a drug overdose to warn them against talking."

"If that's the case, you can add one more murder to the killers' plate," Lily replied.

"It's unfortunate that Paul Decker died," answered Kendall.

"You make it sound like him dying is no big deal. Even though I didn't like him I didn't want him to die," Rose stated walking into the office.

"A child wanders around in your office?" Kendall snarled.

"I'm not a child, I'm fifteen years old practically an adult. Besides this is take your daughter to work day. Why aren't you doing your job and go out looking for Carol and my Aunt Amelia?" Rose snarled back.

"Rose, that was uncalled for. I know you're worried about them I am too, but there is no reason to be rude to someone who will help us find them," Lily scolded.

"She was rude first!" Rose cried, then with a look from her mother she stated maturely, "I apologise. I know we both try to do our part to find my best friend Carol and my Aunt Amelia."

"Your apology is accepted," Kendall responded, sounding sincere.

Rose turned her head to her only her mother and rolled her eyes. Kendall walked away from Emmett as he took a call, making sure he didn't see the look of disdain she gave Rose. Lily thought that was a wonderful idea and it would get Rose away from Kendall, before Lily herself blew her cork at her treatment of Rose. Why wasn't Emmett defending Rose? Should she expect him to? After all they were just dating, but somehow she really thought he'd defend Rose. Rose was looking expectantly at Lily. Had she missed something?

"Can I go get some lunch Mom?" Rose repeated, wanting to get away from Kendall before she said anything else.

"I'll meet you down in the cafeteria, in a half an hour. Today is Taco Tuesday. Please get me a taco too, would you?"

"Sure, mom."

Rose then accepted cash from her mom.

"See you later Emmett. Nice meeting you Kendall," Rose exclaimed to irritate Kendall. Rose then walked away.

"Don't ever speak to my daughter like that again Kendall."

"Okay, mama bear. I guess she's a nice kid," Kendall stated insincerely.

"She is," cried Emmett with feeling, smiling "Let's move on any leads on suspects?" Lily asked.

"We checked out several women, who had been involved with the deceased. They seem to all have alibis," Emmett replied.

"Teresa Brown echoed Emmett's statement," Kendall explained.

"Of course she did. Did you doubt Emmett?"

"No I didn't, but it's procedure to check out everyone's alibi." Kendall explained, then turning to Emmett she said, "No, offence, Emmett"

"None taken," Emmett replied.

"Moving on, we interviewed Teresa Brown's sister-in-law, one Denise Brown, who was spotted outside the school but she was in her car the entire time. Then we interviewed Suzanne Rogers...," Kendall stated, slightly hesitating looking over at Emmett for his reaction.

"You interviewed my sister and didn't tell me?" Emmett asked, angrily.

"Her alibi checked out," Kendall replied nonchalant.

"Of course her alibi did. She was in the hospital. I could have told you that!" Emmett replied obviously irritated.

"Suzy's okay?" asked Lily.

"She's bored. So I bought her a bunch of books on child rearing and got her HBO Canada on my television package," Emmett explained to Lily.

"Good lord, anyone can get pregnant and have a baby it's not rocket science, Can we get back to business?" Kendall demanded cattily.

Emmett frowned and Lily hid a smile.

"That is why you're here Kendall," Lily retorted.

"I don't know why we have to share so much with you, but Emmett insisted."

"Kendall!" Emmett admonished.

"Fine, we also interviewed one, Frieda Abrams. She's the acting librarian at the school. She admitted she was at the school, during the time of the murder and was seen by Denise Brown. In fact they alibi each other. But we also have a report of another man at the school. Funny no one seems to know who he is. We've only a description of a man about five ten, two hundred pounds with dark slicked back hair, and thinning hair in his front," Kendall stated.

"Who does that leave us then?" asked Lily.

"There was some gossip that Dayita Patel, a nurse that works at the local hospital had been involved with Vincent Scholar," Emmett retorted "Also that her brother, Doctor Raj Patel was not happy about it. I believe that came from a conversation you heard, Lily. So we looked into Vincent's background some more and found out that Dayita was married to Mr. Scholar up to a year ago. They were married for three years. Neighbours said he yelled at her a lot about her wearing her..."

"For wearing her head dress," Kendall interrupted taking over.

"The word for it is the Hijab. It's Arabic and it means to veil," Emmett corrected.

"I'll take your word for it," Kendall replied rudely.

"Use the correct term Kendall it's disrespectful. Anyway so the neighbours said they argued all the time. She loved him, but he kicked her out. She's been over to his place, many times since the divorce with a lot of fighting going on."

"Good grief. I'll call it whatever I want. Why are we sharing so much with her?" Kendall stated staring hard at Emmett.

Lily wanted to scream instead she took a deep breath and commented, "You need some sensitivity training Kendall and some education about different cultures, and religions. Perhaps you could look into that."

"And you need to not comment on work matters that aren't any of your concern," Kendall sniped.

"I'm the Crown attorney you need to keep me informed."

"Keep you informed maybe, but not in on the investigation."

"I've sent a patrol car for Doctor Patel and Dayita," Emmett stated, ignoring the friction between the two women. Then he asked, "How would you like to sit in on the questioning Lily?"

"What? She's not a cop," complained Kendall.

"No, as she told you she's the Crown attorney and you should have some sympathy for her cousin has been kidnapped," Emmett retorted.

"All the more reason for her not to question the suspects; she's too close to the investigation," complained Kendall loudly.

Emmett reached out and touched Kendall's arm as if to caution her then said, "Give it a break Kendall. She's sitting in on the questioning."

"I'm going to watch you two in action until a deal is needed, and then you can step in to save the kidnap victims. Is that a deal Kendall?" Lily asked trying to smooth the dissension over.

"I suppose so," Kendall reluctantly agreed, "But it isn't usually done this way."

"Oh, I was supposed to meet Rose downstairs. How could I have forgotten?" asked Lily.

"That's okay, we all need lunch anyway. Let the suspects stew for an hour, we'll go question them. They'll tell us more that way," Emmett explained.

"I'm ready now," Kendall complained.

"Come on Kendall, it could be a long night. We need fuel to grill the suspects. Besides I'm fond of tacos and the company."

Emmett then smiled at Lily, while Kendall frowned. Emmett took Lily's arm and they walked to the cafeteria. Kendall trailed behind them glaring.

~0~

Chapter 20-
Viable Suspects

An hour later Lily, Emmett, and Kendall, went back to the

station to grill the Patel's. Lily looked through the two way glass as Dayita Patel Scholar sat at the interview table, submissively waiting for Kendall and Emmett to tell her why she was there. Only a stray hair that had slipped out revealed her long dark hair, shielded under a blue silk Hijab. Dressed modestly, her arms concealed with a long sleeved flowing shirt, and long black skirt enclosing her legs from view, on her feet black oxford shoes. Her hazel eyes stared at them with fear as she fidgeted her fingers making a noise on the table.

"We know you knew Alexander Scholar. In fact very well, so why didn't you come forward?" Kendall asked leaning forward.

"He was a bad man, in some ways, but I didn't kill him," Dayita stated.

"He was your husband. He shouldn't have cheated on you," Kendall sympathized.

"I divorced him, what did I care?"

"It ate at you, that he was unfaithful. He dated numerous women and told them they were his love, giving rings. You hated that he hurt those women like he hurt you. Didn't you?" Kendall taunted.

"I didn't like his behaviour, but that was none of my concern. I had no say over his doings, even when we were married," Dayita insisted.

Kendall got up and walked around the table.

"He threatened to tell your parents, that you had been married to him?" Kendall chided standing beside Dayita.

"If he did it would do him no good. My parents would forgive me since I dismissed him with divorce. Such a marriage would not be recognized in my culture and he would not exist."

"You do not tell the truth Dayita. Isn't it true that your parents would beat you? Even disown you, if they found out about Alexander Scholar being your ex-husband? That your religion forbids your marriage to someone who is not Muslim?" Kendall rebuked.

"How do you know this? It is not my religion, but my parents who insist on this. Please don't tell my parents," Dayita begged then turned to Emmett, "Please you will keep her from telling my parents? They could kill me for making such a mistake. they search even now for a husband of our faith."

"Did you kill Alexander Scholar, Dayita Scholar? Or did your parents?" Emmett asked softly.

"No, they did not kill him. They didn't know about him. I did not kill him either, for my sins. I love him still. I am a foolish woman. No? He cheated on me. He made me take pills, so I have no children and then he divorced me," Dayita admitted, tearfully.

"You didn't sue for divorce?" Kendall asked surprised going back to sit down.

"No, why would I? I loved him. I love him still. My brother Raj filed for divorce on my behalf, the same day as Alexander did. Alexander had already filed though. He laughed when I told him Raj had filed and not me," Dayita cried. "It was one of those horrible women that took him away. I hate Paula!"

"Paula? Who is this Paula?" asked Kendall.

"Doctor Yates, she can't hold her own man, so she wants mine. That woman is a man-eater."

"You're trying to throw suspicion from yourself. He cheated on you. You hated him. Didn't you?"

"No, I loved Vincent."

"But isn't it true, that he dated your co-worker, Mary?"

"Mary thought he loved her, but I knew better. He would have grown tired of her and then he would be mine again. Let me tell you he could be such a sweet, charming man. A true gentleman," Dayita stated looking into space, smiling at the memory.

Kendall looked stunned for a moment then rearranged her face to look disgusted.

"A gentleman? You actually thought of him as a gentleman? He dated hundreds of women and that made you angry. You killed him, you and your brother!" Kendall shouted.

"I didn't, I wouldn't. Neither would Raj. If he killed him Raj would have brought attention to my relationship with Alexander, Vincent. The last thing he'd ever want. You wrong us." Dayita protested.

Emmett shook his head at Kendall trying to tell her that the technique wasn't working. Kendall frowned at him, but then allowed Emmett to take the lead.

"Where did you meet him?" enquired Emmett softly, trying to get Dayita to trust him.

"I met him when I filled in on a shift in the emergency room, at the hospital. Raj was away at this medical conference in London, Ontario for a week. Alexander came into the emergency room, because he had cut his hand and needed stitches."

"And you got to know him?"

"I went to movies with him. With me, he opened up and appeared charming, sweet, and open. He was what's the word article...what is the word that means knows knowledge?"

"Articulate, the word is articulate." Kendall interrupted.

"Thank-you, yes...he was articulate and knew so much about so many different matters. He was a true renaissance man. That's what most would call him," Dayita gushed.

"A renaissance man, like King Henry the eighth," Kendall stated barely audible.

"How dare you insult him? You do him an injustice. He couldn't help that women chased him. He loved me. I know he did. He may have strayed, but he would have come back to me."

Kendall shook her head sadly.

"You are wrong. He loved me, I know he did. Why else would he have married me, the week he met me?" Dayita cried.

"Hmm," Kendall replied, and then bit her tongue to keep from talking.

"Where were you on the morning Alexander was killed?" Emmett asked softly.

"I was at the hospital. I put in a long overnight shift. A twelve hour shift from seven p.m. to seven a.m., but one of the nurses called in sick. I worked until eight a.m. you can check," Dayita explained.

"Oh we will, and your brother did you send him to kill your ex-husband?" Kendall asked.

"No, I didn't." Dayita protested angrily, "I would never harm my Alexander."

Dayita stood up as if to leave.

"Where do you think you're going?"

"Nowhere."

"Now you might not have harmed Alexander, but your brother would. Wouldn't he, Dayita?" Kendall needled.

"No, he would not. I told you he would not!" Dayita screamed.

"Then where could your brother be found the morning that your husband was killed? Why was he late for his surgical rotation?" Kendall demanded.

"He wasn't late. You lie," protested Dayita.

"Nice try, Dayita, but we've talked to a number of people whom you work with, including Mary."

"You didn't tell Mary, that Alexander was my husband. Did you?" Dayita worried.

"No, but we could," Kendall stated. "That is if you don't tell us the truth."

"I did tell you the truth. Please, I didn't kill Alexander and neither did my brother," Dayita asked exasperated then she begged, "Please don't tell Mary. We are friends, but if she knew about Alexander, it would not be so."

"I don't believe you Dayita. I think you attempt to cover for yourself and your brother."

Dayita shook her head emphatically.

"Now Kendall, maybe she's telling the truth. At least as she knows it," Emmett replied, playing good cop.

"I am. I know nothing of Alexander's murder," Dayita insisted, "You should be speaking to Doctor Yates."

"But you did know of your brother's deceit. Didn't you?" Emmett prodded.

"Deceit? What deceit do you speak of? My brother loves me."

"He loves you, you say? Does he love you enough to kill the man who beat you, and then dumped you?" Kendall asked.

"I don't know what you speak of," Dayita denied.

"You do. You had a broken arm, a broken shoulder, two black eyes, and numerous broken ribs. Why didn't you call the police and report him?" Kendall demanded, "Why didn't your colleagues?"

"A husband has the right to discipline his wife. I told my colleagues, I fell down stairs, twice."

"They violated the law. They have to report spousal abuse," Kendall cried.

"Did your brother know he harmed you?" asked Emmett.

"He would do nothing. After all it is a husband's right."

"I think your wrong, Dayita. It is not part of your religion, or a part of marriage. I have a younger sister and if someone married her and beat her as Alexander beat you, I would want him to pay!" Emmett retorted.

"He didn't...he wouldn't," Dayita stated sounding less convinced.

"He may have you know. He was late to work did you know that?" Emmett asked.

"No he wouldn't. Would he?"

Dayita began sobbing but dried her eyes after a few minutes look thoughtful and asked, "What about that married couple that was with Alexander?"

"What married couple?" Emmett asked.

"I have said too much. I will say no more about Alexander's philandering," Dayita retorted.

"We will be back, Dayita." Kendall replied angrily, "And the next round we might not be as nice."

Kendall turned to Emmett and stage whispered, "She doesn't know anything."

Emmett pointed to the door and said, "Interview paused at two fifteen p.m. I'll get you a drink and we'll continue in a few minutes Ms. Patel."

Kendall and Emmett then exited the room. Once the door was closed they began to discuss Dayita's testimony.

"I'm inclined to believe she doesn't know anything about the murder, but it doesn't mean the brother didn't kill Alexander." Emmett implied, "And by the way, I think your interviewing technique needs work. You riled her up too much (playing bad cop) for her to share anything she does know."

"You wanted me to play bad cop. You think Raj Patel killed Alexander, if so then he kidnapped Rose and Amelia. I think that married couple comment, was a red herring. Something she pulled out to throw suspicions from her brother."

"That's possible. I suppose I could drop it for now. Let's go back in and grill our suspect, Doctor Raj Patel in the next room," Emmett declared.

"Do you seriously think I didn't get anywhere with Dayita?" Kendall asked, dejected.

"Did you notice when she happily talked about Alexander, we got a little more out of her?" Emmett asked.

"I guess," Kendall stated.

"Then remember that as we go to interview Doctor Raj Patel."

"I will remember boss!" Kendall replied.

"Don't call me boss. I'm technically your boss, but I prefer being referred to as your colleague.

"Okay, colleague."

"Earth to you two, can I continue to watch?" Lily interrupted, after speaking to them for a few minutes without either of them hearing.

"Sure, Lily," Emmett agreed.

"Don't interrupt," Kendall cautioned.

"See you in a bit, Lil," Emmett exclaimed.

Kendall and Emmett went over towards the other interview door, stopping outside the door.

"Can I continue playing bad cop? I'm enjoying this role."

"It looks good on you. It suits you," Emmett replied laughing, "But lead our witness to where we want him to go, not into denial."

Kendall then playfully poked him in the side. Lily watched this horse play but didn't like this. They seemed to close, almost like they were attracted to one another.

"Ouch, that hurt," Emmett complained.

"What's matter, are you an old man?" Kendall taunted.

"Save the rhetoric for the interrogation. Something tells me we'll need it with Doctor Raj Patel."

"You think he's a tough nut to crack? I'll break him. You wait and see!" Kendall stated, confidently.

"Want to make a wager?"

Shouts come from all over the station room, "Hey we want in on that one."

"Sorry guys, private bet," Emmett commented.

"Sure five bucks. If I get him to cry you owe me five bucks, if he doesn't you get five bucks from me."

"No deal. If you get him to admit he killed Alexander five bucks, if not you owe me five bucks. I'll throw in an extra fifty if it leads us to where Rose and Amelia are stashed," Emmett declared.

"You're on, but I want Rose and Amelia found as much as you do partner."

"They have to be okay. Lily can't lose anyone else," Emmett replied his voice cracking.

"They will be. We will find them. Raj Patel won't know what hit him. He'll tell us," Kendall declared confident.

Lily felt better about their partnership after this comment. Emmett cared, she knew he did. Emmett turned to Lily and smiled a smile that told her that he was trying.

"What if he isn't the one responsible?" Lily asked.

"Then we will figure it out but he looks pretty good to me for this, doesn't he, Emmett," Kendall reassured, "We'll get him to cop to a plea and then tell us where he stashed Amelia and Rose."

Emmett nodded his head. Lily then watched as Kendall and Emmett walked into the interview room. Doctor Raj Patel did not look worried. He sat calmly starring at the ceiling. His long legs, from his six feet tall frame, tucked below the table did not look uncomfortable. His thick curly black hair, clipped tight to his head, not a hair out of place. An expensive Brooks Brothers, navy blue suit on his thin, fit frame made him look like a businessman. His eyes, their pupils black and slightly enlarged, are the only indication of his discomfort. As the door opened he searched for the lead detective, his eyes centering themselves on Emmett.

"Oh good, you will fix this mistake Lieutenant Rogers," Doctor Patel oozed confidently.

"What mistake Doctor Patel? We brought you here for our inquiries," Kendall exclaimed.

"Oh and you are?" Doctor Patel asked, dismissively.

"I am Sergeant Detective Kendall Evans. I am Emmett's partner and the reason you were brought in here for our enquiries." Kendall replied, coolly, "You've been read your rights?"

"Yes, but I won't need them. Why have you brought me here? Ask me your questions. Do your worst with your questions. I hide nothing," Doctor Patel replied his Indian accent, becoming more prominent.

"I understand that Alexander Scholar was your brother-in-law?" Emmett prodded.

"He was never truly my brother in-law. They married in a civil ceremony. My religion does not recognize such a marriage."

"Then how did he meet your sister?" asked Kendall.

"He met my sister when I was away at a medical conference in London, Ontario. We were conferencing on new surgical techniques. Do you know they have a C.S.T.A.R there? To work with C.S.T.A.R., this amazing piece of equipment; was a dream come true," Doctor Patel declared, going off topic.

"An interesting subject I'm sure, but you are slightly off topic, Doctor Patel. We have more questions pertaining to Alexander Scholar and his death," Kendall stated reining him in.

"Please explain it to me, Doctor Patel. I'd love to hear about it," Emmett interjected, getting a glare from Kendall.

"C.S.T.A.R. stands for Canadian Surgical Technologies and Advanced Robotics. They do all these interesting surgeries with robotic equipment. They train and educate surgeons in minimally invasive surgeries reducing surgical times and scarring. It's the wave of the future now. I want to work in London, Ontario with their team some day," Doctor Patel waxed on the subject.

"So your sister met Alexander Scholar, when you went to this conference?" Emmett asked.

"This would never have happened if she had gone with me as she was supposed to; but she had shifts at the hospital and needed to fill her obligations," Doctor Patel complained.

"So where did she meet him?" Kendall interjected.

"She met him in the emergency room. She filled in there because they were shorthanded. The player which is Alexander Scholar? He comes in with a cut hand. He needed many stitches. He had long conversation with my sister Dayita. He then convinced her to date him, but she brought her friend Angela for chaperone."

"Angela? Who is this Angela?" Kendall demanded.

"Angela Nancy Trippeon. She was Dayita's good friend."

"Where can we find this Angela Trippeon?" Emmett demanded.

"You can't she's dead. She died the week that Dayita met Alexander Scholar."

"How?"

"A hit and run right outside the restaurant, on their third evening together," Doctor Patel exclaimed. "Scholar took advantage of the situation. With no chaperone and Dayita so upset, he convinced her to run off and marry him two days later to save her reputation."

Doctor Patel then stood up and closed his fists as if he wanted to hit Alexander Scholar. Then realizing what he had done, he sat back down.

"It sounds like you hated him," Kendall prodded.

"I hated him, but I would never kill him and make him a martyr in Dayita's eyes."

"A martyr? I don't understand."

"She has created an even greater love affair in her mind, simply because someone has taken him from her," Doctor Patel sighed.

"Did they ever find out who killed Dayita's friend, Angela?" asked Emmett.

"No, they didn't. You police are an incompetent lot. You go about wrongly accusing people and never finding out who the real killers are."

"That's rich coming from the likes of you. You killed Alexander Scholar, didn't you?" Kendall stated trying to get the interview back to Alexander's demise.

"No, I swear on all the prophets. I did not kill such a man, though he sadly deserved it. I could not break Dayita's heart any more than he already had."

"Do you have any idea who could have killed your former brother-in-law, Alexander Scholar?" Emmett enquired.

"It wasn't me and do not call him a brother-in law. My sister severed her tie to him," Doctor Patel protested.

"But you were late that morning. You don't have an alibi do you?" Kendall taunted.

"I admit it I was there at the school. I wanted to tell him to stay away from Dayita. I'd seen him with his other women." Raj admitted. "I was hoping one of them would have taken him out of Dayita's life."

"You expect me to believe that? And was it only the other women? Or did he sniff around your sister again?" Kendall demanded.

Doctor Patel closed his eyes calming himself then explained, "He owed me money, and he came around the hospital, but after his death I found out he dated Mary, Dayita's co-worker. Scholar had begun to see her, to see Dayita again. She hadn't given in to him and gone back to a wedded life with him, but she probably would have. My silly sister loved him. She still loves him. If my father found out he would have ordered me to kill her. And yet, Scholar strutted around like a peacock, with many women following him. I should have severed his man part. Then he would have been useless to all those women," Raj clenched and unclenched his fists and then put them together in a prayer like pose.

"So you were angry. You wanted this man far away from your naive little sister. Didn't you?" Emmett prodded.

"I did, but I didn't kill him. How many times do I have to tell you that?"

"Then what were you doing at the school that morning, if you didn't kill Alexander Scholar?" Kendall demanded.

"I told you I went to see him. I called him the night before and we arranged to meet at six forty-five a.m., but I arrived early."

"I see, you arrived early and killed him. What caused you to kill him? An argument that got out of hand, so you decided to make it look like what a ritual killing?" Kendall exclaimed.

"No, No, No! A thousand times, no! I didn't kill him. He owed me money and he wouldn't stay away from my sister, I admit that. But I would have forgiven his debt and give him more money to get out of town."

"But he wouldn't take the deal so you killed him, cutting out the heart of the problem," Kendall persisted.

"Should I be contacting a lawyer? You seem determined Lieutenant Evans to make me your suspect and the culprit," Raj replied calmly.

"No, not at all Doctor Patel, it appears to have been a little out of line. She's a little green and obviously wants to find the culprit of this hideous crime. Please feel free to ask for a lawyer at any time," Emmett calmed the waters.

"I understand the need to find who did this thing. I admit I hated the man, but I swear on all the prophets I did not take his life."

"Would you like lawyer Doctor Patel?" Kendall enquired.

"No, I don't need one because as I've said many times to you. I did not kill Alexander Scholar!"

"So what happened after you got to the school, Doctor Patel?" Emmett asked.

"I sat in my car awhile, waiting, because I was early. It was six a.m. when I got there. Odd though, the parking lot was full. So many people were sitting in their cars. I saw Denise Brown sitting in her car and I was worried she had taken ill. I went over to her and spoke to her for about a half an hour before going back to my car and waiting."

"And was she ill?"

"Denise had found out the evening before that she had extremely advanced cancer. I didn't think she should be driving anymore and I told her so. She's died, since you know. She died a couple of weeks ago."

"And then what happened?" Emmett demanded to know.

"I went into the school. I saw two students, a boy and a young girl, necking in the hallway. I think one of them was Denise's daughter, Daria. Poor child should have had someone looking after her welfare with her mother so ill. I saw Paula Yates, a doctor from the hospital. I don't know why she was there. Paula cried and leaned up against a wall near the gym. I then walked down to his classroom. The light was dim and the light switch didn't work. I thought he wasn't there yet but then I found him dead. His heart was gone there was no way to save him so..."

"And you didn't call the police? What if the murderer had struck again in the school?" Kendall asked, incredulously.

"I know I should have called but all I could think was that you would think I had killed him. I was worried that the police would say I had the skills, the ability to take out his heart. That I had the...what is the word...oh yes, motive to kill my former brother-in-law," Raj exclaimed.

"You do have motive. Your sister, you look good for this crime to me," Kendall claimed.

Raj Patel blanched.

"Please, I would like to help you find the real killer. I did not kill him. What can tell you?"

"Did anyone see you talking to Denise Brown?" asked Emmett.

"Didn't you see me Detective? I saw you kissing that teacher, Denise's sister, Teresa. Denise pointed it out to me," Raj protested

"You were kissing Teresa Brown?" Kendall whispered puzzled.

"Didn't you read the report? I was cleared. Teresa cleared me. She admitted she kissed me," Emmett commented, embarrassed.

"Oh, I see you hoped to embarrass my colleague and distract from your own motives." Kendall replied recovering, "No one alive saw you, did they? How convenient. My colleague didn't, and he was there."

"That's because he kissed Teresa Brown. That woman goes round," Raj commented, "This is right expression correct? She kissed my former brother-in-law two days before that. I see her in the restaurant at the Pope Hotel kissing Alexander."

"If Teresa didn't have an alibi, than that would be interesting information. Unfortunately Ms. Brown has already informed us, that she dated Alexander." Kendall exclaimed, "So I ask you again do you have an alibi Doctor Patel?"

"I guess not, but I did get to the hospital by seven a.m. You know that Detective Rogers. I performed some of the operation on Rose Brooksfield, with Doctor Thomas assisting. Raj seemed to ponder for a moment then continued, "Wait a minute, I saw Doctor Thomas three days before that talking to Scholar and they were yelling. They have the medical knowledge. He did this deed! He, or that Doctor Yates!"

"And where was this where you saw Doctor Thomas?" Emmett demanded, his eyes narrowing.

"The same hotel, it's the Hotel Pope. I often lunch there in their restaurant," Raj explained. "And two days before that, I saw her lunching with him."

"Who lunched with whom?" Emmett asked, confused.

"Janet Carol Thomas, the principal of the high school. She's Doctor Thomas' wife. I saw her sitting at the table with him and she touched his hand, caressing him. It was the manner, the way he touched her back, I would swear they knew each other intimately," Raj answered.

"That is interesting, I'm still thinking you were at the school and you were at my crime scene. So that makes you guilty," Kendall shouted.

"But I told you I didn't do it." Raj protested.

"You told me you didn't report a crime. I can hold you on that charge alone, Doctor Patel."

"But I didn't do it. Please Detective Rogers, tell her I didn't do it," pleaded Raj. "He was dead. I swear to you on my life, he was dead!"

"I'm going to check this out if we can find someone to verify your story, but Doctor Patel you were at my crime scene. You claim you found your former brother-in-law and didn't get aid. Now that makes you look good for this crime. I have two missing women and they may be connected with this murder...,"Emmett answered.

Raj's face paled and he looked shocked.

"Missing women? Who is missing? I have nothing to do with that. Do not besmirch my good name. I hurt no one. I am a healer. As to women, they are to be revered, protected. I would do nothing to harm women," pleaded Raj.

"Forgive me, if I don't believe you Doctor Patel, but as my partner said we have two missing women and you know them. If I found you have been holding back I will make them going even harder on you," threatened Kendall.

"Tell me who is missing?" begged Doctor Raj Patel.

"As if you didn't know that Amelia Kelly and Carol Banks are missing," Kendall stated.

"I didn't. I wouldn't. I know Amelia and she is a sweet lady, but not this Carol Banks."

"Try another one buddy. This girl isn't buying it."

"What more can I say to convince you?" appealed Raj.

"I think we'll leave you cooling your heels in one of our cells for a little while."

"I want a lawyer now," Raj stated, stopping cooperating.

"Interview terminated at four fifteen p.m.," Emmett announced.

"Here's the phone," Kendall said.

Kendall then placed a phone in front of him and connected it.

"Faisal? I need a lawyer will you come to the Happy Valley police station? Yes I have spoken to them. Oh, thank-you, Faisal. Yes, Faisal, I will wait for you and will say nothing else," Raj spoke into the phone.

"I will wait for my lawyer. He says to say no more, so I shall not," Raj stated turning to Emmett, and not to Kendall.

"Alan will escort you to a cell to await your lawyer, Doctor Patel."

Emmett then summoned Alan who took Doctor Raj Patel's arm to take him to a cell. Emmett and Kendall then went out of the interview room.

"I wondered where Lily went to?" Emmett asked looking around.

"She's getting coffee in the break room," Police Constable Fourth Class Jenni Hayes said as she overheard the question.

"Thank-you Jenni," Emmett answered.

"You don't even notice, do you?"

"Notice what Kendall?"

"The looks the women in this station give you."

"They don't look at me," protested Emmett.

Kendall rolled her eyes, and then commented, "Let's change the subject. That interview didn't go well, I don't think Raj, or Dayita, will ever say anything!"

"I think that's because they have no idea where Amelia and Carol are," Emmett exclaimed.

"They think they can fool you. Let me at him alone. I'll make him talk," Kendall responded, boldly.

"You probably could, but let me ask you Kendall, how did you get to be a Lieutenant on the police force so young?" asked Emmett.

"I worked hard at it."

Emmett gave her an incredulous look.

"I did, but okay since you're my partner and I don't want to keep secrets from you. Now don't let this get around there's a reason I keep it a secret."

"You can trust me. I'm the sole of discretion," Emmett exclaimed.

"My dad is chief of police," she admitted.

"You don't have the same last name."

"I was briefly married out of high school." Kendall explained, "And divorced just as quick."

"But you came up the ranks you had to pass the tests."

"Yes, I did. I've worked hard to overcome the fact that I'm the chief's daughter. You won't tell anyone that he's my Dad will you?" Kendall pleaded.

"No, I won't, but that means Carol is related to you. No wonder you aren't objective," Emmett exclaimed.

"Like you are? I used to babysit that kid. Carol is the sweetest kid. A bit of a know-it-all but...we have to find her. Please, Emmett, whatever it takes. If the Patel's know where she is we have to make them tell us."

Kendall looked scared and Emmett thought about giving her a hug, but found it inappropriate.

"We've overlooked something, I know we have," Emmett exclaimed.

"But what? They didn't say a lot."

"Dayita Patel claimed she saw Alexander Vincent Scholar with someone," Emmett answered, "She also said that someone was married. We have to push her into telling us who. Could more than one person have them? If Raj Patel told the truth the married couple has Amelia and Carol."

"But who? And didn't Doctor Patel mention another couple to look into?"

"There are a lot of married couples at the school and the hospital."

"If it Dayita knew, then why wouldn't she say so?" exclaimed Kendall.

"It's all in how you ask the question. This could be the break we need and if we get them to confirm our suspicions."

"Our suspicions? Who do you think it is Emmett?"

"I'm not absolutely sure and I'd rather not say until I confirm it with Dayita. Then we can get a warrant and send some police to their home to see if there holding them," Emmett stated reassuringly.

"Let's go in Emmett and talk to Dayita again and get that name."

Kendall and Emmett walk into the interview room Dayita is in. Instead they find Lily has already beaten them to the punch.

"I thought you were getting coffee," Kendall griped.

"I think I know where Carol and Amelia are. Dayita told me whom she believes killed Vincent. Let's go. I've already called in a favour for the warrant. You better call out the troops and send them to their address," Lily declared.

Lily then handed Emmett a piece of paper. Emmett grabbed his jacket and Kendall followed.

"What this?" Lily asked, as Emmett handed Lily a five dollar bill.

"Let's say you won a bet."

"Did you bet on my cousin and Carol's lives?" Lily exclaimed, shocked and angry

"No, we bet who would find the information first. It helps to get our minds working on the problem and focus when we are too close to the problem."

"Sorry, I misjudged you Emmett. Let's go find them."

"She's not coming. She's a civilian," Kendall protested.

"You can come, but you have to wait in the car understood?" Emmett demanded.

"I understand, but once they're safe, all bets are off and I'm out of the car," Lily replied.

"I think I hate her." Kendall says under her breath, "Why does she feel the need to interfere in police business? She's a lawyer, not a cop!"

Lily heard her but ignored her only Amelia and Carol's safety was important.

"She got the address for us," Emmett commented.

"I still think she should stay here," Kendall complained.

"You are out voted. I am after all your superior," Emmett explained.

Emmett and Kendall got in the front seat of the police car and Lily got in the back, as they raced to the killers' house. Lily prayed they would find Amelia and Carol safe.

~0~

Chapter 21 - Escape

"I am watching. Now can you spring the lock without

electrocuting yourself?"

"I'm trying. Please, keep looking for them."

Carol continued poking the lock with the nail file.

"Ouch! Ouch that smarted!" Carol yelled, shaking her hand and then putting her finger in her mouth to dampen the pain.

"You should stop now while you are ahead." Amelia responded, "I don't think it's a good idea to get your hand wet when you working with electricity."

"You heard her she wants us dead. She has no compunction on killing us. If we don't get free, we'll die," Carol cried.

"He won't let her kill us," Amelia reassured.

"Dream on Amelia!! He's helped her already. He cut out the heart of a man who may or may not, have been dead at the time; what makes you think he'll spare us, if she wants us dead?" Carol demanded.

"She made him do that. He's a lovely man. You have to understand this is out of character."

"Out of character? He killed a man and took me prisoner and then he helped her keep you prisoner and heaven knows what he did to Daria and her boyfriend."

"You shouldn't take God's name in vain," Amelia scolded."

"I'm sure he'd excuse me mentioning his name seeing as we need all the help, we can get."

"Are you sure you need to pick that lock? I'm sure he'll let us go after she's gone."

"I know you liked the guy, but listen to me, Amelia and genuinely hear me. He's not that nice guy you think he is. He killed someone, or she did. They're in on this together. He's twisted around the finger of a murderess. Do you think he'll stop at killing merely one person for her? Listen through the vent for them and find something, we can use for weapons," Carol retorted, planning ahead.

"Who's the adult here? I guess you are correct. He's dangerous. I loved him, or at least I thought I did but if we want to survive we must arm ourselves. Do you think we can get out of here? We should stay put so they don't kill us," Amelia cried.

"I can't believe you're the adult. I know you're scared. I've been here longer and I'm not letting them win," Carol responded.

"Sorry, I liked the man. He seemed so charming."

"They always do. My dad says they're charming until they bite you on the ass."

"Carol!"

"Sorry the language slips out every once in awhile with my friends and you don't seem like an adult."

Carol kept digging at the lock with the nail file.

"So, you're closer to getting that door open?" asked Amelia changing the subject.

"If I tinker here, move this wire, and connect them here, and voila. Damn it didn't work," Carol exclaimed.

"Damn, we're never getting out of here."

"Tell me how you met him." Carol demanded, "Distract me."

"I went to see my shrink and I bumped into him in the hall. He bought me a coffee and told me he would be getting a divorce."

"Oh, I see."

"No, you don't see. I hadn't had so much fun in such a long time."

"I'm not judging you. I guess he is cute for someone that old."

"Thank-you, Carol."

Carol fidgeted with the wires in the door again. Suddenly she got a smile on her face, and picked up a wire. Weaving it through the other wires she exclaimed "I forgot this wire. There! It worked. The door is open. See, we can escape now."

"Oh, thank-you, Carol. You saved us."

"We still have to get down the hall up the stairs and outside." Carol stated.

"How do you know that?"

"He used a small dose on me and I remember seeing them groggily as we passed by."

"Good that should help. Here you take this lamp and I'll take the other. They'll make good weapons."

Amelia then handed Carol the Tiffany styled lamp. Amelia and Carol crept around the corner, alert to any noise. The central air kicked in and they startled. Realizing they were alarmed by the central air, they laughed and continued down the hall to the stairs. Amelia took the front of the line. They crept slowly up the stairs, being as quietly as they possibly could be. Amelia and Carol listened through the closed door for any sound. Hearing none, Amelia opened the door. Amelia and Carol looked around for the front door and head to it.

"Going somewhere ladies? I don't think so," an unearthly, threatening voice stated calmly.

~0~

Dan Brown and Daria

Dan Brown sat by Daria's bed praying that she'd wake-up soon. He thought back to two weeks before, when he met Amelia Kelly who had now gone missing. Amelia interesting and funny had made him forget about Denise dying, if only for a few minutes. He had wanted to ask her out but how could he? His daughter needed him and he'd recently lost his wife. So he had smiled at her at the meeting, but he still ended up asking her out for coffee.

Could it be that Amelia's disappearance and this sudden drug overdose of his daughter were connected? Daria was always anti - drug none of this made sense. Did Daria know something that put her life in danger this way? Had he neglected his daughter in his own grief? Why hadn't he got her to open up more and talk to him? And that guy she had been hanging out with. Trouble with a capital tee and Dan hadn't even known about him. Now the boy had died been murdered and he had to explain that to Daria. Please God let Daria wake –up even if I have to tell her the boy she loved has died. Wake her up God, so I can make it up to her.

Amelia thought about the same meeting at the same time and wondered if she would ever hear from Dan, if she will be able to escape when she heard the unearthly threatening voice, state calmly "Going somewhere ladies? I don't think so."

Chapter 22- Life is not a soap opera

Two weeks earlier at Lily's home

"**I'**m going now thanks for supper, Lily," Amelia stated.

"We're do you go all these nights?" asked Rose.

Lily shook her head at Rose but Rose continued, "Do you go to your store?"

"Rose...," Lily cautioned.

"I'm off to a bereavement meeting," Amelia explained.

"Bereavement? What is that?" Rose enquired.

"Bereavement means grieving for a loved one," Amelia answered.

"Oh, I'm sorry, Aunt Amelia. Those must be like those meetings, my shrink wanted me to go to for teens and I said I wasn't ready for."

"It's a good way to express your feelings. I have to go now, or I'll be late," Amelia replied.

Amelia then left through the front door.

"Mom, did you hear that Daria's mom died a couple of weeks ago? I felt so bad that I didn't hear until today. I would have said something to her. Apparently they had a private, immediate family only, ceremony," Rose exclaimed.

"No, I hadn't heard."

"I should have sent flowers enemy, or not." Rose cried, "It's horrible to lose your mother."

"You miss her. It's okay to miss your mother."

"I don't want to talk about her!"

"Okay, but if you ever do want to talk, I'm here. Or you can talk to your doctor about her."

"Okay, now let's drop it."

"Do you want me to send flowers from all of us? Amelia, Grandma Katha, you and I?" asked Lily "I'm sure they'd still enjoy the flowers and we could send some food."

"That would be okay."

~0~

Dan and Amelia

Amelia entered the Happy Valley High School, French room classroom, to see it filled with people and she became timid wondering if she truly wanted to be here.

"Hello, my name is Doctor Georgia Jeffries. This is a place where you can talk about your loved ones with no judgement, and share your pain and sorrow. I see we have a great number of new people, so I'm going to ask people to identify yourselves, first names are sufficient." Doctor Jeffries explained gesturing to the lady beside her to begin.

"Uh, hi my name is Roberta. And my husband Fred died."

"Hello Roberta," the group chimed.

"My name is Scott, and my girlfriend Avery died."

"My name is Lark and this is my husband Orville. We lost three babies."

"My name is Dan and my wife died from cancer."

"My name is Amelia and my father, mother, sister, brother, husband, and child were murdered, as well as my employee Megan, and my friend Al."

Amelia heard and saw the faces as she said this, most of them stared at her with shock, others gasped. Amelia almost left as this made her uncomfortable. Amelia hated seeing new groups, this always happened. She could talk to the doctor about one, on one, sessions? She ignored the crowd, as they continued the circle repeating their names, and thought more about leaving.

"I'm so sorry." Dan stated as he quietly sat next to her "My name is Daniel Brown. I worked at that precinct. We let you down, I'm sorry."

"It wasn't your fault, or anyone else's there. He was good at hiding in plain sight," Amelia says "I'm so sorry about your wife."

"We were on the verge of divorce, then she found out she would die. I feel conflicted, you know? I loved her once, but I wasn't in love with her anymore," Dan responded "But I'm so damn angry at her for leaving her daughter, and even me."

"You're at that stage, the anger stage," Amelia commented.

"There are stages?" Dan asked surprised.

"Didn't anyone tell you?" asked Amelia.

"I'm only at this meeting because my boss said I had to go," Dan replied "It was either that or lose my job."

"You're inappropriately angry, huh?"

"That's what the boss said." Dan exclaimed, "How did you know?

"Like I said we all go through that."

"Did anyone ever tell you that you are a sweet lady?" Dan flirted to his surprise.

"Lady you called me lady? That makes me sound like I'm Aunt Katha's age," Amelia answered.

"This Aunt Katha is older? Sorry, I was taught you should always call nice women ladies and of course to watch out for the other ones," Dan replied with a grin.

Doctor Jeffries cleared her throat, as if to admonish them for ignoring the introductions.

"Sorry," Amelia and Dan both said, smiling at each other, while talking to the doctor.

"My name is Annie and I lost my husband Ryan." said the small blonde woman next to Dan.

"My name is Ryan, and I lost my wife Greenlee to a criminal whose name is David."

"Let me see some identification right now," Doctor Jeffries exclaimed sounding annoyed.

Amelia looked astonished and then a nervous laugh slipped out of her.

"Let me in on the joke." Dan said to Amelia.

"It's not funny. Those two people the guy that said he was Ryan and the one that said she was Annie...?"

"Yes, so?" Dan asked.

"They are the names of characters in All My Children, a former soap opera. The characters interact with each other. I don't think these people are here to grieve."

"That's not funny," Dan exclaimed angry.

Dan jumped to his feet and pulled his badge out of his pocket.

"Listen up everyone in this room will show me their identification, but especially you two," Dan demanded, pointedly showing his badge.

"That won't be necessary detective, but I appreciate your help. These people will leave and won't be back,"

Doctor Jeffries exclaimed, pointedly to the two after seeing their identification.

"What kind of people are you? There people grieve and you two come in here, and say lines from a soap opera? Is that how you get your jollies? I should arrest you. I'm sure there is a charge I can lay. You have impersonated a grieving person. You've committed a crime, fraud for one. The charges are endless that I can find for you, two," Dan stated, angrily.

"We are sorry Mister. We thought it would fun, funny even, but it's not. When I heard those real stories, my heart grieved for you all," the woman who called herself Annie stated.

"I'm sorry, sir. Please don't arrest me," the man who called himself Ryan begged.

"Will you two pull this nonsense again?"

"No, never sir. We promise to never, ever do this, again," Annie cried.

"Like, she said." Ryan piped in.

"Fine, Bob. Oh and your real name is Annie," Dan exclaimed, looking at their identification in surprise.

"I'll let you two off with a warning then, but if I ever hear you pulled something like this again then we will lay charges. Is that understood?"

"Yes, sir," Annie whispered trembling.

"Yes, sir," Dan cried.

"Fine then, you two leave now, before I change my mind." Amelia watched as they left and thought that Dan appeared pretty special.

"I don't think I'm ready to spill in front of these people. I'm leaving," Dan stated to the doctor, then turning to Amelia he asked, "Do you want to get a coffee Amelia?"

"Dan I love to." Amelia responded getting up and following Dan, then turned to Doctor Jefferies and said, "Sorry Doctor Jeffries. I think I want to go too."

"I'm sorry those people disrupted our group. I hope you'll both come back next week. Same time," Doctor Jeffries insisted.

"I probably will," Dan and Amelia said together and then laughed because they did. The coffee shop bustled, but Dan and Amelia found themselves laughing and enjoying each other's company. Dan was shocked to feel happy again. Amelia was someone special, he thought.

"Do you have a boyfriend?" Dan asked.

"I am involved with someone, but it's not working out. He says he's getting divorced, but I don't want to be the other woman. He loves his wife, I know he does," Amelia admitted.

"It sounds like he strung you along. You'd be better off without him," Dan exclaimed.

"I think you are correct," Amelia admitted.

"I like to see you again Amelia, on a date," Dan stated.

"What this isn't a date? That would be nice. Here's my number." Amelia replied.

"See you again Amelia, in a couple of weeks." says Dan "I have to go out of town until then."

Amelia then handed him her phone number. She wrote on a piece of paper and said, "Nice meeting you Dan."

Amelia knew she had met someone she could care for. Now she had to break up with Henry. They'd only been on a couple of dates it shouldn't be too hard. Besides Lily, although she didn't say so, was not happy. Henry was still married. Lily was wise when it came to these matters of the heart, even if she hadn't seen in her own two husbands. Lily's disapproval had come through loud and clear, despite her not saying a thing. Lily always thought herself unreadable, but her face was a map of her emotions, except when she was in court. Amelia had seen her there presenting a case once and it appeared like she watched a totally different person.

Henry still seemed awful close to his wife, the wife he said he would divorce! She seen the looks they shared between them in the coffee shop. Amelia had seen them talking, smiling, and laughing. Henry hadn't seen her but she witnessed their affection.

Henry was still in love with his wife. Amelia would not engage her heart with someone who couldn't give theirs back. Despite Dan's recent bereavement, she didn't think his heart was still engaged. She could begin a new period in her life, taking it slow and learning to love again. She merely had to remember though that life was not a soap opera. And she wasn't about to be the heroine who got her heart broke, over, and over, again. She wanted to be strong like Erica Kane but without the heartbreak.

Dan was stable and had a good job. He had recently lost his wife, that wasn't good. On the other hand he said he had filed for divorce and when she found out she was dying he stood by her. So Dan's feelings weren't tied to Denise were they? He was simply being a good guy and husband. Amelia was ready to move on and Dan seemed like a good choice. They'd take it slow and see where it went.

~0~

Chapter 23 - Because I Could

The Present

Dan Brown sat at Daria's hospital bed, willing her to wake up. Dan's mind began to wander. He thought back to the meeting two weeks he had with Amelia and smiled. Did she think of him as often as he did her? An exceptional warm loving woman, he wanted to get to know Amelia, a little better. He wondered why hadn't heard from her. She was as scared as he? After all she had a serial killer stalk her for years who unbelievably happened to be a cop.

Not a good example for his profession especially since Brad Owens stalked her for years. Why would she want to be involved with someone in the same profession? Would Amelia and Daria get along? Daria would probably be none too happy, he wanted to date all ready.

Was it too soon for both of them? Amelia grieved the loss of her husband, and child, still. Probably more than he did Denise. After all he and Denise had been over, before she found out the cancer was back. The only good thing that had come out of their relationship had been Daria.

Dan stared at Daria. Her body seemed small defenceless, not unlike the baby he held in his arms so long ago. But now a machine breathed for her. Her face was pale and lifeless, like Snow White in the fairy tale he used to read her. Like that same fairy tale she'd wake up, except there was no prince to awaken her.

Dan rested his face in his hands and begged God for one more chance and for the chance that Daria would find her prince. He couldn't lose his little girl too. He couldn't. Dan looked up from his prayer at Daria and realized with surprise that she was awake. Daria seemed agitated. Daria's eyes darted from side to side; fear evident as she began to shake.

"It's okay Daria. We won't let anyone hurt you again. I don't know who did this too you honey, but Daddy won't let them near you again," Dan cried emphatically.

Daria motioned for paper and a pen. Dan scrambled to find some and then remembered he had his police notebook with a pen which he hands to her Daria writes on the paper and hands it to Dan. Dan read..., "Amelia Kelly and Carol Banks are in grave danger. They took them."

Dan looked at it and asked "Who took them?"

Daria frantically wrote.

Dan looked at the note and exclaimed, "I'll get them baby don't you worry. You've saved them rest easy. They will pay. I don't want to leave you but I must go to rescue them. I'll be back soon." Dan explained.

Dan then got up from his seat. Daria pulled his arm and wrote again.

"Be careful and come back to me."

"I promise, I'll be careful baby, and I'll call for back-up on the way," Dan responded.

Dan then ran out and told the nurse in the hall, his daughter was awake and alert. He explained he'd be back soon and left the hospital calling for backup.

~0~

Amelia and Carol

At the Killer's house, Amelia and Carol who tried to escape, hear a voice say, "Going somewhere ladies I don't think so."

"It's only a parrot," Carol explained to Amelia.

Amelia and Carol laughed with relief, only to hear another voice behind them say.

"Who do you think taught the parrot? You two aren't going anywhere. I should have killed you when I had the chance. It was easy to get rid of the other two. Why shouldn't it be as easy to get rid of you?"

"What other two?' asked Carol stalling.

"Daria Brown, and that nasty boyfriend of hers, Paul Decker were easy to drug. Daria still lingers, but the first chance he gets my husband, will get rid of that nasty brat," the killer's chilling voice stated.

"You killed Paul? Why?" asked Carol.

"Simple, because I could, that's why. I wanted to get rid of you two, but Henry made me promise not to," she explained. "Henry's such a good person. He has a good heart, unlike me."

"But you'll keep that promise?" begged Amelia.

"I don't know why I should keep my promise. If Henry hadn't taken the heart, we wouldn't be in this predicament.

"Why did he take the heart then?" Amelia enquired.

"I admit I told Henry that Vinnie played with my heart. Henry was always jealous just because Vinnie paid attention to me and slept with me once." she admitted, "Henry gave me this ring. See, isn't it lovely?"

"It looks like the ring that I saw in Lily's files the one he gave to all his women." Amelia blurted, "It's glass."

"He did not give all those women my ring and it's not glass. How dare you lie?"

The woman then stamped her foot angrily and began to walk across the floor. The gun in her hand swung wildly and Rose feared they had made her angrier.

"I'm sorry to hurt you. He was a fickle man. He gave them all rings and promised to marry them," Amelia continued.

"Hush, Amelia," Carol cautioned.

"Lies, all lies. You shut up both of you. I should have silenced your lying tongues, long ago. He loved me, I know he did," she yelled.

"I'm sure he did. Those other women were predators it wasn't his fault. He loved only you," Carol soothed, trying to mollify her and keep her from killing them.

"You are a nice child."

"I'm sorry, he hurt you. You killed Mr. Scholar right though because he did?" Carol enquired.

"I didn't kill him; I wanted to but I knew I could get Henry to."

"Why did you get Henry to kill him?" asked Carol.

"I caught Vinnie with several women. I warned him what would happen if he cheated on me. He lied he said he loved me."

"And I'm sure he did, but he couldn't help those other women fawning all over him."

"I thought so too, but I was wrong. Do you know Suzy Roger's is pregnant with his children?"

"No, he didn't," Carol exclaimed trying to sound like a confident.

"He did and that was the last draw. I've known Suzy since she was a child. She's still child-like and he took advantage of her I'm afraid, so I had to make him pay."

"He sounds like a heel."

"You know I like you. You are not a brat, like that Daria Brown. Now she's a piece of work. Do you know we saw her and her boyfriend having sex in a classroom? And I could do nothing about it, otherwise we would have been found out. That child was evil. I'm not going to jail for killing Vinnie. Purely an accident his death, if he hadn't kept saying he loved her, he wouldn't have died," she stated.

"Who did he say he loved?" asked Amelia, as Carol tried to shush her.

"That woman Dayita, his ex-wife! He claimed he loved her and only her. I wanted to die on the spot and then such a rage came over me I picked up a pen and stabbed him in the chest. Who knew a pen could kill him?"

"But you said Henry killed him," Amelia protested.

"Potato, potato. There wasn't even any ink in the pen how could it have killed him? I must have hit him in the heart. He was bleeding, and bleeding, but then I called Henry and he came and fixed everything. I wanted to take Dayita prisoner and torture her slowly for what she done to me, but Henry stopped that too. He stops all my fun," she replied sounding slightly crazed.

"But how is that her fault? Alexander, or Vincent, said he loved her. She left him. Didn't she divorce him, if she was his ex-wife?" Amelia enquired.

"I thought she divorced him, but I found out he did the divorcing. I thought he would marry me. I was prepared to leave Henry for him, but he had to sleep with any woman who walked this earth," she complained.

Henry entered the room behind her and hearing all this shouted, angrily, "Janet, you were going to leave me? You lying witch! After all I've done for you? After all I've given up for you?"

"Henry, you're mistaken. You've heard incorrectly. I love you!" mollified Janet.

"Love me? You don't love me. I've sacrificed over and over for you. I have swallowed my pride and forgiven your transgressions. I knew about the men who warmed your bed. You said they meant nothing. You said Vincent meant nothing, that you'd made a mistake. That he played with your heart, but that I had always been the love of your life. That he threatened me. For that you killed him. You lied to me, you adulterous slut."

"Henry, please listen to me. I love you, and only you. I'm giving up my career as a principal for you," she pleaded.

"I want to believe that Janet, but your words..."

"You heard wrong. I love you Henry."

"Love? You don't know the meaning of the word. Why did I ever get mixed up with you? "Why did I give you year, after year? I gave you all my free time, when I wasn't saving lives? Why did I throw my life away on the likes of you?" Henry cried with deep anguish.

"Henry, you haven't thrown away anything. I'm here for you always for you. I am your wife, always your wife." Janet placated.

"My wife? But you were always someone else's mistress. You were never mine. That was the lie you sold me," Henry continued pacing.

"That's not true. I loved you once. I loved you the day I married you. Blame yourself for this, it was always the hospital that was your first love I couldn't compete with that," Janet screamed.

"Compete why would you need to compete? I loved you I gave you a million dollar home, the prestige of being a doctor's wife," Henry stated, sadly.

"Did you give me your time? No it was... I have to perform a surgery. I'll be as quick as I can. I'm sorry our vacation is cancelled there is a revolutionary surgery I have to perform."

"Those people needed me. I saved lives," Henry exclaimed proudly.

Henry then held out his arms to her but she didn't fold into them.

"Where were you when I lost our baby? How did you save her? You chose someone else over our child."

"I saved someone's life in surgery. Was it even my child?" Henry asked angrily.

"You dare to ask me that? You dare to spit on the memory of our little girl?"

"You've slept with many men since our marriage haven't you? Why should I believe that the baby was mine? " Henry continued, an ominous tone to his voice.

"How did you know about the others?"

"Know? You thought I didn't know? You thought I did hear the whispers of people talking about my wife? I pretended to myself that it wasn't happening then that it meant nothing. That it would blow over and you would look at me like when we first met," Henry replied, scathingly.

"I'm sorry, Henry," Janet replied, quietly.

"That's the thing though isn't it? You always say you are sorry. You always say you'll make it right! This time you can't make it right, your lies have ruined me. You made me a murderer. You've ruined my life," Henry grabbed her about the throat.

"Doctor Thomas, if you let us go and testify against her she'll pay," Amelia interjected, trying to stop him from killing his wife.

"She deserves to die. I can't let her hurt anyone else, not if I truly love her," Doctor Thomas cried.

Henry kept his hands around Janet's neck tightening slightly as Janet gasped.

"She wanted you both to die. She wanted me to kill you," Henry continued.

"Killing her would make you as bad as she is," Carol explained. "You're a good person. You heal others with your surgical techniques. You could plead temporary insanity after all she drove you to it. You spend a little time in a hospital and then they let you go. She however, would pay for her crime. She planned the murder."

"Shut up you little witch. Don't listen to her Henry. Please, Henry, remember how it was when we first met? How I loved you cherished you. It could be like it once was remember when we first met?" Janet pleaded in a raspy voice, as Henry pulled his hands way.

"You cherished me? The only one you ever cherished was yourself. I remember everything and I should have known from the first, that you loved only Janet," Henry replied, sadly.

"I love you," Janet pleaded. "Henry, you know I love only you. I always come back to you."

"You don't love me. You don't love anyone, but Janet. I thought I could fix you. Heal the wounds your uncle left, but I was wrong."

"I'm whole. I don't understand what you speak of. I have a respectable position."

"You're a teacher a principal of a high school and you killed one of the students who go there. You put another child in a coma. What kind of person kills let alone kills a child? And harms another? If I hadn't stopped you would have killed again two more people. How high does the body count have to go Janet to protect you?" asked Henry, placing his hands again on Janet's slender neck.

"Please, Doctor Thomas, you saved my friend Rose. You're not a killer you're a doctor. Let the courts decide how she pays," Carol begged.

"She tried to kill two children. Children who should be protected and she would have killed you two. One child is dead. I can't let her get away with this. She needs to pay now," Henry answered.

"Please listen to Carol, Doctor Thomas. I know you didn't harm my Daria. She injected them with drugs. She took from your bag. None of this is your fault. Janet fooled you. She fooled everyone. I'm willing to testify on your behalf, take that into account. The coroner said Scholar was dead before you took the heart. He'd been dead probably an hour." Dan exclaimed, coming in the now open front door his gun drawn.

"They'll put me away and I won't be able to bear it. I need to save people. Kill me, as I kill her," Henry insisted.

"Don't throw your life away for this woman she isn't worth it. You'll perform surgery again," Dan replied, "I'll testify for you. I promise."

"You'd do that for me after I took Carol prisoner?" Henry asked incredulously, "She took Amelia."

"Yes," Dan negotiated.

"I can tell Amelia likes you. Look how she looks at you. You're a lucky man. Treat her better than I did. I'm sorry for my part in this."

"I know Janet took Amelia. It wasn't you. You know what a special person Amelia is. You saw it yourself didn't you?"

"She'll pay?" asked Henry listening.

"She's murdered two people she'll pay." Dan responded, "And after what she did to my daughter I'll make it my job to see that she pays most severely."

Henry stopped strangling Janet and took one hand from her neck.

"I've done nothing. It was all him. It's my word against him who will believe him?" Janet lied, putting all the blame on Henry

"You bitch. It always comes down to that doesn't it. Everything is always about you and your needs. Everyone else's needs don't matter. I've finally seen the truth and the truth is you can only love yourself. Isn't that right Janet?" Henry replied, bitterly.

A single tear slipped from Henry's eye.

"That's not true Henry. You can still kill him and I'll kill those two. We will hide the bodies and go away like you planned," Janet pleaded "Please Henry, I love you."

"No you have to die I was right the first time." Henry stated, sadly placing his hand back around her neck and squeezing

"Please don't Henry. Please you don't want to be like her. We will testify too Henry." Amelia says "We heard everything through the vent and everything she said today."

"You do that for me despite what I did?"

"Of course, Henry, you are a good person. I know that." Amelia insisted, "You were coerced by an evil, scheming, woman who used you for her own ends."

"You truly believe that? I can see that you do. I am sorry Amelia. I should have been braver and divorced her. Then I could have made a real life with you. You are a jewel ten, times brighter, than her tarnished fool's gold. Arrest her. I give up," Henry exclaimed, holding out his wrists.

Dan walked over to place the cuffs on Henry but decided to put them on Janet first. Janet grabbed a Taser from his waist and fired at Henry. Henry lay prone on the floor. His arm shook and his legs trembling of their own accord. Janet then fired the Taser at Dan. Dan fired his weapon shooting it out of her hand. Janet screamed in pain and tried to reach again for the Taser, but Amelia stamped on her hand. Janet screamed as those same three fingers now bent the wrong way.

"Need some help, Dan?" asked Emmett who had come in the house, followed by Alan in uniform.

"Could you round up Ms. Thomas? I don't want to touch her. I don't trust myself after what she did to Daria. I don't want Internal Affairs on me."

"Sure, no problem," Emmett exclaimed.

Emmett then placed Janet Thomas' hands behind her back and read her, her rights.

"I'll take her to the squad car and call Jake Barnes, Alan's cousin and partner to take her to the station. I'll take Doctor Thomas to the station."

"No need, I'm here I can we can take it from here. Jake's right behind me," patrolman Alan Barnes exclaimed.

"Thanks Alan. Go easy on the Doc here he tried to stop that evil witch." Dan admitted, "In fact he may need to take a trip to the hospital. She tasered him!"

"No problem, Dan. We've got your back," Alan exclaimed.

Jake and Alan then took Janet and Henry Thomas, out of the house. Emmett watched and was surprised when Dan hugged Amelia and asked her..., "Are you okay?"

"I am now. Thanks Dan for saving me," Amelia replied, smiling.

"Are you okay Carol?" asked Dan.

"I'm fine a few cuts from the wires on the room downstairs, but I'm alive. Will Daria be okay?" asked Carol, looking terrified of the answer.

"I think your cousin will be fine now. She's awake. She's the one who sent me here to rescue you both," Dan answered.

"I'm so glad, she's okay. I worried that they had killed her. I can't believe Paul's dead. He is dead isn't he?" Carol cried. Tears started to streak down her face.

"Paul's dead, but like I said Daria will be okay."

"I'm glad about Daria but I'm sorry about Paul even though I disliked him he didn't deserve to die. Can you call my mom? I want my mom," Carol pleaded.

"Protocol says you have to be checked out by a doctor sweetie, but I'm sure we can get your mom there by the time you arrive," Dan replied.

"I already called her Carol. Lily and Rose know too they will probably meet us all at the hospital after the ambulance takes you," Emmett stated, but Carol didn't seem to hear.

"I want my mom," Carol repeated, shock setting in as she began to shiver uncontrollably.

"I told you honey, your mom's on her way to the hospital. She'll meet us there." Emmett explained, "Your dad's on his way too."

"Daddy's coming?" Carol retorted, surprised.

"Where else would he be? You're his little girl. He harassed the department day and night for us to find you. He even harassed your great-uncle. He's searched high and low himself, with your mother in tow."

"He did?"

"He did!" Emmett confirmed.

Carol smiled

"Okay, but I want you to take us not some ambulance please Detective Rogers?"

"I'll radio it in. Katha, Lily, and Rose, will wait for you there too."

Emmett placed Carol and Amelia carefully in the back seat of his car. He then drove to the hospital with Dan in the front seat as his car wouldn't start.

"I called a tow truck for your car. They'll take it to Mike's garage."

"Thank-you Emmett," Dan replied.

Emmett's phone rang and he apologized to all in the car, as he pulled over to answer it.

"You hot-dogging son of a bitch! Why didn't you call me?" Kendall complained, "You rescued them without me?"

"Kendall?" mouthed Dan as Emmett nodded.

"If you'd answer your phone now and then, you'd know when something goes down," Emmett retorted, angrily, "I must have called you a hundred times."

"I'm going to complain to my Dad about this. It wasn't my fault that my phone was dead," Kendall whined like a little kid.

"You do that Kendall. We have jobs to do. We can't let our phones be out of order. Now in the meantime, I have to go do my job and take the victims to the hospital."

"Wait a minute, tell me what happened," Kendall demanded, "Last I heard you only had an idea you wouldn't share."

"I don't have time. Victims come before chitchat. Goodbye, Kendall," Emmett cried, hanging up on her phone call.

"Sorry about that. Ladies now we'll get to our destination." Emmett replied as Emmett continued driving.

"She sounded real crabby. Will you get in trouble with Chief Stewart? Amelia asked.

"Kendall is always crabby," Carol commented.

"You know her?"

"She's my cousin."

"Oh..."

"Emmett won't get in trouble. My wife was related to Chief Stewart too. I have some pull," Dan answered.

"I guess that's good then, as long as neither of you get in trouble," Amelia answered.

"Come on honey. No worry about others we worry only about you," Dan answered as they pulled into the hospital emergency parking.

Dan and Emmett then helped Amelia and Carol into the hospital.

~0~

Chapter 24-
Epilogue

At her house, Lily paced back and forth. The phone's

shrill ring, jarred her, but relieved her from her worry.

Lily answered the phone, "Oh, thank-you God! I'll let Rose know too. Thank you, for letting us know, Emmett. What? How did Grandma Katha and Terrence find out? Oh, so Terrence got a call from his son the police chief? Then why didn't Grandma Katha call me? She's there with Amelia now?"

"Mom what's going on? What happened? Tell me," Rose demanded.

"They're safe Rose. Thank-you, God, they're safe!" Lily replied, through tears of relief.

"You're sure mom? Aunt Amelia and Carol are safe? Thank-you God, I couldn't go through that again." Rose retorted, "But what about Daria?"

"I thought you didn't care about Daria?"

"Simply because I didn't want to hear nice things about the girl who hit me, doesn't mean I don't care if she lives, or dies," Rose retorted angrily.

"Daria came out of her coma and told her father that Amelia and Carol were in danger and where she thought they had been taken," Lily explained.

"Emmett and you had already figure out where they were so you didn't need that information," Rose stated.

"But Dan got there quicker. Who knows what would have happened to them if he hadn't."

"So it was Doctor Thomas and his wife? He seemed so nice when he took care of me in the hospital. I can't quite believe it. Did you know she was our principal?" Rose asked.

"Yes, but I had no idea the murder was her. This isn't to go beyond these walls, but it turns your principal was involved with your choir teacher. In her twisted mind Mr. Scholar cheated on her so she killed him, That's why she claims she took his heart as a souvenir," Lily explained.

"She took his heart, that's so sick.'"

"Actually the actual cutting was done by Doctor Thomas after the killing. He thought if the heart went missing, they wouldn't blame his wife," Lily responded, "But it seems she didn't let him dispose of it in the hospital bio-wastes and instead kept it in a heart-shaped box."

"Oh yuck, why would you do that for anyone?" Rose asked.

"People do crazy things in the name of love."

"This one takes the cake. Isn't that the expression Grandma Katha uses," Rose asked.

"That is the expression," Lily agreed. "Now let's go see Amelia and Carol at the hospital."

"We're going to visit them at the hospital? But I thought you said they were safe. That they were okay?" Rose asked, suddenly worried.

"They're okay. Emmett says they are fine. It is standard procedure to have kidnap victims checked out at the hospital," Lily soothed.

"Good! You had me worried mom."

"Sorry sweetie."

"I'm sorry, I was so mad at you, before. Accusing you of taking Carol's side wasn't fair," Rose apologised.

"Already forgotten, I love you never forget that my Rosey."

"I love you too Mom, but please don't call me Rosey anymore. I'm too old for that."

Rose then put on her coat and followed Lily out the door to the car.

At the hospital, Lily, and Rose joined Emmett, Katha, and Terrence waited to see Carol and Amelia.

"I've been in to see my girl but I thought I'd give her sweetie and few minutes with her," Katha explained.

"Her sweetie?" Rose commented.

"I guess it's Dan?"

"We don't know any Dan! Dan who?" Rose commented, then looking at a smirking Emmett who pointed to his badge, Rose continued, "Not Daria's dad? Yuck!"

"Rose, Amelia loves him," protested Lily.

"Okay, I'll be nice; but I don't have to like Daria's dad."

"I guess that will do. For now," Lily stated.

~0~

At the Hospital

Dan sat in the cubicle with Amelia, Amelia waited for the

okay from the emergency room doctor to give her permission to leave.

"You should be with Daria, not me," Amelia admonished.

"I'll go up again in minute when I'm sure you're okay. She was fine, a couple of minutes ago. The doctor said she would sleep for a few hours, so I can be there again when she wakes up."

"I know we haven't known each other that long, but you were always on my mind especially when I thought I would die."

"I was worried about you too."

"Good."

"I'd like to date you, if that's okay?" Dan answered, hesitantly.

"I'd like that Dan."

Dan then put his arm around her and hugged her. Rose, Lily, Katha, and Terrence entered room in time to see the embrace.

"Hello, Lily, Rose, and Aunt Katha."

"Would you like to share something with us, Amelia?" asked Lily, surprised.

"I didn't know you knew Daria's Dad," Rose commented, shocked.

"We met a couple of weeks ago. Dan comforted me, it's been an ordeal." Amelia explained.

"Thank-you Daniel, for saving my niece and my granddaughter's friend," Katha replied. "There aren't enough words."

"You already thanked me, Katha. Besides I care about your niece and Carol is my niece by marriage," Dan answered.

"It must be so hard for you to get back to work so soon after losing Denise," Terrence frowned.

"Terrence, we both knew a year ago that Denise was troubled and then she got ill. Daniel stood by her through all that. He could have walked away; after all he had divorced her. He didn't he stood by your granddaughter. He nursed her when she lay dying. You can't ask more than then that dear," Katha admonished Terrence for his coolness.

Then seeing him still frowning at Dan, she added, "Daniel has saved your great granddaughter Rose and my niece Amelia as well. He's a hero in my book."

"I see." mollified Terrence, "I'll try harder to accept this Dan. Katha is correct you did stay by Denise."

"Thank you, Terrance."

"This might not be the right place to do this but I wanted to surprise you all. I want everyone to go to London, England for Christmas."

"Dan too?"

"Of course Dan and Daria too! The whole family, Katha!"

"That's kind of you Terrence but Daria and I are going to my mother's for Christmas. Besides I'm sure you wouldn't want Daria to break her restraining order. We need some time to reconnect. You can come with us too if you want to, Amelia." Dan answered, "If the doctor allows it."

"Oh okay, but if you change your mind..."

"I won't but thank you."

"I think I'm going with my family Dan. You need time alone with your daughter I don't want to mess things up."

"Okay," Dan agreed reluctantly, "If that's what you want I'll see you when you get back."

"Look Katha, I got tickets for Amelia, Lily and of course Emmett (since they're dating and I need another man along, I don't want to be outnumbered) and of course Rose. We can get re-married New Year's Eve. I got them all as e-tickets...that's what you call it when you buy it on the internet right?" Terrence then handed the tickets he'd carefully printed to Katha.

"You did these on the internet? When did you buy the tickets?" asked Katha.

"I bought them about a week ago as a surprise. I found a really great deal. Why?"

"I hate to tell you this but they are non-refundable and they are for a place called London, Ontario. I've been there it's not London England. Haven't you ever heard of it living in Ontario?" Katha replied.

"I guess that explains the price then. That's London in Canada isn't it? I guess that explains the price then." Terrence asked Katha, looking glum, "I've been there too, during the war. Why didn't I read them over?"

Katha bit her lip not to laugh."

"Why don't we all leave Amelia and Dan alone and discuss this in the hall?" Katha asked.

Everyone agreed and they left the room.to listen in the hallway.

"Oh no, I wanted to give you the wedding of your dreams. I'd hoped to be married in a castle," Terrence continued, dejected "Now I've thrown all that money away."

"Were already married dear, remember the justice of the peace at city hall?" Katha stated, annoyed.

"That wasn't the wedding you wanted. You wanted a wedding with family, and I wanted to give you that in England with castles, like a fairy tale wedding," Terrence explained. "And now I've blown it. I bought tickets to somewhere in Ontario, Canada. Our own province! There aren't any castles in this London, Ontario. I know because I've been there."

"This was such a sweet gesture. I do love you big lug. It's still London. Just a different London, then you thought. Let me look it up at the internet and see about it and the area. We should talk to my travel director and then we can find out all about the area and plan this. I love the idea of getting married New Year's Eve. A New Year and a new wedding to remember this will be wonderful."

"So you're not mad at me?" asked Terrence.

"I'm not mad at you Terrence. You thought of inviting my family, and you are so sweet, that's why I'll be happy to be your bride again New Year's Eve. You leave the rest of the planning to me dear. I'm an expert at it."

"I'll be happy to. Frankly, planning gives me a headache," Terrence explained.

"Hey, isn't near Niagara Falls nearby can't we go there?" asked Rose excited.

"Close enough dear give, or take a few kilometres, dear. What do you say Terence?" Katha responded scrolling on her phone.

"Sounds perfect, to me."

"Thank-you Grandpa Terrence. I'm going to see Carol. I'll be back soon."

Rose then left to visit Carol.

"Oh, my goodness, Grandma Katha, we forgot all about the election yesterday," Lily says "Who won?"

"Harold Crimshaw won. I gave it my best. I could have used a couple more votes," Katha remarked.

"Did we lose the election for you?" asked Amelia.

"Amelia, my little love, you were kidnapped you and Carol were more important than any election. Besides if I truly admitted it, I lost by more than a few votes," Katha admitted.

"Oh Grandma Katha, we are so sorry. This was so important to you," Lily comforted.

"Those people are idiots they should have voted my Katha. They'll be sorry that they voted for Harold. Harold hasn't changed he tormented others as a child and he'll continue as a terrible mayor," Terrance cried.

"Oh, no, is he related to you too?" asked Lily.

"Yes, he's my son-in-law."

"What?" Katha cried.

"Sorry, I should have told you, but frankly I don't want to be related to him. I never speak to him. My daughter, his wife, has Alzheimer's. He likes to pretend she's dead that's what he tells everyone."

"I understand, it must be difficult to talk or think about him then," Katha said putting her arms around Terrance to let him know he was forgiven.

"We'll actively work to get him out of office after our honeymoon," Terrence responded. "Don't you worry dear, you'll be mayor."

"I'm not worried, there's another election in four years."

"Carol went home with her mom and dad," Rose complained coming back in the room, "Let's go see Amelia, mom."

"Okay, did you get to see Carol?" asked Lily.

"I did. She's okay, Mom, but she wanted to go home. I'll see her tomorrow."

A doctor came out of the cubicle as they entered. The doctor's name tag said Doctor Abraham, fastened to her white lab coat, walked into the room. She looked at her clipboard examined Amelia and said, "I'll be back in a few minutes. I have to check with my superior but I think you can go after that."

Amelia waited bored and wanting to go home. She looked up as Emmett walked back in.

"Oh good you're still here," he said, "I need you to sign a statement."

Emmett then held out a log book and a pen and Amelia read it and signed. A few seconds later a doctor stuck her head into the cubicle. Fastened to her white coat was a badge which read Doctor Yates.

"I've looked over all the test results Ms. Kelly everything looks fine. The drug left no residue in your blood stream. If you should have any side effects, please come back. But you're free to go, Ms. Kelly," Doctor Yates stated.

"Thank you I just want to go home and be with my family," Amelia admitted.

"See you later, Amelia. I have to go visit Daria." Dan cried.

"How is Daria?" Terrence asked taking Dan aside before he could leave.

"Daria does much better," explained Dan. "The doctor is hopeful. The doctor also said she might be able to go home in a couple of weeks that is if she continues to keep getting better."

"So you got a good doctor?" joked Emmett, overhearing.

"At least this doctor doesn't have a wife or husband, who's a killer." Dan replied. "I know her husband, he's a good lawyer."

"As long, as she's good doctor. That's all that matters."

"Not to worry Doctor Yates, is good. She has a specialty in internal medicine, but she's also a cardiologist. So we have all the bases covered," Dan replied.

Emmett then handed an envelope to Katha. Katha opened it, read a card, and smiled.

"See you later Dan," Emmett retorted. "I'm going to take the ladies home."

"Let's head home ladies." Katha stated looking up from her phone, "We have the wedding of a lifetime to plan."

"What about me?" Terrence asked.

"I'll see you later dear. You can take me to the Pope Hotel for our honeymoon suite. Emmett has given us a night there for a wedding present, the dear man."

"I'll be there with bells on!" claimed Terrence.

"You'd better," Katha exclaimed.

Dan whispered in Lily and Katha's ears and then they collected Rose and left. Terrence hung back wanting to speak to Emmett.

"How did you know Emmett?" Terrance asked.

"I didn't Terrence. I got the card in the gift shop and called the hotel on my phone down there," Emmett admitted.

"Thank-you, Emmett. This is most generous," Terrence commented.

"So I guess. I'll see you later?" Dan asked.

"See you later Dan," Terrence replied, congenially and left following Emmett who was called back to the station.

Dan looked on at Terrence's back, surprised.

"Wow, your Aunt Katha has changed him for the better," he whispered to Amelia.

"As long as he makes her happy, I'm glad for both of them. She's needed someone special since she lost Uncle Kieran."

"Kieran O'Malley is a hard man to replace," Terrence remarked, "But I'm not replacing him. He'll always have a place in Katha's heart and that's okay with me. She's my wife now and I'll make her happy."

"See that you do or you'll have me to answer to," Amelia cried.

"Get better dear. I'll see you later," Terrance said and then left Dan and Amelia.

"So shall we set another date?"

"I'd like that Dan." Amelia answered smiling, "The doctor said I could go home. Will you drive me?"

"Of course I will."

The End or is it?

Read the Kelly's Christmas and New Year's in Ontario, Canada in Betty Blue Lost Her Holiday Shoe, on the next page.

~0~

Betty Blue Lost Her Holiday Shoe

Book 3 of the Kelly Murder Mysteries

A novel

Written by S. G. Lee

Copyright 2016 © Sheilagh G. Lee

First Edition 2015

Published at CreateSpace

Copyright © 2015 by Sheilagh G. Lee

All Rights Reserved

ISBN (13) 9781987977073 (paperback)

ISBN-10: 1987977076

ISBN 9780993653193 (e-book)

Betty Blue Lost Her Holiday Shoe

Chapter 1 - Betty Blue Lost Her Holiday Shoe

Little Betty Blue lost her holiday shoe; what shall little Betty do? Give her another. To match the other. And then she'll walk upon two. Little Blue Betty, she lived in a den; she sold good ale to gentlemen. Gentlemen came every day, And little Blue Betty she skipped away. She hopped upstairs to make her bed, but tumbled down and broke her head~Old English Nursery Rhyme

Rose

T he sun shone brightly and made it feel like it should be summer, but the grass was covered in dirty black sooty snow and the wind was bitterly cold. This tour would probably have been better in summer with green grass and warmer temperatures Rose thought. The bus was warm, compared to the cold temperatures outside of negative four degrees Celsius...or as Grandma Katha always converted it to about twenty five degrees Fahrenheit. Even on the warm bus, Rose shivered.

What was wrong with her this was a happy occasion, a holiday with her family, she should be happy but something inside her felt like something ominous would happen and she couldn't seem to shake the cold that seeped into her very bones. Now she sounded like an old lady, even to herself. Rose shook her head and glanced at Grandpa Terrence and Grandma Katha.

Grandma Katha always had gleaming white perfectly coiffed hair, her brilliant sapphire blue eyes always answered a smile from her loved ones, but when anyone threatened them despite her frail looking appearance she was a pit-bull. This made Rose smile and feel safe.

The feelings that plague were subsiding; they were after all simply left over emotions from all that had occurred in the last year. She was safe, Rose reassured herself. Rose glanced over at Terrence, Katha's new husband, and noted his tall and lanky frame, over six feet tall. He had such nice old world manners, seemed a good match for Grandma Katha.

Even with his hair white and wavy trimmed perfectly, his face clear of any facial hair; he seemed to look like one of those movie stars to Rose.

But what did she know? Rose didn't know him very well. However Grandma Katha loved him so Rose would make every effort to like him. This trip was a good start he seemed to understand how much Grandma Katha adored her family. He'd better continue to treat Grandma Katha right, or he'd answer to Rose. She glanced at them again; Grandma Katha and Grandpa Terrence still had loads of momentum. Where did those two get all their energy? Rose was tired. And people said little kids had energy; Grandma Katha and Her new Grandpa Terrence had more vitality than any child.

A family holiday they'd bounced out of bed early this morning at six o'clock and that was not a normal time to be awake, at least not for a teenager like Rose. She could hardly believe that the whole family was on holiday, for the entire month of December. No school, no books, okay so a little work at night to make up for the time off, but still a month off. That stupid teacher, now acting principal, Mrs. Brown had loaded both Carol and Rose down with a ton of homework. Mrs. Brown insisted and all the teachers from their classes complied. It was like she held it against them that Rose was now somewhat related to her.

Carol insisted that Rose read that into it; but Rose knew she was correct. Mrs. Brown didn't like that Grandma Katha had suddenly married Grandma Katha. How did she think Rose and her family felt?

Carol said she'd do some of her homework, but not all. Rose wanted to keep her A-levels, so she decided to buckle down and do some of it ahead of time. Her teachers really didn't seem to realize how important this holiday was. Rose felt burnt out. This year had been one of the worst in her life and yet everyone expected her to function the same way.

Her school work, the only thing she could control; she kept it up achieving the A's that would eventually get her to a good university. She had a plan she'd be on the honour roll every year and earn scholarships. She wouldn't be a financial burden to her mother Lily. Rose still had to do homework at night to make up for this holiday. Last night she'd stayed up until one a.m., just so she could email her homework this morning to her teachers. But the positive part, Rose didn't actually attend school for a month. Now was ahead of the game, take that Mrs. Brown.

Now nearing ten thirty a.m., Rose flagged, and the two seniors looked fresh as a daisy. It didn't seem fair. This vacation should be amusing, not tiring. A vacation in London Ontario, as well as parts of Niagara on the Lake and Niagara Falls should be fun, even in the cold beginning of December. Rose still thought it funny, that Grandpa Terrence had screwed up the bookings though. Grandpa Terrence had wanted to surprise Grandma Katha, and he booked the tickets. Then he had surprised Grandma Katha, and himself. Terrence thought he booked to London, England, but it turned out with one click on the internet and he had bought them all tickets to London, Ontario, Canada. Poor Terrence, so upset, when he found out he couldn't get his money back.

Katha said she didn't mind, they'd have a wonderful time. Grandpa Terrence went on to say he'd been to London, Ontario and stayed there before, and during the war. Rose guessed he met World War II, as he appeared too young, to have been in the First World War. He must have been really young, when he signed up though, Rose thought. Grandpa Terrence convinced by Grandma Katha, that this would be a great honeymoon trip became excited about the trip. He started adding his two cents where he wanted to go; some of his ideas a little boring. Grandma had countered that by getting him to invite Mom, Aunt Amelia, Grandma Katha, and Rose, with tickets to go on holiday.

Grandma Katha had planned a wedding for New Year's Eve in London, Ontario. That sounded romantic. But romance? They were so old, it was kind of icky! Rose's mind wasn't going to go there.

Carol had been positively jealous at first, until Grandpa Terrence announced that he'd like to bring Carol along too. He almost invited Daria as well, until he remembered the restraining order, and that pesky probation for hitting Rose. Rose had been mad enough to spit about that. How could he have forgotten? So what if Daria had worked weekends and evenings? And had done lots of her community hours? As if Rose wanted to be in the same room with her! It was bad enough she had to see her all the time now that Aunt Amelia and Daria's dad, Daniel Brown dated. Daria had injured Rose by jumping on her and beating her up.

Daria should pay! Rose now had a restraining order against Daria, but she still saw her everywhere.

Daria was lucky, Rose didn't enforce it more, thought Rose. Daria seemed disappointed and hurt that she couldn't come to the wedding. Rose felt bad about that. Ha, ha, no, she didn't, really.

However she didn't want to be mean and lord it over Daria, like Daria would have if the tables were turned; so Rose decided she'd take some nice pictures and post them on Nextagram them for her.

Wouldn't that make Rose seem kind and sweet?

Rose knew she worried about her image too much, but it was hard to combat the image of her family being a pack of black widows and if they found out she was adopted and her real mom in jail Rose would be ostracised. No one, but Carol would speak to her at school. But if she showed them how sweet and kind she was then maybe if they ever found out they stick by her? She wasn't being mean excluding Daria. Daria would have tormented Rose the whole trip. The Nextagram photos would have to do. That didn't seem mean; Daria could then see the wedding as well after all. Not that she friended her, but Carol (Rose's best friend and Daria's cousin) would share them with her if Rose posted them.

The sightseeing bus, touring the Niagara area, had been fun; she had seen a lot of sights. Niagara on the Lake yesterday was amazing and history had come alive for Rose with Fort Henry the day before that. Grandma Katha and Terrence said there wasn't enough time at the fort and they wanted to go back.

Shopping in the village square had been amazing; she had found some unusual Christmas gifts for all of her family. Today however dreary and stopping took forever. She wanted off the bus now. Rose regretted those drinks she had this morning. She began to think that two coffees, three glasses of orange juice, and two cokes, were too much to drink. If they didn't hurry up and stop, she'd explode and embarrass herself. She knew it and those cute guys she'd been eyeing would scorn her.

Come on bus, stop all ready Rose thought.

The bus came to a complete stop in front of a restaurant and rest area and Rose all but ran off the tour bus hurrying to find the bathroom. The front hall of the rest area was open and had pamphlets for people to visit the area. Off to one side was a sign that said washrooms, only the line almost filtered out the front door. There had to be another bathroom in this place. It was a rest stop after all.

Rose searched for another bathroom, and saw a door which said family washroom. This once it wouldn't hurt to use the family washroom. It wasn't like children were waiting and she couldn't wait.

Rose walked down the hall past the other washrooms and tripped over something on the floor.

Picking it up, she looked at it. It was a blue high heeled shoe in a soft suede. Where had she seen a shoe like this one? Oh, right, Betty, whom she met this yesterday on the tour bus, yesterday. Betty was what Grandma Katha called a character. Betty was petite, her eyes blue and her hair blonde and long to her waist. Betty had reminded Rose at first of a cheaper, Dolly Parton; because of the way she always over accentuated her assets. Dolly Parton was classy, but Betty though she tried couldn't achieve that standard. The odd thing though Betty turned men's heads. They always seem to revel in her looks and her soft sweet voice and abundant charm. Betty had introduced herself by saying, "Hi, I'm Betty, but most people call me, Little Betty Blue simply because I'm so small and I am forever, losing my shoes." That sounded kooky to Rose, but Lily had explained the statement when Rose told her. Apparently Betty Blue quoted an old nursery rhyme. Okay, so Rose's mother, Lily knew the rhyme big deal who read nursery rhymes to their kids today?

Betty Blue had now lost a shoe; but how can you lose your shoes and not know that you lost one?

Carol had thought Betty weird too, after all Betty was one of those obnoxious grownups, who talked a lot about themselves and excluded others. Betty had at first droned on and on about stuff that hadn't interested Carol, or Rose. Rose tuned out most of her stories during the trip, only hearing a word or two.

Betty then attempted to win them over, sharing her snacks on the bus. She had even bought cokes, and chips, for Rose and Carol at lunch yesterday. This had endeared her to Carol and Rose. Rose thought that any adult who would share their food could be that bad and Betty did smile a lot! She was like a bedraggled lost puppy that you couldn't turn away.

Come to think of it though, Rose hadn't seen Betty get back on the bus, after the last stop at the winery, or even before that. She didn't remember seeing Betty on the bus, before first thing this morning either. So how could this be Betty's shoe? It must be one that looked like hers. And where was Carol?

She was right behind Rose, a minute ago. Rose jiggled the door of the family washroom. It didn't appear locked, but the door stuck. She pushed harder on the door. The door moved an inch more.

Rose then pushed even harder, and the door seemed to give an inch. She pushed with all her strength. As she stepped around the door, she looked down at what had been blocking the door. On the floor she saw Betty Blue bloodied, a blue high heeled shoe stuck in her head through her eye.

Rose steeled herself. She wouldn't scream, she wouldn't cry! She had to get help. The murderer could still be here. She thought how can this be happening again? One murder wasn't enough for her to find?

The hall seemed to be telescoping, becoming narrow and endlessly long. Rose knew that the family washroom was much further away, than the ladies room, but it seemed she would never reach the other one and people. Rose saw what she believed to be the same endless line of women waiting for the ladies room she seen coming in. In the time she was gone, the line had gotten twice as long. She breathed a sigh of relief and choked back bile. She ran past them all headed for an empty stall to the screams of..., "Hey kid there's a line here."

"Some peoples' children are so rude."

"Oh, she's throwing up; you can excuse her."

Rose proceeded to retch and lost the contents of her stomach. Rose then took the time to pee. As she came out of the stall ashen and shaken, she found her mom waiting.

"Can I help, Rose? Are you sick? Did you eat something bad?" Lily began firing questions at her.

Carol stood beside Lily, listening in.

"Mom, Betty Blue, lost her holiday shoe," Rose whispered, clearly in shock.

"So she'll find it, or she'll have to buy a new shoe,"Lily responded puzzled.

"No, mom, you don't understand,"Rose cried raising her voice. "I did it again."

"You're correct, I don't understand. What did you do wrong, dear?" asked Lily.

"I found a dead body. Betty Blue is dead in the family washroom, down the hall," Rose explained.

"Oh, not again! Sorry, sweetie, that's not fair to you. You found a dead body and I'm saying not again."

"That's okay mom, I did find another dead person. I can't believe those words just came out of my mouth so calm."

"It will be okay, Rose," Lily reassured.

"But what do we do? We are in a different city. Emmett doesn't work here."

"Okay, here's what we will do. You will take my phone and call nine-one-one, and ask for the police," Lily instructed." I will keep people from going down the hall to the family washroom. Emmett may not work here, but people respect him. We'll find him after we make the call, and he can help. We have to keep all the people here in this building. They can't leave. They'll need to be interviewed. We will have to get someone in authority to keep them from leaving the building and driving away."

"Okay, mom," replied Rose, taking her phone and began to dial.

"Amelia, Carol, I know you overheard, so here's what I want you to do. Go find someone in charge, possibly a security guard and get them to keep everyone here." Lily demanded, "While I keep the people away from the crime scene."

"Okay, we're on it!" Amelia and Carol answered at the same time.

"Hello?" Rose stated shakily into the phone. "I'm at the Lazy Rest Stop, on the Niagara Route. I found someone dead."

"Could you repeat that Madame with your name please? We need your location and all the other details," demanded the operator.

"My name is Rose Brooksfield. I'm at the Lazy Rest Stop, on the Niagara Route. One of the passengers on our bus is dead in the family washroom," Rose stated, a little more calmly, but still shaking inside.

"Thank-you miss. May I call you Rose?" asked the police operator.

"Yes, please call me, Rose,"

"How old are you?" asked the police operator.

"I'm fourteen years old, nearly fifteen," Rose answered.

"Is there someone with you?" the operator inquired.

"Yes, of course. My mom, her boyfriend, Emmett Rogers, my aunt, my Grandma Katha, my Grandpa Terrence, and my best friend Carol are all here. Grandma Katha, Grandpa Terrence are still on the bus though."

"Okay, then that's good Rose. Now has someone secured the scene until the police can arrive?"

"My mom has secured the scene. She's the Crown attorney in Happy Valley, Ontario, way up north where we are from," Rose answered.

"Can you describe yourself to me so the officers can recognize you?"

"Okay. I'm five feet four inches tall. My hair is short chin length, in a bob, I cut my hair off two days ago and it's blonde. I have brown eyes. I'm wearing blue jeans with a blue Lady Gaga tee on my top half, and a red winter coat."

"Thank-you, Rose. The police will be there soon. They will present themselves as the Ontario Provincial Police. I'm sure you know them as the O.P.P., but the Niagara police may also respond," the operator stated. "Please stay on the line until they arrive."

"Thank-you, I will," Rose responded. "I hear the sirens now."

"That's good, you're very calm. Now can you go out and direct the officers into the scene?" asked the operator.

"I can do that." Rose stated, still talking into the cell phone.

Rose heard the sirens of police cars approaching the building, and then Rose heard footsteps in the hallway before the washrooms. Rose then saw two police officers in police hats approaching her and turned to greet them. The one was head and shoulders taller than the other although both had broad shoulders and obvious muscle mass throughout their bodies. The shorter one was just under six feet tall the other well over nearing the six foot six mark. Rose shivered a little at the sight of them she was glad she hadn't committed a crime these two were intimidating.

"Ms. Rose Brooksfield?" the taller police officer asked, "I'm Sergeant Detective George Secord and this is my partner Detective Officer Bill Tripp."

"They're here. Thank-you," Rose stated, into the phone and hung up.

"Could you tell us what happened here?"

"I found a woman dead. It's pretty gruesome," Rose commented.

"And do you know this woman?" asked Detective George Secord.

"Yes, and no," Rose replied.

Detective George Secord raised an eyebrow at this answer.

"Don't raise your eyebrow at me. I know how you police officers think; the person who finds the victim is the perpetrator. Just because my father was murdered at the end of the school year and my choir teacher was murdered at in September, doesn't mean I'm the guilty party."

"I see, your father was murdered earlier this year and your teacher in September, you've had a difficult year Miss Brooksfield," Detective George Secord commented.

"You're doing it again, implying that I did something. I met her only the day before yesterday.

My father was murdered by a serial killer, one of your own a cop and my teacher by my doctor and my principal. Can I help it if maniacs target people I know? I'm the innocent victim here I found the body and it's so gross. I think I'm going to throw up again."

Detective George Secord lifted his eyebrow again and looked so expectantly at Rose that she thought he wanted her to confess to the murder. Rose felt sick and wanted Lily. Where was Lily? What was keeping her so long?

"I remember reading about this, George. Her father was the mayor of a small town, up north somewhere and her doctor claimed he was coerced by his wife the high school principal to cut out the heart of her lover, the choir teacher," Bill Tripp recalled speaking in a strong but kind voice.

"Where do you live Peyton's Place?" Detective George Secord exclaimed looking surprised and then hiding it.

"Rude!" Rose said under her breath.

"George!" admonished Detective Officer Bill Tripp then turning to Rose he asked softly, "Could you show us the scene Ms. Brooksfield?"

"Fine if you mean the family washroom, but do I have to look?" asked Rose cooperating.

"Of course, you don't have to look Ms. Brooksfield, but if you could direct us to the scene, the other policeman will be taking statements from the people here."

Rose then directed them to the restroom.

"Do you think you could tell us what happened, Ms. Brooksfield in your own words, and then take us to the scene?" inquired Detective George Secord, "And please, tell us when you arrived here?"

"It was about ten thirty a.m. We were on the bus since we left from our motel this morning, I drank lots. We only stopped for a couple of times at the sights."

"I hope you saw some nice scenery. What were those stops, Ms. Brooksfield?" inquired Detective George Secord.

"I don't know. Some were so boring! I remember a winery and some sort of stand where they sold pies, maple candy, and food like that. Yesterday was so much more fun in Niagara on the Lake. The maple candy tasted yummy today, though," Rose answered.

"And then...?"

"We arrived here and I had to go pee so bad, all those drinks. You know?"

"I've been there," Detective Tripp replied.

"Anyway the washroom line was way too long. Looking for another washroom I found a shoe that looked like Betty's outside of it."

"How did you know it was this Betty's shoe and what does she have to do with your find?"

"I saw her shoes this morning. They were blue and sparkly and the heel was like four inches tall and very expensive. So of course I noticed them. As for what I found first? It was one of those shoes.

"Do you know her last name?" asked Detective Tripp.

"You know this woman?" demanded Detective George Secord.

"Well sort of...I told you that."

"Her name, Ms. Brooksfield, do you know her full name?" demanded Detective Sergeant Secord again.

"She introduced herself as Betty Blue; when she got on our bus the day before yesterday," Rose stated.

"We will get back to that, but for now what happened after you found the shoe?" asked Detective Tripp.

"I pushed the door and it wouldn't move. The door moved an inch. I pushed it harder and the door seemed to give. I pushed it a little harder. As I looked down at the floor and I saw Betty Blue, bloodied on the floor. A blue high heeled shoe, stuck in her head through her eye," Rose whispered her voice barely audible as she recounted what she seen.

"Thank-you Ms. Brooksfield."

"Have you been interviewing my daughter, without a parent present? Did she, or did she not, tell the operator she was fourteen years old?" asked Lily angrily coming up to the policeman.

"She's only fourteen?" Detective Tripp asked, sounding surprised and then spoiling it all by hiding a laugh.

"Emmett, I'm glad you are here. Do you believe it? They were interviewing Rose without me present," Lily complained.

"Gentlemen, I'm sure that this was a mistake. You wouldn't interview an underage girl, without her parent and you wouldn't then hold that cooperation against her," Emmett commented.

"You're correct, sir. We shouldn't have been interviewing a minor child without her parent present. I assume she's below thirteen years of age? I apologise that in our intention to get to the bottom of this we over stepped our bounds." Detective George Secord responded tartly, "And you are Mr.?"

"Sergeant Detective Emmett Rogers, Happy Valley Ontario Police department. I have no jurisdiction here, but I was happy to secure the scene for you," Emmett explained.

"I am fourteen years old." Rose admitted, "They weren't doing anything wrong."

"You told the operator you were fourteen. Did you not?" asked Detective George Secord.

"I did," Rose admitted.

"Then we are within our rights to question your daughter without you present Mrs. Brooksfield and Sergeant Detective Emmett Rogers you know we were within our rights. Now may I have your full name Mrs. Brooksfield?" Detective George Secord demanded.

"Lily Kelly-Wentworth-Brooksfield, the Crown attorney of Happy Valley," Lily answered dutifully.

"Thank-you, Madame. Where were you while your daughter found the body?"

"I waited in line for the ladies washroom with several other women," Lily answered.

"And when did any of you last see Ms. Blue?"

"Yesterday at the motel." they all say at the same time

"Which motel would this be?"

"The Niagara Barrel Hotel."

"Thank-you, Bill, please take over and get all their holiday addresses," Detective Secord declared dismissing them.

"We'll take over now Thank-you for your time Mr. Rogers... er...Sergeant Detective Rogers. We'll be in touch Ms. Brookfield if we have to follow up questions," Detective Secord stated.

"Mommy, please I want to go lie down in our motel, but the bus will go somewhere else," Rose complained.

"Don't worry we'll get a cab," Lily answered.

"I looked forward to the butterfly conservatory."

Carol replied glumly, then looking embarrassed she retorted, "But of course, I'll come back with you Rose."

"Carol, you don't have to go back with us to the motel. You could go with Grandma Katha and Terrence," Lily declared.

"Could I?"

Carol then looked at Rose and asked, "Do you mind Rose?"

"No, go! Take lots of good pictures for me, okay?"

"Let's go get that cab," Lily exclaimed.

"I'm ahead of you. I already ordered one and here it is," Emmett retorted pointing out a cab just pulling up.

Lily, Emmett and Rose then piled into the cab that took them back to the motel.

~0~

Chapter 2 - I'm on Vacation, Damn it!

Rose watched from her hotel window that overlooked the

falls. The Canadian part of the falls was visible and so was the American falls. Mesmerized by the flow of the water for a few moments Rose managed to forget about the horror she'd faced today; but even its beauty could distract her mind for long. Most of her family left in the cab; so she breathed a sigh of relief. She needed time alone to think, however what she wished most was that her mom had gone to the Butterfly Conservatory too. Instead Lily hovered.

Emmett had wanted to stay too but her mother had sent him to buy food, which should keep him busy for awhile. She loved Lily, but sometimes her mom just treated her like a little kid. Didn't she realize Rose had grown up that she didn't need or want protection? Okay, so Rose wanted defending... sometimes, but didn't Lily realize Rose needed to find her own way and to fight her own battles that needed to be waged and won?

Rose lay lounging on the bed, ready to scream in frustration. Mom just had to keep coming in, asking did Rose need anything. Was she fine? Ugh!!! Of course she wasn't fine. Rose had found another body of someone else she knew. She needed to think, or find at least find some distraction from seeing that shoe impaled in Betty Blue's head. It had brought back all the memories she thought she had discarded of Mr. Scholar's dead body. They were supposed to be forgetting all the horrible things that had happened these past months, instead now Rose found a body. She wanted to scream, shout and cry but that would alarm her mother so she held that all inside; instead turning on the television in the motel room.

Despite the images in her mind she fell asleep and before long was in the throes of the nightmare that had taken over again since her dad had been murdered. The nightmare didn't make a lot of sense. In the thrall of it she went from her age now to a small defenseless child. Everything in shadow, Rose hid behind objects as something pursued her. Rose knew she dreamt, but couldn't seem to stop what always came next...hands reaching out and grabbing her wrists and hurting her; mercifully she woke-up gasping and wiping away silent tears.

Looking around Rose thought, Good, mom hadn't heard. Rose could at least hide this from Lily's prying eyes. Thank goodness Grandma Katha, Amelia, and Carol were with Terrence on the Butterfly Conservatory trip, otherwise she'd have those people bugging her too. What did her mom think anyway? She would never be okay again. If okay meant forgetting, Rose would just have to fake it. She'd become rather good at that over the years and these murders wouldn't change that. Her mother Lily, seemed to think visiting a shrink was a cure all and Rose wasn't about to let anyone know how scared she really was even to the shrink.

Dead bodies kept turning up, was it the Kelly curse despite what Grandma said? Or was the true culprit the bad gene she carried in her own gene pool; her real mom's curse, finally showing up for her daughter? Lily, Rose's adopted mom, thought Rose didn't know any of the details of Cordelia, her biological mother's, misdeeds; but what Lily didn't realize how easy it was to get some of the details like that on the internet. Although oddly enough not a lot of information was available about the actual murder and trial afterwards.

Rose knew her mother, Cordelia had killed her pimp/drug dealer. Dad had probably used all his power to crush the story and keep it minimalized and yet Rose still knew. For Rose had been there...at least she thought she'd been there, though all her memories were now jumbled and very foggy. She remembered her mother's hair colour, a pale winter wheat colour and faded blood-shot blue eyes. Those eyes had looked on her with love even in her drug addled states.

Yes, Cordelia Kenney Brooksfield was a troubled woman, of that there was no doubt. Rose had read some of the court documents in Lily's files a year ago before she had been caught in the act. Rose had found out about her mother's childhood abuse beginning at age four at the hands of her father and uncle who were now deceased. Cordelia's brother was in jail for his part in it. The man had participated not only as a teen; but as an adult as well, in the abuse of Cordelia. Cordelia had begun to dull her senses with alcohol at ten years of age and then had graduated to other drugs. She had gone to rehab, gotten herself straightened out and had married Horace, but something in her life with Horace had triggered the slip again into drugs.

Cordelia began to openly use drugs and Horace, Rose's dad had tried to get her to go to rehab again for Rose's safety. Failing he divorced her, taking full custody of Rose. Rose had read the transcripts how Cordelia had never revealed to Horace any of her past. Rose's father had never understood how the woman he loved had slipped into this unrecognizable woman. She grew more and more secretive as she became more addicted. Horace ordered her to leave his house and sought full custody of Rose.

Cordelia started prostituting herself to get the drugs she needed. A pimp took her into his stable. Thus she spiralled into freefall, where she ended up in hospital, a suspected attempted overdose. She finally realized she could die and allowed them to send her to rehab for help. On the road to sobriety, Cordelia had refused to prostitute herself anymore. She rented an apartment and started a new life. Horace rewarded her with access to Rose and she seemed like a new person. Horace even considered taking her back.

However Cordelia's former pimp found her and took her and Rose. Cordelia had missed returning her daughter to Horace. Alarmed, Horace became worried and broke into Cordelia's apartment. Not finding either of them Horace notified the police who put out an Amber Alert for Rose.

The police officers were unable to find them simply because Cordelia's pimp kept them prisoner. Cordelia's pimp drugged her against her will, so she would service the johns he brought to her. Cordelia's pimp appeased Cordelia by bringing Rose toys and candy. He insisted Rose call him uncle. Rose felt fear and revulsion; but she didn't hesitate to call him uncle to protect herself. Despite that the man would raise his hand to her and hit her when the mood struck. Cordelia saw this and planned their escape. She waited her chance after her pimp fell asleep and they had fled but her pimp had caught up to him and she'd shot him dead.

Rose had thought Cordelia heartless and cold, after all, what kind of mom does this in front of her child? But after witnessing the result of two murders, Rose knew that Cordelia had done this to protect her child...to protect Rose. Yet Rose felt torn. Lily had protected and loved Rose more than Cordelia had ever; yet Rose still loved Cordelia.

Twenty years was a long time and that was Cordelia's sentence. She wondered if her real mom would ever see her if she went to visit again at the prison, perhaps when she was old enough? When she was twelve, Rose had tried to visit Cordelia in prison (something Lily hadn't known), but they had said she was underage and must be accompanied by a guardian. They had sent her away and told her to come back when she was an adult. Rose had at first an uneasy feeling like they had kept something from her, but she soon dismissed it as something minor. After all adults did that with anyone under eighteen.

Rose loved Lily did that make her disloyal to her real Mom? Surely her real Mom would understand. Lily was a good mother after all Cordelia had trusted Lily to be her Mother and to raise Rose. Lily could have petitioned to adopt Rose legally without Cordelia's permission, but she hadn't. She had approached Cordelia and got her to sign off on the adoption. So did that mean Cordelia loved Rose pure and simple and had put her first? She hoped that's what it meant. Surely Cordelia would understand that you could love both moms and not be disloyal.

Rose heard the hotel door open and close and knew that time had flown. Grandma Katha, Grandpa Terrence, and Carol were back.

"Rose. Grandma Katha and Grandpa Terrence, Amelia and Carol are back. They want to show you their pictures of the butterfly conservatory," Lily said through the door to the bedroom.

"I'll be right out," Rose answered.

Rose thought of Betty Blue, the woman who was murdered. Why had someone killed her? She seemed so nice. She certainly had been generous with Rose and Carol pointing out the sights, buying snacks and drinks for them. She had also been knitting baby booties. When Carol had asked why she said she would be a grandmother in March. Rose and Carol were shocked she didn't look that old but what did they know. Poor lady now she'd never see her grandchild and her poor daughter had lost her mom.

"Rose we ordered pizza . Your favourite kind. It should be here soon," Katha coaxed through the door.

Rose opened the door and went into the sitting room.

"Look at the fabulous pictures I took," Carol demanded, "I've already uploaded some to Spacebook and Nextagram."

"What about the pizza?"

"It's not here yet you have time," Carol answered.

Rose scanned through the pictures and wished she had felt well enough to go. The place looked amazing.

"That was nice that you could see the butterflies in their winter enclosure." Rose commented to Carol" You took some great pictures."

"You should have seen how big some of them were," Carol answered.

"They do seem a lot larger than the ones we've seen at home. That is if you took the pictures to scale," Rose observed.

"Look at the pictures in the garden. Aren't these flowers something?"

"Are those orchids?" Rose asked.

"Yes, see the purple ones."

"Amazing," Rose remarked and then her mouth turned upside down even though she tried to hide her disappointment.

"I am sorry you missed the floral showcase and the butterflies, Rose," Terrence said.

"Did you speak to that woman, Betty Blue, Grandpa Terrence?"

"I passed a couple of words with her but I was more interested in my honey your Great-Great-Grandmother Katha. She seemed nice enough," Terrence answered.

"She was one of those man eaters. You know the type that comes on to everything in pants." Katha sniped, "Why she even came on to you Terrence."

"Katha there are children present; is this talk appropriate for them?" asked Terrence chastising Katha "Terrence they are young woman and they need to be on the lookout for woman like that," Katha replied "If you say so, dear," Terrence retorted, willing to agree with Katha to keep the peace.

Carol said "Slut shaming" under her breath.

"What was that Carol?" asked Katha.

"Nothing, Carol answered.

"Okay," Katha said thinking she heard something Carol hadn't said.

"Ladies, she was a bit pushy. She wanted to know if I'd come out for a drink. I told her I was taken, that I was with Lily." Emmett agreed.

"Really the nerve, how dare she think she could just pick you up? Pick up any man?" Lily said angrily.

"Someone thought so. I'm sure that's why someone killed her. Don't you agree Rose?" asked Carol.

"Maybe that's the reason, but no one deserves to die. She was nice to us remember Carol?" Rose replied.

"She was nice to us. I remember her knitting baby booties? Oh, no, was she pregnant?" Carol wondered.

"She said she knitted them for her grandchild," Rose answered.

"Oh, that's so sad." Katha commented, "I'm sure the grandchild needed her."

"It is," Emmett remarked, "Those two cops on the case seem like pretty alert cops. They were really making sure none of the evidence was missed."

"You're just wishing you were on the case," Lily replied knowingly.

"I'm not. It's a different city and they don't need my help and I'm on vacation damn it," Emmett answered.

"You are on vacation and don't you forget it," Lily replied smiling and flirting with him.

"Believe me, I know it. Besides I'm doing double duty as best man in a few weeks," Emmett answered then turning from the group to Lily he said, "Maybe we can find five minutes just for us?"

"I think maybe that could be arranged." Lily answered.

"Do you want to take a tour of Ripley's Believe it or not on the strip tonight or perhaps Louis Tussaud's waxworks museum?"

"And then maybe the Movieland Wax museum?" Carol and Rose piped in simultaneously.

"Sounds like a plan Emmett right Katha, and Lily?" commented Terrence.

"It does sound good. What do you think Amelia want to see some wax figures and some world records?" Katha asked.

"I heard they have Johnny Depp in wax," Rose commented.

"That would be great," Carol answered. "Daria said I'd be so bored. Boy was she wrong."

"She's just jealous," Rose answered.

"Rose Brooksfield, don't be petty," Lily admonished.

"Seriously I just found two dead bodies and you're chastising me for speaking of the bully who tormented me. Great parenting mom," Rose answered back.

"I know Daria hurt you and we are sorry for that, Rose. She has been punished. No more talk of the troubles and recriminations; let's just have fun," Terrence said, "After all it is partially our honeymoon, Rose," then he winked at Katha.

"Sorry," Rose said not really meaning it but trying to keep the peace.

"I love you, darling!" Terrence replied.

"Oh you," Katha said. "I love you too, you old fool. Now let's eat the pizza, because that knock at the door is probably the delivery."

~0~

Chapter 3 – Waterpark Wonders

Rose sat at the table in the suite eating cereal and drinking

juice, beside Carol who had already finished.

"That was a riot last night. I mean looking at those wax figures~ so totally fun. They looked so real," Carol remarked.

"I actually got a picture with the statue that looked like Johnny Depp," Rose admitted.

"I saw that on your Nextagram and Spacebook page. Blaise commented that she was jealous."

"I also saw your Nextagram and Spacebook pic with Justin Bieber. I thought you were over him?"

"I am but I couldn't resist a pic with him," Carol answered. "That pic I took with you beside Marilyn Monroe? You looked just like her."

"You're such a liar."

"No really!"

Rose looked at her with skepticism.

"Okay so you're skinner and you weren't wearing the same clothes, but you your hair is the same length and you are as beautiful."

"That's why you're my best friend; you lie so well," Rose commented.

"Do you remember when we were standing near the Terminator wax figure?" Carol continued.

"Yes, and then Emmett jumped when that guard talked to him ....," Rose answered as they both broke into giggles.

"I like the sound of that. It's nice to hear Rose laugh after what happened," Lily said listening from the other room.

"That's exactly why Grandpa Terrence and I would like to treat and distract the girls with these," commented Katha showing Lily tickets at the same time.

"Grandma Katha, you shouldn't have," Lily protested.

"What's a Grandmother and Grandfather for if not to spoil their grandchildren," asked Katha "So is it all right if I give them these?"

"I'm sure they would love that. Please go ahead Grandma Katha," Lily stated.

Katha and Lily entered the sitting room from the bedroom.

"I'm going to meet Terrence for breakfast but Grandma Katha has something she wants to tell you. Oh and here is thirty dollars for expenses for you and Carol, Rose," Lily said.

Lily then left the room, saying goodbye to the girls; while Katha remained behind.

"I have a surprise for you two Rose and Carol. I've paid for you to enjoy all the amenities of the Water Park attached to this hotel. Let see," Katha said reading from a pamphlet, "It has sixteen extreme slides, a massive wave pool, a swirling plunge bowl, a one thousand gallon tipping bucket (whatever that is) and a beach house play area all indoors. You brought your bathing suits didn't you?"

"I didn't think I'd need it," Rose cried disappointed.

"I didn't being mine either," Carol whined.

"Then it's a good thing. I went to one of the stores nearby. Lily thought they were Christmas gifts and I guess they are, but early ones. I hope the bikinis fit because they can't be returned!" Katha said, holding up a bag and pulling out two bikinis, one blue and one pink bikini.

"The pink one is yours Carol, the blue yours, Rose."

"Grandma Katha you're the best!" They both replied simultaneously.

"You're both my granddaughters now and Grandma's spoil their grandchildren," Katha responded.

"Now you two have fun, but don't you leave the waterpark unless you go to back to your room. The adults will visit what you two girls called the musty old fort in Niagara on the Lake. We should be back by five p.m.

"I wanted to see the fort, but the waterpark sounds awesome," Rose replied.

"Oh, I almost forgot here's fifty dollars for you and Carol. Here. Now don't tell your mom I gave you this," Terrence said.

Katha then left the room for a moment to grab her coat, coming back she saw Terrence handing over money to the girls. She pretended not to notice but it made her smile. The old fool had a lot of love in him for her family already.

"Oh and if you have to call us; just call my cell. Bye! Have fun girls," Katha said while looking at her watch, "The bus waits for us with Amelia, Terrence, Lily and Emmett so I'm off."

Carol and Rose soon walked over to the waterpark. Entering the big facility they went quickly to the change room and donned their bikinis.

"Wow, your great-grandmother is so cool," Carol said, "and she's making Great-Grandpa Terence so much more accessible."

"She's your great-grandmother too now!" Rose exclaimed, "We're not just friends now, were family. This is so cool."

"I'm so excited about the wedding. We get to be bridesmaids. Grandma Katha has exquisite taste. We'll probably get fabulous dresses out of this," Carol replied.

"I hope Grandma Katha lets us pick the dresses she didn't do so badly on the bikinis, but dresses? I'd rather try it on and pick my own out."

"Look at this bikini it is so sweet," Rose replied, "And in my favourite colour."

"This is my favourite colour too! How did Grandma Katha know?" asked Carol.

"Gee, I don't know you're always wearing pink?" Rose said sarcastically then laughed to take out the sting which made Carol start laughing too.

"With these bathing suits get lots of guys will look at our hotness," Carol commented.

"I wish I had a one piece. I hate my bust line," Rose said now uncertain.

"Rose it's okay if people look at you. Quit crossing your arms in front of yourself. You have to quit covering up your figure. You aren't asking for anything by what you wear. We, as women, have the right to wear anything we want to. You're not your birth mother."

Rose just wanted Carol to stop talking. Carol received the hint given by the raising of Rose's eyebrow and dropped it.

Carol and Rose then entered the main facility and stared at the waterpark trying to decide where to go next. A young woman with long brown hair to her waist struck a model pose in her barely there bikini near the waterslide. All the male's eyes seemed drawn to her. Carol and Rose gave the woman a disparaging look then started talking about other things.

"Do you think those cute guys on the bus two days ago might be there?" asked Rose.

"Which ones?" Carol enquired.

"The twins Pierre and Michel Charbonneau. Weren't they cute with their stunning blue eyes and blonde hair? And they so tall! Do you think they're close to our age?" asked Rose.

"Michel said they were from Quebec City, Quebec."

"Really? I hope they do show up."

"Michel said he was fourteen years old like us. He also told me that Niagara Falls is puny compared to the Montmorency Falls in Quebec," Carol continued.

"You liked this guy after he thought Niagara Falls puny? He sounds a bit of a braggart," Rose replied.

"No, I accessed the internet on my phone and he told the truth his falls in Quebec are taller," Carol stated.

"So you like him, huh?" Rose asked.

"I just met him maybe?" Carol replied.

"Can you tell them apart?" asked Rose.

"Yes. Michel has a small scar over his mouth if you look close," Carol answered.

"And you looked really close," Rose commented, laughing.

"If you weren't my friend...," Carol replied.

"What about the other guys on the bus? They were older, but cute."

"Nick was so cute. Did you see how his jeans moulded to his butt?" Carol remarked, "And tall he's what six feet three inches. Swoon!"

"Carol!" admonished Rose, "You're objectifying him!"

"Where did you hear that from Aunt Amelia, or Grandma Katha?"

"Grandma Katha!" admitted Rose laughing.

"Well as long as he doesn't hear me. I'm going to objectify him," Carol laughed.

"You are so bad!" Rose laughed again as they entered the waterfall area.

"He's pretty cute too. Do you think he's Nick's brother Gabe?" Rose asked Carol.

"Who do you two speak of?" asked the girl that all the men's eyes had been drawn too.

What a nerve! Why did this girl think she could sneak up on Carol and Rose spy on them and interrupt their conversation?

Rose glared at her, but Carol seemed enthralled and smiled at her making the girl think it okay to continue to speak to them, "I'm Louise Moore also known as Lou."

"I'm very pleased to meet you. I'm Carol Banks and this is Rose Brooksfield, my best friend."

"You were on the tour bus," Louise stated.

"Yes, we were and those guys over there were too," Carol commented.

"Oh, so that's who you were talking about. They are cute. That is if you like them young," said Louise.

"What do you mean young? How old are you?" asked Carol.

"I'm seventeen, but my boyfriend is much older. He's always busy so I think it's only fair that I get to hang out with kids my own age. Of course he doesn't like me speaking about him. But if I happen to ogle somebody, so what!" Louise said, "Oh, there's my friend Michel Charbonneau; see you two later."

Then Louise ran up to Michel and greeted him by kissing Michel passionately.

"She is a strange girl." Carol commented, "Did you see the way she greeted Michel like she wanted to devour him?"

"Yes, I did. Yuck! She did so in public too. What the heck did she say about dating an older man, and then acted like she didn't by kissing Michel? Like we really care what she does! We just met her," Rose said bitterly.

"Let's forget that weird girl. I'd rather focus on the view. Those guys are cute," Carol said fanning herself and looking at the guys again, "They sure are tall in that family. He must be six feet as well. And their hair is sexy as hell. I love the way it waves just so and sits perfectly on their heads."

"That's called hair gel, stupid. But I do like their short hair," Rose admitted.

"Let's stop talking about them before they hear us," giggled Carol.

Rose noticed some young men across the room staring at them. Where had she seen them before? Oh, yes, the bus they had sat at the back of the boss whispering about everyone on the bus. Rose had heard his hateful comments about her bulky coat and sweater. She was a thin body type didn't they understand you had to dress for the cold? Men!! Carol pulled Rose until they were mere feet away from them. The teenage boy, Gabriel Gauthier stared at Rose in a way, which made Rose felt uncomfortable.

"What, or should I say who do you stare at bro?" asked Nick.

"Do you see the girl in the blue bikini?" enquired Gabe.

"Do you speak about the girl in the pink bikini? Yes, she's hot. Dibs bro," commented Nick.

Rose thought what a pig. He divided them up like they were things.

"You shouldn't talk about her that way. You shouldn't talk about any woman that way! It's sexist and derogatory. But she is beautiful. Her name is Rose. I spoke to her on the bus. She's really sweet, too," Gabe replied.

He knew her name? And he wasn't a pig after all. He defended her, called her beautiful and sweet. She wasn't so sure about his brother, however.

"Her name is Rose? I thought that was the girl in the blue one?" Nick asked puzzled.

"Oh, you like the girl in the pink? I was talking about the girl in the blue. But if you like Carol, then you had better smarten up and treat her correctly and with respect. You know what mother says," Gabe replied.

"Be respectful, treat a woman as you'd like to be treated. Remember they have feelings thoughts and they may not coincide with yours," Nick parroted in a weird voice.

"Duh!" commented Gabe poking his brother's shoulder playfully, "The girl you're talking about is Carol. I think they might be cousins, or something."

"Oh, okay, thank-you bro. Do you think I should go over there?"

"In a little while. There's a guy talking to Teri. Do you think she is safe with him? She's only fifteen years old," Gabe said watching Terri standing near Pierre.

"For now, but we should watch him. He better not hurt our little sister, or he'll be sorry," threatened Nick.

"Don't look now, but that other guy is also after one of our sisters. This time it's Erin," Gabe said.

"Where?' asked Nick his eyes narrowing.

"There. Don't worry you know Erin can handle herself. I think his name is George Moore. He was on the bus too. He's Dad's opponent's son," Gabe said, "Did you see his sister Louise. That girl is hot!"

"She's hot, but definitely trouble. That girl is so overly aggressive. She doesn't appeal to me," Nick answered.

"Yes, I can see that. Even if you got her in bed she'd be stalking your every moment, while kissing every guy around."

"I'd like a girl who doesn't cheat."

"Most of the kids who were on that the tour bus are here. You don't think any of them had anything to do with that murder do you?"

"Wasn't that weird, that chick dying? I heard the cop say she had shoe through her eye," Nick stated.

"I thought that cop would never let us go back to our hotel," Gabe complained.

"I still wonder who killed her. It must have been someone who knew her," Nick commented.

"One of those two girls, Carol and Rose found her, but I don't know which one," Gabe retorted, "You don't think they did it do you?"

"No, those girls are so nice and would never commit a crime. I feel sorry for them it must have been horrific discovering the body."

"Yah, if anyone did it. It was probably Louise."

"You don't believe that do you?"

"No, it was probably not someone on the bus. Some strange weirdo killed her. Not someone we know"

"You better keep an eye out for Dad, because if he sees anyone talking to our sisters, he'll go off on them and then us."

Rose watched as an older man about forty-five years old with dark brown hair and eyes about five feet seven inches tall, came over to the slide area. Spotting Louise with Michel Charbonneau he looked angry.

"Why the hell do you think it's okay to wear that tiny bikini, Louise?" shouted the man.

"Really, Alfred, you're not my dad! Mommy bought it for me. What do you want me to do find a swim suit from the twenties?" Louise asked flippantly, "Besides you know you love it."

Louise twirled around and throwing out her ample chest and struck a pose.

"Where's Charlene? You told your father you'd hang out with Charlene and Madeline," asked Alfred grabbing her arm and shaking her.

Rose wondered if she should intervene, but fear of this man held her back.

"Hey, you're hurting me. Please let me go. Charlene is over there with Pierre. See!" Louise said as he dragged her over to Charlene.

"Charlene, you get away from that boy. I should never have allowed her to keep company with the likes of you," Alfred menaced, grabbing her with his other arm while still holding Louise with the other.

"Daddy, I'm just having fun. Please don't do this! Please go away," Charlene begged struggling.

"You will not talk to me that way! And who are you boy? Get lost and stay away from my daughter. Go defile someone else's daughter," Alfred Getts yelled angrily.

Alfred dragged his daughter and Louise off through the pool area while Louise smirked.

"Daddy, please I'm begging you. Please, you're embarrassing me," Charlene stated.

"I'll do more than embarrass you if you don't march yourself to our hotel room and get changed," Alfred commanded.

"Charlene don't struggle. It will just get worse he's on one of his power trips." Louise whispered, (but Rose overheard).

Rose looked on in shock as Alfred's hand strayed across her hip and touched seemingly by chance, but Rose knew it was no accident. Rose felt odd about what she watched. There was a strange under current between Louise and this man. Could Charlene's father be Louise's boyfriend? No, it wasn't possible! An old man with a seventeen year old girl and yet it did happen. Rose didn't trust that man. Rose decided to move herself and Carol away from the action, but where they could still watch in safety. Even if he fathered Charlene, he hurt her and no one stopped him. Should Rose be stepping in? No, he could hurt her if she did. Where was the security in this place anyway?

"Ooh, Al was that on purpose?" Louise asked, seductively.

"Enough of that talk Louise. You will not talk like that to me. Do you understand?" Alfred replied.

"I call them like I see them and you were hot for me," Louise answered wiping her tongue across her teeth and lips seductively.

"Do not including me in your fantasies, Louise, or your Dad will hear from me," Alfred angrily, replied menacingly as he removed her hand from his chest and took both girls to the change room. In you go both of you and don't take longer than fifteen minutes," he commanded.

Fifteen minutes they were all dressed in winter clothing he marched both girls out of the waterpark. Rose listened from some distance away as the two boys talked.

"Woo, thank goodness he wasn't our Dad. What a mean guy," Gabe commented, "That guy ogled Louise and he touched her hip. Weirdo! Doesn't he work for her Dad?"

"Yes, he does work for her father. I think the touch was an accident." Nick commented, watching Carol go down the waterslide.

"That's not what she said. I'm going over to say hello to that girl Rose. Keep an eye on Terri and Erin," Gabe responded.

"They'll be fine. I want to say hello to Carol," Nick answered.

"As long as our sisters don't leave the Water Park we can do that," Gabe replied, "Let's go say hello to the girls and get to know them better."

Gabe and Nick then walked over to Rose and Carol who had just walked out of the pool after going down the waterslide.

"So ...er... Hi. Cute bikini," Gabe mumbled nervously.

"Hi it's Gabriel right." Rose answered smiling.

"Just call me Gabe." Gabe retorted getting more confident, "And this is my brother Nick."

"Oh hi, Nick!" Rose responded then seeing his gaze zeroing on Carol she responded saying, "And this is my friend, Carol."

"Hello, Carol. Say do you want to go somewhere get a coffee something to eat?" Nick asked.

"I'd like that but we're not to leave the Water Park except to go to our hotel room and we're not allowed to have anyone in our hotel room," Carol answered.

"Let's just go Carol," Rose responded, "It would hurt to go for a drink, or coffee with these guys; as long as we didn't go far."

Rose then smiled at Gabe, who smiled back.

"Would you excuse us for a moment guys?" Carol demanded pulling Rose aside.

Carol then grabbed Rose's arm and pulled her a few feet away.

"What just happened there? Who are you and what have you done with my best friend Rose?" Carol whispered.

"I like Gabe and I want to spend time with him. Don't you like Nick?" Rose whispered back.

"Yes, Nick's okay .alright then let's not question this lets just have fun."

Rose took Carol's arm and off they went.

~0~

Chapter 4 - Questions, Questions!!

Katha, Terrence, Lily, Amelia, and Emmett arrived back

at the hotel early, after their tour bus had broken down for the second time that morning.

"What kind of tour did I sign up for? I'm sorry all, I thought the tour firm reliable. They had a four star rating out of five."

"How were you to know Terrence?" Katha commented.

"You have to take my part, Katha, you married me."

"And don't forget that old man. I saw how those ladies were eyeing you."

"What women?"

"Smart move, Grandpa Terrence," Lily whispered.

"It's only three p.m. and we didn't even get to see the fort," Terrence complained.

"I hope at least Carol and Rose can have some fun," Lily commented.

"I would rather have looked at Niagara Falls, anyway," Emmett griped.

"You didn't have to come at all Emmett," Lily said angrily.

"What have you two been bickering about all day? Katha asked, "Maybe you too should go off by yourselves and settle this."

"Sorry, Katha; it's not Lily's fault. I've been grumpy all day because I might have to go back for a couple days to Happy Valley. It seems that quite few cops are down with the flu."

"Oh, Emmett, I'm sorry I've been cross too. I felt guilty for having fun with you when my daughter witnessed another murder. I felt I should have been with her."

"Let's start the day over again. I heard that the Maple Leafs play the Montreal Canadiens tonight in Toronto. We could take the train there or rent a car. I can get tickets on the net now for everyone. My treat, of course," Emmett answered.

"No, you guys should go. Why don't you have supper in Toronto? We ladies can find something to do and have our own fun," Lily commented.

"I agree. Terrence needs some time to relax and he's a huge fan."

"Are you sure Carol and Rose would like to see a hockey game?" asked Terrence.

"You can ask them but I don't know if Rose or Carol are really interested in hockey," Lily commented, "Use my computer. It's right there."

"Thank-you Lily," Emmett said opening the computer and going to the website, "Score. Two prime tickets for the game tonight. I can get two more if the girls decide to go."

His triumph was interrupted by a loud knock on the hotel room door. Lily opened to admit Sergeant Detective George Secord and Officer Bill Tripp.

"Hello gentlemen. Please do come in. Have you news?" Lily asked.

"Oh good," remarked Officer Bill Tripp scanning the room and not answering Lily's question, "Most of you are here."

"Sorry, our girls aren't here. Rose and Carol are next door in the Water Park. Those poor kids needed some fun after yesterday's horror," Katha admitted.

"I understand it this is the first time Rose found a body," Sergeant Detective George Secord stated.

"So she found a body what of it?" Amelia asked defensively, "So have I."

"Do you insinuate my daughter had something to do with this woman's murder? Rose just met her," Lily asked angrily.

"No, Madame...er madams, we were just thinking it must be hard on a child to find one body, let alone two," Sergeant Detective George Secord interjected.

"It has been hard on her, that's why we sent her to the waterpark with her friend," Katha repeated annoyed.

"They just do their job, ladies. I'm sure they know that a child wasn't responsible. The trajectory had to be wrong, from the angle I saw. Rose is not tall enough, or strong enough to have killed her," Emmett stated trying to soothe the waters.

"Actually we have determined that your bus had not even reached the way station before the murder happened," Officer Bill Tripp answered.

"That doesn't make any sense. Betty Blue was on the bus earlier," Lily commented then turning to Grandma Katha she asked, "Was she still on the bus before we got to the rest stop Grandma Katha?"

"I don't remember seeing her after the wine stop, or maybe just before that," Katha replied sounding confused.

"You know none of us did it; so why are you here then?" Terrence asked, slightly annoyed.

"We need any background on the victim you can give us. It seems the victim travelled using an assumed name," Sergeant Detective George Secord announced.

"She was an American. How could she have gotten across the border without passport in this day and age?" Emmett asked, "The Canadian and American border guards are very thorough."

"We aren't aware of what day she came across the border. She must have assumed the name, Betty Blue after her trip across the border," Officer Bill Tripp answered.

"Did any of you talk to the victim?" asks Sergeant Detective George Secord.

"I believe we all did at one point or another. Terrence admitted, "We already told you that she had confided in Katha that she expected a grandchild by her daughter. Both Katha and I told her they were good thing and how lucky we were to know have more blessings from our civil union then we could count."

"I understand you were just married. Congratulations! Did she mention the name of this daughter? Or the age and whereabouts of her daughter?" asked Officer Bill Tripp taking notes.

"If she did say the name, I can't recall. Do you remember Katha?" Terrence asked.

"I think she said something like Betty. Was it Belle, or Bette?" Katha recalled.

"It was Bette. She said that to me too," Amelia agreed.

"So she said her daughter's name was Bette?" Sergeant Detective George Secord demanded to know.

"Yes, I am sure," Amelia stated.

"Okay this is very helpful. Did she give a last name?" Sergeant Detective George Secord inquired.

"No, sorry I never heard one," Amelia answered.

"Neither did I. Did you Katha?" asked Terrence turning to her.

"No, I didn't. Did she say anything to you Lily?" asked Katha.

"She told me she was from upstate New York and that she came across at Niagara Falls, New York," Lily remembered.

"That was a huge help, Mrs. Brooksfield. I'm sure we can now go back and try to find out from the border patrol who fit her description," Officer Bill Tripp commented.

"The children maybe unaware that they have information, do you think we could interrupt the children's fun for a short time to interview them?" asked Sergeant Detective George Secord.

"I don't think that would be a problem provided Emmett and I are present." Lily answered, then turning to Amelia, Katha and Terrence she said, "We'll be right back. Emmett can ask Rose and Carol if they'd like to go to the hockey game while he's there."

Emmett and Lily then left followed by the two police officers and went next door to the waterpark. Searching frantically for Rose and Carol they cannot see them.

"Do you think they've been kidnapped?" Lily asked, hysterically.

"Lily don't jump conclusions. Maybe she's in the change rooms? Why don't you go check?" Emmett reassured.

Lily entered the change rooms coming back a few minutes later agitated, "They are not there. Where can they be? What do I tell Francine? She trusted me with Carol and after the kidnapping too! You don't think they've been kidnapped do you?"

"We'll find her. She probably went somewhere and forgot to tell us," Emmett soothed.

"She was told to stay here!" Lily objected.

"She probably decided while the birds away the mice will play," Emmett pacified.

"She wouldn't do that she's a great kid. She's never any trouble."

"There's always a first time, Madame. She's a teenager," Sergeant Detective George Secord admitted.

"Would you like me to call this in Mrs. Brooksfield or just check around see if we can find them? They are material witnesses to this murder investigation," Officer Bill Tripp stated.

"I'm responsible for both girls. Her mother trusted me to keep Carol safe and she even let her stay after Rose found the body. We have to find them, safe and sound. You better call this in. Better safe, than sorry," Lily said.

"We have two kids missing, two fifteen year old girls, five feet-five and five foot-four respectfully. One blonde blue eyed, one brunette blue eyed. No wants, no warrants. Tell them not to approach them, just radio me when you find them. Thank-you, Karen," Bill said into his walkie-talkie.

"Thank-you. We really appreciate all your help," Emmett said holding out his hand which Bill shook.

Emmett and Lily then returned to the hotel room where Katha, Terence and Amelia waited with Officer Bill Tripp and Sergeant Detective George Secord following behind them. As they entered the room crackling came over Officer Bill Tripp's shoulder mounted walkie-talkie.

"Tripp here!" Bill answered pushing the button.

"Tripp, we have located two females approximate age. One wearing pink sweater, one wearing a blue sweater, both wearing jeans in the Hard Rock Cafe with two young males," Tripp's radio voice said.

"Thank-you Karen. Can you keep this unofficial?"

"Can do," Karen answered.

"Tripp out," Officer Bill Tripp stated, then turning to Lily he said "You heard? We're off to the Hard Rock Cafe."

Sergeant Detective George Secord commented looking at Lily's angry face, "Sounds like two young ladies will be punished for going off from the hotel."

"Yes, they will be grounded." Lily admitted," Emmett, can you stay you here in case they return?"

"Sure, good luck Lily, don't be too hard on her," Emmett cautioned.

Sergeant Detective George Secord and Officer Bill Tripp marched with Lily, Katha, and Amelia and Terrence, to the Hard Rock Cafe.

~0~

The Hard Rock Cafe a short time ago

"**U**nbelievable Rose! I thought that man named Al had escorted Louise to her hotel room, but there she is," Carol exclaimed.

"Whoa, who is that guy sitting with her? He's what in his thirties?" Rose retorted.

"More like in his forties," Carol stated.

"He must be her father. Or her father's friend," Rose answered.

"Yes, that's probably it," Carol replied.

"He's leaving," Rose commented.

"Yes, and he looks a little angry," Carol commented.

"She's leaving too but she went the other way."

"Why are we wasting time talking about her?" Carol asked.

"I don't know. Gabe and Nick are cute. We should be talking about them," Rose said and then giggled.

"But then they'd come back from the washroom and know we were talking about them," Carol stated and started laughing.

Gabe came back and sat down followed by Nick.

"I see you were having a good time without us," Nick said.

"We talked about Louise. She sat over there," Rose admitted.

"Where?" asked Nick.

"That wasn't nice to laugh at Louise. She's had a hard life," Gabe commented.

Carol rolled her eyes and then said, "Good grief what kind of people do you think Rose and I are? We were not making fun of her. Yes, we noticed her; but our laughter was just being happy."

"Sorry, I jumped to conclusions. I just feel sorry for her, you know?"

"I understand that," Rose stated.

"I met that lady that was killed," Gabe said changing the subject, as he drank his coffee the waiter placed in front of him.

"We all did. We were all on the bus," Rose commented.

"She spoke to me too. She said she came to meet her boyfriend. She told me that her boyfriend was married," Carol interjected at the same time.

"Her boyfriend was married, but she said he was the father of her daughters," Rose commented.

"She told me she had one daughter, just a little older than me who was pregnant. She said her daughter would have a baby in March. She knitted booties for it," Gabe replied.

"She kept telling me that her boyfriend (whom she showed me a picture of) was handsome and that he was once young like me. How old do you think the guy was fifty years old?" Nick asked, "I thought she didn't look anywhere near fifty didn't she?"

"No, I don't think she was fifty probably closer to forty years old but she might have had Botox. She told me her daughter that was pregnant was Bette. I think she said the other daughter's name was Bella. Bella, close to my age stayed with her grandmother in...Was it California? Hmm, I wonder who the man she wanted to meet was? I'm speaking of her boyfriend. Do you think he was on the bus?" Carol asked.

"Oh, those poor girls! It's awful to lose a parent. If he was on the bus originally, do you think he murdered her?" asked Rose, "Like Dr. Thomas' wife did?"

"A lot of these killings are to do with personal anger," Carol said knowingly.

"How do you know so much Carol?" Gabe asked.

"We've had some experience with murder."

"Do tell us, when?" Nick asked.

"I don't want to talk about this Carol. I can't understand why you'd want to after what happened with Doctor Thomas."

"Who's Doctor Thomas?" inquired Gabe and Nick, both at the same time.

"Rose and I found our choir teacher, Mr. Scholar murdered at the beginning of the school year," Carol admitted, "Dr. Thomas and his wife (our principal) were responsible for his demise."

"You didn't find him. You were in the same room, and you didn't even see his dead body." Rose protested, "I did!"

"I was the one who was kidnapped by the killer and her husband," Carol complained.

"I was still ill from the appendicitis," Rose complained.

"You were kidnapped?" Gabe asked.

"Wow, sounds fascinating so you've found two bodies Rose. What are you a corpse magnet?" Nick asked insensitively.

"I think we should go now Carol," Rose replied stiffly.

"Nick, that's a little harsh, don't you think?" Gabe protested to Nick then turned to Rose and said, "Excuse my brother. He opens his mouth and inserts his foot. Please stay a little longer."

Gabe then elbowed Nick in the side. Nick responded by saying, "Sorry Rose. Actually that must have been terrifying."

"It was, but I think I was more terrified when they had Carol and my Aunt Amelia. I was afraid I'd never see either of them again," Rose answered.

"So how did you get away Carol?" asked Nick.

"My father's an electrician. So when they locked us in a room, I triggered the lock by connecting the right wires and broke us out; unfortunately those two nut jobs were waiting for us," Carol explained.

"So then what happened?" asked Gabe.

"Well...," began Carol, but then seeing Lily and the two police officers she said to Rose, "Oh, dear; I think were in big trouble, Rose."

"Why did they have to find us?" Rose asked.

"Your mother looks mad," Carol stated.

"I'm sorry Rose. It seems we've gotten you in trouble. Is it because you're with us?" asked Gabe, "Can we do anything to smooth this over? She won't beat you will she?"

"Beat me? My mom? She has never laid a hand on me. I'll just get punished by being grounded or something. She'll probably ban us from watching television and using the computer. Does your mom or dad beat you?" asked Rose shocked.

"Where would you get a silly idea like that?" denied Nick.

"Mom and dad have never lifted a hand to me. Right, Gabe?" Nick said playfully poking Gabe in the ribs to make him agree.

Gabe grimaced then said, "Yes right."

"Rose Cheryl-Lynn Brooksfield." Lily said in a chillingly quiet voice," I like to speak to you and Carol. That is if you can pull yourself away from these young men, for a moment."

"I hope to see you again Gabe. It was a nice afternoon," Rose said before going to her mother.

"I enjoyed the afternoon too. See you tomorrow Rose on the bus," Gabe said as they walked further way.

'Goodbye Nick! I have to go but it was fun," Carol yelled.

"Yes I had fun too. Are you sure all is okay?" Nick asked looking at Lily.

"Lily is very fair. I'm not worried," Carol answered.

"Okay, then see you tomorrow on the bus. Goodbye Carol," Nick said walking over and kissing her on the lips.

"You take liberties, young man," Katha said angrily.

"Aw, sorry?" Nick said.

"You will be if you ever pull a stunt like this again," Katha sniped.

"I'm not sorry I kissed you Carol," Nick exclaimed.

"I hope to see you later, but I may have to finagle it," Carol answered whispering.

"See you later then," Nick replied.

Katha took Carol and Rose arms pulling them over to Lily. Lily then steered them all to another table further over in the corner, where the two policemen waited.

"We will talk about this rules infraction and your punishment later, but right now Sergeant Detective George Secord and Officer Bill Tripp would like to ask you some information about Ms. Blue," Lily explained.

"Hello, Sergeant Detective Secord, Officer Tripp. I'd like to apologize for you having to come and find us I'm sure that's how you found us Mom?" Rose stated.

"Carol and I will tell you anything hare any information we know about Ms. Blue."

"Thank-you, we'd appreciate that. So do either of you know Ms. Blue's real name?" asked Sergeant Detective Secord.

"Betty Blue wasn't her real name?" asked Rose surprised.

"You're so gullible. As if someone's name would be Betty Blue," Carol exclaimed which then earned her a dirty look from Rose.

"But Betty was her real first name. She answered to it and turned her head when called that," noted Rose.

"Thank-you Ms. Banks. That was extremely helpful. So you believe her real first name was Betty," Officer Bill Tripp enquired.

"Do either of you know anything more about her? Did she confide any information about herself to either of you?" asked Sergeant Detective Secord.

"We talked to her about boys and we discovered a few things." admits Rose "She had two daughters Bette and what was that other name Carol?"

"Bella that was the name I heard. She's our age," answered Carol, "She's at her grandmother in California."

"She said that?" asked Officer Bill Tripp.

"Yes," both Carol and Rose say and nodded.

"Anything else you remember her saying ladies? Anything you could remember may assist us in identifying the woman and finding her killer," Sergeant Detective Secord commented, "Maybe she said more about the place in California?

"I don't think I ever heard here say where in California," Rose answered.

"You know I do remember her mentioning a place in California. What was that place?" Lily answered, struggled to remember.

"Oh, I think I remember that now too. She talked about wineries in the Napa Valley. She said her friend was a housekeeper at one, but that she was moving to another state," Carol replied.

"I don't remember that," Rose said, "And I have a really good memory."

"I believe you were snoring...er sleeping Rose, during the conversation," Carol answered, apologetically.

"I was not. I don't snore or sleep on buses," Rose retorted then she turned to Sergeant Detective Secord and said," She said would meet her boyfriend and he was married. Do you think he was on the bus?"

"Thank-you ladies that will be all," Sergeant Detective Secord replied not answering and stood up as if to leave.

"Thank-you officers," thanked Lily.

Rose could hold back no longer she lit into Lily in whispered, "Thank-you for embarrassing me in front of Gabe and Nick. Good grief we were innocently having fun. Do you have to track my every move? I wish you'd never adopted me."

"I want to go home," Carol complained.

"Do you have any idea how lucky the two of you are? You, Carol got to go with your great-grandfather, me because of his lady here Lily Wentworth Brooksfield. She promised your mother she would take care of you. Your mother seems to think I'm a doddering old man who can't look after a fish," Terrence claimed in an eerily quiet voice, and then paused for a breath, "And you, Rose this lady adopted you. She loves you like you were her own flesh and blood and how do the two of you repay her? You break the rule, the one thing she asks you to do. Stay in the hotel complex. Did you think to leave a message where you were?"

"What is it to you? You're my great-grandfather but I barely ever see you. You were always too busy deciding other people's fates," Carol complained.

"I care. I love you Carol. I know I've neglected to spend time with you when I should have, I had hoped to make that up to you. Do you know how many teenagers go missing? I've heard many cases on the bench where they went missing and were murdered. I even have a friend who lost their child and have no idea where she is. These criminals just wait until you defy your parents to grab you. The parents and their families are devastated, broken forever," Terrence said sadly.

"I'm sorry," both Rose and Carol said simultaneously.

"You worried all those who love you here. So that two policemen had to find you. Please, don't do that again," cautioned Terrence.

"Where's Emmett? Is he mad at me too?" Rose asked looking around.

"Emmett and Grandpa Terrence were going to offer to take you to a hockey game in Toronto," Lily commented as she's interrupted by Carol.

"Really, cool! We get to go to a hockey game Rose," Carol blurted.

"No, we don't," Rose explained realizing what her mom meant.

"We don't? Are you sure?" Carol asked puzzled.

"Carol, you and Rose are grounded. That means neither of you get to go to a hockey game. You aren't to leave the hotel room unless you're with me," Lily explained and then she continued, "You had me worried. Once a long time ago, someone else I loved went missing. I couldn't bear it if that had happened to either of you."

"Emmett and Grandpa Terrence were going to offer to take you to a hockey game in Toronto," Lily commented as she's interrupted by Carol.

"Really, cool! We get to go to a hockey game Rose," Carol blurted.

"No, we don't," Rose explained realizing what her mom meant.

"We don't? Are you sure?" Carol asked puzzled.

"Carol, you and Rose are grounded. That means neither of you get to go to a hockey game. You aren't to leave the hotel room unless you're with me," Lily explained and then she continued, "You had me worried. Once a long time ago, someone else I loved went missing. I couldn't bear it if that had happened to either of you."

"I'm sorry, Mom. I'm sorry, I worried you. I'm so sorry I said I wished you hadn't adopted me. Forgive me, please," Rose pleaded.

"I know you are sorry, now. I was young once too believe it or not. I know it's nice to spend time with young men, but you don't even know these young men and I had no idea where either of you were," Lily stated.

"I'm sorry too, Mrs. Brooksfield," Carol said contritely.

"Okay, let's get back to the hotel and have some dinner with Amelia and Grandma Katha. We will decide if any further punishment is required," Lily stated.

"You were right. Your mom is pretty cool. The punishment was deserved, but it won't be too bad. Will it?" Carol whispered, but Lily heard and hid a smile.

"Bad enough that it's a punishment," Rose exclaimed.

"I should never have listened to you, but if I hadn't I would never have met Nick," Carol commented.

"I hope they were worth it," Rose exclaimed.

~0~

Chapter 5 - Grounded

The next morning

Rose sat staring at a television with Carol beside her on the bed. Katha sat in a corner of the room knitting.

"This is so, so boring, sitting around here watching television and staring at four walls," Rose complained loudly.

"It's such a beautiful day out there and we're stuck inside," Carol complained.

"It is child abuse that's what it is," Rose complained.

"You my dears, are very lucky Lily didn't give you a worse punishment. She could have taken away the television privileges too. I would have," Katha said pointedly while looking up from her knitting, "It's pouring cats and dogs anyway."

"It's not snowing that makes it a beautiful day. We don't need a babysitter, Grandma Katha. You could have gone with Mom, Emmett and Grandpa Terrence." Rose insisted.

"Actually it's obvious you do. You two were totally irresponsible yesterday. Lily worried out of her mind searched for you. Terrence, Emmett and I were worried too. Did either of you give a thought to how anxious we'd be?" Grandma Katha

"You were worried?" both Carol and Rose queried seeming surprised.

"Of course, I was worried. A woman was murdered from our tour bus and my great-grandchildren were both missing." Katha says "And you Rose, you should have known better, your mother had every right to be worried considering how her mother went missing when she was young."

"I'd forgotten about that Grandma Katha."

"Huh?"

"My mother doesn't talk about this ever; so you can't talk about it either," Rose whispered.

"I won't just tell me."

"When my mom was nine, she lived in Prague with my grandfather, Peter Kelly who was some kind of attaché or something."

"I've wanted to ask you about that. Your grandparents both had the same last name aren't you worried your mother was interbred?"

"Your mind would go there. You're disgusting Carol," Rose responded.

"I'm sorry. It just popped into my mind and wouldn't let go."

"For your information Carol, my grandfather changed his name in his teens from Kirally to Kelly because he wanted to join the civil service."

"What's wrong with Kirally?"

"I don't know he just changed it. Okay?"

"So tell me your mother's story," Carol insisted.

"Her dad had to be early to the Embassy so her mother drove her to school. She dropped her off at school and the car was found hours later full of blood. Grandmother Heather disappeared never to be seen again," Rose explained.

"Oh, no, your poor mother."

"Your mother has had a lot of great losses. She also lost your Dad this year as well." Grandma Katha added, "But I don't think she'd appreciate you discussing her business."

"Your hearing is phenomenal for your age, Grandma Katha," Carol claimed.

"My age?" Katha murmured under her breath.

"Shush," Rose cautioned.

"What?" Carol said dazed

"We never thought of the fact mom lost my dad, Carol?" Rose said sarcastically.

"No, we just thought your Mom, a stick in the mud and didn't want us to hang out with boys," Carol admitted missing the sarcasm.

"Those boys are quite a bit older, than you two," Katha commented.

"So you're older than Grandpa Terrence," Rose exclaimed, as Carol nodded.

"It's different when you're older," Katha responded.

"That is blatant age discrimination, right Rose?" Carol retorted.

"At least Gabe is only one year older than me. Nick is two years older than you," Rose commented.

"So? He is so cute and he likes me. He even kissed me," Carol stated dreamily.

"Gabe likes me and I thought we'd be seeing him on the bus, but that darn bus broke down and we've been regulated to this room," Rose complained. "We'll never see either of them again."

"Nick will never forget me. You're correct about this show though. It so lame! I think that one guy thinks he's totally now, but he's so yesterday," Carol responded, "I turned the channel."

"What this new program then?" Rose asked.

"Like you don't recognise Much Music. Oooh they're going to have Retro up," Carol asked.

"This actually looks pretty good. Let's watch this for the next hour," Rose commented.

"Okay," Carol agreed.

Katha breathed a sigh of relief and put down her knitting getting her latest *S. G. Lee* mystery out *Dreams Can Kill*. She was just getting to the good part an hour later, when Lily came into the hotel room looking a little annoyed.

"What is up dear you look like thunder and where is my dear Terrence?" Katha asked.

"Terrence drove Emmett to the Toronto Airport." Lily said tersely

"Why would Emmett go to the airport? I thought he had the entire month off and didn't have to go back until after the New Year?" Katha says puzzled.

"Me too, but then he got a phone call. Remember yesterday when he said he might have to go home to work? Today he doesn't say a word to me and then tells Terrence he has to get a flight back to Happy Valley." "I thought we'd gotten close, but he didn't even say goodbye."

"He probably didn't have time dear," Katha commented.

A series of thunderous knocks were heard on the hotel room door.

"Hmm, Terrence is back already?" Katha commented opening the door.

~0~

Chapter 6 - It's All Relative

At the door of the hotel room, a young man about sixteen

years old. He has long scruffy brown, shoulder length hair and the beginnings of a moustache and beard. He stood six-feet-three inches tall. His eyes blue and searched the room. He carried a bulging hiking backpack.

"Is my Dad here?" he asked looking around.

"What is your name dear and who is your Dad?" Katha enquired, puzzled.

Carol and Rose looked on wondering who this hot guy who looked oddly familiar could be.

"My name is Caleb, Caleb Rogers. My dad is Emmett Rogers, is he here?" Caleb asked his eyes still searching the room.

"Come in, so we can discuss this," Katha exclaimed, ushering the teenager in the hotel room.

Lily looked over in shock. So this is what he had been keeping from her. Emmett had a son, a sixteen or seventeen year old son. Where had the boy been all this time? His mother was dead. Emmett had said his wife had died from breast cancer last year. Could Caleb have been sent to boarding school? What kind of man kept this from the woman he dated? Obviously they weren't as close as she had thought. Well it wasn't the boy's fault, that his father was a closed-mouthed snake in the grass.

"You're Emmett's son?" Rose asked surprised.

"Yes. So you do know my dad?" inquired Caleb, "I was told he stayed here."

"They know him well. He's dating her mom," Carol said pointing at Rose and making sure he knew that Rose would be like a sister to him.

"Carol!" Rose admonished.

"I told the truth," Carol said in her own defence.

"Your father was on his way to the airport. I will call him and hopefully he hasn't boarded the plane yet," Lily answered.

Lily dialled his cell phone number from hers, "Emmett? It's Lily..."

"I can't talk now Lily they call my flight. Sorry I didn't tell you that I had to go. I promise I'll explain later," Emmett responded.

"Emmett, your son Caleb, is in my hotel room. Don't you dare board that plane," Lily insisted.

"Caleb's there?" Emmett asked.

"Yes, now come and get your son," Lily sniped.

"I'll be there within the hour. Sit tight until I get there." Emmett demanded, "I promise I'll explain."

"I'm not about to go anywhere. Now just get here," Lily cried annoyed.

Lily then hung up without saying goodbye.

"I'm sorry to be so much trouble. Maybe I should just go wait in the lobby until my Dad gets here," Caleb exclaimed, overhearing Lily's conversation.

"No, Caleb. I'm the one who should be sorry I'm a little peeved at your Dad, but that shouldn't reflect on you. Please sit down and we'll have a pop, coffee, or tea and introduce ourselves," Lily invited smiling.

"If you're sure I'd like a pop, please," Caleb answered.

"I'm Rose Brooksfield and this is my best friend, Carol Banks," Rose introduced, before Caleb even had a chance to sit on the sofa.

"I'm Lily Wentworth-Brooksfield and Rose is my daughter," Lily continued.

"I'm Amelia Kelly, I'm Rose's honorary Aunt, Lily is actually my cousin once removed," Amelia explained.

"And I'm Katha O'Malley-Stewart. I am Lily's great-grandmother and Rose's great-great-great grandmother. I am Amelia's great-aunt and Carol's great-great grandmother by marriage to Terrence Stewart, my new husband." Katha explained, "A bit confusing, but there you have it. We're all related, it's all relative."

Katha then laughed at her little joke as Carol and Rose smirked. Caleb looked dumbfounded but then he turned to Rose and asked, "She must be really old then; so why doesn't she look that old?"

"She's eighty-one," Carol whispered in his ear.

"No, that's impossible she doesn't even look seventy," Caleb whispered back.

"Good genes," Rose whispered.

"Young man didn't anyone ever teach you it is impolite to talk about a lady's age?" admonished Katha; but she looked pleased that Caleb thought she looked seventy.

"I am sorry Ms. Stewart," Caleb said immediately looking mortified then whispered to Rose, "And even better hearing."

"Very well, I accept your apology." Katha said, "But no more whispering children."

"Grandma Katha is very sensitive about her age," Rose whispered in Caleb's ear.

"Rose, what did I say about whispering? It's bad manners."

"Sorry, Grandma Katha."

"Now Caleb, tell us about yourself. Where were you born?" prodded Katha.

"I was born in London, Ontario. My mom moved with her family to London just before I was born," Caleb explained.

"Then how can Emmett be your Dad? He lives in Happy Valley, Ontario, not London," Carol demanded.

"My mom and dad met in high school. My mom is a little older than my dad. She was seventeen and he was only sixteen. They were childhood sweethearts and loved each other very much but ...," Caleb continued.

"And they got together and made you," Carol said bluntly.

"Carol!" admonished Rose "You really should watch how you say things."

"Sorry, you'll find out sometimes my mouth gets ahead of my brain and I blurt things," Carol apologised.

"That's okay," Caleb answered, then continuing he blurted (the story coming out a bit disjointed), "My grandparents didn't like my father's family and therefore they didn't think my dad was good enough for my mother to date. Anyway, when my mother's father and step-mother found out my mother had fallen pregnant with me, they sent her to her aunt's and uncle's almost overnight."

"Wow, that's harsh," Carol stated as Rose tried to hush her.

"Ignore her Caleb, please continue," Rose said.

"They never even told my Dad she was pregnant and then my Great-Aunt and Great-Uncle kept my mother a prisoner in their home in London, Ontario where they moved to. Mom thinks I don't know what they did, even though they've been arrested. Not only that but they hired some super powered lawyer who will probably get them off."

"Off? What crime did they commit?" asked Katha.

"Abuse and some other things I think. My mom wasn't allowed to use the phone, or go to school. A doctor friend of theirs saw to my mother's care during her pregnancy with me. My mother gave birth and my great-aunt pretended I was hers. They even tried to get the doctor to register me as Great-Aunt's child, but that he balked at."

"Wow, what an awful story," Katha commented.

"Your poor mother," Rose remarked, "How did you find out you were really hers?"

"I didn't find out until a couple of years ago, when my mother moved out of the house taking me with her. She told me I was her son and they were not my mom and dad, but my great-aunt and great-uncle. Great-Aunt Selma and Great-Uncle Hiram had the police bring me back. Mom then sued for custody proving she was my mother and won."

"So you found out about Emmett then?" asked Katha.

"My mom refused to tell me who my Dad was, but I found her year book last week. Then I found the love letters she had placed in it. She'd found the letters that her parents had kept from her in my Great-Aunt's jewellery box. My dad wrote her after he obtained our address every year until I was two, then he gave up when there was no response. I found out where my dad lived and I called directory assistance and got his home phone."

"Good thing he hasn't ditched his home phone. A lot of people have. You don't need one of you have a cell phone," Carol commented.

"Yah, anyway I called the number and some lady answered who said she was his house sitter. Turns out she's my Aunt Suzy. When I said I was his son. She asked some questions about my mother and then said dad toured Niagara Falls and wouldn't be back until the New Year."

"So then what did you do?" asked Rose.

"I couldn't believe my Dad was so close I wanted to meet him. So I hopped a bus and scoped out the hotels and motels. I had to sleep in the lobby of one last night, but I finally found out where he stayed and I went to his room. He wasn't there. I asked the desk clerk and they said he'd just checked out. I guess I must have looked crestfallen for he took pity on me and said that dad had spent a lot of time with you, so here I am," Caleb rambled, excited that he had done all this to find his dad.

"Good grief; weren't you scared?" asked Rose.

"Yes, Rose is right. What if your father didn't want you?" asked Carol.

"That is not what I said at all. Don't put words in my mouth, Carol Banks." Rose exclaimed angrily, "I spoke about Caleb taking the bus by himself and sleeping in the lobby of the hotel."

"He is my father. He'll want me," Caleb insisted, not sounding quite as sure as before.

"I'm sure he will Caleb," Lily agreed, "I'm sorry; I'll get you that drink."

"You two quit sowing trouble and leave the boy alone. As for the drink I'm already at the fridge. Here you go, Caleb, is Coca-Cola okay?" Katha asked rummaging in the fridge.

"Can I have a coke too?" asked Rose and Carol at the same time.

"There's one ginger ale and two *Seven-Up's*; which do you want?" enquired Katha.

"We can't drink ginger ale. Carol's allergic. She can't be in the room with ginger," Rose replied horrified.

"That would be good to know ahead of time. Why have you never told me this? I'll remove these drinks from our fridge and I'll notify the hotel in London, so we can protect Carol. They tend to break out the ginger in all the foods and even in candles at Christmas," Katha retorted.

"Emmett is a good man and he'll be a great father. He'll do right by you," Lily continued.

"Emmett is a good man. Did you know your Dad is a police officer?" Katha asked.

"Really he's a police officer? I'm waiting until I'm old enough to go to Police College. I want to be an R.C.M.P. officer. That is so awesome," Caleb answered.

"He is a Sergeant Detective," volunteered Rose.

"So he must be good at his job and my dad dates you?" Caleb asked Lily frowning.

"Yes," Lily admitted.

"Let's watch some television till your dad gets here," Carol offered.

"My mom showed me some old VHS tapes of Much Music it used to be lot better," Caleb commented watching the television.

"How was the show better?" asked Rose.

"More in depth interviews with recording artists and better VJ's," Caleb answered.

"VJ's what does that stand for anyway," Carol inquired.

"Video jockeys," Rose answered smugly.

"Thank-you, Rose. She's so smart ~ off the charts smart. It's really so sad," Carol snidely said.

"Why is sad? I think being smart is great," Caleb stated starring at Rose with a charming grin.

"Oh, so it's like that. You like her," Carol muttered under her breath.

Caleb glanced at Rose and she glanced sharing a smile. Katha looked over at the blossoming friendship going on and said to Lily, "There's going to be trouble there Lily; watch my words."

~0~

Chapter 7 - Election Troubles

Earlier that day

Lily searched for a paper in the lobby of the hotel. She

knew she could read them on line but she liked the physicality of having the newspaper in her hands. Lily watched a tall woman, about seventy years old pacing back and forth. She seemed to be waiting for someone and something about her agitation caught Lily's eye. The women beautifully coifed, shimmered as their short, close cropped, white hair, moved with them. She wore a white blouse neck high, a pleated navy blue skirt completing the look with blue kitty heels.

"Finally you're here Paul, but where is Trent, your campaign manager?" the woman asked the man who came into view.

Lily could help overhearing and noted that Paul stood about five foot nine inches tall and wore a tailored expensive golf shirt, with tailored khaki casual pants. His hair chocolate brown and wavy was short and clipped to his head. The man pulled the woman who approached him into an alcove; but Lily standing nearby could still hear them.

"Mother, I am on holiday with my family. What was so urgent that you had to fly here?" the man clearly annoyed, asked the woman.

"I'm not happy that a murder happened on your tour bus, Paul," the mother began, "It's in all the papers back home. How could you have booked a holiday with that nitwit your so called opponent? And then to have a murder occur....?"

This man was on their bus when the murder occurred? Wait a minute, his mother said something about an opponent; was he running for some sort of office? Lily thought.

"Mother, first of all I do not consult my opponent, David Moore, about where I holiday. However, I think my opponent may have spied on me to find out where I was holidaying," Paul replied "Second of all I am appalled by this senseless tragedy."

"Don't you give me the party line Paul, I wrote it," the mother stated, sounding annoyed.

"Mother, everything is fine. My family and I enjoy a vacation. It will be the last out of country trip, that isn't state business for the next six years so let us relish it," Paul insisted.

"I'll let you enjoy yourself, after you secure your next six year term," the mother exclaimed fiercely.

"We will win, mother. David Moore has nothing on me. I have a proven record. He's a two bit upstart with illusions of grandeur. Come election day he'll have egg on his face," Paul reassured.

"Then your wife is no longer a liability to you?" the mother asked with mock sweetness.

"She spent her time at the Betty Ford Clinic. She's dried out now, mother," Paul cried angrily enunciating all of this.

"She better know her place Paul. If the press found out about her addictions, we could still lose the election." the mother said pointedly.

"She knows, mother. She stumbled, but she wants me to win the election as much as you do," Paul exclaimed.

"Well if she refuses to act the part then something will have to be done about her," Grace cried, viciously.

"Do you threaten my wife, mother? Because you are not in charge of my life, I am! Maria is my wife and my long suffering partner.

She is a good Catholic girl. She'll live up to her marriage vows," Paul stated.

"Don't let that witch wander off into any more bars. If you'd listen to me you'd never be in this fix. I told you not to marry her. You had better keep her in check and keep it in your pants at least until after the election," Grace laughed.

"My opponent is the one to watch. That man is too buttoned down. He probably has one on the side."

"Your man should be looking into that," Grace stated.

"He is. I'm on top of things mother. Never doubt me."

Lily noticed a man searching the room from the front door of the hotel. A bespectacled man about five feet six, with messy and slightly greasy hair. His tailored suit hung on his thin frame looking baggy and cheap. The man seemed to mysteriously fade into the background unless one focused on him.

The man walked over to the arguing couple and asked, "Is there a problem Paul?" then turning to the woman he waxed, "Grace, dear, how lovely to see you. You get more beautiful every time I see you."

"Why didn't you call me Trent?" Grace asked and then air kissed Trent.

"Sorry, Grace, I have been working on keeping the information from the press. We've been liaising with the local cops and staying on top of it."

"Then how did I read about it? Do they have any clue who the murderer is?"

"So far the police have no leads on the murder. In fact they seem puzzled to who the victim was," Trent replied.

"Really? How fascinating. Now has Paul released a statement to the media?" Grace demanded.

"Yes, and it will go out today and be carried by the Associated Press so it will be seen at home," Trent replied.

"I guess I underestimated your abilities Trent. I should have remembered how devoted you are to my son and winning this re-election," Grace declared, "But I still don't understand, how did David Moore and his family ended up at the same resort?"

"He may have used the oldest trick in the book Grace. David Moore and family are devious. Moore sent his daughters Louise, (a seventeen years old and Patricia, a fifteen year old known as Trish) to get the information from Paul's sons. Teenage boys are very susceptible to female charms," Trent answered, "And this girl Louise is a femme fatale. I assure you this will not happen again."

"You assure me? That's like telling me it will never rain or snow again. Like father, like sons! Those apples don't fall far from the tree. They must feed their appetites like their father." Grace exclaimed.

"That's a little harsh ma'am, they are fine young men. They've never been in trouble."

"If you say so; now has Paul been behaving himself?"

"Paul is the model politician," Trent answered.

"I'm not a child mother and I don't need a monitor," Paul declared.

"The election next year is important in our overall plan. One false step and all our plans will go up in smoke," Grace answered sighing as if talking to an inferior, "Then of course it's one more step forward to the presidency."

"Paul will make a wonderful president," Trent replied.

"With you at his side my son will go all the way." Grace announced, "I'm going up to see my grandchildren. Will you see that they are ready to receive their grandmother, Trent?"

"Certainly, it would be my pleasure to I assist you, Grace," Trent replied.

Lily saw Paul mouth 'Thank-you' to Trent. Paul then left the lobby and headed for the bar. Lily then went on her way and spotted her newspaper in a rack by the front desk. She then went back to the hotel room hoping Emmett would have breakfast with them.

~0~

In the bar Terrence sat nursing a scotch. Katha was would meet him soon, but frankly he was bored. He wanted some one on one time with his new wife, when she was surrounded with her 'chicks'. He watched as the man strode in with easy confidence. Terrence noted the man, tall and lean wore a tailored an expensive golf shirt with tailored khaki casual pants. Everything about him spoke money and power. He sat to Terrence's left at the bar.

"Scotch rocks," the man demanded from the bartender.

"My treat," explained Terrence, signalling to the bartender that it was on him, "Just waiting for the wife."

"I've been there. It seems were always waiting for them."

"Even on honeymoon," Terrence griped, getting a text from Katha.

"Congratulations," Paul exclaimed, "To happy husbands."

Paul then clinked his glass with Terrence's.

"Name's Paul, I think I saw you on my tour bus."

"Terrence. Yes, bad business that," Terrence said holding out his hand, "Bad day?"

"Murder is always bad business but yes, I've had a bad day too. Sometimes family can be too much," Paul explained.

"Agreed, sometimes you just need five minutes to yourself; especially after years without them under foot," muttered Terrence.

"But I thought you said you were on honeymoon?"

Terrence then went onto explain how he had invited the whole family on it to please his new wife. Terrence then ordered and paid for two new Scotch rocks for the two of them. Terrence was surprised to find himself talking about his former job as a judge.

This Paul was very personable, Terrence thought and then he realized the man had said nothing about himself. Just as he was about to ask what the man did he saw a tall, lanky, thin man, with blonde wavy hair charging into the bar and then sit down beside Paul on his right side. Terrence wondered who the heck this guy was as he grabbed Paul's arm. He looked like he just stepped off the pages of Surf World except for the fact that he dressed fashionably in Dockers pants with a blue polo shirt. His eyes twinkled when he looked at Paul, like he knew a secret.

"Let me go, Gauthier!" yelled Paul.

"Enjoying your vacation?" David asked letting go of Paul's arm.

"I'd enjoy it more if you hadn't foisted yourself and your family on my holiday." Paul stated angrily.

"Feeling threatened Paul? You better get used to it, because come next November you're work address will change." David volleyed.

"In your dreams, Moore! The election is all but wrapped up in a bow with my name on it." Paul claimed.

"We'll see about that won't we, Paulie," David stated.

"This murder is bad for both of us. We were both on that damn bus. Maybe we should for the sake of both our positions show a united front?" David asked.

"I'm not propping up your flagging ratings. If you think I'll help you with that think again," Paul said throwing money on the bar and gulping down his drink in one swoop.

Terrence was not enamoured of this new man rose and left following Paul intending to go find Katha and go to the shops.

"Thank-you for the drink, Mr.?" Paul commented as Terrence caught up to him.

"Stewart. Terrence Stewart."

"I hope we meet again," Paul said.

"I'm going back to my hotel room; the wife texted me to come back."

Terrence and Paul then got in the elevator.

"What floor?" asked Paul.

"Eleventh," Terrence answered.

"Me, too. I'm in 1104."

"How about that? My family and I are in 1105 and 1106," Terrence answered.

."We're here," Paul said as the elevator reached the floor and he soon was in his hotel room.

Terrence heard voices when he went to the door of his hotel room, "My name is Caleb, Caleb Rogers. My dad is Emmett Rogers, is he here?" he heard.

Emmett had a secret kid? No wonder Katha had been delayed. Terrence decided he wanted no part of this yet. He go to the restaurant have something to eat and come back in an hour, and then maybe this would be all sorted out without all the shouting and bad feelings he expected. Just passing by Paul's door he heard raised voices and stopped to overhear.

"Where is your mother?" Paul asked.

"I don't know she was here a half an hour ago," a young men's voice answered.

"Gabriel did I, or did I not, tell you and your brother, Nick to keep your eye on your mother?" Paul demanded.

"You did sir. I'm sorry it was my fault. It won't happen again." Nick answered.

The sound of something being smacked with an open hand was heard and Terrence wondered if he should knock on the door and intervene. Did Paul hit his son? If he did Paul wasn't the man he thought he was. Should he knock and intervene? No, Paul probably smacked the table in anger.

"You are absolutely right it won't happen again. Where is your grandmother?" Paul demanded.

"At home, isn't she?" replied a young women's voice.

"If I talked to you Erin, you'd know it. Women should be seen not heard," Paul declared angrily.

Women should be seen and not heard? What decade did this man live in? Terrence thought. He needed someone like Katha to straighten him out.

"I'm sorry, father," Erin cowered. "I spoke out of turn."

"So none of you have seen you're grandmother?" Paul asked again.

"No, father," three voices answered.

"Where did that idiot Trent go with your grandmother? He better not fill her head with lies," ranted Paul, and Terrence heard a clicking sound like he put some ice in and then poured another drink.

Terrence felt embarrassed that he listened in and he left to go to the elevator. As he entered the elevator he spotted the other man, David Moore from the bar. Couldn't he escape these people? He tried to hide himself at the back of the elevator as they didn't even notice he'd entered and continued their conversation.

"I'm worried David that the woman knew you," the blonde stylish woman said to David.

"I knew her as Betty Blue, Kelly. I don't even know her real name," David protested.

Holy crap did all of these people know the murdered victim? Terrence wondered, but could help continuing to listen to the whispered conversation as the elevator descended.

"But you know you've seen her before and you didn't volunteer that to the local police if they find that out ....," Kelly broke off sounding worried.

"Should it come to that, they won't be able to prove I know her." David replied

"But you slept with her." Kelly protested.

"I know I did and I have apologized over and over again. The woman is a political groupie she is known in our business as fame bunny to put it politely," David answered, "She probably crossed someone and they did her in it has nothing to do with me or you."

"But David, she could torpedo your campaign," Kelly complained.

"She can tell no one. Besides she had nothing on me," David exclaimed.

"So you say, then looking over at Terrence and noticing him for the first time Kelly asked, "Did he hear us?"

Terrence tried to pretend that he didn't hear them and looked straight ahead.

"No, he's old and probably deaf and we were whispering," David remarked.

Terrence continued to pretend he heard nothing and stared at the wall. The elevator reached the ground floor and the two left. Terrence waited a few seconds more and then left the elevator too, striding towards the restaurant.

~0~

T errence finished a scrumptious snack and wondered if he

should head back to the hotel room, when he saw Paul Gauthier enter the restaurant and zero in on a blonde woman sitting at the bar.

"So you're back, Paul. Did you hear she's dead? You're little whore is dead. You must be so happy all your problems solved. A dead woman tells no tales!" the woman said slurring slightly, like she had been drinking for awhile. Then the woman fell to the floor in a drunken stupor.

Paul took out his phone and dialed saying, "Trent, I need you to call the doctor again, to come and rehydrate the missus." Paul stated, "Yes, and she's done it again. He travelled with us, didn't he? Good! And don't let my mother know, or will never hear the end of it." Then turning to the teenage boys standing next to him he demanded, "Nick help your mother to our room. Look after your siblings and your mother. See that the doctor tends to her in our hotel room and no word gets out. I'm going out to do some sightseeing," Paul demanded,

"Yes father!" Nick replied sounding accustomed to obeying his father.

After Paul left Nick said to his siblings, "You can go to the gift shop Terri and Erin, but don't let him see you and be back as quick as you can to the room."

Terrence felt sorry for the children. Paul seemed like an egotistical jerk, and an abusive father. He put everything on the kids, What an obnoxious human being, expecting others to take care of conflicts; but wasn't that what Terrence did, avoiding conflict and hiding out here in the restaurant? He better face the music and go back to the hotel room. If Emmett had a secret son then Katha, Lily and the kids needed support. He'd step up, he failed his family years ago by focusing too much on his career he wouldn't fail his new family now.

~0~

Chapter 8 -
Campaigning

T errence bored, wondered if he'd made a mistake agreeing

to a honeymoon which included Katha's family. They are very important to him too, but did she have to spend all her time with them? He'd tried to be there when they were all upset about Caleb and she'd shooed him away. Katha had actually said she needed some time alone with Lily. She'd turned to Lily. He was her husband, didn't he count? They were on their honeymoon. What about him?

Terrence stepped into the Casino in the hotel. He'd buy some tickets to the floor show and spend some quality time with Katha and his new family. That would score some points with Katha. He knew when he married Katha that she and her family were package deal, but it would be nice if they could find some time just for themselves. Maybe the tickets would make Katha happy that's all he truly really cared about.

It wouldn't hurt to play some slot machines first. This machine looked like a winner. Terrence played for what seemed like minutes then looked at his watch. Had it really been two hours? Would Katha be angry? No, she seem to understand his need to be alone at times. He won some; lost some, it was time to move on. Blackjack would be fun, but first the tickets to the tribute concert it was for Tuesday after all. Would they still be here Tuesday? He consulted his day planner. Yes, that was tomorrow. He could buy the tickets.

"Eight tickets to the tribute concert Tuesday," Terrence requested.

"You two, huh." The man behind him said.

"Paul?" Terrence replied when he knew he couldn't avoid the man.

"That's correct, Paul, actually I'm Senator Paul Gauthier. We keep running into each other, must be fate," the man exclaimed.

"Of course that's why you seemed so familiar, I've also seen you on television," Terrence answered.

"I hope I have your vote," Senator Gauthier commented, actively campaigning.

"Sorry, I'm a Canadian and not from your state." Terrence explained. "I'm Terence Stewart by the way."

"I'm sorry I get a little excited. Of course you can't vote. I get a little tired of campaigning, but I have to be always on," Paul said holding out his hand.

"I don't believe it don't tell me you gents were buying tickets to the tribute concert too," David Moore claimed slyly appearing behind them.

"I suppose this is just a coincidence? Who's your spy Moore?" Paul asked.

"Gentleman, please, can't you be civil," Terrence insisted.

"You obviously want to keep your activities with this gentleman a secret. Who is this joker?" David demanded to know.

"That's rude, Moore. This gentleman as you call him is a former judge and someone you should recognize from the tour bus you angled your way onto. But obviously this behavior, really nothing new from you," Paul retorted.

David blanched and turned to Terrence and said, "I apologise for snapping at you, sir. He got the best of me. The tour bus trip was horrific for us all." then turning back to Paul he said, "I don't have time to be following you around Gauthier. My family and I enjoy a last big family vacation before the campaign starts in full earnest so you better be on your toes."

"Gentleman even if you run against each other in an election; can't you keep this civil?" Terrence interjected again.

"I'll show you how civil I can be. Mr. Stewart, I'm sorry for all the discontent; to show I'm the bigger man why don't you and your family and party join me for dinner after the concert tomorrow? And you and your family too, David," Paul insisted.

"I'd be delighted Senator and I'm sure my family will be too," Terrence answered then wondered why he agreed.

"And you David?" asked Paul.

"Just name when and where, Paulie. My family will show Mr. Stewart and family who the better candidate is." David answered, "But you do know he's not a voter. Don't you?"

"So what he's good enough for you to associate with then he's good enough for me. Since I can't get rid of you David, how about the revolving restaurant in the Skylon Tower, about nine p.m. provided the concerts over? Terrence Stewart and his family can join us to keep us civil." Paul asked, "The view from the restaurant is incredible; you can see the entire area."

"I'll be there good day, Paulie," David Moore answered.

David Moore then walked away and went through the doors that led to the lobby.

"So can I count on you Terence to keep the peace?" Paul asked.

"I'll be glad to attend. It will be a nice surprise for my family," Terrence answered.

"Sir, there you are," Trent exclaimed interrupting

Trent, a bespectacled man about five feet six, his hair messy and slightly greasy had on a tailored suit that hung loosely on his thin frame looking baggy and cheap. The man however seemed to mysteriously fade into the background unless one focused on him.

"What did you want Trent?" asks Paul irritated

"I calmed down your mother. All is well, sir," Trent soothed.

"Good! I'd like you to make dinner reservations for my family at the revolving restaurant in the Skylon Tower, tomorrow at nine p.m., as well as David Moore's family and Terence Stewart party," ordered Paul then turning to Terence he asked, "How many in your party Terrence?"

"Eight, sir," Terence added adding Caleb Rogers to the number.

"You heard the man, tell them the number and make sure there are enough tables, Trent."

"I'm going to play some blackjack. See you tonight," Terrence announced.

"See you later, Terrence."

Terrence walked over a little farther and stared at the blackjack tables, but from where he stood he could still hear Paul and his associate Trent though they didn't seem to realize it.

"Do you think that you should really dine with the Moore's, sir?" Trent asked.

"I believe it that old saying Trent. *'Keep your friends close, and your enemies closer.'*" Paul exclaimed.

"That Chinese general and military strategist **Sun-Tzu** had a good idea. I really like his other quote. *'Be extremely subtle, even to the point of formlessness. Be extremely mysterious, even to the point of soundlessness. Thereby you can be the director of the opponent's fate,'*" Trent agreed.

"It is a great quote. We will follow that advice and end his career before it begins," Paul stated deviously.

"Yes, sir, this election is in the bag," Trent answered.

"I liked that old guy Terrence and he's not a voter so I don't have to be on at the dinner," Paul retorted.

"A bit of waste of time and resources then, don't you think?" Trent inquired.

"Not really. Betty Blue was found by the young girl in his party. I want to know what they know," Paul then changed the subject and laughing said, "Can you believe that guy, Adam Gregory's father speaking on the radio yesterday? He actually sounded like he thought if his son ran against me as an independent he'd win."

"Too funny sir, independents rarely win against the current candidate." Trent reassured, "Adam Gregory will never win."

"We will win Trent, another term as a Senator and then on to the presidency."

"I'll make it happen, sir and I'll keep any scandals from breaking out on my watch," Trent insisted.

"See that you do," Paul declared.

These two politicians and then press secretary bore watching. Terrence was sure one of them was probably mixed up in that young woman, Betty Blue's murder. Should he really be exposing his family to a dinner with these people? They were probably innocent though. Politicians had a habit of talking in innuendo and supposition. Terrence really wanted to eat in that restaurant and hadn't been able to get a reservation. It was only one dinner; his family would be safe and they'd all have a good time with tantalizing conversation. It would be good for the children to learn a little about politics south of the border. There really wasn't enough history being taught in the schools nowadays.

~0~

Chapter 9 - Old friends and Surprises

Two Hours Before

Emmett paced back and forth, waiting for his flight to

London, Ontario, Canada. He could believe what had precipitated all this one phone call out of the blue on his cell phone. He thought back to the call.

"Is this Emmett Rogers from Happy Valley, Ontario?" a quivering voice asked.

"Yes, this is Emmett Rogers from Happy Valley. Who is this?'

"It's someone from long ago, high school to be exact. I'm Sherry-Anne Mobley," the voice responded.

"Sherry-Anne is it really you? I haven't heard from you since you broke my heart and disappeared in tenth grade." Emmett replied, "Though I did write for a couple of years after that. Your Great-Aunt Selma promised to forward my letters to you."

"I didn't receive your letters until much later and by then it was too late," Sherry-Anne responded.

"Too late? What do you mean too late?"

"I gave birth to our son."

"Our son? We have a child, Sherry-Anne?"

"It's a long story Emmett, but yes you have a son. I'm so sorry I couldn't tell you sooner. His name is Caleb. He is sixteen and a fine boy. So much like his father," Sherry-Anne said in one breath, her voice quivering with emotion.

"We have a son," Emmett answered stunned, "I want to, no; I need to see him Sherry-Anne."

"That's the thing Emmett he's mad. He doesn't understand what happened to me or maybe he does and that's part of his anger. Oh, I don't know; he won't talk to me."

"What did happen to you? Why didn't you write back? Why didn't you tell me about our son?" Emmett asked sounding hurt.

"My father and step-mother found out I was pregnant and sent me to my Great-Aunt Selma and Great-Uncle Hiram who lived in London, Ontario, Canada. My Great-Aunt and Great-Uncle were my jailers. They kept me locked in a room feeding me and letting me go to the adjoining facilities, but I saw no one but them. They kept me prisoner there for sixteen years."

"They kept you prisoner for almost sixteen years? Do they face charges?"

"Okay, so not literally locked up, but they kept close watch over me and I wasn't allowed to leave the house without them, or use the phone."

"My god, Sherry-Anne that's horrific. How did you get away?"

"My cousin helped me and I went to the high school and got Caleb."

"Then you and Caleb were safe?"

"No!! Those two people who are my Great-Aunt and Great-Uncle... people who claimed to be family said I was delusional and that he was theirs."

"Didn't Caleb think it was suspicious that they claimed he was their child?"

"They told him I was his crazy sister and they did that to protect me. He didn't know what to believe. They almost convinced the courts when they claimed custody too. A blood test and a psychiatrist however vindicated me."

"Good grief, Sherry-Anne, this entirely my fault. I should have come looking for you. I'm so sorry. I let you down."

"That's all in the past Emmett. I know I should have reached out to you as soon as I was free, but the psychiatrist said it could harm Caleb. He doesn't know they were arrested you see. The charges might not even stick. I wouldn't let him see the people he thinks are his parents. He then snuck over to their house to go through the things I left behind. When he didn't find any information about you; he searched through my Great-Aunt Selma's stuff and found your letters to me hidden in her jewellery box."

"Is the boy okay?"

"I don't know," Sherry-Anne retorted in a whisper and then started crying.

"What do you mean?"

"I can't find Caleb. You have to help me find him. I'm so sorry, Emmett. I should have told you somehow, but help me find our boy, please," Sherry-Anne begged.

"Don't be ridiculous. None of this was your fault. Where do you think he is?" Emmett demanded.

"I don't know, Emmett. Can you come here and retrace his steps?" Sherry-Anne asked.

"Where is here, Sherry-Anne?" Emmett asked.

"I'm in London, Ontario," Sherry-Anne answered, "How soon can you be here?"

"I'll be on the next flight. Don't worry we will find him Sherry-Anne," Emmett reassured.

"Thank-you, Emmett, I knew you'd help me find our son." Sherry-Anne answered with relief, 'See you soon."

Emmett hung up the phone and dialled his work, "Chief Stewart, please. Emmett Rogers, speaking! Hello, sir, I have an urgent family situation. Yes, sir, no, sir, not your family. No they're just fine. Yes, sir, despite the finding of the dead woman. No, sir, I assure you, it has nothing to do with them. A family member of mine must be found in London, Ontario. I can't come home. No, I'm going to attempt to find them myself. Yes, I will contact your friends in London if I can't find him. Thank-you, Chief Stewart; I'll explain more when I can. Thank-you for understanding."

Emmett stood waiting to board the plane to London, Ontario. He'd had no trouble changing his tickets. He had to find his mostly grown son. His son! He had a son. Would the boy like him? Would he even be able to find him? Kids went missing every day! He had given that kind of bad news constantly to parents in his career.

"Please God." He begged, "Please let me find and meet my son."

If he found his son would Caleb resent Emmett? Would he think his father a heel for abandoning his mother? Emmett grew angry at Sherry-Anne for keeping this from him, but then he realized how unfair that was. She had been held a prisoner. Sherry-Anne had been sixteen years old and pregnant and he hadn't been there for her. Instead she had been forced to pretend Caleb wasn't hers, while her Great-Aunt Selma and Great-Uncle Hiram held her like a prisoner. And it had been Emmett's fault if he hadn't slept with her...

He had been a brash braggart of a football player in high school boasting about how he had made her his conquest. When he thought of it he was ashamed. Sherry-Anne probably hadn't been able to approach him, because of the shame he had caused her. His thoughts turned to Sherry-Anne's Great-Aunt Selma and Great-Uncle Hiram. They had let her down, not helping her in her hour of need, keeping her a prisoner and then pretended Caleb was theirs. He wished them the same kind of pain they'd done to Sherry-Anne.

"Oh please, God let me find him and make this up to him," Emmett prayed to the heavens again.

"Flight 77, to London, Ontario, now boarding at gate 53," the voice over the loudspeaker announced, interrupting Emmett's thoughts. Then his cell phone began to ring. Emmett answered his phone.

"Emmett, it's Lily." Lily started.

"I can't talk now Lily, they call my flight. I promise I'll explain all later," Emmett says "Emmett, your son, Caleb is in my hotel room. Don't you dare board that plane," Lily stated angrily.

"Caleb's there? He's safe?" Emmett asked.

"Yes, now come and get your son," Lily insisted.

"I'll be there within the hour sit tight until I get there," Emmett replied.

"I'm not about to go anywhere. Now just get here." Lily said hanging up.

Emmett was relieved his child was safe but was his relationship? Lily sounded angry. Sherry-Anne... he had to tell Sherry-Anne. He hit redial to call back Sherry-Anne.

"Sherry-Anne, its Emmett, Caleb's safe," he said as he left a voicemail and then hailed a cab to drive him back to the hotel.

Arriving back at the hotel and Emmett practically ran to the hotel room. Knocking on the door, Lily opened it to him and behind here stood Caleb. Emmett looked at his son in wonderment. This was his son? He was taller than Emmett. His son had long scruffy brown, shoulder length hair and the beginnings of a moustache and beard and he stood six-feet-three inches tall. He was extremely thin, but maybe that was because he was still growing. This wasn't a boy but a man.

"Hello." Emmett said tentatively.

"Are you Emmett Rogers?" asked Caleb, eagerly running over to him.

"Yes, I'm Emmett Rogers. Your mother tells me I'm your father and you're Caleb Mobley," Emmett replied awkwardly.

"I've taken my rightful name. My name is now Caleb Rogers," Caleb replied, proudly, but with a tremor in his voice showing trepidation.

"And your how old?" asked Emmett trying to fill the air with words, "Seventeen?"

"Yah, what of it? Do you think I'm not your son? See we have the same nose and eyes." Caleb replied, belligerently and then pointed to his nose.

"I know you're my son. I have no doubt of that." Emmett exclaimed, "I'm just sorry that I missed all these years, not knowing about you. I couldn't be happier that you are my son."

Emmett then held out his arms and Caleb folded himself into them. Emmett hugged his son with a ferocity, like he never wanted to let him go, but Caleb broke away like he was embarrassed for allowing himself to be hugged.

"Can I stay, then?" Caleb asked.

"If you stay for a little while; we need to straighten this out with your mother," Emmett replied, holding out his cell phone.

"What if she says I have to come home now?" Caleb demanded.

"Then I'll talk to her. I'd like to spend some time getting to know my son." Emmett reassured, "If that's okay with you?"

"Yes, I'd like that," Caleb answered his voice sounding choked up with emotion, just as Terrence came in and announced, "You'll never guess what I've got an invitation to dinner for all of us and seven tickets to the tribute concert tomorrow. Wait a minute. Who's this?"

"This is Emmett's son, Caleb," Lily explained.

"Oh, then I better go back soon and tell the Senator there will be for dinner and get another ticket to the tribute concert." Terrence lied, "Excuse me while I go into the corridor and call him." and then left for a few minutes to fake a call that he spoke to the Senator.

Terrence wasn't good with emotional scenes and this looked definitely like one of those. Emmett also stepped away into the corner of the room where he and Caleb sat down and attempted to get to know each other.

"Did Terrence say we were going to dinner with a Senator? He knows I hate politics and politicians are the worst," Katha exclaimed.

"But Grandma Katha, you ran for Mayor, doesn't that make you a politician?" Rose asked.

"She's got you there, Grandma Katha," Lily stated.

"Maybe, but who ever said children should been seen and not heard was right," Katha said, laughing.

"Ah Grandma Katha, you don't really mean that. Carol won't know you're kidding." protested Rose.

"You caught on fast enough Rose, so will Carol," Katha said laughing some more.

"Do you think Caleb is okay?" Carol asked looking over at Caleb and Emmett still talking in the corner of the room.

"He's okay. Emmett is a good man and he'll be a great father to that boy," Katha commented.

"Are you okay with this mom?" asked Rose suddenly thinking about her Mom's feelings in all of this.

"It's a surprise, no doubt about that, but it's not like it's another woman. It's his child," Lily commented, sounding like she tried to convince herself.

"He looks a lot like his Dad; but cuter and younger," Carol commented.

"Carol quiet!" cautioned Rose, "He'll hear you."

"So what?" Carol commented looking at Caleb and smiling.

"Mom, if we're going to eat with a Senator what will we wear? We didn't bring any fancy clothes except our wedding clothes and we can't wear that it's too formal," Rose complained.

"I don't have anything to wear either. I only brought travel clothes," Lily replied.

"I think I can fix that. Terrence got us in to this so he owes us all some new clothes," Katha claimed.

"I don't know that's awfully expensive and these two are grounded," Lily said.

"Can they be let off their grounding to go shopping with their Great-Grandma? And of course I want to take you and Amelia. We can't meet a United States Senator and not be dressed correctly," Katha begged, "Besides it's a grandmother's privilege to spoil her grandchildren."

"Or a great-grandpa. I got the ticket for Caleb," Terrence interjected as he came back in the room.

"That is very generous of you. What do you say Amelia? Should we take Grandma Katha up on her offer?"

"Aunt Katha has exquisite taste and she's offered to pay? What's not to love about that?" Amelia said.

"So we can go Mom please?" Rose begged.

"Yes, I guess," Lily exclaimed.

"If Terrence doesn't mind us using his credit card," Katha said.

"I love to spoil my grandkids. Go get them dresses to make me proud," Terrence said, "And whatever bobbles they need to go with them."

"Let's go shopping now, but we need to rent a car. I think the closest centre would be Toronto," Lily commented as Rose and Carol squealed with delight.

"I heard about this fabulous mall in Mississauga Square One Mall. They have everything. Let's go there," Katha interjected, as Rose and Carol hurriedly googled the mall to find out what stores there they would recognize.

"It's actually Square One Shopping centre, not a mall," corrected Carol.

"Carol, don't be rude, or they won't take us. It's a mall," whispered Rose through her teeth and then elbowing Carol.

"Sorry, that wasn't meant to be rude," Carol said.

"Wow, it is one of the biggest malls in Canada and it has three hundred and sixty stores. One of those has to have a fabulous dress for us," Rose said excited looking at her computer.

"Do you want to see if Emmett and Caleb would like to come?" Katha asked.

"I don't want to interrupt them. I think they'd like some alone time," Lily said.

"Maybe, but I'm going to ask anyway," Katha said then tuning to them she asked, "Emmett, Caleb we're going to the mall in Mississauga. Do you want to come?"

"Caleb it doesn't look like you have a lot of clothes with you and I have a few birthdays to make up. Would you like to go buy some?" Emmett asked.

"Do we have to spend all our time shopping for clothes?" Caleb asked looking glum.

"No way, that would be torture. There's an Apple store there maybe we could go check out the stuff there. What do you say?" Emmett replied.

"When do we leave?" Caleb replied.

"Terrence do you want to join Emmett and Caleb?" asked Katha then realizing she hadn't asked Emmett and Caleb first she enquired, "Would that be okay?"

"Sure no problem, Katha. Right Caleb?" Emmett insisted.

"Shopping? Do I have to dear? I'm rather play some more cards at the casino," Terrence answered

"No dear, but don't lose your shirt, I rather like it," Katha declared, "What time is the dinner?"

"It's at nine o'clock tomorrow at the Skylon Revolving restaurant, after the concert," Terrence answered "Okay then," Katha replied, "I need your credit card to pay for our finery since you're the reason we need new clothes."

"I'd be delighted to pay for the finery, my darling Katha. I think my back account can stand it. I have a surprise for you go into my luggage and in the right hand pocket you will find a MasterCard platinum in your name," Terrence declared, laughing.

"I knew I married you for a reason," Katha answered with her own laugh, "Have fun dear. See you soon. I love you."

"I love too darling, I'm the luckiest man ever," Terrence replied.

"No, dear, I am," says declared, "Goodbye my love."

 "Goodbye Katha. See you soon," Terrence said.

"Come on Lily, we're going to find you something to knock Emmett's socks off," whispered Katha.

"I need to shave but I didn't bring my shaver," Caleb commented.

"Come to my room and use one of mine," Emmett said, then turning to Katha he said, "We'll meet you in a few minutes.

~0~

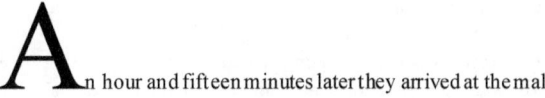

n hour and fifteen minutes later they arrived at the mall
and went their separate ways. Emmett couldn't believe how
handsome his son looked without his scruffy beard. A lot of young
girls at the mall were giving his son a second look as they walked
through the mall. Caleb walked around with Emmett for a while
stopping in the Apple store to purchase a new phone and computer
for Caleb. Caleb was overjoyed and thanked Emmett profusely.
Emmett wondered if he had overdone the generosity; it could be
said that he tried to buy Caleb's love but then he dismissed the
idea. Even if it was true, he owed Caleb a lot more than a phone
and a computer for all the years he'd missed with him.

As they walked through the mall Caleb spotted a pretty brunette
girl. She was tall and statuesque and carried herself with
confidence far behind her years. She wore a red blouse tucked into
a pair of skin tight jeans and black boots with three inch heels that
she strutted in. Emmett was surprised when she licked her ruby red
lips and smiled broadly at Caleb, while also sashaying her hips.

"Hello, handsome," the beautiful brunette girl said to Caleb.

"Hi," Caleb answered.

This girl was trouble with a capital T," Emmett thought and
somehow she looked familiar. Normally he placed people instantly
but where he had seen here escaped him. The girl continued talking
to Caleb following beside him as they walked down the mall
corridor. Emmett tried to tune them out he wished the girl would
go away, so he could have more alone time to get to know his son.
He even at one point hinted this saying, "It was nice to meet you
young lady but Caleb and I need to go shopping." But all that
happened? The girl said, "I love shopping. Let me help you pick
out some chinos, Caleb" and with that he was sold.

Shortly after that he placed where he had met her. He had met her
and her parents on the tour bus...the bus that had also carried Betty
Blue. For a moment he considered whether she could have killed
Betty Blue, but Emmett dismissed the idea after remembering he
hadn't even see this girl speak to anyone, but her parents and her
protective parents hovered. She'd obviously escaped their yoke her

in the mall and now exuded the suppressed sex appeal that she couldn't show around them. Typical repressed teenage girl, with over protective parents.

Emmett stared at the girl again. He had been right in his first impression she was trouble but only if Caleb fell for her. Caleb was flattered by her attentions and granted Emmett didn't know Caleb well but he didn't believe the boy would be controlled by any girl.

The girl, introduced herself as Louise, and actually got Caleb to but clothes. That did impress Emmett as he had wanted to buy some decent clothes for the boy to wear to this dinner but did that mean Caleb fell for this manipulative girl's wiles? Should he be stepping in? Was that what a parent did?

"Would you like to join me for a drink in the food court?" Louise asked pointedly indicating that she meant just her and Caleb.

Caleb gave his dad a look like please, can you get lost. Emmett didn't want to, but Caleb whispered, begging, "Please dad. Give me hour to have a coffee with her or something to eat."

Emmett remembered how it was to be a teenage boy and have a pretty girl pay attention to you. It wasn't like Caleb would be with this girl much. They were almost done with the touring by bus. A little harmless fun having a coffee, or something to eat with this girl wouldn't hurt. How could he say no? He wanted to get this kid to like him and putting his foot down and playing firm parent wouldn't cut it. He decided to let Caleb go. Emmett nodded and Caleb all but jumped for joy.

"I'll meet you in front of the Apple store in an hour okay, Dad?" Caleb exclaimed.

"Let me put your new phone number in my cell first," Emmett insisted and Caleb did so quickly and then in the blink of an eye was gone.

~0~

Louise and Caleb

"**S**o where are you from?" Louise asked.

"London, Ontario," Caleb answered.

"Where's that?"

"Halfway between Detroit and Toronto," Caleb answered.

"That makes no sense. Detroit is in my country. You can't be between two different country's cities," Louise exclaimed.

"It has to do with the way the border was drawn up and the Great Lakes," Caleb explained.

"Oh, okay," Louise said faking that she understood, but it was obvious to Caleb she didn't understand.

"So what's an American doing here? Are you a tourist?" asked Caleb.

"I'm visiting and seeing the sights."

Caleb didn't know what else to say. He wasn't much of a talker and it wasn't until the last year that girls had even looked at him before that they had thought him a skinny pock-faced runt. A little growth spurt had made him grow from five foot seven to six feet three in less than a year. A trip to a dermatologist who had prescribed medicine that had cleared his face and now girls were actually speaking to him. This girl was hot and he didn't want to say the wrong thing and chase her away.

"A little tongue tied? That's okay I'm not much for the small talk anyway. I get enough of that at home."

"Why?"

"My dad's a politician running for the senate."

"Oh, that must put you in the press a lot. I wouldn't want that either."

"You're really nice and you don't talk a lot it's kind of restful," Louise said.

"Ah, thank-you..."

"Sometimes are words are too much. I'm bored want to join me? "Louise asked holding up a condom she pulled out of her pocket.

"Where?" Caleb asked, intrigued.

"Follow me," Louise answered licking her lips seductively.

Caleb followed her to a family washroom where she pushed him and then entering herself she locked the door behind them. A half an hour later they exited Louise doing up the buttons on her red blouse; so her red lace trimmed blouse was covered. Caleb zipped up the fly of his jeans after realizing his shirt was tucked into the zipper.

"That was fun, sugar," Louise exclaimed, kissing him on the lips and then sinking her teeth lightly into his bottom one.

"So it was good?" Caleb asked.

"You weren't bad for a virgin," Louise claimed.

Caleb reddened and looked crestfallen.

"Don't be so upset. It will be better next time," Louise claimed.

"Will there be a next time?" Caleb asked.

"Maybe. I must rush I have to meet the units and I'm late. See you around, sugar," Louise cried.

She then kissed a stunned Caleb one more time grabbing his crouch one last time and then walking away. Caleb pulled himself together willing himself to rid himself of his erection and went to meet his father hoping that Emmett wouldn't guess what his son had been doing. Caleb felt ashamed that he had been drawn like a moth to a flame with this girl. He had all but prostituted himself with her.

He should have listened to his mom when she said the first time should be special with someone special. Now he had all but made it disgusting and dirty. Louise wasn't special and what she said made it obviously she'd been around and yet he wanted to see her again. What the hell was wrong with him? The condom couldn't have been faulty and he could get and STD or have made Louise pregnant. He was an idiot wanting a woman who didn't give a damn about him.

~0~

Chapter 10 - Dinner with the Rich and Famous

Lily looked at her dress that she'd got at the mall. It was a

robin's egg blue and matched her eyes. Her long brown hair was pulled up in a sophisticated knot at the nap of her neck. As she put the finishing touches on her make-up she thought she didn't look half-bad, if she said so herself. Emmett would love it too it was his favourite colour.

Amelia wandered in and said, "I can't reach the zip on this dress can you zip me?"

"No problem, Amelia. That dress is lovely. Red is your color," Lily answered.

"Thank-you Lil. I've never seen a more lovely dress on you." Amelia stated, "It ought to knock Emmett's eyes off his ex."

"I'm not worried about her!"

"Just keep an eye on her if she shows up you'll know she wants Emmett," Amelia insisted.

"I will."

Amelia then dropped the matter and went over to the full length mirror and admired her reflection.

"Mom, are you ready?" Rose asked through the closed door.

"Yes, are you and Carol?" Lily enquired.

"Yah, and Grandma Katha and Grandpa Terrence are too. Oh and here's Emmett and Caleb. They're ready too."

"Good, tell them Amelia and I will be right out," Lily exclaimed.

Lily came out of the bedroom just in time to hear Caleb say to Rose, "Wow, you sure know how to shop. That dress? Smoking."

"Thank-you Caleb," Rose replied blushing.

"Your dress is pretty too, Carol," Caleb stated diplomatically.

Lily started to think Katha was right, this budding relationship between Rose and Caleb could be trouble as they walked to the Skylon restaurant. She'd have to speak to Emmett about this. But Caleb must not know it came from Lily. She wouldn't want to embarrass Caleb. Arriving to the restaurant they told the waitress they meet with Senator Gauthier.

"Hello, I'm so glad you could make it. I'm Senator Paul Gauthier. This is my mother Grace Gauthier and these are my children, Nicholas, Gabriel, Theresa and Erin. I'm sorry, but my wife is indisposed and will be unable to dine with us this evening," Paul stated standing up.

"Paul, dear, you forgot to introduce your opponent and your aide," Grace prodded.

"Quite correct mother, do forgive me. This is my aide, and press secretary my right hand man Trent Bryant, and this my esteemed opponent David Moore."

"This is his wife Kelly and their children George, Patricia, and Louise Moore," Paul answered, "And this is his aide Alfred Getts"

"Excellent introductions, son. Now please tell me who are these people? And why are they here?" Grace whispered.

"I'm Katha O'Malley-Stewart, retired law school teacher, lawyer and hospital board this my husband, Terrence Stewart, former CEO and owner of Terrabond and a former sitting judge. This is my niece Amelia Kelly, and these are my great granddaughters Lily Wentworth-Brooksfield, and Carol Banks and my great-great granddaughter Rose Brooksfield," Katha explained and this is our dear friend Emmett Rogers and his son, Caleb," Katha announced in a chilly voice having heard the whisper.

"Katha is too modest; she just ran for mayor of our fair city and almost won. She only lost by four votes in the recount," Terrence bragged.

"Really? Well done son these are our kind of people," Grace whispered to her son then turning to Terrence and Katha she said regally, "How do you do?"

"It's very nice to meet you all," Lily responded when the usually gregarious Katha didn't.

Lily could tell that Grandma Katha was annoyed and really didn't want to be here; despite her showing a polite face.

"Yes, it is," Amelia added politely.

"Thank-you for having us," Katha added finally in equally regal tones.

Paul pointed them to their seating, and sat Amelia next to him. Grace frowned at this, but said nothing. On Paul's other side sat his aide Trent and next to him, Paul's mother. They soon all ordered and silence was heard as their meals were delivered and eaten.

"So you're running for re-election, Senator what makes you the better man?" Katha asked as they finished their meal.

"Senator Gauthier, in the last six years, has done a lot for his state. He has increased and steered a great deal of federal money toward projects in our state for roads and funding for our manufacturing plants and jobs. He has had previous experience as a town selectman and assessor. As a practicing attorney, concentrating in real estate law and serving as defense counsel in the Judge Advocate General Corps of our state's Army National Guard. He can use that knowledge to help our state and guide it to prosperity," Trent replied proudly.

"Not that I know a lot about it because I'm a Canadian, but I did google your boss. It seems he has done a lot for your people," Emmett answered.

"I believe I can do a lot more good for our state. Gauthier's pork barrelling has harmed our state's good name. No whitewashed sites can launder away the damage he's done. He's campaign contributions for nefarious characters are well known. I can do a lot of good for our state without harming our state's good name," David Moore answered.

"You take that back Moore!" Trent insisted, "Or I'll have our lawyers slap you with a slander. How dare you defame Senator Gauthier?"

"Yes, how dare you talk about my son that way? If you can't be civil then maybe you should leave!" Grace Gauthier insisted angrily.

"I think that's a good idea. We don't have to stay here and be insulted David!" Kelly Moore stated loudly, and then stood up and walked across the room.

Kelly Moore than stood by the door waiting for her husband and the rest of her family.

"Let's go, please Daddy," Trish begged.

"I don't back down," David answered.

"It's not backing down, sir. We deserve to be treated with respect," Alfred his aide cautioned.

David Moore stood up and threw some bills on the table saying, "That should cover my share of the bill. You'll not charge my family's meals to the state. I won't be compromised."

Then he turned to Lily, Amelia, Katha, Rose, Carol, Terrence, Emmett and Caleb and said, "I hope you will view my qualifications before deciding on your vote in February."

"We can't vote young man. Weren't you listening, Terrence told you we're Canadians," Katha reiterated then she whispered to Terrence, "Terrence this man doesn't really listen. Do we really want to be here?"

"It will be fine, my dear. A little initiation into another countries politics will be good for the children," Terrence answered.

"If you say so...I guess we can stay for now. After all I want desert," Katha whispered back, clearly not happy to stay.

"Now that Mr. Moore has left maybe we can enjoy some desert?" asked Paul congenially, overhearing Katha and calling for the desert tray.

Rose sitting between Gabe and Caleb seemed to enjoy their flirtation and rivalry for her affections while Carol enjoyed the attentions of Nick.

"Please mom, can we? I would like some of that delicious cheesecake, and so would Carol. Right Carol?" Rose begged, her eyes pleading with Carol to agree.

"Okay, we will stay for desert but we insist on paying for our dinners," Lily declared.

"If you wish you may pay for your own dinners," Paul said.

"Like I need his permission," Katha muttered under her breath.

"I have to go sir," Trent exclaimed.

"Very, well, I hope you'll excuse my aide, ladies and gentlemen," Paul retorted.

"I hope you'll excuse me too. I find I have a headache, but it was lovely to meet such charming people. Goodnight," Grace said getting up and leaving.

"That woman is plain rude," Amelia whispered to Lily.

They finished their deserts and Lily and Emmett reluctantly pull Rose away from Gabe and Carol from Nick.

"Goodnight Rose. I hope I'll see you tomorrow on the bus," Gabe said.

"I'm sure you will but she'll be sitting with me," replied Caleb boasting.

"Actually, I'll be sitting with Carol," Rose said, suddenly annoyed that they treated her like a piece of meat.

"That's right, Rose sits with me, but I'm sure you boys could sit across the aisle or behind us on the bus provided you get there first," Carol said, "Goodnight guys!"

The night air is crisp and cool and Lily pulled her coat up around her neck.

Lily heard Carol said to Rose, "How did you manage that? You have two boys fighting over you?"

"Be quiet Carol; Caleb will hear you," Rose cautioned.

"We will talk about this in our room later," Carol insisted.

"Dad...do you mind if I call you that?" whispered Caleb.

"Not at all, I'd love that," Emmett stated pleased.

"Do you know a lot about girls because I don't understand them!" Caleb retorted, "Why is Rose mad at me?"

"I don't think any man does, but we have to respect them and treat them as we want to be treated," Emmett answered.

"I don't understand what you're getting at Emmett...er Dad," Caleb commented.

"You didn't ask Rose to sit beside you, you just told her she sat with you. Would you like someone to tell you where you can sit?" Emmett asked.

"I didn't think of that. Do you think she'll forgive me?" Caleb inquired.

"Maybe if you treat her better and you give her space tonight." Emmett explained, "But you do realize she's too young for you?"

"Yes, but I still like to be her friend. She's easy to talk to, you know?"

"Yes, I understand that," Emmett answered.

"I know. Thank-you for the advice, Dad. I'll try to treat her better and you give her space," Caleb said they walked behind the women and Terrence.

Arriving at the hotel and exiting the elevator, Lily declared, "Goodnight Grandma Katha, Grandpa Terrence. Goodnight Caleb and Emmett we'll see you in the morning," echoing refrains were heard from all as they reached their room doors. Rose, Carol, and Lily then entered their suite next door to Emmett's.

"I'm glad Emmett was able to get a rollaway bed for his room. This hotel is booked solid." Lily commented, "Did Emmett and Caleb seem to get along okay tonight?"

"Yes, they did get along. Caleb's lucky Emmett's a great guy. Emmett accepted Caleb as his son right away," Rose answered, "It has to be hard finding out you had a dad and you were kept from him. Let alone finding out your grandparents are not your parents and that you're real mother is the woman you though was your sister."

"Caleb seems to have adjusted to the idea."

"Mom, sometimes you are so naive it's scary. Caleb puts on a brave face, but he's terrified. His whole world fell around him. It's not quite that easy to move on." Rose stated, "I feel sorry for him."

"Of course, it's not that easy. Why did I think everything would be rosy, now that he met his dad? How did you get to be so grown up and smart?" asked Lily.

"You're just lucky, I guess." Rose stated, "We're going to bed. Night mom! Come on, Carol."

"Night, pumpkin. Goodnight Carol. I'll come to bed in a few minutes," Lily commented.

~0~

Chapter 11 - I hope you have a good alibi

The next morning

Lily, Amelia, Rose, Carol, Katha and Terrence eating breakfast together in Lily's suite heard a knock at the door. Lily answered the door and ushered Caleb and Emmett.

"Emmett come in, you too Caleb. We're just about to eat breakfast. Come join us. There's lots of food." Lily invited.

Caleb heard the word food and turned to his Dad and said, "Can we? I'm starving."

"Okay, if you're sure you have enough, Lil. You have coffee, don't you?" Emmett asked.

"Of course we do, what's morning without coffee?" Katha answered.

Emmett looked over at Lily and wondered if she had grown angry at him. He hadn't really explained anything to her. Would she hold this against him? She seemed to accept Caleb; but was it all an act to hide her anger? Crap, he really couldn't take all of this in. He was a father and not just father, but a dad to a seventeen year old man.

Looking over at Caleb Emmett smiled at him and Caleb smiled, shyly back. Caleb seemed like a really nice kid. Sherry-Anne had done a pretty good job of raising him to be polite and respectful to adults. Caleb seemed happy to be with him and very respectful, but what did Emmett know about teen boys? Only his own experience and he had to deal with his alcoholic father.

Caleb would never be subjected to that Emmett had vowed a long time not to drink like his dad. It was probably genetic though maybe he should tell Caleb about his grandfather's problem. It would all be okay, the kid was a very polite, respectful young man. The only problem he saw right now was his crush on Rose. She was fifteen years old to the boy's seventeen. If this crush kept up he have to talk to Caleb about the difference in their ages and the fact she was jailbait. Emmett remembered those raging teenage hormones. He knew that's why he had a seventeen year old son. Quite frankly he was sure that Lily and he didn't want to be grandparents just yet, although maybe he pulled ahead of himself?

No, he wasn't, he thought as he looked over and saw Caleb grinning at Rose with a silly smile on his face. Emmett then watched as Caleb sat down next to Rose touching her arm. That talk would have to come today, but now, right now he'd have breakfast and enjoy being with his son.

"Earth to Emmett," Lily said.

"Sorry, my mind was on Caleb."

"I noticed," Lily commented.

"You're not mad at me?" asked Emmett whispered so Caleb didn't hear from across the room where he's at the table.

"Mad at you? You thought I was mad? I admit I was surprised to find out you were a father, but then so were you. I admire the way you stepped up for your son immediately," smiled Lily.

"You know you're a pretty special lady yourself," Emmett retorted.

Emmett began eating, conversation flowing freely about the bus trip today to the Welland Canal. When they are all almost done their breakfasts, a loud knock is heard at the hotel room door.

"I'm sure it's not Nick." Rose cried, "It's too early."

"I think it's him," Carol shouted and ran to the door.

Carol opened the door to a police officer dressed in an R.C.M.P. uniform.

"Is there an Emmett Rogers in that room?" asked the policeman, as his partner appeared beside him.

"Just a moment please," Carol replied, swallowing.

Carol suddenly felt frightened and didn't know quite why.

"Emmett..., I mean Mr. Rogers, sir. I don't what has happened, but there are two police officers at the door who want to speak to you," Carol cried, over her shoulder.

"Please, officers, come in.," Emmett said opening the door wider, "I am Emmett Rogers. How may I help you?"

"We'd like you to accompany us to Police headquarters and help us with our enquiries," retorted the other police officer.

"Not to be disrespectful officer, but I'd like to see some identification," Lily demanded.

"Certainly, I am Sergeant Detective Peter Brooks and this is Sergeant Detective Gordon Downie," The first police officer answered showing his badge and Sergeant Detective Gordon Downie also showed his.

"What happened to Sergeant Detective George Secord and Officer Bill Tripp? I assume you're on the case of that poor woman who was murdered?" Katha asked surprised.

"They been reassigned Madame," Sergeant Detective Peter Brooks answered, and then gave an unspoken command to his partner, Sergeant Detective Gordon Downie who nodded in agreement.

"You're with the R.C.M.P.? Why have you been called in?" Katha asked.

"Names, please," Sergeant Detective Gordon Downie asked.

"Katha Kelly-White- Kent-O'Malley-Stewart and this is my husband retired judge, Terrence O'Malley, former CEO and present owner of Terrabond. This is my great-niece Amelia Kelly, and these are my great-granddaughters Lily Wentworth-Brooksfield, and Carol Banks and my great-great-granddaughter Rose Brooksfield," Katha explained.

"Thank-you, Madame and thank-you for helping us out by offering all of your names," Sergeant Detective Gordon Downie answered.

"You've come to speak with our dear friend, Emmett Rogers? "I don't understand either the O.P.P. or the Niagara Police have jurisdiction. Don't they Emmett?" Katha interrupted as the policeman started to clear his throat to say more.

"And the boy?" Sergeant Detective Gordon Downie asked.

"Oh dear, I did forget Caleb. This is Caleb, Emmett Roger's son. But you won't need to speak with him about the murder on the bus. He wasn't on it."

"This isn't about that murder and since we find you are all here. I'd like your alibis where were you from nine thirty p.m. last night until six a.m. this morning?" demanded Sergeant Detective Peter Brooks.

"It isn't about Betty Blue's murder?" Katha asked perplexed.

"Has something happened?" Terrence enquired.

"We will get into that after alibis sir; your first name sir, for my records?" Sergeant Detective Gordon Downie demanded.

"I am an attorney and former acting Judge Terrence Aloysius Edward Stewart." Terrence replied putting his shoulders back.

"And where were you sir from nine-thirty p.m. until six a.m. this morning?" Sergeant Detective Peter Brook enquired.

"I walked back to the hotel with this bunch; then my wife Katha and I went to bed. I got up at six-thirty and watched some television in my living/sitting room, Then Katha joined me a few minutes later. Then at seven, or seven-thirty we came over here," Terrence stated looking at Katha for collaboration. Katha nodded.

"And your wife collaborates this, sir?" Sergeant Detective Peter Brook demanded, ignoring the nod between them.

"I certainly can officer and it was seven-thirty a.m. that we came over here. As I said, I am Katha O'Malley Stewart. My husband was with me from nine-thirty p.m. last night until now," Katha answered indignantly.

"Thank-you, Madame, and sir." Sergeant Detective Peter Brook retorted then looking straight at Lily he asked, "Now you, Madame?"

"I am Lily Wentworth-Brooksfield. I am the Crown Attorney of Happy Valley, Ontario. I walked to my hotel room with my daughter and her friend. We share a hotel room and we all spent the night in our room," Lily answered.

"Is that true ladies?" Sergeant Detective Downie asked, standing closer to the girls.

"Yes, sir, absolutely, we got ready for bed and then mom came in," Rose retorted.

"Thank-you ladies, and you, young sir?" Sergeant Detective Downie demanded of Caleb.

"I walked home to the hotel with everyone here and then spent the night from about ten pm to seven-thirty a.m. on a cot in my Dad's hotel room. Dad called me then to come here. We were going to take them to breakfast but they invited us to eat here," Caleb answered.

"Your full name and your parent's names?" Sergeant Detective Peter Brooks demanded.

"My name is Caleb Rogers and my father is Emmett Rogers, my mother is Sherry-Anne Mobley," Caleb retorted.

"You're mother isn't here?"

"No, sir, she lives in London, Ontario," Caleb answered politely.

"Mrs. Stewart said but you weren't on the bus...why?"

"My son joined me yesterday. He's my alibi as well," Emmett explained, as his phone rings. He ignored his phone and it rang again.

"Maybe you should answer that, sir," Sergeant Detective Downie insisted.

"Oh, okay," Emmett obeyed.

"Hello. Yes, this is Emmett Rogers. Yes, I'll hold for Chief Stewart. Hello sir. Yes, sir. Of course sir," they all heard Emmett say into the phone.

"What is it Emmett?" asked Lily as he handed his cell phone to Sergeant Detective Downie.

"It seems I have been asked by the Happy Valley Police Department to liaison with the Royal Canadian Mounted Police to assist them." Emmett explained, "It turns out that Betty Blue is actually the daughter of a former Senator. Her father was William Renfrew. Of course they don't really need my help, but the U.S. State department insists, (because of the crimes we solved this year) that I should help them."

"But what does Betty's murder have to do with us having alibis'? Why did we need an alibi for last night? Has something happened then?" Lily asked.

"Yes, and it is part of the reason that the State department got their way," Emmett retorted, "Two other people were murdered last night."

"Who was murdered?" Katha asked sounding horrified, "Not someone else we know?

"Trent Bryant and Alfred Getts were murdered." stated Emmett.

"But they're the aides to the Senators." Rose cried shocked, "Who would have murdered both of them?"

"That's what we're looking into," Sergeant Detective Downie, "Your alibis check out so we feel that you can help us with our enquiries ladies and gentlemen. But we'd really prefer your assistance Lieutenant Rogers," Sergeant Detective Peter Brooks said.

"Someone murdered them somewhere between the hours of nine-thirty p.m. last night to six a.m. this morning. They'll know better once the autopsies are completed, as the time period is just a guess," Emmett answered ignoring the R.C.M.P. officers.

"Lieutenant Rogers!! You shouldn't be sharing this information," protested Sergeant Detective Downie.

"These people are like family and none of this information will go beyond this room," Emmett insisted.

A chorus of "No's and of course we won't say anything", met this statement.

"Nonsense one of these people could have committed the crime Lieutenant Rogers," complained Sergeant Detective Downie.

"They didn't, besides I have a duty to my son, despite your agreement with my chief, I don't know if I can help you. My son and have lost a lot of time and need to learn to know one another."

"You have to go Dad. They need your help," Caleb demanded.

"I want to spend all my time with you. We have a lot to catch up on," Emmett insisted.

"Dad we'll spend time together after you wrap this up. I'd like to brag that my dad caught the murderer that killed these people," insisted Caleb.

Emmett looked torn.

"Caleb, can go with us. It is okay if we continue to Welland on our bus tour; isn't it? We'll be back by five p.m.," asked Lily.

"That will be fine Madame," Sergeant Detective Downie answered.

"As long as Caleb wants to go?"

"It sounds interesting," Caleb answered.

"Then I'll try to assist you in any way I can," Emmett agreed turning to the police officers.

"Thank-you, sir." Sergeant Detective Downie, "And we appreciate your help, Mrs. Brooksfield so that Lieutenant Rogers can assist us. Follow us please," Sergeant Detective Brooks responded.

"Goodbye, ladies, Terrence, and Caleb. See you later," Emmett said and then left with the two men.

After Emmett left Lily, Rose, Caleb, Carol, Katha, and Terrence went the stop to catch the bus which would take them to the Welland Canal.

"May be we should fly home. We can get remarried in Happy Valley. The children have been through enough," Katha retorted.

"Grandma Katha we want you to get married at your fairy tale castle in London, Ontario." Rose and Carol answered.

"I don't want my great-niece and great-grandchildren in danger," insisted Katha

"We're not in any danger. We hardly know these people." Rose countered, "And you deserve the wedding of your dreams; not that hole in the corner civil ceremony you had when we weren't there. No offence Grandpa Terrence."

"None taken, Rose, dear. Katha you do deserve your family at your side and a beautiful wedding. Will you let me give that to you, dear?" Terrence asked.

"Terrence you are such a romantic. I do want my fairy tale wedding. I bought a new dress," Katha said, "Just as long as the children are safe."

"We will keep them safe dear. I love them as much as you do. They are my family too," Terrence answered, "Besides Emmett's on the case now. He'll find the culprit."

"That's why I love you Terrence; you always make perfect sense," Katha responded.

"I love you too, Katha. Now let's show these children what the Welland Canal looks like," said Terrence.

Outside waiting for the bus to arrive, Lily grasped her head. Katha looked at her in alarm.

"I have a terrible headache," Lily insisted to Amelia.

"Oh dear, is it one of your migraines, Lily?" solicited Amelia.

"I think it is. This isn't good. I can't see straight," Lily stated sounding worried.

"I heard that Lily. I think you should go back upstairs and lay down," Katha answered.

"Yes, go Lily. We'll be fine," Amelia insisted.

"You can't handle three teens and Grandpa Terrence and Grandma Katha can't either," Lily insisted.

"Oh can't I? I looked after two, what's one more? Besides I'll have Terrence and Amelia with me. You heard Amelia we'll be fine. Go!" Katha demanded.

"She's right Lily. No, don't look at me like that...march. Go upstairs and lie down," Amelia commanded.

"Thank-you, you two. This is much appreciated," Lily stated gratefully

"See you later," Amelia said waving goodbye.

"I didn't even get to read my paper." Terrence grumbled.

"You can read on my cell phone. That is if you want to Mr. Stewart," Caleb offered "We got a really good deal and I have internet on my cell."

"That's kind of you Caleb, but the print is too small," Terrence answered.

"Oh, sorry, I can make it bigger on my phone," Caleb offered.

"Thank-you Caleb, but I like the feel of newsprint anyway," Terrence explained.

"That was really nice Caleb," Rose stated taking her seat on the bus as the others followed. Caleb then sat across the aisle from them seating with Amelia.

"Yes, that was," Carol commented.

"Where did you get the rad phone?" Rose asked.

"My Dad got it for me at the mall yesterday, plan and all! He said it was to make up for all the Christmases he missed," Caleb says proudly leaning into the aisle to speak with Rose.

"Emmett is a pretty nice guy. You're lucky to have him for a dad."

"So do you think he likes me?"

"Likes you? He loves you, not only because you're his son, but because you are so well adjusted."

"And if I wasn't well adjusted?"

"He'd still love you. Emmett is pretty cool for an old guy." Rose claimed, "Are you screwed up?"

"Maybe a little inside. The people who raised me and I loved lied to me and kept my mother from acknowledging that I was her son, not theirs."

"That's the pits. Sorry that happened to you. But at least you have both your parents. Want to know a secret?"

"You have a secret? You, who has a family who loves and adores you?"

"My family is really my family at least not by blood."

"You're adopted?"

"Yes, my mom, Lily adopted me when she married my father."

"And your dad died."

"Yes, he was murdered in earlier this year."

"Murdered?"

"Yes, my dad was the mayor of Happy Valley. A serial killer decided he loved my Aunt Amelia stalking her and us and when he found out my dad cheated on my mom...,"Rose choked up here and wiped away a tear.

"I'm sorry, Rose. I think I read about this when I researched about my dad. You shot at the killer."

"Yes, I shot at him and missed."

"But none of this is the secret. Promise you won't tell anyone?" Rose asked whispering.

"I promise," Caleb agreed looking around to see if anyone listened, then nodded to tell Rose that no one could hear.

"My mother is in prison. She murdered her pimp. When I'm eighteen I can visit her," Rose whispered.

"Why would you want to?"

"Are you shocked?"

"You told me this to shock me. I'm sure they are extenuating circumstances, I bet. Did they put her in prison for something she didn't do?"

"No, she did it. She took drugs and got involved with the wrong man who put her into prostitution. She got clean and walked away. Her former pimp grabbed her and me and forced her back into the life. He tried to sell me, when she killed him."

"Holy shit, Rose. Are you telling me the truth?" Caleb demanded.

"I told you a secret that I never tell anyone and you ask me that?" Rose asked, "Only one other person besides my family knows and that's Carol. Why did I tell you?"

"I'm sorry Rose. I should know better than anyone life is stranger than fiction."

"Life is weird. I think I'm under the Kelly curse even if it isn't in my blood. I lost my dad in April and in September I found my choir teacher dead...murdered...and now Betty Blue. I've seen four dead people this year if you count the dead cop. I hope I never see another dead person as long as I live."

"I hope so too," Caleb commented.

"You're very easy to talk to Caleb," Rose commented.

"I find you easy to talk to too. I should tell you a secret in return. I did something stupid yesterday; I let my guard down and she took advantage, or maybe I did."

"You? You'd never do anything wrong you're a boy scout," Rose scoffed.

"Maybe I shouldn't tell you this. You might think less of me."

"Nah, people make mistakes."

"This is a big one. I don't even know why I was so stupid. It's just she was so beautiful and available," Caleb continued whispering.

"She?" Rose asked blushing.

"I'm sorry. I think I'll change the subject," Caleb stated.

Rose didn't know how she felt about this it almost sounded like Caleb treated her like one of the boys, and yet she wanted to be friends with Caleb. This was a type of friendship Caleb was offering, opening up to her as she had done with him she had to hear him out even if this sounded like it got into territory she didn't like to hear about.

"Caleb, don't leave me hanging here. I told you my secret tell me yours."

"I met this girl she said she meet me her today on the bus. I even thought I saw her outside the bus but I was wrong. See here's her pic," Caleb said, showing Rose a picture on his cell phone.

Rose looked out at the girl he pointed out and was surprised to see it was Louise Moore. Her brown hair flowed in waves to her shoulder and she struck a model pose in the picture.

"Her?"

"You say her like that's a bad thing. Do you know Louise?"

"I met her a few days ago at a waterpark. She was also at the dinner last night briefly."

"She was? I didn't see her. I would have spoken to her," Caleb complained.

"Louise is a very forward kind of girl."

"Forward? She gets around?"

"I don't want to hurt you."

"I know. Why would some girl, who looks like that, like me?"

"Any girl would be lucky to have you as a boyfriend Caleb. I just think she's a rather a high maintenance woman."

"Yes, I know I'm a fool. I just met the girl and I... Yet she promised to meet me here and she doesn't answer my texts or my calls."

"I'm sorry Caleb; maybe she has an excuse, but I doubt it. I've seen her with several guys since I met her. Forget her, Caleb. She's already forgot you," Rose advised.

"Thank-you for listening Rose and sharing with me. I appreciate the friendship you're offering me."

"Friendship?"

"I can't screw up my relationship with my dad. You're his girlfriend's daughter. That's like incest in my dad's book and besides your jailbait."

"Thank-you for clarifying that, maybe I should move away from you. I wouldn't want to screw things up."

"Rose...please," Caleb begged.

"I yanked your chain. I'm not interested in you other than friendship," Rose said laughing.

"Friends," Caleb asked offering his hand.

"Friends," Rose agreed taking his hand in hers.

Their conversation was interrupted as Nick and Gabe sauntered up the bus stairs, Nick and Gabe then took the seat in front of Rose and Carol. Their sisters Terri and Erin followed shortly behind arguing under their breath. Terri five-foot-four inches tall very skinny, and had long light red hair. Her sherry coloured eyes searched as if looking for someone before she took a seat across from their brothers. Erin's long caramel hair swung back and forth as she followed her sister and then sat down beside Terri. Rose noted that the two sisters are roughly the same height.

Rose tried to remember the next group getting on the tour bus which ended in Betty Blue's death and remembered the Charbonneau twin brothers and their sister Madeline. The brothers took the seat in front of Gabe and Nick. Madeline's dark red corkscrewed hair swung as she boarded. Madeline's eyes flashed like sky blue diamonds and her mouth turned up in a smile, when she spotted Gabe as she sat across from her brothers.

"So you had to bring the dud?" Gabe commented, pointing to Caleb, but also sharing glances with Madeline.

"Calling Caleb names will not endear yourself to me," Rose stated angrily.

"Good grief, how the frig old are you? You talk like a little old lady," joked Terri.

Rose frowned as she also heard Madeline chuckle under her breath.

"Calling Caleb names will not endear yourself to me," Nick parroted in a singsong voice.

"Shut-up asshole. Don't you dare talk to Rose that way," Caleb said menacingly.

Madeline didn't even try to hide her laughter at this as it pealed out like little bells making Rose even angrier.

"Like he could take either of you!" Madeline continued.

"Nick cut it out," protested Gabe.

"Yes, Nick, knock it off," cautioned Carol, "Rose is my best friend and now that her grandmother married my grandfather we are also related. You both act like jerks," then she turned to Madeline and said, "As for you mind your own freaking business."

"Who are you to tell me anything, biotch?" Madeline shouted getting out of her seat.

Caleb jumped up out of his seat and got between Carol and Madeline.

"Carol, it's okay," Rose intervened.

"It's not okay, Rose," Carol stated then turning to Madeline she said, "I'm warning you for the last time, biotch. Leave Rose alone or you'll be very sorry."

"Madeline, please sit down for me and ignore Carol. She's mad at me, not you," Gabe retorted.

"You sit down first, Carol. You don't want to be removed from the bus because she's acting like a psycho biotch." Caleb instructed, "If she continues standing she'll look like the aggressor she is."

"I'm not antagonist. How dare you?" then she said, "Fine, I'll sit down; but only for you, Gabriel. Rose's psycho friends don't scare me."

Gabe quickly sat in the seat Caleb had vacated when he got up. Caleb looked like he wanted to fight Gabe for the seat but then sighed after looking at Rose and mouthed, "Be careful friend." Caleb then walked over and sat beside Amelia and started looking out the window.

Gabe turned to Carol and explained, "Don't mind Nick. He's upset about Trent. That guy adored my Dad would do anything for him and because we were his sons he spent a lot of time with us. He was like a second dad to us. I still can't believe that someone would kill him."

"I'm sorry Gabe, Nick. It's hard to lose someone close to you," Rose said sympathetically, "But that doesn't give either of you an excuse to treat people badly."

"What would you know about it?" Nick asked, belligerently.

"Actually if you were listening, when we talked to you Nick, a lot," Carol interjected, "This is Rose's first Christmas without her dad. He was murdered a few months ago."

"What?" Nick said.

"You heard me," Carol said.

"I'm sorry Rose," Nick apologised.

"We didn't even want to go today. We just didn't feel like it." Gabe says "But my dad is so upset and my mom is drinking, again."

"Gabe!" Nick said censoring Gabe.

"I meant she drank coffee," Gabe covered.

"I'm sorry Nick. That's got to be so hard," Carol replied.

Katha noted the fighting ongoing and started to rise from her seat.

"Aunt Katha, you must not interfere you'll embarrass both Rose and Carol."

"But those children are bullying them," Katha protested.

"Leave them be. Gabe likes Rose he won't let them bully her for long," Amelia answered.

"Fine for now, but if I think Rose or Carol need protection I'm going to step in."

"I remember when you stepped in with Lily and I; we were embarrassed for weeks and the bullying became worse," Amelia commented.

"But it got better?"

"Yes, it did, Thank-you for caring Aunt Katha."

Amelia and Katha continued to watch Rose and Carol.

"Hey Rose, switch seats with Nick will you? Then he can sit beside me. Will you please?" Carol begged.

"Fine, if you insist," said Rose not too thrilled with the idea, since she's still annoyed with Gabe.

"We will soon be arriving in Welland." the tour guide Shelley Turcott announced, "In Welland we will be touring the Canal by boat. The Welland Canal runs twenty-seven miles or forty-two centimetres from Port Colbourne on Lake Erie to Port Waller Ontario. It's part of the St. Lawrence..."

"That doesn't make any sense! The St. Lawrence seaway is way up near my home province of Quebec," Michel Charbonneau complained.

"Yes, the St. Lawrence is up near Quebec, but this waterway connects with it. It allows the ships to avoid Niagara Falls," Shelley explained, "In fact it allowed the cities of Montreal, Detroit Cleveland, Windsor, and other industrialized cities to have growth and receive the goods they need. They could then ship things back the same way for oversea places." Shelley continued.

"Wow, this is actually interesting." Madeline declared.

"You would find it interesting," her brother Pierre, Michel's twin brother commented, sarcastically then continued by asking, 'Where's Louise? I thought she came today. She promised me. I thought she liked me."

"Liar, Louise said she would appear for me."

"You jerk; you knew I liked her," Pierre said putting his twin in a headlock.

"Enough cut it out. If dad finds out you were fighting we'll be all grounded," Madeline complained pulling them apart.

"Sorry, Mads," Pierre said.

"Yes, sorry Madeline," Michel said.

"Where's Charlene, Charlene's not here, either," Pierre complained.

"Of course not; her father is dead," Michel announced.

"Hey Gabe," Nick cried as he motioned for Gabe to bend over so he could stage whisper in his ear, "That girl, Madeline is smokin hot. I love dark red corkscrewed hair and her eyes are like sky blue diamonds. I'd like to do her."

"Shut-up you pervert. Don't you dare speak about our sister that way," Pierre and Michel cried, overhearing.

"Boys I appreciate the defense but I can handle this. I wouldn't look at a pathetic, wimpy geek like you in a million years. So get your tongue back in your mouth and tuck your tail between your legs and saunter back to girls in your own status. I think there's a couple right there."

Madeline then pointed at Rose and Carol. Rose looked over at Carol. Madeline was a bitch there was no doubt about that but Nick was worse. Carol tried not to show it, but it was obvious Nick had hurt her feelings. Carol had thought Nick liked her and so had Rose. Rose vowed to make him pay for hurting Carol.

"I'd like my seat back now, Gabe," Carol stated.

"Oh, okay." Gabe answered surprised then turning to Rose he said "Nick and I will see you two later?"

"I'm not sure. Carol and I could be busy. Right Carol?"

"If I'm not I'm sure I can find something," Carol replied.

"Carol, why don't you and Rose join me?" Caleb offered, whispering.

"Thank-you. We'd like that wouldn't we Rose?" Carol answered.

"You do know where going on tour with Grandpa Terrence, Grandma Katha and Amelia?" Rose whispered back.

"Yes, but they don't know that. Take my arm ladies and will show them how to treat you properly," Caleb whispered back.

Rose smiled and took his arm allowing him to help her down the bus steps. Nick rushed his siblings off the bus to follow behind them. Gabe tried to catch Rose.

"Please, Rose. We're sorry." Gabe pleaded.

"That's nice. I'm busy," Rose stated.

"You have a free hour before the tour of the Canals begins on the boat. Remember though we will be leaving promptly at nine a.m.," the tour guide, Shelley continued from outside the bus.

Rose watched as a woman of about forty years of age petite, with perfectly coiffed blonde hair showed up in a rental car. The woman was followed out of the car by a man about fifty perfectly tanned, even though he has a shocking bright red hair short clipped closely to his head and a perfectly trimmed moustache and beard. The man looked like a businessman, the woman like a trophy wife, Rose thought.

"Michel, Pierre, Madeline, and Genie we made it," the woman said, "Come have lunch with us."

Rose realized that they must be the parents of twins, Michel and Pierre and Genie their thirteen year old sister. Genie was a skinny thirteen year old girl about five-foot-two inches with glasses and red hair in plaits. Madeline grabbed Genie's arm and walked over to her parents. Her parents looking as snobby and nasty as Madeline, Rose thought peeking over at them. Rose hated that Madeline appeared like a fashion model with her brown hair and the way she carried her thin frame, but seeing her mother it now made sense. The father herded them into a nearby restaurant as the mother followed behind like a sheep. Rose was just glad she wasn't part of that family.

Terrence and Katha got off the bus slowly their movements showing their advanced age. Waiting for Amelia, to exit, they watched as other people embarked the bus. The newly wedded Denise and Anna Purdy got off the bus ahead of Amelia and Caleb. Denise and Anna Purdy kissed on the steps of the bus as they got off.

Most of the other passengers smiled at them realizing that they were on their honeymoon, but a few pedestrians passing by commented, "I can't believe that they are both women and they kissed." Denise smiled looked at her wife Anna who nodded and took off her winter coat revealing a shirt that said, "Yes, I am a woman and no you can't watch!"

"What is so funny?" asked Terrence hearing people laughing and being the last person to get off the bus after the Purdy's and not seeing the tee-shirt.

"Some intolerant people were shown up," stated Katha, "Maybe they'll realize that their attitudes are archaic."

"Uh, okay!" Terrence replied, not really understanding but dropping the conversation, "We've got an hour; I wonder if I can find a financial paper and a coffee."

"We'll find you both a coffee and your paper. How about you ladies and Caleb would you like a snack before the boat tour of the Canal," Katha asked.

"Sounds good, I'm starving." Caleb replied, "Rose said we were eating lunch together."

"I did not and you ate six pancakes a couple of hours ago," Rose blurted, "How can you be hungry?"

"My mother says I'm still growing." explained Caleb.

"He is pretty skinny," Carol stated.

"I'm not that skinny," protested Caleb.

Caleb stared at the older man he looked tired and seemed older than Katha and yet he knew that wasn't possible. He might as well ease the old man's pain. It was probably travelling with all these women that were tiring him out. He'd help the old guy out and get in his good books.

"Where the heck is a toonie?" Terrence asked finding a paper box

"Here's a two dollar coin, I have one," Caleb replied bending over and putting it in the coin slot to get Terrence's paper. Caleb glanced at the headline of the Toronto Star and said, "That was the woman you found? It can't be her..."

"Are you okay Caleb?" asked Rose.

"I don't know...," Caleb answered, walking quickly to a bench and sitting down.

~0~

Chapter 12-
Sherry-Anne

Lily lay prone on the bed, her head pounding. She closed

her eyes and fell into a dreamless sleep, awakening only to the knocking at the outer door of their hotel suite. Lily ignored the thumping preferring to snuggle into the blankets and the pillow.

The banging continued followed by pounding. Lily then wondered who could be at the door and jumped up in alarm. Could something have happened to the children Carol, Rose or Caleb? Or had something else happened to Amelia, Grandma Katha or Grandpa Terrence? Had something happened to Emmett?

Lily felt she could no longer procrastinate; she had to answer the door. She threw on a robe over her tank top and panties and ran to the door. Opening the door she was stunned to find a woman who looked so much like herself that she could be her twin.

Examining the woman, she realized that the woman was actually about five years older than her. Her hair curly and blonde worn in much the same style Lily wore, when on vacation for some reason unnerves Lily. The woman's hair was even the same length. The women's eyes met her as they were oddly enough the same height. If it wasn't for the colour of her eyes it would be like looking in a mirror. That's when Lily noticed the woman's chocolate brown eyes sparkled with anger.

"Are you deaf lady? I asked you a question." stated the woman in an angry tone.

"I'm sorry what did you say?" Lily asked embarrassed, "I apologise I didn't hear you, I have a headache."

"I'm sorry too. I got you out of your sick bed and then berated you. That wasn't very nice of me. I've just been so worried. I should apologise I just got in after taking the Greyhound bus and I'm tired." the woman explained then appeared to lose her train of thread.

"The question you asked. What was it?" Lily asked trying to get her to repeat the question.

"I asked if Emmett and Caleb Rogers were here?" she asks looking around the suite.

"No I'm sorry, they aren't. Who are you?" Lily demanded, curious.

"I'm Caleb's mother, Sherry-Anne Mobley and you are?" the woman asked imperiously.

"Oh, I'm sorry. I'm Lily Kelly-Wentworth-Brooksfield. Please come in," Lily invited opening the hotel door wider.

"That's a mouthful," Sherry-Anne muttered under her breath.

"So where did they go? When will they be back?" Sherry-Anne asked.

"Emmett was called back to work and...,"Lily tried to explain.

"So he just took my son back to the Happy Valley without even asking me?" complained Sherry-Anne.

"No, sorry I didn't explain that well. Someone on our bus was murdered and then two others were murdered last night. So we were asked to stay in the area as they don't know yet if the two are connected. Emmett however was asked by his boss and the State department to work with the R.C.M.P. to find the murderer or murderers," Lily stated.

"So where's my son then?" Sherry-Ann demanded, "Emmett didn't take him on the job did he? And what the hell? There has been a murder? My son wasn't exposed to a murder; was he?"

"I don't blame you for being upset hearing there was a murder. Caleb was not present when it happened. Caleb is safe. He went with my daughter, Rose and her cousin, Carol, my cousin, Amelia and my great-grandmother and great grandfather in Welland," Lily explained.

"What the hell is wrong with Emmett? He must have really changed dropping off our son on strangers," Sherry-Anne yelled.

"We're not strangers. I'm Emmett's girlfriend," Lily stated.

"Really and is this new development? Emmett didn't mention you," Sherry-Anne quipped.

"I don't plan on discussing our relationship with you." Lily simply answered and thought about kicking Sherry-Anne out, but that would be petty so instead she said, "Your son Caleb will be back by five o'clock. You're welcome to remain here and wait."

"Thank-you, I think I'll take you up on that," Sherry-Anne replied then sat down on the sofa in the sitting room, "So do you know the person who was murdered? That must have been scary."

"Yes, it was. I met the first lady who was murdered on our tour bus and my daughter was the one to find her," Lily answered, "And the other two we met the night before they were murdered."

"I hadn't heard anything about any other murders when did this happen?" Sherry-Anne says her eyes narrowing in anger, then fear.

"The first one occurred Thursday. I think the politicians were able to keep it quiet so the papers didn't get any of the information until yesterday for print today."

"Politicians?"

"I think it was in the *Toronto Star* this morning," Lily replied, handing Sherry-Anne the paper.

Sherry-Anne took the paper and as she glanced at the headline she turns ashen and in an anguished voice said, "Noooooo!!!! They said it was an unidentified woman it can't be Betty. Not Betty!!Where's the picture?"

Sherry-Anne examined the picture below the headline and paled. Her knees seem to buckle and she grabbed the wall for support.

"Did you know her?" Lily asked, gently worried about Sherry-Anne's reaction.

"Know her? Do I know her? Of course I know her, she is my sister. Are you sure there's no mistake this is who they found?" Sherry-Anne demanded, "Why didn't Emmett recognize her? He met her once years ago."

"I'm sorry so there's no doubt Sherry-Anne?"

"I can't believe this just when we'd be able to be together again...,"

Sherry-Anne then began crying huge tears that Lily maliciously noted made her eye make-up run. Lily almost smiled, and then she realized she shouldn't be so small taking delight in her disheveled appearance the woman just found out her sister had been murdered. She needed comforting. What would Grandma Katha do? She'd make tea. So Lily put on the kettle and handed Sherry-Anne tissues. Sherry-Anne dried her eyes while Lily fixed the tea and then Lily handed her a cup of tea.

"But what is this ridiculous name, Blue? That's not her last name," Sherry-Anne complained, pointing to the newspaper.

"Your sister used the name, Betty Blue," Lily stated gently.

"I had forgotten ...when we were young daddy called her his Betty Blue. That was her nickname. She loved the color Blue, but when she was little she was obsessed with the Blue Boy pictures. She got Daddy to buy her a replica of the Blue Boy painting that she hung over the head of her bed," Sherry-Anne answered sadly, "Daddy also used to quote a nursery rhyme at her because she always misplaced her shoes. It went like this I think~ Little Betty Blue, lost her holiday shoe; what shall little Betty do? I don't remember the rest."

"Actually Betty did; she quoted the nursery rhyme to my daughter. So what was your sister's real name?"

"Her real name is...was Elizabeth Anne Renfrew. Our father is William Renfrew."

"But your last name is Mobley," Lily protested.

"Mom divorced Daddy. When my mother divorced my father she made me change it to Mobley, from Renfrew. I stayed with mother and Betty stayed with Daddy, but not for long. Daddy had rules and if you didn't follow them you were out the door. Then mom married the bastard. The bastard and mom sued for custody of me. Of course, daddy wasn't any better, he married her and heaven forbid you should embarrass him in front of his society friends by getting knocked-up."

"I'm so sorry."

"My father left me with my mother and my stepfather. Then I met Emmett and when they found out I was pregnant they sent me back to my dad. My dad then sent me to his Aunt Selma and Uncle Hiram in London. They made me give birth in their home in secret. That awful woman convinced Daddy to keep my son from me, telling him they were his parents. My mother never spoke to me again after I became pregnant. I don't even know if she knew I gave birth to Caleb. She moved from her last address I have no idea where she lives and neither did Betty."

"I'm sorry that sounds horrific," Lily commented.

"My family is screwed up; what more can I say? And now Betty who was the only sane one is dead, murdered. How could this have happened? She's the only one that loved me," Sherry-Anne stated then regaining some control and then dabbing her eyes with a Kleenex she said belligerently, "Why am I sharing anything with you? You're a total stranger! I don't know what came over me."

"I am so sorry Sherry-Anne. When did you see your sister last?" Lily asked.

"What's it to you?"

"I'd like to tell the police officers then maybe they can apprehend her killer."

"That's the thing; I haven't really her in about seventeen years. Not since Caleb was born. She did send gifts and postcards, but I wasn't allowed to respond to her. The last postcard I got ten years ago. She put a phone number on it and I called her when they left the house. She came and helped me. She provided money to fight them."

"When was the last time you heard from her?" asked Lily.

"A week ago she called me. My sister told me she had big news for me. She said she would be married. She also said I would be a great-aunt," Sherry-Anne explained.

"Do you know to whom she planned to marry?" enquired Lily.

"I don't know to whom. She kept that man's name, pretty close to her vest. She said he was married, but he would leave his wife. I know it sounds like the oldest story in the book; but she claimed he was her daughter's father and now they could all be a family finally. Do you think this man killed her?" Sherry-Anne asked.

"Maybe, but I don't really know. I do know this though, I trust Emmett and I think he'll find the killer of your sister. When you tell him that the victim is your sister it will make him work even harder to find the killer. You have to share everything with him," Lily stated.

"You're very nice. I don't know that I would be so welcoming to my boyfriend's ex, the mother of his child. Thank-you for being so nice especially since it's obvious he still has a thing for me," Sherry-Anne answered.

"Whatever would give you the idea that he still has a thing for you? I told you he's my boyfriend," Lily asked, flabbergasted that Sherry-Anne would say such a thing.

"Just look in the mirror, honey. We look so much alike we could be twins; except my eyes are more beautiful, because of the sherry color," Sherry-Anne stated.

Sherry coloured? The woman was blind, her eyes were a dull brown, Lily thought.

"So you said they'd be back at five? It's what ten p.m. now? This could take a while. I'd like to talk to the police about my sister but I'll be back by five to retrieve my son, make sure he's here honey. Oh, and thank-you for the sympathy, but Emmett and I have lot of catching up to do, you might not see him for awhile," Sherry-Anne said slyly.

"I just bet you do," Lily replied under her breath.

"Did you say something?" Sherry-Anne answered.

"I just wished you well, that's all," Lily covered.

"Aw, thank-you then, goodbye, Lily," Sherry-Anne answered leaving headed to the police station.

Lily decided she didn't like Sherry-Anne, not one little bit. The woman thought she could just waltz in and take Emmett back after eighteen years over Lily's dead body. Why did she just lie down and let that bitch run over her? Yes, Sherry-Anne had just lost her sister, but that didn't give her the right to come by after (what seventeen or eighteen years) and think she could wiggle her finger and Emmett would leave his present girlfriend and be with her? She didn't like Sherry-Anne Mobley, not one little bit.

~0~

Chapter 13 - Talking to Emmett

Lily had tried to get her anger under control it had been

hours since Sherry-Anne had arrived and left but the more she thought about Sherry-Anne, the angrier she grew. She knew she should feel really bad that Betty Blue was Sherry-Anne's dead sister.

All she could selfishly think was that Sherry-Anne would have an excuse to get closer to Emmett...to be with Emmett. It was bad enough Sherry-Anne came up with a surprise child but now she could help with the investigation while she Lily was left out of it. Added to the fact Sherry-Anne looked a lot like Lily. Did Lily hold the place for Sherry-Anne in Emmett's subconscious? No, he cared about Lily. Didn't he? Lily shook herself. What the hell was wrong with her? The woman's sister had died. Emmett said he cared about Lily and if he let Sherry-Anne in then he wasn't the man for her.

Lily gave and expected fidelity. Emmett was a good man he would stick around. She didn't have to worry did she?

Lily paced beside her bed in her hotel room wondering if she dared race down to the police station. That sounded desperate and Lily Kelly-Wentworth-Brooksfield was far from desperate. She had never let a man push her around and she wasn't about to now. Did the fact that Horace and William cheated on her and she hadn't known affect her feelings on this?

Did she now suspect Emmett before the fact? Is that the kind of example she wanted to set for Rose? A suspicious shrew? Lily felt like she was been torn in two different directions. She had just started having real feelings for Emmett. Not that she had talked about it a lot with Emmett. Yes, they had kissed many times; but it always seemed like they were surrounded by people and frankly that would never change.

Rose had needed her so much the last few months. And she felt she couldn't have time for herself when her daughter had suffered so much.

Then there had been the other fact the fact that Horace, Lily's husband of seven years had only be murdered six months ago. How could she think about moving on so soon she had asked herself? Emmett was an incredibly giving man and had taken what she had been able to give him. She worried though that even the most patient man must get frustrated and wondered what he waited for when the woman he cared for had admitted that she too, had feelings for him. Sherry-Anne was a complication she hadn't counted on.

She hadn't been fair to Emmett it was time to tell Emmett her true feelings for him and before Sherry-Anne got there and messed everything up. But how?

Lily had his cell phone number she'd call him tell him Sherry-Anne had dropped by and might be on her way there and invite him for lunch. Maybe she shouldn't mention Sherry-Anne he'd find out about her soon enough and if she mentioned Sherry-Anne he might want to invite her to lunch; but then again Emmett would be mad if she kept things from him.

"Hello, Emmett?" Lily said into the phone as Emmett answered.

"Is this important Lily? I'm kind of busy here; we're interviewing some people here," Emmett answered, tersely.

"Sorry, for interrupting Emmett. I just wanted to give you a heads–up Sherry-Anne was here and...,"Lily explained, before being interrupted by Emmett.

"Sherry-Anne was there, but I thought she said Caleb could stay with me until we got to London, next week,"Emmett complained puzzled.

"I don't know what your agreement was but she seemed puzzled you weren't here...that Caleb wasn't here. Then she saw the paper and...,"Lily tried to explain as Emmett interrupted again.

"She saw there had been a murder, no murders and she doesn't think he's safe; so she wants him to come home doesn't she?" Emmett blurted.

"Emmett, please, would you let me get this out? I have something important to say," Lily stated perturbed.

"Sorry, Lily, I guess I was a little sharp. Please finish what you were saying," Emmett apologised.

"Sherry-Anne saw the picture and recognized Betty Blue," Lily blurted out.

"She knows Betty Blue? She knows who she is?" Emmett enquired.

"You might who? Did you ever talk to her about her family when you two were together?" Lily asked surprised.

"I'm very embarrassed that in the two weeks we were together the only thing we did was make Caleb. Talking never really came into it. I may have met a sister of hers. I can't remember what she looked like though, I was too busy mooning over Sherry-Anne," Emmett answered, sounding mortified,

"You were a young teenage boy I guess that could happen," Lily commiserated, "Betty is related to Sherry-Anne."

"Betty is related to Sherry-Anne?" asked Emmett.

"They're sisters," Lily answered, "I think she's the sister you met."

"But how is that possible they have different last names. Are they half-sisters?" Emmett exclaimed, "And isn't Betty Blue from the United States?"

"Sherry-Anne said they were full sisters. Her name however, is Betty Renfrew. Her mother divorced Senator Renfrew and she took her mother's maiden name, Mobley and they moved to Ontario, Canada where her mother was from. Betty was all grown up and kept her last name for legal purposes, but went by her nickname Betty Blue," Lily explained.

"Oh no, how will this effect Caleb? If she's his aunt," Emmett exclaimed.

"I'll help you Emmett. But I don't know how well Caleb would have known her. Sherry-Anne hadn't seen her in years, but if necessary Rose has had to deal with a lot of loss, she can help too," Lily offered.

"Thank-you Lily. I appreciate this," Emmett stated.

"Do you think we could meet for lunch?" Lily asked.

"I love to Lily, but it's not going to be possible tonight. I promise you and I will get a nice lunch just for the two of us really soon. "Emmett explained, "I have to go. See you tonight, sweetheart."

Well that went well Lily thought as she hung up her phone. Did she sound desperate? No, she hadn't and she had given Emmett all the information he needed. She just wished she could have made a lunch date with Emmett. Sherry-Anne had better not try to put her hooks in Emmett, it wouldn't work.

Emmett called Lily sweetheart. He loved her. The man was really focused on solving this murder; he didn't have time for Sherry-Anne's games. Whoever committed the murder had better watch out, because soon Emmett would have them in his sights.

In Welland

Terrence fumbled for a coin to put in the paper box. He wanted that paper and he wanted it now with his coffee.

"What the heck? A Toonie?" Terrence asked, reading the paper box instructions "That's expensive. I'll have to ask Katha."

"Here let me. I have a two dollar coin," Caleb bending over and putting it in to get Terrence's paper. Caleb glanced at the headline of the Toronto Star and said, "This was the woman you found? It can't be..."

"Do you know her son?" Terrence asked surprised.

"Yes, this is my Aunt Betty. Aunt Betty was outside the hotel Thursday morning when I arrived, it was five am. She said she wanted a smoke break. I recognized her right away though I hadn't seen her since I was seven years old. Aunt Betty asked me why a teenage boy wandered at five a.m., in the cold, in front of a hotel. I told her I was looking for my dad."

Aunt Betty said "I know you don't I? It's Caleb my nephew. Does your mother know where you are?" "I'll call her Aunt Betty. I promise," I answered.

"See that you do mothers worry when their chicks are missing," *Aunt Betty had replied. "Besides I want your mother well rested to be my matron of honour at my wedding," then she asked me, "Now where is your dad?"*

"Here in this hotel. I think," I told her.

"Then go find him and then call your mom," Aunt Betty demanded.

"I came in to the lobby. I then found out from the desk clerk my dad's room with a lot of work, but it was too early and I didn't want to wake him. So I sat down on the sofa and closed my eyes for a moment. The next thing I knew, the clerk woke me up and it was ten a.m. My dad had gone out, so I went to get something to eat and came back and then waited and waited. Then I figured that maybe my dad had moved onto another hotel so I went up and down all the hotels looking for him. Then when I got back I was tired I sat on the sofa and I fell asleep again it was late when I awoke too late to call my dad's room; so I waited another day and here I am," Caleb explained.

"I think we have to tell Katha and the girls this and miss the boat tour of Welland Canal; the police need to know this." Terrence answered," I wonder where I can rent a car?

He turned slightly and spotted a car rental agency. He started walking over there, but turned and said to Caleb, "Go tell all to the ladies we're going back while I rent the car to get us back to the police station in Niagara Falls."

~0~

Sherry-Anne

Sherry-Anne entered the cab and told the cabbie to take her

to the police station. Angry and shaking, she knew that life went on for everyone the last eighteen years; but Emmett had always been hers at least in her mind. In her dreams he had languished, wondering where she had disappeared to (the love of his life) wondering how he could go on. Instead he had replaced her with someone who looked so similar they could be twins. Could it be that he thought of only her as the ideal woman? That this snooty Lily Kelly-Wentworth-Brooksfield was just a pale substitute for her, Sherry-Anne? She smiled thinking that that was the real reason. She still loved Emmett, after all these years her heart hadn't changed.

Sherry-Anne felt guilty. She here she worried about her own life when Betty had none. Her sister Betty had had battles over the years. Different battles then her own, but no doubt caused by the terrible parenting. For whatever reason, Betty seemed to gravitate to the wrong men. She sought money mistaken the men's lavishing on her as love. Sherry-Anne had tried to tell Betty to guard her heart, but it appeared like telling a waterfall not to flow.

Sherry-Anne loved her sister, Betty. She'd been looking forward to seeing her. Though they had communicated only through letters, Facebook and email it just wasn't the same as having your sister by your side. How could it be that Betty, irascible Betty was dead? She had been so bright, so bubbly, so loving. And now some evil person had stolen her life taken her away from all that loved her. Did Bette and Belle know about this? Poor Bette following in her mother's and aunt's footsteps having a child without the father.

Why was her family so unlucky at love? Betty loved deeply and look where that had gotten her... murdered. She had told Sherry-Anne that she would marry the love of her life. This was the man who had held Betty's heart for two decades. Sherry Anne hated him. The man had obviously taken advantage of Betty's good nature and then killed her. A married man Betty had not said his name; but from Betty's hints Sherry-Anne knew he was a politician. Now two politicians were here in Niagara Falls at the same time her sister had been murdered. A coincidence? Sherry didn't believe so. One or both of them, had conspired to get rid of Betty. She was sure of that, as sure as she was that Caleb was her son. Even if they hadn't sullied their own hands one, or both of them had killed her sister and she would make them pay!

Betty had been there when she had needed funds to sue for custody of her son and Betty had also testified that Caleb would be better cared by Sherry-Anne his own mother. She had been only twenty-two years old but knew that without Betty's funding and testimony she would never have gotten custody of her son. Betty had also given her enough money to go to school and become a nurse. That career had helped her get custody of her son. She had then proven that her father and his dreadful wife conspired with her Great-Aunt and Great Uncle to steal her child. The same career now kept Caleb and her, with a roof over their head and food on their table.

Sherry-Anne had thought she would see her sister more after that, but Betty had told her that she had to keep away from her sister for Sherry-Anne's and Caleb's protection. She hadn't said to whom she was frightened of but she said that she hadn't wanted to put them in danger. Why hadn't she been so frightened? Why hadn't she pushed for more...for Betty to come stay with her? Betty had told Sherry-Anne that her lover's marriage was finally over. She had said her sweetheart would be announcing he had divorced his unfaithful wife. In a short time he would marry her and she would be a politician's wife. But which one of them had committed the crime? She had given Sherry-Anne no clue to her lover.

Emmett would find out who! Emmett would help her. Wouldn't he? For months after she had been taken away to London, Ontario she had believed Emmett would find her. He was even at sixteen intelligent and very adept in solving puzzles. But Emmett had let her down he wouldn't let her down this time he owed this too he. He would find Betty's murderer. She just wished they had the death penalty here in Canada. She had never wanted to support the death penalty before but in this moment she wanted the person who had taken Betty's life to die a horrible death or to at least suffer. Maybe a long prison sentence would do that?

When the person who committed this heinous act knew they would never have their freedom again? Yes, that's what she wanted they had caused her pain her family pain, they should know the same. Sherry-Anne hadn't spoken to her mother in seventeen long years not since she had told her she was pregnant and she had been sent away against her will to her Great-Aunt and Great-Uncle's. Did her mother know about Betty? Did she care? Or was she still the same mother who looked at her daughters as an embarrassment? Did Sherry-Anne really want to see her again? Even a terrible mother deserved to know she lost a daughter. Sherry-Anne knew she should try to find her. Sherry-Anne fingered the letter that had arrived from Betty this morning. She hadn't had a chance to read the letter yet, maybe it would give her some insight about Betty's life. She opened the letter and began to read it. She gasped.

Maybe she should keep this to herself, this could be the reason Betty died and Sherry-Anne didn't plan to join her. She couldn't share this with anyone not even Emmett unless he wanted to endanger them all.

The cab arrived at the station and stopped at the curb. Sherry-Anne paid the cabbie and stepped out from the cab. Her high heels catching on the curb she almost tumbled, but someone caught her.

~0~

Chapter 14 - Taking Note

"Hello Sherry-Anne, long time, no see," Emmett

said as he righted her.

"I missed you, cowboy," Sherry-Anne cried kissing him full on the lips just as Katha, Rose, Carol, Amelia, Terrence and Caleb arrived to see this.

"Are you a police officer?" a man asked touching Emmett's shoulder, as Sherry-Anne finished her kiss.

"Would you excuse me Sherry-Anne, I'll be right back." Emmett exclaimed moving the man further away from Sherry-Anne to talk to him as well as to keep the conversation private.

The man painfully thin, wore a crumpled suit coat with pants torn at the knees. He was tall and very lanky. It looked and smelled to Emmett, like he'd been in the clothes for weeks.

"Yes, sir, I am a police officer, but not in this jurisdiction," Emmett replied. "If you follow me into the police station, I'll be happy to find someone for you."

"I'm an American. Are you one like me?" the man enquired.

Emmett puzzled why the man seemed so fixated on him and why he wanted him to be American. Emmett started to wonder if this man is one of the people who have gone by the wayside, let down by the medical association. Was his mental illness keeping him on the street? Was he a vet in need of help? Did he need help to go home?

"I've got to trust someone with this man and I choose you," the man continued.

"Trust someone with what?" Emmett asked softly.

"I saw something the other day near the hotel on the strip," the man announced, "You know, the day that same lady was killed."

"Did you see Betty, the victim?" Emmett enquired taking out his notebook and a pen.

"See, I knew you were the right man to talk to. You don't use one of them new-fangled answer machines thingies. You take notes with paper and pen. Much more reliable, then them electronics," The man commented. "And you'll ask the right questions."

"You saw something strange? Mr.?" Emmett prompted.

"Mr. Parcell. Fred Parcell. It was Thursday. I did my rounds, you know to find some food. The kitchen at that hotel they put out some good eats and they did that day...but not today. Say, I'm really hungry; you don't have anything I can eat do you?"

"I'll find you something to eat then we'll talk. Excuse me a second would you?" Emmett exclaimed.

"Don't go too far. I need to get this off my chest," Fred Purcell insisted.

"Katha, I'm so glad you're here. I assume you have something you want to tell me but right now I have to speak with this gentleman. Could you bring some coffee and a donut back for Mr. Parcell and then wait for me with Sherry-Anne getting to know her?" Emmett begged.

"No problem, Emmett. I love to get to know Caleb's mother," Katha said.

"Emmett, are trying to shuffle me away to strangers like did you with your son? Shame on you!" Sherry-Anne shouted.

"I'm sure you realize that Emmett is a policeman. If he says he needs to speak with this man then we need to give him a few minutes. He won't be long dear and I really don't bite. Now I'm Katha O'Malley-Stewart you must be Sherry-Anne Caleb's mom. Please come and have a cuppa with me," invited Katha.

Katha then smiled widely.

"I guess I could if it will help you, Emmett," Sherry-Anne conceded smiling back and falling under Katha's spell.

"Just don't give her the third degree, Katha," Emmett cautioned as he then went back to the homeless man.

"Now would be the fun in that?' asked Katha winking at Sherry-Anne and then turning to her and saying, "Men!"

"Come on mom. I'll buy your favourite hot chocolate," coaxed Caleb.

Caleb then took his mom arm and dragged her into the coffee shop.

"I was worried sick about you Caleb. How could you scare me like that?" Sherry-Anne asked.

"I'm sorry Mom. I just wanted to meet my Dad," Caleb explained.

"I can understand that, but you should have talked to me about this. You disappeared. What was I supposed to think? I thought someone had kidnapped you."

Sherry-Anne stated, "You're coming home with me today. This is a dangerous place."

"I said I was sorry mom. What more do you want, my blood?" Caleb sniped back.

"Caleb! That is no way to speak to your mother. If you were my son I'd be worried sick too," Katha exclaimed.

"She always treats me like a five year old. I'm tired of it."

"Caleb, I treat you like a seventeen year old boy. The seventeen year old boy you are and I do have the right to worry about you. You're my son, the son I was denied for years. I'm not about to let anything happen to you."

"Why didn't you tell me about my father then?"

"Your psychiatrist warned me not to," Sherry-Anne explained.

"Mom, other people can hear," Caleb protested.

"It's not a sin to see one; especially after what happened to us," Sherry-Anne stated.

"I see one. After my father dying I needed one," Rose admitted.

"I need to tell you something Caleb...alone," Sherry-Anne insisted, pulling Caleb into an alcove.

"If it's about Aunt Betty, I know!" Caleb announced.

"You know that the woman who called herself Betty Blue, the murdered woman...was your Aunt?" Sherry-Anne asked shocked.

"Mom, I saw her that day."

"You saw Betty the day she died? You haven't told anyone?" asked Sherry-Anne.

"Why? She was so kind to me Mom. She even recognized me. She asked me where you were. I told her I ran away to meet my Dad. She told me how much she loved you. She gave me heck and told me to call you. She gave me the key to her room and said use her phone and call you," Caleb explained.

"Did you see Betty after that?" Sherry-Ann asked.

"No, but she told me a secret," Caleb then whispered in his mother's ear.

"No, you're wrong that's impossible she would have told me," Sherry-Anne says "Don't repeat this to anyone."

"I won't Mom. I promise," Caleb whispered.

A sound like fireworks rippled through their ears. The echo of that sound seemed to go on and on reverberate in their heads.

"Oh my god, Emmett's out there. That noise was the sound of gunshots. Call 911, Caleb," Katha yelled from a nearby seat.

Everyone ran to the windows of the coffee shop to see Emmett and the homeless man lying in the street. A huge pool of blood flows from beneath the two men. Sherry-Anne ran to Emmett and tried to stem the blood flow.

~0~

Chapter 15 – I'm
His Son

T errence gripped the wheel of the rental car tightly as he

came closer to the hospital in Toronto. The people in the car were all grim and scared and he was one of them. He rather liked Emmett he was a good sort, besides Katha had said it was Emmett that had convinced her to marry Terrence.

"You're sure this where they took my father?" Caleb asked from the front seat.

"Yes, this is where they flew the two men to in that helicopter, we saw."

"But the Greater Niagara General Hospital was closer why didn't they take them there?"

"This is a trauma hospital, son. Sunnybrook Health Centre has been taking care of trauma, since the Second World War. They know what they have they best doctors and staff.

Caleb unhooked and bounded out of his seat the second he car stopped.

"Caleb wait," Sherry-Anne called.

Caleb however didn't wait and went straight through the emergency department doors, leaving everyone behind. Lily who had arrived at the police station just as the shots rang to find Sherry-Anne stemming the blood flow out, also bounded out of the car, and followed by Sherry-Anne tried to catch-up to Caleb.

Caleb waited his chance and snuck back into the hospital emergency rooms. He searched rooms hoping to find his father. As he passed a room he glanced in and saw the staff working on a man.

".01 Epinephrine Nurse." the doctor demanded working on the man as the nurse handed over the amount and the doctor plunged into the man's heart. Caleb gasped as the doctor was unable to save the patient.

"Time of death, twelve hundred hours," the doctor declared.

"Kid you shouldn't be here," an orderly said suddenly appearing beside Caleb.

Caleb shook with fear, but reaching down deep he found the strength to ask, "Sir, please help me. I'm looking for my Dad. He came in with the guy that died. The paramedics wouldn't let us near my dad and then they flew him away in a helicopter over an hour ago. I have to know, if he's okay."

"Listen kid you can't be in here without permission; I'll look around for you, kid, but you have to go out in the waiting room. I'll come out and let you know when I find him," the orderly insisted, "Tell me his name."

"Emmett Rogers is my father's name. Lieutenant Emmett Rogers. He's a cop," Caleb answered.

"A cop why didn't you say so. Your name kid?" the orderly asked.

"My name is Caleb Rogers, thank-you sir," Caleb retorted.

"Okay kid, go out and sit tight and I'll come find you as soon as I know where your Dad is. I'll get the doctor to come out and talk to you, too. I promise," the orderly says taking him back towards the door into the waiting room.

Caleb then exited still staring back into the exam rooms.

"Did you find your Dad, Caleb?" asked a worried Lily and Sherry-Anne at the same time.

"Yes, did you?" Carol, Rose, Katha and Terrence asked suddenly appearing.

"No, but that man promised me he'd find Dad and let me know how he is," Caleb answered.

"The waiting will kill me," Sherry-Anne stated, "Why don't they let us know anything?"

"He hasn't been here that long. We have to let the doctor's work on him," Katha exclaimed.

"He has to be okay. He just has to be," Lily said not hiding her fear.

Katha wrapped Lily in her arms and then gently took her to a seat, making her sit.

A few minutes later a doctor came out to the waiting room saying, "I'm looking for his son, Caleb Rogers. Are you he? I'm Dr. Frank Nightshade."

"I'm Caleb Rogers," Caleb said coming forward.

"Do you have someone with you son?" Doctor Nightshade asked.

"Yes, these people are all with me," Caleb indicated Katha, Terrence, Carol, Rose, Lily and his mother.

"I need some medical background. Has Mr. Roger's suffered a trauma to his head recently; that is besides today?" asks Doctor Nightshade.

Carol started laughing.

"Carol what's wrong with you?" Rose asked, "Emmett is hurt; this isn't funny."

"He called him Mr. Rogers," Carol laughed.

"You're an idiot Carol, that's his name," Rose sniped.

"Your sense of humour is most peculiar, young lady," Katha admonished.

"Sorry Grandma Katha. "I'm sorry when I get stressed I laugh," Carol explained, "You know this Rose.

Grandma Katha continued to glare at Carol.

"Grandma Katha, in Carol's defense I forgot she does this when she's nervous," Rose admitted.

Grandma Katha then smiled at Carol who then began to relax.

"You were saying Doctor, before you were interrupted," Lily prompted.

"I asked if Emmett had a head injury recently," repeated Doctor Nightshade yet again

"He was hit over the head about six months ago," Rose answered, "He had a concussion. Right mom?"

"Yes, he did. He got it in the line of duty. You do know he's a police officer?"

"Yes, so I was informed. Mr. Rogers suffered a bullet wound to his upper arm. He has suffered another concussion; this one is a little more serious. Obviously these are acute conditions. Mr. Rogers has been taken up to an operating room where we removed the bullet. We will be pumping antibiotics and fluids into him. Bullet wounds are serious, as are concussions, but we will take good care of him.

Mr. Rogers will be taken up to a room on the four floor in a few minutes. Then you can see him," Doctor Nightshade explained.

"So he'll be okay?" asked Lily and Sherry-Anne at the same time tears in their eyes.

"If everything continues to mend and there are no complications we anticipate a complete recovery. Please be advised that there is a limit of two visitors at any time. Mr. Rogers will be groggy and need his rest," Doctor Nightshade insisted, "My nurse, Nancy will be happy to take you to his room follow her."

Caleb, Sherry-Anne, Lily, Carol, Rose, Grandma Katha, Amelia and Terrence all follow Nancy, the nurse. As they exit the elevator and follow Nancy to Emmett's room. Caleb and Lily attempt to enter, but Sherry-Anne shoved Lily out of the way.

"Ladies, please my patient doesn't need any stress," Nancy cried, "Which one of you is his wife?"

"Neither. My granddaughter Lily is his fiancée." Katha lied.

"Very well, you can go first Lily and you Caleb, because you're his son," Nancy announced, "The rest of you can wait in the room down the hall."

Nancy then pointed and waited while they went to the room. Nancy then escorted Lily and Caleb into the room. Lily grabbed Emmett's hand.

"I'm okay. It is sweetheart," Emmett reassured as Lily wiped tears away, "See, Caleb knows I'm okay. Right son?"

"Yes, he'll be fine soon, Lily and he won't get shot up again will you Dad? "Caleb agreed, though worry crept in his voice.

"I can't promise that, but I'm sure I've used up my quota of work accidents this year." Emmett joked then getting serious he exclaimed, "How's my witness? Doctor Nightshade wouldn't tell me."

Caleb looked at Lily and shook his head as if to say don't tell him.

"So he's dead?" Emmett asked sounding pained, and catching on, "Damn, poor guy and I didn't even get any information out of him."

"I'm so sorry Emmett," Lily sympathized.

"Are you sure you're okay, dad?" Caleb whispered.

"I'll be right as rain in a couple of days I have great recuperative powers," Emmett stated.

"Mom's worried too. No offence to your girlfriend, but she should see you, too," Caleb insisted.

"Send her in son," Emmett commanded.

"Can I?" Caleb asked Nurse Nancy who stood at the door.

"One of you will have to leave and your mother can only stay five minutes tops. My patient needs his rest," Nancy stipulated.

"I'll go but I'll be back later, Dad," Caleb stated.

"Love you son. Don't worry I'll just be sleeping and getting better here," Emmett responded.

Sherry-Anne came in the room crying hysterically and putting on a show. Nancy looked disgusted pulled her aside and said, "Calm yourself, because if you upset my patient you can leave now and not come back."

"I won't I promise, nurse," Sherry-Anne stated wiping away her tears. Then running to Emmett she exclaimed, "They wouldn't let me into to you and I was so worried!"

"I'm fine now Sherry-Anne. Why don't you take my credit card and get room at the hotel for you and Caleb and stay there for a few days until I get better. I'd like to spend some more time to get to know my son," Emmett begged.

"I do have some days coming to me. I guess I could call the hospital and get the time off. After all you're going to need some nursing care when you get out," Sherry-Anne replied her long red finger nails racking over possessively over Emmett's arm. Then she looked over Emmett's head and smiled maliciously at Lily.

"It's time to take for this patient to get some sleep," Nancy claimed sensing the tension, "You ladies are welcome to come back and visit in a couple of hours after we get him settled in and he has a little rest."

"Actually ladies if you would come and visit during visiting hours this evening that would be better. I'd like the patient to get some rest," Doctor Nightshade said coming in.

"Okay, see you later Emmett, darling." Lily stated claiming him and kissing him passionately on the lips.

"Goodbye darling," Emmett replied hiding a chuckle and smiling back.

Sherry-Anne leaned over and whispered, "I can't understand why your with that milk toast, but maybe this will make you think twice." as she kisses him full on the lips, "I'll bring your son back later."

"How is he, Lily?" asked Katha as she spotted them.

"He's a little better, but I need to get some hotel rooms nearby. I'm not leaving him."

"Of course you're not. Don't worry it's a couple of weeks to my wedding. I already rented hotel rooms for us at the Toronto Downtown Eaton Square Hotel."

"I have to get a room for Caleb and me," Sherry-Anne exclaimed.

"Sherry-Anne and Caleb I rented rooms for everyone for the next two days our treat." Katha answered.

"Thank-you that is very generous. Are the rooms nearby?" asked Sherry-Anne.

"It's about twenty-one minutes by car, but the hotel is first class. It's the Toronto Downtown Eaton Square Hotel," Katha explained.

"I guess that will do." Sherry-Anne answered, "Thank-you again Ms. Stewart. We'll see you much later."

Sherry-Anne then left with Caleb and hailed a cab outside the hospital.

"I like Caleb but I don't like that woman," Rose whispered to Katha.

"You know what they say dear, 'Keep your friends close and your enemies closer.' Katha stated then turning to Lily she said "Wasn't that from Sun-Tzu a military genius form 400 B.C.?"

"Yes it's a favourite quote of mine. Now I know where I got it from." Lily laughed.

"Let's go get a late lunch at the hotel, people," Katha said to Carol, Rose, Lily and Terrence.

"Or slupper," Rose improvised.

"Sounds, good. Whatever the meal, I'm starved," Carol replied.

"But you've been eating all kinds of stuff from the vending machines," protested Rose.

"I'm still hungry. Junk food doesn't count and it certainly doesn't fill you," Carol insisted.

They all laughed at this statement and Carol looked on in bewilderment.

"What? What did I say?" Carol asked.

"Nothing Carol," Rose stated hiding a smile, "Let's just get some lunch. I'm hungry too!"

Terrence retrieved the car and they all got into the car driving towards the hotel.

"I'll check us in and then join you in the dining room. Get a great table, Terrence." Katha cautioned as they reached the hotel, "Let me out here."

"See you there darling. I'll have some tea waiting for you." Terrence agreed, "Come on children. I'm starving let's park the car and go rustle up some grub."

~0~

Chapter 16 - Concentrating On My Holiday

"Shots rang out near the Niagara Falls Regional

Police Department. A visiting police officer, Emmett Rogers from Happy Valley, Ontario and an identified man were struck by bullets fired from a passing car. Orange was called and flew the two gunshot victims to Sunnybrook Health Sciences Centre trauma unit. No word yet on their conditions. Police ask the public for their help in identify the car and its occupants in this grainy video. Please call the Niagara Falls Regional Police department with any information," was heard over the radio.

"What have you done?" asked the voice.

"Nothing, I did what needed to be done. Did you think I wouldn't protect you? Don't I always protect your interests," the other voice answered patting the bed.

"I didn't need protection. I did none of this. Don't you start blaming me!" the voice insisted.

"Good, keep practicing that. They have to believe that, should it come to that," the other voice reassured.

"Do you really believe that I killed three people?" asked the voice.

"Of course you didn't. You killed two indirectly. They were a threat and you had someone eliminate the threat," the other voice soothed.

"You know me so well," the voice confessed.

"I do, don't I?" the other voice agreed.

"I miss him," the voice admitted.

"Of course you do. You knew him for such a long time," the other voice soothed.

"Why did he have to turn on me? We could have gone so far together," the voice exclaimed.

"He loved you he thought I would lead you astray. Foolish man! Did he really think you'd turn on me?" the other voice laughed, "Or that you would be his lover?"

"He was loyal up to that point," protested the voice.

"Loyalty does not waiver. It does not threaten those closest to you," said the other voice.

"What can we do? This has gotten terribly out of hand," asked the voice.

"I have a plan. Don't I always have plan?" the other voice demanded.

"I can always trust you to help me," the voice replied sounding relieved.

"Yes, you can. The first part of my plan is already in place. It might take a little bit of prodding. You have nothing to fear," the other voice reassured.

"Good, then I can concentrate on my holiday. I need to relax," the voice replied.

"And so do I." said the other voice giggling while undressing.

"Have I told you how much I love you?" asked the voice.

"No you haven't recently. I want to hear you wax about me," the other voice exclaimed.

"I adore you. A loyal giving person, you complete me," the voice cried.

"And?" the other voice prodded.

"And I love you," the voice answered.

"I love you to mi amore," the other voice said.

The man took the woman in his arms and stripped her clothes off one by one. Caressing each piece of flesh he tenderly laid her on the bed then tied off her hands and wrists to the bedpost with two scarfs he pulled out of his pockets.

"Oooh, kinky," she cried happily.

They spent the next hour satisfying their desires, before going their separate ways.

~0~

Chapter 17 - Eliminating the Threat

Sherry-Anne after spending time searching on her

computer, paced back and forth in her hotel room.

"Mom, what's wrong?" Caleb asked looking up from his television show.

"Nothing is wrong," Sherry-Anne lied.

Caleb frowned but said nothing. Used to his mom's mood swings, he knew questioning her more would yield no results. The hotel phone rang and Sherry-Anne jumped on it.

"It's for you. It's that woman's daughter, Rose Brooksfield," Sherry-Anne exclaimed sounding angry.

"Mom!!"Caleb admonished, "She'll hear you."

"Hello, Rose," Caleb said picking up the phone.

"The hotel is next to a mall. Isn't that cool? Carol and I want to go shopping for a present for your dad. Do you want to come?" Rose asked.

"Sure, but I have to check with my mom first," Caleb answered setting down the phone for a moment.

"Let us see, Rose wants you to go somewhere?" Sherry-Anne laughed.

"Yes. She wants me to go to the mall next door with her and Carol." Caleb admitted, "Please can I go? I'd like to get something at the mall for Dad."

"I guess that would be okay, but could you find something for me to give to your dad?" Sherry-Anne asked, handing Caleb three twenty dollar bills.

"Sure, I can do that. How much of this is for me?" Caleb asked.

"Here have another twenty. You can have forty dollars. Try to find something nice from me for the other forty, okay?" Sherry-Anne demanded.

"Thank-you mom," answered Caleb then picking up the phone again he said, "I can come I'll meet you in the lobby in ten minutes Rose, "I'll be back in a couple of hours."

Caleb then left. Sherry-Anne waited a few minutes then dialed a number on the telephone.

"Hello?" Sherry-Anne said.

"Hello." the voice stated on the other end of the phone.

"Did you really think you could get away with this?" Sherry-Anne asked angrily.

"Who is this?" the voice demanded.

"It's your daughter, the daughter you've never acknowledged .Your dirty little secret," Sherry-Anne exclaimed, angrily

"My daughter is a teenager. Who in the hell is this?" the voice asked.

"Really, you're going to pretend you don't know. I guess the next thing out of your mouth will be that you don't know my mother," Sherry-Anne cried bitterly.

"Who is your mother?" asked the voice sounding, genuinely puzzled.

"Oh we're playing that game, are we? You think your favourite entertainment and amusement, the game of secrets begins now." Sherry-Anne continued, "Except your game ends now."

"Are you threatening me?" the voice asked.

"Take it any way you want, but if you think I'm going to let you get away with murdering my mother and shooting my son's father; you can think again. I have your letters to my mother," Sherry-Anne sniped.

"I killed no one. I really don't understand. Who is your mother?" the voice complained.

"You claim you killed no one? And I suppose Emmett wasn't shot and almost killed today? Fine, shall I give you a hint daddy, dearest?" Sherry-Anne asked, "It seems we have a family system of lying about who all our fathers are."

"You insinuate that I'm your father; so I ask again; who is your mother?"

"My mother is...was...Betty 'Blue' Renfrew. She posed as my sister. Does that ring any bells for you?"

"Betty was your mother? And you have a child? How old are you?" the voice asked sounding shocked.

"You didn't know did you? How did she hide it from you? You must have impregnated her in high school." Sherry-Anne stated, "Like mother, like daughter I guess."

"You say I know this Betty 'Blue' Renfrew, the woman recently murdered and not only that you claim you are my daughter by her?" the voice asked.

"That's right daddy, dearest," Sherry-Anne said sarcastically.

"Even if any of his were true what do you want from me?" the voice asked.

"Nothing, I'm just warning you your career is over and you won't go get away with this. I will make you pay for killing my mother and wounding my son's father," Sherry-Anne cried, "I don't care who you were."

"This is all very entertaining dear; but really if you had any proof of this you'd have gone to the police all ready. Now wouldn't you have Sherry?" the voice said manically.

"So you did know who I was? My name is Sherry-Anne; not that you'd care."

"I'm hanging up. Now don't call here again or I'll have to resort to measures you wouldn't like," the voice insisted.

"Oh, I wouldn't do that daddy. You see I have proof of everything I'm saying."

"Like I said you have no proof, or you'd have gone to the cops already."

"Maybe for genetics sake, I'd like to protect my father; but a little monetary compensation for all those years you neglected me wouldn't be refused," Sherry-Anne answered.

"Oh, you are your father's daughter then, aren't you? I do rather like your forwardness. I'll be in touch Sherry-Anne." the voice cried.

Sherry-Anne then heard two clicks as he hung up and wondered if somehow had overheard their conversation? No, she was on edge and imaging obstacles and villains. She spoke with her father he'd back off now because he thought she wanted money. Frankly that was the only thing her biological father understood; that and power; but she had a back-up plan that would protect them all.

As soon as she set up a meet with her father she'd contact Emmett's colleagues. They could fit her with a wire and nail her father to the wall for Betty's murder. He wasn't getting away with Betty's murder.

The letter had said that she was marrying her lover and had hinted that he was famous yet again, and that she had a secret she wanted to divulge to Sherry-Anne. Even still it had been a huge shock when Caleb had whispered that Betty was her mother. Sherry-Anne had heard whispered rumours before from her Great-Aunt but everything she said was a lie so how could it possibly be true. So Sherry-Anne dismissed all that. The truth? She had just been afraid to ask Betty.

Poor Betty, she knew what her parents were like and how they treated Sherry-Anne when she told them she was pregnant, she could understand why Betty had been force to keep this hidden. It was hard to go against them and she had probably not wanted to harm any good memories Sherry-Anne had of them by letting her know they were really her grandparents. But how she wished she could have known when her mother was alive. To be able to thank her mother for all the wonderful things Betty had done for her. She wouldn't have custody of Caleb or a career if it wasn't for her mother.

Sherry-Anne had remembered Betty talking about her lover. How he was famous how they had gone to high school together. Sherry-Anne had searched Spacebook pages for the high school after reading the letter. Some nostalgic people had posted pictures from their yearbook and several pictures of different people in her school years. Sherry-Anne then had scrutinized those pictures and had been able to narrow down who the man who had slept with Betty had been.

This man who had been her mother's long term love was Sherry-Anne's father she was sure of it; but could he also be her killer? Was Sherry-Anne right about that? He had denied it; but he did say he'd be in touch. Did that mean he was guilty? If he was he would pay! He wouldn't get away with killing Betty she'd see to it. She had sister's too, full blood sister that had been denied their mother's love. The murder would pay or her name wasn't Sherry-Anne.

~0~

Three hours later

Sherry-Anne wondered why Caleb had not returned. He

said he would be a couple of hours, but here it was three hours later and no sign of him. She remembered how it felt to be a teenager and be with the one you had a crush on and frowned. Did it have to be the witch's daughter? She would just steer Caleb to a more suitable girl.

The girl with that family, the Kelly's; they were all pure trash. Crap, she sounded like her mother...scrap that her grandmother. She called Caleb again and got his voice mail immediately. Darn, he must have turned his phone off, or forgot to charge it again. Something couldn't have happened to Caleb could it have? No, she was sure he just forgot to charge his phone; being in puppy love did that. Wait a minute, surely Rose had a phone? She'd march up to that woman Lily's room and get her to call her daughter. Lily must be expecting Rose back too and didn't want unexpected consequences for her daughter.

How old was that kid anyway? Could Caleb get himself into a pack load of trouble? She couldn't be younger than sixteen was she? Then she started to think of her experience and she thought, I don't want to be a grandmother yet, I have to break the circle of children born to teens. I have to find Caleb and maybe I should talk to that boy about consequences.

Sherry Anne looked over and saw her winter coat and realized in her hurry to get to Emmett's side, she brought both her fall winter coats from the hotel. She loved her long puffy white winter coat, but the red long wool coat also to mid-calf length was also attractive. Why did she think about coats? She should be heading up to Lily's hotel to get that number, so Caleb could come back to the hotel room. Sherry-Anne walked quickly to Lily's room and knocked loudly on the door.

"Who could that be?" wondered Katha, "I hope they don't wake up Terrence; his sugars are too high. He needs to rest and recuperate."

"I'm sorry you two had to share the suite with us and that Terrence felt unwell," Lily answered.

"He hasn't been following his diet and there's too much stress. He should know better with his diabetes," Katha cried angrily but Lily could tell she was worried.

Lily hurried to answer the door.

"Sherry-Anne, please come in," Lily said answering the door.

"I didn't want to bother you but Caleb said he'd be back an hour ago," Sherry-Anne blurted.

"Kids, there always saying they'll be back at a certain time and then you wait and wait," Katha commented.

"Rose is usually really good about getting back in time. Why didn't I realize she wasn't back yet?" asked Lily of Katha

"Well if you could call her, I'd really appreciate it. Caleb must have forgotten to plug in his new phone and it must be dead because it goes straight to voicemail," Sherry-Anne exclaimed.

"I'll call her right now," Lily said picking up her cell phone.

"Her phone goes straight to voicemail too. And so does Carol's. That's odd. The mall is right next door, let's go look for them," Lily stated.

"Okay, but it is cold out. You should grab your coat and I have to go get mine." Sherry-Anne commented.

"Oh no, I forgot my coat in Niagara Falls with the hurry to get here," Lily realized.

"I brought both of mine. I don't know why I did that. We're about the same size, why don't you borrow one of mine." Sherry-Anne offered, "You can come to my room and borrow my white calf length one it has a hood."

"Thank-you Sherry-Anne," Lily replied.

Sherry-Anne and Lily then went to retrieve the coats before going next door to the mall to search for the kids.

~0~

In a dark sedan driven by a mysterious driver a person sits brooding and putting together a high powered rifle.

Bitch! Who did she think she was? Did she really think she could threaten a politician and remain unscathed? And to claim she was his daughter? He was much too young for daughter so old and yet mathematically it was possible. If Betty Blue was Sherry-Anne's mother that figured, the woman acted like a slut. Goodness knows she seen Sherry-Anne, the filthy whore flirting with that policeman who was so obviously with that other woman.

The woman called him daddy. Being a father was more than sleeping and producing a child. He wasn't her father. She had gotten rid of that problem of that evil bitch, Betty Blue. She just have to do it again a little more creatively. She hadn't really meant to kill Betty when she went to meet her at that truck stop, but when that bitch was there coming out of the family washroom, Betty said such awful things about him. How dare she say such filthy things about him?

Needless to say her temper had gotten the best of her. Betty had said he strung her along, not Betty. How he had three children with Betty.

That he loved Betty!!! Lies, all lies out of her filthy, disgusting, pouty, mouth. He loved her! He said she was his true love that he would be with her forever. She slept with him put up with his disgusting sexual fantasies. Did everything he wanted and more and yet that evil bitch, Betty dared to say he left to marrying her. Betty had dared to say just open your eyes and see. Well she had opened that woman's eyes.

Tee hee. Silly woman always losing her shoes it had been nothing to pick up that six inch heel and poke out her f***ing eye. She'd laughed when she realized it sounded like that old nursery rhyme that stupid woman went around quoting, "Little Betty Blue lost her holiday shoe; what shall little Betty do? Give her another. To match the other and then she'll walk upon two."

Only she'd never be walking on two shoes ever again. And if she had her way neither would this woman Sherry-Anne Mobley.

"Pull up here and wait; but remember I've paid you well and we know what happens to people that cross me," the woman said to the driver.

"It was never about the money." the driver answered, "You know I would protect you with my life."

"Good then this is settled, we wait for her," the woman answered back.

"I didn't sign up for this," the driver said unhappily.

"Don't you want me happy," she said running long red fingernails across his arm.

"Of course I do but this? This is murder," the driver exclaimed.

"Miguel, don't you forget our game."

"Game?"

"Where you pretend to be the kitchen staff." she continued.

"I am the kitchen staff at the Pagett Hotel Toronto. Where you meet your lover," Miguel stated.

"Silly, I know that and one day we will be together. Did we not talk endless hours over the internet? Did I not get you the job driving for him?" She lied placating him.

"One day you will burn the fire in someone so deep you won't be able to put out the flames and you will get burnt," Miguel whispered.

"There! There she is. I recognize her horrible white coat." she said.

The woman took her automatic rifle, took aim and shot through the window striking her target. Then she instructed the driver to quickly drive away.

~0~

Chapter 18 -
White Coat,
Brilliant Red

Lily lay on the ground in front of the hotel, Sherry-Anne's

white coat spread out in a fan around her. Lily's life's blood seeped out slowly, turning parts of the white coat into a brilliant red as Sherry-Anne looked on in horror.

Sherry-Anne quickly dialed 911 telling them, "A woman has been shot and needs an ambulance."

"Could you tell me the address please?" the operator asks

"Address? How hell should I know? It's in front of the Toronto Eaton Square Hotel. Oh god, I just realized we didn't have to go outside. We could have exited to the mall from the hotel. Why did we go outside?" Sherry-Anne said setting her cell phone on the ground beside her, leaving it on speakerphone. She then took off her coat and long sleeved shirt and pressed the cotton sweater into Lily's wound.

Was it gang warfare? Were they in danger from other shots here? Or something else more sinister? Sherry-Anne thought.

"Please listen, Madame. Is the patient breathing?" the operator asked.

"She's breathing, but she's bleeding so much and it hit her chest. I think they've nicked an artery. That can't be good. She won't have long if you don't hurry," Sherry-Anne answered.

As Sherry-Anne waited for the ambulance her phone beeped, she put the emergency call on hold and answered instinctively, "Caleb?"

"No, not Caleb but I know where he is." the voice she recognized as her father said.

The number was from his hotel room she recognized it. He couldn't have shot Lily mistaking her for Sherry-Anne. Could he? Who did this? And why had he mentioned Caleb. Had he done something to Caleb?" she thought.

"Where is my son, you jerk?" Sherry-Anne yelled.

"Now, now that's not very lady-like language. He is safe for now...with his two little girlfriends. Lusty little devil isn't he? Must take after his grandfather. Don't worry, I won't harm a hair on his head. He is my grandson after all; unless he's mother won't give me the evidence she holds," her father said.

"You can have it all, anything you want just give me back my son Caleb and the girls," Sherry-Anne cried, terrified.

Lily heard this and even though she was struggling to stay conscious with her wound she demanded, "You know who did this? They have the girls too?"

Sherry-Anne nodded and looked apologetic. Lily grappled with the pain from her wound, and the spreading realization that she could die. Frankly, she is terrified. This can't be happening. Not again. Now Rose could be motherless all because Sherry-Anne held onto a secret. Lily sucked back the pain and bit her tongue to find some clarity. Trying hard to hold back her anger and as she felt her chest tighten and blood oozed from her wound; Lily scrambled and found a solution to save the children.

"Pretend you are shot. He will let kids go," Lily whispered and then lost consciousness.

Sherry-Anne let out a scream of pain and in an act which should have won an Oscar, she dropped the phone then grabbed it up saying, "Why Daddy? Why did hire someone to kill me?"

Sherry-Anne then dropped the phone again and left it on as she put it next to Lily; catching the sounds Lily's body made suffering from her bullet shot wounds.

"Who shot you? Oh god, not again. Don't die on me Sherry-Anne. I should have told you I love you. You're mine, my child. Don't die. Daddy will make her pay," is heard from the phone on his end. Ambulance's sirens blared as Sherry-Anne disconnected the phone.

~0~

Chapter 19 - Taken

Rose couldn't believe how easy it was for someone to take them. Men coming up behind all of them and then have guns jabbed in their sides and told them not to fight back. Like something out of a movie. It was totally unreal. Yet no one screamed and called for a security person; as they marched ahead of the gunmen guns in their sides. No one even seemed to see their distress.

Caleb, Rose and Carol pushed into a waiting van and then gassed, all without raising any alarm. Now they were awake and tied to chairs. Rose could see that Caleb was tied in a chair beside them. Rose recognized Carol by the heavy breathing and snoring she heard behind her; so Carol must be tied to a chair there. Rose acknowledged with some surprise that she alone appeared to be awake; maybe because she had covered her face with her hoodie and hadn't breathed in as much of the gas. What Rose did know was that they had to somehow get untied and get out of here before whoever had taken them came back. Rose bent her wrist at an odd angle.

"Sometimes it was good to be double jointed," she thought as she twisted her fingers as well. Her hands were free soon her feet and ankles were added as she quickly untied them.

"Carol wake-up," she whispered in Carol's ear.

"What? I'm tired; go away Rose. We'll do whatever you want to do later, I promise," Carol replied.

"Carol we are prisoners. We have to get away wake-up," Rose stated.

"What do you mean we're prisoners?" Carol cried, her eyes opening and then she realizes she's tied, "Again? I've got to stop hanging out with you."

Rose untied Carol and said, "Very funny Carol. Now we have to wake up Caleb and get free him. You get his ankles I'll get his hands."

"I knew you both liked me, but this is some dream," Caleb muttered still half asleep.

Rose and Carol suppressed a laugh and then began to loosen his bonds. Caleb awoke with a start.

"Wow, it wasn't a dream? We're prisoners?" Caleb enquired, "Have you seen our captors?"

"No, we haven't seen anyone and if they come in cover your eyes. If we see them, they'll probably kill us," explained Rose, "I think our best bet is to escape now."

"Does either of you have a nail file, or something sharp?" Carol enquired, "I think if I had something slim I could pick this lock. It is really an older lock and easy to pick with the right tool."

"Will this do?" asked Rose, taking a bobby pin out of her hair

"That just might. Thank goodness your bangs are growing out and you needed that booby pin," Carol answered taking the booby pin and inserting it into the lock.

"Can she really do that?" Caleb wondered.

"Yes, her dad's an electrician, but her grandfather on her Dad's side is a locksmith." Rose answered, "And she spent a lot of time with both of them so she's good at that stuff."

"Got it," Carol announced as she showed them an open door.

"Where do you think we are?" Caleb asked.

"Darned, if I know." Rose answered.

"Is anyone out there?" Caleb enquired.

"It looks like a hallway. It has to go out somewhere. Come on we won't get caught if we go slow and quietly," Carol stated.

"Don't forget to hide if you see someone," Rose cautioned.

Caleb, Rose and Carol crept silently down the hallway. Halfway down the passage they heard a voice and then looked around the corner to see a man speaking on the phone. Caleb motioned with his hands for Rose and Carol to join him on their hands and knees and crawl past the man. Crawling quietly they passed the man without him noticing. They moved a short distance away where Carol in the lead then spotted a door.

"I think that might be the front door," Carol whispered.

Carol, Rose and Caleb opened the door slowly trying to keep it from squeaking. Exiting the building they realized they were now in an industrial part of a city.

"Do you think we're still in Toronto?" asked Rose.

"Yes, see it's there in the distance. The one all lit up, I think that's the CN tower," Caleb answered.

"Which way should we go?" Carol enquired.

"If the CN tower is that way, then I think it's that way to the hotel," Caleb said pointing.

"We need to run; once they find out we're gone they'll chase us," Rose said.

Running down the unknown street trying to put distance between them and the building, darkness overwhelmed them. The sky shone like black velvet, with no stars showing and the street lights seem dim in this part of town. Passing darkened homes they are reluctant to go to any doors in case someone worse lay behind the walls.

Finally after what seemed like hours of wandering, Rose spotted a variety store and motioned for the others to follow her inside. In the store they turned to the store clerk; who stared at them with distrust and disdain.

"We've been kidnapped, please call the police," they all begged.

"I don't know what you're trying to pull, but I'm not going to be part of it. Now out, with all of you," the clerk replied.

"We're telling the truth. Listen to us! We were kidnapped from the Eaton's Centre this afternoon," Caleb stated.

"If you had been kidnapped you would have been mentioned on the news. Get lost with your wild story," the clerk argued.

"Just turn up the radio please," begged Rose, "I'm sure you'll hear all about it."

An announcer broke in with the news... *"In breaking news, last night a shooting downtown near the Eaton's Centre has taken a life. Sherry-Anne Mobley thirty-two of London, Ontario died as result of her wounds. In unrelated news the police have issued an Amber Alert for Rose Brooksfield and Carol Banks. Rose Brooksfield is described as five foot five, or six inches tall, one hundred ten pounds, with blonde bobbed hair and brown eyes. Carol Banks is described as blonde hair to her shoulders and blue eyed five foot five inches tall. They may be accompanied by a young man seventeen years old, six feet, one hundred and sixty pounds going by the name of Caleb Rogers. If you have seen these two girls or the young man, please notify police."*

"What? Did I hear that right did they just say my mom was shot? That she's dead?" asked Caleb reeling, "No, I heard wrong, didn't I? They would have said I was her son and that the two were related."

"Oh Caleb, I'm so sorry," Rose cried, "I can't believe this happened."

"Caleb, I'm so sorry. This is awful," Carol stated.

"Then I heard right? My mom is dead?"

"I'm so sorry it's not fair that this should happen to you and your mother. I know it's not the same, but I lost my Dad to murder about six months ago and I know how awful it can be. If there is anything you need, please let me know."

"I called the cops you kids better be telling the truth. Or they're going to lock you up," the clerk announced.

"Good grief! Didn't you hear the Amber alert for us?" Rose asked.

"What Amber alert?"

"I suppose you didn't hear the other announcement either, about the woman being shot near the Eaton centre?"

"I heard that. I'm not deaf you know," the clerk complained.

"Then do you mind giving us some peace? Caleb just heard his mom was murdered," Carol demanded.

"That woman who was murdered near the Eaton's Centre, was that your mother?" the clerk enquired.

"Yes, that was his mom. Now please give him some space," Rose commented as Caleb tried to hide his face so no one would see his tear streaked face.

Sirens were soon heard and police officers with drawn guns entered the store.

~0~

Chapter 20-
Secrets Can Kill

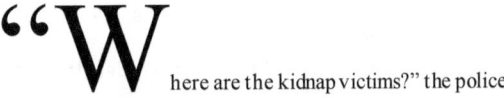

" " W here are the kidnap victims?" the police

officers asked as they enter the variety store guns drawn as the clerk pointed to the girls, the police yell at Caleb, "Hands over your head. Now! Down on the ground! Legs spread," the police officers commanded.

Caleb complied, puzzled and scared as the police officer placed his arms at his waist level and then put him in cuffs. The policeman then roughly pulled him to his feet.

"Hey, don't hurt him. He was kidnapped too," Rose shouted.

"Let me get this story straight. All three of you teenagers were kidnapped?" enquired one of the patrol officers coming over to Rose.

"We were."

"Okay, details please one at a time. What is your name, young lady?" asked the patrol officer.

"My name is Rose Brooksfield. This is Carol Banks and Caleb Rogers. I'm sure my mom, Lily Kelly-Brooksfield would have put an Amber Alert on us by now. Besides we heard over the radio that there was an alert; so why aren't you up on it?" Rose answered.

"Bernard, there's an Amber Alert out on these kids," said an officer coming in.

"See? What did Rose tell you? Now can Caleb get those cuffs off?" Carol asked.

The other police officer then took Rose and Carol to one corner while they spoke with Caleb in another.

"Sorry kid," the patrol officer said, removing Caleb's cuffs.

Caleb rubbed his wrists and politely replied, "Understandable, gentlemen, you thought the girls were in danger. I like to speak with Sergeant Detective Downie or Sergeant Detective Brooks of the R.C.M.P., they are working with the Niagara Falls Regional Police Department and try to solve the murder of Elizabeth Renfrew, also known as Betty Blue. I think my mother Sherry-Anne Mobley and my grandmother, Elizabeth Renfrew were killed because of my grandfather."

"Betty was your grandmother?" Rose and Carol cried, shocked from the other corner.

Carol turned to Caleb her eyes lit up with curiosity, she shouted across the room, "So who is your grandfather?"

"Everyone who knows my biological grandfather is now in danger; so I'm not saying anything until I see Sergeant Detective Downie, or Sergeant Detective Brooks." Caleb insisted, cryptically, "Know this though; that man will pay for killing my family. I will not consider him any kind of kin."

"Now don't be taken things into your own hands, son. Right now we need the information on your kidnapping," the police officer demanded.

"We could stand her and tell you all about that, but I want to get to my mother's body. I already told you I believe that all of this started with the killings of my mother and grandmother," Caleb replied, bravely putting aside his sorrow.

"We need more information," Bernard insisted.

Caleb's mask slipped, he wiped back tears and then pleaded, "Please can I go to the hospital first and say goodbye to my mother?"

"I'm sure that can be arranged, son; now about the kidnapping?"

"I can tell you what happened. We were minding our own business in the mall, the Eaton's Centre Mall, when these three guys come up behind us and stick guns in our sides outside. They demanded we come with them," Rose stated stepping across the room and standing beside Caleb. Carol joined her a few seconds later.

"We do what were told they shove us in a van outside the mall and gas us. Next thing I know Rose untied me from a chair, in a warehouse," Carol commented.

"Yes, that's about right, Carol. But I pulled my hoodie up and covered my mouth when they gassed us, so it didn't keep me out as long. I was kind of in twilight zone when they carried us in. They placed us in these chairs and tied us up, but I was still kind of out of it. It took me some time to realize what they'd done; but when I did I untied myself."

"How did you manage that, miss," the police officer asked.

"I'm double jointed. See?" Rose exclaimed as she bent back her fingers.

"Oh yuck! I hate when you do that Rose," Carol cried.

"You ought to be glad I can do this. If I wasn't double jointed I could never have got those ropes off," Rose sniped.

"And that what happened, miss?" prompted the policeman.

Caleb looked at the two girls amazed at how quickly they spoke and still managed to tell the whole tale. He took a breath to continue the story, but Rose beat him to it.

Oh well, Rose was the heroine she had saved them all by untying them and then Carol saved them by picking the lock. It kind of made a fellow feel useless. These two fourteen year old girls were amazing.

"While I got the rope off behind my back, I untied my feet. Then I untied and woke up, Carol...sort of at the same time. Carol helped me wake up Caleb and untie him. Then the three of us snuck out of this old abandoned plant they took us too. We crept down the hall until we go to this door that was closed. We heard some guy talking on a cell phone so we crawled by the door and then we went out the front door. Then we ran and ran. It must have been fifty blocks. Of course then we spotted this store," Rose explained.

"Wow, that's quite the story." the other policeman acknowledged.

"I don't like he said that. Are you insinuating we're lying," Carol asked

"No, of course not. Thank-you, miss," replied the police officer then turning to Caleb he said, "Is that how it happened, son?"

"I can't add anything to that. That's what happened!" Caleb replied.

"Okay then," Gerald stated putting away his notebook.

"My boss says you have to all be checked out at the hospital," stated the other police officer coming back.

"We're fine," protested all three.

"We've got to follow the rules. You were gassed after all," the police officer answered directing them to his car and then putting them in the back seat.

"Fine, but then I must see my mother and say goodbye. Please, take us to the same hospital her body is in. It's probably Sunnybrook Health Centre." begged Caleb.

The two policemen conferred and seconds later the one police officer said, "Okay, son, we can do that. I'll radio in to get some more information on the shooting."

"Thank-you," answered Caleb.

The police officers radio reacted and told him to take the teens to Sunnybrook Health Centre. They were placed in the backseat of the police car while the police officers drove to the hospital in silence. Caleb, Rose, and Carol arriving at the emergency room and were escorted into it by the police officer. He signalled to the staff and a nurse let them in through the locked door and into the emergency rooms.

"But I need to see my mom, now," Caleb protested to the nurse.

"Sorry son, rules are rules. You need to be assessed and cleared before we can take you to your mother," the cop said, "I'll wait for you, children outside."

"Children? Did he call us children?" Carol asked outraged.

"Be quiet Carol. Can't you see Caleb is upset? Have some sympathy," Rose insisted.

"Sorry, Caleb, I kind of forgot for a second," Carol commented.

Caleb muttered something, but neither girl heard him, or pursued the information. A nurse handed them gowns and directed them to separate cubicles near one another. She then instructed them to put on and they waited for a doctor to see them.

"I've never be so scared in my life," Carol said through the curtain.

"It ranked up there with when you were taken prisoner by Dr. Thomas and his crazy wife," Rose exclaimed.

"You were taken prisoner before?" asked Caleb.

"We were taken prisoner a couple of times actually; but the last
time I was kidnapped, when our crazy principal killed her
boyfriend. Her boyfriend was our choir teacher and she took it in
her head to kidnap me and Rose's Aunt Amelia," Carol explained.

"Carol picked the lock while been held captive there, too. She used
some wires to open it. She saved herself and my Aunt Amelia.
She's very resourceful and brave."

"How did you two get away?" Caleb asked.

"First I tried to sympathize with our evil principal. If they see you
as one of them they might like you and then they won't kill you.
Rose taught me that when we were taken before."

"Rose taught you that?"

"Yes, we were kidnapped before by a crazy serial killer and that
helped."

"You were both kidnapped by a serial killer? What kind of crazy
place is Happy Valley?"

"It's not a crazy place. We've just had bad luck," Rose
commented.

"Okay, so then what happened with that crazy principal that
kidnapped you?"

"Her husband came back in and heard her confess how much she
loved our choir teacher."

"Don't forget to tell him they murdered him."

"Yah, that too; anyway he was so angry. I thought he'd kill us
immediately and my now Aunt Amelia, too. I talked to that weirdo
doctor and made him see the bitch principal used him."

"Carol, language!" Rose cautioned, "We're in a public place."

"Gee Rose, quit being the language police. So Caleb, the principal
didn't care about her husband at all. She wanted what she wanted
and would use whoever and whomever she needed to get her own
ends. I'd almost convinced him to turn evidence against his crazy
wife. I still can't believe she was our principal."

"Really? She was your principal?" Caleb commented.

"Yah, and I almost had her husband all on our side; like I said but then that woman grabbed a Taser."

"A Taser... she had a Taser?" Caleb cried.

"Oh, yes." Carol commented. "But Aunt Amelia's boyfriend Dan (the cop and my uncle) came in and shot the Taser right out of her hand."

"Then what happened?"

"Aunt Amelia and I gave a victim statement when they both pleaded guilty, a few days ago. He received ten years. She got life," Carol answered.

"Carol's a heroine," Rose cried.

"Rose is modest about her own achievements. You saw how she saved us untying us from those kidnappers just a little while ago. When Rose's Dad was murdered Rose burst in like Annie Oakley and saved her whole family," Carol claimed.

"Carol, don't tell him any more about that," admonished Rose embarrassed.

"She's a crack shot. She charged in when this serial killer guy had nothing to lose. After all he'd killed her great-aunt, great uncle, four cousins, and her uncle without being caught. He'd also recently killed her father."

"This is the man who killed your father? Were you crazy Rose?"

"Yes, probably, but I couldn't let him hurt them."

"He took her family...prisoners," Carol explained.

"My mom's gone...I'll never see her smile again," Caleb commented his voice breaking.

"I'm so sorry Caleb," Rose answered, "It's not the same as my dad, but I do understand and how much that hurts."

"What did you do after that man took them prisoner Rose?" Caleb asked changing the subject.

Rose didn't answer and Carol continued to explain, "She went into the house her gun blazing."

"You had a gun?"

"It was Brad's bullet that hit the bad guy not mine," Rose explained, "I'm not a killer.

"You actually used the gun?"

"My dad taught me how to shoot a gun. If I hadn't been so scared; maybe I would have aimed better," Rose complained.

"Who was this Brad and I can't believe you shot a gun and then missed him?"

"My bullet went into the wall and missed Sergeant Detective Brad Owens, the serial killer," Rose explained.

"You fired a gun at a cop, who turned out to be a serial killer? I think I remember reading or hearing something about a cop being arrested, but I didn't realize it happened in Happy Valley," Caleb repeated, shocked.

"She wouldn't have fired if she didn't have to," Carol protested.

"I didn't want to lose any more of my family," Rose cried.

"Holy crap, a serial killer cop. No wonder they had a hard time catching him; unbelievable that you were able to get away from him in one piece."

"Your dad helped me," Rose protested.

"My dad seems like a pretty good guy; that's why I can't understand why he dumped my mom..."

"There's probably more to the story that you don't know about."

"Probably, but I don't want to talk about them. You've been through a lot, but you got through this," Caleb said, "I just want this exam over so I can see my mom. I won't believe it until I see her and get to say goodbye. Then maybe it will seem real and then

I can check on my dad. I can't believe they were both shot. It still hasn't really sunk in that my mom...my mom is..."

"I'm so sorry about your mother, Caleb; losing my Dad that way, was the hardest thing I've ever faced, but with my good friend, Carol, I got through it. We will be there for you Caleb. We'll help you when you need a friend."

"Thank-you, Rose that means a lot to me, especially when I'm going to have to tell my dad. I mean he's laid up and I have to tell him that I'm his for good. That he's stuck with me," Caleb answered.

"He's not stuck with you. He's lucky to have you for a son," Rose answered.

"Yes, he is," Carol chimed in.

"Thank-you Rose and Carol." Caleb answered. "Any ideas on how to tell him?"

Their conversation was interrupted by the appearance of a doctor in Carol's cubicle and then to Rose's and Caleb's cubicle. Checking them all over and listening to all their lungs he gives them the okay. Dressing quickly they exited the room to find Sergeant Detective Downie and Sergeant Detective Brooks waiting for them.

"Ms. Banks, Ms. Brooksfield and Mr. Roger, would you please come with us?" Sergeant Detective Downie and Sergeant Detective Brooks demanded.

"I want to see my mother. Now! I'm not waiting any longer," Caleb countered.

"We will be happy to take you to your mother, Caleb, and then the three of you can fill us in on your kidnapping," Sergeant Detective Downie said.

"But we already told the other cops," protested Carol.

"Then you'll be able to recall all the details for us. Besides I understand Caleb has some other tidbits he'd like to share."

"Yes, I do," Caleb answered.

"After you, Miss Brooksfield, Miss Banks, Mr. Rogers," Sergeant Detective Downie.

The police officers take them on an elevator to the fifth floor and down a long hallway.

"This can't be the way to the morgue," Caleb protested.

"Just trust us and follow us Mr. Rogers," Sergeant Detective Downie insisted.

At the end of the hall they are met by Katha who hugged them all and cried, "Oh, thank-you, God. You're all safe."

"I need to see my mom." Caleb demanded.

Before his shocked eyes his mother appeared hearty and whole.

"Mom? You're alive? You're really, okay?" Caleb blubbered, tears streaming down his face.

Sherry-Anne also crying hugged him tight to her chest unable to say a word.

Caleb pulled himself out of her embrace and cried, "I don't understand Mom. They said you were shot. That you were dead."

"It wasn't me that was shot. Lily wore my coat," Sherry-Anne answered.

"No, not my mom. It can't be. I can't lose her too!" Rose gasped and covered her mouth and looked to Katha for confirmation.

Seeing the evidence that Lily had been shot in Katha's eyes she turned ash white and grabbed the wall for support. Carol reached out and grabbed her hand.

"It's okay, Rosey baby. She's not dead. She's a Kelly woman she'll beat this," Katha said grabbing Rose's right side to upright her.

"What kind of damage? Does she have bullet in her arm like Emmett?" Rose asked hopeful, "They faked Sherry-Anne's death, right? But my mom's fine. It's just a minor flesh wound?"

"Baby girl, it's a little more serious than that," Terrence said gently, as Katha turned to hide her face and tears that she hastily wiped away.

"Lily is a fighter. She had a bullet in her chest that hit some ribs and went into her lung. It nicked some arteries, which they managed to repair; but your mom lost a lot of blood. So until her body can realize that's the blood's been replaced; she's going to have a hard fight," Terrence explained.

"Mom's critical?" Rose asked, seizing the hidden words.

"She won't be on the critical list for long. Like I said your mother's a Kelly," Katha stated.

"Can I see her?"

"You can see her for about ten minutes an hour; the nurse said you could go in when you arrived. Stick to the ten minutes or they'll restrict your visits," Katha cautioned.

Rose went in by herself noting the machine that breathed for her mother. Her mother was so still; but she was alive. Lily wouldn't leave Rose. She couldn't! She grabbed her mother's hand and patted it gently.

"Fight mom," Rose advised, "I'll be back in an hour but you get better mom. I need you."

Rose then exited the room to find Caleb still waiting to go see his dad. She sat down on the sofa next to Katha, and Carol. Rose noted Grandpa Terrence was on a phone in the hallway.

"My mom will be here soon. She's really angry. I think she blames your family and then I'll have to go home. We'll you be okay, Rose?" Carol asked.

"Yes, I have Grandma Katha and Grandpa Terrence."

"You're not going home Carol. I spoke to your mother after you did and she has agreed that I can take care of you. In fact I gave her an all- expenses paid trip for her and your father to an inclusive resort in Mexico," Grandpa Terrence said stepping back into the room.

"What? But they hate each other."

"No, dear, they love each other so as I said I paid for a trip for the two of them. They were going to be in London for the wedding but your dad has to work, the first of January to make up for this trip so he didn't want to fly back so fast. They'll be back in Happy Valley before New Year's Eve, but for almost the next two weeks they're incommunicado; unless there's an emergency."

"Oh, thank-you Grandpa Terrence. I do love you," Carol answered

"That settles that. But who did this? Who had us kidnapped?" asked Rose.

"I think I know who did it," Caleb answered.

"This was your grandfather, Caleb?" asked Rose, remembering what Caleb had said to the cops.

"I suspect it was Rose. I promise I'll tell you who he is later," Caleb answered, turning to Sergeant Detective Downie he said, "Before I tell you all this I'd like to see my Dad. Maybe then, I'll have to tell you both, only one time."

"I guess we can get your statement later Ms. Brooksfield, Ms. Banks," Sergeant Detective Downie said motioning it to Sergeant Detective Brooks.

"Let go see your Dad and Ms. Mobley, you will join us," Sergeant Detective Downie demanded.

"Yes sir," Sherry-Anne said.

Caleb and Sherry-Anne followed him as they walk to Emmett's room.

"Can we go see Emmett first tell him about Lily? It's entirely my fault that Lily was shot and I know he cares about her," asked Sherry-Anne.

"Yes, I guess that's possible but when they get to the nitty-gritty of the story come and get me," Sergeant Detective Downie commented to the other police officer.

"Thank-you, sir," Caleb said.

"Hello, darling, Emmett," Sherry-Anne purred.

"Hello, Dad," Caleb said with a slight hesitation in his voice.

"Finally I though those nurses had chased everyone off. A slight fever and a little double vision and they get a little pushy," Emmett commented.

"You've had a fever and double vision? What did the doctor say about that?" Sherry-Anne asked, sounding worried.

"They just restricted me to quiet and wouldn't even let me watch television." Emmett whined.

"Men! You're all big babies when you're sick," Sherry-Anne commented.

"Okay, you two you're barely looking at me. I'm not that sick, tell me why you have an escort? What's up?"

Caleb and Sherry looked at him but said nothing.

"The stress of not knowing will make me more unwell," pleaded Emmett.

"Dad..."Caleb began.

"Caleb was kidnapped, but as you can see he is free now and safe," blurted Sherry-Anne.

"Caleb was kidnapped? Thank god you're safe. You're okay son?"

"I'm okay dad but..."

"Something else happened and it's my entire fault that all of this occurred," Sherry-Anne cried tears falling from her eyes.

"Sherry-Anne, please don't cry. Whatever it is we can make it right." Emmett comforted, "Our boy is safe. That's all that matters."

"You don't understand," Sherry-Anne cried, "It really is all my fault."

Sherry-Anne began hiccupping with tears continuing to run down her face.

"When Caleb, Rose, and Carol went missing we went to find them. I loaned Lily my white coat. They must have thought Lily, was me... I mean I...oh I don't know how to say it," Sherry-Anne continued.

"Just spit it out, Sherry-Anne," Emmett demanded.

"They shot her, Emmett. They shot Lily, she's in critical condition."

"Lily has been shot? I have to go to her," Emmett cried, trying to get up out of bed getting dizzy. Caleb rushed to his father and helped him back in bed even though Emmett protested.

"It should have been me, Emmett. She wore my coat. I spoke to my dad trying to get him to confess..," Sherry-Anne said.

"I don't understand how could your dad confess? What has he got to do with this I thought the senator was dead?" Emmett said.

"It's a long story, but it's my entire fault."

"Enough of this, Sherry-Anne. Quit nattering on, and repeating yourself; for Pete's sake pull yourself together and get me a wheelchair. I'm going to Lily if it kills me."

"They say Lily's holding her own, dad, but she has lost a lot of blood. The senator you mentioned? That's not my grandfather." Then turning to Sherry-Anne, Caleb reproached, "Tell him mom, as you seem to know all about this and you have been holding out on me."

"It seems that Betty was not my sister, but my mother and my dad visited here her in Canada. He's a politician and he doesn't want anyone to know he has an illegitimate daughter from a long term lover. He thought if they had their affair here the press wouldn't find out. I believe he killed my mother and shot Lily," Sherry-Anne explained.

"And now he's targeted you, but Lily got in the way? The children were kidnapped because of this too? Do I have the gist of this story?" Emmett demanded.

"Yes, you do. I know I should have taunted him, but I couldn't help myself I told him I had my mother's letters as well, and this was his answer," Sherry-Anne continued.

"Did you tell Sergeant Detective Downie this information?" Emmett asked.

"He's waiting outside the door to hear all this," Sherry-Anne answered.

"Bring Sergeant Detective Downie in, Caleb. Let's get this all out there so they can nail this bastard. Then I can go to Lily."

~0~

Chapter 21 - Cold Blooded Killers

T he woman worried that he was so angry with her. She

sought to protect him and show her love over and over again. Was he angry she gave in to the driver? How else was she to get him to obey her when she shot that bitch who threatened his career? He should be grateful that she had the gumption and the ability to protect him. Using her body to get her way meant nothing; after all he slept with his wife and it meant nothing. It was only the means to the end...to protect him. She had killed two political aides to protect him. One of them she had known and loved once upon a time. Shouldn't that loyalty count?

So many killings. She had betrayed all of her principles for him. But she loved him and he had promised if she could wait that in a few years they would be married. He had to worry about his career and his campaign, divorcing his wife could end that now; but in a couple of years he would divorce his wife, or she would kill her. Either way would be his new wife.

Now though he was angry, not just angry...furious with her...like had disobeyed him. Was it because she had killed the woman who threatened him? He had called this woman Sherry-Anne, his daughter. How was that possible? That woman must have tricked him. She couldn't be his daughter. He would have had to be in high school when he met her. It had to be that lying bitch, Betty's fault. She had convinced her skanky daughter that she was his. How could she convince him that she did all for him? The phone rang and she scurried to answer it after all it could be him.

"Hello."

"Sit tight I'm coming over," her lover said.

"You can't we'll be found out," she answered, forcefully.

"No, we won't, darling. Meet me then," he ordered.

"Where?"

"The Pagett Hotel, Spark Street, room 141," he demanded, "Seven p.m."

"I'll try no promises," she answered.

"Please, come to me, I miss you," he coaxed

"If I can sneak away I will," she promised almost cooing.

"Come my darling," he pleaded.

"Oh you, I can never refuse you. I'll be there. Goodbye darling."

"Goodbye, my love."

She was pleased he loved her. He'd confirmed it. All was right with the world. She'd meet him and they'd spend hours together without a care in the world.

~0~

The Pagett Hotel

She had become a liability. She had lost her mind. He couldn't believe she had killed his daughter, before he had even got to know her. Betty had given him pictures over the years, but he had always kept his distance for fear the press would get wind of their relationship and use it against him. Sherry-Anne would have come around if only she had given her the time. He would have convinced her to protect her father. After all he had money, prestige and power. Surely she had been like him and desired these things; she did share his blood. Why couldn't Sherry-Anne have just backed off?

Now that stupid bitch had killed her. His mistress to polite a name for her; must have lost her freaking mind.

Why had that little the bimbo killed? She kept insisting she had done it all for him, but each killing brought the police closer to him.

It had to be that she had begun killing so much, simply because she now enjoyed it. That had to mean madness had taken over. It was time to cut his losses, before she took him down too. He would mourn her smile, her luscious curvaceous body, but not her possessiveness.

Her obsession with him and his career, hurt him and now the police were getting closer and closer to him.

One whiff of scandal and his career was over. She had to go. He had to call the Fixer. He picked up the phone.

"It's done she's coming to Room 141, the Pagett Hotel Toronto, seven p.m." he said and then sighed, "Call me when it's over and leave no trace."

"I'm a professional she won't know what hit her," replied the Fixer.

"Is it done?" his wife asked.

"Yes." he said, sighing again.

"It had to be done dear. Your little bimbo was about to ruin my life too. Do you think she'd stop there? My life would be forfeit next. I warned you not to let your aberrant behaviour get in the way of our run for the senate," his wife commented.

"Don't you talk to me like that!"

"Sorry dear, unlike your bimbos, I know my place. But don't let one of your bimbos forget, my place is by your side with an open checkbook," his wife commented.

~0~

Chapter 22 - Heather

The hospital

Katha seated in Lily's intensive care room, half dozing

looked up to see Terrence at the waiting room door. Katha wondered why he had come back? He had told her he would go back to the hotel to sleep and he had ushered Amelia and the girls Rose and Carol back to the hotel, but now he was back. The sweet man must be worried about her and Lily she concluded. Going to the doorway, she saw that he blocked a woman standing behind him. Katha felt the bile rising up from her stomach and she rose quickly to her feet going to the door.

"Why is she here? Where have you been?" asked Katha belligerently.

"I've been around," the woman countered.

"You little...,"Katha cried grabbing the woman's arm as if she wanted to hurt her.

Terrence pulled Katha off the woman and then insisted, "Let's take this down the hall into that family room. We don't want anyone else to hear this."

"Fine, I don't want Lily disturbed," Katha admitted.

Katha was silent until they entered the private family room and shut the door. Terrence locked the door so they wouldn't be interrupted and then Katha began speaking angrily, "Years it's been years."

"I've kept tabs on you, both," the woman explained.

"You haven't been around me, or Lily, have you? You haven't spoken to us in person. Bully for you," Katha retorted bitterly.

"Please, there's so much you don't know," the woman pleaded.

"I know enough. I know how much pain Lily has felt because of you."

"Katha, dear, please hear her out," Terrence demanded.

"How did you know to come here?" Katha enquired.

"Terrence called me," the woman answered.

"You knew Terrence? You knew that she..." Katha barely able to speak in her rage, "And you kept this from me?"

Katha looked at him with anger and disbelief. Then with fury Katha began to pummel Terrence's shoulders.

"I'm sorry Katha I couldn't tell you. My son was involved in her disappearance. He worked for the agency then, but he's since retired. When I married you, they approached me. I didn't want to keep this from you; but they told me that if you knew you too could be in danger," Terrence explained.

"If you only knew how many nightmares that child had. How many times she cried out for that woman," Katha cried, "And what she exposed her to."

"Exposed her to?" Terrence said, sounding surprised.

"I did what I did to protect my family. I had no other choice," the woman attempted to explain.

"We always have a choice and you made the wrong one. Don't you dare excuse yourself," Katha stated.

"Please let me see her before I have to leave. Who knows I may help her get better," begged the woman.

"Over my dead body," Katha cried.

"You act like you are the Madonna. That you've never made a mistake with the company you kept. What about my mother, Florence? Do you think she had a good life with my grandfather? Weren't you happy when he died?"

"He wasn't your grandfather," Katha admitted.

"I suspected that. Who was he?"

"Someone, I won't talk about... with anyone. So don't even try to press me."

"The man who you married was an asshole."

"He was, but he was also not my choice. If I wanted to keep Florence, I had no choice but to marry him."

"What he did to my mother..."

"I didn't know and when I did I put a stop to it. I left him. He had too many connections and no one would believe us," Katha stated.

"He's not my grandfather, but my father you know that."

"I didn't know."

"So that makes it all okay?"

"No, I'm doing penitence for my sins of ignorance."

"I trusted you with my daughter despite all of that."

"I got her by default."

"No, you didn't I made a plan and I followed through. Why do you think she ended up with you?"

"Because Peter gave in," Katha answered.

"Peter couldn't handle raising a child. He's all about his career. I knew he'd give in."

"You couldn't have known that."

"I married him to provide for that girl. He's not her real father but he's a father that she could look up to. I've always done right her. You always underestimated me. I provided for my daughter, even when I couldn't do it myself. Make no doubt about my intentions, they were always good."

"Bullshit, Peter is her father and she cried for you night and day. You know something bad happened to her. You exposed her to that."

"I made mistakes, everyone does. You are far from perfect. Now I'm telling you. I need to see her. She's out of it. She won't remember I came. But maybe even if she thinks I'm a dream it will help her recovery to know I was there."

"Fine, but if you hurt her...,"Katha answered.

"I won't."

"Don't let her see you. Don't let her realize you are real. I can't bear to see her cry and dry her tears; when she realizes you abandoned her all over again," Katha pleaded.

"When did you grow so hard?" asked the woman.

"I became watchful and cynical the day you betrayed the love and trust of my granddaughter. She was an innocent young girl and you brought her into a seedy world where she could be harmed," Katha replied.

"People who live in glass houses shouldn't throw stones, old woman. I'm going in now and seeing my daughter. I've asked you nicely, but I've had enough. You can't stop me old woman," said the woman.

"If I wanted to I would have stopped you, but so help me God if you hurt her in anyway...."Katha threatened.

"I won't, not now, not ever," the woman answered.

"We'll see. Your type always claims they don't harm; but the darkness they bring is forever in the background just waiting to pounce," Katha responded.

Katha then opened the door to the family room and allowing the woman to enter the same room with Lily. Katha watched as the woman slowly walked over to Lily's bed and tenderly stroked Lily's hair.

She then took Lily's hand gently caressed it and said, "Baby, I'm here and I love you pumpkin. You have to fight, Lily. You have your own daughter to worry about. Don't leave her, like I left you. Fight darling! Please fight, and win this battle."

Wiping tears from her eyes she then kissing Lily on the cheek, she left the room, only to stop outside the door and stare back in through the glass partition.

Katha followed her to reproach, "You don't have it in you to stay. You're always leaving. I don't care what your reason is. Lily deserves better. I won't speak of you, to Lily."

"It's probably better that way," the woman sadly exclaimed.

"For whom would it be better? You?" Katha said her voice dripping ice.

"Goodbye, my baby," the woman said. She looked at Katha as if she wanted to say something else, but staring back once more at Lily she turned on her heel and left.

"I won't say goodbye. Despite everything I still love you, Heather," Katha whispered to the departing back of the woman.

Katha then dabbed tears away from her eyes. Walking back to Lily's bedside Katha wondered if she had made a mistake not forcing Heather to stay but a few seconds later Lily stirred and whimpered Katha breathed a sigh of relief and reconsidered. Lily would be happier this way and heal. Katha protected Lily the only way she knew how. It would have to be okay. Katha hurried to her side bent over to hear what Lily said. She then heard Lily say, "Mama?"

Lily opened her eyes wiping her eyes, looking around hopefully she asked, "Was my mother here?"

"No, baby doll. It's Grandma Katha, here. Rest easy, sweetie. Your Grandma Katha will always be here as long as she can breathe," Katha replied soothing Lily's brow.

"But I thought...," Lily broke off here shaking her head.

"What did you think sweetie?" Katha asked.

"I thought my mother was here. I smelled her perfume. The old country roses scent, which she always wore," Lily said, drowsily.

"You must have been dreaming, sweetheart. It's understandable that you wanted your mother, but you know she's gone," Katha answered.

"But it seemed so real," Lily protested.

"They have you on some powerful pain killers, honey and your mind must have conjured your mother up," Katha lied again.

"I'm going to be okay, Grandma Katha?" Lily asked try to feeling her wound.

"Now don't do that Lily. They have you all bandaged up," Katha stated, "You're going to be just fine. You are a Kelly after all."

"The children and Sherry-Anne, are they okay?" asked Lily.

"The children are fine thanks to you. You thought quickly and having them think Sherry-Anne was the victim worked," Katha answered.

"Oh, okay," Lily said drowsily.

"You have one brave daughter, it does a great-grandmother proud," Katha said.

"Why, what did Rose do?" Lily asked.

"Nothing, she's just such a joy," Katha covered.

"Don't lie to me. You're hiding something. Did something happen to the children?"

"Don't get excited, dear. Everything's just fine." Katha stated, "The kids were kidnapped, but they're okay. They're free and unharmed."

"Kidnapped? Again?"

"Yes, but this time Caleb was taken as well. There's nothing for you to worry about."

"How did they get free? They did get free?"

Katha made a face and then tried to pretend she hadn't heard.

"If you want me to relax and get well, then you better answer me."

"They're free and safe. Rose covered up her face with her hoodie when they gassed them."

"Gassed? Are you sure they're okay?"

"I wouldn't lie to you. They really are fine. Rose didn't breathe in as much, so she was able to untie all of them and get everyone free.

Carol then picked the lock. Carol should be made an honorary Kelly. That girl has gumption," Katha chuckled.

"Wow. That was smart," Lily said, "So if everything is okay then why isn't Rose here?"

"Rose was tired; so I made her go back to the hotel along with Carol. You're not to worry about Emmett either. Emmett rests comfortably in his hospital room. He wanted to come to you; but the nurses said they'd have to wait until tomorrow. Now rest and get better. I'll bring the girls and Caleb to see you tomorrow, as well," Katha said as Lily closed her eyes and drifted off, "Sleep, my darling girl."

Katha went into the hall to speak to Terrence.

"I'm not going to tell Lily about her visit."

"That's probably best. I don't think Heather will be back. The nurses will bring you a cot, my dear," Terrence stated.

"I should say thank-you, but don't think this gets you a get out of jail free card," Katha replied, tersely "I know your still angry Katha, but I'll make it up to you. I'll never keep anything from you again," Terrence promised.

"You'd better not," Katha replied.

The nurse put a cot near Lily's bed.

"Well that's a start." Katha stated, "Now go back to the hotel and get some rest like I'm going to."

As Katha lay down on the cot and went to sleep. Terrence covered her gently with a blanket, kissed her on the cheek and then left to get a taxi to take him back to the hotel room.

~0~

Chapter 23 - Checkmate

Earlier across town at the Pagett Hotel Toronto

T he young woman lay naked and prone across the hotel

bed. Should she put her sexy nightie on now, or when he arrived? She thought he would have been here already. Where could he be? Maybe she should go down to the front desk and see if he left a message? It was almost seven-thirty p.m., where was he? She jumped to her feet and shimmered into her tight black mini dress. She then grabbed the hotel magnetic room card and thought I'll take the stairs one floor down to the front desk.

In the elevator, a man his phone wedged to his ear pushed buttons on the elevator panel locking it on the floor, "Boss I'm just getting off the elevator. I had some car trouble; but I'm on my way to the room now," he said.

The man exited the elevator and walked down the hallway to room 141. He knocked on the door. Hearing no answer, he looked around and seeing no one, he took out a device. The device beeped and the door opened. Finding a woman's coat he smiled wickedly and searched for any trace of her. He took apart his case and put together a silencer and waited for her return.

At the front desk the woman asked for any mail, or messages.

"Sorry, miss, I don't think so, but let me check," the clerk answered.

She shuffled from foot to foot nervously waiting.

"Sorry, miss, this wasn't filed properly," the clerk said handing over a message.

She read it and smiled wildly.

My darling girl, she read and smiled, then continued to read the rest of the letter,

You are an integral part of my life. I can't live without you. I may have not said enough but I appreciate all that you have done for me. I know with you by my side we will go places. I promised you my freedom and you shall soon have it if you stick but my side.

P. S. I will be a little late but please order whatever you want to eat. I will be there by eight thirty p.m.

Love your Snookums

The woman started to walk to the stairs, but decided to order a tray of food to be sent up. To save time she entered the kitchen in the basement and began to prepare the food.

"Miss, we deliver the food. People don't take their own food from the kitchen." the kitchen worker protested with a Spanish accent.

She smiled as she recognized Miguel who had driven her before and whom she had slept with before she secured her lover's favour.

"Please? I'll be happy to pay a little extra," she cajoled playing the role Miguel liked so much.

"This is for someone special?" Miguel asked.

"It is and I want tonight to be a night he'll remember; but I wish it could be you," she said with naughty smile.

"He is one lucky man." Miguel answered.

"Yes, he is but I wish things could be different," she retorted.

"No, miss. He is truly lucky for he has you," Miguel exclaimed.

"You are so sweet, to pretend that you don't know me. You are truly gallant. I wish things could have been different, but the heart wants what the heart wants."

"I have moved on," Miguel claimed.

"You're a peach. I wonder do you have silver tray I can present the meal on? You know one of those with a lid. As I said I'll be happy to pay extra," she begged.

"Certainly, for such a lovely lady and her paramour, I can do so," Miguel answered, but his eyes lingered on her and he licked his lips and he touched her arm seemingly, accidently.

She hid her glee that he still cared for her and waited patiently for the food. If only things were different and he had the power, the money and the prestige. Then maybe her heart would have chosen him and they could have been together. The food prepared, Miguel presented it to her with a flourish.

He handed her a tray, an ornate silver tray. She smiled at the rose in the vase on the cart and the fillet mignon that Miguel had prepared at her urging. She was sure her lover would adore it and would forgive what he thought of her transgression... killing his so-called daughter. She had killed she should feel bad, but instead she felt elated, like a drug it filled with euphoria. She felt more alive than she ever had before but she needed him. They would eat this luscious meal and then they could dig into the cheesecake, his favourite dessert and then they would top it off with her the real dessert.

"Thank-you, Miguel," she said smiling, "You don't know how much this will mean to me."

"Perhaps I do. One day you will tire of him and be mine," he muttered under his breath.

As she left the kitchen, she marvelled at how he had sent her this love letter. He wasn't one for gestures and yet he had declared his love for her in a note. He had said she was an important part of his life. Just thinking about it made her smile. It was the first one he had ever sent her. And he had signed her Snookums, her pet name for him. He did listen to her and loved her. She held the letter to her chest for a moment incredibly happy. Then she kissed the note and folded it tucking it into her pocket.

She decided to take the elevator. As she pushed the cart with the heavy tray into the elevator the elevator started moving and she hurriedly pushed her floor. She exited the elevator to see a man impatiently looked out of her hotel room. What was someone doing in her room? The man spotted her coming down the hall and raised his gun; but she saw him in time throwing up the tray and pushing the cart in front of herself.

As he fired again she managed to shield herself. She backed into the elevator pushing the cart in front of her and closed the door. Shots come through the door as it closed striking the tray. Scared and angry, she worried the shooter would beat her to the first floor as the elevator began to move. Someone was trying to kill her.

The only person who knew she was in the hotel was him. How could he turn on her after everything she'd done for him? She needed another way out, but where? She pushed the first floor button and then with second thoughts, she then pushed the basement button instead.

Reaching the basement, she looked both ways. Stepping out the silver tray both top and bottom in her hands she yield them like shields. The tray had several dents in it from bullets; but no holes and it made excellent armour. She made her way to the kitchen and accosting Miguel, she said, "You saved my life with the tray. Thank-you."

"Someone shot at you? Those dents were made by bullets?" Miguel asked.

"Yes and he'll be here soon. If I don't move soon; he'll catch up with me and kill you too. Is there another way out that the gunman would not know?" she asked.

"Come, I will save you, my love. He will not harm you," Miguel answered.

"Where can we go?" the woman asked.

"To the laundry room."

"The laundry room?"

"Yes, it's through the tunnel and it exits to the outside. The door is hidden. He won't find us," Miguel explained.

"Thank-you Miguel. I am a foolish girl I trusted him you see," she stated sighing.

"When one is in love, one trusts," Miguel commented.

"I should have known. He's married," she explained sadly.

"The married man, he betrays you both," Miguel stated, "He is not worthy of your love."

"He said he'd leave her that we'd be together. That it was only his job, that kept us apart," she cried.

"I loved a woman once. She too said she loved me. She was in love with a married man. She said that she leave him. But now he's found us both," Miguel answered.

"Oh, Miguel, I'm so sorry I strung you along for so long. I should have chosen you. This man I thought that loved me. I should have known he's a two-faced, no good politician. They all lie," she said then thinking ahead at what she will tell the police she continued," I think he killed his first lover and his campaign aide and another man. He also killed his own daughter."

"He killed his own daughter?"

"Yes, and now he tries to kill me all, because he thinks I had figured out all of his crimes. But I didn't know. I really didn't," she cried dabbing tears from her eyes, "If only I left him a long time ago for you."

"Quiet, my love. That is in the past. We must not let this man find us," Miguel says "You know that I love you, I will not pretend anymore. I would not let him harm you."

"Sorry, of course I can trust you," she said drying her tears, and then continuing she asked, "How far is it from the hotel to the police station?"

"Not far couple of blocks. I will take you," Miguel insisted. "I will show you that a man can protect you."

"I do care about you Miguel," she stated, "And maybe someday I can love you."

"I know you will but until the day we can still be together. I'll protect you and now we will turn him," Miguel answered.

They crept out of the hotel through the side door. Sure the gunman looked for her at the front of the hotel, she felt safe. She recognized the shooter as the man known as The Fixer. He had sent him. Why had he betrayed her this way? She had believed that he loved her. Hadn't she sacrificed for him? She had proven her love for him. She had killed for him. Then he had tricked her with false flowery words trying to lure her to her doom. He obviously forgot who he dealt with. She wasn't a foolish bimbo!

He had betrayed her threatened her life. If she hadn't been so smart and outwitted The Fixer she'd be dead.

He would pay for this. She had planned ahead just for an occasion such as this. She hadn't believed that he would do such a deceitful thing; but she knew she must always protect herself. She smiled certain that she could convince the police that he had done all of these killings without her knowledge. He would pay!! And pay big!

His career was over, his marriage was over. His life would be in ruins. She wished she could take his life; like he had tried to take hers. Yet again maybe this revenge would be better still. He would lose everything and spend the rest of his life in jail. That would be justice indeed, no politics and prestige for him only a locked room and Bubba to keep him company. And she would have Miguel and laugh at his plight and flaunt in his puny little pug face.

She searched for him, looking behind them at different times; hoping she's escaped her lover's hired killer. They exited the hotel taking a back street behind the hotel to get to the police station; running through streets always feeling the gunman at their backs. She saw the police station and smiled with relief. He would pay now. She would make him pay for his traitorous act. As they attempted to enter the front of the police station she heard cacophony of sound and then she saw Miguel fall down. She heard more sounds like firecrackers and then felt a slight pain as a bullet pierced her skin and she collapsed on the steps.

~0~

Chapter 24 - Revenge is Bittersweet

"**B**oss I'm sorry she got away. She went into the

police station before I shot her. I don't know how much they know," the Fixer stated, then continuing he asked, "Did you did get the package that I sent you?"

"I did receive the package. Your money has been wired to the usual place," he answered, "This is goodbye."

"Boss, please, we've had a long relationship. I know I've failed you this time. I'll make it up to you. I'm good for it," the Fixer uncharacteristically begged.

"You are always and will always, be my associate. This is not goodbye, but adieu for now," the boss stated tersely fingering three typed envelopes.

"Thank-you sir. You can count on my loyalty."

"I know I can."

"Bye," the Fixer said.

The man then hung up the desk phone.

"Brian," the man shouted.

"Yes, sir," Brian answered.

"Mail these would you? I'd like them personally delivered. I'm on my way out."

"Will do. Where can you be reached?"

"That information is unnecessary, but in an emergency I can be reached on my private cell phone. Thank-you for all your hard work and stepping into this job. I know it's not easy taking over details hereto unknown to you from a murdered colleague, especially when we're all still grieving," he enthused.

"Well, thank-you, sir. I will try to be the best aide you've ever had sir," Brian cried with surprise.

His new boss waved and then exited the room. Brian thought maybe this job would be so horrific after all. If he worked for the man for a while and the man turned out to be the ass everyone said the man was, at least he'd have some great job prospects with this job on his resume

.~0~

Sometime later at Toronto's Sunnybrook Hospital

“ **S** o how is she?” demanded Sergeant Detective Peter

Brooks of the emergency room staff.

“Are we allowed to give that information out? I mean aren't we suppose to follow privacy laws?” a staff member asked.

“He is a member of the police force. I think we can make an exception,” the nurse insisted.

“You go ahead, but I want no part of this. I'm not breaking the privacy laws and losing my job.” complained the other nurse, she added, “She's underage, sir. I don't think you can question her unless she has a parent, or a lawyer.”

“That's actually a misconception. I can question her if she's over fourteen years old. In fact I believe she's closer to eighteen, is she not? She is of an age to understand her rights,” Sergeant Detective Gordon Downie insisted.

“Besides she has been the victim of a crime. We need to speak to her so we can catch the perpetrator,” Sergeant Detective Peter Brooks stated.

“Okay, then, I guess we can tell you. She has through and through in her leg and a through in through in her shoulder. She's very lucky. We're taking her to her room soon. The doctor feels she can go home with antibiotics and pain pills possibly tomorrow,” the nurse admitted.

“Has she had any pain pills now?”

“No, not yet.”

"Can you take us into her cubicle?" Sergeant Detective Peter Brooks asked.

Emmett Rogers followed behind him propelling himself in a wheelchair.

"Are you sure you're well enough for this Emmett?" asked Sergeant Detective Downie.

"I can manage. I won't interfere; but I want to know what she has to say," Emmett responded.

"She due for a pain pill in a few minutes; I take it you want us to delay that while you question her?" the nurse asserted.

"That's if it doesn't harm her physical well-being."

"It won't," the nurse answered and directed them to the patient.

Sherry-Anne arrived breathless, carrying a letter she held out followed by Caleb.

"I want to talk to her Emmett," Sherry-Anne demanded, "You should read this letter."

Emmett read the letter quickly while Sergeant Detective Downie the entered the cubical.

"After she gives a statement Sherry-Anne, we'll nail her. These cops are top notched she won't get away with this," Emmett stated, handing Sherry-Anne back the letter.

"Emmett's correct, Ms. Mobley," Sergeant Detective Peter Brooks acknowledged then turning to Emmett he said, "If she sees or hears you, Sherry-Anne, or your son, Caleb this could change her testimony. So stay out of sight and be quiet."

"Fine, then I'll wait with Caleb outside in the hallway in that alcove, but nail her Emmett," Sherry-Anne stated.

Emmett spoke briefly to the nurse and the nurse escorted Sherry-Anne and Caleb into a waiting room.

"How are you?" asked Sergeant Detective Peter Brooks drew the curtain around her bed for privacy, as he Emmett stepped in the cubicle and joined Sergeant Detective Gordon Downie. Sergeant Detective Peter Brooks pulled out an I-Pad and added a foldable keyboard to it.

"Nice tool," Emmett commented.

"Yes, I'm very fortunate," Sergeant Detective Peter Brooks stated.

Emmett felt stupid for commenting on it. The three policemen looked over at the young woman and saw her left arm in a sling, and her left leg peeking out from under the blanket, bandaged at thigh level.

"Better now, thank-you. I take it you would like a statement about what happened. I still can't believe that lovely man, Miguel who helped me is dead," she spouted covering up her thigh.

"We would like a statement, but before you do that we'd like to advise you of your rights. Strictly procedure but we must follow that. Mustn't we?" Sergeant Detective Peter Brooks stated.

"Go ahead, I have nothing to hide. I've decided to tell you everything," she admitted.

"You have the right to remain silent and refuse to answer questions. Anything you do say may be used against you in a court of law. Do you understand?" Sergeant Detective Gordon Downie asked.

"This seems tedious, but yes," she answered.

"You have the right to consult an attorney before speaking to the police and to have an attorney present during questioning now, or in the future. If you cannot afford an attorney, one will be appointed for you before any questioning if you wish. Do you understand?" Sergeant Detective Gordon Downie continued.

"Please just finish it all and I'll just nod." she answered.

"I'm sorry for the record. I really need a yes." Sergeant Detective Downie.

"Fine, I'll answer, yes. Anything to get through this and tell you what happened." she whined.

"If you decide to answer questions now without an attorney present you will still have the right to stop answering at any time until you talk to an attorney. Knowing and understanding your rights as I have explained them to you, will you answer my questions without an attorney present?" Sergeant Detective Downie asked.

"Yes. God damn it!! " She cried angrily, "I don't need, or want a lawyer, but I do want immunity from any unintended crimes."

"We'll see about immunity; first though we need to hear you out and see if it's worth immunity. So in your own words could you tell me what happened Miss Moore and speak into my recorder?" Sergeant Detective Downie enquired.

"I think first we need to get the pesky details out of the way Gordon," Sergeant Detective Peter Brooks insisted.

His lips turned into a smile, which disarmed Miss Moore and made her smile back. His hands ready on his computer keyboard typed the conversation so far.

"Pesky details? I don't understand," answered Miss Moore.

"Your name, birthdate, etcetera, those details," Sergeant Detective Peter Brooks said.

"Oh, okay my name is Louise Celina Moore. I'm seventeen years old. I turned seventeen two weeks ago. I was born on December eleventh, nineteen hundred and ninety eight. I am an American citizen living in the U.S., I'm just visiting this country. My father runs for Senator, against my lover Paul Gauthier for state senator," Louise stated.

She waited for the shocked faces, but was disappointed as the cops including Emmett showed no emotion.

"I must say you don't look shocked. I thought you'd be more surprised," Louise continued.

"We've heard lots of strange things before, Miss Moore," Sergeant Detective Peter Brooks quipped, "This will be nothing new."

"Somehow, I doubt that. Now call me Louise, Miss Moore is too impersonal and I like to get personal." Louise replied openly flirting with Sergeant Detective Peter Brooks.

"For politeness sake, I'll call you Louise, but please stick to the facts. When did this relationship start?" Sergeant Detective Peter Brooks demanded.

"The relationship started about four and half years ago, when I was almost fourteen. We went places together, slept together, every time he could get away. He seemed so worldly so dynamic and exciting. I couldn't believe it he was interested in me," Louise waxed smiling.

"That is a crime," Sergeant Detective Downie admitted.

"And what has this to do with your shooting?" asked Emmett, feigning boredom.

"Oh, it has everything to do with it. He took advantage of me and yes, it's a crime," Louise cried angrily.

"Senator Gauthier could be charged with statutory rape, but it's not our jurisdiction and therefore that has to be handled in your home state, where the crime took place," Sergeant Detective Downie insisted.

"Oh, why don't you just shut-up and listen. Paul Gauthier has killed several people. He's a serial killer. He killed Betty 'Blue' Renfrew, Trent Bryant, Alfred Getts, a homeless man named Fred, and just yesterday Sherry-Anne Mobley. Then he shot Miguel killed him and tried to kill me just today."

Emmett whispered to Sergeant Detective Downie and Downie nodded and demanded, "Really and what evidence have you of any of this Miss Moore?"

"Lots, but it's a long story and I'm a foolish little girl. I was duped. I had no part in any of his crimes. I want to make that clear," Louise cried making her voice seem like an innocent small child's.

"Okay, talk and we'll listen," Sergeant Detective Downie insisted.

"I did have an affair with him. He told me he left his wife and I believed him, crazy little girl that I am. We continued our relationship for four years and half years."

"And no one knew you were with Mr. Gauthier?"

"No, no one knew. Paul was careful to make sure no one saw us together."

"What has this to do with the murders, Louise?" Sergeant Detective Brooks asked.

"Everything! The night my father's aide was killed, Paul and I we're in bed together in Paul's hotel room. His wife and kids were out so Paul thought it would be safe; only his aide Trent Bryant came in and caught us in bed. Trent started yelling at Paul and then me. He was so mean."

"What did Trent say to the two of you?" Sergeant Detective Brooks asked.

"Horrible things," Louise answered, shaking her head and then squeezing fake tears them out of her eyes.

"What kind of horrible things did he say?" Sergeant Detective Downie asked sympathetically.

Louise reached out and touched Sergeant Detective Downie's arm and looked like she wanted to throw herself in his arms.

Louise looked up with doe like eyes and continued in a small whispering voice, "He was so angry and shocked he yelled, *"How could you? Don't you know what this could do to your career if you are caught with this little slut? Her father could use this against you."*

"I yelled back that I wasn't a slut. That Paul loved me. But it hurt so bad that anyone would think that of me."

Trent then continued, *"You stupid little girl. He's using you. You can't believe he loves you."* then addressing Paul he said angrily *"Isn't it enough that you killed your lover, Betty Blue. Do you have any idea how hard it was to cover up the evidence for that?"*

"For the record, you say that Trent Bryant confronted Senator Gauthier with evidence of his crime," Emmett demanded.

"This is hearsay and not really proof of anything," Sergeant Detective Brooks stated.

"But it's the truth. All of it!! Trent said that he knew all about the murder," Louise insisted, her eyes rolling back in disgust that they didn't believe her.

"Now why would he do that in front of you?" Sergeant Detective Brooks said sounding doubtful and narrowing his eyes.

"I think he forgot I was there." Louise answered, "Do you doubt me?"

"No, of course he isn't. Please forgive my partner and continue," Sergeant Detective Downie said soothingly.

"Paul got so angry at Trent took him aside and then Trent left. Paul started being so nice. Kissing me and telling me how much he loved me. He promised me that he would leave his wife, after he won the election. He begged me to forget, what I heard from Trent if I loved him. He said Trent was mistaken, but he looked so different. His face was wooden and I almost believed he'd killed Betty. But I dismissed the idea immediately. Someone I loved couldn't have killed someone."

"Different how? Besides his facial expressions how was his behaviour atypical?" Emmett asked.

"He acted like he could kill...anyone!! He was angry and his fists were always clenched, but as I said I dismissed the idea. Then I found out Paul got Trent to leave us alone, by promising him money. Money he could ill afford that he would have to defraud his donors to give Trent," Louise admitted.

"How do you know all of this and how much money was promised?" Sergeant Detective Brooks asked.

"I found a record for the money on his computer when he went to the bathroom. I think it was a hundred thousand dollars put in a Swiss bank account, and I heard him offer him even more for the following week," Louise answered.

"So then what happened to make you think that Paul Gauthier killed Trent and Alfred Getts?" Sergeant Detective Brooks demanded.

"I didn't think about that until later when Alfred came in a short time later. We had started making love again when Alfred walked in. He said that Trent had told him that Paul was unavailable but he'd seen us together and he had to see for himself whether we were lovers. He seemed shocked and he said, "I can't believe what I saw. You're a married man. Even if you weren't you're a senator and that is a child. Pervert!!!"

"I told Alfred I wasn't a child, that I loved Paul. Alfred dismissed it and asked what would my father say? Paul tried to reason with him. Paul said he loved me and that I would be eighteen in a year and he'd divorce his wife and marry me. Alfred wanted to go my father and then to the press. Paul begged him to reconsider and pleaded telling him that this would ruin his career. Paul then offered him a job with him and a salary increase. Paul got dressed and went out with Alfred."

"And then what happened Miss Moore?" Emmett asked.

"I was tired and fell asleep. When he came back I got up got dressed and went towards the door. I didn't want my father to find out and use it against Paul in his campaign. At the door putting on my shoes, I saw his shoes were freshly covered with blood. I was stunned and horrified. I didn't want to believe he had done anything; so I dismissed the idea until I heard that they were both dead the next day."

"Why didn't you turn him into the police and tell them about his shoes?" Sergeant Detective Brooks asked.

"Let me get to that. I confronted him with all of my suspicions and he denied it, categorically. I wanted to believe so bad, that he hadn't done any of this. I loved him. I'd loved him for years, believed in him, and supported him. I wanted to be his wife. I believed I was mistaken...that he couldn't have done any of this."

Louise stopped here and wiped a tear, "But he had...he really had done all of the murders."

"And how did you know that Miss Moore. Was it only the blood on his shoes? How do you know he didn't cut himself shaving?" Downie said scoffing.

"Do you think I didn't think of that? I racked my brains trying to find any other explanation, but it soon became clear, he had killed them."

"I repeat again. How do you know this?"

"It's bit of a story," Louise began.

"Just spit it out. We've got time," Sergeant Detective Downie insisted.

"Okay fine, what made me understand was when he got a phone call on his hotel phone. We were in bed and he answered the phone right in the middle of...well you know. There was this woman on the phone, Sherry-Anne Mobley, and she said she was his daughter. She said she knew he had killed her mother and that he was her father. I had met her and I was shocked to find out that she was his daughter. I felt sure she was mistaken. I mean she's what thirty-two? He would have to have had her in high school. But as I listened, I realized she believed she told the truth. Not only was she his daughter; but she alleged he killed her mother."

"For the record you're saying Sherry-Anne Mobley told her father that she knew he killed her mother?" Detective Sergeant Downie asked.

"Yes. Paul threatened her on the phone if she revealed his existence as her father, but he did say he believed her and wanted to meet her son. Then he left and the next day I hear that Sherry Anne Mobley's dead. I couldn't believe it, still I wanted to ask him about it. So I called him and begged him to convince me, he hadn't killed his daughter."

"You really wanted to believe him," Sergeant Detective Downie stated softly.

Louise nodded her head and continued, "Paul insisted he hadn't killed anyone, but asked me to meet him at the Pagett hotel Toronto room one hundred and forty-one at seven p.m. last night. So I go to the hotel and he doesn't come on time. I go down to the hotel desk and the clerk gives me a message. It was a sweet love letter. See!!"

Louise stood up pulling the sheet around her like a skirt; she bent down to the bottom of the bed wincing and holding her side. She then produced the letter from her clothing. She then handed it to Emmett who read it then passed it to Sergeant Detective Brooks. Sergeant Detective Brooks read it and then passed it to Sergeant Detective Downie.

"I believed him at the time. I really did," Louise claimed.

Louise paused for effect here and wiped away a stray tear.

"So you were convinced he hadn't committed any crimes at this point," Emmett sympathized.

"You do understand? Good! He loved me. He wanted to be with me. I wanted it to be special; so I went to the kitchen and got a special dinner; the fillet mignon special little potatoes and cheesecake for dessert. I even requested that Miguel retrieve a sterling silver serving tray for presentation."

"Yes, we found the tray complete with bullet holes," Sergeant Detective Downie commented.

"I know thank God, it saved me. I put the food on the cart and went to go up back to the room. When I got off the elevator someone shot at me. I dumped the food using the trays to protect me I got back on the elevator and rode it to the kitchen where Miguel helped me through the laundry tunnel to the door. Then we ran through all kinds of streets, until we reached the police station. As I went to go through the doors shots rang out."

"Is that when Miguel was killed?" asked Sergeant Detective Downie.

"I guess, because when I looked down Miguel lay bloodied on the ground. A bullet hit me and went through my leg and arm."

"Did you see the gunman?" Sergeant Detective Downie enquired.

"I saw the bastard. Paul sent him."

"How do you know that?" Sergeant Detective Downie demanded.

"I arrived at Paul's hotel room a little too early and fell asleep in the bed. Paul came in and kissed me and said he had some business on the phone in the other room to conduct, enjoy my nap. I don't know why, but I became fully awake and went to the bedroom door as he ushered a man in. The bedroom door was ajar and I listened peering in and saw that man, the shooter. Paul offered him an envelope and the man opened the end of it revealing a number of hundred dollar bills. He called the man the Fixer and he told the man that the money was a down payment on the next killing."

"Did you hear what this was a down payment on?"

"No, but shortly after that Trent was dead and while he talked to the man he called the Fixer, Paul said he was happy Betty was dead; that he had killed her himself."

"You've stated that Paul Gauthier contracted to kill Betty Renfrew, Trent Bryant, and Alfred Getts, Sherry-Anne Mobley, Frederick Parcell, and Miguel Torres as well as the attempted murder of yourself?" demanded Sergeant Detective Downie.

"Yes, I am. Paul Gauthier and the man he called the Fixer are responsible for all those murders," Louise answered.

Sergeant Detective Peter Brooks stepped out and then came back in a few minutes later.

"Did you get all that Pete in your notes; as well as this recorder?" asks Sergeant Detective Gordon Downie of Sergeant Detective Peter Brooks.

"Yes, and I had the nurse connect my I-Pad straight to the printer. Ah, here she is. Would you sign this statement Miss Moore," stated Sergeant Detective Brooks as the nurse handed him the printed statement.

"Thank-you," Sergeant Detective Brooks.

"Is this correct Miss Moore? Sergeant Detective Downie enquired handing her the statement.

"Yes, that's all correct," Louise commented dipping her head and hiding a smile as she took the pen from Emmett. Louise completed it with a smile and a flourish. Louise jumped as the curtain around the cubicle is drawn back angrily, by long fingers topped in red nail polish.

"You lying little bitch. Everything out of your mouth is a lie. For one thing I called my father after you shot at me," Sherry-Anne screamed and then before the policemen could stop her slapped Louise across her face.

Emmett pulled Sherry-Anne off Louise and cautioned her about assault and arrest.

"You're alive? Oh thank-you, God," Louise stated.

"You're not fooling anyone, sweet cheeks. Give up the act," Sherry-Anne cried angrily fighting to get free from Emmett.

"Oh no! Did he kill someone else they mistook for you?" Louise continued her voice sounding like an overacting teen.

"You're good. I'll give you that. You almost had me fooled," Sherry-Anne cried.

"I don't know what you mean!" Louise puzzled.

Sherry-Anne got free from Emmett and started clapping then commented, "Bravo award winning. Want your Oscar now, sweetie?

"You don't actually believe this crap? Do you Emmett? I mean Detective Rogers. She's the liar!" Louise claimed.

"She signed a statement," Emmett commented, passing the signed document to Sergeant Detective Downie, and then he whispered to Sherry-Anne, "I know she lied."

"Then you can nail her."

"Do I have to be subjected to this? I feel sorry for you I really do, but the same person that shot me shot you. And now I'm injured and you hit me? I think I've been nice to you but I want you to leave," Louise stated.

"Actually that isn't quite true," Emmett commented.

"What? What do you mean?" Louise asked feigning innocence, but still managing to look worried.

"He means this, bitch. My father, the senator killed himself tonight, but before he did he sent three letters out. One to letter to his wife Maria, one went to me and the other one to the police. I don't know how you thought you could get away with this," Sherry-Anne cried shaking her head.

"Paul's dead? You rotten liar! He would have sent one to me, not Maria. So I know he's not dead." Louise claimed.

Louise stared at Sherry-Anne the realization that Sherry-Anne told the truth shone in her face as she took on a grieving widow persona, wiping her eyes, and looked grief stricken, "I loved him; but he killed so many people I can't forgive him. I'm sorry for your loss, however."

"You obviously weren't listening he told me and other about all of his crimes in his suicide note.

Louise looked first shocked and then frightened.

"Here let me read it to you, *"My darling daughter, Sherry-Anne. I'm sorry I denied your existence on the phone and appeared to threaten you. Things were not as they seem. Yes, I wanted to retain my power and prestige, but I had hoped to get to know you without risk to my career. Even my beloved wife understood my love for you, but alas Louise did not. Louise eliminates obstacles to what she wants and you were the biggest one. Louise wanted all of my attention and adoration and that made you her main target.*

I was overjoyed to learn through my sources that you are alive. It probably means nothing to you; but I do love you. You are my daughter and despite my outrageous behavior, I will always love you.

I have committed grievous sins. The first sin as I've stated I denied you and your sisters as my daughters. This denied me the chance to get to know you and your sisters. I took advantage of your mother's love promising her as I did others; that I would leave my wife Maria. The truth is I could never leave Maria. If I'm truly honest, I love her as much as a selfish narcissist like me could. Maria loved me, as no woman has ever done sticking by me despite my many failings. Maria knew what others did not, she knew deep in her heart I would never leave her, for Maria was always the one I adored.

Though I have often strayed; Maria has forgiven supported me and loved me. She understood my needs and my peccadillos. She allowed me to stray as long as I kept her in the dark as much as possible and offered me the money from her trust fund to finance my campaigns and ambitions.

"Liar! He didn't love her! Shut up you crazy bitch!!"Louise interrupted.

Louise tried to get to Sherry-Anne and throttle her but Emmett held her back.

"Don't you want to hear the rest Louise? Too bad. Listen up little girl, this will make you cry," Sherry-Anne taunted and then continued reading...*Four and half years ago, Louise Moore was my rival's daughter and as such it seemed like delicious irony to seduce and sleep with his daughter.*

She told me she was eighteen years old and starting college. Foolishly, I believed her and started a relationship with her. When I found out her true age, I was ashamed of myself and tried to break it off.

Louise however had made a secret video of our tryst and threatened me with exposure, unless I continued our affair. I gave in, but I have to admit I was secretly flattered that she wanted me an aging Lothario. I took what she offered and felt fulfilled, and yet that was never enough for Louise. She always wanted more. She was a drug to me. The more she rallied at me the more I felt alive and challenged.

I take full responsibility for my foolish behaviour. I could have stepped down and not submitted to blackmail; but I continued with our affair savoring every moment and promising her (through lies and presents) that when she reached her majority I would divorce Maria and we would marry.

Betty was still in my life and my bed and I struggled to juggle both her and Louise without either of them finding out about the other. Louise meanwhile spiralled more and more out of control demanding more and more of my time and energy. I found myself indulging her as you would a child; even planning my trip to Niagara Falls because she wanted to be with me there and secretly taunt her father. I grew tired of her but I was trapped in my own lies and actions. I didn't want to lose my career, and power. Most of all I refused to lose my beloved Maria, who had taken to drink because of my actions. Your mother, Betty called me shortly after we arrived in Niagara Falls, unfortunately Louise intercepted the call. Louise was devastated to find out she had another rival for me. Louise decided that Betty was at fault. That Betty had enticed me and interfered with Louise's and my relationship and was a liability to my campaign. She wouldn't tolerate someone else rival for my affections. She killed her with Betty's own shoe, all the while pretending to be an innocent bystander.

I have to admit I honestly didn't know it was Louise who killed her ~ at least not at first. When Trent and Alfred found out about

Louise and my affair, he threatened to tell her father of our trysts and destroy me in the press I told them I would break it off to save my career. Louise decided that wouldn't work and she took steps to kill them both. She took them out for a drink individually then drugged them and shot them both. She then found out about you my beloved daughter, you Sherry-Anne and hired a driver to drive herself to a vantage point where she could shoot you in front of the mall. I had already taken steps to keep you, Sherry-Anne from coming forward and exposing me; by kidnapping my grandson and his girlfriends. Louise knew nothing of my plans and went ahead with her own, before I could tell her. When I heard she'd killed you I wanted to die. I knew it was my fault.

Hearing that you had been murdered along with a homeless man that I knew, I decided I had to put a stop to Louise's murderous tendencies. I had condemned all of my family to slaughter if Louise still lived. I hired someone to shoot her; unfortunately they were unsuccessful. Louise's horseshoe like luck held out. You deserved a better father then me. I should have protected you. I have sent the police all the proof they will need to prosecute Louise. She cannot continue on her murderous rampage. The innocent have to be protected.

I have sent them my bloody shoes (she put of mine on her feet; her brown hair still attached to them.) She wore these shoes to kill my sweet, Betty.

Louise thought she was clever; but I paid a waiter to give the glasses (which she put the drug in to drug the aides) and the gun she used to kill them. I also have sent the written, witnessed testimony from the first driver she used to go kill the senators' aides, (whom the police will never find for I advanced him funds to flee). I sent the shotgun used to kill the homeless man and to shoot and strike Lily Brookfield, instead of you Sherry-Anne. I am so sorry for not stopping that in time. I know you thought I had committed this horrific crime, but I did not. You almost had me convinced it was you, until I tapped into my sources and found out the truth.

I pray that Lily Brooksfield recovers (for I know her child lost her father earlier this year to murder and no child deserves that).

I have also sent law enforcement a recording in which she confessed to me her culpability. Louise needs to be held accountable. She is not an innocent victim in any of this. Louise lies as easily as she breathes; but evidence trumps deceit. I trust *justice will now be served. I sent funds to Miguel's family. The poor man got snared as I did and now he's dead thanks to Louise.*

I am sorry from the bottom of my heart to bring all this shame upon my children. I love you all. But the only way out is for me to pay for my crime, is with my life. I pray that society will not bear the sins of the father upon his children; for my children are blameless in all of this and through some luck of genetics have not received the evil genes that propelled me to such perfidy.

I hope that after my death that my other children might get to know their oldest sister and someday forgive their flawed father. Please Sherry-Anne feel free to share this letter with them and be kind to Maria she will grieve my passing.

Your loving, but always absent father

Paul

"Where did you get that? There's no way Paul wrote that. He loved me he wouldn't turn on me. You wrote this! He didn't love Maria he loved me. ME!!!" Louise shouted, "I didn't kill any of those people and no amount of manufactured proof by you could prove I did."

"So you don't want to take any of your so called statement back, Miss Moore?" Sergeant Detective Brooks asked.

"I'm innocent. I'll have you up on slander charges if any of you dare to repeat this nonsense." Louise cried indignantly. "I stand by everything I said. She's lying."

"Miss Moore you're under arrest and as we already gave you your Miranda; please be advised that anything you've said since then can and will be held against you. Now are you sure you want to stand by your statement?" Sergeant Detective Peter Brooks demanded.

"No! What? You can do that. I want you out of here now. Anything I've said can be put down to shock and pain. A good lawyer will get me off." Louise said, "Besides I'm underage, you're not allowed to take statements from me even if I did sign it, it was under duress."

"That's not true Louise. You agreed to speak with us and you made a sworn statement," Sergeant Detective Gordon Downie insisted.

"I'm ill. I'm not going to jail. Tell them I'm not going to jail," Louise maintained, then turning to the doctor coming in.

"Miss Moore, you're free to go. We don't think you need another day after all," the doctor said, totally missing Louise's statement, "Here are your scripts for pain and antibiotics. Please rest and come back in a week's time for a check-up. The nurse will help you dress."

The police officers and Sherry-Anne stepped out for a moment while the nurse helped Louise get dressed and then when she was finished they went back in the cubicle.

"Do not pass go, go directly to jail," Sherry-Anne exclaimed.

"What? Shut-up you're not in charge!" Louise shouted.

"It is time to go to jail, Miss Moore," Sergeant Detective Brooks stated slapping a handcuff on one wrist then the other.

"I can't go to jail! I get a phone call. I want a lawyer! I want my Daddy!" rattled Louise cried, hysterically.

Sergeant Detective Brooks slapped cuffs on her one wrist then said, "Thank-you for your help, Lieutenant Rogers, we will be in touch."

"Wait, come here, Ms. Mobley."

Sherry-Anne curious wandered over to Louise. Louise bid her bend over, so she could whisper in her ear, "I did the deed with your son." Louise whispered, "I hope that image haunts you. So think on that you, bitch."

"What did she say to you?"

"Nothing, but more falsehoods. Get that filthy, lying bitch, out of here."

"Let's go Miss Moore," Sergeant Detective Brooks replied.

Sergeant Detective Brooks then sent Sergeant Detective Downie to retrieve their car. Sergeant Brooks then marched her to the elevator and out of Emmett's sight.

"It's over Emmett. That crazy bitch will go to jail. Is there something wrong with me? I should feel sorry for her. She's only slightly older than Caleb," Sherry-Anne stated.

"I felt sorry for her too, but I feel sorrier for her victims. There are five people who are dead because of her and Lily could have been one of them," Emmett said.

"How is Lily?" Sherry-Anne asked, "Is she any better?"

"Better since she's seen the kids. She was really scared for Rose, Carol, and Caleb," Emmett answered.

"I know and I know it was my fault. I should have come to you, instead of talking to my father," Sherry-Anne remorsefully.

"It's okay Sherry-Anne, we all make mistakes," Emmett replied.

"Can I see Lily?" Sherry-Anne asked.

"I think she'd like that," Emmett answered.

"I'll take you to see Lily and then you're going back to your room to rest," insisted Sherry-Anne, "I got you into this Emmett. I'm not about to let you wear yourself down and get sick and die before you even get to know your son."

"She's right dad, you need to rest," Caleb stated.

"Fine, with both of you ganging up I'd better listen; but first I'm seeing Lily."

"I'm your chauffeur," Caleb stated.

Chapter 25 - Life moves on

Lily's Hospital Room

"I'm so glad you're getting better mom. You're in a

regular room, so when can you leave here?" Rose demanded.

"In a couple of days as long as I rest," Lily answered.

"Good," Rose stated, "Do we go home then?"

"Grandma Katha wanted to cancel the rest of the trip and her wedding, but I insisted we continue," Lily answered.

"Mom, are you sure?"

"I want to go to something happy and it's still a week and a half from now."

"I'm looking forward to the wedding and Grandma Katha said we'd have fun in London, Ontario. They have a Victoria Park there which they decorated for Christmas and even has an ice rink," Rose said excitedly, "Oh, but you'll be alone at the hotel I'm being selfish."

"No, you're not!! You and Carol should have fun. Besides Emmett needs to rest too he can spend some time with me."

"Good. I can't believe that it was Louise Moore who committed all these murders," Rose commented.

"We met her at the Water Park. She was very flirty with all the boys there," Carol said.

"I thought it was weird how she mentioned her older boyfriend, like he had a job that was special," Rose commented.

"She said that Michel Charbonneau was her friend, but that wasn't the way you greet a friend kissing them on the lips," Carol observed.

"Mom I'm betraying a confidence here, but...," Rose broke off.

"You hate betraying a friend. It's not really a betrayal if it's told to protect a friend."

"I am worried about them."

"Then tell me Rose. I'll keep the confidence as much as I possibly can and only tell what I need to help them. Carol can you give us a moment; maybe go in the hallway for a moment?"

"I guess," Carol answered, peevishly.

Carol then left the room and went into the hallway.

Rose waited then said, "Caleb told me something...,"

"What did he say?" Lily asked.

"I maybe reading more into this, but I think he was involved with Louise."

"Involved with Louise? But how did he even know her?"

"He met her at the mall in Mississauga and she was at the dinner with those politicians for a few moments."

"And?"

"I think he..."

"He what?"

"He slept with her."

"But Emmett was at the mall with him."

"Mom, don't be so naive."

"Naive. It's a mall; how could that even happen? You shouldn't know about these things. What kind of boy would share these disgusting things with a vulnerable young girl?"

"Mom, good grief you act like I'm nine still. Besides Caleb didn't actually come right out and say he slept with her, it was more implied. He said he had made a big mistake. The point is Caleb suffers. He almost feels like it's his fault you and his dad was shot, because he got involved with Louise."

"She took advantage of Caleb; but he obviously has the morals of his mother."

"Mom!!!"Rose admonished, "I like Caleb."

"I don't trust her," Lily commented.

"You don't like Ms. Mobley?" Rose laughed.

"I know I don't like the way she acts around Emmett."

"Me neither. She fawns all over Emmett like she owns him. She hasn't seen him in years and he's your boyfriend."

"She doesn't seem to register that Emmett is my boyfriend."

"She knows, she just refuses to acknowledge it; but don't worry she'll go home and get out of our hair. Caleb will visit his dad while she lives in London. I like Caleb, he's very like Emmett. He's a sweet boy, but he's had a hard life," Rose claimed.

"Boy?"

"I know he's older than me; but he's like most men very immature,"Rose commented.

"I like him too and I'd like to help him grow into the fine young man he could be...as a friend of course, not as his mother, for he has one of those,"Lily commented.

"So you'll help me show him that Louise's actions weren't his fault, without revealing that I told you?"

"Of course, Rose."

"Let's table this then, here comes Carol, Terrence, and Grandma Katha."

"Okay," Lily agreed.

Carol, Terrence, Grandma Katha walked into the hospital room.

"Where's Amelia?" asked Lily.

"She had to fly home to tend to her shop. She'll join us in a couple of days," Rose answered.

"So did you tell Rose?" Grandma Katha asked.

"Tell me what?"

"I'm leaving the hospital today."

"Really? I'm so glad," Rose said excitedly.

"If you could all wait in the hall, I'll get dressed," Lily said.

Carol, Rose. Katha and Terence stepped into the hall to wait.

I can't believe that it was Louise Moore who committed all these murders," Carol commented.

"And the guy she killed Alfred Getts (the aide that worked for her Dad) he seemed a little too forward with her. I think she had something going on with him," Rose exclaimed.

"That's probably why she killed him. He probably didn't want to share her with the Senator," Carol concluded.

"Young ladies shouldn't speak the way you're speaking," Terrence admonished the girls.

"Really Terrence, dear you're behind the times. Young ladies today need to understand what goes on in the world to protect themselves from predators. Sadly women like Louise are everywhere," Katha stated.

Terrence looked thunderstruck then gulped and apologised, "Quite right, Katha, dear. Forgive an old fuddy-duddy, girls."

"I forgive you dear; after all I married you for your old world charm," Katha answered.

"I had no idea it was that young woman," Terrence commented.

"I really didn't guess it was her, either. I suspected the Senator and his opponent David Moore. How did Mr. Moore take the news that his daughter was a serial killer?" Katha asked.

"David Moore and his wife Kelly are devastated. They are also in denial about their daughter. They claim they had no idea about the long term affair or any of Louise's outrageous behaviour," Emmett answered.

"Do you believe them?" Katha asked.

"I do. David Moore was obsessed with himself and his career and his wife, Kelly is obsessed with him. Kelly Moore further claims Louise is in treatment for a bipolar illness. She also says that Louise was abused as a child by someone hired to look after her, so if (and in her mind it's a big if) Louise committed any crimes she's did so not in her right mind."

"That poor child."

"You can still have sympathy for her Katha?" Emmett asked.

"She's a broken soul and Senator Gauthier abused her, no matter what his suicide note says. His opponent was a public figure. Public figures children's ages are well known. He either knew, or chose not to know, that she was fourteen years old, when he took up with her. He is not an innocent party. He took the easy way out instead of facing up to the music and now who will suffer for it? His family will suffer," Katha replied vehemently.

"I think they already are, Grace Gauthier sues for custody of the children from Maria," Emmett stated.

"Why? Nick's mom did a good job," Rose exclaimed, "It's not their fault, their father was a cheat."

"I think there's something else wrong there. I need to tell you Mr. Rogers, but with all that went on I forgot to tell you," Carol said sheepishly.

"What else do you think is wrong there Carol?" Emmett asked.

"Gab and Nick denied but I think their father hit them, and maybe here siblings Erin and Teri too."

"You have good instincts Carol. I was just about to tell you before you and Rose interrupted that Grace's custody suit wouldn't have a leg to stand on. Paul Gauthier confessed in his suicide note to Maria that not only had he been a bad husband to her; but he had followed in the footsteps of his mother's abuse of him and had abused his wife and kids. He asked Maria to forgive the beatings that drove her to drink and the mental and physical abuse at his hands and his mother's for her and his children. He apologised for the police officers who lost her paperwork on his orders," Emmett explained

"Gabe and Nick must have been hiding this for a long time," Carol replied.

"I didn't see any signs they were abused," Rose commented.

"Your father had his arm broken by his mother as a child, Rose and it seems that Paul had that happened to him as a boy as well. Grace Gauthier denies it all of course. She threatened the police with libel and slander; but it seems Paul had all his ducks in arrow. He had doctor reports that he had suppressed with his money and power of his abuse of his wife and children and those of his own at his mother's hands. I think he knew with his death, his mother would seek to get custody of his children and he couldn't allow that," Emmett stated.

"Well at least he did something right," Lily said joining the conversation and them in the hallway.

"Something was up with Caleb. He seemed upset do you know anything about that Rose and Carol?"

"You know don't you, Rose?" Carol stated.

"I can't reveal what he told me," Rose said.

"Please, Rose. If I did something to hurt Caleb you have to tell me," Emmett implored.

"It's something really personal and has nothing to do with you. You didn't do anything wrong," Rose claimed.

"Are you sure?"

"I'm sure he'll tell you if he wants to."

"How do you know and I don't?" Carol asked, "Tell me, Rose, and whisper in my ear, if you don't want all to hear."

"I keep confidences. No amount of pleading will make me tell you Carol Banks," Rose exclaimed.

"You told your mother. I know you did," Carol commented.

"Shut-up, Carol," Rose shouted.

"Don't fight girls," admonished Lily, "Let's head to the car," then turning to Emmett she asked, "Will we meet up with Caleb and Sherry-Anne at the hotel?"

"Caleb and Sherry-Anne had to go to the airport." Emmett replied.

"They went to London all ready?" Lily asked getting on the elevator while Katha pushed the buttons to reach the ground floor.

"Yes, they went home early because Sherry-Anne's younger sisters Belle and Bette are coming to visit her. Bette is lucky she hasn't got to the stage of pregnancy where she can't travel yet." Emmett answered.

"They will be nice for the girls to meet with their Aunt. After a death family needs family," Katha commented.

"Speaking of pregnancy, my sister doing well. They're still keeping her in the hospital. The twins are due March twenty-fifth still, but she and the doctor insist that everything is good," Emmett continued.

They exited the elevator went out the door and to the car park. There they climbed into a van. Lily sat beside Emmett while Carol and Rose sat behind them. Katha sat in the passenger seat and Terrence climbed into the driver's seat.

"You're sure you don't need to fly home Emmett?" Lily asked, "I'm on the mend now. We could drive you to the airport that is if you need to be with Caleb."

"Lily, you're not getting rid of me that easy. I'll see Caleb soon; but he needs to be with his mother and other family right now. As for you, you scared the heck of me getting shot. I'm not leaving your side for awhile," Emmett answered.

"Now you know how I felt," Lily said looking at Emmett's arm in a sling.

"Christmas day will come soon. Do you girls want to go Christmas shopping while your mom and Emmett rest?" asked Katha turning around as they pulled into the hotel parking lot.

"We should stay here with mom." Rose said wanting to go but still worried about her mom.

"I'm fine, besides I really want a fabulous Christmas present," Lily said laughing.

"Are you sure Mom?" Rose asked.

"I'm going to take a nap. How about you Emmett?" Lily asked.

"I'm going to veg out and watch some television," Emmett answered, "See you later, Lil"

Emmett then went to his room.

"I'll pick up some presents for you for Rose and Carol and Caleb. Did you want me to get you something to give Emmett?" Katha whispered to Lily as she helped her to the hotel room.

"I brought some presents with me, but yes please pick some more up for me would you Grandma Katha? I'd love to have something for Caleb," Lily answered, "Maybe some stocking stuffers, too?"

"Will do. We'll have a fabulous Christmas and then the wedding can take place in London New Year's Eve," Katha reassured.

"Are you sure you don't need me to stay?"

"I'll be fine. I'm going to sleep. Goodnight Grandma Katha." Lily said as Katha tucked her into the bed.

"Goodnight, my sweetheart. Sweet dreams," Katha said watching Lily from the door.

Katha went back out to the van looking torn.

"She's going to be okay, honey," Terrence stated, knowing what Katha thinks.

"I almost lost her Terrence," Katha cried, wiping a tear away

"Now, now, you'll upset the children. You didn't and she's fine." Terrence said, "I never thought I say this but let's go to the mall. My credit card is getting cold."

~0~

Chapter 26 - Bad Memories

After Katha left and Lily fell asleep a lone woman slipped into the hotel room using a stolen card. In Lily's doorway of her room the woman watched her sleep.

"I'm so sorry I left you, Lily. Thank-you God you'll be okay, baby doll. Even if you don't know, I'll always watch over you and keep you safe," Heather Kelly whispered softly.

She crept in and kissed Lily's brow softly. Lily stirred, but didn't wake continuing to slumber as Heather swept out of the room quietly and left locking the hotel room. She left the hotel as quickly as she came, so that Grandma Katha would not catch her. No one would notice a woman dressed as a maid. Her superiors were not happy with this visit as it was she could risk more exposure. She had an assignment and they expected her to leave the country and get on with it

~0~

At the mall Rose and Carol wondered off on their own promising to meet up in an hour while Terrence and Katha go to the nearest restaurant. In the restaurant they entered a booth.

"I'm still angry that you knew about Heather and didn't tell me," Katha stated "But I understand you thought you were doing what is best, so I can forgive you."

"I'm sorry you feel I betrayed your trust. She won't be back. I reached out to some of my contacts she's been reassigned." Terrence answered.

"Let's be honest the woman is spy. That's no kind of life for a mother. Her actions and duties could impact Lily."

"No, they won't. That is why she has distanced herself from Lily. Everyone thinks Heather's dead; there is no strings or connection that can lead to Lily or anyone else in your family."

"You think I'm overreacting, but I'm not Terrence. I want to tell you why I reacted this way. When Heather left their home and Peter with that man, Lily was devastated. Her mother suddenly was gone no explanation to Lily. Then Heather came back and drove Lily to school. Lily was over the moon, deliriously happy. She was sure her mother was back. Lily doesn't remember that her mother ever left at all and she definitely doesn't remember what happened next."

"Armed gunman took them hostage. Lily was blindfolded and kept for days in a room without food, or water. Her mother was threatened they wanted Heather's lover and they said they would kill Lily. Lily heard all of this and feared for her life. Lily pried a window screen off a window and escaped after three days. She came home, but she wasn't the same. She felt guilty for saving herself, but not her mother. "

"We went to the home, but by the time we reached the place where they had kept Heather she was gone. We were all sure her mother was dead and then the police came and Lily despite any of our assurances thought they were blaming her father for her mother's disappearance. She stopped eating, she stopped drinking. Lily was a mess."

"We took her to a psychiatrist and the doctor treated her in hospital for six months in Switzerland. He said something else had a happened to her, but she wouldn't even admit to herself what happened. The only way she could cope was to block out the kidnapping and only remember her mother leaving her at school. Not the kidnapping and anything else that happened. Peter couldn't cope. He was always busy with his job as an attaché. Also they his bosses were hounding him for information he didn't have on Heather. I begged Peter to let me have custody and to take her back to my home for a year. He agreed after talking to the doctor."

"A year later went by and he had moved on and was in a relationship and Lily didn't fit back into his life. Lily thrived with me and I continued raising my darling girl. When she was a little older, Amelia joined us. She still doesn't remember what happened and the doctor warned me not to talk to her about it. Her psychiatrist (as a child) told me that it's probably better that she never remembers and I want it to stay that way. Seeing Heather could trigger all those memories and destroy Lily I won't have that. Heather maybe my granddaughter, but her selfishness harmed her daughter and for that I can't forgive her," Katha explained.

"I didn't know that Katha. I was told they rescued Heather from the gunman and took her into protective custody." Terrence stated.

"She was saved. Lily had to save herself. You're forgiven. But remember Terrence, no more secrets ever," Katha insisted.

"Never my love. Now I have to go shopping. I want the best Christmas and wedding gifts for you, ever. I'll meet you at the front doors at five p.m.?" Terrence stated finishing his coffee.

"See you then," Katha answered, "But you'll have to wait until Christmas to see that my present is better."

Terrence placed some bills on the table, kissed Katha on the cheek and then left the restaurant.

~0~

Chapter 27 - Christmas in Toronto

Christmas Day

Katha happily tucking blankets around Lily, as Lily

lounged in her bed, at the Toronto Eaton Square Hotel.

"Are you sure you're comfortable Lily?" fussed Katha.

"I'm very comfortable Grandma Katha. Quit worrying the doctor said I could travel in the next couple of days," Lily answered.

"That's like telling me not to breath. I have to worry about you. It's my job," Katha answered.

"Sorry, Grandma Katha. I worry about Rose the same, so I do understand," Lily replied.

"It's Christmas." shouted Rose and Carol excitedly coming into the sitting room dressed in jeans and warm sweaters.

"What no pajamas?" Lily asked.

"We can't have Emmet see us in our pajamas," Carol answered.

"Emmett, isn't here yet?" Rose asked looking around.

"Emmett will be here soon," Katha said.

"And Grandpa Terence?" asked Carol.

"Grandpa Terrence is still wrapping his presents," Katha answered smirking.

"Grandpa Terrence hasn't finished? Why didn't he do that all ready?" Rose asked.

"He's never wrapped he's own before and he wanted them to be perfect," Katha replied, smiling.

"Ah that's sweet," Carol and Rose exclaimed at the same time.

"Yes, it is isn't it?"

"I'm so glad we get to see you marrying him again, next week. We really wanted to be part of the ceremony," Lily stated.

"I'm sorry you girls weren't there the first time. Terrence caught me at a weak moment swept me completely off my feet and before I knew it we were married at City hall. I should have had you all there I'm sorry," Katha apologised.

"No, that was my mistake, dear. You shouldn't take the blame. I was in such hurry to make you my bride I wasn't thinking about how our family should be there. That's why my lovely bride we re-marrying in one week's time. We'll be surrounded by all the love and family you deserve," Terrence exclaimed.

Terrence's arms were so full of presents he could barely hold them and his face was not visible. He set the presents under the tree, all except one. Emmett entered the hotel room at the same moment carrying his own armful of presents.

"Here my darling girl, open this I can't wait." Terrence said handing her a misshapen badly wrapped present.

Katha opened the package to reveal a gold necklace with a K & T etched into a gold heart.

"Oh Terrence it's so beautiful," Katha cried trying to put it on.

Terrence stepped up and helped her fasten the clasp around her neck.

"I hope you will wear it when you commit to being my wife again," Terrence stated.

"I'd be honoured to. Now enough of me everyone get to unwrapping your presents. I want to see some smiles," Katha exclaimed.

The presents pile up in tee-shirts, jeans, blouses and other clothes for Rose and Carol. Lily and Amelia also piled up presents of clothes.

"Lily, here this one is for you from me," Emmett said handing it to Lily.

As she opened the small package and gasped Emmett dropped to bended knee and said, "When I found out you had been shot, my heart felt like it stopped beating. My world stopped revolving. I couldn't picture a world without you. I love you Lily Kelly-Wentworth-Brooksfield. You make every day an adventure. Please Lily will you marry me?"

Lily stared at the perfectly cut diamond. It had a perfect princess cut and gleamed in the sunlight flowing into the hotel room.

"Oh Emmett," Lily answered, not quite sure what to say.

"Is that a no?" asked Emmett, dejected.

"I don't know I have to think about this. This is a big surprise Emmett and a huge commitment. Can I have some time to think about this? I mean what will people think? I've only been widowed for six months," Lily stated.

"They'll think you're a lucky woman?" Emmett quipped.

"Can we talk about this in the bedroom without witnesses? "Lily asked getting up and walking slowly to the bedroom.

Emmett followed her to the bedroom shutting the door shut they continue the conversation.

"I don't know Emmett. I care about you I think I might even love you, but what if there really is a Kelly curse? My last two husbands were murdered, I don't want to make it three," Lily stated sadly.

"Lily, I understand your fear. I really do but I think we could have a wonderful life together. I want you to know I love you and I want to marry you. And I could be a great stepfather to Rose," Emmett insisted.

"I need more time. Can I have some time?" Lily begged, "Must you have an answer to your question today?"

"I'll give you a week to think about it but I want an answer New Year's Eve," Emmett declared then kissed Lily and started to put on his winter coat.

"Do you go somewhere?"

"I'm going to London to visit with my son Caleb, now. That will give you the time you need without pressure. See you New Year's Eve. Caleb and I are going to spend some guy time the next week, while Sherry-Anne entertains her sisters."

"I do love you Emmett," Lily exclaimed.

"I love you too, see you New Year's Lily."

"Goodbye Emmett," Lily said.

Emmett then left the hotel room.

"You'd be a fool Lily to throw that man away," Katha stated as Lily came out of the bedroom.

"I need some time Grandma Katha. I may love Emmett, but I still love Horace and he is still in my heart," Lily explained.

"Terrence understands that Kieran will always be in my heart. Maybe you should give that boy some credit too that he can understand that." Katha stated.

"I hope so but Grandma Katha I have to be sure," Lily answered.

"Don't pressure my mom; she needs to take her time, Grandma Katha," Rose protested.

"I know Rosey, but Lily I know that if it's right you'll know it in your heart." Katha stated, "Why don't you get some rest Lily and we'll have Christmas brunch in about two hours."

"Thank-you Grandma Katha. I love you," Lily said wiping away tears.

"I love you too, my lillypad,"Katha answered.

Lily then when back into the bedroom and shut the door.

"Grandma Katha she will marry him, won't she?" Rose asked.

"Your mother has to make her own decision and follow her heart," Katha stated.

"Fine, but Emmett better make her happy. I think Emmett can," Rose answered.

"I know dear mine too. He'll make a fine addition to this family, too" Katha stated, "Now let's clean up this mess. You too Carol, the wrapping paper is everywhere."

"But that's what the maid is for," protested Carol.

"We don't make extra work for anyone."

"Fine, I'm cleaning. See," Carol answered.

"Me too. Merry Christmas Grandma Katha and Grandpa Terence and thank-you for all the lovely presents," Rose cried.

"You're welcome dears," Terrence said, "Merry Christmas to all of us and to all a good night."

"But I'm ready for lunch." Carol complained.

"Let's go eat Carol," Rose commented, "First one to the restaurant is a dirty egg."

"Save a good table for us," Terrence said pushing Lily's wheelchair.

~0~

Chapter 28-
London Calling

Four days later

M

"om, have you made up your mind? It's okay if you

don't want to marry Emmett."

"I didn't say that. Don't you want me to marry Emmett?"

"I do and I don't. I like Emmett, but I don't want you to forget my dad."

"I'll never forget Horace. I loved him, we had a very happy life together and he's your father."

"Okay so, what will you tell Emmett tomorrow night?" Rose asked.

"I wanted to talk to you about that," said Lily.

"I hope that includes me too?" Katha enquired.

"Yes, of course," Lily replied.

Terrence and Carol looked on expectantly, as if to ask are they also included.

"You're all included. Are you all happy now?" Lily asked.

"Not until you let us know what your answer will be," Rose quipped.

"I've thought long and hard about this. Emmett is a wonderful man a wonderful father. I like to think he could be a wonderful stepfather to you too Rose," Lily answered.

"So you're going to marry him?" Rose demanded.

"I'd like to marry him. I love him and I think he'd make a good husband. I know I want to spend the rest of my life with him, but only if it's okay with you Rose."

"Mom, I miss Daddy and I know you do to. I think Emmett can understand that we will always love your Daddy. I know he will always love his dead wife, Jenna. He spoke to me about her. She seemed like a nice lady and Emmett has been so good to me. He's been like a friend, but also like a step-dad to me already, so if you want to say yes, just do it. I'd be happy and proud to have him as my step-dad. Even if it will be odd to have a stepbrother," Rose declared.

"Thank-you Rose. I want you to know how much this means to me."

"Will you make that poor man wait until tomorrow? He must be on pins and needles," Terrence commented overhearing the conversation from his easy chair in the corner.

"We'll be in London tomorrow." Lily answered, "I wish I could do it today, but tomorrow will have to do."

"I have surprise for you all. How would you like to see Emmett today?" Terrence demanded jumping to his feet.

"What's the surprise Terrence? How can she see Emmett today? Our flight to London, Ontario isn't until tomorrow," Katha exclaimed.

"I cancelled our flight yesterday."

"You did what? Terrence you should have consulted me," Katha complained.

"I thought Lily would be more comfortable travelling by limousine, or rather by Robert Q. The Robert Q Company said tomorrow was their busy time, but they had an opening for our number and they're coming in about an hour to take us to London," Terrence announced, smiling.

"An hour? We have an hour to be ready? How can we ever be ready in time?" Katha stated. "Men?? Have you any idea how much we have to pack?"

"If I know you Katha, you'll be ready," Terrence said.

Then going into drill sergeant mode Katha barked, "Girls start packing, or will never be ready in time."

"I know what you're going to say I've changed our reservation at the same time for the Delta London Armouries. I opted to rent our rooms for four days instead of the three. We all go home January second anyway. The Robert Q bus will pick us up at three a.m. on the second and drive us to Pearson Airport for our ten a.m. flight," Terrence explained.

"Thank-you, dear, but now you better get in our bedroom and start packing," Katha instructed, "I can't do everything."

"I'm already packed," Terrence declared which earned him a dirty look from Katha.

An hour later they were on the road and a couple of hours later the Robert Q bus arrived in London. They then took a taxi to the hotel.

"Wow, Grandma Katha this hotel does look like a castle," Rose commented walking up to the front door.

"It's very pretty, but it doesn't look like a castle to me," Carol responded.

"You're not looking at it the right way Carol. Look at the side there," Rose pointed out.

"Wow, I was wrong it does look like a castle Look at the turrets."

Lily and Katha just smiled at the girls as Terrence retrieved a luggage cart.

"It's known as London's fairy-tale castle." Terrence stated preparing for a lecture, "The Delta London Armouries was originally constructed in 1905 as a training location for Canadian soldiers in World War I and II. Then when it was in use anymore they decided to save its historic significance by incorporating it into this hotel."

"How does he know all this?" asked Katha, "I made the original reservations in his name."

"I showed him how to use Google and he probably used it to look up its history," Carol responded.

"Ha, I was here in the war, and so was Kieran at some point. A lot of troops were moved through London. I told you all that," Terrence quipped, "I know it must contain some wonderful memories for you Katha. I'm glad that those memories of Kieran O'Malley will be with us for our wedding."

"You don't mind?" Katha asked surprised.

"He must have been a great guy to have kept your heart all those years. I only hope that somewhere he smiles at us being together. I'd like to think he loved you so much, he pointed me your way," Terrence answered.

"I think he did send you to me," Katha declared.

Katha then kissed Terrence fully on the lips.

"Hey get a room, you two," Carol cried laughing.

Terrence stepped into the lobby and went to the desk retrieving the room cards for everyone he passed them out.

"So do you know what room Emmett's in?" Katha asked.

"He said he was in room, three hundred and five," Lily answered.

"Why don't you leave all your bags with us. We will get your luggage to your suite and settle in the girls. In fact Terrence and are were thinking of taking a walk. We're taking the skates we bought the girls for Christmas and walking over to this Victoria Park. I believe there's an outdoor ice rink there," Katha stated.

"Really?" squealed Carol and Rose excitedly.

"Yes, really. Now go speak to Emmett, Lily and give him your answer. In fact why don't you get a key from the front desk and go surprise him. "Katha says "Already, done here. I'm paying for the room as your Christmas presents; so they gave me a spare key when I asked," Terrence said smiling and handing Lily the key card.

"Thank-you, you are the best great grandparents ever," Lily responded.

"And don't you forget it," Katha declared.

"You look happy," Terrence professed.

"I am now, so let's get rid of the bags and go see this magical park. I heard they put the lights on at night," Katha commented.

"Good, because it's almost dark," Terrence said, "We'll get some exercise and be ready for a nice family dinner when we come back."

"I love you, Terrence."

"I love you too, Katha. Now let's get moving. We can show this young people how young we are when I twirl around with you on the ice."

~0~

Chapter 29 - Heartbreak Hotel

Lily entered the elevator and pushed the third floor. She

was so excited. Lily and Emmett had much to celebrate and the time to do with Rose, Carol, Grandma Katha and Grandpa Terrence at the park.

Reaching room three hundred and five she excited and put the key card in the door and opened it. She noted that Emmett appeared to be sleeping in the bed. She'd soon change that. He'd make a great husband and stepfather to Rose. Her heart overfilled with love for this man. Lily walked over to the bed and realize as she touched Emmett's bare shoulder that someone else is also in the bed as the sheets move. Lily looked on in surprise as a woman's bare shoulder, and then a bare breast is exposed, above the sheet.

With shock Lily recognized the face which popped up above the sheet, as Emmett rolled over and embraced the woman lying there.

"You bastard Emmett! How could you?" Lily yelled then ran out of the room crying and slamming the door.

Lily ran to the elevator and taking it to the first floor to retrieve her room card. Wiping her tears as the elevator door opened, Lily attempted to hide her distress from strangers, but she failed to halt the flow of tears. Stepping off the elevator through a veil of tears, she bumped into a man.

"Oh, I'm so sorry," Lily cried, as the man, reached out to her to keep her from falling.

"That's okay, I don't know when I've had such a lovely woman fall into my arms." he chuckled and then smiled as he spoke with a lilting accent Lily couldn't quite place.

Lily looked up at the man through long wet lashes. She saw a devastatingly handsome man. His short black wavy hair sat perfectly on his head, his eyes clear and a azure blue twinkled with concern for her and he stood over six feet tall. He appeared to be about thirty years of age. As he smiled, at her she realized why he looked so familiar he looked like a younger Pierce Brosnan.

"Is there anything I can do?" he asked solicitously.

"No, I'll be fine. Thank-you anyway," Lily answered, dismissing him and walking over to the front desk.

"Okay, but you can always join me for a drink I'll be in the bar area. My name's Dafydd. "

"Thank-you, but no," Lily answered.

The man then turned and left entering into the restaurant area. Emmett suddenly appeared and Lily so ducked into the restaurant/ bar area to avoid him.

"We seem destined to be in the same place today. Would you like to have lunch with me?" Dafydd asked, standing up at his table when he saw Lily.

"I don't even know you," Lily protested.

"What better way to get to know me?" charmed the man, "I'm harmless, I promise."

"I guess I have to eat," Lily replied.

"That's quite the endorsement," Dafydd laughed.

"I don't even know your full name."

"My name is David Jones, it is spelled D.A.F.Y.D.D.," Dafydd answered.

"I'm Lily Kelly-Brooksfield," Lily introduced herself and looked around.

"Do you avoid someone?" Dafydd asked.

"Truthfully yes, I'm avoiding someone," Lily admitted.

"Should I be worried?" Dafydd asked arching an eyebrow.

"No we're done," Lily stated.

"That bad huh?"

"I trusted him and I was wrong. End of story," Lily answered.

"I'm sorry. I've been on the receiving end of that. I came home from work a year ago and found my wife with another man. I thought I'd met someone charming a month ago, but that didn't work out either. Now I'm celebrating since my divorce was final yesterday." Dafydd said, "Should I say congratulations, or I'm sorry?"

"Let's just move on."

They ordered lunch and continued talking.

"So where are you from?" Dafydd began.

Emmett appeared from nowhere at their table looking devastating and Lily almost felt sorry for him.

"Lily we need to talk," Emmett stated.

"I think that scene I walked into said it all," Lily answered, ignoring him and turning her head.

"Please Lily, hear me out for our friendship?" pleaded Emmett.

"Fine! Excuse me Dafydd. This might take a few minutes. But it was nice meeting you," Lily said placing money on the table to pay for the meal she ordered.

"Later," mouthed Dafydd smiling.

"Lily, please sit down over here," Emmett asked motioning to a table further away.

Emmett asked a waiter for two coffees. After receiving them he began, "I know what you walked in on but it wasn't what you think."

"Really? So Sherry-Anne wasn't naked beside you in your bed, which my great-grandfather had paid for?" Lily replied sarcastically.

"I'm sorry Lily. I would never do anything to hurt you. I love you. I want to marry you," Emmett answered.

"That's funny way to show it," stated Lily angrily.

"I'm sorry Sherry-Anne and I talked over old times. Sherry-Anne and I must have had too much to drink because the next thing I know I'm waking up beside Sherry-Anne, and you're running from the room," Emmett admitted sheepishly.

"Your honor sir; it really wasn't my fault I had too much to drink. Do you think I haven't heard the felons tell the judge that in court? You disgust me Emmett Rogers. You knew my husbands had cheated on me. You knew I had trust issues; but you still slept with your high school girlfriend, Sherry-Anne. Over-indulging in alcohol is no excuse. You made your choice."

"I didn't..."

"You didn't sleep with Sherry-Anne?"

"I'm sorry," Emmett stated.

"When I met her I thought it was a coincidence that she looked like me. Ha! Joke's on me. You were only attracted to me, because I looked like her," Lily replied, snarling.

"That's not true Lily. She's the substitute; you're the real thing."

"That's too bad for you then, because you blew that when you slept with her. I came to tell you that I wanted to marry you; but I've changed my mind. I never want to see you again Emmett Rogers as long as I live. And don't bother coming to my great-grandmother and great-grandfather's renewal ceremony tomorrow. I'll make your excuses. Now please go!" Lily stated, "Or I will."

"Please Lily. Please don't do this," begged Emmett.

Emmett reached out and grabbed Lily's arm preventing her from standing up and walking away. Lily pale skin leached from her face, but she stuck to her guns and demanded loudly, "I want you to go!"

"I believe the lady said for you to go," Dafydd said coming over to the table.

"This isn't over Lily. I'll see you back home in a few days." Emmett retorted getting up to leave.

"No you won't! There are stalker laws even a cop knows that," Lily shouted to his departing back.

Lily grasped her chest and then reached into her purse for a pain pill which Emmett with his back to her and now retreating to the elevator didn't see.

"Are you okay?" asks Dafydd.

"I'll be fine. I had major surgery about two weeks ago, that's all," Lily answered.

"That's all? You should be resting," Dafydd answered.

"You sound like a doctor," Lily replied.

Dafydd blushed.

"You're a doctor?"

"I have a medical degree," Dafydd said without explaining, "come back and eat your food. It finally came to the table and you paid for it."

"Okay, I guess. I'm in safe hands," joked Lily.

Lily walked over to the table but before she reached it she turned very pale and collapsed on the floor.

"Do you want me to call a doctor or an ambulance?" the waiter asked.

"Not right now. I'm a doctor." Dafydd cried, "I'll let you know, but I left my bag at the front desk could you retrieve that for me."

"I'll do that," the waiter cried running.

The waiter returned in seconds with Dafydd's doctor bag and Dafydd dove into it as he attended to Lily. Katha entered the restaurant followed by Terrence, Amelia, Rose and Carol. Katha spotted Lily on the floor and the man kneeling beside her and ran.

"Lily, are you all right? What do you do to her?" shouted Katha.

Dafydd did not reply but pulled out a stethoscope and listened to Lily's chest.

"Dafydd is that you?" Terrence asked.

"Oh hello, Terrence." Dafydd replied distracted, "Sorry, busy here. This woman collapsed."

"Is she okay? Is Lily, okay?" asked Terrence trembling.

"You know her?" asks Dafydd.

"She's our great-granddaughter." Terrence and Katha answered.

"Is my mom, okay?" asked Rose coming in with Carol and Amelia.

"Her pulse is okay. She said she had major surgery before she collapsed. Do you know what that surgery was?" Dafydd asked.

"She was shot in the chest. She lost a lot of blood and had to have several blood transfusions." Katha answered.

"Her heartbeat is good and solid. Has she been resting?" Dafydd asked.

"Yes, I have been. Sorry to scare you all. I don't know what happened." Lily replied, "Maybe stress?"

"Have you eaten today?" Dafydd asked.

"No," Lily answered sheepishly.

"Okay then doctor's orders, you need to eat now. I'm sure they'll box your food up and you can take it to your hotel room," Dafydd said

The waiter overhearing this scurried to find boxes to put the food in.

"If Lily's okay we can take her to her room," Katha replied, "Or should we be taking her to the hospital?"

"I think she'll be okay; if she eats something and rests for the rest of the day. I'm in room 410 if she needs anything come get me. Or page me within the hotel here's my cell number," Dafydd replied, "Make sure you see your doctor when you go home, okay?"

"Thank-you for all your help Dafydd it was wonderful to meet you," Lily replied.

"If you want to thank me, then eat something." Dafydd said and then added, "See you at the wedding tomorrow."

"He's coming to your wedding?" Lily asked.

"I invited him," Terrence answered.

"Let's get you to your room and get something in you," Katha stated helping Lily to the elevator.

"Mom you should have eaten. You're always telling me breakfast is the most important meal of the day," Rose scolded.

"You're right. I'm sorry," Lily answered, sheepishly.

"Should I call Emmett?" Rose asked.

"No. I'm not speaking to him," Lily answered.

"What? Since when?" Rose demanded.

"Tell me what happened," insisted Amelia.

"Quit pestering. Lily will tell you both when she ready and right now she doesn't need the stress."

"Grandma Katha's right; here it is for all of you. I'm not taking any questions. Emmett and I are over. We broke up. I'm not discussing this so don't ask," Lily admitted.

As they exit the elevator door they saw Sherry-Anne enter the opposite elevator. Lily paled and looked very angry. Katha saw the anger and guessed the reason.

"I'm sorry dear I can see we were all very mistaken about Emmett. Damn that boy!" Katha stated vehemently, "That's it. Terrence will now find a new best man. Won't you dear?"

"I'm sure Dafydd will fill in in a pinch. I'll ask him then tell Emmett's out as my best man," Terrence agreed.

"Do we have to talk about this?"

"We will talk later Lily, but I'll drop it for now. We all will. Won't we, Aunt Katha, Uncle Terrence," Amelia answered.

"You all need to get something to eat. You have to be hungry and cold after being outdoors skating," Lily replied, changing the subject

"I'll order pizza but you'll eat this food just like your doctor ordered," Katha commanded, helping Lily to the sofa and then setting up her food on the coffee table she pulled over.

"You should have seen it mom the rink is huge and there was Christmas music still playing. Apparently they turn the Christmas lights on after six p.m... I want to see them," Rose began excited, "And they had these bells that were made in the Netherlands. They were a present to thank the Canadian soldiers for their liberation of their country during the Second World War."

"Yes, that was cool, Rose. The chimes played this song 'It's a small world after all'. They were so beautiful. It was really fun. Aunt Amelia promised to take us back to see the lights again, after the wedding," Carol stated.

"That sounds wonderful I'm glad you had a good time," Lily stated sounding distracted.

"So what's the story on the good doctor, Uncle Terrence?" Amelia asked.

"He is my godson. His grandfather was my very best friend. His grandfather's name was Alexander. He was a wonderful man, but he died much too young of a triple aneurysm. But because his son Andrew worried that he could have passed that on to him he begged me to become his son's godfather. Good thing he did because he was killed in a car accident when the boy was in medical school. Though the boy has an uncle with loads of money, he needed me for advice and guidance. "

"It's a good thing he had you then," Amelia exclaimed.

"I've got news for you all. Dafydd will be the new coroner of Happy Valley replacing Coroner Dr. Andrew Piper who's retiring."

"He's a coroner?" Lily asked, surprised.

"Yes, he prefers solving crimes to practicing medicine with live people," Terrence answered.

"The hunky doctor follows you home, Lily," Amelia said, as Lily blushed.

"Let's watch some television," Rose said not happy that Amelia talked about setting her mother up with this new person.

Katha sat watching the television show, but her mind was on Lily. Damn that Emmett Rogers. How could he have broken Lily's heart? She looked over at Lily and noticed her nodding off. She signalled to Terrence and they helped Lily into her room. There Katha tucked Lily into the bed and then kissed her on the cheek and turned out the light.

Doctor Dafydd Jones sounded like a real charmer maybe he'd be a better fit for Lily. She wanted Lily happy and supported like the kind of support she, Katha had with Terrence. Terrence had given her the wedding of her dreams tomorrow and she could hardly wait. Katha only hoped that Lily could try to be happy tomorrow. She knew it wouldn't be easy, but maybe a friend like Doctor Jones would make it easier for Lily.

~0~

Chapter 30 - For
Your Protection
Earlier three days before New Year's

Sherry-Anne went into the bathroom and took the item out

of the bag. Peeing on the stick she waited. After a few minutes she starred at it in disbelief. The second time she slept with anyone and the plus sign said pregnant.

Sherry-Anne couldn't believe it she'd met the father of this baby a month ago at the hospital. A brief hello, until they danced at the Christmas party, four weeks ago. At the party they'd drank and danced and drank some more. Then Sherry-Anne had broken her self-imposed rule of never sleeping with anyone. In her drunken stupor the likewise drunk doctor had looked so much like Emmett she had given him herself body and soul to him.

Now she was pregnant and he was gone. She had confessed to him that it was all a big mistake, weeks ago and he told her he was moving away to a new position out of town. She hadn't even listened to him when he told her where. Sherry-Anne was pregnant and alone again raising two children.

Why now? She had the love of her life back in her life. Mind you there was an obstacle Lily Kelly, or whatever the hell that woman called herself. The woman if the internet was too believed was a black widow. Two of her husband's had been murdered by a serial killer and her mother had died mysteriously in Prague when Lily was a child.

The woman was cursed, even if she didn't want Emmett for herself; Sherry-Anne would never allow Lily to ingratiate herself, more into Emmett's life and endanger not only Emmett, but Caleb. Caleb deserved a full time father and since Sherry-Anne was not about to give custody to Emmett that meant Emmett must live with her.

That simpering Lily Kelly thought Emmett was hers. Lily had even received a proposal from him. That lucky bitch hadn't even answered him right away. What kind of woman does that? The wrong kind, that's who! But she knew Lily would cave, Emmett was a catch and where would that leave Sherry-Anne?

Sherry-Anne had hoped to woo Emmett on her own time; but between this baby and Lily, her plans would have to be moved up. Something had to be done about Lily, but what? It wasn't in Sherry-Anne to kill Lily. Though she had to admit it briefly crossed her mind, but then thinking about Caleb stopped her. He couldn't have a murderess for a mother. No, the truth was she couldn't harm anyone. She had a nursing degree and helped people, but this baby wasn't going anywhere. This baby needed and deserved more than Sherry-Anne could provide. If she could somehow convince Emmett that this was his baby he'd marry her, not Lily. But time was short and Lily could seize her opportunity tomorrow if she hadn't already.

Sherry-Anne dialled the hotel hoping to find out when Lily would arrive. Pretending to be Lily she asked, "My name is Lily Kelly. I have a reservation for your hotel made by my grandfather, Terrence Stewart. I'm afraid he didn't tell me the date for my arrival."

"He just changed it this morning Ms. Kelly. He said you would arrive tomorrow afternoon between five and six p.m."

"Thank-you, see you this afternoon then," Sherry-Anne said hanging up.

Now what? How could she stop Lily in her tracks and convince Emmett that this baby was his? She could drug him nothing that would harm him but a little rohypnol, commonly called a roofie would make Emmett and Lily think Emmett had slept with Sherry-Anne. Most victims did not have the drug still in their system after twelve hours so it would be undetectable in Emmett's urine then. But how could she do this? She couldn't endanger her nursing career by taking this drug from the hospital. What about her career if she were caught it would mean the end of it. No, she'd do it if she took all the right precautions they'd never find out what she done.

She remembered a dealer she treated in the emergency room. He had said he owed her a favour and he'd give her the drug. He'd even given her a card with his phone number on it. At the time she'd wondered why she'd kept it but the man was cute and his rakish smile had reminded her of Emmett.

Every man reminded her of Emmett. She couldn't lose him again not when she was this close to getting everything she ever wanted. Sherry-Anne made the call and met up with the man. He handed over the rohypnol telling her to make sure she allowed enough time for the drug to work. Sherry-Anne planned for Caleb to spend the night with his aunts.

Calling Emmett she lied and said she was working late, but could she meet Emmett at his hotel room perhaps at two a.m. Emmett balked saying that was too late, but Sherry-Anne pressed saying there was something she needed to urgently discuss about Caleb. She had hoped he agreed. Now she had hours to prepare her plan and make sure it would work. But she would achieve her ends. This was her chance to change history and make both her, the new baby and Caleb a happy family. She deserved this, for all those years she was cheated of happiness and so did Caleb. She would do this she had no choice.

THE END OR IS IT?

Thank-you for reading these books, if you enjoyed these stories please think about leaving a few words for me at your favourite retailer

~Sincerely S.G. Lee

Look for the next book in the series, 'What Will Robin Do?' Coming 2017!

www.ingramcontent.com/pod-product-compliance
Lightning Source LLC
Chambersburg PA
CBHW070532030726
47505CB00001B/10